BLOOD AND RUST

RAVEN

THE FLESH, THE BLOOD, AND THE FIRE

S. A. SWINIARSKI

DAW BOOKS, INC.
DONALD A. WOLLHEIM, FOUNDER
375 Hudson Street, New York, NY 10014

ELIZABETH R. WOLLHEIM
SHEILA E. GILBERT
PUBLISHERS
www.dawbooks.com

First Omnibus Printing, March 2007
1 2 3 4 5 6 7 8 9

DAW TRADEMARK REGISTERED
U.S. PAT. OFF. AND FOREIGN COUNTRIES
—MARCA REGISTRADA
HECHO EN U.S.A.

PRINTED IN THE U.S.A.

Raven

The literate parts of this are dedicated to
Robert E. McDonough.

The bloodthirsty parts of this are dedicated to
Susie Kretschmer.

Acknowledgments to
Astrid, Susie, Charlie, Levin, Mary, Bonnie, Geoff, and
Paula for doing their best to eviscerate this novel in the
manuscript. I also give thanks to Mr. Poe
for the obvious reasons.

PART ONE

PREMATURE BURIAL

Thank Heaven! the crisis—
The danger is past.
And the lingering illness
Is over at last—
And the fever called "Living"
Is conquered at last.
                    —"For Annie"

1

I dreamed of blood, and I awoke in a frozen darkness, wondering why I was not yet dead. As my blood-red dreams faded, cold wrapped my body in a grip severe enough to tear flesh from bone.

"Shit."

My painful whisper was loud enough to frighten me down to my soul.

My back pressed against a wall of curving concrete. Water rushed over me, up to my waist. I opened my eyes, and could barely see a darker shadow where the rest of my body was. The water numbed my body, and my frozen hands couldn't feel the ice on the walls.

My senseless hands slid over the concrete as I tried to push myself upright. When I finally stood, I heard the rip of my clothing tearing from where it had frozen to the wall. When the wall released me, my head slammed into the low ceiling, and dizziness overcame me. I had to crouch and dry-heave until my gut ached and my eyes stopped watering.

I was so *cold*.

My mind flew in chaotic tumbles, the cold and the vertigo making it easy to lose my concentration. My thoughts took a supreme effort to retain, and it was some minutes—too many minutes in this icy tomb—before I had overcome my disorientation long enough to think about where I had awoken.

Once I could concentrate, it was obvious that I stood in a storm sewer somewhere. But I had no idea where it was, no memory of how I got here.

The more I tried to force my memory, the more traitor my mind became. As I groped for some impression, some image of my life before this icy hell, my mind was gripped by a headache that shot sparks of color before my eyes.

I was in serious trouble. I had no memory. Everything before my awakening, and a sense of a dream, was a void. I felt a sick impression of what was there, like sensing the definition of a forgotten word, but the substance of my memory was gone.

Not only couldn't I remember how I had come to this place, but I couldn't remember who I was.

I put a hand to my head, and while I couldn't find an injury—all parts of my skull throbbed equally—my hair was clotted with frozen blood.

Not good. Possible head injury, nausea, dizziness, amnesia, nightmares—and I was probably going to die of exposure and hypothermia down here. The thought of dying down here, with no memory of who I was, terrified me.

I started downstream, hoping for an exit before the cold finally claimed me. As I duckwalked through the knee-deep current I tried to force a memory of how I'd gotten into this mess.

Had I fallen through an open manhole? Had I collapsed into a drainage ditch to be washed underground? I could not focus on what had happened. Nothing emerged from my memory beyond the impression of violence done to me.

However I had come here, I could not imagine it happening more than a quarter-hour ago. The cold was deadly. It was a miracle that I had not yet died from it. However long I'd been submerged in this icy water, any longer, I felt, and I never would have woken up.

For a moment I took some comfort in being able to think clearly now. That comfort brought an unbidden thought, *If I am brain damaged, would I know I was thinking like mushy cabbage?* I pushed away the idea.

I slogged downstream, the rushing water cold, deep, and painful. I felt sick that I might have survived whatever accident brought me here only to die of hypothermia, or lose my legs to frostbite.

For some reason, that brought an involuntary laugh which made me dizzy and surprised me by showing me my own breath. My eyes had adjusted to what little light there was, and I could see my misty laughter before me. I hugged myself for warmth—gaining little from it—and slogged on.

The laugh had been for the word "accident."

The word was soaked with irony despite the fact I could remember nothing of what had happened. My subconscious knew, however, that "accident" was the last word to describe what had occurred. What had happened to me was violent, purposeful, and intentional. This had been done *to* me. No faces, no memory of the act itself, only the certainty that some asshole had tried to kill me.

My anger made me a little warmer. So did the movement, the effort easing some of the chill. It helped when I finally walked into a chamber tall enough for me to stand upright.

By now I could nearly see, and I was fighting to stand upright against the current pushing me. The water was up to my chest before I found a ledge lining the tunnel that was high enough for me to stand out of the water. I climbed up on it and stood, shaking, cold, and wet. Sensation, searing cold, returned to my numbed lower body.

I don't know how long I'd walked down that sewer pipe, or how long my legs had been submerged, but when my legs were exposed to the air, cold as it was, it felt as if someone were torching them. The pain was bad enough to make me gasp and nearly pitch headfirst into the torrent below.

Looking down at the water, I couldn't believe I had fought my way out. Now that my eyes could make out this gray subterranean world, I saw how close to death I'd been. The water roared, carrying logs the size of my thigh and battering them against the walls. As I watched, one slime-blackened log slammed into a swamped shopping cart that was wedged against the walls. The sound of the impact echoed through the sewer, and the cart was dented and knocked loose, to clatter along the wall and out of my sight. If I'd been struck by that log, it would have cost me some ribs or possibly my spine.

I must have been unconscious and swept down the sewer by this torrent. Miraculously I hadn't drowned or had parts of me bashed to pulp against the walls.

I felt my head again. Maybe part of me *had* been pulped.

I suddenly realized that I had stopped breathing.

Panic gripped me, slamming the headache back into my skull. I thought I was having a stroke. But once I thought about it, my chest shuddered and I started breathing again. I sucked air in great gulps that had to originate from psychological rather than physical need. I hadn't been consciously holding my breath, and I hadn't stopped long enough for it to cause any pain or discomfort.

It scared me.

It scared me worse than amnesia or possible brain damage. It scared me because I hadn't realized it was happening. I was terribly conscious of my own breathing as I made my way down the storm sewer.

I inched along that concrete ledge, sliding along walls of brick, concrete, and eventually corrugated steel. I managed to avoid immersing myself again.

It seemed an aeon before I finally made it out of that frigid little hell. Logic told me that the time I spent underground must have been subjective. Had I actually spent the hours down there that I felt I had, I would have been a frozen corpse long before I reached the sewer's outflow.

The outflow I came to emerged from underneath a highway. The echo of traffic reached me through corrugated steel long before I saw the opening. The exit itself was hidden around a bend until I stepped in front of it.

It opened onto a swollen river that snaked away into a frosted ravine. Snow-covered ice began a few feet from the opening, an unbroken blue plain, shimmering in the moonlight.

I inched out of the sewer opening, stepping on rocks and downed trees, trying to avoid dunking myself again. It was colder out here, under a clear black sky, the air sharp enough to shave with.

I pulled myself onto ice that could support my weight, holding on to a tree growing out from the lip of the ravine, and looked up the wall from which I had just emerged. The storm sewer outlet was set into a sloping hillside that went up for maybe a dozen or twenty feet, topped by a guardrail. As I watched, a lonely car sped out of the darkness, passed me, and disappeared back into the darkness, chased by its own bloody taillights.

I moved to the edge of the ravine, holding on to the branch above me until I was certain that I was on firm ground rather than snow-covered ice. Seeing the highway lifted something in me, as if it was a confirmation of my survival. I was going to make it through the snow and the cold. I was going to live, however unlikely that was. I shook in the cold and told myself that I had, finally, made it. I had gotten out of the pit alive.

Whether or not I was in one piece, that was debatable.

I felt around my head again, now that it wasn't throbbing constantly. My hair was a tangled mass of frozen blood. No dangling flaps of skin, no bumps, no holes, no abrasions. I was comforted until I thought that I might have suffered an injury that had frozen under the mat of hair I was prodding. It was cold enough out here to numb anything, and I'd been in the water way too long.

I had to get inside and warm myself up. My legs felt asleep. I thought my pants had dried, but when I felt them with my numbed hand, I found them frozen stiff.

I scrambled up the slope toward the highway, putting my share of bruises on my numbed shins as I started a dozen mini-avalanches. When I got to the top, I had to scramble over the guardrail and six feet of snowplow ejecta. I rolled into the breakdown lane.

I got up and started walking.

As I walked, I searched myself for clues to where I was, what had happened to me, and who I was. I felt desperate for some item my ragged brain could hang a memory on.

I wore well-worn steel-toed work boots—if they didn't have to chop off my toes it was thanks to them—a pair of terribly abused blue jeans, a denim work shirt that, like my hair, was ruined with frozen blood—mostly on the chest and collar—and a black, fleece-lined trenchcoat that would probably never be usable again. Everything had been soaked and frozen stiff. I made cracking and grinding noises when I moved.

My wallet, if I'd had one, had either been stolen or had been lost in the sewer. Same for a watch, or keys. No rings, or any jewelry for that matter. My pockets were almost completely empty.

For a time I felt as if I had been robbed. But something in my void of a memory made me feel that what had happened had been more than a simple mugging.

My hands were clumsy and numb, and found it difficult to manipulate my frozen clothes, which is why one of the last things I discovered was the empty holster. It was clipped to the rear of my belt, hidden from view. I didn't know what I had found until I'd unclipped it and looked at the thing.

It gave me my first memory of something before the icy sewer. I could see the gun that belonged in the holster, a mental image of a blue steel Colt Police .38. It was more than an image. I felt how much it should weigh, how it should fit in my hand. I knew what it was like to load it, by hand and with a speed-loader. The shock of the impressions made me drop the holster.

What had I been doing with a gun?

I bent slowly, my frozen clothes abrading my skin, and fished the holster out of the slush in the breakdown lane. I shoved it in a pocket, for the first time suspecting that I might not be an innocent victim.

No one is innocent, I thought.

I resumed my stumbling progress toward the lights of what I hoped was civilization. I continued examining my pockets, my search taking on an edge of desperation.

I found only one other thing, besides the holster. I felt something in the breast pocket of my shirt. The pocket was buttoned shut and gummed with blood, but I tore it open. Inside was a small plastic card. At first I thought it was a credit card, but there was nothing embossed on the surface.

It took a moment for me to realize that it was a key. The print identified the place as the Woodstar Motel. The key carried a weak visual impression with it. A view of a garish neon sign that could have been as much my imagination as memory.

There was an address on the card and that cheered me, but only for a moment. I had no idea where I was, much less how to find this motel. I looked up and stared down the four lanes of unused asphalt. How did I know I was going in the right direction?

I had yet to pass so much as a sign identifying this road. I pushed my way along the shoulder, leaning into a wind that cut like a razor, dragging my feet through dirty brown snow.

By now, on top of the cold, I was feeling pretty damn weak. I had lost even the pins and needles that reminded me that I still had legs. My fatigue was a dangerous sign. I felt as if I could lie down upon the snowbank and take a nap; the idea was tempting even though I knew I'd never awake from such a nap.

I forced myself to march along the breakdown lane, my boots growing heavier with each step. I had gone maybe another dozen yards when I saw the trees lighten in front of me. I saw my shadow reach out ahead of me, and I turned to see a pair of headlights bright enough to make my eyes water.

Incredibly, my first instinct was to hide from the approaching car. It was an insane impulse, since I was certain to die if I spent much longer out in this cold.

Instead, I gathered my coat about me to hide the bloody shirt I wore, and waved the car down. The car passed me and rolled to a stop on the shoulder. I watched the narrow brake lights ease back toward me as my eyes recovered their night vision. The nearer the car came, the more I was gripped by an insane ambivalence.

I was frightened of being discovered, and I had no memory of why I should be.

The car was a late model Cadillac, black or dark blue in color. It had Ohio plates, Cuyahoga County, up-to-date tags, and a five-digit number. I also noticed the small Enterprise Rent-A-Car logo. I was cataloging all these items by rote before I realized that I was doing it. By then the plate number was fixed in my head.

The Cadillac came to a stop about ten feet away from me. For a few moments I was unable to force myself to move. My hesitation was brief. The wind picked up, driving needles into my exposed skin. If nothing else, the cold pushed me toward the car.

I walked up and opened the passenger door, letting out a blast of heat and the sound of Creedence Clearwater Revival. The driver turned to face me. He was an old Asian gentleman with snow-white hair that contrasted with a very dark face. He wore a dark blue suit that was conservative enough to be three or thirty years old.

He took one look at me and said, "My word . . ."

His accent wasn't foreign, but it wasn't Midwestern. It was only slightly offset from the universal newscaster accent, but it made me think Canada. "Sir," I said, doing my best to sound harmless, "I've had an accident, I need to get back to my motel."

The way he stared at me made me realize just how terrible I must have looked. "Of course," he said. "Certainly. Come in."

I slipped into the passenger seat and pulled the seat belt around myself. In the warmth of the car, my skin began burning, fiery needles racing across my flesh. My clothes began melting immediately.

"Are you certain that you don't need an ambulance?" my benefactor asked. "I can drive you to a hospital—"

"No," I said. It was a reflex, and I said it much too strongly. He turned to face me, and I saw the beginnings of suspicion grow on his face. After a pause, I said, "Look, I'm all right—"

"You don't look all right." I could see his face harden, and I could feel him beginning to perceive me as a threat. His fear began to fill the car like a fog. I could almost breathe it.

On the radio John Fogherty was singing about bad moons rising. . . .

I started talking even before I knew, consciously, what I was about to say. I ran my fingers over clotted hair and said, "Look, this is embarrassing. I lost my job you see—laid off, downsized, whatever you want to call it—got cut off with no benefits, no nothing. Car's totaled, sent the damn thing into a ditch—black ice. But my insurance lapsed, and hell—I never had any medical insurance to begin with . . ."

I amazed myself by the facility with which the lies came out. I fell into a natural patter where the hesitation stops gave me time to think of the next sentence. It only took a few glances into this guy's eyes to tell I had him convinced.

"I understand," he said, "but don't they have to take you at an emergency room?"

I laughed humorlessly. "Yeah, and what they'd charge'd wipe out what savings I got left. Then I'd probably be arrested for no insurance on that wreck I totaled. I do *not* want to look for work with a suspended license."

"Head wounds can be nasty."

I nodded. "I can go to the free clinic tomorrow. They'll take that long to get to me in an emergency room anyway."

The look of disgust on the man's face now had nothing to do with me. I had sold him, completely, on a story that I'd constructed out of whole cloth, on the spot.

Who in hell was I?

I felt my head again and wondered why I was so terrified of going to a hospital. *"Head wounds can be nasty,"* said my Good Samaritan. The idea did not make me feel good.

"The health care system in this country is insane," he muttered. "Where's your motel?"

I fished in my pocket and retrieved the card key. I read off the address of the Woodstar Motel in the dim glow from the dash.

"Can you give me directions?" he asked.

"No," I said, "I'm from out of town. I was following up a job prospect." The lies were almost easy, as if the conversation was a puzzle and all I had to do was fish out the pieces to fit. He eventually had me fish out a map from the glove compartment. At least I now knew exactly where I was. We were westbound on Route 322, east of Cleveland, Ohio, just outside of Cuyahoga County.

None of that information held a whisper of a memory for me. All I knew for certain was that everything I had told my benefactor had been a lie.

The song changed to "Fortunate Son."

The drive turned out to be a short one, which was fortunate. Even in the warmth of the car, my breath was shallow, my head throbbed, and I seemed to have no feeling below the waist. More than once I reconsidered my attempt to avoid a hospital, but I never voiced my second thoughts. I was going to follow my instincts all the way, and pray that there was a reason for them.

Eventually the neon-chrome sprawl of the motel emerged from the drifts beside Route 332. The neon sign merged with the memory my card key had inspired.

"Here you are," my benefactor held out his hand and said, "My name's Park. Lee Park."

"Damien Castle," I said automatically, knowing it wasn't my name. "Thank you for the lift. I think you saved my life."

He shook my hand and his expression darkened. "That remains to be seen, my friend."

I nodded as I slipped out. The cold was so searing that I nearly collapsed by the car. It was an order of magnitude worse now that my clothes had partially melted. Immediately the moisture on my skin began to freeze again.

The Cadillac drove away and I stumbled through a recently plowed parking lot, realizing that I had no room number. I gripped the key in a numbing hand, and realized that there was no guarantee that I still had a room here. I had the sick feeling that I might have only delayed the inevitable.

The wind sucked my strength as I tried to think. I stumbled toward the motel, leaning on a dirty Chevette that had been half-buried by a snowplow, and was overwhelmed by a sudden stab of aloneness. The night gripped me in a silence so total that I wanted to scream.

Just as suddenly, the sense of isolation was gone, leaving me shaken and empty. I tried to calm myself, to push back the tide of panic that was making it difficult to think.

I looked around the lot, and noticed something. The Chevette was the only car that was buried so badly. It had been here a couple of days at least.

My car, perhaps?

Even better, I looked down and saw that each room had a parking space marked for it. Room numbers were painted on the curb in front of the spaces. The curb by the Chevette was hopelessly buried, so I kicked away the snow around the empty spaces to either side of it.

The numbers were 222 and 224. That meant the Chevette belonged to room 223. It was worth a try. If I was wrong, I'd just have to try every single door until I found the one where the key worked.

I raised my head and began looking in vain for room number 223. I felt a blurry panic when I didn't see that number on any of the doors facing the lot. It took a minute for me to see a set of stairs leading to a balcony and a second story of rooms.

I ascended the stairs, the only sound the crunching of salt under my boots. I passed two doors and stopped in front of 223. My numbed fingers fumbled with the card, and I felt the panic begin again. What if this was the wrong motel, what if the room had been given to someone else?

The card chunked home and a small diode blinked green from the lock.

Behind me, one of the streetlights illuminating the parking lot buzzed and went out. For the first time I noticed that the sky had lightened from black to a deep aqua.

As the door creaked open, the wave of heat that blew from the room felt like a furnace. My refrozen clothes began to melt again. I spared one more look at the lightening sky.

For some unfathomable reason I felt as if I had made it just in time.

I stumbled into the darkened motel room on legs that felt like stilts carved in ice. I slammed the door shut behind me, not caring if someone else was in the room. Though, even in the near pitch black, with the shades drawn, I was sure the room was empty.

I took a step and stumbled over a suitcase. I was shivering violently, and salt was stinging my eyes—sweat or thawing blood.

Ass on the floor, and in total darkness, I began stripping off my frozen clothes. It was a process that felt as though it ripped skin and hair as much as cloth. Wrestling off my boots ignited deep burning pain in my feet, especially my toes.

For a moment I sat there, naked, shivering. Fiery pain washed over me, leaving bone-deep aches in its wake. Ice trickled down my back as my hair melted.

I crawled to the bathroom, not bothering with the light. I could feel my consciousness ebbing. There was actually a bathtub in the bathroom, not simply an abbreviated shower stall. I turned the hot water on full and half climbed, half fell, into the bathtub, barely worried about scalding myself. I felt the steam filling the bathroom.

My last coherent memory of that first night was of killing the water when the tub began to overflow, thinking I was probably going to die.

2

For the second time I woke up in darkness, submerged in cold water.

For an instant I thought I might be caught in some vicious cycle of hallucination—doomed to traverse some private circle of hell, waking in that sewer and stumbling to the motel over and over and over. . . .

I had to clamp down hard to keep myself from flipping out.

Calming down took a minute or ten. It took that long for me to realize that I was still alive. I hadn't stopped breathing in the night. I hadn't slipped down into the water and drowned. I'd avoided hypothermia. My headache was gone for the most part. And, when I conducted a prodding search of my extremities under the tepid bathwater, I could actually *feel*. Sensation was back in my fingers and my lower body.

All things considered, I felt better than I had any right to feel.

I probably *looked* like hell.

I heaved myself out of the tub, carefully, expecting a wave of vertigo that didn't come. I was waking up. I felt alive, alive in a way you can only feel after coming pretty damn close to the alternative.

I stood in the darkened bathroom, dripping, thinking how badly the boys who tried to off me had screwed up. I was going to find them and—

"Calm down," I whispered to myself. It was hard. Like the panic that had surged in me before, thinking about my hypothetical attackers gave vent to a deep well of raw emotion. A visceral anger gripped me, abnormally intense even after what had happened. Especially since, with my hole of a memory, I couldn't say for certain that I was the victim of *any* sort of attack.

The problem was that I *was* certain.

I shook my head and tried again to force a memory. The strain was almost physical. I clenched my fists and felt a bead of sweat roll off my brow.

I remembered a brief sensation. A smell like rusty leather, and a heavy wet sound of something falling on. . . .
On what?

That was all the memory that would come, the smell of ferric leather and that incongruous, ominous sound. Nothing more would come to me, and my subconscious left me with a deep rage and a feeling that I had been, in some sense, raped.

"Maybe I don't want to remember." I took a deep breath. "Stop talking to yourself in the dark, people will think you're nuts."

I groped for the light switch. A frosty fluorescent flashed a few rattling strobes before it came on.

The bathroom was a mess. Worst was the bathtub. The water was black with dirt and blood. Water had slopped over and drenched the hex-tile floor, streaking it red and brown. A few towels were sopping in the midst of the mess on the floor.

I walked over to the tub and hit the lever for the drain, its only response an anemic gurgle. I had to pull out a tangle of hair and twigs from the drain to get the thing to start. I shook my hand off into the john and glanced in the mirror—

—and got a stabbing pain straight through the temples that made my eyes water. I immediately looked away, as if I'd been blinded by a bright light. The pain faded.
What the . . . ?

I looked into the mirror again, slowly raising my eyes—

When the second headache faded enough to allow me some awareness, I was staring into the sink in front of the mirror and gripping the sides of the counter so tightly that my arms were vibrating. The idea of brain damage came to me again.

But I had felt *fine* until I had looked directly at the mirror.

I cast a furtive glance at the mirror without raising my head. I saw my naked waist sliced by the lines of the sink. I saw my hands, veins standing out on their backs, knuckles white.

I didn't quite have the courage to raise my head all the way.

I thought furiously for a moment and came to the conclusion that it was an effect of the light reflecting off of the mirror. Bright lights could trigger headaches. Strobes could start seizures in epileptics. Maybe some weird angle of reflection hit me just the wrong way when I looked directly in the mirror.

That decided, I grabbed a dry hand towel from the rack and, without looking, hung it up over the bare fluorescent tube that ran along the top of the mirror. Once I was sure it was secure, *then* I slowly raised my gaze.

No migraine struck this time, if that's what had sliced my skull open a few minutes ago. The towel didn't cover the whole mirror, I could see myself from mid-chest down.

On the parts of my body I could see, there was no injury, nothing that looked like frostbite. That was good—or not so good, because that left only one place for all that blood to have come from.

The drain in the tub gurgled as it finally emptied out.

I prodded my skull—with the towel in place I couldn't see my head—and found my hair a crusty mess. No area felt particularly sensitive, but I wasn't going to find any signs with all that clotted hair in the way. I shrugged, sighed, and stepped back into the shower.

After a long time pulling gunk out of my hair, I emerged from the shower. I felt about as good as I could ever remember. Which, of course, wasn't saying much.

As I dried myself off with the only clean towel left in the bathroom, I looked at the hand towel I'd draped over the mirror. I found it disturbing. It was the one concrete sign, other than my memory, that there *was* something wrong with me. I might not have found so much as a bump under my clotted hair, but it wasn't normal to have migraines just from peeking into a mirror.

Maybe it'd just been a temporary aberration.

Yeah, like the blood. If the blood came from you, that bleeding aberration was pretty damn temporary. Wasn't it?

I reached over and touched the corner of the towel. Two ways to test this, lift gently, or yank it away.

I began to lift it.

Slowly, it revealed my shoulders and a scar on my left pectoral. Then my neck, the cords standing out as I clenched my teeth. My chin, dark with a few days' beard. My mouth, pressed into a hard, bloodless line. A nose broken once, severely, and reset. My . . .

. . . eyes . . .

"GOD!"

The pain dropped me on the floor this time. It was as if someone had fired a high-powered laser through my eyes and burned all the way to the back of my head. My palms pressed into the orbits so hard that I felt I might fracture my skull.

It took a while for me to think straight.

As the pain faded, I stared at my hands. I became very conscious of my vision. It seemed normal. Nothing was blurred, nothing doubled, the colors seemed right.

Nothing I remembered seeing in the mirror clued me in either. The reflection that had looked at me, despite the grotesque contortion of pain it had caused, seemed normal. Even the eyes—green, I remember—couldn't account for the blinding stab I'd felt when I made eye contact with my reflection.

It struck me as some sort of psychotic pathology, and that really scared me.

It scared me because I had no obvious injuries. That left me with the strong possibility that the blood wasn't mine. I had refused to be taken the hospital. I was afraid of something. What if it was the police I was afraid of? I was missing a gun. Was it possible that I had killed someone?

I climbed, shaking, to my feet.

Amnesia could be psychological as well as from a blow to the head.

Was I insane? Could I be a serial killer with a few dozen bodies to his credit? Was I—

I put my hands over my face and told myself to cut it out.

I pushed out of the bathroom to get away from that damn mirror. I might be on shaky ground, mentally speak-

ing, but it wasn't time to be sized for a white jacket that
buckled up the back.

Fumbling for the light switch, I told myself that, for all
my erratic behavior, nothing I'd felt or done yet was more
out of line than the situation I found myself in. I needed
to give *myself* the benefit of the doubt, since I didn't think
anyone else was about to.

I found the lights and flipped them on, hoping that something in my room would pull loose a memory. But the only
thought that crossed my mind upon seeing my motel room
was that the place had been tossed by amateurs.

There are two ways to search a room: thorough and subtle. Subtle is supposed to leave the room so the owner
doesn't know it was touched. Thorough is just like it
sounds; you don't give a shit, you trash the place and sift
through the pieces.

This was neither.

I tried to push the thought away, blame it on paranoia,
but the certainty gripped me and wouldn't let me go. The
feeling grew as I rummaged through a pair of suitcases
for clothing.

As I dressed, I began cataloging the details that told me
the room had been searched. Furniture had been moved.
The legs of the end table, the wheels of the bed frame,
both were slightly off the divots they had worn in the motel's carpet. The cushion on the one easy chair had been
compressed by a succession of rear ends, but the cushion
only sat loosely on the chair itself, as if it had just been
placed there. The runners that held the carpet down at the
front door and the bathroom were loose. The suitcases had
been gone through and hastily repacked.

At least the clothes fit me.

Dressed, I went over the motel room more thoroughly.
The closer I looked at anything, the more evidence I found
of tampering—shiny scratches on dull screw heads, an absence of dust on the back of the TV set, nicks on the sides
of drawers where they'd been forced off their tracks and
replaced.

I couldn't check around the mirror above the dresser
until I thought of putting on a pair of dark sunglasses I'd
found on the night table. The sunglasses prevented eye contact with myself, and that prevented the pain.

Once I could check the mirror, I found the tampering there as well. Along the edge of the mirror, scratches circled the plugs capping the screws that held the mirror to the wall.

I got the feeling that whoever had done this—and it was obviously not the cops, or, if cops, seriously bent cops—had been rushed. Maybe not amateurs, maybe seriously rushed pros. That didn't make me feel any better.

Then I had a sick paranoid thought to add to all the others. What if all of this was my doing? I had no memory. It could as easily have been me as anyone else. If it had been, what had I been looking for?

Presuming that there was something to find, I proceeded to toss the place myself. I hoped desperately for some clues to who I was, to who searched this room, to what had happened to me. . . .

I checked the doors and windows first and found something truly strange. White crumbs were ground into the carpet by the front door, as if someone had stepped on a cracker. By the window that faced the garage I found another cracker, white, about the size of a Ritz. It lay on the sill where the window opened, and I had to reach behind the chair to retrieve it. When I saw the image of the Lamb embossed on the surface of the thin wafer, I realized what it was.

I held in my hand a holy wafer. Someone, probably myself, had placed the Eucharist across the entrances into this room.

"Why?" I asked. My voice felt hoarse from lack of use. I backed from the window, confused and fearful. Looking at the wafer in my hand, I heard a voice out of my memory—

". . . it is something evil. It is evil and I fear for my daughter's soul . . ."

There was little in the room that gave me any clue to who I was. There was much, however, that implied what I did for a living.

In the closet I found a camcorder, a high-end model with interchangeable lenses; next to it an empty tape case for videos. With the camcorder was a voice-activated microcassette recorder. Again, an empty tape case for the cassettes. I found a very expensive pair of binoculars.

And in the bottom of the closet was a briefcase, aluminum and covered by a matte-black vinyl veneer. It weighed more than it should have. When I placed it on the bed, the mattress sagged. The latches had combination locks set to 537.

When I tried the latches, it opened. Whoever had opened this last hadn't bothered to relock the case. I suspected that my visitors hadn't cared after they'd finessed the combination.

Inside the case, resting on a foam rubber cushion, was a two-thousand-dollar monster: a Desert Eagle and two boxes of shells to go with it.

Its presence scared me more than the missing thirty-eight. The revolver was a reasonable weapon, but a fifty-caliber Desert Eagle is bigger than any handgun had a right to be. It'd throw a magnum bullet through someone, through the guy behind him, through the wall, and crack the engine block on the car parked outside. No one had any business carrying this thing outside a combat zone.

Scarier still was the way my hands knew the weapon, checking the slide and the magazine. The gun was fully loaded, and so new it shone. In the closet hung a shoulder holster that could fit it and an extra magazine.

I would have preferred some form of photo identification.

But in the remainder of the room I found no papers, no keys, no wallet, no checkbook. The closest I came to my identity was in the drawer of the nightstand. Three hundred dollars in cash was weighted down by an expensive-looking watch. I picked up the watch. It was shiny, and old enough to show some wear. On the back was an engraving, "Happy Birthday. Love, Gail."

Something clogged my throat. It came from the same blank place where the anger and the fear had been coming from.

"Gail?" I whispered, not enjoying the sound of my voice.

I put the watch on my wrist. I wondered why I had left it here. Fear of losing it, maybe?

When I lifted the stack of crumpled twenties out of the drawer, something clattered back into the drawer. I picked up a wedding band.

"*. . . Kate, I'm worried about you and Gail—*"

A sigh comes from the other end of the phone. "You're always worried about Gail. That's what your work does to you."

"This is different—"

"It's always different. I'm not like you, I can't live in fear all the time. That's why I left you. . . ."

The memory burned, but even so, I tried to hold on to it. I couldn't and I felt sick and ashamed that I couldn't. I had a family somewhere, and I was certain that I had done evil by them.

I sat on the bed, staring at the night table, trying to remember anything. But forcing did me little good. I sighed and looked at the phone.

For once I seemed to have some luck. The message light was on, I had some voice-mail waiting for me. I picked up the receiver and punched up my messages, hoping for some sort of revelation.

The first message was a voice that was achingly familiar though I had no memory of ever hearing it.

"Okay, Kane, you owe me. I got the information on Childe you wanted. Call my beeper, 216-3839. *Not* my apartment or the station. You better get this cleared up before Internal Affairs eats me alive for not handing you over."

Internal Affairs? That implied police, and that I was dealing with a cop who was risking something by talking to me. Was I wanted for something?

But I had a name now. Somehow that lifted some of the weight off of my soul.

The second voice was still familiar, but I had a more ambivalent feeling about it.

"It's Bowie. We gotta talk. Not over the phone. Meet me at the Arabica tonight, seven. There's talk on Coventry that you've got to hear."

The voice sounded frantic, but I didn't understand anything he said. Arabica and Coventry were just words to me, though my traitor memory decided to give me an image of the speaker. I saw a thin man in a leather jacket wearing a jet-black ponytail.

The next message was a repeat of the first caller.

"It's Sam again. Where the fuck are you? Call me."

Now I had a name for my policeman friend. I tried to

remember him, but my memory seemed to resist it. I couldn't force a memory, they only seemed to come when I wasn't prepared for them.

The next message was like a fist in the gut.

"Dad?" A young woman's voice on the verge of breaking into tears. "Sam gave me this number. Please, talk to me. You're hiding because you think you're responsible for what happened to Mom. Call me. Damn it, I love you. I love you. . . ."

"Gail," I whispered into the phone.

Kate my wife. Gail my daughter. That, my memory would give me. I could feel that something bad had happened, but what I didn't know. I sat there, stomach boiling, wishing that Gail had left her number.

But that would be something I was supposed to know.

The messages ended, and I slammed the receiver down on to the cradle.

I called Sam's beeper, left my name, and waited.

He called back within ten minutes. I grabbed the receiver before the first ring faded.

"Hello?" I said, my voice wrapped in an asphyxiating uncertainty.

"God damn it, Kane! Where the fuck have you been?" It was the same voice that had left the message. Sam's voice.

"Sam?" I said uncertainly.

"Yes. What the hell were you thinking, falling off the Earth like that? You want everyone to think you're dead? Please, at least tell me you've called Gail."

"I got her message. I had—"

"Christ, and you're just letting her worry about you? After what happened to Kate?"

A flash of a memory hit me, a bad one—blood-red and violent. I saw torn, ragged flesh. I remembered the sickening reek of disinfectant that just failed to cover the smell of blood, the almost subliminal smell of death.

Lo! Death has reared himself a throne. . . .

"Kane? Are you there? Hello?"

I choked back something. The receiver shook in my hand. *Why can't I remember?*

"I had an accident," I said. "I've had some problems." It was an effort to get the words out.

Sam's voice changed. "What happened? Are you all right?"

"I think someone tried to kill me."

The response was silence.

"Hello," I said. It was beginning to sink in that here was someone who knew me, someone who might tell me what happened.

"Who?" Sam said, earnestness replacing the anger in his voice. "Was it Childe?"

Childe. That name again. "I don't know. I can't remember—" I hesitated. Something inside me didn't want to admit how badly off I was. "We need to meet."

"Where?"

My mind was a blank. I tried to force an image of a place to meet, but forcing my past to the surface was like trying to build a snowman out of water. No memory would come when I wanted a memory.

On impulse I parroted one of the other messages, "How about the Arabica?"

"Which one? Shaker Square, University Circle, Coventry—"

"Coventry," I said. Perhaps I could find Bowie.

"When?" Sam asked.

"Give me three hours or so."

"Okay, 10:30."

I nodded. There was some hope that I would find out what the hell was going on.

"Are you all right? Do I need to send help out there?" Sam asked.

"No, I'll be fine." I said it even though I didn't believe it. "Do me a favor and call Gail and tell her that I'm okay?"

"Sure, but why don't you—"

"Tell her I love her," I said, and hung up the phone, my hand shaking. Somehow, memory or not, I had meant it.

What had happened to my wife? Presumably I was going to find out. However, from the wisps of memory I was getting, I was not sure that I wanted to know.

I needed to find this Arabica before 10:30. I looked at my watch and saw that it was pretty late already. I needed to get going if I was going to find Sam.

I walked up to the window and drew the shades aside. The night was ink-black with solid clouds. The street lamps were globed by halos of wind-whipped snow. It was as if the day had never happened, as if the sun were gone for good.

I looked down and saw the Chevette was still snowed in. It seemed to be my car, but did I want to use it?

I drew the shade and decided to call a taxi.

3

There were a few things I needed to check with the manager here, before I left. I stepped outside and tried not to think of the Eucharist crumbs that dusted the doorway. The idea that I might have been the one to grind the wafer underfoot made me uncomfortable.

The denim jacket I'd found wasn't up to the weather. The wind cut under it, and the snow abrading it made an audible patter. I counted my blessings. I'd been lucky I'd packed more than one jacket. I had, in fact, packed a hell of a lot.

All the signs seemed to indicate that I was running from something, something that had caught up with me at least once. Which made me feel more than lucky that this jacket was large enough to hide the Eagle and its holster.

I trudged through a growing snowstorm to the front of the motel and entered the manager's office. The woman behind the counter was easily sixty-five, wore thick glasses, and had hair the color of FD&C Red # 5. She glanced up at me, then went back to reading the book in her lap.

I walked up to the desk and cleared my throat.

"Can I help you?" she asked in a bored voice.

I opened my mouth, and for a moment I had difficulty speaking. I was suddenly overly conscious of a lot of things: the buzz of the unnaturally white fluorescents, the weight of the gun in my armpit, the smell of stale coffee from a mug on a counter, melting snow dripping down my neck. . . .

The sense of hyperawareness passed. "I need to check how long my room's paid for."

The woman gave a hostile sigh and put the book face down on the counter, cracking the spine. She looked up, her eyes magnified grotesquely by the glasses she wore.

"We don't give refunds for—"

"Yes?" I said. Her distorted gaze had made me realize that I'd still been wearing my sunglasses. I'd been taking them off when she paused.

"Yes?" I repeated. I was becoming uncomfortably aware that she was staring into my eyes. It was an intense and disturbing contact that made me wonder what she was looking at. Somehow I gained a very deep feeling of how boring she found her job, of how lost she felt here. Somehow I knew this woman regretted missing the chance to be something other than she was. The wave of empathy was like a blow.

I was drawn, leaning forward. Something pushed at me, something that wasn't a memory. Something more like an instinct.

She interrupted me by saying, finally, "What can I help you with?"

Her entire manner had changed, she wasn't looking through me any more. I could swear that what I saw in her eyes was lust, a lust that didn't make me nearly as uncomfortable as it should have.

"I'm in room 223. I need to know how long I'm paid up for."

"Yes, certainly." The hesitation in the way she breathed as she spoke made my interpretation of her expression unmistakable. So much so that I felt immense relief when she broke eye contact to rummage in a card file next to the phones.

"Do you have a phone book I could use?"

"By the pay phone, dear."

I glanced around the office looking for the pay phone. I found it back in the hall I'd come through. I left her to search in her files while I stepped outside. The hall was little more than an air lock, with glass doors to the outside and the office. The only things in it were the pay phone and a pair of newspaper machines.

For a few moments I stood there and tried to regain my composure. I was washed by a sense of disorientation. Rationally, I knew that all I had seen and felt about the woman behind the desk had been manufactured by my own mind, but I had to tell myself that none of it was real.

The roiling in my gut was real, though. The feeling of need inside me, a reciprocal and distorted version of what I thought I saw in the woman, that was real. The fact that I stood there with muscles tensed to where they felt as if they'd tear from the bone, that was real, too.

For the first time I truly considered the possibility that I might be psychotic.

My absent memory provided a fragment of a poem;

> *From childhood's hour I have not been*
> *As others were—I have not seen*
> *As others saw—could not bring*
> *My passions from a common spring—*

The sense of being totally alone gripped me again. I clutched the sides of one of the newspaper machines and forced myself to take deep breaths. If nothing else, the effort and concentration that took calmed me. When I felt as if I had rejoined the real world, I picked up the Yellow Pages.

As I called the cab, I started watching outside. Once I'd calmed down my inner world, I began thinking about the threats that might exist in the outer. There were people out there who had left me for dead, and I was beginning to feel much too overexposed behind this wide expanse of glass.

The stretch of Route 322 that I could see was all snow-cloaked shadows. I saw nothing threatening until I'd hung up the phone.

It was a small thing, off in the distance. Out there, by the side of the road, I saw the glow of someone lighting a cigarette. It was far enough away that it shouldn't have concerned me. Except that spot of road had an overview of the motel's entrance, the parking lot, and the door to my room.

I didn't stare. If that distant smoker was watching me, he had a very good view right now, as well-lighted as I was. I didn't want to tip off the guy that I'd seen him, not until I had some idea who he was. For all I knew he could be a cop, or my imagination could be running away with me.

I returned the Yellow Pages, and pulled out the White Pages to try to find an address for an "Arabica," whatever that was. The listing said it was a coffee house, but I couldn't find an address for "Coventry." I had to hope the cabby would know what I was talking about.

I walked back into the manager's office, avoiding obvious glances outside. "Four days, dear," said the woman behind the counter. I jumped at the sound.

"You're paid through Wednesday," she finished.

I realized that I didn't know what day of the week it was. "Wednesday? Morning or evening?"

She returned to her book, but she kept staring at me over the spine. "Morning. Checkout time is at 10:30."

It was Saturday.

The taxi took twenty minutes to show up. Despite the snow, I waited for it outside. I didn't want to spend the time in the office alone with that woman. When the cab came, I was covered with snow, and almost used to the cold.

It was ten minutes toward the city before I was positive the taxi was being shadowed. It wasn't easy for me to make the car. This stretch of highway was without streetlights, and the snow was getting worse. Most of the time the only visible signs of the car were the twin cones of headlamp-stirred snow.

However, not all pairs of headlights are created equal, and my tail was marked by a clump of ice by the right edge of the bumper that warped the lower right corner of its headlight. The car faded behind us two or three times as the cab made its way deeper into the snowbound Cleveland suburbs. But each time headlights reappeared behind us, it was the same car.

I resisted the impulse to have the cab pull over, or to change my destination. I wanted to keep track of these guys as much as they seemed to want to keep track of me.

I wondered if they were the same people who had tried to kill me. That didn't make sense. By all rights, the people who dumped me in the sewer should think I was dead.

I was beginning to have problems with the idea that someone had tried to kill me. If all the blood that had frozen on me was my own, where was the injury that had bled so much? All I had to go on, really, was a gut feeling that didn't even have a memory to support it. From the evidence, it could have been me killing someone and wandering into the sewers to escape. . . .

By the time the cab passed the border into Cleveland Heights, Route 322 had turned into Mayfield and we had passed deep into well-lit suburbia. The general lack of traffic made it hard for my tail to hide. They made a valiant effort, but they only had one car, so no matter what they did, I could eventually pick them out.

The car was a little too old to be totally anonymous. It was a tan Olds that was made prior to the streamlining of the nineties. Mid-eighties was my guess, though they never let me have a good look. Best I could see, there were at least two people in the car, both large males. Nothing much else I could make out through snow and distance.

I finally lost track of them when the cab turned to Coventry. I suspected they'd held back at the intersection of Coventry and Mayfield. By the time the cab went a block, I had lost the intersection beyond a white fog of snow.

It was two blocks to the next tangled intersection when the taxi stopped. It confused me for a moment before I realized that we had made it to my destination. I had to squint past a snow-draped courtyard to see a storefront, but the neon sign was lit up reading "Arabica."

I paid the cabby and stepped out into the snow.

I stood ankle-deep in a snowdrift in the center of the courtyard and stared through the windows into the well-lit shop. Looking in, I felt a nagging sense of familiarity. This place meant something—a lot of teenagers, more punk than anything else. I saw a lot of weird hair and body piercing. I also saw a lot of the bearded-poet type, the kind of folks who wear dirty army jackets, write longhand on yellow legal pads, and quote Nietzsche a lot.

I knew this place.

At one of the tables near the window, a lanky kid with a blond ponytail was having an animated discussion with a shadowy-eyed girl. They both wore abused leather jackets.

I stood there a long time before I walked to the door. The familiarity frightened me, as if this place might make me remember something that I didn't want to remember. But after a few minutes the cold drove me inside.

Stepping from the empty night street into the babble of humanity crowding the coffee shop was a shock. A wave of irrational enmity froze me in the doorway. No one actually looked in my direction, but I felt as if everyone in this place were paying attention to me, weighing me.

I forced myself to walk to the counter. *It's just the crowd. I'm not used to crowds.* That's what I told myself at least.

I was certainly in the midst of the largest group of people I'd seen since walking up *sans* memory. It was only natural to find it disturbing, after what I'd been through.

Of course that was just me bullshitting myself, but it helped to steady my hands as I took a cup of espresso and two horrendously-priced Danishes to one of the few free tables. The table was way in the back, in the smoking section. It was somewhat dark, and smelled like an ashtray, but having my back to a wall helped steady my nerves.

For a while I just sat there, cradling the warm mug in my hands, letting the cold retreat. I forced myself to moderate my paranoia. While some of the patrons gave me some odd looks, I was sure that they were the ones who gave everybody odd looks. I didn't look terribly out of place here, it just felt that way to me.

At the table next to me, two chain-smokers were playing chess. I classified the young clean-shaven one as an eternal grad student, the middle-aged bearded one as another unemployed poet. I didn't know where the assumptions came from, but it reinforced my impression that I had been here before. . . .

It made me wonder if being here was a good idea. If the cops *were* looking for me, and someone here recognized me—

I lowered my gaze. My sunglasses didn't seem much of a disguise.

As if spurred by my thought, someone slapped my back and said, "Hail Eris, you bastard. How goes the hunt?"

"Huh?" I said. I put down the espresso without drinking from it. I turned around. The speaker wasn't Sam or Bowie, I could tell from the voice.

I looked at him hoping for some twinge of memory. He seemed like someone I should remember. He had wild blond hair and wore at least seven earrings, though his ears were all he had pierced. He wore a denim vest over a linen shirt whose drawstrings left the neck open on a pentagram necklace. He wore a pair of John Lennon glasses with slightly blue lenses. He looked like an avatar of the sixties, though he couldn't be more than nineteen years old.

He awoke no memories. He didn't even awake a sense of dejà vú.

He slid into the chair opposite me, folded his arms on the table, and asked, "Find her yet?"

I was glad for my sunglasses. If he had seen my eyes, he would have seen my confusion. "No, I haven't," I said. "Do you have anything new to tell me?" It was a strange question, but one that came to me automatically—a rote question, something a policeman might ask.

My guest sighed and leaned back. "How'd I know you were going to ask that? Sorry, my friend, nada. I haven't seen them since that open circle I told you about. Not her. Not Childe. But you've been asking around; you know that. Vanished, poof." He flowered open his fingers, "Good riddance."

I nodded.

He held up his hand. "Not the girl, you understand—but that Childe freak. Just gave the fundies and the cops something nasty to have us confused with. Hey, but that's why I like you."

I looked up at the guy, feeling lost. "Why do you like me?"

"You never came in with that Satan-cult bullshit."

"Why would I?" At this point the questions were becoming a defense mechanism, to keep him answering questions so he wouldn't ask me any.

"Hey, man, you're *rare*. Most people, if you say you're a pagan, they think you're out torturing cats somewhere. Take any fundie and talk about any non-Christian spirituality, *boom,* you worship the devil. Somehow pointing out that Satan is a Christian invention doesn't seem to faze them. Childe's as close to the devil as I've ever been."

I still couldn't give him a name. However, as I talked, I got some feeling that I knew his community, that I had brushed against it before. His words held a familiarity that he did not.

And there was that damn name again. "Is there anything else you can tell me about Childe?"

He shrugged. "That I haven't told you already? Not really. English accent, snappy dresser, on a power trip that'd make

Alister Crowley and Anton Le Vay look like altruists." He sighed. "Hey, I want you to find this girl. I don't like the idea of anyone stuck with Childe. If there was anything I could do. . . ."

He trailed off.

Behind him, the chess game continued. I heard a slap-ding as the grad student slammed the top of a timer next to the chess board. The poet immediately moved his queen and made his own slap-ding.

"What is it?" I asked. My companion seemed to have lost himself in a thought.

"Are you as open-minded as you seem?"

"I try to be."

He grinned, "Then perhaps I can offer some sort of aid." He fumbled in his pockets and retrieved a bag. Behind him I heard the timer again.

Slap-ding.

From the bag he pulled a stack of cards. Slowly he began shuffling. "You're not someone who comes believing the oracle, are you?"

I glanced at the cards. "You mean fortune-telling?" What came to my mind when I thought of divination was more con artistry than the supernatural.

The kid shuffled cards and said, "More than that. We attach complex symbols to the cards, manipulate them, arrange them into patterns. The patterns they form are reflections of the patterns around us. This is as much us truly seeing as it is the cards telling us anything." He looked up and gave me a disarming smile. "Sounds pretentious, doesn't it? Just started reading up on chaos theory and emergent behavior." He placed the cards down on the table between us; a slap-ding echoed his motion.

I decided if this kid was about to try a con on me, that would probably tell me more than any oracle. "Go ahead, it can't hurt."

"Form a question in your mind, something for the cards to focus on. Then cut them for me."

I reached over and cut the cards. As I did so, the only question that would come to mind was, *Who am I?*

"Do you want to know the question?" I asked.

To my relief, he shook his head. "Sometimes the reading

is more profound if only *you* know what is being asked. At this point I am only helping you to see."

He drew the top card, laying it on the table between us. There was a look on his face I did not like. The card I liked even less. On it a corpse lay facedown, pierced through the back by ten swords. "The Ten of Swords." He swallowed. "This card is the past, the basis for what is to come. You've come through something tragic and unpleasant. Relationships have ended, maybe badly. You've perhaps felt a feeling of abandonment. Things have not gone as you planned or wished them to. . . ."

He took another breath and laid down a card above the first. This one showed a man upon a throne, holding a sword. "This card represents you, and the situation surrounding you. The King of Swords, not a great surprise since he deals with law enforcement. You have a determination to overcome the obstacles that confront you. There is a lot of stress around you, you're fighting your way uphill, but you are fighting."

He laid down a card above the other two; this one showed a woman on a throne, holding a staff in her right hand and a flower in her left. The card was upside down, her flower pointing down at the king's sword. "Ah, this represents your hopes or fears. In a sense, it is what you are looking for. A woman, I suspect that Cecilia that you've been asking about, though the Queen usually has blonde or red hair. The Queen of Wands, reversed. A troublesome woman, vengeful, she may turn on you or others.

"Your immediate past. . . ." He flipped over a card to the king's right. "Whoa."

A skeletal horseman bore a black banner toward the king. Corpses fell across the steed's path. "Death," he said needlessly. "Not necessarily a bad card, but you are in the midst of some change, a major severance with the past. With the swords I see a lot of struggle, but the change is powerful and won't be denied.

"The forces arrayed against you, the obstacles you must overcome. . . ." He turned over a card and laid it across the king. A bat-winged demon squatted on a pillar, raising his hand toward me.

Behind the kid, the chess players went on. Someone hit

the timer again. Slap-ding. We sat there, quietly for a moment or two before he went on with the reading. Most of the lightness had gone out of his voice. "The Devil," he said quietly. He placed his cards down and ran his hands through his hair. "Evil forces are blocking your path, and escape from them seems doomed to failure. . . ." He looked up at me and said, "Do you want me to go on with this?"

I nodded, not trusting my voice. His anxiety was infecting me, even though I found it hard to credit the idea that cardboard rectangles could say anything about me.

"The immediate future," he said, slowly picking up the deck. He turned over a card, looking at it for a long time before putting it down. The color drained from his face. I wondered what could be worse than Death or the Devil.

He slowly placed the card down on the other side of the king, opposite Death. "The Tower," he whispered. Lightning struck a lighthouselike structure, people tumbled off the precipice, and flames danced from the windows. "Chaos, disaster. Your upheaval has yet to end, and the tribulations you are about to face will be worse than what you've already endured."

He shook his head. "That's enough, man. I just don't like seeing those cards." He began picking up the spread shoving the cards back into his bag. "Look, I'm sorry. It was a bad idea."

"Don't worry, I don't believe in it," I told him.

He stood up and touched my hand. "Man, I know where you're coming from. But even if I didn't believe it, that kind of spread would freak me."

With that, he left me.

Who am I? I thought.

He was right. Even though I didn't believe it, those cards bothered me. I turned to ask him another question, but he had disappeared into the crowd.

The student and the poet had set up a new game. The poet was busy arranging pawns. Smoke hung low in the air, like fog on a battlefield. *Change, evil, and disaster. . . .*

"Yeah, I have seen her," said the blond pagan. His name is Neil, but he calls himself Sunfox. He hands back the picture I showed him of a dark woman named Cecilia. She is missing, and I've been paid to find her.

"Where did you see her last?" I ask him.

"A week ago last Sunday. She came to a few open circles. She's one of those people who're looking for something, but they're not sure what. The kind of kid that Childe bastard's supposed to prey on."

"Childe?"

"Yeah, that was the last time I saw him, too. A bunch of us got together and asked him to leave. . . ."

The memory evaporated with a slap-ding from the next table.

I tried to hold on to it, but that made it escape all the faster. The young man in my memory was the same one who read my fortune in his cards. Again I was hearing Childe's name, again I was looking for someone. . . .

Am I a cop?

". . . The King of Swords, not a great surprise since he deals with law enforcement . . ."

The poet moved a pawn. Slap-ding.

I cradled my espresso in my hands and thought that Sunfox had given me a lot of information outside of any debatable tarot reading. I looked into my cup and felt a wave of thirst and hunger wash over me, an intense and weakening feeling.

I took a bite of Danish and my first sip of espresso.

Queen takes pawn. Slap-ding.

The coffee slammed into my stomach, constricting my throat. The liquid hit my stomach as if someone had napalmed my abdomen. My gut started spasming violently.

Knight takes queen. Slap-ding.

I managed to drop the mug on the table without spilling it all over myself. I had my hand over my mouth. I knew that I was going to throw up. It felt as if someone were slamming me with an ax handle.

Rook takes pawn, checkmate. Slap-ding.

I stumbled the dozen feet to the rest rooms barely in time. I could feel the contents of my stomach rising as I pushed open the door. I was kneeling over the bowl before the door had swung shut behind me. It took me ten minutes to expel that single mouthful of coffee; it felt like an hour.

The worst part of all was the steely taste of blood that came with it. I couldn't ignore it, much as I wanted to.

Streaking the bowl, swirling with the ugly liquid mass, were trails of bright crimson. The sight of it made me nearly too weak to stand.

As I got unsteadily to my feet, I knew I could no longer pretend that I was okay. Okay people don't vomit blood.

I turned around and leaned over the sink. My eyes refused to meet the mirror, even though I still wore my sunglasses. Despite all the evidence to the contrary, I still felt a perverse thread of denial. It was only a little blood, after all.

I laughed, though I didn't feel at all amused. I was in serious trouble. However well I felt when I woke up, right now I was light-headed from hunger, and probably thirst. My gut was too torn up to handle anything without puking. I needed a doctor.

I ran water into my cupped hands and drank a tiny amount. It washed the taste from my mouth, but from the tightening in my stomach I knew that drinking any more would send me back to the john.

I had a longing thought about the three bucks' worth of pastry sitting back at my table, and almost threw up again. I finally raised my face to look at myself in the mirror.

"Kane," I whispered, "you look like shit."

Part of my face was obscured by a "Silence=Death" bumper sticker. But what I saw showed that, whatever was wrong with me, it must have been getting rapidly worse. I certainly didn't remember looking this pale back at the motel. The stubble on my chin looked black against my skin, and my lips were almost white. Shadows carved out too much of my skull on my face.

I backed out of the bathroom.

Behind me I heard a familiar voice say, "Kane, what the hell happened to you?"

I turned around to face Sam. I was expending what little exhausted effort I had to keep from shaking. I knew him, and the sight of his face inspired a feeling of trust that managed to find its way past my lack of memory. I knew this man was a friend, even though I couldn't remember him.

"Sam," I said. "Get me out of here."

4

Sam helped me out of the coffee shop. I was past embarrassment or any worries about being noticed. He supported me even though he was a head shorter than I was. It wasn't until we were outside and the snow was biting my face that Sam asked again, "What happened to you?"

"Get me to a car," I whispered. "I need to see a doctor."

The whole world felt distorted, *wrong*. I still tasted my own blood, and I felt as if blood tainted my other senses. Colors were too vivid. The street lamps shone like magnesium flares. Each windblown snowflake was a pin piercing my skin. The only warmth I felt was from Sam's neck against my hand.

He lay me against the side of a red Saturn and began fumbling for keys. As he did so, a question came to me, unbidden. "How's Gail doing?"

"She's as well as she can be after losing her mother. We've a car watching her." He pulled the passenger door open and said, "She's worried about her dad, and so am I. What's wrong? This isn't just a missing kid anymore, is it?"

I slipped into the passenger seat and placed my face in my hands. "Kate is dead, isn't she?" My voice had degraded to a whisper. "My wife is dead."

Sam gripped my shoulder. "Christ, what's wrong with you? You identified the body—"

The smell of blood somehow reaches me through the smell of disinfectant and alcohol. She lies on a stainless-steel table like dozens more I've seen before. I haven't had to see this since I left the force. I never wanted to see this place again.

Seeing Kate here is almost unbearable. It would be unbearable even if they hadn't torn at her body. There is an awful stillness, a motionlessness that's perverse and unnatural. Sam is there, holding my arm. He is the only reason I haven't fallen to my knees.

"Kane?" Sam shook me out of the memory. "Are you with me? Are you going to tell me what the problem is?"

I looked up at him. I wiped the blur out of my eyes and said, "I don't know. I can't remember. I can't remember anything."

We sat in his idling car as I told him what had happened. He listened quietly, nodding occasionally. After I finished, Sam said, "This is just great. You know once we get you to the hospital, we're both in the shit. You *know* that?"

I shook my head and said, "No, I don't."

He pulled the Saturn out into the street. The car slid a little. The snow was wet and heavy, the kind that was hell on driving. The wind whipped it into a white wall that erased everything more than half a block distant. Once he'd pulled away from Coventry, and the businesses clustered there, we were the only car on the street.

Sam focused his concentration on the road ahead, "I've been covering your ass when they wanted you in for questioning. You could have been in protective custody by now."

He gritted his teeth, and I could feel his stress at driving in this mess. "Now you've made yourself look like a suspect, and that makes me look like an accessory—"

"Can you please tell me what's going on?"

He looked at me. I felt the car slide, and he looked back at the road. "The way you keep things close to the vest, and you think I know something? God that's what I hated about you when we were partners." He sighed. "What I know? Two weeks ago a high-class hood hires you to find his missing kid. You find some connection between this kid and a guy, alias 'Childe.' You find something going on, and you refuse to tell me about it. They go after your ex-wife, and you insist on going off on your own after this Childe person—and somehow you convince me to let you." Sam pumped the brakes to bring the car to a slow sliding stop at a red light. "That's 'what's going on.' "

"Am I a cop?"

"Christ, you don't remember anything? Do you?"

I shook my head.

"Damn, I'm glad you asked to go to the hospital. I'd hate to try and convince you to do anything you didn't want to. Look, your name is Kane Tyler, you're forty-five years old. You're the most stubborn man I know. You were a cop for nearly fifteen years. Since then you've been freelance, finding people's missing kids."

"Tell me about my family."

The light turned green, and Sam spun the wheels for a while before the car started moving.

"You have the daughter I should have had. Don't worry about Gail, I did manage to swing some police protection for her. I have a detective sitting with her in Oberlin."

"Oberlin."

"She's eighteen, goes to college there. Is any of this helping you remember?"

I gritted my teeth and balled my hands into fists. All of this and no memories surfaced. All I had was one last lingering image of Kate's corpse. I couldn't even picture my daughter's face. I felt a deep rage for the people who had left me in that sewer. They had taken my life from me, just as surely as if they had killed me.

My gut ached, and I felt very cold. I stared down so all I saw were my pale fists shaking in my lap. "How could this happen? How could I forget everything?"

"The doctors will help you."

I slammed a fist into my thigh. "But *how?*" I looked up at Sam. "There was nothing wrong. All that blood, and I didn't find a wound—"

"Calm down," Sam said. "I don't know what happened to you, but you're frightening me. You could be bleeding inside. You should have gone to a hospital immediately."

"How long has that van been there?" I said, interrupting him. A black van, little more than a shadow, was behind us. It was gaining slowly through the snow. The windows were black, and I saw no sign of a license plate.

"I don't know, two or three blocks?"

"Call for backup," I said, staring at the van. Something else had joined the anger and frustration—fear. I knew that van, even without a memory of it, just as I'd known Sam as a friend the first moment I'd seen him.

"What . . . ?"

"Call! Now!" I could feel that it was nearly too late. The van was accelerating toward us. Something, either my tone of voice or the fact that I drew the Eagle, convinced Sam.

He got on the radio and started calling, "Officer needs assistance."

As if in response, the van slid behind us, and thudded against our rear bumper. We blew through the next intersection without even slowing for the red light. Sam's knuckles were whitening on the steering wheel.

"Pull away from them."

"I'm trying—"

The van kept with us, as if it were tied to our bumper. I leveled my gun at the grille of the van, and fired. The sound tore at my ears, so much it seemed that it was the gun's report and not the bullet that shattered the rear window. Gun smoke filled the cab for a moment before it was sucked out by the sharp winter wind.

"What the fuck are you doing?"

I didn't answer. The van was like a wall behind Sam's car. I fired into the grille again. The van didn't slow or pull away. Snow bit my face.

The world began wailing and pulsing red as Sam turned on the siren. With that and the tearing wind, I could bearly hear him yelling into the radio.

Out of the corner of my eye I saw the sliding door on the side of the van open. I tried to shift my aim, but the van rammed the rear of the car, throwing me against my seat. It knocked what little breath I had out of me, and I suddenly had more panicked thoughts about forgetting to breathe.

This is a bad time to start losing it.

I forced those thoughts away and pumped another shot into the front of the van. The shot went wide of the mark and one of the headlights shattered. Without that glare in my eyes, I saw a shadow slip out of the side of the van, out and up.

"What the. . . ."

Something thudded on the roof of the Saturn. I raised the gun and was firing through the roof before I realized what I was doing. Sam jerked, swerving the car toward the left curb. *"What are you doing?"*

I never had a chance to answer him.

The driver's window shattered. I barely had time to see an arm reaching down from the roof to grab the wheel, before the resulting skid threw me against the passenger door. My gun clattered into the foot well.

The car jumped the median, sliding sidewise. Sam fought for control of the wheel and the arm let go just in time for the van to plow into the side of the car. The van stopped, and we kept going, spinning out to crunch into a parked pickup truck, slamming to a halt with a lurch that tried to ram my stomach through my throat.

For a few moments, the world was cloaked in a ghostly quiet. The siren had died, leaving only the crimson strobe of the flasher. The engine had ground to a halt. For a few seconds all I heard was the ticking of cooling metal.

Then I heard a step on the roof.

How could anyone . . . ?

I scrambled to reach my gun. Someone jumped off the roof of the car before I had gotten to where my gun had slid under the passenger seat.

"You?" I heard him say. His voice was harsh and rough, like the grinding of millstones.

I turned to face him and saw a kid; he couldn't be more than eighteen. He wore black, and the only highlights I saw on his clothes were the studs on his leather jacket. There was no sign of the fact he'd been riding on the roof during a near-fatal skid.

He leaped up to squat in the shattered rear window. It was a leap of unnatural dexterity. I kept fumbling under my seat until my hand felt the butt of the Desert Eagle.

The kid looked at me with a monochrome face intermittently tinted red by the oscillating police flasher. He smiled at me with lips that appeared alternately black and soaked with gore. "Aren't you dead, my friend?"

I got my hand around the gun. I pulled it out and leveled it at the kid's chest. Even though I grabbed my wrist to brace it, the tip of the gun still shook.

"Don't. Move." I said. My head throbbed, I felt weak. I felt as if I moved through molasses.

The kid laughed at me. "You really don't want to shoot me, Mr. Tyler." He leaned forward slowly, looking me in the eyes. The kid had black irises. I couldn't see any pupils, just black, bottomless holes that tried to suck me in. Everything slowed as he reached for something in the back seat. I could feel his breath on my cheek.

My finger felt like lead when I pulled the trigger.

The sound was like a grenade going off in the back seat. The kid flew backward out the rear window, disappearing behind the rear of the car.

The world went quiet again. "Sam?"

I kept looking out the busted rear window, and I saw nothing but flying snow. "Sam?" A note of hysteria leaked into my voice. I turned to look beside me.

"Shit." It was little more than a whisper. The wind tore the words away. Sam was slumped in his seat, unconscious. Blood streamed from his nose and mouth. The sight of it froze me.

So much blood that it steamed.

I reached over and felt for a pulse. It was there. He was alive. My hand came away covered in livid crimson. The heat of it sank into my fingers. I held my hand in front of my face, the blood almost seemed to glow. . . .

The sound of sirens broke me out of whatever trance I was in. I got loose from the seat belt and pushed open the door. Leading with the gun, I inched my way around the wreck. When I rounded the rear fender, I leveled my gun at the pavement—

The kid wasn't there.

I started looking around maniacally until I saw him dimly, through the snow, jumping into the van. He was carrying something. By the time I had the gun steadied in his direction, there wasn't anything to shoot at.

"Missed," I whispered. "Must have missed."

I stumbled around to the driver's side, which was a crumpled mess. Sam was still breathing, but the blood looked even worse on this side. The blood pulsed crimson in time to the light on the dash, like something alive, like a beating heart.

I slid to my knees next to the door, my head level with Sam's. My knees hit the slush, but it felt as if I'd never stopped falling. The world kept spinning and spinning, and I lost all sense of time or space. For a few minutes all I knew was that red pulsing light. . . .

Sam's coughing brought me back to reality. He was on the ground, next to the car, and I was crouched next to him. I had no memory of prying open the wrecked driver's side door, or of pulling him out of the car. My face was barely inches from his.

His eyes fluttered open for a minute and he looked into mine. "Where the fuck did you learn mouth-to-mouth?"

I didn't respond because I was trying too hard to keep the world from spinning out of control. Sam's face was covered with blood. I could taste it on my own lips. I had a horrifying suspicion that I hadn't been trying to resuscitate him.

Sam coughed again, turned away from me, and spat up a mouthful of blood. The sight tightened something inside me. I began nervously wiping the blood from my own face, and sucking it off my hands. I knew it was Sam's blood, but I did it anyway.

I became afraid of what I might do. This man was a friend of mine, and all I could do was watch his life leak out of his body and feel a sick hunger, picture my lips on his, taste the blood again. . . .

I needed to see a doctor. I was having some sort of psychotic episode. What I was feeling was not sane.

Sam had called for backup. Where the fuck were they?

I pushed myself upright, consciously trying to wipe the blood off my hands in the snow. Sam would be fine, fine as long as I didn't do anything more. But all I could think of, all I smelled and saw, was that damn blood.

"Don't think of it," I was almost pleading with myself now. I needed to concentrate on something else, anything else. For once my memory provided something on command.

"Gaily bedight, / A gallant knight, / In sunshine and in shadow, / Had journeyed long, / Singing a song, / In search of Eldorado." I chanted the stanzas like a mantra. With each word I was trying to force the blood away from my sight. "But he grew old— / This knight so bold— / And o'er his heart a shadow / Fell as he found / No spot of ground / That looked like Eldorado."

Minutes it had been, only minutes since the van had forced us off the road. It already felt as if I had spent most of my life here. The taste of blood was still in my mouth as I spoke.

Something about my distorted state of mind made my

senses unnaturally sharp. I was aware of everything—the bite of individual snowflakes on my cheek, the crunch of salt under my feet, the rattle of the power lines in the wind, the sound of a car's distant engine, and the noise of its tires crunching the snow.

I looked up and saw headlights in the distance, through a swirling wall of white. The headlights and the emerging silhouette were familiar. It was my tail from the hotel.

I kept chanting, trying to calm myself. "And, as his strength / failed him at length, / He met a pilgrim shadow—"

It was an Olds, and it pulled up next to the wreck. Three people got out of the car. One bent over Sam, the other two walked toward me. My first thought upon seeing them was: *They're dressed like lawyers, not cops. But lawyers don't drive seven-year-old Oldsmobiles.*

A pair of them stopped in front of me. They were dressed to match, dark suits, wine-red ties, and charcoal-gray trench coats. The one in the lead was tall, black, and completely bald down to his brows. His friend was a wea-selish man with a razor mustache and slick hair, who would have looked more at home in a brown shirt and jackboots.

Their hands were empty, but I got the impression that the white guy at least had a shoulder holster under his trench coat.

I whispered, " 'Shadow,' said he, / 'Where can it be— / This land of Eldorado?' "

"Mr. Tyler?" The tall one spoke with a Jamaican accent that was at odds with the snow-whipped landscape.

I nodded, not trusting myself to speak. My senses sharpened with the tension, my eyes carved razor edges on everything. But my heartbeat, if anything, slowed.

"We represent Mr. Sebastian, your employer."

When I didn't respond, the Jamaican continued, "Mr. Sebastian wants you to come with us. He is very emphatic about police involvement in his daughter's disappearance."

I could feel myself being backed in a corner. "But, Sam, he's—"

"We understand your relationship with him, and granted you some latitude. But Mr. Sebastian does not want you questioned by the police. He does not want official investigations. Especially after what you've unearthed already."

What have I unearthed? "You bastards stole my tapes."

The Jamaican's partner, the one I'd been thinking of as Mr. Gestapo, smiled. His teeth were gray. The Jamaican nodded slightly, acknowledging my statement but not granting it any importance. "You disappeared," he said.

"You mean I managed to shake your tail and you panicked." It wasn't time to be lobbing verbal grenades, but anger was welling up and it was hard to contain.

Mr. Gestapo stopped smiling.

"Perhaps," said the Jamaican, "but if you'd been killed, Mr. Sebastian needed to know what you knew."

"So now you know what I know—"

"If you would come with us, please." The Jamaican held a long arm up to the Olds. "Do not worry about your friend. We'll leave a man here to tend to him until an ambulance arrives."

I didn't move. "What if I wish to stay and wait for the ambulance?"

The Jamaican lowered his arm. "Mr. Tyler, we will not force you into the car. But I should remind you that Mr. Sebastian has many friends in the police department. Friends who are quite aware how emphatically he does not want you questioned. If you were to fall into police custody, the consequences would be unpleasant for all concerned." He motioned at the Oldsmobile. "Now, may we please offer you a lift away from here? You do have Mr. Sebastian's daughter to find."

I smiled, shook my head, and got in the car. I felt more and more like the knight in the Poe poem—

> *"Over the Mountains*
> *Of the Moon*
> *Down the Valley of the Shadow,*
> *Ride, boldly ride,"*
> *The shade replied,*
> *"If you seek for Eldorado!"*

5

They put me in the back seat of the Olds, which was good. It gave me some chance to hide how strung out I was. My hands shook, my head throbbed, and my thoughts were racing around in circles, trying to deny that anything odd had happened with Sam.

I needed a doctor more than ever. But some sense of caution kept me from telling my escort.

The Olds pulled away just as the police flashers began emerging from the snow behind us. When the flashers stopped by the wreck, it was a few moments before the snow reclaimed them, turning blank and gray behind us.

"You've caught up with me," I said, forcing my voice to sound more stable than I felt. "Now what?"

"We stay with you, Mr. Tyler. It's because of you that Mr. Sebastian knows what we're dealing with, and he feels very strongly that you should continue—"

"And continue under Mr. Sebastian's leash. I see."

Mr. Gestapo chuckled at that one. "I see you understand. Mr. Sebastian does not wish you to disappear again."

You bastards, my life is falling apart. How the hell can I collect the pieces with you guys riding my tail?

Worse, I was beginning to think I might need a psychiatrist, and not just for my amnesia. There was a less than subtle threat that if I went to the police, I would find it unhealthy. I doubted that Mr. Sebastian would be any more sanguine about me talking to a doctor.

I racked my stumbling brain for questions I could ask that didn't reveal my ignorance. "What exactly does Mr. Sebastian think we're dealing with?" I asked. "What does he know about what's going on here?"

"An old evil, Mr. Tyler. An evil that goes far beyond

idolatry and false gods. An evil that threatens his daughter's immortal soul."

I shook my head. That kind of language prompted thoughts I didn't need to be having.

Pumping these guys for information wasn't very effective. The Jamaican was only slightly less laconic than Mr. Gestapo, but his answers were just as uninformative. Hiding my amnesia hampered my questioning. Even so, I got a few solid facts.

It was Saturday the fifteenth, and I'd started this hunt for Sebastian's daughter on the first. My ex-wife had been killed on the eleventh, and Sebastian's people lost track of me on the thirteenth—a full day before I'd opened my eyes in a storm sewer.

I asked them annoying detailed questions about what they were doing when, and most of my solid information I got from the context of their answers. The subtext of their answers, never actually stated, was that I'd been under Sebastian's surveillance nonstop from the point I took his job. . . .

"Where are you taking me?" I asked.

"To Mr. Sebastian. He wishes to hear from you what happened between seven on Thursday and nine this evening."

Great. "Why did you take so long to pick me up?"

"I wasn't certain about your identity until you met with Detective Samuel Weinbaum."

Whatever I had been hired to do, I had to lose my escort and get some help. I felt certain that whatever sickness gripped me was pulling me toward something dark. "I have a meeting," I told him.

"What?"

I removed my sunglasses with a shaking hand. I had been wearing them all night, and removing them flooded the world with light. The Olds seemed to drive through a tunnel of glowing white motes. "I have to meet someone at the Arabica."

I saw him glance at me in the rearview mirror. "You were just leaving there with Detective Weinbaum."

I smiled a little weakly. "I'm not supposed to meet him

until closing. He's paranoid about cops, I had to talk to Sam first—"

He kept glancing between the mirror and the road. "I find this sudden revelation somewhat hard to credit, Mr. Tyler."

"The *van* was a sudden revelation. This was just an attempt to get things done with too little time. Or don't you want me to do my job?"

"But why did you and Detective Weinbaum leave—"

"We were going to the hospital to pick up some paperwork."

"What kind of paperwork?"

What kind of paperwork? I was stuck for a moment.

"Mr. Tyler?"

"My wife, damn you," I let my shakiness, frustration, and my anger find my voice. "Blood tests, the contents of her stomach, where they cut into her body. . . ."

I stared at his eyes, and felt my own begin to blur. The frustration and anger were real. I was lying, but my tears were for my wife, and because it hurt not to remember.

He looked away from me. "Forgive me, Mr. Tyler. We'll go to your meeting."

I felt some sense of victory. It was muted because I didn't know what I was going to do when we got there.

Mr. Gestapo stayed with the Olds, and the Jamaican accompanied me inside. Before we entered, I said, "Take a table near the front. I told you this guy's paranoid. If he sees you with me, he's liable to spook."

He didn't look pleased, but he nodded.

I stepped inside, and the lights were so bright that my eyes watered. I replaced my sunglasses. The smell of coffee made me uncomfortably aware of my stomach. I gave the counter a wide berth.

No one seemed to go out of their way to notice me. The blond pagan who had given me a tarot reading wasn't here. The poet and the grad student had abandoned their chess game. There seemed about half the people here that there'd been when I left.

I had until closing to think of something.

I kept walking farther into the coffee shop, hunting for some sort of inspiration. As I closed on the smoking section, I began to notice that there was more to this place than was visible from the front. The room curled around the bathrooms like the tail of a snake, and I followed it to a smoky alcove that was almost a separate room from the rest of the coffee shop. There was a whole other section back here, dim and smoke-filled.

The walls were dotted with fliers back here: a feminist flier announcing a pro-choice rally, some New Age thing about pagan open circles, a Communist tract about the liberation of Peru; but what captured my attention was a poster for a band called "The Ultraviolet Catastrophe" who were playing at the Euclid Tavern.

The concert poster disturbed me. Most of the 8½ x 11 page was taken up by a black-and-white line drawing. It showed a tanning bed, and on it was a cadaverous man, with smoke rising from his mouth and eyes. In his hand, dangling to the ground, he held a bottle of something that could have been a Molotov cocktail.

The artist's interpretation of the band's name, I supposed. It made me uneasy. It made me feel that Death had walked from his tarot card to sit back here with me.

I turned away from the poster to focus on something more relevant. There was a fire exit all the way to the rear. Dull gray metal with a crash bar labeled "for emergency only." It was obviously wired to an alarm, so my escort would know as soon as I ran for it.

But I walked to the door and considered whether or not I could outrun him. I figured that he wasn't going to give me more than half a minute to think about it before he walked back here to check on me. If I was going to do it, I should do it now.

I put a hand on the crash bar—

"Kane? Is that you?"

I turned, surprised. Two people were sitting at a table next to the fire door, a man and a woman. Somehow I hadn't even noticed them when I'd turned the corner. I was farther gone than I thought.

The man spoke again. "Kane? Christ, what happened to you, man?"

I recognized the voice from the phone. "Bowie?"

He nodded. He was tall, thin, and wore a long black ponytail that hung to the small of his back. He wore a black motorcycle jacket and blue jeans. His only concession to the weather outside was a pair of gray wool gloves, under the fingerless black leather ones that covered his palms.

I looked at him and felt familiarity. Not the sense of trust I'd felt with Sam, but I knew that I had dealt a lot with this person recently.

The woman, a redhead who was between seventeen and twenty-one, brought me no sense of recognition whatsoever. She was looking at me, as if she wasn't quite sure of who I was.

Makes two of us, I thought.

"That is you, Kane?" Bowie asked.

"Yeah," I said.

"You look dead," he said.

"Thanks, that makes me feel better." I took the conversation as a cue to sit. The smoke, and the scent of heavy perfume underneath it, made me feel a little dizzy. I wondered when it would stop being disorienting simply having people recognize me. I glanced around, and, as I expected, my shadow had moved to another table, one in view of the alcove I'd retreated to.

"Let me introduce you," Bowie said. "Kane, this is Leia, Leia this is Kane Tyler."

"Oh, the gentleman who finds missing children." She had a high, slightly breathy voice, with a very distinct English accent. She had a habit of touching the collar of her turtleneck when she spoke. "An admirable pursuit." She held out her hand and I shook it absently. It wasn't until I saw a quarter smile cock her lips that I realized she had meant me to kiss it.

I looked back to the Jamaican. He was still there, pretending to read a newspaper. *At least if nothing else, I have met with someone.*

"So how's it going? Haven't seen you in days." He looked at Leia, and they exchanged an unreadable glance. "And what's with the sunglasses?"

I rubbed my temples. "Light hurts my eyes. Lights and mirrors." I glanced up and both of them were staring at me. "I know how it sounds." It sounded like any number of things, the most probable being that I was stoned out of my mind. I was getting to the point where I was going to start to search my own arms for needle tracks. "I need a doctor," I whispered.

Bowie and Leia exchanged glances again, and Bowie asked me, "Why don't you get one?"

I looked at him and then at the Jamaican. This was a noisy place, and I was certain that he was out of earshot. "I need to get away from a friend of mine."

Bowie looked off in the direction of the Jamaican. "What, you need some help?" Bowie laughed, and he leaned in conspiratorially and whispered, "Why sure, man."

He was grinning and I felt compelled to say, "This isn't a game, Bowie."

I felt a light touch on my hand. I looked up at Leia. She stared at me in a way that made me realize just how attractive she was. She had a very seductive whisper. "Mr. Tyler, I am certain that Bowie realizes what is a game and what is a not. You need to seek medical attention." She patted my hand. "We will get you to a doctor."

I felt a slight unease in trusting these strangers, but when it came down to it, everyone was a stranger to me. I looked at her and said, "How?" I had the feeling that if I did make it to an emergency room, the police would become involved.

"We know a doctor who can help you." Bowie was still smiling. "Don't we, Leia?"

She looked at him and shook her head. "My grandfather is a physician." She pulled something out of her purse and slid it to Bowie. "I'll page you when my grandfather's ready and I can pick you up."

She stood up to leave and I whispered, "Wait, what about him?" I cocked my head slightly in the direction of the Jamaican. He was still pretending to read the paper.

"I'll take care of him," she said. "Just, whatever you do, stay with Bowie." Leia walked away from the table.

"What is she going to do?"

Bowie chuckled and said, "You see the same ass I do and you can ask that question?"

She walked past the Jamaican's table, leaned over, and whispered something. I had no idea what she said, but in a matter of a few moments, the Jamaican wasn't paying much attention to our table.

Bowie backed out along the wall, toward the fire door. I saw where he was headed. "What about the alarm?"

He grinned broadly and slipped a tiny pry bar from inside his jacket. "The alarm is set when you push the bar—" He slid up to the door, and I didn't know how the Jamaican could miss him. "—not when you jimmy the latch." He put the pry bar between the door and the jamb and said, "That's the theory anyway."

I watched my shadow, back by the entrance to the smoking section. He wasn't looking our way.

There was a small creak as Bowie levered the bar, but no alarm. The door swung out, and I felt a chill wind hit my face. "Come on," Bowie urged.

I didn't need to be told again.

6

We ran, and for once I was happy for the snow. In the whited-out landscape, we were out of sight of the rear of the coffee shop before we had gone two hundred feet. Even if the Jamaican had come after us the instant we'd left, Leia had bought us enough time to get out the door and lose ourselves in the blizzard.

We ran behind buildings, across side streets and through parking lots, until we came to the intersection of Coventry and Mayfield, a couple of blocks north of where we started. We emerged in the parking lot of a Dairy Mart after jumping a chain-link fence.

Bowie led me across the street and away from the intersection, away from the Dairy Mart, away from all the businesses. Coventry Road on the other side of Mayfield was a residential accumulation of apartment buildings. It was also less well lit, cutting down visibility even more.

"Follow me," Bowie said, darting toward a brick apartment building with me following. Once inside, he opened the door to the basement with the explanation, "Lock's broken."

In a few moments it was obvious that this building wasn't our final destination. We passed a pair of apartments, a laundry room, wove our way through ranks of storage lockers, and came out of a door to the rear of the apartment.

Bowie darted across the asphalt behind the apartment, straight for the garage in back. I followed him out a small door in the rear of the garage.

We walked along an unlit path, calf-deep in snow. To our right were garages facing away from us, to our left was an old chain-link fence. After we'd walked passed two or three garages, I finally spoke, "I think we lost him. Where're we going?"

"I know this chick in East Cleveland, she owes me money. We can crash there till Leia calls and picks us up."

"Uh-huh." I assented without letting any of my reservations show. I needed that doctor. I felt a pain in my gut that never quite went away, combined with a hunger bad enough to make me giddy. If I didn't know better, I'd think I was starving to death.

I don't know any better, do I?

"What's over there?" I asked, waving my hand toward the chain-link. It was impossible to see a few feet beyond the fence; whatever was beyond was unlit.

"Lakeview, I think. We passed the rear of the Jewish place a bit back."

Neither explanation helped me, and I kept glancing off to the left. *Golf Course? Country Club? City Park?* Of course, none of those explained having a separate entity for Jews. It stumped me until I caught sight of a shadow on a hill just beyond the fence. An obelisk stood, a darker shadow against the blowing snow.

"A cemetery," I whispered.

"What?" Bowie asked over his shoulder. He was busy navigating himself over a pile of snow covered garbage someone had dumped back here.

"Nothing," I said as he gave me a hand over a dead refrigerator.

"Bowie, you acidhead!" The "chick" Bowie knew was a little upset with him.

We were a few blocks into East Cleveland, and this building was still on the border of Lakeview Cemetery. We had gone up to the third floor, Bowie's friend had opened the door, looked at both of us, and pulled Bowie into the apartment. I had enough of a glimpse to see short black hair, a tank top, and a livid red skull tattooed on her bicep, before she slammed the door in my face, leaving me alone in the hallway.

I was left to listen to their argument through the closed door, feeling less inconspicuous by the moment.

"Christ, Billi, he's my friend—he's in trouble."

"Do I come to your place so *my* drugged-out friends can crash?"

"He isn't—"

"Have you looked at him? It's almost midnight, in a snowstorm, and he's wearing *sunglasses?*"

The only bright spot was the fact that this was only one of two raging arguments going on in this building, and covering the noise of both was a loud party downstairs. I was the only person in the hall, and I did my best not to look like I belonged to Bowie's argument.

"You can't do this to me, Billi. I need to—"

"I don't."

"You owe *me,* Billi."

Any sane person would have made a graceful retreat by now. But I was feeling worse by the minute. The blizzard outside was rattling the windows loud enough to be heard over the chaos in the apartments, and I did not want to go out there again. The cold felt as if it was sucking the marrow out of my bones.

On top of everything else—

I leaned against the wall and stared at the ceiling. If someone showed for me—police, Sebastian, or Childe—I wouldn't put up much of a fight. It was hard for me to believe that when I had gotten out of that bathtub I had felt fine.

What the hell was wrong with me?

"No, Bowie, you're not holding that over me."

"Billi, if it wasn't for me, you'd be out on the street."

"You know I'm going to pay you back—"

"Yeah, right now."

"Bastard."

My view of the rust-spotted ceiling was blurred through the condensation fogging my sunglasses. A bead of melted snow slid across my field of vision as the door to the apartment opened.

I took off the sunglasses to get my first good look at Bowie's friend, Billi. She was as tall as I was, almost as tall as Bowie. But where Bowie was stick-thin, she had an athlete's body. She was wearing sweatpants and black tank top that might have been sexy if she didn't look so pissed.

"Come in," she said.

I stepped through the door, and she quickly slammed it shut behind me. She turned, as if to launch into another high-volume argument. More raised voices I didn't need; my luck was pushed as it was.

"I'm sorry to put you through this," I said. I did my best to sound conciliatory.

She looked at me as if she was about to say something, then shook her head. "Yeah, whatever." She ran both hands through her hair, a gesture of frustration.

We stood there, paused, in the entryway to her apartment. Neither of us wanted me to be here. "All I need is to rest a moment, talk to Bowie— When our ride calls, I'll be out of your hair."

She looked at me with an unbelieving expression. "Don't even talk to me. I'm doing this for your bastard friend."

I nodded and rubbed my temples. On top of everything else, I was beginning to feel feverish. I tried to tell myself that the apartment was just too hot.

I stumbled inside.

I am going to get some medical attention. I'll be fine once I see this doctor. That was becoming as difficult to believe as everything else.

Our hostess left us in the living room. The place was sparsely furnished, a sagging sofa surrounded by shelves made with cinder blocks and milk crates. Spiral notebooks and loose-leaf paper covered every available surface. I took it all in with a glance, then I collapsed on the side of the evil green sofa that wasn't in line with the windows. The cushion sagged halfway to the ground.

Bowie sat on the arm opposite me. He was perched so close to the edge it looked like he was levitating. I closed my eyes, because without the sunglasses the light in here was giving me a headache.

It was hard not to give in to the feeling of helplessness.

"We need to talk," I said.

Bowie shook his head nervously. "Yeah, yeah— You gotta tell me what happened to you." He took a pause, and, very uncertainly, he said, "Was it Childe?"

The pause in his speech made me feel a little sicker. "Damn it, I don't know! I'm barely keeping what's left of my head together. If you're supposed to be my friend, you tell *me* about this Childe guy."

"I don't have a hell of a lot more—"

"Tell me *everything* you know. I need to get it straight in my head. You have no idea how scrambled my mind is."

"Maybe I do. . . ." He looked at me, and our eyes locked

briefly. "Maybe I don't." He gave me a funny look then he shrugged. "Okay, everything *I* know about the guy. He showed up about five years ago, hanging around the neo-pagan scene here. He'd just show up at their rituals, circles, whatever you call them. Everyone describes him as tall, bearded, English accent. None of the pagans I talked to liked the guy. He gave everyone the willies—bad karma, smelly aura, or something. Half the people I talked to described him as predatory."

"Childe a real name or an alias?" I asked.

Bowie looked at me as if I should have known that. I probably should've. But I was long past my limit as far as feigning an intact cerebellum was concerned.

"Almost certainly an alias," he stared at me. "The pagan crowd has a thing for renaming themselves. Not that this guy was ever part of the pagan crowd."

I stared back. "Not part of the crowd?" I thought of my errant fortune-teller.

"No. The pagans are a good crowd, throw good parties. Childe wasn't there for the parties."

"What was he there for?" I was getting an odd feeling about the conversation I was having with Bowie. Something was happening.

"He was a predator." Bowie had nearly ceased moving, and a lot of the inflection had gone out of his voice. Looking into his eyes, I could see his pupils dilated nearly all the way. If I hadn't been watching him all this time, I could have sworn he had just taken some heavy drug.

"Predator?" I asked.

"It took a long time for them to notice what Childe was doing. See, they had open rituals, circles, whatnot, where anyone could come and see what they were doing. Childe would pick people, the curiosity seekers. Never one of the regulars, the serious pagans."

"Young teenagers, usually girls?"

"Yes. But boys, too. Anyone who left with Childe never returned to any of the public gatherings. Since these were always strangers to the pagans, it took them a long time to notice."

"But they did notice." I had the eerie feeling of knowing everything Bowie was telling me, and the associations weren't pleasant.

"They barred him from their functions—and he disappeared, along with a large number of confused teenagers."

I rubbed my knees and noticed Bowie imitating my motion. He blinked when I blinked. We were breathing in sync. I had to repress an urge to shudder.

What was happening?

"This is where I came in, isn't it?"

"You were looking for this girl, Cecilia. Childe is still the last person to be seen with her, until you made the tape."

"What tape?"

"The tape you made of the sacrifice—"

Memory slammed into me. A *real* memory, as unexpected and violent as a sledge to the back of my skull.

I stand behind a screen of leafless scrub, calf-deep in frozen mud. Ice cuts into the upper parts of my calves. The night is clear, the air sharp, the moon full. I'm facing a wide clearing, a flat spot bordered by steep, snow-dusted hillsides.

Facing me, a hundred yards away or more, is a flood-control dam, an angled wall of concrete sloping up about a hundred feet into the dark. The runoff forms a creek snaking the left side of the clearing. I'm hidden along the shores of that outflow.

I'm aiming my camcorder at the right side of the clearing, toward a smaller hill nestling by the right corner of the dam. There are structures built into the hill—

That's not what I'm looking at. My camcorder has drifted away from my eye, so there is nothing left between me and what I am looking at.

Between me and the small hill is a semicircle of a dozen people. They stand in a patch of snow darkened far beyond the depths of their bluish shadows. The snow they stand in is black.

The blackness smears what portions of their skin I can see. It dots their jackets, their hair, their jeans. The blackness almost completely obliterates the crumpled form they surround, making it no more than a lump in the shadow.

What they surround used to be human. The spreading blackness is its blood.

One of the circle looks directly at me. The blood carves a black hollow in his face. He smiles and I cannot see his teeth for the shadow.

I jerked out of the involuntary memory as if an icicle

had been shoved into my aorta. The image came with a legion of emotions: disgust, fear, and—-it turned my stomach to think of it—something akin to lust. I sat there, shaking, staring into Bowie's dilated impassive eyes, and decided that I must really be insane.

I ran from that scene, I know I ran from it.

But he had seen me—

"What am I involved in?" I said. My voice was barely a whisper.

"Something you don't understand. Even the Le Vey Satanists shy away from these Childe people."

Looking at Bowie scared me. It was almost as if he had become some sort of automaton. It was hard to tell if I was really talking to Bowie, someone who knew me, or if I was talking to some warped part of my own mind. The sense of knowing what he was about to say just before he said it didn't help.

It began to sink in that these people had slaughtered Kate to warn me away. The sick, feverish feeling overcame me again, and I blacked out for a moment.

The next thing I knew was I'd broken eye contact with Bowie, and I was trying to throw up again. I was on my knees on the floor, my stomach trying to slam through my diaphragm, and nothing coming up but a few bits of sour blackness.

"God, you all right?" Bowie's voice sounded normal again. I barely noticed.

He dragged me toward the bathroom. I didn't fight him. As he led me, one bony arm around my waist, he kept talking. "It'll be all right. We're going to get you to that doctor."

The door opened to the bathroom, and suddenly I was faced with a mirror and searing pain. "Lights!" I managed to croak.

Bowie understood me, and hit the light switch, breaking the molten eye contact I had with myself. I turned away from the medicine cabinet and sat on the lid of the john. I waved him away.

His silhouette hovered in the doorway for a moment and he asked, "Are you going to be all right?"

No . . .

"Yes."

He closed the door to the windowless bathroom, leaving me in near-perfect darkness. The only light came from the cracks around the door, filtered through the edge of the hall carpet. It was a dusty, anemic light that carved a thin strip of visibility across the walls.

I was no longer retching, but I felt empty, violated. I felt as if something had been cored out of my being, leaving me with just the husk. I fingered the ring on my finger.

My wife. My daughter. And I couldn't remember. . . .

7

It took me some time before I had gathered the strength to turn on the light. I was careful to keep my back to the mirror until I had replaced my sunglasses. Even with my eyes covered, I winced when I saw my reflection—not from pain, but from the ravages written on my face.

I wasn't looking at the same person who had stepped out of the bathroom of the Woodstar Motel. My face was lined and hollow-looking, worse even than the pale shadowed mask I had seen in the Arabica. My skin wasn't just pale now. It was translucent. The bare bulb above the mirror carved the outline of a skull on my face.

Four hours ago, in the bathroom of the motel, I had looked perfectly fine. An hour ago, maybe less, I had looked in the mirror at the Arabica and saw someone who was ill.

Here I looked like death.

I reached up and touched my cheekbone, under the edge of my sunglasses. My skin felt dry, thin, and cold. As I drew my finger down my face, it left a streak of gray compressed skin behind it. I stared at that strip for a full minute before it returned to the anemic color of the surrounding skin.

Death was a kind word for what I saw in the mirror.

My hands shook, and it began to dawn on me exactly how loose my clothes felt. My jeans were hanging on my hips, the denim jacket I still wore felt like a tent on me, even my holster felt loose. It felt as if I'd lost twenty pounds since the motel room.

I raised my arm so the sleeve fell away from my watch. The watchband—which was snug when I'd donned the watch—was loose on a wrist much bonier than I remembered.

"No way," I whispered. This was an impossibility.

I looked at my hands and saw that my nails had lengthened, just like they were supposed to on a corpse.

I backed away from the mirror and grabbed for the door. My heart felt frozen in my chest. I couldn't sense it beating. And, like during my journey through the storm sewer, every breath I took was a conscious act.

I stepped through the door and into a dim hallway. I took a few steps and leaned on the wall where I could see into the living room. Bowie was there, in a corner, talking on the phone. "Yeah. He's here, locked in the bathroom. . . . Yes, urgent, he looks like shit . . . what? I don't think he's fed at all. Just look at him. . . ."

Hearing him tore at the inside of my head. I wasn't thinking quite right. Whatever help Bowie and his friend were offering, a torn part of my mind was telling me that I was beyond medical attention. Could some doctor who was used to dealing with junkies and overdoses do anything for someone who was turning into a walking corpse?

"Look, just get over here. We'll worry about that when we get him straightened out. . . . Dangerous? . . . When was the last time you were as strung out as he is?"

I was suddenly very afraid of doctors, and what they might find. I needed desperately to get away from Bowie, to get away from the help he was offering. I edged along the wall of the hallway, toward the entranceway, senselessly afraid that Bowie would turn around and see me.

"Yes, that would be easier. . . . If you want me to I will. But all this we've gone through was to avoid that. . . . You know what I mean. . . ."

Somehow I inched all the way to the door. I watched Bowie, and I was frozen for a moment when I saw my reflection in the night-black windows behind the couch. Bowie faced away from me, staring out the glass at the storm.

Either it was the angle, or something he was watching outside, but he didn't notice me. "You didn't tell anyone about him, did you? . . . No, I just noticed this guy standing outsi—"

I stumbled out of the apartment, closing the door on Bowie's conversation.

Even with the sunglasses, the lights in the hallway hurt my eyes. I sagged against a wall, the light a weight on my shoulders. The hall was hot with a heat that didn't reach beneath my bone-dry skin. Cold was deep in the core of my body, as if my chest was packed with snow.

I shook my head and forced myself to walk. I needed to get away. My body was screaming its need at me, and it was a call that was impossible to ignore now.

My eyes refused to focus on the hall ahead of me. My gaze darted to shadowy corners, where the painful light didn't reach. In the darkest corners, the ones of impenetrable black, I could imagine something glistening and wet.

The wall abraded my shoulder like sandpaper, even through the denim, and the sound was like tearing canvas. Snow rattled the windows in the stairwell, like an unwanted visitor scratching to gain entry. . . .

" 'Tis the wind and nothing more,' " I muttered. I almost laughed. I could feel an inappropriate glee surge like a tide, an alien desire to shout the lines from Poe's poem—

"Nevermore," I choked out, grabbing the railing for balance. I was losing it. My mind was as erratic as the snowstorm, feverish neurons firing at random. My grip on the banister was crushing the skin on my hands.

I stared down the center of the stairwell, all four floors to the ground. The sunglasses slipped off my face and tumbled slowly to the concrete below. They broke when they hit, the lenses fragmenting into a dozen pieces of glittering plastic.

I let go of the railing and jerked back as if I'd been hit. My back slammed into the wall behind me. I heard the plaster crack.

I'd been going *up* the stairs.

I looked up the stairs, where I'd been going, deliriously. Now, listening, I could hear it. The argument upstairs—one I had heard upon arriving here—was continuing, or had renewed itself.

I could just see the door of the apartment up at the next landing. Number 401. The door seemed to swell in my vision. Even with my back to the wall, I was still inching toward it. I could feel it from where I was, a half-flight down. It felt as if it was the open door of a blast furnace. Not heat. Anger. Fear.

"You don't play me like that, *bitch!*"

I could make out the voices now, like a tiny river of lucidity in a feverish desert.

"Please, Tony—" Woman's voice cut short by an impact and the sound of something breaking.

I stood in front of door 401. It was razor sharp in my vision, everything else had blurred away. The entire apartment building melted away, everything but the door.

"You think I'm *stupid?*" Tony was shouting through the door. "You think I ain't got eyes?"

"Please—" a timid, frightened voice, nearly inaudible.

"Do you?"

I tried the doorknob.

"I'm going to kill you if you don't tell me who the fuck he is."

I was breathing again, sucking in hot coppery air. Something in that air shriveled my gut into a hard little knot. The door was locked, but that barely mattered to me. My body was an automaton.

I heard a sound behind the door, a strangled gurgle.

My shoulder slammed into the door. It hit hard enough to break bone. It was the doorjamb that broke. Wood splintered, and the door jerked as the security chain caught it. The chain barely held a fraction of a second—

Then it gave.

I stumbled into the living room. The door crashed into the wall, cracking plaster, and slowly swung back shut.

The room was a mess. Chairs were overturned, a glass coffee table was smashed, blinds had been ripped from the windows, and there was a hole in the drywall where someone had thrown a telephone through.

The only light was from a floor lamp in front of me. Sprawled on the ground, its shade askew, it cast crazy inkblack shadows on the walls.

"What the *fuck?*" Tony was shirtless, wearing only a pair of dirty blue jeans. His girlfriend was naked, and only supported by his hand in her hair. There were bruises across her back, and she was bleeding badly from a broken nose. Badly.

The smell of blood was rank in the room. I sucked in the smell, and the colors in the room seemed to get deeper, the light brighter.

"This ain't your business, scarecrow. You better leave or I'll have to fuck you up." His hand left the woman's hair, and she slid to the ground, unmoving.

Her bruises shone like crimson flares, her blood was like a river of fire, but where her blood splattered Tony it was like a black taint of leprosy.

Tony stood before me, muscles flexing in a display of intimidation. "You deaf, motherfucker?"

None of this meant much to me at this point. I was quite mad. I was in free fall. The only thing that anchored me to earth was the magnificent flare of emotion standing before me. Looking at Tony right then was like looking at the sun.

And I was cold inside.

"What you staring at?" Tony took another step toward me. His face was reddening, a tide of blood washing over his expression. *"You been fucking with my woman?"*

It began as an angry shout, but it trailed off as I drew the Eagle from its holster.

"Hey, man, don't do something stupid—"

I leveled the gun at Tony's head. "Once upon a midnight dreary—" The poem came unbidden to my lips, some mad urge to taunt the last shred of my sanity.

I was halfway into the stanza when Tony said, "What the fuck are you—"

I whipped him across the face with the overlong barrel of the automatic. His face snapped to the side, his mouth sprayed blood, and he almost fell to his knees. Almost, but not quite. Tony was a strong kid. Strong, and so full of anger that standing in front of him was like standing in front of a bonfire.

His shocked eyes stared into my own, blood streaming down his face. I could tell his blood from hers. His blood burned my eyes with its inner life, while the places where her blood had touched him were dead, dormant, and black.

The shock in his eyes slowly drained away as he looked at me. I whispered, " 'Tis some visiter,' I muttered, 'tapping at my chamber door / Only this and nothing more.' "

Where the woman's blood had been rivers of fire, the blood on Tony's slackening face was the mouth of an open volcano. Heat, where I was so, so cold inside.

I took a step forward, still quoting, whispering, staring at the transfixed Tony. I lowered the gun because Tony was no longer moving. I was close enough to feel his breath on my face. The only thing separating the two of us was the lamp, a narrow rod on the floor.

Upthrust shadows crossed his face, devouring his eyes, leaving empty wells to stare at me.

"Then this ebony bird beguiling my sad fancy into smiling, / By the grave and stern decorum of the countenance it wore."

I remembered the sacrifice, the memory of a gore-stained face, smiling. Tony's mouth was like that now, blood-covered and black with shadow.

" 'Though thy crest be shorn and shaven, thou,' I said, 'are sure no craven, / Ghastly grim and ancient Raven wandering from the Nightly shore—"

I could feel the same bizarre lust I'd felt during that memory. It struck me full force in the chest, and the groin, an aching hunger that had drawn me to this room even in my delirium. I dropped the gun.

" 'Tell me what thy lordly name is on the Night's Plutonian shore!' "

I raised my arms to embrace Tony. He didn't move.

"Quoth the Raven,"

I stepped on the lightbulb. It popped, plunging the room into darkness.

" 'Nevermore,' " I whispered.

I kissed him, tasting the blood. I felt his heat, and I wanted it. Needed it. The blood that had drawn me here lit a dark fire in my belly. Even as eye contact was broken, and Tony began to move again, I didn't let go.

He bucked and struggled, but from somewhere I found the strength to lift him off the ground. He screamed, but it was muffled by my own mouth. His breath forced life into my own lungs. The fire inside him flared into a nova.

His head whipped from side to side. I felt flesh tear. Warmth spread across me, inside me. As he thrashed, I bit into the heat, drank it in, absorbed it.

Then my delirium snapped, the fever broke, and I became aware that I was holding a corpse. I dropped Tony, now only so much dead weight, and I could think clearly again.

What I thought was, *I'm a fucking nut. I'm a homicidal maniac. I just killed a man.*

I backed away from the scene, until I felt my back pushing the front door completely closed. The room in front of me was dark, but my eyes had adjusted well enough to see both crumpled bodies. Only one breathed.

I tensed myself, and walked back into the living room, stepping over Tony's body. I checked the woman. Even in the dark I could see that she'd been severely beaten. Even as my mind tried to use her to justify what I did, I felt the same perverse lust when I smelled her blood.

As when I smelled Sam's blood.

I knew that in the state I'd been in, if she'd been the only one in this apartment, she would've been the corpse. Tony had died not for any moral decision on my part, but because he had attracted my attention.

What was happening to me?

I stood by the woman and, thankfully, felt myself in control despite the feelings her blood kindled in me.

At first I thought she was out cold, but when I touched her, she winced and curled up tighter into a fetal position. She was sobbing, but so low that I could barely hear her.

"It's all right," I told her lamely. "It's over."

As I whispered meaningless reassurances, I wondered how much she'd seen. By all rights she should've been running away from me, screaming for the police. Right now I didn't much care. I had a totally selfish desire to get her away from Tony's corpse.

It took a little encouragement to get her to stand up; fortunately, she didn't stand up facing the door, or Tony. "That's it," I said. "We've got to get you into bed."

She shivered against my arm, which was around her shoulders, supporting her. "I didn't," she whispered. "I don't do things like that."

"I'm sure you didn't." I maneuvered her down the hall toward what I hoped was the bedroom.

"Where's Tony? I have to tell him—"

"Tony left," I said a little abruptly.

She half-turned toward me, as if suddenly realizing I was there. "Who are you?" A note of panic slipped into her voice.

"A friend," I said. I tried to put all the reassurance I could in the word, and it made me feel like a fraud.

She stared at me through a right eye that was swelling shut. The emotion leached out of her voice as she said, "It isn't his fault."

I turned away and kept her moving toward the bedroom.

"He loves me," she said.

I felt sick.

When I laid her out on her bed, she looked up at me and asked, "What's your name?"

Something inside made me say, "Raven."

She smiled, weakly, and I told her to go to sleep. She did as I told her.

By the time I had gotten her—I still didn't know her name, and I didn't really want to—to bed, I was pretty sure that no one in the building had noticed our little disturbance. With what I had broken in on, if anyone had noticed, they'd ignored it.

Flash of a memory, more an amalgam of images and impressions than any single scene from my past. Women all of them, I had met dozens of them, but they all felt like the same woman. Most were clients who wanted help rescuing a child from an abusive runaway spouse. On a few more agonizing occasions, the women were the ones who illegally swiped the kids. . . .

Sometimes the law is a poor parent.

Every time it's the same question. The neighbors hear the yelling, the fights, the beatings—Why don't they ever do anything?

I rubbed my temples. A corpse was a high price for a piece of my past.

But, thanks to the stoic ignorance of the residents here, there were no police, no ambulances, no one even knocking on the broken door to ask what was wrong.

I turned on a still-intact table lamp, to get a good look at Tony. He had collapsed facedown, and I prodded a shoulder with a boot to flip him over.

I took a step back, and almost fell over.

The lower quarter of Tony's face was gone, flesh ripped down to the bone. Torn flesh ran down the right side of his neck to the collarbone. The bite-marks did not come from human teeth.

I raised my hand to my face, and it came away bloody.

I looked down at myself, and Tony's blood covered me, coating the front of my shirt. Tony looked as if he'd bathed in it. I wanted to feel sick, but the sight failed to raise a single twinge of nausea.

I knelt by Tony's head and examined the bites.

I knew I had been the one who savaged Tony's face, I remembered doing it, but there was no way my teeth could have produced the wounds I saw. I traced a line above the worst of it, drawing my finger across the intact skin over Tony's cheekbone. It left a small trail of blood, and the skin beneath turned an even paler white with compression. The color refused to return—

A realization came to me.

I ran to the bathroom, my eyes lowered until I had my hand up to shade my reflection's eyes.

Under the smears of blood, my face looked perfectly normal. There was none of the pallor that I had seen earlier, none of the paleness, none of the desiccation. My body filled out the clothes I wore. The weakness, the disorientation, all the symptoms that had me in a near-panic, they were all gone.

I was more convinced than ever that I had lost my senses. The physical transformation I had seen in myself was flatly impossible, and the only explanation I had was that I'd been in a state of homicidal derangement ever since I had left the bathroom downstairs.

That's a lie. There's at least one other explanation.

I tried to push the thought away.

Lust for blood, an aversion to mirrors. . . .

It was insane.

Someone placed a Eucharist upon my doorway—

It wasn't as if I'd reacted to it.

That sacrifice, the blood—

"Stop it. Stop it. Stop it," I whispered. My mind didn't stop gnawing on the possibility—the impossibility—but I tried to ignore it as I did what I could to clean the blood off myself.

Fortunately, the mess had confined itself to my shirt-front. The shirt was a total loss, but the rest of my clothes had gotten by with only a few minor spatters. My shoes, face, and hands, I washed off. I was hampered by my reflection and my lack of sunglasses, but it was surprising how easily I became used to not looking myself in the eye.

I left the bathroom, and the bedroom door was still closed. Tony was where I had left him.

I sat, shirtless, on the edge of an askew couch, and considered my options. I had until the woman woke up to do something. The best course—for humanity, if not myself—seemed to be to sit around and wait for the cops, since I appeared to be a psychopath.

For some reason, that option didn't appeal to me.

Neither did just leaving Tony the corpse here. Not only did that woman, whoever she was, have enough to deal with, but if I was serious about avoiding the police, Tony was one hell of a calling card.

So how to dispose of the body? That was the question.

Packing Tony for storage was easier than I expected. It was helped by the fact that, while the corpse was covered by blood, there was none of the spraying I'd have expected from someone missing half his neck—

You know what happened to most of the blood.

—The blood was pretty much confined to Tony and the carpet beneath him. Another lucky break was the fact that the carpet in the entryway was a loose Oriental-style rug resting on the wall-to-wall, and the blood hadn't yet soaked through.

I managed to find duct tape in the kitchen, and rolled Tony and my bloody shirt up in the carpet. It wasn't perfect—his legs stuck out below the knees—but it managed to get most of the evidence in a single package.

I found a garbage bag and stuck that over Tony's dangling feet.

Then I went through the apartment collecting his spoor. It was her apartment, so finding Tony's possessions wasn't too difficult. In a few minutes I'd found his shirt, boots, wallet, keys, and a handful of cheap male jewelry. Most of it was in the bedroom, but the woman slept so deeply that most of my caution in collecting the remains of Tony's life was unwarranted.

Tony's car keys were important. I'd been hoping—praying—for the keys. I couldn't exactly call a cab to pick up me *and* the corpse.

The last thing I retrieved was my gun. Picking it up brought home the complete insanity of what had happened. I had dropped the gun to *bite* the bastard.

What I could make no sense of was that he had *let me*. If he had had any sense at all, he should've dived for the gun the second I'd dropped it. But he had stayed there, fixated on me—

Just like Bowie. . . .

I was avoiding that line of reasoning, so I looked out the kitchen window, searching for Tony's car.

8

It wasn't easy moving Tony by myself. It didn't matter how strong I was, or how strong I thought I was. Carrying a corpse was different than carrying any other two-hundred-pound object. It wasn't just dead weight I was dealing with, but it was loose, jointed, dead weight that insisted on bending and sagging toward the ground. Picking Tony up was like trying to swing a two-hundred-pound sack of wet cement over my shoulder.

I felt incredibly exposed as I descended the fire escape. Even though, by my watch, it was after two in the morning. Even though the snowstorm was still whiting-out everything beyond a hundred feet. Even though I couldn't see another soul. I felt as if I were being watched during every step I took.

It was a harrowing descent. The metal fire-escape had accumulated a layer of snow over a coating of ice. Each step was uncertain and felt as if my foot would slide out from under me. Tony didn't help. Every time a gust rattled through the metal around me, Tony would catch the wind and try to pull me off my feet. Ice motes buffeted my face, but I barely felt them.

In the lot behind the building, everything was blue-tinted monochrome, black, blue-grays, and whites. The cars were hard to discern. A half a dozen sat back here, and all I had to go on were Tony's keys, which went to a Chrysler. Instinct led me to the large, unaerodynamic pile of snow that had no hubcaps.

With one hand, I wiped snow away from the rear of my chosen car, and saw it was a Plymouth Duster. In a final test I fumbled out Tony's keys from my pocket, trying not to let him tumble into the snow.

I shoved the key into the ice-coated lock on the trunk.

It slid in, but wouldn't turn. In frustration, I forced it. The key turned and the trunk popped open.

It was Tony's Plymouth.

With a sense of relief, I let Tony's corpse roll off my shoulder and into the trunk. The car was an old model, '76 at the latest, and the cavernous trunk swallowed all of him without complaint. I slammed the trunk shut, thankful that no one had seen me.

My thanks came too soon.

"Sir, you show some instincts that will stand you in good stead."

I whipped away from the trunk, to look for the speaker. I heard him before I saw him. It may have been because of the clothes he wore. It was a few seconds before I saw a white-suited figure emerging from the blowing snow. It was disorienting to watch. I faced the rear of the apartment, and I could see it barely as a shadow within the blue-gray wall of wind-whipped snow.

The speaker appeared between me and the apartment, as if he were emerging from an invisible distance, as if the apartment building had never been there.

"Who are you?" I asked.

"My chosen name is Gabriel." He spoke with a thick Southern accent. He was past middle age; he looked to me to be in his late sixties or early seventies. His hair was white, and blew around his shoulders. He wore a white suit that was more fit for the Bahamas than Cleveland. He walked with a long cane whose shaft was silvered. He had large hands, the hands of a pianist. They completely enveloped the head of the cane when he leaned upon it.

For a long time I stared at him. Then I asked, "What are you doing here?"

Gabriel smiled. "Ah, it has been a long time since any youth had the temerity to question my right to be anywhere. It is my question you ask, sir. One I would be addressing to you—" He motioned to the trunk with his cane. "—if I had not already known your business."

I began to look for a likely escape route. Unfortunately, all of them—the building, the driveway, and the alley opposite the driveway—led past Gabriel. He didn't look threatening, but there was something about his bearing that made me loath to test him. "So you've called the police already?"

Gabriel laughed. "If you were not so obviously ignorant, I should take that question as an aspersion on my honor. I keep my Covenants, sir. Even with those who know no Covenant."

I shook my head; none of this was making any sense to me. "What are you doing here?" I repeated. "What are you talking about? What's going on here?"

Gabriel frowned slightly. "Learn some respect for your elders, Mr. Tyler—"

"You know me?"

He pointed his cane at me. "Keep your peace for a moment and perhaps your questions might be answered. Now, may I speak without interruption?"

I nodded.

"I knew of a man, a man named Kane Tyler. This man was a hunter of children. In time he was hunting one of the Covenant, the one known as Childe. It has come to be that those of the Covenant hunt Childe as well."

He paused for a time and I nodded, still not understanding all of what he was saying. "So you're looking for Childe, too?" After a beat, I added, "Sir?" There was something about him that did command respect.

Gabriel smiled. "Childe has allowed his blood to disregard the Covenant, and for that he must be found and disciplined."

I shook my head. "I don't understand. What's this Covenant that you talk about?"

Gabriel looked at me for a long time. "Who is your master that would send you into the world without that knowledge at least? Is it Childe that spawned you?"

I stared at him.

"You are ignorant, sir." Gabriel took one step, and suddenly he had closed the distance between us. One of those pianist's hands gripped my chin, cradling my face. He held his face within an inch of my own, staring into my eyes. "Do not feign ignorance that you do not possess. I am lord of my blood, and you may not deny who it is that owns you."

"I don't know what the fuck you're talking about!"

Gabriel grimaced, and I saw anger burn there. It was an anger that never left the eyes, but it was a fury that made Tony's bonfire rage nothing more than a birthday candle.

My feet lifted off the ground before I realized what was

happening. "Witless thrall!" Gabriel said as he flung me toward the apartment. I was in the air nearly a full second before my back slammed into the railing of the fire escape. My head snapped back with an impact that felt as if it broke my neck. I tumbled forward, and fell six feet to land face first in the snow. The impact had stunned me so much that I couldn't raise my arms to protect myself. My face slammed into the snow-covered asphalt.

I lay there for a long time, feeling warmth trickle down my cheek.

"Get up." I felt a boot push my shoulder, turning me over.

After that impact, I shouldn't have been able to move, much less get to my feet. To my own surprise, I found myself standing. I stood, shaking, as the wind froze the blood on my face.

Gabriel held his cane in both hands, horizontal at belt height. I could finally see the head of the cane, the head of a serpent or dragon worked in pewter. Set in the serpent's eye was a red stone, a ruby at odds with the blue-gray world around me.

"You have exhausted what license youth and ignorance grant you. I am not here to answer your questions, and you have no leave to challenge me. The only respect due you is the respect due your master." He twisted the head of his cane and slowly withdrew a blade from it. "You *will* tell me who your master is, and your chosen name. If you do not, your master shall find his thrall less than worthy."

I took a step back, toward the building. I reached for my gun, but the holster was empty.

Gabriel shook his head. "You disappoint me. Perhaps I was wrong about your instincts." He kept walking toward me. "Many as young as you would have abandoned the body after such a feeding. I must deal with such violations too often." He raised the blade of his cane to my neck. It felt even colder than the wind. It was sharp enough that I could feel skin part under the pressure. I feared that he would open my jugular.

"Answer me. Do not force me to mark you."

I gasped. "I don't know what to tell you. I don't know what you're asking. My name is Kane Tyler, and if I have a master, I don't know about it."

"If you lie . . ." Gabriel stared at my face, and then at where the blade met my throat. He removed the sword and held it up so that a bead of my blood rolled down its edge. My own blood looked black in the dark, nothing like Tony's.

Gabriel turned the blade, examining the blood. His nostrils flared and he touched the edge briefly to his lips.

He stood there immobile for a moment, looking at me. Then he took a handkerchief from his breast pocket, wiped his mouth and the blade, and replaced the blade within the cane.

He then shocked me by making a low bow. "Sir, it seems the humble servant before you has done you a wrong."

"What . . . ?" The question refused to form itself.

"You are of free blood. I ask your pardon, sir. Such prodigies are rare." He withdrew a card from his breast pocket. "This is not the place for our discussion, and I have withheld you too long. Please come to me. Childe must be found."

He held out the card, and I took it. There was no name on it, only an embossed address, and a single phone number. As I read the card, Gabriel said, "Perhaps then I might answer some of your questions and redeem myself for this unfortunate business."

"Wait, I have some questions now. The first of which—"

I raised my head and Gabriel was gone.

"—why the sudden change of heart . . . ?" I whispered to the snow.

The only sign of Gabriel's presence was the card he had handed me, and a pair of footprints that were already filling with snow. I wiped the snow off my watch and checked the time.

It was 2:30.

I wondered what had happened with Bowie and Leia. I also wondered what their doctor would have found if I'd gone to his office. With all of the reference to blood, insane as the idea was, I was beginning to suspect that the doctor would have found something very unusual.

I pocketed the business card and walked back to Tony's Plymouth. The keys were still dangling from the trunk. Also sitting on the trunk was my Desert Eagle.

*   *   *

Tony's Plymouth had seen better days. Its left rear fender occupied the back seat. Fortunately, it started. I was nervous as I pulled the Plymouth out onto Coventry. I was the only vehicle on the road. I felt as if I were driving under a follow-spot. All I needed was a bumper sticker, "Body in Trunk."

What now? I asked myself as I drove away from the apartment.

Everything was different now. I'd killed a man. I had little memory of my life before this, but I could feel, in my gut, that I was not a killer. I had carried a badge, carried a gun, but I wasn't a killer. . . .

The first real memory of Kate hit me—

"Are you sure you want to do this?" she asks, massaging *the back of my neck. She's using the tone of voice that asks, "You're not just doing this because I want you to, are you?"*

I shake my head, massaging the scar on my chest. "I'm getting disability leave now. I think it's time for me to get out."

A guilty silence fills our bedroom. Kate thinks she's driving me to this decision, and I can't do much to dissuade her. Still, I try. I take her hand and turn to face her.

"Look, I know it's what I've done for fifteen years. But I still see that kid's face before I shot him—"

"He tried to kill you," Kate objects. Her mouth is downturned and I know that she could never accept me as a cop again, not after what we've been through. She says that she'll support my decision, but I know if I put my life on the line like that again, she couldn't handle it.

I hug her. "I don't want to face those decisions any more, I don't want to see any more kids' faces when I sleep."

I gripped the steering wheel hard enough that the whole assembly was shaking. I could remember shooting the kid who put a thirty-two slug through my left lung. I could remember his head snapping back.

Worse, I could picture the funeral. I could picture his mother as clearly as if she were sitting next to me. She hadn't cried, or cursed me. That would have been easy. That must have been what I had been looking for, attending the funeral within days of my own hospitalization. All she had done was sit still, staring straight ahead, blind to everything but her son in that coffin.

Tony's family wouldn't have even that.

My thoughts were jarred when the Plymouth jumped the curb. I had to brake in the middle of a snowdrift. I looked madly around for cops. But any cops were lost far behind the blowing snow. I looked at my watch, and I felt another wave of memory—

"Happy Birthday, Dad." Gail smiles at me. In that moment I see so much of her mother in her, in the long red hair, in the freckles, in the smile. The wrapping falls away from the little crystal box that holds the watch.

"Hey," I said, "are you trying to say something here?"

"Try not to keep so many late nights," Kate says from behind my right shoulder.

"We miss you, Dad," Gail says and hugs me.

—I'd already been driving over an hour.

I cursed my memory. I cursed it for showing me fragments of a life that I could now no longer go back to. The man named Kane Tyler had died in that apartment as surely as Tony had. The man driving Tony's Plymouth was a cipher that I knew nothing about, other than that this man was capable of tearing out the throat of a stranger.

I rocked the Plymouth back and forth, freeing it from the mess I'd put it in. When I got it free, I drove the car west, toward the city.

9

By four in the morning, I'd driven out of the snow and out under a clear sky. The layout of the city was coming back to me, and that gave me some hope—good or ill—for the rest of my memory.

The city slid by me on skids of gray ice. I was surrounded by the deadest part of the night. Tony's Plymouth was the only vehicle on the road other than the occasional snowplow.

The city was an eerie landscape painted in cold colors. White streetlights, bluish snow, purple sky, and buildings made of gray and black shadows. The only warm color I passed came from the traffic lights.

Cold, still, and empty. Even the snow had stopped moving for the night. It gave me a weird sense of superiority to be out at this time of night, as if the city were mine, as if I owned the broad expanse of Euclid unrolling before the Plymouth. It was a spooky feeling, and one that felt as if it came from the same part of my mind that had made me go into apartment 401. That made me nervous, and I turned on the radio.

Some college station was playing an album side from Blue Oyster Cult, *Fire of Unknown Origin*. It fit my mood perfectly. I drove through an empty Downtown accompanied by "Joan Crawford."

I'd spent too much time in this car. I needed to dispose of it and the body. I think I'd only delayed the inevitable for this long because the destruction of the evidence of my crime was as irrevocable as killing Tony in the first place.

At this point there was still some dim possibility that I could argue that Tony's murder was justified, that I was protecting the woman. I did not believe it, but if I turned to the police with that argument, I was still part of human society.

Destroying Tony's body would be an admission that I believed that I'd left that society.

Instead of crossing the Cuyahoga River, I drove Tony's Plymouth down into the Flats. I didn't drive toward the darkened restaurants and bars lining the mouth of the river. I drove away from the development, toward the remains of industry.

I took a turn that carried me under a bridge. Under the snow the tires of the Plymouth left the pavement. I paralleled a rusted chain-link fence that separated what used to be a road from a field dotted with piles of broken asphalt and old tires. I pulled to a stop in a lot dominated by one of the massive pillars supporting the bridge above me. Despite the storm earlier, there was little snow here.

I wiped off the wheel and stepped out of the Plymouth.

Behind the field of debris, a broken hillside rose toward the city. Everywhere down here were piles of concrete, fallen from the bridge above as if it were some gigantic creature shedding old skin.

Further up, where the road finally ended, sat a broken gate in the fence. Just inside was a small brick shack, no more than a shell. The windows were glassless, and it was roofed only by a single girder as ocher as the bricks that supported it.

I stood in a world as dead as a graveyard.

I opened the trunk and searched my pockets for Tony's possessions. I tossed his watch, wallet, and his jewelry into the trunk with Tony, after wiping them for prints. His lighter, a gold Zippo with an eagle engraved upon it, I kept—wrapped in a wad of tissue paper.

" 'Yet if Hope has flown away . . .' "

I left the trunk open, and backed away from the right rear fender of the Plymouth. I gave it a decent clearance, twenty or thirty feet. Then I looked around for anyone observing me. The only witness I saw was a lone crow perched on a metal post by the fence. It seemed to be watching me.

I looked away from the bird and out over the black waters of a river that had once burned. Across the river, a few lone smokestacks released white smoke; one black chimney breathed fire. The sky was black and starless, the only lights red ones—ruby diadems crowning the smokestacks. I stood upon the night's plutonian shore, if I stood anywhere.

The night was quiet, the air still, cold and sharp as a blade. I drew the Desert Eagle out of its holster. I drew the slide, checked the action, and leveled it at a spot behind the right rear tire.

I braced my wrist and fired.

The shot echoed, its flash illuminating the underside of the bridge. I saw there, in an instant, that the girders under the overpass were massed with crows. Hundreds, maybe a thousand, of the birds took wing in response to the gunshot. They exploded out above me, a black cloud cawing a demonic avian chorus.

For a moment I was deafened amid their roar, and by the sound of their wings tormenting the wind. Then, like a dream, the birds were gone, slipping through the girders of the bridge, into the sky, like a handful of sand slipping into the ocean.

When they were gone, I could hear the sound of liquid spilling to the ground. I lowered my gaze. My bullet had torn a hole through the gas tank of the Plymouth. The smell of gasoline sliced though the air toward me. Under the rear fender, a stream of liquid melted the snow. Gas dripped from the bottom of the fender and from the bumper.

The ground sloped in my direction, and a snake of melted snow was weaving its way toward me.

I holstered the Eagle and took out Tony's lighter.

The Zippo's flame was small and blue. It danced weakly in the little wind the night had left. The flame ignited the tissue wrapping the lighter, and I tossed it all into the gasoline. The tissue flew off toward the sky, but the lighter landed in the puddle. The little blue flame escaped and raced to embrace Tony and the Plymouth. When they met, the gas tank unrolled itself toward the sky with a burst of ruddy light and hellish wind.

When the smoke reached the bridge, I was already walking away.

It was after four-thirty when I walked out of the Flats. I was cold, alone, and empty. I had walked all the way to

Public Square before I heard the sirens responding to my conflagration. I couldn't feel much of anything other than fatigue and a sense of loss.

Where did I have to go? What was it that I could do?

Everything seemed to be falling apart, slipping away from me. Things had spun out of control. I needed things to stop, to slow down, if only for a while. I wanted to go home, to rest.

I wanted to go home, but I had no idea where home was, or if I still had one.

I needed to find a phone book. The night was leaking away, and I was afraid of the coming dawn. However, I had some little time left. When I reached the intersection central to Public Square, I saw the lights in the lobby of the Terminal Tower. The transit station down there was open, and somewhere inside would be a phone.

By five, I had an address and I had a cab.

The West Side was more familiar to me than the Heights area. I knew the streets the cab rolled down. I knew when the cab was just around the corner from the house where I had lived the past ten years of my life.

The last five, alone.

I told the cabby to drop me off a fair distance back from the intersection of two one-way streets. I paid him and stepped out into a virgin expanse of snow. The cab continued down the street, its taillights the last thing to vanish as it turned away, looking for a main road.

I stood alone on the street for a long time. The cross street ahead of me was Allan Drive, a three-block-long street that was barely a lane wide. Just looking at it caused tiny flares of memory—

Under the snow, the street is brick and hell on the suspension.

The green house on the corner is home to an old woman with way too many cats.

Kate doesn't like the neighborhood, but she wanted her own house since Gail was born, and she bears it with the same grace that she bears my profession.

Gail caught the bus to the high school on Detroit, three blocks away.

Until Kate left me, that is.

Fragments, disjointed facts. They hit like tiny sparks from an abused piece of machinery. I stared at the wedding band on my finger. Why did I keep it? Did I have some hope of one day coming home and finding Kate there . . . ?

Something is wrong—

I stared at the ring. Kate had left me five years ago. Five long years. I had kept the hope that she'd return. Just like I had kept this ring. . . .

I come home, and I see the house. I know something is wrong—

A memory wanted to come, a memory that filled me with a sick dread. I wanted to call back the taxi. Call it back and have it take me to someplace else, anywhere else.

But the taxi was gone, and I was committed.

I looked up and down Allen Drive. I couldn't see my house from here, and every other building was darkened and closed. There was a dim threat I felt, unfocused, trapped within my frozen memory. The feelings made me cautious, made me worry that my house might be watched.

There was no reason to stake out my house, but I worried. If there were police here, they had yet to see me. I approached from the back. Somewhere a dog barked at me.

The way the backyards and driveways interconnected on these narrow blocks, it was easy for me to approach my house from the other side of the block. The neighborhood became increasingly familiar as I walked up my neighbor's driveway toward the back of my house. When I reached my backyard, I froze for a minute. No footprints marred the snow, no tire tracks marred the driveway. Everything was still, silent. The wind had ceased.

Recognition struck like a blow. From the gutter sagging beneath the ice to the too-loose storm windows, I knew this place. I knew the kitchen window that was painted shut, and the half-assed addition someone had tacked to the back porch in the fifties. I knew that the second-floor window facing me was for the rear stairs, and if the light were on, I would see the top of the bathroom's door frame. I knew Gail's room overlooked the driveway, Kate's and mine overlooked the front of the house and my office was opposite Gail's room. I knew the glass block on the basement windows was expensive as hell, but necessary since the darkroom equipment in the basement was even more so.

I knew the attic was reached by a trapdoor that stuck in summer and shouldn't be opened unless you really liked the feel of fiberglass insulation on your skin.

Even as I remembered, I had to revise the memory, correct for the history of the past five years. Nothing was Kate's and mine anymore, except maybe Gail—and she was more Kate's. Gail's room was storage now. . . .

I had walked up on the porch, feeling something wrong. I was on the porch before I realized that all the shades were drawn. I like the light, I almost always leave the shades open. The door—

The memory left me again.

"God," I whispered.

I approached the rear of the house. When I reached the back door, I stopped. Covering the door and the jamb a few inches above the doorknob was a yellow sticker— "Sealed by Order of Cleveland Police Department."

The door was locked, and I didn't like the implications of that sticker. Something *was* wrong here, and not just within my errant memory.

I was about to try breaking in, but I remembered something about the back of the house. I walked away from the door, about ten feet to my left, stopping in front of a mound of snow that sloped against the rear of the house. I started kicking the snow away to reveal a pair of storm-cellar doors. These didn't need a key. The sloping doors were shut with a combination lock.

There was no police seal here, but I had to kick ice away from the lock before I could open it.

While I crouched, I had a few nasty minutes when I couldn't remember the combination. I squatted, fingers numbing on the metal lock, for close to five minutes before I began turning the dial. The numbers finally came, one at a time. With the ice, the lock needed to be forced, but the numbers were right, and I managed to tug it open.

I slipped it off and dropped it into the snow.

The door came open with the grinding sound of breaking ice. The opening revealed concrete steps descending into a darkness the moon didn't reach. At this point, familiarity should have been reassuring, but it wasn't.

The front door is ajar. With the shades drawn, none of the morning light reaches inside the house. I had run here, driven madly, expecting something. I draw my thirty-eight—

I had been driven to come here, driven by fatigue and an aching hole of a memory. But now, as more memories came leaking to the surface, the idea of entering the house filled me with nauseating dread. I felt an urge to run.

I stepped down into the storm cellar.

My eyes quickly adjusted to the feeble light down here. At the bottom of the stair was a flimsy door, unlocked. I stepped through into my basement.

The feeling of familiarity was overwhelming. The past fogged this place, like a choking perfume—a perfume hiding an uglier scent.

I looked around without benefit of the light; the bluish moonlight streaming through the glass block was enough to see by. I found the darkroom I expected, in a walled-off corner of the basement. I stepped in and finally had to turn on a light to see.

I groped in the dark and finally hit a switch that flooded the room with red light, as if the room had been sunk in blood. In addition to the trays, the chemicals, and everything else, there should have been pictures in here. Negatives and prints should have been here. Someone had taken them.

Sebastian's men? The police?

The police, I thought as I found traces of fingerprint powder on one of the trays.

What was on those pictures? Why were the police dusting here for prints? The ugly feeling grew in my stomach. Something bad was going on here.

I push the front door open with my foot. I sweep the living room with the gun. It's dark and empty. I step in to cover the dining room—

I forced myself to act calmly, to move deliberately. I knew I was nervous about what was going on. If there were important pictures, I knew that I'd stash them somewhere.

I knelt down, almost unconsciously, and pulled a plastic jug of developer out from under the table. Underneath it was a small drain. The grate came up easily. A layer of scummy water sat an inch under the grate. I stuck my fingers in, not quite sure what I was feeling for, but I knew it when I touched plastic.

I pulled a slimy Ziplock bag out of the drain. It came out with a slurp. Inside was a plastic film canister. I had no idea what was inside it, but I peeled open the bag and removed the container. I opened the cap on one and saw what I'd expected to see: rolled-up negatives. I put the cap back on and pocketed it.

I shoved the empty bag back in the drain, and replaced everything else as I'd found it.

I was stalling. Eventually, I killed the light and headed upstairs.

Halfway up the flight, I had to stop. The feeling of dread was like a weight holding me back. By the time I had reached the door to the kitchen, it seemed to take an hour just to reach up and turn the knob.

I could smell it even before the door opened. It tore into me, ripping the shroud from a memory—

"You should not pry into things which are not your business." The voice on the end of the phone had been female, barely. The sound was harsh, violent. There were scratching noises in the background.

I'm remembering the call as I sweep the living room with my revolver. My pants are still muddy. My camcorder is back at my car. The call had come on my cell phone as I'd driven madly away from Lakeview.

The voice had said, "You are being punished. Then you will die." There were moans in the background, someone in pain, barely conscious.

I am remembering the moans as I turn, covering the dining room. I am remembering the inhuman laugh that was on the other end of the phone—

The door to the kitchen sticks on something, but I keep on pushing. The smell hits full force.

I remember the noises, wet noises, as my eyes adjust to the gloom shrouding the dining room—

The smell is of old blood.

10

I stepped into the kitchen, unable to separate memory from the scene before me.

I stumble into the kitchen, breath ragged and dizzy from the scene in the dining room. I'm frozen at the chaos in here. The overturned dishwasher, the broken table, the dented stove— Everything ignited fragments of my weak memory. *Blood is everywhere. Pooled on the stove, speckling the table, coating the sink. Stab marks*—now dutifully circled by the forensics team—*gouged holes in the walls, as if the house itself were being attacked, bleeding*—central to it all now was the surreal contribution of the police, the strings leading to blood spots on the walls. Their attempt to map flying blood cast the kitchen in a giant spiderweb.

"Kate," I managed to croak out.

I edged away from the kitchen, filled with a sour rage that was nearly as sickening as the carnage in front of me.

I backed all the way into the dining room before I turned away from the scene. When I turned away, the rage burned itself out, blown out by the impact of the full memory, complete and ugly.

Ever since she had left me, I had the dim hope of someday coming home to her. Childe had granted my wish.

I barely escape that scene in Lakeview. I drive away from the scene of that carnage, numbed. Then the car phone rings. It beeps insistently. I don't want to pick up the phone, but my hand reaches for it.

"Kane," says the ragged voice on the other end of the phone. I don't know who it is—the voice is distorted beyond recognition—but I know what *it is, what is represents.*

"You killed her," I whisper.

"Hardly," the voice laughs at me. "You should not pry

into things which are not your business." The voice on the end of the phone is barely female itself. The sound is harsh, violent. I hear scratching noises in the background.

"You aren't going to get away with this:"

Laughter, endless mocking laughter. Then the voice tells me, "You are being punished. Then you will die."

I hear moans in the background, someone in pain, barely conscious. I can almost recognize the voice.

"Come home, Kane Tyler, someone is waiting for you." She hangs up.

I race the car into the dawn, in a near panic. I know what waits for me, but I keep some desperate hope that I can make it in time. As I drive, I call the police, then I call Sam.

Something is wrong at my house.

I arrive before the police do. I walk up on the porch. All the shades are drawn. The front door is ajar. With the shades drawn, none of the dawn light reaches inside the house.

I draw my thirty-eight, and push the door open with my foot. I sweep the living room with my revolver.

I remember the noises, wet noises, as my eyes adjust to the gloom shrouding the dining room.

The strength goes out of my legs. My breath catches in my throat and I almost drop the revolver. Blood is everywhere. The air is so rank with the smell that my brain doesn't want to identify it.

"Kate," I manage to croak out. Breathing in the blood-tainted air makes me sick. My stomach wants to rebel, but after what I've already seen tonight, all it can do is spasm quietly.

They had crucified her on the dining room table. The violence was so bad that I could not be certain if she had been alive when they had tied her there.

The memory dropped me to my knees. It was so vivid that I almost saw the body on the table there in front of me. Even though Kate had long ago been taken away.

In the moonlight it was hard to make sense of the stains, the strings, the marks left behind by the policemen in their investigation.

The stains formed a vaguely cruciform outline on the table. Markings by the police gave it a human shape. The table was scarred, knives perhaps, maybe even claws. I saw wires that could have bound legs and arms. Some of the strings led up to bloodstains on the ceiling.

"No." I whispered again, trying not to see it.

The memory came, in incoherent, unwanted pieces. My gaze fixated on the head of the table, where a single beam of moonlight picked out a shape. I stared at it, trying to make sense of the tiny black knot in the black bloodstain. I edged around the table, irrationally drawn to it.

When my back was to the window, I finally understood what it was. I stared at a finger-sized clump of my wife's hair, glued to the table by her own blood.

I had a memory from after the medics came, when they had finally moved the body out of the tacky blood. I had seen her head nod limply as that knot of hair was tugged from her skull. No one had seemed to notice.

I had loved this woman, loved her past the end of our marriage. How could I grieve for her with my wounded memory? I finally began to cry.

I still have a daughter, I thought.

If anything, that made things worse. Gail had lost her mother because of me, and she was in the process of losing her father. Not only was my memory crippled, but there was blood on my hands. I was a murderer.

A murderer, and maybe something else.

I wanted to see her—desperately—but forcing me upon her after what had happened to me would be needlessly cruel. Better that she should bury me with her mother.

I reached out to touch the table, gripped by a torrent of conflicting emotions—grief, anger, and a hollow sense of failure. My finger brushed a strand of long red hair.

A murderer, and maybe something else.

Why did I insist on maintaining that possibility? Was it some sick way to moderate the guilt of Tony's death? Thinking that was sabotaging my own sanity. Insisting that I was infected by some supernatural entity was insane.

But if it was insane, why did all my feverish symptoms, the delirium, the *hunger,* all vanish when I had killed Tony? I had physical symptoms. I had *needed* that blood. I had needed it when I was in that accident with Sam.

I walked out of the dining room, swamped with fatigue.

Behind the blinds in the living room I could see the sky lightening with the coming dawn. I had a reaction to the light, a visceral fear that I couldn't damp by telling myself it was irrational.

I forced myself to walk to the front windows, and separated the slats of the blinds with a shaking hand. Through the blind I stared at the sky, which had lightened from purple to a deep aqua.

The fear flared into a barely controlled panic. My hand dropped from the window and I turned away. I faced the dining room and felt a different fear grip me. I had stopped breathing again, just as I had in the sewer. I had no idea when I had stopped. I had suffered too many shocks in the past few minutes for me to pick out one that could have knocked the breath from me.

If that insane possibility were right, if I were somehow the walking dead, did I *need* to breathe?

I ignored the panic, and kept holding my breath. I waited for my chest to tighten, for my body to protest the lack of oxygen. I waited for my vision to darken and for a feeling of giddiness.

Nothing.

I stood, and waited for five minutes, then ten, as the room around me began to lighten slightly with the approaching dawn. The light began to take a yellowish tint.

Something had happened to me. Something that had driven me to tear the throat out of a man and drain his blood. Something that had removed the necessity for breathing.

I had yet to see daylight, ever since I crawled out from underground. I turned to see the predawn glow shining from behind the blinds, and I felt the terror of having to.

I needed to get away from that light.

It was insane to think what I was thinking. But it was either that, or I had lost the ability to trust anything that happened. And, if I had completely lost touch with reality, what difference did it make what I thought? If I had lost touch with reality so completely, I could believe I was a leprechaun for all it mattered.

Of course, no one made movies about leprechauns bursting into flames and crumbling to dust at the first touch of direct sunlight.

I couldn't leave this house. And there was only one place here I knew the rays of the sun wouldn't reach. I ran through the remains of my dining room and kitchen and took the stairs to the basement two at a time. It was no longer hypothetical. I had stopped playing what-if with myself. I had stopped telling myself that the idea was an insanity.

I dove into the black womb of my darkroom knowing what I had become. As the rush of fatigue crashed over me, I felt the card in my pocket and knew that I was going to talk to Gabriel.

Somewhere in the not-quite-sleep that gripped me, I remembered things. Remembered them, or dreamed them. Maybe both.

The guy I'm talking to is known as Switz. Not his real name. The name has something to do with his excessively Aryan appearance. That's my guess at least. He's blond, blue-eyed, and has a motto in German Gothic tattooed on his bicep. I suspect he's a Nazi, but I don't know and don't ask.

He's not a friend, and I'm not talking to be social.

We're standing in a parking lot somewhere in Richmond Heights. Behind us is a vast expanse of snow-covered Mall, after hours, empty. We're standing behind Switz's car, a brand-new white Mercedes sedan that's at odds with his military-surplus clothing. Switz has just pocketed a large sum of money.

He pulls out the keys and opens the trunk. Inside is an aluminum briefcase covered in black vinyl, which he also opens—

"There she is, Kane. Mother of all handguns, the biggest thing I got."

The gun is massive, a forty-five on steroids. I pick it up, heft it. It seems almost cartoonishly large in my hands. "Fifty-caliber? You have shells for this?"

"Fifty-cal magnum." Switz nods at the case, "I've enough shells." He smiles. "What you planning to drop with that thing?"

I clear it, check it, put it back in the case. "You don't want to know, even if you'd believe me."

Switz snorts, "Whatever it is, you shoot it with that, it'll drop."

"*I hope so.*" *There's a trembling note on my voice.* "*Is it clean?*"

"*Clean? It hasn't even been fired.*"

"*Where's it from?*"

"*A collector gave himself a 12-gauge lobotomy. His estate got thinned a little. This was still in the packing crate when I got it.*"

I nod and close the briefcase and take it. "*Wish me luck,*" *I whisper.*

"*With that thing you don't need luck.*"

Kate and I are having one of our uniquely formal lunches, something that has become a tradition with us since she left me. Dinner was too significant a meal, so it was always lunch at some inexpensive restaurant downtown.

Today we're in the Arcade downtown, sitting at a table next to the mezzanine railing. The light from the glass ceiling is too white with the snow collected up there.

We've just finished discussing Gail's tuition.

Kate reaches out and touches my hand, as physically intimate as we've been for the past five years. "*What's wrong?*" *she asks.*

I shake my head.

"*Tell me. Something's been bothering you.*"

I drink some Styrofoam coffee to avoid answering. But there's little coffee left, and it doesn't last long. I stare into the empty cup. "*My job,*" *I finally say in response.*

"*What about your job?*" *I look up and see the concern in her eyes. I am uncomfortable with the idea that she might still worry about me. She had been the one to leave me. I should be free of her concern—*

Life is never that simple. "*I called someone a rotten parent today.*" *I shake my head at the self-evident hypocrisy of the statement.*

"*You deal with rotten parents all the time,*" *she says.* "*Mostly stealing their kids from each other.*"

"*This is different.*"

"*How so?*"

"*There's this gentleman—I use the term loosely—named Sebastian. I know him from my days in the force. Not as a colleague.*"

"*Uh-huh?*"

"He's done well for himself. He was a two-bit punk we'd pick up every other month when I knew him. Since then he's done five years, made some connections inside, and come out a businessman. Now I'm pretty sure he's got a finger in every drug-laced pie in this town."

I crave a cigarette, even though I haven't smoked since I left the police—or, more accurately, since I took a bullet in the lung.

"And he's the rotten parent?"

I nod, *"He's got a family now. And a daughter about two years younger than Gail."*

"And she's missing."

"Bingo." I crumble the cup in my hand. *"He's not a man people say no to. But I said I didn't want to touch his money. When he got insistent, I told him that a man who did what he did wasn't fit to be a father—"* My voice chokes off.

"You were angry—"

"I saw his eyes. I think I'm the first person to have hurt him, really hurt *him, in years. I'm surprised he didn't have one of his bodyguards shoot me there."*

Kate looks at me and I can see her read me. It's something she is still too damn good at. *"You're nothing like him."*

"Then why aren't we still married?" I whisper.

"One of the reasons is you have a tendency to compare yourself to your clients."

"He's not a client."

"Isn't he?"

After five years, she still reads me too well. I find missing kids for a living. Doing that compensates for a lot of moral ambiguity.

"Twenty-five hundred retainer, nonrefundable. Five hundred a day, plus expenses."

The man on the other side of the wide antique desk smiles weakly. *"Somewhat mercenary, aren't you?"*

"I always quote the price first, Mr. Sebastian." I sit in one of the leather chairs facing the desk. The whole office seems lifted out of the last century, which makes the off-white PC with the rounded corners all the more incongruous. *"Too many times the parents know exactly where their kid is, they just don't want to deal with cops or lawyers."*

"*The money's not a concern. I* am *somewhat surprised at your change of heart.*"

"*I have a daughter myself, Mr. Sebastian.*"

"*I'm aware of that.*"

"*I find missing kids. That's who I do this for. I deal with a lot of parents I don't approve of. I let our prior relationship get in the way of my job.*"

Sebastian nods. "*I understand.*" He turns around one of the pictures on his desk and says, "*You will find my daughter.*"

PART TWO

DESCENT INTO THE MAELSTRÖM

Lo! Death has reared himself a throne
In a strange city lying alone
Far down within the dim West,
Where the good and the bad and the worst and the best
Have gone to their eternal rest.
There shrines and palaces and towers
(Time-eaten towers that tremble not!)
Resemble nothing that is ours.
Around, by lifting winds forgot,
Resignedly beneath the sky
The melancholy waters lie.

—"The City in the Sea"

11

I never completely lost consciousness. Even as I was kept company by returning memories, I never lost awareness of the concrete floor I lay upon, or the faint chemical smell of developer. Hours passed, and I never lost those two sensations.

I rested—but I never slept, and I never truly dreamed.

Somehow I knew when I was supposed to rise. It was as if the unseen sun were a weight on my body, a weight that lifted when the sun left the sky.

When I stood, I knew who Kane Tyler was. I had built a mosaic of myself and I could see the broad outlines of the man I used to be. I had been driven, obsessive. Kate had married me, but she had married me when my obsessions had an external focus. I quit the force to save our marriage, and in doing so I had destroyed it.

I knew more about Kane Tyler than I wanted to know.

I knew almost nothing about who I'd become.

There weren't any police in sight out the front. I didn't really expect any. No one had entered the house during my twelve-hour slumber, and the Cleveland police didn't have the manpower to waste staking out my house.

Still, it'd been a stupid risk coming here. I berated myself for not thinking clearly last night. Distressed or not. Memory or not. It was an easy exercise in hindsight to think I should have realized that I'd rented that motel room for *some* reason.

I should have left as soon as I'd seen the blood—if the dawn hadn't trapped me here.

Risk or not, here I was, and no one knew it. Once I left this place, I wasn't going to come back. So I gave myself one more hour, to pretend I still lived here.

Still, I did not turn on any lights, and after checking the front of the house, I avoided windows.

I went upstairs and showered. I did it mechanically, in the dark. I was cloaked in numbness. I'd felt the panic when I'd fallen from the precipice, but I was in free fall now, and a long way from the bottom. Almost everything had been burned out inside me.

Too much had happened to me, too much to absorb, too much to react to. But this was the first true pause in which I had time to think. With my rest, the logical part of my mind started working again.

Childe was central to a cult, a circle of youths that were into dark rituals that offended even people who were into the occult. I remembered only fragments of my investigation, but I could remember that the distaste for Childe was universal throughout the whole neo-pagan community.

I remembered another odd fact now. Within the neo-pagan community, with their elaborate taxonomy of belief systems separating wiccan from druid from followers of the Golden Dawn, and with their disparagement of Satanism as a uniquely Christian perversion, not one of the pagans or fringe-pagans I had talked to had given me even a tentative classification of what Childe actually practiced. They classified *him:* predatory, sadistic, cold, charismatic, and in many cases, evil, but they never classified his belief system. It was as if they never even heard any rumors of what it was he did.

"Childe runs a tight little group," I whispered as I left the bathroom. I said it, but it did not jibe with what Childe's cult seemed to be doing now.

They had killed my ex-wife in a manner almost designed to call attention to itself, killed in a manner that would club the police over the head with its ritualism.

With my healing memory, I was almost certain I could place the leather-clad teenager at last night's collision at the "sacrifice" I had videotaped. His face had been the one to smile at me.

Childe's group was low-key enough to work for years around the fringes of the pagan community without once leaking any hint of its internal structure. That didn't fit with Kate's death or ramming Sam's car.

I had worked with cults before; it goes with the territory.

And a true cult is almost always organized around a central charismatic figure. Because of that, because they're an extension of its leader's personality, cults don't change their behavior very often. And if they're inner-directed, they do their best to cut off the outside world almost completely.

I was beginning to understand why I'd been talking to Sam. I had had these thoughts before, and they had led me to the same conclusion. I needed to find out Childe's history.

And now this investigation wasn't just a matter of finding Sebastian's daughter, Cecilia. It was a matter of finding myself.

"Yes," said the voice on the other end of the phone, "We had a Detective Weinbaum here. But his injuries were minor. He was released after twelve hours of observation."

"Thank you," I said to the receptionist, and hung up.

University Hospitals had been the second place I'd called after the Cleveland Clinic. At least they'd given me good news. It was bad enough that I had Tony on my conscience, I did not need to find out that I'd somehow worsened Sam's condition.

I sat on the edge of my bed in a darkened room, holding a phone on my lap. I could see perfectly well by the light from the streetlight outside. Everything was blue-gray and black, a gloom that choked the room like smoke but somehow didn't obscure my vision.

I'd gotten dressed in the dark, so no one would notice my house being occupied. I now wore a tie and a black suit, with shoes to match. Not my first choice, but it was clean. On the bed next to me lay my gun, my old clothes, and an old tan trench coat I'd found in the closet.

An address book sat on a table next to the bed, and I flipped through it. When I reached my daughter's phone number, I read it with the strange déjà vú of seeing a number that I hadn't known I'd memorized. I wondered again how long things would taunt me with their familiarity.

I dialed the phone before thinking of what I would say. It rang four times.

"Please, Gail, answer. . . ."

After the fifth ring I heard Gail's voice. "Hey! You have reached—*me*. If you're calling for someone else, you've gotten a wrong number. Otherwise say something at the beep."

The receiver was shaking in my hand. I could see her face as I heard her voice on the machine. I pictured her smiling, with her freckles and her mother's long red hair. So much of her mother in her, except her eyes. Even as a baby, everyone had said she had her father's green eyes.

After a long pause, the beep surprised me. I had to gather myself to leave a message. "Gail? It's Dad. If you're there, pick up the phone. If not, I'll do what I can to call you back tomorrow." What could I say to a machine? "When I call you again, it'll probably be late. I'm sorry, I know you have classes, but I can't really avoid it. Good-bye."

I set the receiver back in the cradle. I tried not to feel the press of worry, but it was too late. It wasn't something I'd *ever* been rational about. I had always been overprotective, and every time I had a nasty missing-person's case, even after the divorce, I always had to reassure myself about Gail.

Sam said he had gotten her police protection, and she's in Oberlin, far away from all of this.

But it was 7:30 on a Sunday. Where was she?

I told myself that she was at a movie, or was out with friends, or in the shower. . . .

"Stop doing this to yourself," I whispered to myself. "You do this every time you get her machine—"

I smiled, because I was right, and I could remember it, at least partially. But recognizing it as rote paranoia didn't change the fact that there was a real danger out there—a real danger that I still knew woefully little about.

I had rebuilt some sense of self out of my amnesia, but I was remembering generalities. I still had little or no memory of specific facts or events. Especially frustrating was the gap between the eleventh and the fourteenth, the three days between Kate's death and my waking in the storm sewer—

My God, who's doing the funeral arrangements? Have they done it already? The cops would have to have the body for autopsy, but that'd be done by now. . . .

"Monday, if they haven't held it already. Maybe Tuesday at the latest—"

I realized that I wanted to be there—and if I couldn't face daylight, I couldn't be.

I stood up and walked to the windows, staring out the blinds at the streetlight. I took deep, unnecessary breaths. My attention was scattering when I needed to think straight. I still carried the phone. I had one call left to make.

I pulled Gabriel's card out of my pocket. Here, at least, I might have some answers to the darkness that had claimed my life. If nothing else, even if he was completely insane, Gabriel knew something of Childe—and Childe was central to everything that had happened to me.

The card had a single gold embossed number upon it, and when I called it I received a nasal computer-generated voice.

"You have reached an automated voice messaging system. At the sound of the beep, speak your own name slowly and clearly. If your response is unclear or unacceptable, you will be disconnected."

The machine beeped at me.

"Kane Tyler," I spoke slowly. I was nonplussed at dealing with a machine, but it did seem to fit with someone who wouldn't put any identification on a business card.

The machine digested my response, and after an electronic pop I heard Gabriel's voice, Southern accent and all. "Greetings, I am pleased you decided to call me—"

"Yes, I—" I started to say, when I realized that this message was as automated as the computer. Gabriel had recorded a message for me. I sighed.

"—assume you wish to meet with me," the recording continued. "At twelve this evening I shall be awaiting you at the address embossed upon the card. If this is inconvenient, please leave a message for me. I await the pleasure of your company, sir."

Midnight, three hours to kill before I talked to him. I sighed again.

The computer voice returned. "To replay this message, press one. To reply to this message, press two. To—" I hung up.

Three hours, which gave me time to find Sam and ask him a few questions—especially about Childe's history. I set the phone back on the nightstand, and pocketed my address book.

Outside I heard a car slow and turn up a driveway.

My driveway.

I grabbed the Eagle from where it lay on the bed, amidst my old clothes. I heard the engine idle, and I heard a car door open and slam shut. I edged up to the bedroom window, but it didn't offer me a view of the driveway, the roof of the porch was in the way.

I could hear the car, though, almost feel its presence.

I backed out of the bedroom, grabbing the holster and the trenchcoat with my free arm. It looked as if I might be leaving fairly shortly. When I'd backed into the hall, I could hear someone messing with the front door downstairs.

Who was it? The police?

I slipped into Gail's old room, so I'd have an overview of the driveway.

A wave of disorientation flooded me, making me realize I'd been too comfortable with my returning memory. I had stepped into her room expecting a bed with a flowered comforter, and shelves of ceramic animals that she had made. My memory had laid a nasty trap, I didn't realize I was expecting the little multicolored dragons and horses until I had bumped into the first pile of filing boxes that was stored here.

The box fell with a rustle, spilling 1993 over the bare hardwood. Dust balls flew away from the impact like frightened mice.

"Fuck," I whispered. I had to be more careful. Assuming that I knew something could be more dangerous than ignorance.

I froze, listening for a reaction. Below me, I heard the front door opening. I heard footsteps. I could almost swear that I could hear someone breathing—

The breathing wasn't me, I had stopped when the car pulled into the driveway.

Whatever else this darkness had done to me—whether it was madness or a supernatural affliction—it did grant me an acuteness of sense that I knew I had not possessed before. I could picture the shoes of the man who tread below me, I heard their rubber soles on the hardwood, and I heard the change when he stepped upon the carpet. I heard his breathing, steady but elevated, the breathing of a man tense but not yet excited.

I heard his footstep upon the stair, and if I concentrated, I could hear the beating of his heart.

The door was closed behind me, but I'd know when my visitor was behind it. I leveled the gun at the doorway and backed next to the window. Outside the window, I could hear a dog barking, and distant traffic. One of my neighbors was watching television. I heard canned laughter.

I glanced down through the blinds. Parked, idling in the driveway, was a familiar tan Oldsmobile.

How did Sebastian find me?

The phone, it had to be the phone. I had been working for this man for two weeks. He was rich, and he was driven. He had hired me and had me followed. I had no trouble believing that he might have tapped my phone as well.

"Damn it, for once we're on the same side," I whispered.

There was one driver. I could see a flash of pale skin and I decided that he was Mr. Gestapo. The one walking up the hallway toward me had to be the Jamaican. They'd cornered me.

I glanced at the window and thought of the teenager who had somehow landed on top of Sam's car. I drew the blinds on the window, and opened it.

I knew the Jamaican now stood without the door.

My exit was blocked by an old storm window. When I heard the doorknob rattle, I raised my foot and kicked at the bottom of the storm window's wooden frame. The window swung out, hinging at the top where hooks still held it in place. But those fasteners were over forty years old, and I heard metal snap, liberating an explosion of paint flakes.

After that snap, gravity took the window and it slid down like the blade of a guillotine.

Behind me I heard the door burst open and a Jamaican voice said, "Stop, Mr. Tyler—"

I'd already jumped out the window. Below me, the ancient storm window crashed into the hood of the Oldsmobile. The wood splintered, and glass exploded like a crystal grenade. The crash was like an explosion.

It had been Mr. Gestapo's first clue that something was wrong.

My jump ended half a second after the window's impact. Mr. Gestapo had only time to open the door when my feet hit the hood of the Olds. The impact felt as if it had broken both my shins, and had torn every one of my leg muscles from the bone. I should have collapsed and rolled off the hood, but I kept my balance, and I managed to unbend my knees.

I pointed my Eagle through the windshield and said, "Get out."

By now he had a gun out as well, but he looked at me and froze. He stared at me long enough that I had to repeat myself.

"Get out."

Slowly, he backed out of the car. Above me, I heard the Jamaican say, "Stop this, Mr. Tyler!"

I looked up and saw the Jamaican holding his own gun down on me. I stepped off the hood, continuing to cover Mr. Gestapo. I smiled up at the Jamaican. "I'm afraid I am going to have to borrow your car."

"I can't let you do that."

I looked down at Mr. Gestapo and said, "You really want to drop that." He did as he was told.

I looked up at the man covering me. "You have a name?" I asked.

"My name is Bishop, Mr. Tyler." He called down and I could see his breath fog. He didn't seem nervous or out of breath, unlike his partner. "I'm afraid you have to come with us."

"Odd name for one of Sebastian's hoods," I said.

Bishop smiled at the remark, his gun didn't waver. "And you, Mr. Tyler, have an odd name for a policeman."

"What do you mean?"

"Wasn't Cain the first murderer?"

I shook my head. "Well, Bishop, have you thought out the logistics of this situation?"

"What do *you* mean?"

"Your man down here is covered, and you are two stories above me. I see three options open to you. You let me take the car. You shoot me now. Or we stand here for an hour until the police show up and you explain a B&E on *my* property."

"Why do you think I won't shoot you?"

I looked up at him, "Because I'm looking for your boss' daughter, still. I am doing my job, *and I can't do my job if I am attached to you guys at the hip!*"

I could almost feel the options running through Bishop's mind. Eventually, I heard him say, "Go, but don't think this will happen again."

I smiled grimly and walked to the side of the Olds. I told Bishop's friend to get down on the ground, and I took his gun and tossed it in the car with my coat and my holster.

The key was still in the ignition.

It was a pain getting out of the driveway one-handed. But I wasn't putting down the Eagle until I was out of sight of the house.

12

Sam lived on the East Side, so on the way I stopped the Olds at a BP station downtown. I chose my vantage carefully, to be in sight of the approach from the police station and be a short U-turn from the I-90 on-ramp. I didn't want to be cornered again.

The police station was an old sandstone building. Pollution had turned the walls black. If not for the fluorescent lights shining through the windows, it wouldn't be out of place on an English moor.

It was early in the evening, quarter to nine, but it was Sunday and the traffic on St. Clair, between me and the station, was light. I idled next to the pay-phone and rolled down the window. Despite parking myself where I had an easy escape route, the black-and-whites made me nervous.

I dialed Sam's apartment and didn't get an answer, so I dialed the station.

After a couple of rings I heard, "Detective Weinbaum here."

"Hi, Sam. We need to talk."

"Goddamn it," Sam's voice dropped to a harsh whisper. "I told you not to call me here. Where the fuck did you disappear to?"

"My employer offered me a ride. I need what you have on Childe."

Sam's voice lowered. "Are you seriously still in this? After I saw you last time—"

"I'm handling that, Sam."

"Okay. Where are you?"

"Look out your window."

Sam ran across the street, a folder under his arm. I let him in and pulled the Olds in a quick U around the BP parking lot. The green-lit logo was receding down the on-ramp behind us before Sam asked. "What the hell's going on, Kane?"

"I'm trying to find out—"

"No, I mean with you. Yesterday you were a basket case. You were shaking and asking for a doctor. I was scared shitless that you'd wandered off on your own after the accident, the Heights cops have a bulletin to look out for you, and I'm in no end of shit because I have to explain how you were in my car in the first place—" Sam had to stop to breathe.

He didn't sound too good, and I looked at him. His nose was buried under a pound of gauze, his skin was pale, which made the shadows of his bruised eyes even more violent.

"I'm sorry about that. I don't want to get you into trouble."

He shook his head and patted his chest. "No," he coughed. "I can deal with my problems. I do get some slack because Kate's my case. It'll stay that way until you do something that makes me look real stupid."

We rolled onto the Shoreway and Sam asked, "Do you still need a doctor?"

"I said that I was taking care of it."

"That's no answer."

"I know." Before Sam could bring up any more questions, I added, "I have enough of an idea of what's wrong with me to know who to see about it. But it's not something I can tell you about."

"Damn it, I was there when you were shot—"

"I know, but please drop it."

The Oldsmobile plowed east along the Shoreway, street-lights sweeping us like an intermittent strobe. A dusting of snow started to drift down, and I turned on the wipers.

"Okay, but you're worrying me."

I nodded. "Sam, Childe is central to this, so I need to know what you were going to tell me."

He nodded and opened the file on his lap.

For all the effort expended, almost all Sam had on Childe was disappointing. Sam explained that everything they had had come from overseas when he had followed up the suspicion that Childe wasn't native to this country. Indeed Scotland Yard had a record of Childe's alias, and his addresses and activities in and around London from the late forties.

His passport photo looked much younger than that implied, but I had some suspicions why. Childe's name in London, which remained when he immigrated to this country, was Manuel Deité.

"Five to one it's another alias," Sam said.

"Why?"

"Manual Deity—hand of God—I think our Mr. Childe has a high opinion of himself."

Mr. Deité had been the subject of extensive investigation mostly under the direction of a Chief Inspector Cross. When Cross had begun the investigation wasn't in the papers that Sam had ordered from the Yard. However, it was clear that there were three decades of files on Deité and not one scrap of evidence—physical or circumstantial—that tied him to any crime, real or alleged.

The Yard's investigation ceased with Cross' retirement in the mid-eighties. However, with the name, Sam had managed to work forward through immigration and find a passport photo that matched the papers faxed from London. Sam even had an address for Mr. Deité in Cleveland.

Just like London, however, there was no scrap of evidence that connected Childe to any crime here, real or alleged. All I had myself was hearsay evidence placing Childe with Cecilia—and Sebastian had not reported her missing to the police. Considering his desire to keep the police out of things, it was unlikely he ever would.

"That's it?"

Sam nodded. "I've yet to convince a judge that we even have enough to get a warrant for his house."

"You're kidding."

Sam turned to me and said, "Do I look like I kid? What are we looking for? A bunch of missing kids that no one' reported missing? It's a fishing expedition—and even if I got a warrant, what I have is so thin that it'd last about three minutes at the hands of a court-appointed public defender, and wouldn't even get through the door against a lawyer Childe could afford."

"Thank you for reminding me why I don't miss the orce."

I pulled off the Shoreway at the tail end of MLK Boulevard and drove around under the highway, pulling into a darkened lot facing the lake. I stopped the car. For a few moments I sat there and listened to the metal knocking.

"I do have something that's unofficial."

"What?" I asked, not very hopeful.

"Manuel Deité seems to be missing."

I sat up, suddenly interested. "What do you mean?"

"I mean that I did some unauthorized snooping in his credit and bank records, and called his house a few times. He hasn't spent a cent since January 26th, when he filled the tank of his car at a Shell station out by the Metroparks. I can't get hold of him by the phone to his house, or by his two cellular numbers."

"The 26th wouldn't happen to have been a Sunday?"

Sam nodded.

That coincided with the last witness I had to see Cecilia. Three weeks ago. All I could think of was that he had gone to ground somewhere when he realized people were looking for him.

But I hadn't been hired until the first.

There *were* other people looking for him. I wasn't sure what Gabriel represented, but it seemed something worth hiding from.

"Okay, what about the van that hit us?" I asked.

Sam shrugged. "I don't know. Hit and run. Some sort of warning."

"What did they take? I thought I saw one kid steal a package out of your back seat."

Sam looked surprised. "Is that what happened to that? I guess that gives us a bit more circumstantial evidence pointing at Childe, then." He shook his head.

"What do you mean?"

"I had a lot more from England on this guy. That's what they took, the bulk of Cross' files from Scotland Yard." Sam nodded to himself. "Yeah, this gives me something on Childe I might be able to use. . . ."

"What?"

"Who else would have motive to swipe them? If I get a judge in a decent mood, I might swing a warrant to search for the van and those files. With that, I might turn up something."

I nodded, wondering. What was in those files? Why take them when all Sam had to do was make another call to Scotland Yard for more copies? The more I learned about what was going on, the less sense it made. I could discern no reasonable motives for what Childe and his people had done in the past three weeks.

That bothered me.

For a while we sat in silence. I stared out, toward the horizon. The sky hung low, its clouds heavy above a black lake frozen into stillness. No moon, no stars, the only lights out there were the small red flashers on the breakwater and an ice-white spotlight near its end.

Lake Erie was serene, melancholy, and still. It was the kind of stillness that made me wonder what kind of ugliness might lie beneath the surface. If I had not woken when had, would I have first opened my eyes under that sheet of endless ice?

"Sam?" I whispered.

"Yes?"

"The arrangements for Kate—what are they, who's handling it?"

"I—uh—her sister came in from Chicago to handle it. I've been helping, what I can do."

"When are the services?"

"Tuesday."

A half hour later, the Olds was driving up I-90, back the way we had come. Most of the way, we traveled in silence. It was a long time before I asked, "Gail is coming?"

Sam nodded, sighing. It was as if the statement had released a pressure that had weighed on him ever since we'd left the lake.

"Tomorrow?"

"Evening, yes. We were arranging all this while you were missing. I said she could stay at my place."

"What about police protection?"

Sam looked at me, squinting over the bandage on his nose, "*I'm* a cop, remember?"

I nodded. "You know, if there was any way she could stay with me. . . ."

"Of course I know. You could let *her* know—"

"I tried calling."

"She'll be here tomorrow, and she wants to see you."

I didn't answer. I drove off I-90 filled with conflicting thoughts. I wanted to see my daughter. I needed to see her survive the wound of losing Kate, but I was afraid that she may have already lost me also. How could I talk to her, reassure her, comfort her, when I had passed so far beyond the pale myself?

I felt that if I touched my daughter, some measure of the corruption infecting me would infect her as well. Beside that, the possibility she might reject me for my role in her mother's death was almost comforting.

"Kane?"

"Yes," I said. "I need to see her, don't I?"

"Are you all right?"

"No. You'll be home tomorrow?"

"I sort of have to be, don't I? I plan to be working around the funeral. All day tomorrow, and then after the funeral."

"Sorry this is screwing with your investigation."

"She was my friend, too." Sam looked out the windows at the black sandstone station emerging from the shadows. "Besides, talking to the survivors goes with the territory. You know me, I'd try to be at the funeral even if I didn't know her."

"Yeah, I know." I pulled the Olds to a stop about a block from the station. As Sam stepped out of the car, I asked, "Can you do me a favor?"

He turned and said, "What?"

"Give me twelve hours before you serve that warrant."

"Why?"

"Sometime tonight I want to pay Childe a visit."

"I didn't hear that, Kane." He tossed the file folder on the passenger seat. "Just in case you need that information, those are all copies."

He shut the door. I rolled down the window and shouted after him, "Can I have the time?"

Sam turned around and said, "I didn't get that." He looked at his watch. "I got to get back and wait for a judge to wake up so I can get this Childe warrant issued." He smiled and resumed walking toward the station.

He'd given me my twelve hours. And sitting on the passenger seat was Childe's address. I wanted to go there now, rush in, and demand explanations from whomever I found there—

However, I felt the need for some sense of caution. If there was a possibility of me confronting Childe, I wanted to know something more of his nature.

Also, I had the gnawing suspicion that—Sam's warrant aside—there would be little to find at Childe's residence. I suspected that Gabriel would have information as basic as Childe's address. If Childe was to be found there, I doubted Gabriel would still be searching.

What was at Childe's home would be what was left behind when he disappeared with Cecilia. There might be something there useful to me, but if that was so, it would stay there while I met with Gabriel.

13

Waiting for my midnight conference with Gabriel gave me an hour to think. I drove around trying to reason out the unreasonable, attempting to distill some rational sense out of an irrational situation. The unreason went beyond my search for Childe and Cecilia, and the disintegration of my life—

I forced myself to think the word that was at the core of my dilemma.

Vampire.

The farther Tony's corpse receded in my memory, the more it seemed that all the events I'd experienced, however bizarre and unwarranted, were more than the products of my own derangement. What had happened to me that insisted on that peculiar interpretation?

Fear of the sun, holding my breath. . . .

I was driving the Olds east up Superior, through some of the uglier parts of the East Side. The night turned a blind eye to me, the streets snowbound and empty, the storefronts shuttered in metal or plywood. Ragged men, young ones and old ones, hovered at corners, wrapped in their own secrets.

I felt a need to prove something to myself, before I delved any deeper into something that could just as well be a delusion. I needed some physical proof, some tangible stigmata. . . .

I pulled the Olds over at the corner of E. 55th. At the moment, the only animate things in sight were a few snowflakes dancing in the wind. I stepped out of the car and gathered my coat about myself.

It was closing on eleven, and it felt as if I stood in a world abandoned. In the far distance, I heard a siren. Other than that, the only noise was from the streetlights rocking in the wind.

I crouched and examined the sidewalk. It was a mass of gray slush, but it wasn't too hard to find what I was looking for. The neck of an abandoned beer bottle stuck up from a mound of grime-spotted snow. I withdrew it and upended it, loosing its unfrozen liquid to splatter the slush at my feet.

Stigmata, I thought. If I had truly died, if somehow some supernatural darkness had claimed my soul, my body should not be as it was. It would not act as a living body would. My breathing, my eating, both showed some physical transformation, if they weren't symptoms of some derangement.

I stepped to a storefront, and set down the bottle to roll up the sleeve of my left arm. I made a fist and held out my arm, about half of my forearm exposed.

"Going through with this is not going to argue for my sanity."

I paused a bit after saying that. However, at this point, after all I'd been through, that was no reason not to. The only reason not to was the fear that my hypothesis was wrong, and I *was* delusional.

I knelt down and grabbed the neck of the bottle with my right hand, while I clenched my left. On my exposed forearm, the veins came into relief under too-pale skin.

I shattered the body of the bottle against the metal cage imprisoning the storefront. Before I could reconsider, I drew the jagged end of the glass in a powerful slash across my forearm. I felt its bite as it tore skin. I felt the sour stab of the alcohol contaminating the glass.

The flesh parted across my wrist, the wound deep enough to sever the veins and slash the tendons. My fist shook and opened and I felt as if a brand had been applied to my wrist.

I saw the lips of the wound, ragged and black, before blood oozed to fill the wound. For a moment I felt an exquisite agony, as if the skin had been torn from the wounded area—

And suddenly the pain was no longer there.

My too-black blood no longer seeped from the wound. The blood sat mute, demarking the line where the insult had occurred, little more than would have been there had I suffered a scratch from an angry kitten.

I dropped the neck of the bottle and wiped the blood from my wrist. Beneath it, the skin was whole. No scar, no sign of injury, nothing but the blood on the fingers of my right hand. I no longer had any doubts that something had changed me.

I stumbled back to the Olds, my mind consumed with thoughts of the undead.

I couldn't decide when I had first suspected Childe of vampirism. There was a good chance—I was beginning to think—that I might have started suspecting him and his cult before I had lost my memory. I couldn't be sure of that, because those last days were still one of many black holes in my memory.

But I had seen a blood-drenched ritual, and I had made tapes of it. Damn Sebastian and his people for swiping them.

It was looking more and more as if I had been the one to place the Eucharist upon my own threshold. There seemed to be a peculiar irony to that, since if I was now a member of the undead, the Host seemed singularly ineffective.

I hoped it had at least helped me sleep nights.

Had I had discovered something? The true nature of Childe's cult? Its location? Childe's true identity? Had my investigation unearthed something that had prompted them to violence that, according to the absence of police records, was uncharacteristic?

I still couldn't pin down a motive.

Maybe it's something about their nature that's making me miss something. . . .

Undead. Vampire. Ghoul. Zombie. A thing that survives its own demise, to feed on human flesh and blood. A monster, pure and simple.

Unfortunately, pure and simple monsters didn't accede to logical examination. Pure and simple monsters don't need motivations to act. And if my experience showed anything, if such monsters existed, they were neither pure nor simple.

As far as I could tell, supernatural manifestations or not, the worst blood-drinking fiend still started human, and that meant that I still dealt with human nature. That meant that Childe, and his followers, were still doing things for reasons and were acting in expectation of some result.

The obvious interpretation was that somehow my investigation was getting too close to Childe, and his followers were reacting violently to protect him.

Because that conclusion was obvious, I distrusted it. I also distrusted it, because if shielding Childe were the goal—if that was why they had killed Kate, and why they'd stolen those records from Sam—their effect was exactly opposite what they intended. If anything, they were calling attention to themselves.

As I pulled into Cleveland Heights, I had one more unanswered question to ponder.

Until Cecilia disappeared, Childe had never excited interest from anyone but Chief Inspector Cross at Scotland Yard. Presumably, Childe had been seducing vulnerable teenagers into his circle for decades. Until now, he had never taken anyone that someone missed.

I don't know exactly what I expected from the address Gabriel gave me. It was in Cleveland Heights, which I generally thought of as middle suburbia. However, I knew that I wasn't headed to a typical middle suburban household. Gabriel lived on a street nestled behind Euclid Heights Boulevard and overlooking University Circle.

When I saw the house, I knew it had been there when streetcars rode up and down the hill behind me. This had been here when most of Cleveland Heights had been a golf course.

The house was a massive structure, the front a forest of Doric columns two stories tall, giving the facade the appearance of two Grecian temples set side by side—the house's entrance set between them. The entrance, the windows, almost everything else about the house was dwarfed by the columns.

Like Gabriel's dress, the house was white, and its nineteenth-century appearance wouldn't have been out of place on a plantation. At 11:55 I got out of the Olds and walked up an immaculately shoveled walkway, to the front door of the house.

When I reached the door, it opened for me. The action

gave me pause for a moment, and I stopped before I reached the threshold. A figure stood in the doorway, but not one I expected. Gabriel wouldn't have surprised me, nor would've a butler or other servant. Instead, I was greeted by a tall, dark woman dressed in a purple gown that looked as if it could have been worn in the latter half of the previous century.

She regarded me a moment, and said, "You are expected."

I stepped through the threshold, still suspecting that I had somehow mistaken the address. "I'm here to meet with Gabriel," I said.

She shut the door behind me. "I know. Come with me."

The woman was a striking example of exotic beauty, pale as marble and as finely carved as any Grecian Aphrodite— but it was a cold beauty, withdrawn and wary. If anything was out of proportion in the otherwise perfect face, it was her eyes. Even in their half-closed scrutiny of me, her eyes were of startling size, dominating her features. When she turned to lead me, it was her eyes I remembered.

She took me through the house. Despite the high ceilings, the broad corridors, and the lights shining everywhere, the overwhelming impression was one of gloom. There was something oppressive about the decor, and about the placement of light. The disturbing part of it was the elusiveness of the mood the house evoked. I couldn't find a source for the mood that pervaded the house in any particular part. It seemed to be part of the *gestalt*.

My hostess didn't say a word.

"Is this Mr. Gabriel's residence?" I asked to break the silence.

"Just Gabriel," she said.

"Okay. Is this his house?"

"While he is here, it is here he resides." She looked back over her shoulder, and I noticed a small turn at the corner of her upper lip, as if she found my confusion amusing. "This house belongs to Gabriel's circle. This is where he stays when he is in town."

I noted that for future reference. It explained the identityless business card, as well as the voice-mail system. "Circle," was also an interesting word, it implied some sort of societal unit.

"Are you part of Gabriel's circle?"

She laughed. The laugh matched her appearance, lovely and cruel. "So impertinent." She stopped to turn and brush my face with her hand. She touched me with a heat that didn't quite reach her skin. "So," her eyes stared into mine as she appeared to search for a word. Her eyes drank me in, and it felt as though she pulled something out of me as she stared. "Raw. Yes, so raw you are. So unschooled. Perhaps you need a teacher. . . ."

She drew me toward her, and I felt such a hot rage of desire that it numbed out every other sensation. Everything but those too-large eyes, so violet that they were almost black. She bent and briefly touched her lips to mine.

"Please," I said. Somehow I managed to keep my voice steady.

She released me, a ghost of a smile on her face.

"I'm here to see Gabriel."

"Of course you are." She turned with no explanation or apology, and resumed walking down the hall. "To answer your impertinent question. Of course I am of Gabriel's circle. My chosen name is Rowena, should you care to remember it."

I was still recovering from that near-kiss. I could still feel her lips, as if someone were holding a candle too close to my face. I also felt it in places that I didn't know vampires were supposed to feel anything.

"Why was it an impertinent question?"

"Why is it impertinent for a peasant to interrogate his prince?" She stopped before a large oaken door and knocked. Before she left me she said, "But then you aren't quite a thrall, are you? Pity."

From beyond the door I heard a Southern voice say, "Come on in, Mr. Tyler. Come on in."

I pushed open the door and entered Gabriel's office. I stood for a moment in the threshold. If the rest of the house was designed to have an effect on the mood, that effect was all focused in this one odd-shaped room.

The room was a huge pentagon, the door at one vertex. The entire wall opposite the door was a vast window. Through the window, the city lights were filtered through gnarled trees as old as the house itself. The other walls were of golden wallpaper that fit some garish nineteenth-century motif, embossed so that the shadows formed shifting geometric patterns that changed depending on where I stood relative to the light.

To the left of the great window, an Egyptian sarcophagus stood against the wall, surrounded by a box of glass. On the other wall hung a full-size reproduction of the center panel of Hieronymous Bosch's *The Garden of Earthly Delights.*

My addled memory gave me the name and the artist without telling me where I had learned of him.

"Come in, my friend. Have a seat." Gabriel stood behind a desk of black wood. And motioned me toward a waiting chair.

I sat down, looking at Gabriel. He had a look of wild authority about him, with his cane, his lined face, and his long white hair. Authority and passion that made his gray-blue eyes seem less the color of ice than the color of a gas-jet.

He sat, his long hands enveloping his cane. "Again, I offer my apologies, sir."

I clutched my left hand. "I am still trying to understand what is going on here. No offense, but I don't know who the hell you are or what you have to do with what's happened to me."

"We are here to illuminate each other's ignorance." He leaned forward. "We shall have a fair exchange, question for question. I shall give you the first two as compensation for our prior misunderstanding."

Misunderstanding? This person, who looked to be seventy, had thrown me through the air fifteen feet—one-handed. That had to be one pretty big misunderstanding.

"Let's start there, then," I said. "Exactly what was your misunderstanding? You were threatening me one minute, and the next— What brought on the sudden change of heart?"

"A mistake about your status, Mr. Tyler. I am not infallible. I knew that you were mortal when I first began the search for Childe, and I knew, when I saw you last, that the thirst had claimed you. The thirst could not have been upon you for more than a few days. The possibility that you could have been masterless never occurred to me until I tasted the strength of your blood. You do not have the blood of a thrall, which is what I treated you as."

I didn't feel as if I understood things any better. I shook my head. "You'd better start describing the society I've stepped into, because I don't know anything about masters or thralls, other than what the words usually mean."

"Now that is a broad question, but I did give you two." He paused in thought for a moment.

"We keep a Covenant, sir. That is the first law we hold to. Without the Covenant, our race would swiftly die. There are three things the Covenant holds us to. First, no one who holds to the Covenant may slay another who holds to it. Second, no one who holds to the Covenant may act so as to reveal those of the blood, or allow the revelation of those of the blood. Third, a master is responsible for the actions of all of his blood. Any of the blood who don't hold to the Covenant, even those who are not part of it, forfeit their existence."

I nodded. It made a certain amount of sense, too much sense. It reminded me of the code of a Mafia family: don't kill family, keep your mouth shut about family business, keep your own house in order.

"Our society is larger than the Covenant, but I think of the Covenant as central to it. Within my circle, my duty is to enforce the Covenant—" He looked at me and shook his head. "I suppose I need to explain that as well." He raised a hand and began tracing circles on the desk in front of him. "We are a race of hierarchies. . . ."

14

It seemed that we spent hours in that room. Gabriel spoke of hierarchies, and explained them at length, and I saw the master-thrall relationship mirroring itself throughout the whole society Gabriel described.

A thrall was the lowest someone could be within the society, little more than the animate property of his master. In terms of relationships, a thrall was treated almost as if he were an indivisible part of his master.

The thrall's master was usually the vampire responsible for creating him. According to Gabriel, almost all vampires began as humans chosen by a vampire in search of material for a thrall. Those choices were consciously made; no thrall was ever created by accident.

A thrall remained bonded—physically and psychically enslaved—until his master chose to free him, or until the master was destroyed. From what Gabriel said, I wondered if it was an unusual occurrence for a thrall to end up killing his master. Even if the enslavement was as much mental as physical, I doubted that it could be maintained permanently, or vampire society would stagnate. If there weren't an implicit threat of eventual rebellion, there would be no incentive for any master to ever release a thrall and create a new one.

Though the Covenant forbade masters from slaying one another, a thrall operated under his master's responsibility. If a thrall killed his master, it was the master that was responsible—essentially suicide. I noticed that Gabriel said nothing about any of that. It was probably a touchy subject.

What he talked about, at length, was the web of associations among those of "free blood," as he called it. Just as with any culture, there was a definite pecking order, high to low. The circles that Rowena mentioned were levels of power, or—more accurately—associations of vampires who had roughly the same status. It seemed that individuals could gain status on their own, or the circle as a whole could rise and fall, a combination of a political party and a noble house.

Gabriel explained the relationship between higher and lower, and I began understanding why Rowena would consider my question about her circle impertinent. Vampire society seemed divorced from the material world. The more so the closer to the center you came. In such a society, information was a valued commodity. Information about relationships within the community, especially.

In a way, Gabriel was telling me how grave his mistake was in the way he had first shaken me down, and at the same time telling me how well he was making up for that mistake.

After information, what this society valued was reciprocity—in all its forms. A favor granted meant a favor returned. A wound inflicted meant a wound repaid. It went beyond that, into areas that were hard to understand in one sitting. Favors were exchanged like gifts, but status and power dictated who could initiate such an exchange. Offering something to someone of a level much higher than my own could be seen as a bitter insult, while asking anything of that person could disadvantage me, incurring a social debt that I'd be obliged to repay.

After he was done with his lengthy description, I was taken by one question that he had not answered. "Where do I fit in this? I've been dropped in here without a script."

Gabriel held up a hand. "This is your third question, sir. You must give me leave to ask you one of my own."

I understood what he was doing now. By allowing me those first two questions, he had expunged a debt between us, a debt that he'd incurred by his "misunderstanding." Now we were in a game of reciprocal questions. I nodded to him, "Fair's fair."

"Who was it that granted you the thirst? Someone must have taken your mortal life, or have fed upon you before your mortal life was taken."

His gaze held me, and I felt the distinct fear of disappointing someone more powerful than I was. "I don't know."

"You don't know?"

"If I do know, it's a memory that's inaccessible to me at the moment."

Gabriel looked at me, and I had the uneasy feeling that those blue-gray eyes could see if I lied. "It is an answer of sorts," he said. "My own answer, to your question: You do *not* 'fit' into our society. You have not pledged yourself to the Covenant. You have taken no name. You are a rogue as outside us as is the human from which you sprang. You are of the blood, which means I must respect you. But you have no status, high or low. I treat you as a peer because I disadvantaged myself to you, but others will treat you as is their fancy."

That disturbed me. It meant I was at a considerable disadvantage in dealing with others of my kind.

"My kind," I whispered, surprised at the form my thoughts had taken.

"Pardon me, sir?"

"No, nothing. This has all been a little much for me. I had a life—"

Gabriel shook his head. "You *have* a life, Mr. Tyler. Don't mistake what has happened for death; those who do taste the true death before long." He leaned back. "But that was not a question."

"No, it wasn't." I sat up a little straighter in my chair. "How *could* I fit into this society?"

"You need to accept the Covenant and choose your Name before us. However, you need one of us to accept you, and such a boon will not be granted lightly or freely. Some measure of responsibility shall attach—not absolute, your sponsor did not create you—but enough that your actions will reflect well or ill upon the one granting you this. Something in return will be asked, and only someone great in his own position would not demand some indenture."

"Someone has to open the door and take responsibility for letting me in."

Gabriel nodded.

"Your turn."

"I presume you've seen Childe's thralls at one point. Describe the last time you saw any of them."

"I can't be certain who his thralls are, but if they are the teenagers he's supposed to be collecting, the last time I dealt with any of them was yesterday. They rammed a van into a car I was in. . . ."

The question game went on for hours. I answered Gabriel's questions truthfully, not because I trusted him—I didn't—but because he never asked anything that was worth it to risk a lie. The only personal questions he asked me were about me becoming a vampire, the sequence of events immediately afterward, and about Tony.

Everything else was about Childe, directly or indirectly.

I learned as much from Gabriel's questions as I did from my own. It was clear that he hunted Childe for some violation of the Covenant. Specifically, Childe bore the responsibility for his thralls' violations. His thralls—apparently the people identified with Childe's cult—had broken the second law of the Covenant, "revealing those of the blood." I had the uncomfortable feeling that I was the one, through my investigation, to whom things were revealed.

Listening to Gabriel, I had the sense that he had some personal stake in finding Childe, beyond the fact that Childe seemed to have violated the Covenant. He seemed to view Childe with the same distaste that the neo-pagans did, and I could not figure out why he would feel that way. However, Gabriel's attitude toward Childe raised my suspicions.

I felt Gabriel was too ready to convict Childe, especially now that I knew the nature of the Covenant. The Covenant now made it even harder for me to fathom what Childe's people—his thralls—were doing. I couldn't account for it even as some sort of mass rebellion, a slave revolt. That wouldn't explain the outward-directed violence. It didn't explain the attention drawn in Childe's name. A thrall rebellion would have at its focus the master.

I wondered what Gabriel gained by dealing with those who violated the Covenant. What did he gain in status and power? I wondered if his gain was roughly proportional to the level of the person he brought down. I didn't question

Gabriel about these points. I didn't want to allow him into the routes my own mind was taking.

My questions were more basic to my immediate survival. I kept asking questions about vampirism in general. I didn't want Gabriel to think of me as a fellow investigator. The more he saw me as a neophyte, the safer I thought I was.

So I asked if I had to kill.

Gabriel said it wasn't necessary. Life was the important thing, not death. He explained that I had been in such a diminished state when I had taken Tony that I had no choice but to take all he had to give.

How much blood?

The answer depended on too many things, from innate physical strength to the level of exertion.

Garlic, crosses, and holy water?

He gave me an amused smile and a comment about superstition. "Belief is all you have to fear," he said. "Yours and your adversary's."

Stakes, decapitation, and fire?

Such things would be anathema to any being.

The sun?

Gabriel's expression turned grave as he said, "The light of the sun is insidious. A more spiritual person would say it drives the soul from the flesh where it is bound. From my point of view, it is simple death. Exposed to that light for any length, and you shall become a corpse."

"Speaking of that light," I said, "there are things I must do before dawn."

He nodded at me. "I appreciate all your answers, Mr. Tyler. Your information may yet help me find him, or at least make the case that he must be found." He stood and extended his hand.

I stood and clasped his hand. I didn't know what to make of him now. His comment came uncomfortably close to what Sam had said about getting a warrant. I didn't trust Gabriel, or his motives.

"I apologize for the gaps in my memory," I said, hoping that I had at least gotten as much out of him as he had out of me.

"As I said, what you do know may yet help me." He smiled at me, a smile that managed to condense all the darkness in this house into a single facial expression. "I'm sure you can find your way out."

When I drove away from the house, it was nearly three in the morning. When I arrived at the Lakewood address of Manuel Deité, a.k.a. Childe, it was closer to four. It wasn't that it took an hour to drive from Cleveland Heights to Lakewood. I just needed the time to digest what I had learned—and what I thought I'd learned—when I talked to Gabriel.

Childe had an Edgewater Drive address, and at first I thought that he lived in one of the ranks of ice-tray apartment complexes that claimed the view of the water. However, one look at the address told me that he resided on the other side of Edgewater. The apartment buildings on that side were stone and brick as opposed to concrete, and a few decades ago, these would have had the view of the water—

Now they just had the view of apartments that were more expensive, newer, and uglier.

The building had a parking lot in back. I pulled the Olds up over a hump of snow and looked up at Childe's building. It would have been at home overlooking the Rhine. Most of the buildings on this side of Edgewater would. Childe's building was a Tudor study in stone detailing and leaded glass.

His apartment number was 1000. Probably a place of prominence, tenth floor, facing the front. I left the Olds and walked around the building. When I rounded the front of the building, I saw what *had* to be Childe's apartment. One corner of the building was rounded, almost like a castle turret. On the top floor, the entire outer circumference of that stone curve was fitted with a huge leaded glass window. The window had to be ten feet wide and half again as high. It was hard to tell, since the room beyond was dark, but I had the impression that the inside was hung with heavy drapes.

Now all I had to do was get in.

I continued to circle the apartment building, looking for an entry point. The usual entrances were secure. I could have tried to have someone buzz me in, but I didn't want to announce my presence like that.

When I completed my circuit, I saw my way in.

Above the rear door, overlooking the parking lot, windows looked in on a rear stairwell. The door itself sat within a Gothic arch topped with an elaborate stone shield. I looked around, to assure myself that I was unobserved; then I ran up and jumped at the door. I grabbed hold of the top of the arch, around the projecting shield.

Levering myself up to the window was easier than I expected. I thought of the litany of aches and pains this should have ignited, and now that I was thinking of them, I noticed the lack. I lived in a forty-five-year-old body, but I don't think I could have pulled myself up so easily when I was eighteen.

I remembered jumping out a second-floor window. My body seemed capable of more than healing a slashed wrist.

I stood on a small stone prominence, looking in on the stairwell. The window I faced was locked, but I saw no sign of any alarm system. All that held it shut was a small tab of metal, screwed into the wood of the frame. My first thought was to break the glass, reach in, and unlock the window, but I reconsidered.

If I pulled myself up here so easily, how easily could I force the window?

I grabbed the bottom of the upper frame and started tugging it down. It tried to move, and through the glass I saw the metal of the lock levering upward in response. I saw that it had been painted shut. Paint flaked from the lock.

Then, abruptly, it gave, and the top half of the window slammed down in the sash. A small twisted piece of metal sailed into the stairwell, clattering down the stairs. I stood there for a moment, waiting for someone to react to the noise. No one did.

I climbed though the top of the window, closing it as firmly as I could behind me.

At Childe's door, I wished for some lock picks, or at least a credit card. I was reduced to drawing my gun, looking both ways down the hallway, and kicking it open.

The door blew in after I slammed my foot next to the inner edge of the doorknob. The room beyond was dark. I covered it with the Eagle as the door hit the wall. Even before my eyes adjusted, I knew the apartment was empty. I could *feel* it.

I stepped in, still covering the room with my Eagle. Feelings aside, I wasn't going to let my guard down until I *saw* the place was empty.

I did a quick sweep of all the rooms. All were dark, all were unoccupied. Then I holstered the gun.

I went back to the front and closed the door to the apartment to ward off the curious. By now I could see fairly well, even in the near-complete darkness. Well enough to read titles on the bookshelf across from the grand, draped window. Another of the fringe benefits of vampirism.

I started searching Childe's rooms at the bookshelf. The titles weren't helpful except in confirming Childe's interest in the occult. Many of the books were old, and the majority weren't in English. I noted titles such as *Directorium Inquisitorum, Ordinall of Alchimy, Heaven and Hell, De Quinta Essentia Philosophorum,* and *Iter Subterraneum.* I noted authors from John Dee and Alister Crowley to Thomas Aquinas.

The remainder of the living room, dominated by the great curtained window, was less remarkable. Childe had a predilection for antiques, and I had the feeling that most of his furniture, as his books, must have traveled here from England.

What was striking was what was *not* here. Childe didn't own a television, or a stereo. The only sign that he acknowledged the century he lived in was the presence of electric lights, and a telephone that occupied a table to itself in one corner of the living room.

I examined the phone and found an answering machine. The machine held half a dozen messages.

The first message was a gravelly voice that sounded slightly familiar, though I couldn't place it. "I hear you look for a woman of certain qualities. There will be one at the ritual tonight, I've told her to look for you." There was a computerized date-time stamp on the messages; this one had been left at 6:15 p.m. on Sunday, January twenty-sixth.

The next message had been left over a week later, after I had already begun my search for Cecilia. The voice was unquestionably Gabriel, requesting a meeting.

The next two messages were also from Gabriel, no longer

requesting. The last of Gabriel's messages was a virtual demand for Childe to explain himself. The dates of the calls were portentous. One corresponded to Kate's death. The next corresponded to my own disappearance.

The last two were from Sam, leaving a name and number. I noticed that he didn't identify himself as a policeman, and that he left the number of his pager.

I worked through an empty and unused kitchen and a dining room, finding little of Childe left behind. It was as if no one had ever really lived here. The furniture was all in place, but most of the drawers I opened were empty. Nowhere did I find any papers, bank records, checkbook, opened mail, phone bill, anything.

The only sign that this was anything more than a mail drop was in the bedroom. The room was huge, and central to it was a canopied bed, which was curtained with heavy black velvet. The curtains had been drawn aside, revealing that the bed held no mattress, no bedding. The bed frame supported a flat wood panel.

Even though the windows were curtained, I noticed immediately that this room was darker than the others. Dark enough to give my now-exceptional night vision difficulty. It was as dark down here as it had been in the sewer.

When I pulled the curtains on the window aside, I saw why. The glass had been painted so that no light could leak into this room. I backed up to the door, and checked around it. There was a curtain rod mounted just above the door frame, and more heavy curtains hung to the side, ready to be drawn across a closed door—a door that would be held shut by a pair of heavy dead bolts that could not be unlocked from the other side.

Childe was serious about not having his rest disturbed.

However, I had the feeling that there were a number of other places in the city where Childe slept. This one, I felt, was here for the people who were looking for Childe, and the outfitting of the bedroom was secondary, in case Childe needed a dark place to sleep.

It was frustrating, but not unexpected. I knew that there'd be little to find before I'd come here. Childe had been doing what he'd been doing for decades at least. There was no way he could go so long without learning how to cover his tracks.

No papers, no mail. . . .

Now there was a thought. If Childe had truly disappeared with Cecilia, his mail here would have been accumulating for three weeks with no one to pick it up. Even if this was only a front, at the very least, Manuel Deité had to pay a phone bill.

No matter how many places Childe might have, Manuel Deité only had one address in this town.

I slipped out of the apartment and checked the time. I'd been quick, it was only four-thirty. I had some time before I had to worry about the sun.

I descended by the rear stairwell, where I had entered the building. It may have been because I had left Childe's apartment, or because I'd found nothing there, but I let my guard down for a moment when I reached the first floor landing. I began opening the door before looking down the hall. I saw my mistake immediately, but it was too late.

The hall shot the length of the building, from this stairwell across to the front lobby. The mailboxes were set in an alcove about midway down the hall. In front of the boxes stood a beefy man with slate-gray hair, who was busily jimmying one of them open. A younger man stood next to him, watching.

I am no believer in coincidence, and I could pretty much guess which mailbox he was opening.

The younger one saw me, shouted something, and they both started running toward me. I had a split-second to decide if I was running up the stairs or down. I ran up the stairs, hoping that at least one of them would head for the obvious exit. As I rounded the landing where I had broken in, I heard one of them yell, "Police! Freeze!"

15

Time slowed. The thought that I ran from the police might have made me hesitate. But it was too early to be Sam. I never got the chance to stop.

One of them said, slowly and very deliberately, "He's going for a gun."

I heard a gun go off. A bullet struck me, a twenty-pound sledge in the side of my chest. I fell into the window next to me. It shattered as my shoulder smashed against the frame.

"Shit!" One of the cops said, a different voice than the one who said I had gone for a gun.

Another sledgehammer slammed into my shoulder, and the windowframe collapsed around me. The dry wood gave way under my weight, and I felt the bite of winter air as my momentum carried me sidewise and my feet slipped out from under me.

The cop's gun barked a third time, the bullet hammering my gut. I fell across the sill of the window, tumbling forward. There was little I could do to stop my fall.

I pitched out the window before I felt the throb of the first gunshot. Everything felt distant, as if I were watching it all from a remove. I tumbled through space for an endless instant, my body rolling so I faced the sky.

My wounded shoulder plowed into the ground first, grinding into a mixture of snow and glass. I collapsed into a heap below the window, immobile.

I felt so cold.

I wasn't breathing, and I couldn't feel my own pulse. I could feel the cold, and I could feel the empty holes where bullets had ripped chunks from my body. Oddly, I felt little pain, just an odd pressure in my chest, my stomach, and my shoulder. The wounds were like pits, and I felt as if I was draining myself down into them.

I could almost feel my body shriveling, and my torso tightening in response.

I knew when they came out the rear door, into the parking lot. Not because I could see them, I felt as if I couldn't turn my head, but because I felt a sense of distant warmth. The police radiated an inner warmth that tightened my gut.

"You shot him!" one of them said, the cop who had spouted the profanity. I suspected it was the younger man, though I didn't see him. My eyes were focused on the sky and the wall of the apartment building in front of me. Above me, the window gaped like an open wound.

"Damn straight I shot him."

"Is he dead?"

A face leaned over me, its heat and emotion rippling toward me through the wind-torn air. I could feel parts of my body, inside me, moving in response to the warmth.

The gray-haired cop was ugly and rumpled, and looked at me with an expression of disgust. He still had his gun out as he knelt next to me. I could hear—I could *feel*—the younger one pacing behind me. The old cop placed his fingers on my neck and the feeling of pulsing heat was as intense as an orgasm.

"I put three bullets into him. He'd *better* be dead."

The fingers stayed on my neck for a long time, and my body drew the heat—and something else?—from them. "Fuck," the old cop said, yanking away his fingers. "He's cold already."

With the touch I felt a dreamlike realization that I *could* move if I tried. My anger was building, as if I had to collect the shattered pieces of the emotion and piece it into some coherent whole. The shock was wearing off. This cop had tried to kill me. Hell, this SOB tried to *murder* me. He taken me down without a single hesitation, even down to the lie about me going for a gun.

"This ain't good," the young cop was saying to my right.

"Look, kid, this was a clean shoot. You ever say different, you'll be in shit you don't even know exists." The old cop transferred his revolver to his left hand and felt around my chest until he found my holster. "Bastard doesn't even bleed—" the cop mumbled.

"What?"

"I said, 'Look at this fucking cannon.'" The old cop held

up my Desert Eagle with his right hand. Its barrel glinted in the streetlight as he clicked the safety off.

"Just plant the gun so we can call this in," the young cop said in a disgusted tone of voice.

"I ain't planting it. It's *Tyler's* gun." I noticed the old cop was wearing surgical gloves. He began pressing the Eagle in my right palm.

I could see what this was now. These were Sebastian's men. No, that was kind. These were bent cops on Sebastian's payroll. This guy had probably shot me because there was a hefty sum for keeping me out of police custody.

Thinking that allowed the anger to break my paralysis. I screamed. It was an inarticulate, primal scream that sounded as if it were torn from the throat of some wounded animal. My hand clutched the Eagle.

The sound of the gunshot was like an explosion going off in my hand. The old cop cursed, and the young one screamed. I whipped my head to the side to see the young cop collapsing. The wild shot had caught him in the upper right thigh, and the fifty-caliber bullet had shattered his leg.

"Shit!" The old cop's right hand was missing the last three fingers. He was yanking his right hand in toward his body and leveling the revolver at me with his left. Steaming blood stained the snow. Its scent was a dagger into my forebrain.

Something was happening to me.

I got up, and everything I saw seemed to have been carved out with a razor. Blood was glowing fire, turning back at the edges where it soaked into the shimmering violet snow. The old cop scrambled away from me, pointing the gun. His skin glowed, heat and fear and anger rippled off of him, distorting my view.

I could feel my body changing, my bones shifting as I stood. My skin emitted nothing, no heat, no emotion. If anything, it was a gaping *lack* that surrounded me, a desperate hunger.

I dropped the Eagle.

The cop's gun fired, licking a tongue of flame at my abdomen. I felt the bullet as a blow to my midsection, but there was no blood. I could feel the slug pass through my body, tearing its way through, but that was little compared to the tearing my body was doing to itself. I felt muscles ripping and knotting back together; my skin stretched, tightened, gave way, and then regrew; the bones of my face moved of their own accord.

I should have been screaming in pain.

The cop put two more slugs through me before I reached him. I felt a hiccup of fluids as the first bullet shredded my right lung. And, when I was nearly upon him, I was blinded by the flash when he put a bullet through my right cheek. I could feel my jaw cave in with the impact, and I could feel my flesh and bone shred behind me.

All of this happened, and I was only really aware of the hunger.

Still blinded by the muzzle flash, I grabbed for the cop. I could sense where he was, his fear—*his life*—was like a beacon. I felt my hands, fingers much too long, grab the sides of the cop's head. I felt the barrel of the thirty-eight rammed underneath my chin. I heard the click as a hammer fell on an empty chamber.

My vision cleared as I felt the flesh of my face reknitting itself into a new pattern. I felt the sharp curve of new teeth as my jaw rebuilt itself.

The cop looked at me with terrified eyes. "Holy Mother of God."

Nothing was left of my conscious thought. All I had was sensation, and the hunger to posses what this man possessed: heat, blood, life.

I snapped his head back, hearing a crack in his spine. Then I buried my teeth in his exposed neck. My rebuilt jaw easily covered the entire area, and my bite severed both jugulars. None of the blood was spilled on the ground.

When I finally gained control of my actions, I was leaning over the second cop, the young one. He was curled in a fetal position below me, whimpering, "Don't kill me . . . please, don't kill me."

I stood at the edge of a pool of black slush. The snow smelled of blood, a scent like molten iron. Most of the blood came from between the cop's fingers, where he was trying to hold his shattered thigh together.

There was no question in my mind that I was about to kill this cop, just as I'd killed his partner. Then, suddenly,

I was in control again. The *need* had receded for the moment. I actually felt warm.

I stood there, paralyzed by what had just happened. The events had the feverish intensity of a hallucination, but even now, as I felt perfectly lucid, I could feel my body shifting inside.

Bones moved inside me with the persistent pressure of a dull toothache. I stared at my hands.

My hands were inhuman. Their skin was tough, leathery, and nearly black. The fingers ended in curving black nails that were almost talons. As I watched, the fingers shortened, the skin softened and regained its color, and the talons withdrew back into my fingers.

I uttered some profanity, but the word came out as a low slurred whistle because my mouth was rebuilding itself. I put my hands to my face and it was like touching a bony waterbed. I felt what could have been a muzzle retract into my skull.

I turned around to face the other cop.

There was the window, blown open where I had fallen through it. There was the glass, and the remains of the windowframe. There was the imprint in the snow where my body had fallen. An imprint with no blood inside it. There was my fifty-caliber Desert Eagle, dropped on the ground.

And there was the dead cop.

He was sprawled in a half-sitting position, his back to the wall of the apartment building. His right hand was across his waist, fisted into a ball around the missing parts of his fingers. His left hand still clutched the thirty-eight. His face was slack, and as blue as the snow he sat in.

His neck had been torn open down to the bone. Muscle, windpipe, everything between me and the vertebrae had been torn out as if mauled by an animal. The sight should have been gory, but it wasn't. The living cop, next to me, was much worse with his bleeding leg. The dead cop, with the exception of a few trails from his wounded hand, had spilled no blood at all.

My body had stopped changing, and I looked down at myself.

I saw five bullet holes in my shirt, two showing powder burns. I felt underneath, and my chest was intact.

Of course, it's intact, I thought.

"Please don't kill me . . ." the cop behind me whimpered again.

I felt sick over everything that had just happened. I had just killed a cop—a bent cop, but still a cop. The guy with the wounded leg had watched every minute. Shadows moved at windows above me, and in the distance I heard sirens wail.

The man beneath me was the only witness to what had happened. And by Gabriel's Covenant, I had to kill him. He had seen what I had done. If I left him to witness against me, I'd have more than the police after me.

I knelt down and pulled him up to face me. I held the sides of his head like I had his partner. . . .

He was sputtering and tears of fear and pain ran down his cheeks. I felt his terror. Whatever I had become, I couldn't kill him. Not like this, and not in cold blood.

There has to be another way. There had to be, Gabriel had told me that it wasn't necessary to kill for blood. How then did any vampire take blood without revealing his nature?

It was a combination of impulse and memory that made me shout at the terrified cop, "Look at me!"

The memory was of Bowie's reaction when he looked into my eyes. Everyone seemed to have a reaction to my uncovered gaze. The impulse was totally unlike me, possibly inspired by my talk with Gabriel. I remembered thinking, *who is this man—this* human—*to defy my will?*

He looked at me, and when our eyes met, his gaze didn't shift or turn away. He didn't even blink. "You did not see who shot you," I said to him, bludgeoning him with the words. "You saw nothing of what happened. You do not know what happened to your partner. Tell anyone what has happened here, if you even remember it yourself, you shall surely die. . . ."

I felt a flash of memory, someone's stony voice saying, ". . . *if you even remember it yourself, you shall surely die* . . ." I was gripped by the feeling that this had happened before.

I had no time to dwell on it. The sirens were closing on me. The young cop nodded like a zombie, and I let him slide to the ground. I ran back to the building and grabbed my Desert Eagle and its one spent casing. Luckily for me, the cop was using a revolver and I didn't have to go hunting for his brass.

After holstering the Eagle, I grabbed the collar of the dead cop and dragged his corpse to the Oldsmobile. I tossed him in the back seat because I didn't have the time to wrestle with the trunk.

I drove away, relying on whatever psychic impression my will had made upon the young policeman.

16

It was almost five in the morning when I drove out of Lakewood with a corpse in the back seat. I didn't pass any police cars in my escape. I only stopped once, on a side street, to steal a manhole cover. I was caught up in a rush of action which gave me no time to reflect.

The central part of the Cuyahoga River had yet to freeze, and the cop's bloodless corpse found its home in a plunge from the Detroit-Superior Bridge. He slipped under quickly. His legs were bound to the stolen manhole cover with the Olds' jumper cables.

When he had slipped beneath the dark waters of his ultimate dim Thule and I had driven away, my mind was free to think beyond the next five minutes of my future.

I began to appreciate what had happened. I had slaughtered one policeman, and shot out of the leg of another. It had been Tony all over again.

I ran my hand across my face. I was shaking.

"What have I become?" I whispered.

I had no justification for killing the policeman. His bullets could not harm this thing I was. I had been in no danger from him, and I had known it when I had risen from the ground. I couldn't see the circumstances to rationalize dropping my gun and mauling his neck. It was all too much like what had happened with Tony. I had murdered Tony, and I had murdered this cop.

There was one major difference between the cop's death and Tony's. With this man I didn't even have the excuse that I didn't know what I was doing. I knew what I was, and I had known what I was capable of, and I did not stop myself.

I felt as if, on some level I had killed both of them, Tony

and the policeman, because their existence had *offended* me.

I pulled the Olds to the side of Superior, just past Public Square, because I had begun driving erratically, and the last thing I needed was to draw the attention of any more police. Once the car was parked, I put my face in my hands feeling that I had lost Kane Tyler completely.

When I bent over, something small and black tumbled onto the passenger seat.

It was a thirty-eight slug, or the biggest part of one. It was flattened and coated with a thin layer of gore.

I picked up the slug. It looked as if it had struck bone on its way through, a bone that should be broken and splintered. It was covered in my blood, but the only holes were in my clothing, not my body . . .

I had left the human universe, physically as well as morally. I thought of Gabriel's society and wondered how anyone could live like this, live in that world, and remain sane.

Perhaps sanity was only a human concept—

"Stop it," I whispered. "We all come from the same place, all of us." I *was* still Kane Tyler, a Kane Tyler who had undergone a physical transformation of some sort, but I was still the same man.

Thinking that only made the deaths that much worse.

Wind whistled by the car, the sound low and loathsome. Garbage rustled by the car, scuttling across the snow in front of the Olds. I thought of the cop slipping into the black waters of the Cuyahoga and wondered if he had any family. Was there a widow out there, perhaps a son who was trying to understand where his father had gone?

As Gail was trying to understand why her mother had gone?

How could I face my daughter, when I was becoming what I was hunting? I sat in the car a long time, wondering if this life after life was worth what it was eating out of my soul. I sat trembling as I stared at the sky, which had lightened from purple to a deep aqua.

According to Gabriel, all I would need to do was await the transit of the sun, and this would all be over. I would have no more blood on my hands. . . .

The sky ahead of me, to the east, began to take a yellowish tint to the clouds.

I couldn't do this. My life didn't belong to me. I couldn't make Gail an orphan, and I couldn't abandon Cecilia to her fate. If I gave up now, the deaths on my conscience really *would* be pointless.

I revved up the Olds and started down Superior. Now that I'd changed my mind, the coming dawn filled me with a growing fear. I needed to get inside.

I drove through the shadows provided by the buildings downtown, but a furtive glance in the rearview mirror showed me the first molten light washing the tops of the skyscrapers downtown. The eastern faces of the towers were washed in gold, and reflections off the mirrored glass seared my eyes. The sight burned like a brand, scattering purple dead-spots across my field of vision.

I was driving *toward* the sun.

The Olds swerved as I blinked my eyes clear. Twice-reflected dawn sunlight—*Cleveland* dawn sunlight, in *winter*—was as blinding to me as a magnesium flare.

In a matter of minutes, the long shadows of the buildings would crawl across the Olds, leaving me bare to the sun. Worse, something in the ambient light, the light that reached into the shadows, was hot, numbing, and brought with it a crushing fatigue. I felt an urge to pull to the side of the road and go to sleep.

I turned off of Superior to find a darkened bolt-hole. I found an underground parking garage that offered all-day parking for ten bucks. When I pulled into the driveway, the sunlight had reached the second floor of the building. I waited by the gate and peeled off a fifty from the cash I'd liberated from the hotel room.

There was a guy sitting in a booth by the gate, and I waited for him. And waited. And waited.

When the sunlight reached down to the top of the garage's entrance, I laid on the horn. The guy in the booth to my left looked up and gave me a sour look. He didn't move. I laid on the horn again.

He stepped out of the booth and yelled at me, "We ain't open till seven-thirty."

Fuck. I looked at my watch. It was fifteen after.

I rolled the window down the Olds and tried to shout at the guy, but it came out as a wheeze. I panicked for a moment before I realized that I had to consciously start breathing again. As I did so, I tempered my anger. "Come on, I'm only a little early—"

The guy looked peeved, but he stopped yelling, "Look, you have to wait."

"Only fifteen minutes." The dawn was drawing across in front of me, a blinding curtain of light washing across the front of the garage. I could feel my skin tightening. I wanted to shrink into the shadows the Olds provided. But I leaned out the window and flashed the fifty at the guy.

I looked him in the eyes.

The guy squinted as a line of sunlight began crossing his face, "I don't know, my boss'd can me."

I extended the fifty. "For a few extra minutes? Come on, open the gate."

We stared at each other as the sunlight crept toward my hand. I wanted to flinch, but I sensed withdrawing the fifty—or any sudden move—would break whatever spell I was trying to weave.

"I don't know. . . ." Blinding light toughed the edge of the fifty. Light so bright that I was surprised that the bill didn't burst into flame.

It was slow, so damn slow. It seemed an age before he said, "Okay," and grabbed the fifty.

I snatched my hand back, but as I did, I felt the brush of sunlight across its back. The touch of direct sunlight was not as dramatic as I thought it should be. My hand didn't burst into flame, or crumble into dust.

What happened was frightening because it was so subtle in comparison. I felt my entire hand flare with pain, fall asleep, and go numb. It was as if I had plunged my hand into a vat of boiling Novocain.

As the gate opened, I had to drive with one hand. My left hand was limp, paralyzed. I drove into the darkened garage as if the gates of hell were behind me.

Whether I was entering or leaving was open to question.

I found a space in the lowest level of the garage, a place that had never even seen reflected sunlight. I maneuvered the Olds into a dark corner, into a space half-concealed by a concrete pillar. I was as far from the elevator as I could get.

Once I parked, I looked at my hand. The skin was white and numb. It could have been an inanimate lump of meat for all I could do with it. I was still staring at my hand when fatigue crashed over me.

More memories, older ones, kept me company as I fell into my not-sleep.

I don't want to be in this man's office, I resent it. Haven't I've been through enough? Dad's dead. What the hell is this guy supposed to do about it?

"Hello, Kane," the doctor says. "I'm pleased to finally meet you."

"I'm glad someone's enjoying this."

"Your mother thinks you need someone to talk to."

I sigh. "You mean she wants me to talk to someone. What if I don't have anything to say?"

"I find that hard to believe," the doctor says. He glances down at the desk in front of him, where he keeps his files. "You seemed to have a lot to say to your classmates— enough to get you suspended."

I shook my head. "That wasn't me talking."

The doctor makes a note in front of him and asks, "It wasn't you? Are you saying that you did not step up on a desk in your physics class and shout poetry?"

"I'm saying that those weren't my words. Mr. Franklin asked what something meant. *I quoted something that seemed to apply."*

The doctor makes another note. "Mr. Franklin felt you were being disruptive."

"Sometimes the truth is disruptive."

The doctor nodded, but I didn't make the mistake of thinking he agreed with me. I was here because no one seemed to agree with me. Somehow I was wrong. We were all supposed to accept death, and pain, and loss. Give it some higher meaning, and go on.

"So what was it you quoted to Mr. Franklin that got you in so much trouble?"

"It's by Edgar Allan Poe. 'The Conqueror Worm.' It's part of a short story he wrote."

Another note. "How does it go?"

I sigh. I'm surprised that the doctor doesn't have it in his files there in front of him. But then, I am here to perform.

Why disappoint him? I stand and recite the poem from "Ligeia," first stanza to last.

" 'Lo! 'tis a gala night / Within the lonesome latter years! / An angel throng, bewinged bedight / In veils, and drowned in tears, / Sit in a theater, to see / A play of hopes and fears, / While the orchestra breathes fitfully / The music of the spheres.' "

As I speak, the doctor scribbles, I find that annoying. He requested this, he should be giving undivided attention to it. I raise my voice a bit.

" 'Mimes, in the form of God on high, / Mutter and mumble low, / And hither and thither fly— / Mere puppets they, who come and go / At bidding of vast formless things / That shift the scenery to and fro, / Flapping from out their Condor wings / Invisible Wo!' "

Scribble, scribble. He was worse than Mr. Franklin, who had stood in the midst of his cosmology to stand looking at me agape. He was worse than the other students, who had laughed at things that weren't funny.

" 'That motley drama—oh, be sure / It shall not be forgot! / With its Phantom chased for evermore, / By a crowd that seize it not, / Through a circle that ever returneth in / To the self-same spot, / And much of Madness, and more of Sin, / And Horror the soul of the plot.' "

Damn him. Listen. Stop that infernal scribbling. I climb onto the chair in front of him, as I had in Mr. Franklin's class. The doctor is like the others. He just refuses to see.

" 'But see, amid the mimic rout / A crawling shape intrude! / A blood-red thing that writhes from out / The scenic solitude! / It writhes!—' " *I begin shouting,* " 'it writhes!— with mortal pangs / The mimes become its food, / And seraphs sob as vermin fangs / In human gore imbued.' "

I jump upon the doctor's desk to grab his attention. Finally he looks up from that infernal notepad of his.

" 'Out—' " *I shout.* " 'out are the lights—out all! / And, over each quivering form, / The curtain, a funeral pall, / Comes down with the rush of a storm, / While the angels, all pallid and wan, / Uprising, unveiling, affirm / That the play is the tragedy, "Man," / And its hero the Conqueror Worm.' "

The doctor looks up at me and asks, "How did you feel when your father died?"

*   *   *

"Dad!" *she says to me. Her expression shows exasperation, as if she doesn't understand.*

"Where the hell were you?"

"With friends—come on, it's only one o'clock."

I'm standing out there, more angry at myself than at Gail. I'd just gotten home from a bad day, a really bad day. I look at her, feeling powerless. "I'm sorry, I overreacted. You weren't here and. . . ."

Gail looks around me and says, "Where's Mom?"

Now I feel guilty as well. "She's upstairs, we had a fight."

In her face I can see she understands now. I see her take an unfair share of the weight between me and Kate. "Oh, Dad—it was about me, wasn't it? I'm sorry, I should have left a note or something."

"Shh—"

Gail pushes past me, her hands balled into small fists. "I don't want to give you and Mom something else to fight about."

"No, no," *I reach out and place a hand on her shoulder.* "It's not about you. It's me."

"I'm sorry," *she says.*

"It's not your fault." *I say.* "It's never been your fault."

As I hold my crying daughter, I can't help remembering the girl I'd found today—a girl no older than Gail, who had slowly died on a filthy mattress in a condemned hotel. She had died clutching a dirty needle. In the end, she had lacked the strength to force the needle through her paper-thin skin.

I'd been thinking of Gail ever since I'd told the parents.

I look up from my daughter, and I see Kate framed in the stairwell above us. Our eyes meet and I know our marriage has ended.

17

I wasn't going to put Gail through what that dead child had put her parents through. I wasn't going to put Gail through what my father had put me through. I would see her, and somehow I would make some explanation.

I sat up and felt a tug on my left arm.

I looked down.

I'd been slumped against the driver's door allowing my left arm to slip between the door and the seat. My left hand was snow white, and its thumb was caught in the metal under the seat, twisted at an ugly angle. I stared at my hand for a long time, stared at the white, waxy skin.

I didn't feel a damn thing. My thumb was bent back past the wrist, a position that meant a sprain, a dislocation, or even a break, and all I felt was the tension in the muscles of my arm.

The shock of the sight brought back the memory of sunlight on my skin.

I used my other hand to free my thumb from its trap. Touching the skin of my hand was like touching ice. I leaned back in the seat and rested my hands on the wheel, comparing them. I couldn't move my left hand at all; it was only some residual elasticity in the tendons that pulled my thumb back into position.

The skin was dead-looking, slightly puffy and taut. If I hadn't known how it had happened, I would think frostbite. The sight was scary, not just for itself, but because the injury was still there, still affecting me.

Everything else that had happened to me since I had come out of the ground had healed, everything from bullet wounds to the slashes on my wrist put there with a beer bottle. But what the sun had done—that had lasted through the day.

What was I supposed to do? I couldn't quite go into a normal emergency room and tell them what was wrong with me. I doubted anyone at the Cleveland Clinic had vampirism as a specialty. Once again I was forced to drive the Olds one-handed. It made me thankful that it was an automatic.

The sky was still a light azure when I pulled out of the garage. The streetlights were just coming on. It was barely quarter after six, and the city was still wrapped with people. It was Monday afternoon, and the people, and the traffic, made me feel part of the world for a while.

It was too easy to become lost in the night. Too easy to feel alone. I missed the light.

I'd left the downtown area, and was driving past the Cleveland Clinic. Sam lived in University Circle, that's where I was heading. I needed to see Gail, but my hand was becoming harder to ignore.

The base of my thumb had begun to discolor. It was only the color of a bruise, but in contrast to the blank whiteness around it, it was as livid as an open wound. I still felt nothing.

How was I supposed to deal with this? I needed to find out, before it became any worse. I pulled over and got out of the car next to a pay phone. I only knew one source of information who might know how to handle this. I called the number on Gabriel's card.

I stood there, holding the receiver with my shoulder. It rang a few times, and then I heard the familiar electronic voice. "You have reached an automated voice messaging system. At the sound of the beep, speak your own name slowly and clearly. If your response is unclear or unacceptable, you will be disconnected."

In response to the beep, I said, "Kane Tyler."

Up until then it had gone just as before. But in response to my name, it said, "I am not able to respond to 'Kane Tyler.'" It was my voice, complete with traffic noise in the background. The machine clicked, and I heard a dial tone.

"No . . ." I hung up and tried again. I hoped that I just hadn't spoken clearly enough for the machine to recognize me. I got the same response a second time, and a third.

I slammed the receiver down on the cradle. The bastard

had cut me off. Damn Gabriel and his preoccupation with status. I could see his thinking. In his eyes, it wasn't proper to for *me* to initiate a contact with *him*—and that was annoying as hell.

I looked at my hand. Annoying? It might be deadly.

Fuck. I wasn't going to let them lose me that easily. People hung up on me all the time. I had something better. I had an address. That house of Gabriel's held more than Gabriel, and somewhere there was someone who would talk to me.

"What about Gail?" I whispered.

I stood there on the curb staring at my hand. Snow fell, and when the snow touched my left hand it didn't melt. I felt no pain, no cold. My hand didn't even feel part of my body anymore.

I told myself that it had happened twelve hours ago, and the effects hadn't spread beyond my hand. I doubted spending some time with Gail could make things worse; the damage was done.

I shouldered the receiver again and fished out another quarter. I called Sam's apartment. The phone barely rang once when I heard Sam's voice, "Gail?"

I stood there, frozen by all the possible evils that onc word could mean. Gail wasn't at Sam's like she was supposed to be. Sam was worried, I heard it in his voice. That meant . . .

I didn't even want to consider what that meant.

"Hello?" Sam said.

I had to force myself to breathe so I could get the words out. "What's happened, Sam?"

"Christ, Kane, why aren't you at the motel?"

"Gail—" My voice sounded strangled. "Where is she, Sam?" I asked in a hoarse whisper. My breathing was so shallow that my voice didn't even fog the air.

"She was supposed to drive here with the cop—"

"Fuck 'supposed to!' What in hell *did* happen?"

"She took her own car, Kane. I'm sorry."

"My God, what kind of protection is that? How did— Where—"

"She slipped away from her cop. The only word was a message she left on my voice mail; she's coming to see you."

"How? She doesn't know where I am—" I stopped. The phone slipped out of my fingers.

"Kane? Kane?"

"The motel," I whispered. "She's going to the motel." Gail knew where I was *supposed* to be staying.

The receiver swung free as I ran back to the Oldsmobile. She knew about the motel. I needed to get there before she met anyone else who knew about that motel.

I raced back to the motel. I drove with my bad hand, pressing the palm to the wheel and steering by friction. I was making it worse, but I wasn't giving up any of the time it took to drive one-handed. I sped most of the way there, slowing only when I actually saw a cop.

My mind was tumbling with ugly emotions, fear, anger, anticipated grief. I knew that if Gail was harmed, the person responsible would be torn apart at my hands. I tried to tell myself that she would be there, and fine, but Sam's voice . . . he knew I wasn't at the motel, that meant he had been calling. She wasn't there yet. Or she had been there already and—

The shift lever bent in my hand, and I tried to force myself to think of driving.

It was ten after seven when I skidded the Olds into the parking lot of the Woodstar Motel. The Olds threw a shower of snow across the parked cars as if it were a two-ton figure skater. The moment the car stopped moving, I grabbed the keys and dived out into the cold night air.

I looked at the lot, checking the cars. The Chevette, my car, was still there, buried up to the fenders. The Olds blocked it in now, parked cockeyed in the center of the parking lot.

Also here was Gail's car. I knew it the minute I saw it. It was an ancient lemon-yellow Volkswagon Rabbit with an Oberlin College sticker in the rear window.

"Maybe she just got here," I whispered.

I edged up on the Rabbit and placed my right hand on its hood. The hood was cold, and the snow dusted the car evenly. I looked back, up the street. I didn't see Sebastian's men. I looked toward the front of the motel, at the glass-fronted manager's office, and saw no one inside.

There was nowhere left except my room.

I felt my heart beat, much too slowly for how I felt. I fished the motel key out of my pocket one-handed as I ran up the stairs. When I closed on my room, I slowed. I could see lights glowing around the shades in the window.

I inched toward the door, listening.

The TV was on in there.

Gail? Would she've been able to talk her way in? I looked down at the doorknob and saw the fresh scratches of a real amateur jimmying the door open.

When I saw that, I pocketed the motel key and drew the Eagle.

I took a deep breath and kicked the door open, leveling the gun at the room. The door slammed into the room, jingling broken hardware.

There was Bowie, on the bed, beer in his hand, watching the motel's piped-in pornography. He looked at me and said, "And where the fuck did you go?"

I almost shot him right there. Instead I yelled at him, "Where the hell is Gail?"

Bowie looked as innocent as I suppose he was capable of. "Who?"

"My daughter, you bastard!"

He shrugged and sat up, chugging the beer in a way that made me feel sick to my stomach. "Why would I know?"

"Because you're here," I leveled the Eagle at him. "And if you don't explain what you're doing here, I am going to decorate the wall with parts of that skinny torso of yours."

Bowie spread his arms wide and said, "Whoa, whoa, whoa! Hold the phone, I was supposed to be helping you, remember? Doctor and all that."

"What are you doing in my room?"

"Looking for you. You ran out on me and Leia. Where else do I have to look for you, huh?"

"You make a habit of jimmying the doors of people you're trying to help?"

"Fuck it, Kane." Bowie grimaced at the can, crushed it, and tossed it out the door, through my legs. "Did I know what state you were in? You could've been catatonic on the floor for all I knew." He shook his head and said, "Why don't you come in here and put that cannon away?"

I looked at him and decided, even if Bowie weren't completely sincere, he wasn't immediately threatening. I holstered the gun and pushed the door shut with my foot.

The door closed crooked and left in a draft. Luckily, the latch still caught, even after the violence done to it. I leaned against it, and looked at Bowie, keeping my eyes averted from the mirror on the bureau.

Bowie had made himself at home. The remains of a six-pack littered the floor, and he had moved the TV away from the bureau so it sat at the foot of the bed.

"I'm going to ask you again," I said. "Where's my daughter?"

"I'm telling you," Bowie said. "I. Don't. Know."

"Her car's outside—"

"She never came here, man. I been up here almost since you slipped out on me. . . ."

I looked for the phone, it wasn't on the night table anymore. "And you haven't picked up the phone?"

"They're your messages. I was trying to keep a low profile."

"Yeah, right. Where is—" The phone began to ring before I had a chance to ask. The sound was muffled, and it was hard to tell where it was coming from.

"Under the bed," Bowie said.

"Under the—" I knelt and the phone was there, wrapped in a pillow.

"Too many calls, man." Bowie explained. "The noise was distracting."

I grabbed the phone out on the third ring, "Hello."

I was expecting Sam's voice. Instead I heard, "Dad?"

"*Gail?* Christ, baby, where are you? You have no idea how worried I was."

There was a pause as she took a breath.

"What's wrong?" I asked.

"Dad, I'm sorry, I think I've screwed things up."

"Whatever it is, I forgive you. You're all right?"

"Yeah, I think so."

"Now where are you?"

"Bratenahl."

"*Bratenahl?* You're in Bratenahl? How did—" I paused for a while as it sank in. My employer, Mr. Sebastian, had an estate in Bratenhl. "Oh, no," I whispered. "What does he want?"

"He said that you were just supposed to come down here. He wants to talk to you real bad."

"If he hurts you—"

"He's been nice, really."

"Nice?" I shouted into the phone. "That bastard's a god-damned drug-dealer. *He kidnapped you!"*

There was a long pause.

"Gail? Gail?"

"Look, Dad, I'm sorry. He didn't kidnap me."

"What?"

"They said that they'd give me a chance to see you. You weren't answering your phone, and you already disappeared once. And you *are* working for him, aren't you?" I could hear the tears in her voice. "I fucked up again, Dad. I'm sorry."

"Shh. It's all right, I'm coming down there, okay?"

I heard her sniff. "Okay. He wants you to come alone, with his car."

"I'll see you soon, baby."

"Yeah, Dad. Love you."

"Love you." I waited to hear the click of a disconnection. Then I slammed the receiver back on its cradle hard enough to explode the phone's plastic shell.

"You bastard, Sebastian!" I yelled at the walls.

"What's going on?" Bowie asked.

"I'm going to see my daughter," I said, yanking the broken door open. I left Bowie to his beer cans and his pornography.

18

The ride gave me time to think, not necessarily a good thing. Feelings washed over me in cycles: first anger, then black depressive guilt, then numbed fear, then rage again. It was very hard to hold my mind together. Whatever I thought about, I kept coming back to Gail, and what I had become.

I kept blaming myself for involving her in this. I had the sick feeling that somehow my job was responsible. I was, or I had been, a private investigator hunting missing children, runaways, parental kidnappings. How could I do that for a living without somehow dragging my own daughter in? I had seen Gail in every case I worked; that had been what destroyed my marriage. . . .

My own obsession blamed itself for her involvement, as if my perpetual worry were a self-fulfilling prophecy.

God, I had entered this line of work because I thought it was *safer*. It was as thankless a job as being a policeman, especially in the custody cases, but it had been supposed to be better. The bullet that pierced my lung made me believe that working on the force was too reckless for a man with a family. So I took a job that destroyed the family that I was trying to protect.

Sebastian had hired me to find his daughter Cecilia. He had put me under surveillance, and I was certain that the cops who had tried to kill me were on *his* payroll. At this point I didn't know what he was capable of. Now he had *my* daughter.

And I *worked* for him.

My vision blurred, fuzzing the streetlights. With all the strangeness going on in my body, I found the tears reassuring.

This had to stop, somehow. It was bad enough that Gail

had run into the human part of this travesty. I had to do everything within my power to prevent her from becoming ensnared in the undead half of everything. It was a sick thing to think, but with Childe out there—with his cult out there—maybe being with Sebastian was the safest place for her.

It was nearly eight when I reached Bratenahl, a suburb of walled estates, gatehouses, and garages bigger than my house.

Sebastian lived in a Rockefeller-era mansion of gray stone. The cobbled drive was flanked by a pair of bronze lions gone white with frost. There was no gate barring the Olds as I followed the circular drive to the front of the house, but I noted more than a few anachronistic security cameras panning along the wrought-iron fence surrounding the property. The cameras hung from the eaves, poked out from odd bits of landscaping, and one even nestled in the arms of a century-old oak that dominated the lawn between the mansion and the gatehouse in front.

I pulled the Olds to a stop at the front door. The main entrance was a Gothic stone arch filled with a massive pair of oak doors, and flanked by an acre of leaded glass.

In '77 I was a rookie, and I had busted Sebastian for a dime bag. Somewhere between then and now I had retired, and Sebastian had done five years at Lucasville. Now he lived here, the home of a millionaire with a few zeros to spare.

I opened the door and slid out, shoving my bad hand in the pocket of my jacket.

The massive doors opened, and Bishop and Mr. Gestapo stepped out to greet me. "Welcome, Mr. Tyler," said Bishop. "Mr. Sebastian is eager to meet with you, finally."

I nodded, not trusting myself to say anything that wouldn't sound like a threat. As choked by anger as I was, I still knew I didn't want to antagonize anyone needlessly.

"The weapon, if you please?" Bishop held out his hand. I wasn't in a position to argue. I drew the Eagle and handed it over to him. Bishop took it, gave it an admiring glance, checked the safety, and slipped it into his waistband.

Mr. Gestapo was much less polite. He held out a sweaty palm and said, "Keys."

I looked at him, tempted to toss the keys at his feet.

Again, though, there was little profit in antagonizing people right now. I dropped the keys into his hand.

"Come with me," Bishop said. As he led me toward the massive doors, Mr. Gestapo drove the Olds away toward the gatehouse.

Bishop led me through a central hall dominated by a massive staircase. The stairs sat below tall windows that faced north, toward the lake. In daylight it must have been a seven-figure view, but right now the windows were blank, an acre of dead black broken only by the reflection of the chandelier.

Bishop took me along a broad corridor leading off the entry hall. He delivered me into a library that could have comfortably fit most of Childe's apartment inside it. The ceiling was eighteen feet high, and the fireplace, currently roaring away, could have doubled as a garage.

Sebastian stood facing away from me, the fireplace, and the door. He was looking out a set of French doors that opened up on a slightly lesser darkness than the windows in the entry hall.

"Sit down." Sebastian's voice was a perfect Midwestern null. The voice was at odds with the rest of him. He had dark curly hair, and swarthy Mediterranean features. He had the look of old-world Europe about him.

"Where's my daughter?" I said.

"Where is *my* daughter? *Sit down*, Mr. Tyler."

I sat down on one of two leather chairs facing the fire. I noticed the bullet holes in my shirt. I pulled my coat over to hide them. The damage to my trench coat was less obvious; the bullet's damage was hidden in the midst of all the other damage I'd done to my coat.

"I'm *looking* for Cecilia," I said. "My job, remember?"

I had to half-turn to see Sebastian, who remained staring out the windows. When I turned, I ignited a new ache in my left wrist, still wedged in the pocket of my jacket. I tried to adjust my body to ease the pressure on my hand. I didn't try to remove it from my pocket.

"I've tried very hard to hate you, Tyler," he said. It wasn't what I expected from him. I felt the need to say something, but I had absolutely no idea what it could have been.

Facing out the window, fiddling with his hands, Sebastian talked on as if I weren't quite there. "When you first turned me down, I tried to hate you. Your accusations, 'How could something as evil as I, a drug dealer, be a decent father—' You have no idea of the anger I felt. What I felt because I still *needed* you."

"You're not helping by taking Gail—"

Sebastian raised his head, as if he were talking to a bird perched on the transom of his door. "Am I? I've seen those tapes. Your daughter needs protection, as my own daughter needed protection."

"I appreciate the vote of confidence."

Sebastian didn't seem to hear me. "Hate is not an easy emotion for me, Mr. Tyler. I don't hate the police. We both have jobs, and I accepted the risks of mine, just as they did theirs. Like them, if I have to draw a weapon in my line of work, something's gone wrong. And despite my anger, I can't hate you, Mr. Tyler. I understand you too well."

Sebastian turned to face me, and I saw a rosary in his hands. My throat tightened.

"You hold me guilty of too much. Can you hold that *I* am evil after you've been touched by it yourself?" The firelight carved dancing shadows on his dusky face. The light reflected in his eyes made him look a little mad.

I wanted to tell him exactly what I thought he was guilty of. All I needed to think of were dead-eyed junkies dying of AIDS, or reed-thin teenagers selling what was left of their bodies so they could buy a rock. Something in his eyes kept my mouth shut. The sight of the rosary held my attention.

"If I wasn't a father to my Cecilia, it was because I was kept from her the second five years of her life. And afterward, what could I do after Rosa died?" His eyes welled up and he crossed himself. I had to turn away. It was becoming as difficult to watch Sebastian as it was to see my own eyes in a mirror. If I needed any confirmation as to what was happening to me, the uncomfortable proximity of Sebastian's faith was it.

"I didn't know how to be a father. She was lost to me before she was taken."

Sebastian had walked in front of me, but he was staring into the fire. "I have seen those tapes you made. I have seen them too many times. I have seen the—the—*being* who was once my daughter." Sebastian turned to look at me. "Do you understand?"

I nodded.

"You *made* those tapes. Do you understand the evil I am talking about. The true *evil* here?"

"I think so."

"I do not hate easily. But this Childe, him I hate. He has mortgaged my daughter's *soul*. So she is not only lost to me, but to our Savior as well." Sebastian kissed the rosary and put it in his pocket. I felt better without the beads in view. I felt that I could speak again—

"What about *my* daughter, Sebastian?"

"I need you to lead me to my daughter, and Childe. I need your mind focused, and I need to keep track of you." He stared into the fire and said, "I do not hate easily. But I have hatred for the creatures responsible."

Sebastian's profile, rose-colored in the firelight, appeared as if it were carved out of the shadows around him. "Lately I've had to ask myself, Mr. Tyler, if you are part of the evil that took my daughter."

"What?" My voice was a near-whisper, but the shock in it must have carried to Sebastian. He turned his head to look at me. Half his face ruddy-lit by the dancing flames, the other half a featureless black shadow. But both his eyes locked on my own, and I could see a fire in them that wasn't wholly reflected from the fireplace.

"Are you a part of this evil?"

"No," I said it confidently, but there was a squirming doubt in my gut.

"Perhaps." I saw him fingering the rosary in his pocket. "Only perhaps. If you were to succumb to the evil, though, I would be less a man if I allowed that to harm your daughter. . . ."

There was something in the eye contact, I could tell. The same thing that had drawn Bowie out when I questioned him, the sense that my own words could have some physical effect behind my opponent's eyes. This, however, was different. What was behind Sebastian's eyes was armored by something impenetrable. The light I saw was the reflection of something deep and solid within the man, which could not be moved.

Whatever it was, it was strengthened whenever he fingered the rosary in his pocket. Sebastian shook his head and walked back toward the window. For a long time he stared outside. Finally he said, "Your daughter is lucky, she has her soul."

"What do you want from me?"

"You are going to lead me to Childe, so I can wipe this abomination from the face of the Earth."

"I've been looking—"

"There is no more search. You have what you need. I've listened to your notes. You've known this evil, and you knew enough once to track the evil to its heart. I do not believe your ignorance."

He turned around to face me. He was silhouetted by the reflection of the fireplace in the windows behind him. It looked as if he were walking out of the fire. "I don't know what stays your hand: fear, or something else. But by our Lord, your hand will move. You have no choice."

I stood up and Sebastian looked at me with his hard, fiery eyes and said, "If you are part of the evil that consumed my daughter, I will destroy you." He turned back to the window. "Bishop will lead you to the gatehouse and give you a few hours to think."

19

Bishop locked me in a set of rooms that originally were part of the servant's quarters. These had long since been converted to a set of small apartments on the upper floor of the gatehouse. One of the first things I noted after the door closed behind me was the fact that the iron scroll-work outside the windows was a bit more functional than it looked.

I'd been cornered again.

What had Sebastian done with Gail?

I collapsed on a couch in the living-room area, and felt a renewed ache in my wrist. Not my hand, which was as insensible as ever, but in the area of my wrist that seemed to separate the damaged flesh from the rest of me. The pain was deep into the bone, and made me stand up before I had completely seated myself.

Even without the pocket cutting into it, the ache persisted.

I tried to shake my hand loose of the pocket, but it didn't come free. I had to peel the fabric of my coat away with my right hand as I pulled my hand away. In addition to my hand, I had liberated a smell. A faint overripe smell, some sweet fruit which had just gone a little mushy.

I wrinkled my nose and looked down to my hand. It had changed color. The ugly black at the base of my thumb had spread to the meat of my palm extending into a vague imprint of the Oldsmobile's steering wheel. The back was crossed by a purple-black diagonal stripe where the seams of my jacket pocket had bit. A webwork of coppery-green streaked the white skin. My whole hand had swollen, asymmetrically in some places.

I touched the black area by my thumb. The skin gave with a soft mushy sound and the color seeped a little into the surrounding area—like ink bleeding under my skin. I took my finger away, and a dimple stayed in the blackness, where I had pressed. The smell had grown much stronger in the interim.

"Oh, fuck."

I pushed up my sleeve, and saw the line where the dead flesh—in my gut I now knew it was dead—met my own.

When I joined the force, I had some basic first-aid training. I wasn't a medic, but I could recognize a few basic things; burns, fractures, shock—and when my nose is rubbed in it, I could recognize gangrene.

At the edge of the dead tissue, where the ache in my wrist began, there was a definite line of discoloration. It was reassuring to see the diseased flesh stop at that line.

I walked into the apartment's kitchen and washed my hand off. It was a futile gesture. The smell came from inside the flesh, and when the rot reached the surface of my skin, nothing would stop it. I scrubbed maniacally, my left hand cold, limp, and mushy. I must have washed for five minutes before I came to my senses. Mercifully the mushy fruit smell had receded beneath the lemon scent of the dish soap I was using.

My hand was dead, period. It had to be amputated before the gangrene spread.

"Dad, are you all right—"

I spun around, suds from the dish soap splattering the linoleum of the kitchenette. Gail stood in the middle of the living room, on the other side of the only furniture, a couch and a glass-topped coffee table.

She stared at me. I stood there, gaping a few moments, suds dripping from my dead hand.

"Dad?"

"Where did you come from?" I finally asked. "You startled me." I reached across the sink and grabbed a dishtowel, more to hide my hand than to dry it. It wasn't something Gail needed to see.

She bit her lip as she looked at me. My memory was still playing traitorous games with my mind. When I looked at her, I kept wanting to see a thirteen-year-old who made pottery horses and dragons. Gail wasn't supposed to be an adult. She wasn't supposed to be taller than Kate.

In answer to my question, she gave a halfhearted wave

toward an open doorway on the other side of the apartment. Beyond, I saw the corner of a bed. She stood there looking at me for a long time, then she shook her head and whispered, "No. I refuse—" Her voice choked off the words.

"Gail, don't—"

She looked at me and moisture was streaming down her cheeks. "My God, Dad. What's going on here? You're the one who disappeared, and you give me that damn *look,* as if I was some criminal—and, and, and. . . ." She collapsed on to the couch, putting her face in her hands.

"Oh, no, honey." I sat down next to her, putting my good arm around her shoulders. "I never thought that, I just worry about you—"

Gail sat upright and glared at me with her tear-streaked face. "You worry? What about *me?* I'm not allowed to worry about you? You disappeared, Mom dies, and you let me go on thinking the same thing—" Her words caught and she looked away from me, the anger bleeding from her voice. "That the same thing might have happened to you."

I hugged her. In that embrace I felt a profound sense of loss, perhaps as deep as the loss Sebastian felt. I was here, with Gail, but I had already started down a path that she couldn't follow.

"That isn't going to happen," I said weakly.

"Is there any particular reason I should believe that?" Gail asked. "I have a right to know what's going on here—what happened to Mom."

"I don't want to get you involved in this."

Gail shrugged out from under my arm and stood up. "You're incredible, Dad. Mom's dead. I spent a week with a cop. I'm here because I wanted to see you. Dad, I'm involved whether you want me to be or not."

"You don't know what you're saying."

Gail turned around and yelled at me, *"Whose fault is that?"*

We stared at each other, and, stressed as I felt, I found my gaze searching out her eyes. I wanted to force her away from the subject.

When I realized what I was doing, I turned away. My gaze landed on my reflection in the glass top of the coffee table. The vision brought only a slight twinge; my face was cloaked in shadow, and my eyes were invisible. "I don't want you hurt."

"It's a little late for that."

The words stung worse than the sunlight. They had a similar effect, leaving me numb and dead inside. "I never wanted Kate to—"

Her voice softened. "I never said that." She sat down on the arm of the couch, facing me. "But you've already tried to protect me from what you do. Anytime I ask you details, you close up. It's time you stop it." Gail sighed. "You can't protect me from my own life."

I turned away, nodding. "It would have been better if you didn't have me for a father—"

Gail sighed.

"What?" I asked.

"Nothing. You just always end an argument by blaming yourself. I never could stand that."

Perhaps, but it didn't mean what I said was any less true. Yet Gail was right as well. She had a right to know. But what could I tell her before she decided I was crazy?

"Have you talked to Sebastian about any of this?"

"I asked him what was going on."

I nodded. "What did he tell you?"

"He's crazy. Did you know that?"

I turned back to face her; this time I did look into her eyes. Her eyes were so much like I had remembered my own. "What did he tell you?"

"He told me stories about Gothic paranoia, spirits of evil, and the threat to my immortal soul. He showed me a video." Her voice changed tenor. "He *is* crazy. Isn't he?"

"What did he say threatened your immortal soul?"

Gail grimaced and began turning away, but her eyes kept locked on mine. "You, Dad. He said you might threaten me." She reached into her collar and pulled out a rosary she was wearing around her neck.

Strangely, I felt no effect from this rosary—nothing like the one Sebastian had been handling.

"He gave me this thing to protect myself."

I looked at the cross and asked, "What video did he show you?"

Gail described it in hushed tones that sparked my own memory.

*   *   *

The wide expanse of a dam, the circle of figures. . . .

Ten people in the semicircle, facing away from me, toward the structure set in the hillside. The building is stone, its one doorway a shadowed black hole. It looks like a mausoleum.

A woman is led from the mausoleum by a figure cowled in black robes. I feel an awful certainty that the cowled figure is Childe, even though I see none of his features, or much of anything beyond the robe.

The woman, however, I recognize. Her white dress contrasts against the surrounding night and her Mediterranean features. She is Cecilia, Sebastian's daughter.

Something catches in my throat as she opens her arms to the surrounding horde, as if to embrace them.

Childe's people descend upon her—a chaos of motion. I see claws and fangs appear from nowhere. The attackers' bodies distort, backs arch unnaturally, limbs extend. During the frenzy the creatures tearing into Cecilia are no longer human. Cecilia is invisible behind the demonic mass. Only glimpses of her white dress are visible.

And, with each glimpse, over the space of half a minute, her dress darkens. The snow around the attack darkens as well, until the mass breaks off from around her. Cecilia is now only an inert form on a field of black snow.

They appear human again, and then the teenager stares at me with a face covered with night-black blood.

He smiles.

Before I turn and run for my life, I see something else as well.

Childe bends over Cecilia. In the glimpse I see only a pair of pale arms extend out of the sleeves of his robe, over the corpse.

Before I run, I see Cecilia move.

"I made that tape," I whispered. The whole episode could have been staged to drive Sebastian insane. I wondered if it had been.

"Are those bullet holes?" Gail asked. I had leaned back, remembering, and Gail was now leaning forward, staring at my shirt. The rosary now dangled free from her neck. "Dad?"

She looked up at me, and I could see fear in her face. I

could feel it welling up from wherever she had hidden it. "He's wrong, isn't he? On the tape those were just shadows right, you're just looking for some nut-cult, right?" She grabbed my shirt and said, *"Right?"*

I shook my head and stood up. I couldn't stand her touching me, touching what might as well be her father's dead body. The dishtowel fell to the ground and I shoved my left hand into the pocket to my coat.

"Your hand, what happened to your hand?"

I stood, back to her, and said, "I caught a little sun."

"No." I heard her voice tremble. "You can't say he's right. You *can't!*" I heard her move, and her hand pulled my shoulder around to face her. "I love you, Dad."

She hugged me, burying her face in my shoulder. I patted her on the back. "I *love* you, too."

"He wants to put a stake through her heart," I heard her whisper into my shoulder. "His own child."

I shook my head. "He's not right about everything," I told her. I felt the rosary digging into my sternum to no ill effect. "He's not right about everything."

"Are you . . . ?"

"Shh."

"And his daughter?"

"I don't know about Cecilia, but it seems that way."

"What happened to you, Dad?"

"I don't know, honey. I'm still figuring it out myself."

There was a long silence as she rested her head on my shoulder. Then she backed up and said, "I have an Ace bandage in my purse. Do you think that would help?"

I knew it was pointless, but I nodded, "Sure, honey."

She ran and fetched her purse, leaving me to wonder what she must be thinking about me. She returned with the bandage and I told her, "I think I better do this myself."

I turned away and wrapped my hand completely, thumb and fingers together. When I was done, Gail put her hand on my shoulder and asked, "You can't be damned for something you can't control, can you?"

"I don't think—"

I was interrupted by the sound of a gunshot.

Gail broke from me and said, "Dad?"

I grabbed her and dived with her into the kitchenette, flattening myself against her behind the half-wall separating

the kitchen area from the living room and the front door.
"What?" Gail said.

"I don't know."

The gunfire came from the hall outside. It climaxed with
one last, much louder, gunshot. The explosive sound resonated the tile in front of me.

Something slammed against the door hard enough for
the walls to shake. One of the pots hanging on the wall
clattered to the counter, and fell to the floor. My grip on
my daughter tightened.

There was a second or two of silence. I was about to
move us from our minimal cover, when the door to the
apartment exploded into the room. The force of the door
swinging into the apartment scattered yard-long pieces of
the doorframe. Pieces of door were immediately followed
by Bishop, falling backward with such speed that I doubted
his feet touched ground until he landed on the coffee table,
blowing glass everywhere.

Bishop held a nine-millimeter Beretta, or something similar, in his right hand. Falling out of his left hand, as he
skidded across broken glass, splintered wood, and chrome
table legs, was my Desert Eagle.

Bishop was unquestionably unconscious, if not dead.

I stepped away from my slight cover, putting distance
between me and the door. I held up my hand to prevent
Gail from following me into the open.

Following Bishop, walking through the remains of the
door, was Bowie. He turned to face me and I saw a large
bullet hole in the front of his leather jacket. I stared at him
for a second, speechless.

"You waiting for an invitation? Come on, let's move it!"

20

Seeing Bowie here stunned me a moment. Gail stared at me from the corner of the kitchenette, watching me for a reaction. I was still trying to digest the fact that Bowie was a vampire. There wasn't much else that could explain the gaping hole in the front of his shirt, or how he'd taken out Bishop unarmed.

What the hell was happening here?

"Come on," Bowie said. "Before these fucks get their act together!"

Bowie's entrance didn't give me much of a choice. I ran for my gun.

Outside, the night was waking with the sounds of men and dogs. I cursed.

"Come on!" Bowie urged. He shook like a coiled spring.

I holstered the Desert Eagle and held my good hand out to Gail. She hesitated briefly, then took it.

Then Bowie took off down the stairs, out of the gatehouse. I pursued with Gail. "How . . . why . . ." I began. I stopped when we reached the driveway.

Gail bumped into my side, and stared. Next to the road lay the guy I thought of as Mr. Gestapo. His body was immaculate, and the same blue-white as the snowdrift he'd fallen in. I saw the edges of a wound, but most was hidden because he'd fallen face first into the snow.

"Bowie, damn it! I'm supposed to be working *for* Sebastian!"

"Not since you joined the dance, my friend," Bowie yelled, without turning or slowing.

Behind me, too close, I heard a canine growl and the scrabbling of claws across the driveway. I started running again, pulling Gail along and pushing her ahead of me.

I dropped back a few feet, so the dog reached me just

as Gail reached the gate. Bowie was through it, ahead of her, when I heard a growl directly behind me. A Doberman, out of nowhere, clamped its jaws on my right wrist. The sudden pain ignited a flare inside me, a coal of rage I'd been husbanding since Sebastian had taken my daughter.

I growled back.

I turned. For a moment my gaze locked with the animal's. The dog's eyes were empty of everything, like the eyes of a machine. My will burned through those eyes, flashing through the tiny space that was the animal's mind. The dog froze under the onslaught. Something that might have been an abortive whimper died in its throat, behind my arm.

In response, I whipped my right arm toward one of the concrete pillars marking the edge of the gate. The dog's jaws remained attached to my wrist, even as its feet left the ground. It hung on until its back slammed into the pillar. I heard a crack as, about four feet off the ground, the corner of the square pillar put a mortal crease in the Doberman's spine.

All the strength left its jaws, and my wrist ripped free. I ran through the gate as the dog fell to the ground. It hit with a spastic jerk and ceased moving.

Gail wasn't running; she had turned and was staring at me.

I grabbed her as I passed and I heard her whisper, "The world's gone crazy."

I silently agreed with her.

My car, the Chevette, was sitting at the curb, idling, the door open. Bowie was already behind the wheel. He began shifting gears as I shoved Gail in the back seat. Bowie floored the accelerator as soon as most of my own body was in the vehicle.

A Chevette wasn't meant to attempt screaming acceleration on icy pavement, but somehow Bowie managed it. I had to hook my left arm over the passenger seat to keep from tumbling out of the car. My legs dangled over the curb, and the door tried to slam shut on them without quite succeeding.

I managed to lever my legs inside. "What the hell are you doing? Sebastian is—"

"I know, I know." Bowie kept staring ahead, as the Chevette swerved. The passenger door swung widely, but I had my hands full holding myself in place. I kept staring behind us, waiting for the Olds, or some other car, to slide out of Sebastian's estate after us.

"Shut the door, no one's following us."

"How do you know?"

There was a snick next to me. I turned to see Bowie holding an illegally long knife. "Hard to drive with four flats." With a flip of the wrist the knife disappeared.

"What's going on?" Gail finally said with all the angry confusion I felt. "Who is this guy?"

"Friend of your father, sweet-cakes." Bowie said.

I slammed the door shut. "That remains to be seen. This is one hell of a bonehead stunt. I should throttle you for endangering my daughter."

"It's my life, Dad." Gail said. "*I'll* throttle him."

"Hey, man, it's *your* skin you should worry about. You were in there with the man most likely to drive a stake through your heart." Bowie looked at me. I stayed quiet. "You're damn lucky I followed you."

"Was that man dead?" Gail asked.

"What man?" Bowie asked.

"The man, back there, in the snow."

Bowie laughed. "Of all the— Of course he's dead."

"Why did you have to kill him?"

"He was an asshole, he shot me, and I was hungry. That's two more reason than I needed."

"What about the Covenant?" I asked.

Bowie gave me another look, as if he was measuring me. "What about it?"

"You know what about it. The second law, 'No one who holds to the Covenant may reveal those of the blood.' "

Bowie smiled. "You been talking to people, ain't you?"

"Damn it, you've left corpses all over the place and you're blabbing all . . ."

"All this in front of your all-too-human daughter? Tsk, tsk."

I looked back and saw Gail shrink back a little in the seat. She was pressed all the way behind my seat, as far away from Bowie as she could be within the Chevette.

"Look man, first off, I am not leaving 'bodies.' I left one body for Sebastian, who is already too aware of what's going on, and who certainly isn't going to anyone else with the corpse. He'll probably decapitate it, stake it, burn it, or something. Second, you got the abridged version of the Covenant."

"Abridged?"

"Fuck, yeah. Three lines are easy to remember. But we're talking about something older and longer than the Magna Carta. Whoever enlightened you probably saw no profit in describing all the exceptions."

"Like?"

"Like, humans can join the Covenant. Hell they have to if you don't want them to have one hell of a shock when you bring one over."

"Lord, you have no idea," I whispered.

"I knew what you were going through when you stumbled into the Arabica. The doctor I was going to take you to, he's Leia's grandfather."

"Why?" Gail said from behind me.

"Why what?" Bowie asked.

"Why are you helping my dad?"

"Kane's hunting down a guy named Childe." Bowie's face got a serious cast then. "Got my own thing with Childe."

"What?" I asked.

"Personal," Bowie said flatly. "You find him, so would I."

I rubbed my forehead. We were rolling out of Bratenahl, and back toward Cleveland Heights.

After a long pause, Bowie asked, very gravely, "What do you remember about being brought over? Who did it?"

"I don't know."

"You don't know," Bowie repeated slowly.

"You said you knew a doctor?" Gail asked.

Bowie nodded, still looking askance at me, as if he didn't trust my answers.

"Then you've got to take Dad there, he needs help. His hand is injured."

"What?" Bowie asked. When I pulled my bandaged hand out of my pocket, Bowie added, "What the fuck is that smell?"

I noticed it as well. A sweet-rancid odor was suddenly very noticeable. It was thickening in the air, and when I looked down, I could see a damp stain spreading on the elastic bandage covering my left hand.

Gail started coughing.

"My hand," I said. Breathing in the odor made me gag.

Bowie rolled down the window and leaned away from me. I stared at my hand. It was swollen and misshapen under the loose bandage, except where the stain centered around the base of my thumb, where it appeared the flesh had collapsed.

"What happened?" Bowie shouted into the wind.

"Sun?" Gail said, speaking through her hand.

I rolled down the passenger window.

"Of all the idiot things—" Bowie coughed. "Yeah, sweet-cakes, we're going to see the doctor."

Bowie drove through Cleveland Heights, and into Shaker. He pulled us to a stop in front of a large brick house set about thirty feet back into its lot. It had large windows and a Tudor design that reminded me of Childe's—or Deité's—apartment building. Even though it was a common style—a lot of the buildings in Shaker and Cleveland Heights wouldn't be out of place in Lakewood, a lot of them built around the same time—the similarity put me on edge.

Bowie parked my car on the curb. He piled out as soon as he killed the engine. I could smell why. Without the constant wind through the open window, the reek from my dead hand was overpowering. The bandage was crusted with seepage and the form underneath was only barely hand-shaped.

I stumbled out, and Gail followed with her hand over her face. "My God, Dad." She looked on the verge of throwing up, and the tears in her eyes had to be as much from the smell as from sympathy.

The ache in my wrist had gotten worse, and I was rubbing it unconsciously. I could feel an ugly give to my skin, even though the sleeve of my jacket.

"Come on," Bowie said. "Got to fix that hand." He made a face when he said it.

He walked up to the house, and I was disturbed when I realized that the place was familiar. More than the accidental similarity to Childe's apartment. The place in Lakewood was just another building. I felt as if I had been here. However, with the holes in my memory, I had no idea if the familiarity was significant. I didn't know if it represented something that had happened in the last two weeks, or if the feeling came from some fragment of the prior four-and-a-half decades that I had yet to remember fully.

"What kind of doctor?" Gail asked. He voice was muffled under the handkerchief she held to her face.

Bowie chuckled, "Someone with an interest in our kind."

I wondered what kind of medial school someone went to, to specialize in "our kind."

My unease was becoming difficult to ignore. What did I know about this place? What was I trying to remember? I felt my good hand moving toward my holster as Bowie leaned on the doorbell. After a minute or so the door inched open. A redheaded woman looked at Bowie through the crack, Leia.

"Yes?" she said in her high, breathy, English voice.

"Leia? Could you get your grandfather for me?" Bowie nodded back toward where I stood back from the doorway. I stopped reaching for the gun.

She looked past Bowie, at me. "You found him!" Her accent made me think about Childe again, redoubling my sense of nervousness. She looked about the age Childe was supposed to prey upon. My hand found the butt of my gun. "Who's the girl?"

"His daughter— Look, we got to do something about his hand."

She looked at me, and I saw something alive in her eyes. Not the fires I felt in Sebastian's, or the machinery I felt behind the Doberman's, but something moving, living, and writhing in pain. When she spoke, her hand went to the collar of the black turtleneck she wore. A single blocky earring glinted from underneath a tumble of red hair. "What happened to his hand?"

"Bad dose of sun," Bowie said.

She nodded, and I lost sight of those pained eyes. I felt no desire to see whatever those eyes had seen. "I'll get Grandfather. Wait here," she said, closing the door.

As we waited, Bowie said, "Good looking babe, ain't she?"

"Hadn't noticed." That wasn't quite a lie. I repeated

Gail's question, "So what kind of doctor is Leia's grand-father?"

"He was a medic in World War Two, when he got involved in—"

The door opened again. Standing there was a broad, white-haired man in a blue bathrobe. "This better be good, I was—"

He had begun by addressing Bowie but as he spoke he slowly turned, and I could see his nose wrinkle. "God," he said. "How much tissue is affected?"

He addressed the question to me. "My hand," I said. "About six inches up the wrist."

He shook his head. "Come around back. I don't want that smell infecting my house."

PART THREE

—

THE CONQUEROR WORM

By a route obscured and lonely,
Haunted by ill angels only,
Where an Eidolon, named Night,
On a black throne reigns upright,
I have reached these lands but newly
From an ultimate dim Thule—
From a wild weird clime that lieth, sublime,
            Out of SPACE—out of TIME.
                        —"Dream-Land"

21

Bowie nodded and waved us along. I followed. As we walked up the driveway, we passed a black BMW with vanity plates, "Ryan 1."

"Ryan's first or last name?" I asked Bowie.

"Last, I think. Always call him Doc Ryan."

We came up on a patio around back, and stopped at a pair of storm-cellar doors abutting the house. The doors were new and set in fresh cinder block that appeared to have been built in the past two years or so. Bowie stopped by the doors, which—conspicuously—had no external handles.

"Come here often?" I asked.

"Doc's been practicing a lot longer than I've been nocturnal."

Not a real answer, I thought. "So how long have you been 'nocturnal?' "

"Half a year or so."

"Who 'brought you over'?"

Bowie looked at me askance again. "If we get the time, I'll tell you the story."

Gail spoke up from behind us. "Is this Doctor Ryan one of . . . one of you?" she asked Bowie.

Bowie shook his head. "No, the Doc ain't one of us. I thought I mentioned that."

"He's not?" I said.

Bowie shrugged.

"He knows what he's doing?" Gail asked.

"I suppose so," Bowie said. "The gentry pay him enough for services rendered."

Gail squeezed my shoulder. I felt her concern. But, it was *my* hand and I couldn't help feeling that it was wrong for her to be here. Even if there was some family exemption, some loophole in the Covenant that let her be here, it was wrong to drag her along—

But what choice did I have? Did either of us have?

With Bowie's little asides, I felt my daughter being ensnared by the same nocturnal society that had ensnared me. Bowie, with nearly every sentence, was dropping references to a culture I barely knew and Gail was totally ignorant of.

Ignorant of, and already trapped within. Just the fact that she knew meant she was ensnared in the web of relationships Gabriel had disclosed to me.

Which made me wonder where Bowie fit within that web. With the easy way he talked about the Covenant, he must have a role within that society. Being only six months a vampire meant he was almost certainly a thrall to some older vampire. Which meant that, when I dealt with him I wasn't dealing with Bowie. As far as the social rules were concerned, I was dealing with Bowie's unknown master.

A master whose name he'd avoided mentioning.

I had an awful thought. What if Bowie belonged to Childe?

Before I could worry any further, a short buzzing sound escaped from the doors. Then, after about two seconds, they swung outward. The wood exterior panels were only veneer. On the inside, the doors were thick, plastic and metal, with a rubber gasket surrounding the edges—airtight and soundproof.

At the foot of the concrete stairs stood Doctor Ryan. He had dispensed with the bathrobe. He now wore jeans, a flannel shirt, and a long white lab coat. He still wore a pair of slippers.

His hand rested on a metal box mounted on the wall, pressing a green button. Bowie led us down the stairs and once we all cleared the doors, Ryan pressed a red button and the buzz repeated itself, louder this time. The doors shut behind us with a hydraulic whisper of air.

It wasn't any warmer down here than it was outside. Combined with the white tile walls and the stark fluorescent lighting, the place felt like a morgue. *If he treats vampires, maybe that's what this is.*

"What's your name, son?" Ryan asked with a puff of visible breath.

"Kane," I said.

Ryan looked a little disappointed with my name. "And you, miss?"

"Gail—can you help my dad?" She was still talking through a handkerchief.

"I'm certain I can." To Bowie he said, "You go upstairs, I don't need company while I work."

"Sure, Doc. Maybe Leia can get me something to eat." Bowie grinned and left before Ryan could answer him.

To Gail, Ryan said, "You should go with him."

Before I could raise an objection, Gail straightened up and said, "I'm not leaving my father."

Ryan looked at her and said, rather gravely, "This is not going to be pleasant." When she showed no sign of backing down, Ryan said, "Well, stay out of my way."

He led us down halls that were all concrete and white tile. Every ten feet or so we passed a blank stainless steel door, like the door to a commercial-sized freezer.

"Quite a setup," I said, cradling my hand and trying not to inhale the smell.

Ryan seemed preoccupied. "What I do can be quite lucrative with the right patient." We stopped in front of a door like the others. "Now I need to see that hand."

He opened the door. I expected to see lines of meat-hooks, hanging slabs of beef, or the like. Instead the room looked fairly normal, if stark. It was populated by stainless steel cabinets, chromed fixtures and spigots set into the walls, carts of medial equipment I couldn't identify, and an examination table under an intricate-looking set of operating lights.

"Sit down," Ryan said, motioning to a chair in the corner of the room, also fitted with lights and equipment. I sat.

"You," he said to Gail. "Come with me."

While I did my best to get comfortable without touching my hand to anything, Ryan went to the wall and began flipping switches. Gail stood next to him and cast nervous glances back over her shoulder at me.

Lights came on around my end of the room, and the whir of a ventilation fan started up. That was good, because once we'd stopped moving, the odor from my hand had quickly built to intolerable levels.

Ryan handed Gail a surgical mask and said, "Tie this on and stand over there." He indicated the far corner, away from the chair where I sat.

Gail tied on the mask and backed over to the corner that Ryan had indicated. Ryan laid out an equipment tray on one of the carts, tied on a mask, and began scrubbing at a sink across the room from me.

"Are germs really a problem?" I asked, thinking of alleged vampiric immortality.

Ryan laughed softly, with an ironic lilt to it. "Depends on the germ. I can tell without looking, for instance, that under that rag on your hand, a herd of anaerobic bacteria are having a festival."

"Ugh," Gail said. From here I could see some of the color going out of her face.

" 'Ugh,' is right." Ryan shut the faucet off with his elbows and began the delicate procedure of retrieving a pair of surgical gloves from a tray near the sink. "You're new, aren't you."

"Why do you say that?" I asked.

"Experienced vampires do not go around nursing advanced cases of solar necrosis. They usually have enough sense to feed right after the initial injury, before circulation shuts down completely." He pushed a cart toward me with his foot. It bore an ugly selection of surgical instruments. "Take off your jacket and roll up your sleeve for me, would you?"

I did as I was asked, doing my best not to smear the contaminated Ace bandage against my clothes. The bandage itself was now stained, streaked with red and black, and every time my hand brushed something I could hear an ugly liquid sound.

" 'Feeding' would have stopped this?" I asked as I manhandled my jacket. I left the holster and gun in place, and the Doctor didn't comment on them.

"Most of the time, if you survived the sun in the first place. Fire's a different story," Ryan nodded.

I noticed Gail edging across the room to get a better look at what was going on. Ryan paid no attention to her. He kept talking, "But, you see, after the bacteria has a chance to do gross damage to the tissue, that's something else. Would you place your hand over here?"

I did as he asked, placing my bandage-covered hand on the examination tray he indicated. He picked up a pair of scissors from his pile of instruments and began cutting away the bandage. "Don't move."

"I can't." My hand was an inanimate lump of meat.

Ryan talked as he worked. "If I had been doing my work in a research hospital, I'd know more than I do. Forty years as an individual doesn't match ten in a well-equipped—This is bad."

Gail's eyes widened, and her hand went up to cover her nose and mouth.

Ryan had just peeled away a length of bandage with a pair of forceps. Beneath, my hand was pockmarked by greenish-black lesions that swelled up under the skin. The skin had broken in places, weeping thick noxious fluid. The meat where my thumb met my palm was entirely eaten away, leaving a moist ragged crater where the flesh had liquefied down to the bone.

"A human would've probably died of blood poisoning by now." Ryan paused a moment, arrested by something other than the sight of the wound. The pause only lasted a minute before he began rambling again. "Now I was going to explain this to you, without getting into the spiritual gibberish—"

Ryan carefully removed the remains of the bandage as he spoke, dropping them into a stainless steel tray. He then retrieved another tray, slipped it under my hand, and used a bottle of clear liquid to wash the discharge erupting from the sores in my hand. I felt nothing.

"Aren't you just going to cut it off?" I asked.

Gail made a strangled noise and turned away from the scene. I could hear her sucking deep breaths through her mouth.

When I looked down again at my hand, I couldn't take my eyes off of what Ryan was doing. He would rinse a fleshy crater, then attack it with a small sponge clamped in his forceps. Each sponge only lasted a dozen seconds before he'd toss it in with the scraps of my bandage.

"Again, if you were human." A sponge tossed. "The infection that created you—I was about to explain—has some pseudo-regenerative capabilities." More rinsing.

"Infection?"

Fresh sponge. "Vampirism is a result of, or a complex related to, an infectious entity somewhat akin to a virus." Swab. "Unlike a virus, it doesn't destroy the cells it infects, quite the opposite in fact—it can infect dead tissue and revive it. I've never had the resources to analyze it properly, I don't even know if it is alive, or simply some extremely exotic collection of proteins." Toss. "But this entity infects every cell of your body now, and every cell needs it to survive." Wash.

"That caused this?" I still stared at my hand. It looked as if I'd run it through a garbage disposal. It was puffy, discolored, and perforated by sores that sank though flesh, muscle and bone.

"The dissolution of that pseudovirus caused it." Ryan said. "This thing is photoreactive. UV B breaks it down fairly quickly, and direct sunlight can trigger a chain reaction from the surface all the way down to the bone. All tissue along the way dies off, and the natural decay process starts."

He dried parts of my hand with a final sponge. He retrieved a scalpel. "It's medieval to do this without a local, but I've never found an anesthetic that works properly."

"I don't feel anything in my hand."

"Not yet," Ryan said, and began cutting. He cut around the worst of the lesions, slicing ragged black flesh away from the lips of the wounds. I finally looked away, toward Gail.

She was facing away from us, leaning on the examination table. I felt a wave of empathy for her; she shouldn't have had to be here for this. As I watched, she turned around and waved weakly at me, as if to say she was all right. I noticed that she kept her gaze locked on my face, never looking down toward my hand.

Doctor Ryan never stopped talking. "What I have to do now is isolate whatever tissue in your hand that hasn't had its gross physical structure destroyed. That tissue can be revitalized back to something like life."

"Something like life?" I asked and looked back at him. I caught sight of the bones in the base of my thumb. They appeared to be eroded. I turned away again.

"Infected cells are hardier—survive everything but destruction of the cell membrane—they can radically alter their own function, but they don't reproduce."

"How can my body replace tissue that dies off—" I was about to say "naturally," but there was nothing natural about this.

I suspected the answer before Ryan provided it. "Human blood, living whole human blood. You ingest it, the blood itself is infected and incorporates itself into your own tissue. Blood's the only medium that's readily absorbed, but any properly suspended solution of intact human cellular material could do as well."

"Has to be human?"

"Nonhuman cellular material can be infected, but can't be absorbed. There are a few species that can be carriers, but none are suitable for feeding from. And as far as I know, the infection results in vampirism only in humans—and then only in select cases."

He kept cutting as he talked. I felt nothing but the occasional twinge along my wrist where the living tissue stopped. I kept glancing back to see him removing ragged strips of red-black, unrecognizable as flesh, and dropping them into the waste tray. The smell was beyond belief. I had to cease asking questions because breathing made my eyes water.

I kept looking back at Gail, occasionally forcing a smile. By now she had backed away from the smell herself, back to the corner Ryan had put her in.

Somehow, Ryan managed to stand the smell, talking all the while. "With no intervention, the infection only thrives in a particular type of host—and then only after death. And *then* only if death follows swiftly after infection. In most humans this entity can't survive the first twenty-four hours in a living host. Though, if another infection weakens the immune system, the entity can survive much longer." Ryan's voice took on the same distant tone it had had when he'd mentioned blood poisoning. I had the feeling he was remembering something specific.

He turned my hand over, resting the perforated back on a gauze pad. He began working to excise the rot from the meat of my palm. "If a susceptible host does die while infected, the infection spreads like a brush-fire through the whole body. Much faster than the normal decay process. Often too fast for rigor, or even lividity, to set in. The infection actually reanimates the tissue."

I looked up at him as he set down the instruments. He looked at my palm. He nodded to himself and looked back at me. "So far so good."

I lowered my gaze to what was left of my hand. I had trouble accepting it as part of my body. Large patches of flesh had been eaten away down to the bone, as if it had melted. The edges of the wounds were now razor-sharp, thanks to Ryan's scalpel. There wasn't nearly enough blood, and any remaining skin was now snow-white with occasional streaks of discoloration.

"The structure of the remaining tissue should be intact enough to allow reinfection. If all goes well, your hand should reform itself and expel the remaining damaged tissue."

Ryan took the tray of waste and dumped it into a metal door set into the wall. An incinerator, I supposed. He stripped off his gloves and tossed them in after the waste. That done, he returned to the sink and scrubbed again, and replaced his gloves.

"This is where this may begin to hurt," he said as he picked up a large hypodermic needle.

He swabbed my right arm, and sank the needle into a vein. "I have to use fresh, infected blood," Ryan said. "The patient's own is always the best to use when the damage is this grave." Then, slowly, he withdrew blood from my arm. The blood didn't look quite right to me. It seemed thicker and darker than it should've.

That wasn't the part that hurt.

What hurt was when he began injecting the blood into the remaining flesh of my dead hand. I felt nothing at first, as he slid the needle through the edges of the largest wounds. But at the third injection, the permanent ache in my wrist began traveling down toward my fingers. Sensation began returning, a pins-and-needles sensation of restricted circulation.

Then, as the hypo was emptied of its blood sample, leaving white trails of flesh pock-marked with needle tracks, I began to feel the raw ends of the nerves.

"God," I gasped, breathing again.

"Dad," I heard Gail say. She ran toward me.

My hand twitched. It was on fire. I could feel it burning everywhere Ryan's scalpel had cut. I could feel the blood he'd injected, rivulets of lava running under my skin.

I stared at my hand, teeth clenched, and watched as Ryan's miracle happened. Pink color began to creep down my arm, past my wrist, and to the strips of flesh still connected to my hand. My wounds began to bleed.

I felt the now-familiar sensation of skin tightening and flesh flowing. The lips of the wounds stretched and flowed across naked bone and tendon, knitting together with their neighbors. It felt as if my skin were being torn off my hand, and then stapled back into place. If I hadn't been riveted by the sight of newly vital flesh, the pain might have made me black out.

But, after a subjective eternity, I sat, exhausted, with an intact hand resting on a gauze pad soaked with blood and plasma. I stared in disbelief as I clenched it into a fist.

"Good Lord," Gail said from my side. She had seen the entire process.

Ryan leaned over and swabbed off my hand. "Let me see," he said.

I let him take my hand and prod it. As he did I marveled at the sensation of feeling in my hand again.

22

Doctor Ryan's treatment, and his nonstop dialog, answered many of the physical questions about blood and regeneration. Even so, for all his scientific jargon, his explanations seemed incomplete. I was a vampire because I was a susceptible host for the vampiric pseudovirus, and had "died" shortly after being infected with it.

But what made Kane Tyler a host susceptible to vampirism? Ryan could offer me no clear answer beyond the fact that it involved the time since infection, the physical state of the host, and environmental factors up to and including the state of mind at the time of death. A susceptible host was a rare phenomenon, and that was how the vampiric pseudovirus could evolve, and propagate without destroying the host population.

At least until social forces overwhelmed the evolutionary ones. Ryan mentioned, almost off-hand, that most vampires were now made as the result of a conscious decision by their creator. Apparently, any human, susceptible or not, would become a vampire with a sufficient infusion of infected blood.

Ryan indirectly answered a few of my more obvious questions. Regeneration or not, "dead" or not, most of the organs in my body performed the same functions as they did before, only at a much lower level of activity. The infection impregnating my flesh took up most of the slack of a slowed metabolism, and my blood now had the duty not just of oxygenating tissue, but of replacing it as well.

A stake through the heart, as long as it remained in place preventing regeneration, would pretty surely kill me. Same for decapitation. My body could withstand an extreme amount of purely mechanical damage—a gunshot, stab wound, a broken arm—and rebuild itself. But anything that destroyed large masses of tissue—fire, acid, or sunlight—would cause my body no end of grief.

To hear Ryan speak, the whole subject of vampirism had no claim on the supernatural. Ryan had a ready answer for all the physical stigmata, and what he said fit well with what Gabriel had deigned to explain about the subject.

But there were things that Doctor Ryan did not explain and, with his point of view, things I doubted he *could* explain. He didn't explain how I could look into someone's eyes and push his or her mind in a particular direction. He didn't explain the fire I had seen behind Sebastian's eyes, or why I felt an unease around his rosary and not my daughter's. He didn't explain why I couldn't look at myself in the mirror. He didn't explain why I could see blood as a luminescent fire that turned slowly black as it died.

He did not explain why I could sometimes feel the emotions of people around me, like ripples carried upon the wind.

After all the poking and prodding, Ryan released my hand. "I've done all I can tonight. Nerves take more time to regenerate than other tissue. If you could stay here the night, I'd like to look at it in the morning."

I took my hand off the tray and clenched it a few times. There were a few aches deep in the bones, and it trembled when I moved. It was gaunt and skeletal, but a miraculous achievement all the same.

"You might want to wash that off," Ryan waved over to the sink. He yawned. "I'll tell my granddaughter to set up the guest rooms for both of you."

I looked at Gail and said, "Just for me. My daughter won't be staying."

"Dad," Gail said at me in a harsh stage whisper. I looked at her and shook my head aggressively. "No."

Ryan didn't seem to notice the exchange between me and Gail. He yawned again and nodded. "I'm too old to keep these hours," he muttered.

He waited for me to wash my hands before he led us up. He locked the door to the basement after we emerged. "I'll let you see your daughter out yourself. I must see Leia and get some sleep."

Once Ryan was out of earshot, Gail glared at me. "I go through all this to see you, and you're sending me away? How can you do that?"

I put my arm around her shoulders and started walking her to the door. "I don't know if you're safe here."

"I thought you were friends with that guy."

"Please, Gail, I don't know everything that's going on here." I took her out the front door and led her up the walk to the Chevette. "But I do know that I've been mixed up with people who've killed your mom, and who would've killed me but for some fluke, and I'm no longer sure who those people are."

When we reached the Chevette, she looked at me and said, "Then come *with* me, Dad. We can both leave here, get away from Sebastian and everyone else."

I shook my head.

"Why? Why are you going to stay here? He fixed your hand. It's all right now—"

I kissed her on the firehead. "I need to find Cecilia, and Childe."

"But her dad wants to put a stake through her heart."

"Then I have to find her before Sebastian does, don't I?"

We stood there for a long time. Her breath trailed off into the night. The air from my own lungs was nearly invisible. She reached down and took my left hand in her own. "You're so cold, Dad."

"I've been colder."

"I don't think I believed it until I saw your hand. Whatever I said, it wasn't *real* until that happened." Her grip was tight, as if she were afraid I might run away. "They did this to you, the same people who killed Mom?" She looked at me with shiny eyes.

"I think so," I said. "I don't remember what happened. The . . . *transition* left some gaps in my memory."

"God can't damn you for this, can He? You didn't have a choice."

It wasn't a question I expected from her. I didn't know how to answer her; there were times in the past three days that I felt my soul descended to near-irredeemable depths. "If we're damned, it is for our actions, not some opportunistic infection."

Gail didn't let go. "What have you done, Dad?"

"I don't know what you mean."

"Yes, you do," Gail said. "I can see the weight in your face, the way you look at me. You can carry guilt like a badge."

Silence stretched for a long time. The only sound was the wind crying through the branches of the naked trees. Somewhere above, a crow cawed after something.

How could I lie to her?

"I've killed two people."

She stared into my eyes, and I saw in there a glowing warmth. It was both like and unlike the fire I had seen in Sebastian's eyes. The light in her eyes had the heat and intensity of Sebastian's, but not the fearful violence. Instead of a barrier, it was a welcome.

"Were they innocent?" she asked me.

"What?" I was drawn back by the question, enough that my hand pulled free of her grip. "What kind of question is that?"

"You killed two people because you were a vampire?" Gail asked, looking at me with a warmth that seemed to melt down her face with her tears.

I nodded, two deaths that should have never happened.

"Were they innocent?"

I stood aghast at the question. What the hell did it matter? I had two people's deaths on my hands. "My God, Gail, they didn't deserve to die. You can't play God with human lives."

She grabbed me, "Damn it, Dad! You're not an evil person. I know you. Who were these people? What were they doing? Why did you . . . ?"

I looked into her eyes. Had I turned into a monster or not? I had made the difficult admission already, hadn't I? "I—"

"Who, Dad? How did it happen?"

"Tony," I finally said. "The man's name was Tony. I broke into his girlfriend's apartment. He was. . . ."

"He was what?"

I shook my head. "You can't justify this."

"He was what?"

"Beating her, okay? That's not the point."

"Damn it, it *is!* If you were still a cop, could you have shot him?"

"Maybe, I don't know . . . just drive to Sam's, would you? Use the cellular to call ahead and give him some warning."

Gail backed up and wiped her eyes. "Okay. What should I tell Sam?"

"As little as possible."

She opened the door to the Chevette. "You're not going to be at Mom's funeral, are you?"

I shook my head. "Not unless they have it after sundown."

She took my hand again. "I forgive you."

"Thanks." I started to walk back to the house, but she kept hold of my hand.

"For everything," she said.

I took my hand back and said, "I love you, Gail."

"I love you, still," she said.

I began walking back to the house. Behind me I heard the Chevette start up. Over the engine I heard Gail shout at me, "I still loved you, even when you shot back." Then the engine revved and started to fade in the distance.

I rubbed the spot where the bullet had emerged from my lung, back when I was still a cop. I stood in front of the door for a long time before I could wipe my eyes and enter.

I took refuge in Ryan's den, trying not to think about Gail, and Kate, and trying to keep from going into an emotional tailspin, I stood in front of the French doors, staring at the snow beyond. My own gaunt face stared back at me out of the glass. Shadows made my eyes invisible, a pair of black holes in my face that caused me no pain.

"Can I get you something to drink?" came an English-accented voice from behind me. I turned around to see Leia, Ryan's granddaughter. I didn't hear any irony in her voice.

I shook my head, suppressing an internal shudder. Ryan had told me that the drain my injury caused to my body's resources would require me to feed pretty soon. Ryan had said I could eat and drink normal foods. However, I couldn't digest them, since acid production in my stomach was now about nil. My stomach lining would become more and more sensitive the longer between real feedings.

However, I didn't want to think about blood, or real feedings, not with my last two victims fresh in my mind.

"No, thank you," I said. "Your name's Leia, right?"

She nodded and I caught the scent of a strong perfume. The perfume was the only thing about her that was overstated. "Yes." she said. "Did—" there was a slight pause as she bit her lip. "Did Grandfather help you?"

"Very much," I said. I flexed my intact left hand, still skeletal and trembling. "He saved me from a rather stupid accident."

"Good. I'm glad he could help you." She smiled, but it didn't reach her eyes. Something deep in there told me that she was very unnerved by my presence. I'd be unnerved, too, considering her grandfather's clientele.

"You don't need to be afraid of me." Fear didn't seem the right word, but whatever empathy I had wasn't providing me with convenient labels. I sensed confusion, wariness, caution, expectation—some or all of which may have been me rather than her.

"I'm not afraid." Her smile faded with a sharp feeling of a nerve being brushed. My comment had struck a chord, what one I didn't know. Almost as if she'd seen me notice, she resurrected her smile and said, "What's there to be afraid of?"

I nodded. "Indeed. What?" I turned my gaze back out the French doors. She had caught me within my own fears.

" 'For, alas, alas! with me,' " I whispered, not really aware that I was quoting aloud, " 'The Light of Life is o'er.' "

"What's that from?" Leia asked.

I cleared my throat, embarrassed at having quoted the verse aloud. "Edgar Allan Poe, a poem. It's about death." I lowered my head. "Everything he wrote was about death."

I heard her moving around behind me. "You don't seem the type to spontaneously quote poetry."

I turned around to face her; she had taken a seat in a recliner facing the hearth. She sat, legs crossed, looking at me intently. The low fire brought out livid copper highlights in her red hair.

"I read a lot of Poe in high school. It comes back to me every once in a while." Once in a *bad* while. Ever since my father died. Poe came back when death was near.

"How does it go?" she asked.

"Hm?"

"The poem, how does it go?" There was something in her eyes that drew the poem to the surface.

"It's called, 'To One in Paradise,'" I said. "Thou wast that all to me, love, / For which my soul did pine— / A green isle in the sea love, / A fountain and a shrine, / All wreathed with fairy fruits and flowers, / And all the flowers were mine.'"

I paced as I recited the poem from memory. I had to stop and catch my breath, because my throat was tightening up.

"'Ah, dream too bright to last! / Ah, starry Hope! that didst arise / But be overcast!'"

I turned away from Leia to face the French doors again.

"'A voice from out the Future cries, / "On! On!"—but o'er the Past / (Dim gulf!) my spirit hovering lies / Mute, motionless, aghast!

"'For alas! alas! with me / The light of Life is o'er! / No more—no more—no more—

"'(Such language holds the solemn sea / To the sands upon the shore) / Shall bloom the thunder-blasted tree, / Or the stricken eagle soar!'"

I leaned on the windowsill and whispered the final stanza.

"'And all my days are trances, / And all my nightly dreams / Are where thy gray eye glances, / And where thy footstep gleams— / In what ethereal dances, / By what eternal streams.'"

I ended with my forehead touching the glass and the sensation that everything behind my chest had fallen away.

A long silence followed before Leia said, "I'm sorry."

I collected my thoughts enough to say, "What for?"

"That poem's difficult for you, isn't it?"

I tried to dry my eyes as subtly as possible as I turned around. "It's not the poem."

She stared at me, and I got the feeling she was seeing into an uncomfortable depth. "No," she agreed. "It's not."

"So you live here," I said to change the subject. "With your grandfather?"

She nodded.

"What about your parents?"

"They died, a long time ago."

"Sorry."

She shrugged.

"Are you friends with Bowie?" She looked to be about Bowie's age.

She laughed. "Hardly what you'd call our relationship. Let's just say I associate with him. Are *you* friends with him?"

"I don't know. Where is he? There are a few questions I have to ask him."

Leia shrugged. "Bowie has gone, to do the things that Bowie does. Are you sure about me getting you something?"

I felt an unnatural clarity in the air, as if every sense had been honed to a scalpel edge and was cutting into my brain. Brushfire emotion had consumed everything inside me, and sensory input rushed in to fill the void. The light burned my eyes, Leia's perfume stung my nose, and the ebb and flow of my own blood was a hammer in my ear.

Hunger was suddenly a deep ache inside me. Leia stared at me knowingly and said, "Are you *sure?*"

The offer violated me, as if a stranger were viewing my own private perversion. She looked at me and I felt the thirst swell inside me—

I felt a wary sense of self-preservation. I did not fully trust this place, and Gabriel had impressed upon me that everything freely offered carried a price along with it. I shook my head. "No. Thanks."

She frowned briefly, as if something was wrong. I didn't know what. I was able to push the sudden wave of hunger away. The need wasn't yet strong enough to make me lose control. From talking to Ryan, who opined much more freely than Gabriel, after two victims I should have at least a week—if it hadn't been for the drain because of my injury. As it was, I could go one or two days before I reached the state where I became uncontrollable.

I pushed the urge away, but the taste lingered in my mouth and the light was still bothersome. I walked over and dimmed the lamps to a tolerable level, where they barely competed with the glow from the fireplace.

I looked at Leia, seated in the recliner, looking at me with a faintly curious expression. Who was she? Why had she been seated with Bowie the first time I'd seen her?

Like Bowie, she was young enough to be recruited by Childe's cult. . . .

"Do you happen to know anything about a man calling himself Childe?" I asked.

Her face darkened, but she showed no surprise at the question. "He is not a man."

"You know him, then."

She stood. "Evil. Pure distilled evil. Everything he touches turns to rot sooner or later." She walked until she was nearly touching me. The smell of her perfume was overpowering. She ran a finger under the collar of her turtleneck as she spoke. "You should leave Childe be while you still own yourself."

I shook my head. I couldn't back away now, even if I wanted to, even though the farther along I came, the less certain I was of what was happening.

She stepped back. "Don't think your losses make you special, my poetic friend. Revenge is not a happy pursuit." Leia stepped around me and out the door. "The guest room is upstairs and to the right."

I stood in the doorway and watched her ascend the stairs, a spectral figure. The black sweater and pants soaked up the darkness, with only her flowing red hair to mark her humanity.

Revenge is not a happy pursuit.

That woman had been hurt by Childe. I wondered how her parents had died, and how her grandfather had gotten into the business of treating the undead.

23

I didn't go to the guest room. I didn't think I could sleep normally now if I tried, despite feeling the burden from Ryan's ministrations. My hand had drained me, and dark thoughts had drained me even more. More than my hand, the events of the past three days wearied me. I had been pulled along this path nonstop, and more than my body, my mind was tired.

I needed to relax, if only for a few hours. So, after Leia's departure, I rummaged through Doctor Ryan's bookshelves. Ryan's library was a much lesser and more pedestrian affair than Childe's, but in it I found something familiar: a small cloth-bound volume entitled simply, *Tales and Poems*. Under the title was the name, "Poe."

The memories it sparked were melancholy, but so were the tales, so were the poems. Right now I needed the familiarity, the feeling that something of myself was still mine, unchanged. As always with Poe, I needed the feeling that I had company in the darkness.

I pulled a drape across the French doors, shutting out the rest of the world, and settled in the recliner, which still held a whisper of Leia's perfume. I opened the book at random. The first line my eyes fell upon were within the opening paragraph of "The Masque of the Red Death."

"No pestilence had ever been so fatal, or so hideous. Blood was its Avatar and its seal—the redness and the horror of blood."

It was as if the two decades since my father's death had never happened, and Poe's words were still talking directly to me. I let myself be taken to Poe's realm because, somehow, it vindicated my own. . . .

In a few hours I had passed from the Prospero of the Masque to the Fortunate of the Cask—from Doom to Revenge. I had passed into a blackness now wholly literary, and therefore a little lighter.

The first tier of masonry had but been laid within the text when a noise drew me out of the story. I looked up, not sure what I had heard. The winter night was deathly silent, a blanket of snow soaking up stray sounds.

I convinced myself that it had been the house creaking, or something popping within the hearth—a few shadowy embers still glowed there, the last ghost of a fire.

Just when I returned to reading, I heard the noise repeating. I heard it, again—a very distinct knocking coming from in front of me. Something about the rapping frightened me.

Lightly tapping, the noise repeated itself.

I told myself it was nothing, the wind . . . But there wasn't any wind.

I slowly placed the book on an end table. A Raven, embossed in gold leaf, looked up from the cover.

I stood up and walked toward the heavy purple curtains I'd drawn across the French doors. It was those doors from which the sound came. Someone gently rapping on the panes to gain admittance.

"Bowie?" I asked, even though I knew it wasn't him. Bowie would not cause me such dread.

The rapping continued. I felt certain that whatever was outside those doors represented death. The sense was so strong that, as I reached for the curtain, I felt as if it could be Kate beyond, risen from the stainless steel cart from which I'd last seen her.

I flung open the curtain.

The feeling of fear and present death did not cease when I saw the man who had been knocking at the door. If anything, my feelings deepened.

The man did not have the appearance to inspire terror. He was, in fact, attractive in an androgynous fashion. He was dark-skinned, but any attempt to put his face in a set racial category was doomed to failure. His nose was European, his eyes could be Asian, his hair was Indian, his skin African—but none of the terms fit him. He was not a marriage of separate races. He was of a race of himself.

"Come with me," he said. His voice did not fog the air. I doubt it was even audible inside the house, beyond the glass, so softly was it spoken. I heard it nonetheless, and I found myself unable to refuse.

I opened the door with the feeling that this was a particularly vivid dream. The cold and my feet sinking into the snow only slightly dispelled the illusion.

I never felt so much power tied into a single entity. Standing next to him was like standing next to volcano that was about to erupt. There was nothing about his appearance, absolutely nothing, that gave that impression. Physically he was less imposing than I was.

"You will walk with me," he said.

I didn't have much choice. Even if I had felt able to refuse, this man's bearing and his sudden appearance would have demanded some sort of attention in spite of the intimidating presence around him.

I followed him away from Doctor Ryan's house, and into the night-emptied streets of Shaker Heights. Once out of sight of the house, he addressed me again, "Ask your questions."

"Who are you?"

He glanced at the sky and said, "Another spirit bound in chains of flesh. No names for me, Mr. Tyler, I am not here."

The denial of one in power. I could feel the tug of secrecy behind this visit.

"You know me," I said, half-question, half-statement.

"I have an interest in what you are involved in." We stopped and he gave me a searing look. "You are an outsider."

"I know. Why are you here?"

"You question my presence?" His stare became a holocaust, I could feel his gaze stripping layers from inside me. I knew now what Gabriel had told me about power, and status. I was standing in front of a vampire as far beyond Gabriel as Gabriel was above a Thrall.

Still, under that invisible assault, I managed to whisper, "Yes, I am."

The first trace of expression crossed his face, a slight upturn at the corners of the mouth. "Strength," he said to himself. He turned and continued walking along the sidewalk.

"Perhaps I'm here to offer you Indenture."

"Indenture?"

He turned around and extended his right arm beyond the sleeve of his jacket. It extended for an unnatural length. "You feel the hunger upon you, don't you?"

In response, I felt the ache begin in my stomach, in my brain. The raw need consumed every vein in my body. A death chill frosted every nerve. The night focused into razor clarity, every angle slicing into my brain. Every sense amplified a dozen times, including the ethereal sense that told me of the power this creature before me held.

This creature, now, burned like a pillar of divine fire. I saw within him a heat, a power to take away the hunger, the need, the pain. More than enough. More than I could take in a dozen lifetimes. His life burned infinitely brighter than that of the human souls I had seen.

And before me was his extended arm, the life within nearly too bright for me to look at, the heat within burning the frozen skin of my face. The skin of his arm was bare before my face, and as I watched, the skin laid itself open to me. A slit appeared between the bones of the wrist, above the vein, traveling up the arm and pulling apart.

Blood spilled out of the wound, fire-red, leaking on to the ground. The smell drew me, and my lips were almost upon the spilling wound before I whispered, "No."

I knew what drinking would mean, I knew there was a tie in the blood beyond what Ryan suspected. No one had to tell me that, I could feel it. I felt it rippling from the blood that spilled from his arm—its life, powerful, seductive, and not my own. Accepting this from him would form a bond that I did not want to make.

I was still leaning forward, the need, the lust, pushing me. I repeated, "No," and pushed the arm away. The blood drew a black arc in the snow. It was the hardest thing I had ever done.

When I turned away, everything returned to a sense of normalcy. I expected him to be angry, at the very least. But, from behind me, I heard the whispered word again, "Strength."

I turned to face him. He was no longer a god offering communion. He was a figure of purely temporal power.

"Who are you?" I asked, my voice unsteady.

"No one to trifle with." He extended a now normal-looking arm ahead of him. "You have some strength. Do not confuse it with power."

He began walking, and I had no choice but to follow him. I began to think that, had he wished me to drink, I would have drunk. My victory had only been over myself, my own desire. Apparently that was enough for now.

"What did I refuse?" I asked.

"Security," he said. "Comfort. No small bit of power. That, and slavery."

It was the blood. Ryan's pseudovirus transmitted itself through blood, taking over the flesh, controlling the flesh. Somehow the mind controlled Ryan's bug—

"You think you understand." His words made me feel naked, as if my thoughts were exposed in his presence.

He laughed and it was terrifying to listen to. More terrible because I knew what he was laughing at. "Such desperate clinging, Tyler." His eyes burned when he said it, heated from the internal fire that had nearly consumed me before. "The doctor has buried himself in the flesh, as have you."

He reached over and gently touched the edge of my chin. "Do not think describing the Mystery, in whatever detail, will explain it."

I was frozen, staring at him. I almost wanted to believe I was held in place by some mental power, but I knew that it was awe that held me there. His face was a fusion of the angelic and the diabolical, shaped like a man's face, but no longer remotely human.

It stroked my cheek as if comforting a child.

"Blood is All. But the All is not simply blood. It is Life, Spirit, Soul. *Our* Mind, *our* Soul, everything *us* that transcends the physical is chained within us, has become part of the flesh chaining us to this world. It lives with the flesh, dies with the flesh. It controls the flesh and is controlled by the flesh. Ryan is not of *us*. He does not see the mind within the blood, the soul within the blood. He cannot see what we see, or understand that there is anything unphysical about us." He looked deeply into me and said, "You have seen the soul within the blood, tasted it."

I couldn't bring myself to speak, so I nodded.

"You have seen the maelstrom of faith within a righteous man."

I thought of Sebastian and nodded again.

"You cannot look into the daemon within your own eyes."

I nodded again.

"You have left the world of men. The human being you once were is dead, and the remnant spirit has remolded your flesh. You must set aside the beliefs you once had; such things can only hurt you now."

"But—"

A stern edge crept into his voice. He dropped his hand. "You think like a human and you will die like one."

I backed away. "Why are you here?"

"Because of your ignorance, your novelty, your potential importance. Because you are a rogue. The first such born to us in half a century to survive the day of his creation. Because you are of use to me."

The sense of otherworldliness seemed to recede. The cold I felt was real, and the colors I saw belonged to Shaker Heights, not a higher, or lower, realm.

"What use?"

"You have no master. No one has given you what I offered you." He gestured with the arm he had brandished earlier. It was intact, no sign of wounding now. "You have a freedom that few have until centuries after their birth."

I was glad of that, at least. I didn't relish having a master, of any sort.

"No Master. No Teacher," he said. "A rogue is dangerous, especially to himself. You have no status, no role, no protection. You honor no kin. You have no Name."

"This makes me useful to you?" I asked.

"Yes, Kane Tyler. It does." He steepled his hands in front of him, as if consciously withdrawing all the intense impressions I had felt around him, as if he folded his sprit back within his body. "I am older than you can imagine, and my power is such that even a thrall to me is a force few would contend with. But I cannot move incautiously, my acts bear too much weight for me to make an ill move."

"Are you asking something of me?"

He laughed, "I am offering something."

"Something with a price."

"All things have their price. Can you accept the Covenant?"

Could I? Perhaps, more importantly, could I reject it? Gabriel had labeled me an outcast because I had not accepted the Covenant, and had said that someone would want much for "granting me that boon."

"What do you want in return?"

"The conclusion of the troubles that have come to this city."

"Childe?"

He laughed softly, "It is not for me to accuse. For me to express myself, rightly or wrongly, in this matter would do worse damage than is being done now."

"Then what do you want from me?"

"Those who search for the truth in this are blinded. I wish your eyes. I wish to commend upon you the duty of vengeance."

"I thought that was Gabriel's job."

"Such it is. But I shall not wrongly demean his status if he is blameless. You shall be my agent, but you shall not be me. Shall you accept the Covenant and provide this for me?"

That gave me all sorts of questions about Gabriel's role in all of this. I found myself nodding even before I had decided to do so.

"Again, shall you do this, refusing the option to turn back?"

"Yes."

He placed a hand on my forehead, and I felt a burning there. "Between me and the night," he said, "name yourself."

The word was pulled immediately from my lips, as if it wasn't me talking, but something speaking though me. "Raven," I heard myself say.

"Raven it is, and shall ever be. As Jaguar, I am witness to your entrance to the Covenant, speak your name now, and it will be known of what you are a part."

I opened my mouth to ask a question, one of a tumult of questions about Childe, and Gabriel, and even Bowie. However, before I had taken breath to speak, he had removed his hand and had stepped backward into a shadow.

Though my eyes never left him, I could not see where he went. When I looked down, I only saw my own set of footprints.

"Jaguar," I whispered, naming the apparition.

He had been right. Neither Ryan nor I had come close to the mystery. Or the Mystery.

24

I took my vampiric nonsleep in Ryan's windless guestroom. For once I wasn't tormented by memory. I simply rested, barely aware of my surroundings or the passage of time. The sunlit hours of Tuesday passed without me.

I came to full consciousness with someone knocking on my door. I felt a weird sense that the day had not fully passed, and that I had just laid down upon the bed. A glance at my watch told me that the day had indeed passed. It was nearly seven.

I sat up feeling fatigued and hungry. I rubbed the sleep from my face as the knocking continued. "Coming," I said.

I stood up, feeling as rumpled as my clothes looked. I picked up my holster and put it back on before I unlocked the door. I opened it to found Leia standing outside. She'd traded her black turtleneck for a navy blue one, and her perfume was as strong as ever. "Grandfather wants to see you in his office, to look at your hand."

I nodded. "I'll be down in a few minutes."

I had a memory flash, and as she turned to leave, I asked, "How long have you been here?"

"Here? With my grandfather? All my life."

I shook my head, "No, in Cleveland."

She shrugged. "Six months or so, why?"

"Just curious. I've noticed your accent."

"Oh," she said.

Still thinking of England, I asked, "Does the name Cross mean anything to you?"

"Should it?" she asked.

"I don't know."

"You enjoy asking questions, don't you?"

"It's my job."

She gave me a half-smile and said, "In my experience questions are often far more interesting than answers. Pardon me, but I have errands to run."

She left me abruptly enough for me to feel that I had hit something significant. What, I didn't know. However, I was too much a detective to discount Leia and Childe's common nationality as coincidence.

I met with Ryan in his office downstairs. It was a study in whitewash and stainless steel. However, it was aboveground and a much more pleasant environment then the morgue in the basement. The room felt as if a person worked and lived there. There were pictures on the wall, a reassuring clutter on his desk, and a spider plant hanging in one corner of the room.

I sat for the doctor as he poked and prodded my left hand, which now bore no sign of yesterday's gangrene. There was, in fact, little now to distinguish it from my right hand.

Ryan, as he'd shown last night, was a talker. As he flexed my hand and dragged little pointed implements across it, he'd talk all about what he thought was going on inside me. He talked about how much resources my body had used up during the night. How it had expelled or reabsorbed the dead tissue. He talked about a lot of chemical esoterica that I couldn't understand.

Most important to me was the fact that he talked. It wasn't very hard to change the thread of his conversation.

"So," I asked as he tested the reflexes of my pinkie, "how'd you get into treating vampires anyway?"

"The war," he said without missing a beat. "I was a volunteer medic. I was in London, treating civilians during the Blitz." He nodded absently to some pictures on the wall, many were black and white, showing a young Doctor Ryan. "During the worst part of the bombing, there was an epidemic of unexplained deaths. All in a single ward, all in the middle of the night. We weren't equipped for autopsies, not to mention the lack of personnel." He rolled up my sleeve and began prodding my wrist. "So I stayed up to watch the men in the ward. That night I saw my first vampire. The creature must have been caught in the bombing, much of the soft tissue had been burned away. The face was little more than a charred skull."

He paused for a while, looking my hand over. "Sunlight is bad, but fire is worse. Destroys the tissue immediately. This thing's skin was like charcoal. It rustled like dry leaves when it moved. And when it moved, its skin cracked, showing livid red tissue." Ryan shook his head. "The mass of blood it would have needed to repair that damage would have been twenty or thirty full grown men. As it was, with me and the orderlies there, once we overcame our shock and saw it begin feeding, we restrained it—and inadvertently killed it."

Ryan put down my hand and pronounced, "Your hand is fine, Mr. Tyler. My suggestion is to feed, rest, and build up your strength. You should be as good as new."

"Thank you. What can I do to repay you?"

Ryan smiled. "Money usually suffices. If you're low on funds, a blood sample once you've fully recovered."

"More research?"

Ryan nodded. "Feel free to remain my guest here as long as necessary."

"I appreciate the offer." I also had the suspicion that it was too generous. "Do you think you could answer a few of my nonmedical questions."

"I'll do my best, Mr. Tyler," he folded his hands. "It's actually refreshing when one of my patients has an interest in what I have to say."

"That's unusual?"

Ryan chuckled. "Very. What do you want to know?"

"I was interested in what you could tell me about some vampires I'm interested in."

"What about them?"

"What you've heard, what they're like—"

"I suppose I'll be more forthcoming than your kinsmen, for what little I know about the figures in your society."

You're part of that society as well, I thought, *you have to be to do your work.* "Tell me what you know about one named Childe."

Ryan shook his head. "He is old. He came out of central Europe about four hundred years ago. Childe is very—" He wrung his hands as if groping for a word. "Inner directed, I suppose you could say. He uses people. Uses them up."

"You know him, then?"

"No," Ryan said quickly. "I know *of* him."

"From England?" I asked.

Ryan gave me a blank look and then he nodded. "Yes, from England."

I nodded. "Your granddaughter said you left England about six months ago. Why did you leave?"

"Huh?"

"You were there since the war?"

Ryan nodded.

"Why return to the States now?"

"Oh. The last of my wife's family passed away. There was nothing left to hold us there." He glanced up at the wall and said, "I thought you wanted to know about vampires?"

"Do you know of a gentleman named Gabriel?"

"Gentleman," Ryan smiled. "Appropriate word. He's one of those Americans that become so enamored of aristocracy that they become more class-conscious than the British. He's pre-Civil War, and he slipped into the society as if it were made for him. He would hate Childe."

"Why?"

"Because Childe has no use for any rules of society, human or otherwise. He's fond of quoting Alister Crowley, 'Do what thou wilt shall be the whole of the law . . .' The fact that Childe is older, more powerful, and has more status than Gabriel does would be almost a perpetual insult."

Ryan stood up. "Now, if you please, I have business to attend to."

I stood and extended my hand. "Thank you for your help, and for fixing my hand."

"It's my job." Ryan shook my hand. "As I said, feel free to use our guest room."

"Thank you, but I think I should be moving on soon."

Ryan got up to leave, and I asked, "How come you're still human?"

"What?"

I stood up myself. "You must have been tempted, doing all this research, to become one of us." The phrase, "one of us," came much too easily to me.

Ryan shook his head. "Never."

"You could, though, couldn't you?"

He nodded. "Yes, I could infect anyone I wished to, via-ble specimen or not. But I have never been tempted. I've seen what it can do."

Ryan, somewhat hurried, left me there. I could tell that I had hit a nerve or two. I also could tell he was lying through his teeth about not ever meeting Childe.

I glanced at the wall with all the pictures. Many shots—wartime England, a primitive-looking hospital, Ryan doing this, Ryan doing that, Ryan with the hospital staff, a color picture of Ryan and his granddaughter with a modern London background. I took a step back from the wall and was struck by a feeling that something was wrong here.

The sound of someone clearing his throat interrupted me. I turned to see Ryan standing at the door, waiting. "I'd like to lock up, Mr. Tyler."

I nodded. "Sure," I said, slipping out the door past him. I still felt something was not quite right about that office. I just wished I could figure out what it was.

I called Sam's number once Ryan and I were through with each other. Gail answered the phone. "Hello, Weinbaum residence."

"Gail?"

"Dad?"

"Yes. What are you doing answering Sam's phone?"

There was a pause before she said, "Hoping you'd call. How're you doing?"

"Hand's mostly better," I locked my lips because a hunger was nagging at me as well, something I needed to take care of soon. I never again wanted to push myself to the point where something like my attack on Tony became inevitable. "How did things go at . . . how'd things go?"

She paused for a long while before she answered. When she spoke, I could hear the stress in her voice, "It went well, I guess." I could tell she'd been crying.

"I wish I could have been there."

"So do I." She sucked in a deep breath. "I'm going to miss Mom."

"I miss her, too." *I've been missing her for five years.* "Is Sam around?"

"Sleeping," she said somewhat abruptly.

"He's asleep?"

"You make it sound like an accusation."

"He's supposed to be protecting you."

"It's not his fault."

She seemed on the verge of tears again. "I'm sorry," I said. "Look, I'm going to take a cab down there—"

"You don't have to do that."

"I need the car."

"Oh. I'll be here, I guess."

The strange conversation lasted a few more minutes, talking about nothing in particular, and I hung up the phone and realized that I still had a family. Despite everything else, they hadn't taken *that* from me. When I called for the cab, I rummaged through my pockets for what was left of money I had liberated from my hotel room.

In fishing for cash, I found something that I had totally forgotten about—a small black film canister with a gray cap. I hadn't slowed down long enough to look over the negatives I had found in my house. Whatever was on them still belonged to one of the black absences in my memory.

As I gave the dispatcher Ryan's address, I popped the gray cap and withdrew the negatives. There were a half-dozen strips of various lengths, all high-quality black and white, 35 millimeter. When I hung up, I uncurled them and held them, one at a time, up to the light.

The stills were from long-distance surveillance. They weren't unusual in themselves, documenting people and places. What was unusual was the sense of menace that pervaded the images, images that were otherwise mundane. It was a visceral response that had little to do with what was actually in the pictures.

Without a magnifying glass, some of the pictures were indecipherable. However I had very clear pictures of a number of cars, most focusing on the license plates. One was of a dark van with no plate that could have been the same vehicle that'd slammed into Sam's car.

Another was a dark BMW with a vanity plate, "RYAN 1."

I had also taken pictures of Ryan's house. There were other houses I'd photographed, some of which seemed run-down and abandoned, but the only place that I *knew* was the doctor's.

I had also photographed people, young people for the

most part. I suspected they were either members or candidates for Childe's little cult. In addition to faces that I could not remember, there were three faces that I did know. I had a picture that was recognizably Leia, and on a separate roll I had a picture of the same leather-clad teenager that had jumped onto Sam's car.

My short-circuited memory made a series of connections—

In front of a mausoleum, standing upon a field of black snow, a teenager smiles at me with a mouth invisible under night-black blood . . .

With a millstone voice, the same teenager speaks from the shattered window of Sam's car, "Aren't you dead, my friend?" Washed by the car's flasher, he smiles at me with lips that appear alternately black and soaked with gore.

That same gravelly voice speaks from Childe's answering machine. "I hear you look for a woman of certain qualities," it says. "There will be one at the ritual tonight, I've told her to look for you."

A van plunges out of the darkness and sideswipes me. I'm thrown into a drift.

I'm dragged into the van, and the same stony voice says, ". . . if you remember us, this, anything, you shall surely die . . ." After which I smell rusty leather, and hear a heavy wet sound. . . .

The fragments wrapped within my memory to place this teenage vampire in a role as the leader of Childe's thralls. Childe's lieutenant, I thought. He was at the right hand of the black-cowled Childe at the mausoleum. He had called Childe to deliver Cecilia. He had led the attack on Sam's car. Somewhere in my black memory, he had attacked me, made me what I was.

All that made it even more troubling to me that, in the picture, this kid was clearly talking to Bowie.

25

Outside, the cab honked its horn for my attention. During the wait I had searched for any sign of Bowie, and had found none. When I went out to the cab, I was still racked with contradictory memories. I still recalled little of the time between Kate's death and my own subterranean waking. However, I now remembered the first time I had talked to Bowie.

I told the cab to go to University Circle. I sat in the back, staring at the lightly snowing evening.

"I've seen you talking to Childe's people," I tell him over a cup of Arabica coffee.

"And you think?" He shakes his head at me. "You don't know how wrong you are, man."

"Why are you talking to these people then?"

"You're supposed to know your enemy, ain't you?"

"Childe's your enemy?"

"He fucked with someone I care about. . . ."

Even as I remembered it, I found that I wasn't so ready to believe him now as I had been then. Though, if he was Childe's tool, why had he helped me as far as he had? If he wasn't, why did I now have the impression that his message on my voice mail had set me up?

Thralls did occasionally kill their masters. Perhaps Bowie *was* Childe's, and had killed him off. Loss of a leader could do strange things to a cult, perhaps even spark a flaring of atypical violence.

That didn't explain why Kate and I had been targets. Had I been close to finding out something? If they had been trying to conceal their vampire nature, they'd done a lousy job of it.

"Maybe Childe's still around, and they're setting him up," I whispered. His own thrall had picked out Cecilia as a potential victim. As far as I could see, she was the first of Childe's people to have disappeared with someone to miss them. Everything since seemed to have been designed to draw Sebastian's attention.

The taxi pulled up in front of Sam's building, and I paid the cabby off with the little cash I had left. I entered Sam's building, thinking that I had almost figured out what was going on.

Gail opened the door a crack to talk to me. The funeral had been hard on her, I thought. Her face was pale and drawn. "Hi, Dad," she said through the crack in the door.

"How are you dong?"

"Not too great," she said, shaking her head.

"I'm sorry."

"It's not your fault."

"Can I come in?"

Gail looked back into the apartment and paused. "We should let Sam sleep."

"Is there something wrong?"

She looked at me and said, in a voice thick with irony, "I don't know, Dad, Mom was buried today, what should be wrong?"

I felt sick at what I said. The new sense of empathy I had—the sense of a psychic wind carrying emotional heat and cold through the aether—carried ripples of confusion, of grief, and of sadness from Gail. I had a sense of clarity beyond anything I'd felt before, and with it came a feeling of loss from my daughter beyond any I had felt myself. "Forgive me, it was a stupid thing to say."

She stared at me, and I felt a sense of something that Gail wanted to say, and wasn't saying. "Whatever happens, I love you, Dad. It isn't your fault . . ." I stood there, waiting for some revelation. Instead she said, "I forgive you."

"Okay."

"The Chevette's in the lot out back. Go find what you're looking for, okay?"

"Okay?"

She closed the door leaving me with a feeling of unease.

I was unsure where my normal parental concern ended, and my paranoia began. I wanted to break in the door and ask her what the problem was, but I told myself that I'd seen her, and she was all right, and she was safe with Sam.

When I left, the press of my hunger was bad enough that I could almost smell blood.

I was sick for blood, and I didn't want any more lives on my hands. I needed to take care of it immediately. I had an idea I wanted to test, so I drove by University Hospitals. I parked the Chevette on the street, straightened my jacket to cover the holster and the bullet holes in my shirt, and headed for the emergency entrance.

I walked in, past a reception desk and into the hospital proper, concentrating on projecting an aura of belonging there. I don't know if it was my attitude, any vampiric powers, or simply that the nurses running the desk were too overworked to notice me, but I slipped in without hearing any comment or objection.

A security guard paced the halls, but he faced away from me, and I followed the corridor in the opposite direction from him.

So far so good, but I soon found that at least one part of my plan was ill-conceived. I had intended to slip into the hospital and steal some of their whole blood supply. That was easy to say in the abstract, but now, as I wandered the night-emptied corridors of the hospital, I found it a little difficult to follow through on the premise when I had no idea where anything was. I could feel hunger eating away inside me, making it harder for me to think clearly.

I ran across a few directory maps, but none had a convenient label saying "find blood here."

After about half an hour of random searching, all I had succeeded in discovering was that I could do a pretty good job of mentally convincing inattentive humans that I wasn't there. That was useful, but it didn't help my hunger, which had grown even worse with my mental effort. The hunger was an ache in my joints, a pressure at the back of my skull, a fire searing behind my eyes.

I wandered deep into the hospital complex, away from the constant activity around the emergency room. This corridor was empty enough that I must have let my guard down for a moment, because, just as I was washed with a stunning wave of hunger that near-doubled me over, a tall woman stepped in front of me.

"Pardon me, but can I help you?"

The woman confronting me was thin, and maybe an inch shy of six feet tall. That, combined with her intense gray eyes, invested her with a quiet authority. I glanced down to her name tag, stitched on her white coat over her left breast. "Dr. Nicholson."

I felt warmth, heat, and life inside her. I knew—I could feel—that what she carried within her could fill the void that was eating a hole inside me. We were separated by six feet, but I already felt the strength of her pulse under my fingers. Something savage inside me told me I wanted to grab her right there and sink my teeth into a vein.

She was becoming impatient with me, I could sense irritation rippling within her. "Can I help you find something?" There was a note of demand in her voice that almost hid the subliminal fear. She knew I wasn't supposed to be here, and the strength of my hunger was so intense that even she had to feel it on some level.

I took a few steps forward, and she said, "Sir, I'm going to have to ask you to leave."

I took another step.

"Do I have to call Security?" The fear was reaching her voice now. I felt a tidal pull toward her.

I stared into her eyes and felt my words push into the deep gray pools I saw there. "That won't be necessary."

I felt a spike of fear accompany her answer. "No, it isn't."

"Don't be afraid."

I heard her swallow. "I'll try." I felt the emotion dim somewhat, but it didn't disappear. That was interesting. What exactly was I doing? If it was control, it wasn't absolute.

She kept staring at me, as if fascinated. *I can take her here,* I thought, *and she won't resist. She'll feel panic, and fear, but she won't stop me.*

I almost reached for her—

Then I heard Gail's words, *"Were they innocent?"*

Instead of grabbing her, I spoke. "I need whole blood. Take me to where you keep it."

She nodded. "Follow me."

As she led me off, I tried to imagine what was going on inside Dr. Nicholson's mind. I still fought the frightening impulse inside me that made me want to take all of what she had inside her. When she finally took me into a darkened lab and opened a refrigerator for me, I got a nasty surprise.

Of the bags of whole blood I saw filling the refrigerator, none of them bore the heat of life. I was desperate in my hunger, and I grabbed one of the bags. The fluid inside seemed black and dead to me, I gently bit into it, to taste the contents.

I heard a sharp intake of breath from the doctor, who still held the refrigerator door open.

The taste of the blood made me gag—like bile in my mouth, like death. I threw the bag down in frustration, and a tiny stream leaked out of the hole my tooth had made. It made a black trail on the linoleum floor.

I looked up at the doctor, and the sense of the life within her was overpowering. As was her fear. "I'm sorry," I said.

There was no way around it, I had to drink from a living person. All I could hope for was, as Gabriel had said, it didn't have to be fatal.

"What are you going to do?" she asked.

We stood apart, the light from the refrigerator the only barrier between us. I could feel the pull of her blood, and I could feel the skin begin to tighten around my jaw. "I won't hurt you," I said, with difficulty. I hoped it wasn't a lie.

I stepped forward, and she let go of the refrigerator door. It closed neatly all the way, leaving only a sliver of light between us.

I touched her neck, and felt the shiver of a racing pulse. "Please calm down," I said, as gently as I could manage.

"I can't," she said.

I felt for her, for her vulnerability. She didn't deserve this, but my own remade nature insisted that nether of us had a choice. I leaned forward.

My lips almost brushed her neck, but I held myself back. I didn't want to injure her. "You take blood, show me the vein you use."

In the ghost-dim light I saw her shake her head. Her

arms were folded across her in a protective gesture. My will was holding her here, but she was afraid. I didn't blame her.

I took her hand, gently, and drew it out in front of her. "Show me. Please." The heat this close to her body was intoxicating. I could smell the life, and every vibration of her pulse sent a tremor through my own body.

After a long pause, she reached down and rolled up her sleeve.

"Forgive me," I said. I leaned over and kissed the crook of her arm, the vein a hot brand against my tongue. My remade teeth bit into the skin almost on their own. Her life, her warmth, filled my mouth. I heard her breath come in shuddering gasps as I drank.

The blood filled weaknesses I hadn't been aware I'd been feeling, the nagging pain evaporated, the fatigue drained away. As soon as I realized that the thirst no longer was a weight within me, I forced myself to stop. It took an effort to pull myself away from her arm, but I managed it. I had refused temptation on a much grander scale last night.

As I pulled away, I was grateful to find that my victim was still standing. As I broke, she sighed and collapsed against me. I had to scramble to keep her upright.

I was beginning to worry when I heard her whisper in my ear. "Who are you?"

"No one important," I said, walking her into the light out in the hall. I looked down at her arm. It was pale and still bleeding, but not badly. I sat her down on the first chair we came to.

She was conscious and seemed to be all right. She looked at me with a wistful expression that made me nervous. "Who are you?" she repeated.

We were out in a corridor, apparently alone. "Just a random nut," I told her. "You should forget about me."

She nodded. She had her arm bent upward, and was putting pressure on the wound. Whatever I was doing mentally, this woman was still in possession of all her faculties. Again, I wondered what was going on inside her mind.

She looked up at me and nodded. "But will I see you again?"

I was stunned by the question for a moment. In response I just shook my head and said, "I don't know." Then I got out of there as quickly as I could.

*   *   *

I wasn't thinking about much of anything as I wove my way back out of the hospital. I wasn't concentrating on not being seen. I passed a small alcove of vending machines, and shortly afterward I heard feet running after me. "Kane? Kane Tyler? Is that you?"

It was a female voice that I barely noticed as familiar. I had conflicting urges to draw my weapon or run, but I turned to face the person.

My first thought was, *what is* she *doing here?*

She slowed to a stop, still holding a Styrofoam cup of hospital coffee. "I thought that was you. If you're here to see him, you missed visiting hours. He's asleep anyway."

I stood there blankly staring at the woman. I knew her, though I could not remember her name. She was in her early thirties, blonde, and wore a dark flowered print dress that was at odds with the weather outside.

She was Sam's girlfriend. Seeing her here gave me a sick feeling of who she was talking about. "What happened?"

"Oh," she looked surprised. "You didn't know? Well, don't worry, the doctors say he'll be fine. They managed to deal with the blood loss in time."

I wanted to shake her. "What blood loss?"

"From the accident. They let him go home and one of the sutures burst open while he slept."

I shuddered. "*When?* When did this happen?"

"Sometime last night—"

I was running for the car before she finished her sentence.

Gail wasn't there to buzz open Sam's apartment. At this point I had lost all concern for subtlety. When she didn't answer, I kicked in the door to the lobby. I ran up the three flights to Sam's apartment, cursing my own stupidity. I had known something was wrong, I had felt it, and I had left her there.

I had even smelled the goddamned blood.

I pounded on Sam's door and received no response. I drew the Eagle and tried the doorknob. It was unlocked. I felt the copper taste of fear in my mouth, a taste that reminded me of blood.

I pushed the door open with my foot, covering the apartment with the Eagle. The living room was empty, but the smell of blood was there—ferric and sharp-tasting.

"Gail!"

I received no answer as I swept the apartment with my gun: living room, kitchen, bathroom. . . .

The blood-smell came from the bedroom. I stood in front of that door a long time before I had the courage to open it. I couldn't take it, not if Gail. . . .

I kicked in the door to Sam's bedroom. It was dark and motionless in there, but my night eyes quickly adjusted. The bed was soaked with blood, blood that was cold, dead, and black.

Gail wasn't here.

"You bastards!" I yelled at the walls. "Where is she? What are you doing?" My voice spent, I whispered, "Why did she lie to me?"

Looking around, I could see the chaos made by the paramedics when they'd grabbed Sam. From the bloodstains on the bed, I could picture the opening of the wounds in his face, spilling across the pillow.

I couldn't picture it as accidental.

I tore the place apart, looking for some clue to where Gail had gone, but I found nothing of hers in Sam's apartment. The only thing I did find was on the floor next to the bed. It was a dirty, folded, piece of paper that looked as if it had spent a long time in someone's pocket, only to slip out when its owner knelt over Sam's bed.

I unfolded it. It was a map of Lakeview Cemetery.

26

I drove away from Sam's apartment building knowing that to find Gail, I had to find Childe's people, his thralls. A knot of rage burned through my gut, at myself, and at them. I had to get to them before they harmed her—

I couldn't complete the thought. The emotion made it hard to think clearly, and I needed to think clearly. I only had two things to act on. I had a map of Lakeview, and I had a memory of dams and mausoleums. I had a memory of running from the teenager with the blood-black smile, of Cecilia's animate body on the blackened snow, of the mausoleum from which she emerged, and of the flood-control dam that had hovered over the whole scene like some gigantic memorial.

Clearly marked, on the map of Lakeview, was the location of that dam. At the moment, that was all I had.

As I drove up Mayfield from University Circle, I passed a large wrought-iron gate that said, "Lakeview Cemetery." My destination.

I felt pressed for time, and parked opposite the gate as soon as I saw it. The cemetery was shut up and dark, long past closing. The sidewalk on that side of Mayfield was deserted. The dark quiet beyond the fence seemed to have reached out to claim Mayfield as part of itself.

As I got out of the car, I glanced up toward the well-lit intersection of Coventry and Mayfield, with its BP station, its bars, and its people. All of it bustled in the distance. From where I was, cloaked in the silence next to the cemetery, it looked like another world. They even seemed to have less snow up there.

I dashed across Mayfield, and up Lakeview's driveway, stopping at the gate. The gate was large and wrought iron, flanked by shorter fences. I walked to the right of the main gate, staring into the darkened foliage beyond the fence, and waited for the traffic on Mayfield to die off for a moment.

During a pause in the traffic, I took a step up and vaulted over the fence. The ease with which I did it—the fence was seven feet tall—surprised me. Somehow I was exploiting both the energy of my anger and of the fresh feeding.

God help anyone who harmed my daughter.

I came crashing down in the snow-covered mulch on the other side of the fence. I stood still for a time, listening for signs that someone had seen me cross the fence. I heard nothing. The snow absorbed the sounds of traffic.

I slipped through the naked winter bushes and into the cemetery. The sense of entering another world was complete. I stepped out into a world of naked trees, rolling snow-blanketed hills, and a total absence of people.

There were footprints here and there, where people had visited, or tended a grave. But, like the graves themselves— mostly marked only by blank humps of snow—the signs of people seemed distant and irrelevant when weighed against the omnipresent stillness.

The silence allowed it to sink in, what had happened. The worst of my fears, the fear that one day I would be hunting down someone's child only to discover the child was my own. My fears *had* been a self-fulfilling prophecy. I had brought all of this down upon us, and it wasn't hard to believe that my own anger was the only thing keeping the guilt from paralyzing me.

I followed the map as well as possible in the darkened cemetery. More than once my haste threw me down on an ice-slicked road. In my blind rush, when I did see a ghostly figure emerge from the woods, I had drawn my gun and almost shot before I realized who it was.

I held my gun upon the white-clad figure and stared for a moment before speaking.

"Gabriel," I said in a puff of fog.

"Indeed, sir. Now, Mr. Tyler, would you put aside that weapon."

"Give me a good reason."

"You try my good graces, sir. You're in no position to test me."

"Am I not?" My hand was shaking. "I had the impression I left whatever grace there was between us when I stepped out of your house."

"You try my patience, Mr. Tyler—"

I steadied my gun with both hands. "You pedantic, pretentious—You have about five seconds to explain why you're here or you'll feel what it's like to have a fifty-caliber bullet pass through that smug expression."

"You're threatening *me?*"

"It won't kill you, but I'm curious about what might happen to your motor skills."

"Mr. Tyler!"

I took a step forward, staring into Gabriel's eyes. They were closed and dead to me, almost opaque. Even so, I looked into them and poured all my anger into my words. "You're so fond of form. My chosen name is Raven."

Gabriel shook his head, "I don't believe I can accept you as a peer, sir."

"Fuck what you believe. Tell me what you're doing here, *now!*"

I don't know if it was the force of my anger, the threat of the gun, or the blessings of Jaguar, but Gabriel backed up.

"Don't you *dare* move," I shouted at him.

His glare raged with a fury mirroring my own, cold where mine was hot. "All right, Raven, ask me what you will."

"What are you doing here?"

"The same as I was doing when first I crossed your path. I felt the intensity of a feeding. I came to investigate."

"Looking for Childe?"

"Looking for Childe."

"Why?"

"Because he breaks the Covenant—"

I shook my head and felt a glare colder than the snow that soaked into my shoes. "Everyone looks for Childe. He's convenient, isn't he? No one seems to pay attention to the radical change in behavior his thralls have undergone. Or that he disappeared with his last recruit, the first person he's taken that anyone seems to have missed. Childe's been around too long for all this to happen at his hand."

"What are you implying?"

"Isn't it obvious? Childe's being set up. And at the very least you're looking the other way. At worst—"

"Mind your accusations. You do not know what you're dealing with."

I closed the distance between us and pressed the gun barrel to his temple as he had placed a sword against my neck. "You don't know who you're dealing with. My daughter is in the hands of those people. Childe, or the people who're scapegoating him. If I find you're involved, I will tear out your heart. What's down the hill?"

"Nothing you should concern yourself with." His face was remarkably calm.

"Let me be the judge of that."

"There's a young woman down there with a tale to tell."

Those words were enough to send me scrambling down the hillside, toward a fenced-off access road that led to my destination. "Don't pursue this," Gabriel called down after me. "Let Childe sink under the weight of his excesses."

I ignored him as I jumped over the gate blocking the snow-covered road. I didn't know what Gabriel was, but at the very least he acted like a cop who simply ignored inconvenient evidence. He disgusted me.

"You've made an enemy today," he called after me at last. I couldn't have cared less.

I ran down the road to a large bowl-shaped valley close to the center of Lakeview. I emerged on the floor of that valley. Towering to my left was the wide concrete face of the dam.

It was just as surreal as I remembered it, a wide slope of concrete hovering over a flat field of snow marred only by one paired set of footprints.

Near the base of the dam, opposite a tiny, snaking river escaping from its base, huddled a small hill next to the wall of the valley. The footprints pointed me directly at that hill.

As I'd remembered, mausoleums were set into the side of that hill. As I ran out onto the dam's flood-plain, following Gabriel's steps, I noticed no sign of graves on the field between me and the hill. The mausoleums down here had to predate the construction of the dam.

My memory of Cecilia's sacrifice kept replaying itself in my mind. I received no new insights, only more and more vivid shots of adrenaline. Little had changed down here, down to the blue-tinted moonlight.

I had to stop between a pair of barren trees, because it

was the spot where I had seen Sebastian's daughter die—
and perhaps be reborn. I was directly in front of the tomb
from which I'd seen her emerge. Gabriel's footsteps led
directly to the tomb's door. And so did others.

It was hard to tell, but where the flood-plain had been
virgin except for Gabriel's footprints, here, by the hill, there
were signs of two, or maybe three other people walking
around the site. I felt even more unease when I remembered why Gabriel said he had come here.

A feeding.

More footprints led to the mausoleum than left it.

This mausoleum seemed typical of the other half-dozen
granite boxes set into the hillside around it. It had the same
peaked temple roof supported by two polished granite pillars flanking the single door. The door was gated by a lat-
ticework of eroded green bronze. The only decorative
carving on the tomb was an Egyptian sun-disk on the lintel
above the door. I was certain that this was the place from
which I'd seen Sebastian's daughter emerge.

What disturbed me was the fact that this tomb bore no
name.

I glanced to the tombs to the left and to the right,
"Forbes," on the one, and another name, illegible in
shadow, on the other. The place I faced was unique. It
must have been built just before the dam, just before they
stopped using this place where the dearly departed could
be washed away the next time they opened the sluice.

I glanced at the dam. Close as I was, it filled half the
world, ground to sky, at an oblique angle. I felt as if I had
fallen into a surrealist painting. Some element didn't belong
here, the dam, the hill, the nameless tomb, myself. . . .

Not a place I'd chose to be buried. Not a place I'd choose
to die.

I stared at the footprints leading to the door of the nameless mausoleum. I felt the same dread that I had felt when
approaching Sam's bedroom.

It seemed an eternity before I had gathered the courage
to walk up to the gate in front of the door. I stared in, past
the green metal scrollwork, trying to see through the one
window in the door beyond. The darkness was impenetrable, even to my sensitive eyes. The little windows set into
the recessed door seemed to be painted black.

Just like the bedroom in Childe's apartment. Perhaps for the same reasons. It was easy to believe that all my answers lay beyond the bronze scrollwork in front of me. I listened for a few moments, trying to sense if anyone was here.

I let the silence hover a little longer than was comfortable. I felt alone. I hooked my fingers into the cold metal scrollwork, next to the lock, and pulled.

The gate flung open, unlocked. I expected the mechanism to protest more upon opening, but it glided open on well-oiled hinges.

I now faced a heavy, studded, wooden door.

I looked around and listened again. This time I heard something—

I backed, slightly, and began raising my gun. I wasn't quick enough. The door was yanked open from inside. A stench of rotting death billowed out, piercing the cold, worse than anything my gangrenous hand had emitted— the warm, wet smell of decayed meat.

The smell pushed me back like a fist. I saw the source of the smell and wondered if the gun was going to do me any good.

I saw its clothes first, maybe because I didn't want to see the rest of it. What I saw was typical teenage Gothic-punk. Black jeans, black T-shirt, black leather, black everything. At least everything *used* to be black. Everything was torn, ragged, splattered with mud and darker filth.

It emerged into the moonlight, following its smell, a first-hand example of someone who did not wear vampirism well. Its hair was gone except for a few random patches. Feral red eyes burned inside sockets sunk into craters of tattered white flesh. Black sores pockmarked its skin. I saw tendons working through holes in its cheek and the backs of its hands. Fingernails and teeth were absurdly long.

It hissed like an angry cat.

I leveled my gun and tried to stare it down—a move that had been successful lately. But, behind those bloody eyes I didn't see much I could influence. And what was there was dedicated to being permanently pissed off.

The thing leaped at me, screaming something shrill and inarticulate. I ducked to the side just in time to avoid having a bite taken out of my left shoulder. I felt its hand brush by me. Its touch felt unclean.

Before I'd turned fully around, I felt claws rake across my left hip. I backpedaled and saw the thing trailing bloody pieces of my shirt and my jacket. It was fast.

It advanced toward me, a moving corruption.

I fired the Eagle. The zombie and I were connected for a microsecond by a tongue of flame, then it fell backward into the snow, a ragged hole kicked into its chest. Of course, it started getting up again. I walked closer and fired again, this time into his head. Its face caved in and chunks of skull blew into the snow. It stopped moving.

I knew, despite appearances, that I hadn't finished it off. Looks weren't anything. It had looked dead *before* I shot it, and I'd survived a bullet in the face myself.

Though, looking at the mess in the snow, I realized that the bullet *I'd* taken was not into the brain-case, and hadn't been fifty-caliber. From the look of things, at the very least I'd slowed it down a bit.

The mausoleum still hung open, behind me. I ran back up to it.

The first thing I saw, as my eyes adjusted to the gloom, was that Sebastian had left his spoor here, in the form of two dead soldiers. The two crumpled bodies cluttering the marble floor, dressed and armed as they were, were unlikely to have come from another source.

As Gabriel had said, a woman sat here. In the darkness I was allowed one momentary illusion. I almost whispered, "Gail!"

Then I saw through the shadows and saw the face of Cecilia, Sebastian's daughter. She didn't look as bad as the thing I'd pumped lead into—the corpses on the floor didn't look *that* bad—but she didn't look good.

She sat at the far end of the tomb, one of the corpses crumpled at her feet. She glared at me and demanded, "Who the fuck are you?"

Nice Catholic girl, I thought. I glanced at the bodies on the ground and said, "Someone who isn't working for your father." Saying that severed whatever ties I had left with Sebastian. It felt better than it should've.

"Like the last guy?"

I heard a rattle and as I stepped forward, over the first corpse. She was handcuffed to a wrought-iron bench set into the narrow far wall.

"Are you a cop?" she asked. "I told everything to the guy with the cane."

I bent over and rolled one of the dead men onto his back. I didn't know him, but the wound was familiar. His neck was half gone, the wound a black crater in the darkness. In one hand he clutched a rosary, in the other a thirty-eight. Neither appeared to have helped him much.

I picked up the rosary, which didn't seem to hold any special power. Maybe he hadn't gone to church enough.

"Who are you?" she repeated.

"Where're Childe's people? Where're the rest of his thralls?"

She shook her head. "I don't know what you're talking about."

I rolled over the second body, whose wounds were less severe, smaller, and just as fatal as the first's. Two generic hoods with the job of scouting locations for Dad. "How long ago?" I asked.

"What?"

"How long since you and the zombie feasted on these two?"

"I didn't —"

I knelt down in front of her. "No games. I know what you are. This guy has most of his neck, unlike the zombie's dinner. That, and you're pretty damn fresh for someone who hasn't had a drink for a long time. How long have you been here? Since Childe's little ritual? You should be starving."

"Stop it! Stop it!" She was crying, and I backed off. She looked down at her feet and whispered, "I was insane with it. Dominic—" she indicated the corpse "—was dead before I realized I knew him." She sobbed. "I've had to sit here with him for a whole day."

Sebastian had had over twenty-four hours to realize his hoods were missing. I looked back out the door. I could see the bloodless zombie out there on the ground, looking even more cadaverous and thin even though his chest had reconstructed itself.

In the distance I heard sirens. My gunshots had not gone unnoticed.

"You have a choice, Cecilia. I can leave you here for the cops, or I can take you, and you tell me what I want to know." I stared into her eyes, and I didn't know if it was vampiric persuasion or the unambiguous options that made her say, "Take me."

I holstered the Eagle, reached down, and pulled the handcuff chain apart.

27

Fortunately, I was able to lock the mausoleum shut on the corpses. I collected my brass and left zombie-boy where he was. I pulled Cecilia along, through the cemetery, without running across Gabriel again. And, despite the sirens, we reached the gate before any police showed themselves.

I pulled her over the fence and we dashed across Mayfield to the Chevette.

"Who was that he left guarding you?" I asked. I wanted her talking.

"Joey," she said. There was a long pause. "At least I think he's still Joey." Her voice was small and leeched of any of the earlier bravado. I suddenly felt for everything she was going through.

Despite the wave of empathy I felt, I had to remind myself that she was one of Childe's thralls now, which meant she was involved in whatever happened to my daughter. "How did Gabriel get by him?"

"Who?"

"The man with the cane."

"I don't know. He just looked at Joey, and Joey didn't move."

Rank hath its privileges. Apparently Gabriel had better luck staring down the opposition than I did. "I need you to tell me about him, and Childe's people."

She looked up at me, and I stopped next to the Chevette. I wanted her in the car. Her dress was gore-stained, black with dried blood, and I didn't want anyone to see her. "They have my daughter."

"I'm sorry," she said.

I opened the passenger door and set her in the car. "Talk to me."

"I met Joey once, before. . . ." She shivered. "I had no idea that would happen to him. He wasn't happy, even before all this. He thought he was a bad person," Cecilia said.

"He thought Childe was a bad person?"

"No, he thought *he* was, Joey. He saw himself as evil."

"So you knew these people a while before you ran away?" I made my way around to the driver's door of the Chevette. I was feeling strain from standing still. I wanted to wring Cecilia's neck, get her to tell me where they were *now*. But I knew pushing her might make her clam up, and I needed her talking.

"Friends," she said. "I thought they were friends. They aren't people."

Neither are we, Cecilia, I thought. "Go on about Joey."

"He started following Childe before I met him. I don't know what he was like before then. When Joey was in a good mood he would talk about what an evil bastard he was—saw himself as—about all the people he was angry at. When he was in a bad mood, he would sit and sulk. I think he amused Childe."

"Amused him?" I said as I slipped in and started the car. I didn't know how tight control between master and thrall was, but I felt that there was a good chance that this woman was directly under Childe's control. I was lucky she was volunteering information.

Whatever that control aspect was, my experience with my own influence, especially with Doctor Nicholson, seemed to be less absolute domination, and more of an erosion of the victim's will—or desire—to resist suggestions.

After being locked up with Joey, Cecilia probably didn't feel any excessive loyalty to Childe, or to Childe's thralls. If I was right about the way things worked, I could probably deal with her up until she met Childe again, and the domination reasserted itself.

"People amused Childe—" She shook her head. "I tried to leave him before. . . . Who are you?"

The sudden shift startled me. I was driving carefully, away from Lakeview, keeping an eye on the rearview mirror. "My name's Kane, Kane Tyler."

"Why is that name familiar?" She seemed to ask me and herself.

"I arrested your father once."

"You *are* a cop!"

"*Was,* a long time ago. I retired when a twelve-year-old blew a hole through my lung."

"Sorry," she whispered and touched my bicep. "Were you hurt badly?"

"I've been hurt worse since." I turned the wheel, more to escape her hand than to maneuver the car. Her touch made me uncomfortable. "You said you tried to leave Childe. Why didn't you?"

"He convinces you. That's what he does. He convinces you to do things, and once he does that, he owns you. Once you go with him, you can't go back; no one else would have you if they knew what he'd made you do."

"If someone forces you—"

"That's it. He doesn't force. Everyone's free to go, they just *can't.*" She bent over, palms pressing into her temples. "You can't imagine—" She stopped talking for a while, and just shook.

"I wanted to kill myself," she finally whispered. "You know why I didn't?"

"Why?"

"Because of what he has us do to the bodies."

Then, in a massive rambling lump, she let it all come pouring out.

Cecilia had been sucked into Childe's group because she was quite consciously searching for something diametrically opposed to her father's Catholicism. In a sense, the neo-pagans that populated Cleveland Heights were just too good-natured for her.

In other words, she was exactly the kind of person Childe looked for. Childe pulled his followers to him by appealing to something evil.

Childe offered power to his followers, in return for their absolute slavery to him. Somehow the inherent contradiction of Childe's offer was overshadowed by his demonstration of blood-magick. His charisma was such, and his appeal so visceral, that no one who entered his inner circle ever left. He called himself Satan's agent on Earth, and the people he targeted were so alienated and nihilistic that such a proclamation was attractive, especially after Childe demonstrated the ability to transcend death.

Cecilia told me of a time when Childe offered a revolver and a box of ammunition to a doubter named Eric. Within a circle of twenty people, Eric loaded the revolver, and pumped off three rounds point-blank into Childe's chest. Childe's robes erupted with gore, and Cecilia remembered seeing, briefly, the walls of the wound going deep into Childe's chest. Childe smiled, took the gun, and fired a single round into Eric's head.

Eric had not taken Childe's sacrament; Eric died. After that demonstration, it was easy for Childe to order his followers to descend on Eric and feed—even those who had not yet become his thralls.

The pattern Cecilia related was common for all of Childe's followers. He would pull the victim in, gradually force the person to sever all ties to family and friends outside the group, show some demonstration of power, and slowly pull the person into steadily more degrading acts. Each event would increase Childe's power over the individual, until, by the time Childe decided to take the final step and grant his own blood to the victim, the person was already psychologically enslaved.

According to her, she had been locked in that mausoleum for two and a half weeks prior to the ceremony. She only had water. She was nearly driven mad by hunger and isolation—but Childe had done enough of a job on her to keep her from crying out.

When they opened the door for her, she had no choice but to walk out. But according to her, after the door opened, she had no memory until waking up, inside the tomb, with the zombie.

There were things in her story that didn't ring true. There's a difference in the way people tell their stories. And when I listen I can tell the difference between someone who's telling me something for the first time, and someone who's rehearsed. The pauses are more conscious. There's more awareness of the audience. I can see the words flow by as if by rote.

It doesn't matter how emotional or inarticulate a person is, I can see when they know the next word they're going to say. I suppose it was all those times hearing the difference between what people said during interrogation, and what they said on the stand after being rehearsed by their lawyer.

Listening to Cecilia made me wonder if she had been talking to a public defender.

But I had other worries. "So where can I find them?" I asked.

"You don't want to find them."

I slammed on the brakes and skidded the Chevette to the side of the road. Clouds had rolled over the moon, and a light snowfall was captured by the streetlights in front of me. Cecilia was curled up in her spattered, ragged, dress, staring at her lap.

"They have my daughter!" I shouted.

She winced and I softened my voice as much as I was able. "Cecilia, I *need* to find her."

"Too powerful. . . ." she whispered. I had to struggle to keep from grabbing and shaking her.

After the silence became too long, I said, "Lead me somewhere she might be, Cecilia."

She nodded. "I can't go in with you. You can't make me face him."

I placed a hand on her shoulder. "I wouldn't make you do that."

Slowly, very slowly, she said, "There's a house where he kept us—"

The house was in East Cleveland, on the economic down-slope from the hills of Lakeview. I was expecting her to lead me to something a little less mundane. Instead, I pulled up across the street from a three-story brick duplex that had seen better days. The yard was fenced-in chain-link, the gutters were sagging, and I saw a few major dips in the roof. All the windows were dark, and in the sodium glow of the street lamps, I could see newspaper covering the insides of most of them.

"There?" I asked, looking at the dead windows.

Cecilia nodded without looking at the house. "Don't make me go in there," she whispered.

To me, the house looked empty. At least it was a hell of a lot emptier than its neighbors. There was loud rap music from at least two nearby houses. Lights blared from a party on our side of the street. Teenagers were crossing the street from house to house, ignoring the snow, ignoring us.

The clock on the dash read 1:30. The house across the street loomed in silence like a tooth missing from a smile. I looked at Cecilia.

She looked terrified. I could feel the waves of emotion from her even without looking in her eyes. While that sixth sense felt the warm tide of fear, an older sense—a gut instinct that had hung with me ever since I was on the force— smelled a setup.

They had tied Cecilia out there for someone. Sebastian maybe. Maybe me.

I'd been able to bust the handcuff chain with no problem. If she had fed recently, wouldn't she be capable of a similar feat? Why had Gabriel left her there?

"What did you tell the man with the cane? What did you tell him that you haven't told me?"

"Nothing else," she whispered.

I wondered if that meant Gabriel was here. It was probably a mistake, but I couldn't gamble with my daughter's life. Still, I was second-guessing myself even as I said, "Don't leave the car."

I locked the Chevette behind me, leaving her curled up and hidden behind the snow-dusted windows. I stepped out into the slush in the middle of the road and looked around me.

It was so damn *normal*—obnoxious teenagers drinking, partying, and playing loud music. Change the black kids to white, and the rap music to neo-punk grunge, and this could be *my* neighborhood. The alienation I felt from that normalcy was crippling.

I walked to the one empty house, conscious of exactly how quiet it was. I was figuring geography in my head as I stepped through the snow-covered, carless driveway, so I wasn't surprised to see the rusty fence at the rear of the house, the woods beyond it, or the fresh-cut hole in the chain-link.

The ends of the cut wire were shiny, and fresh tracks marred the snow in a path between it and the rear door of the house. Too many tracks to tell if the most recent were coming or going.

It had taken me a while to figure, but it was clear to me now that this property bordered on Lakeview. Beyond that fence was part of the cemetery. Lakeview was a huge suburb of the dead, bordering Cleveland Heights and East Cleveland, as well as Cleveland proper.

Of course Childe would own a house that bordered on the cemetery's property. The question in my mind was, *was anyone home?*

The house gave no clue. It was silent and dark, most of the first-floor windows covered by wood or newspaper from the inside. If it weren't for the glittering wound in the rusty fence, and the trail at least as fresh as the last snowfall, it would appear totally abandoned.

I looked to the lighted yards on either side of this one, and saw no one watching me. I drew the Eagle and walked to the back door of Childe's house.

I tried the door. It was locked. I slowly leaned on it, forcing my shoulder between the lock side of the window and the doorjamb. I thrust with my legs, concentrating on using whatever paranormal strength I had.

The dead-bolt gave with surprising ease. Dry-rot showered me as the wood of the jamb gave. The lock broke as I'd wanted it to, with a bare snap. It didn't look or sound as if I had kicked the door in.

A metal object glimmered a moment, and I caught it with my left hand before it clattered to the ground. It was the half of the dead-bolt that I'd torn loose from the wall, screws and all. I pocketed it to avoid making any more noise.

I listened at the doorway for movement inside. I could sense some dim life—not heard, but felt as a dim wave of barely conscious emotion. The only thing I *heard* was the loud music next door.

I slipped in and shut the door behind me.

I found myself in the rear stairwell of a two-family home. Stairs before me led down into an ink-black basement. The stairs up led to the rear of the first floor apartment.

Where first?

I wanted to follow the impression of life I felt upstairs; it could be Gail. But I had a long instinct for not leaving my backside exposed. I descended into the basement, going slowly down the stairs to give my eyes a chance to adjust. Even my extreme night vision had problems seeing in the near-absolute darkness.

I held the Eagle before me, and before I made it halfway, I could smell the blood. At the foot of the stairs I had to pause for a long time before I could understand exactly what I saw.

At first all I saw was an abstract pattern of shapes piled against the cinder-block walls. I saw blotches of shadow, and deeper shadow, and oblong and round patches that rose out of the shadow. My gaze locked on a circular patch of off-white formed of symmetrical shadows.

I must have stared for at least half a minute before I realized I was looking at a skull, jawless and upside down, perched on top of a pile of other remains.

It was the same conceptual shift I remember from those optical illusions where suddenly a vase becomes a pair of faces. Suddenly I saw the random shadows as bones from maybe half a dozen human beings. Other piles resolved into scattered piles of sneakers and jeans.

I stopped breathing.

Blood dotted the walls like rust-stains. Odd bits of clothing, reduced to rags, were scattered everywhere. Ragged lumps of bone lay here and there. Most appeared to have been gnawed.

I began to see movement in the piles of remains, and I nearly shot, before I saw a fleshy patch-furred thing trailing a naked tail.

Rats.

If I concentrated, I could hear their claws scratching on the concrete. They followed the edges of the basement, scratching and gnawing. But I saw them now, dead-eyed things, the smallest the size of my fist.

Central to the basement, extending the width of the room between the sinks and the rusted-out water-heater, was a table. I saw the stains, the marks, and the chains meant to restrain. I was overcome with memory.

The stains form a vaguely cruciform outline on the dining room table. Markings by the police give it a human shape. The table is scarred, knives perhaps, maybe even claws. I see wires that could have bound legs and arms. Some of the strings lead up to bloodstains on the ceiling.

The table was the same here, the same as the dining room where Kate had been killed. It served the same purpose, for many more people. A deep rage filled me, and fear for my daughter that bordered on agony.

28

As I ascended to the first floor, the air warmed, freeing something dead in the air. I bent close to the door on the landing and listened for movement. I heard the scratching of rats below me, the music blaring outside, little more. I stood for a few long moments, before I reached for the doorknob.

The knob spun loosely in its socket. I pulled gently. It slid out of the door. The door creaked open a fraction, and in the crack I saw a slice of the kitchen.

The scrabbling of rats continued, and the smell grew worse.

I pushed the door open with my foot, keeping the Eagle leveled at the dark kitchen. A rat the size of a brick exploded out of a pile of garbage by the door, shooting between my legs.

I froze, listening for reaction from the rest of the house. Nothing but the sound of music blaring outside and rats scratching inside the walls.

Yellowed newspaper sealed the kitchen's one window, filtering the only light. Piles of garbage, mostly clothing, covered cracked linoleum. The refrigerator, doorless, gaped at me, revealing an interior splattered with black stains. There was no stove.

I dropped the doorknob in the filth choking the sink, and inched deeper inside.

The place was empty, but I counted a half-dozen mattresses in the two bedrooms, where the windows were painted black. The walls in the living and dining rooms were covered with writing, or symbols, or something. Predictably, the marks were written in blood.

The bathroom was where most of the smell was coming from.

I dreaded approaching that place, but when I came near enough I realized that, whatever it was in there, it had been there since long before Gail had disappeared. It hung from a pair of handcuffs to the rear, over the bathtub. It was vaguely humanoid, and quite dead. About half of it had spilled into the bathtub.

The fact that it wasn't Gail was faint reassurance. The deeper into this place I walked, the more the fear gripped me. I backed out of there quickly, and retreated for the stairs.

I could feel that more was here besides me and the rats. What I felt came from upstairs. I mounted the steps, climbing to the second floor. I expected more of the same.

I was wrong, very wrong.

The first sign was that the door was locked. It wasn't a great lock, it broke when I put my shoulder to the door—but just the fact that the door was locked at all was a signal that the upstairs was different.

After the door broke, a security chain went with it, swinging and jingling as the door rebounded off of the wall.

I stood there, the Eagle covering a relatively clean kitchen with refrigerator, stove, and empty sink, and I listened. This time I heard more than scratching rats and Dr. Dre lyrics in the background. I heard a high-pitched whine. . . .

The sound stopped me in my tracks. It was something that might have come from a leaky radiator. It had the same weak breathless quality. But the tone of that sound struck me on an entirely different level, something that tore at the bowels, that made me want to curl up into a ball and shake.

The sound did not end. It droned on and on and on—

I thought of Gail and my stomach tied into a hard little knot. It was that thought that gave me the courage to move. The thought ran over and over in my head, *I woke something up.*

The doorway between the kitchen and the dining room was blocked by a heavy red drape. The sound came from beyond that. I steeled myself, and pushed it aside with my gun.

It was as if I had left this century and entered the previous one. I entered a twisted parody of Childe's apartment.

The walls had been knocked out, down to the structural supports. Most of the second floor was now a giant velvet-draped space. Candles guttered everywhere, and threadbare Victorian furniture weighted stacks of balding oriental carpeting. Incense fogged the air, barely covering the smell of rot.

And over that, came that whine.

Ahead of me, across a room furnished from a nineteenth-century garbage heap, was a trunk, or a table, concealed underneath a tasseled red cover. Gold thread had come loose from the cover, leaving random stitches as almost-comprehensible hieroglyphs.

I took a step and I saw one of the tassels move.

That sound, an exhausted anguished cry, came from under that cover. And something underneath it was moving.

"Gail?" I whispered so low that I didn't hear my own voice.

Whatever the covered object was, it was set so its top was at waist height. It was at least seven feet long, maybe a yard wide. I approached it, hands shaking, feeling perspiration for the first time since the sewer.

I saw that the object was not perfectly flat. The edges were higher than the center, some sort of frame . . .

Within a foot the smell was almost intolerable. Not just from the incense-burning braziers that flanked this thing, but from the rot the incense was trying to cover.

The sound died. It didn't trail off so much as sever itself. Something pushed the red cover, brushing it slightly from underneath. It was a weak motion, and only the thought of Gail kept me from backing away.

I lightly tugged the cover away from the rectangular object. It only took a slight tug before the cover slid off under its own weight.

The object uncovered was as much a discard from the last century as the rest of the room. But it belonged in an insane asylum, or a torture chamber.

I reeled from the box, as the thing inside began keening again.

It was a flat cage of wood and iron, two feet by three feet by seven. The box sat, like an offering, on an antique table supported by a set of cracked jade dragons. The creature imprisoned within could not move more than a few inches in any direction.

It wasn't my daughter; the thing inside that cage had been trapped for much longer. . . .

Exposed, the thing within began thrashing and jerking, screaming louder. It was naked, and reduced to nearly a skeleton. Ragged holes were worn in its flesh, and the skin in its face had tightened to form a rictus grin. The eyes had sunken too deep in the skull for me to see more than shadowed holes. Its teeth were fangs, and its fingers formed six-inch claws—

I kept backing away from it.

It shook as if having a seizure, the claws on its hands slashing its sides. As I watched, the wounds tried to heal, seal themselves shut. However, the flesh would fester and boil instead, and leave another crater in its skin.

I had retreated all the way to the kitchen door when the caged thing arched its back and tore at a gaping wound that scarred most of its shriveled abdomen.

It screamed as it sank claws into its gut, and when its hand withdrew and slapped against the bars, it dropped something that fell through the bars and to the carpet. It was a rat, coat slick and black. It scurried off into the darkness to join its brethren.

I wanted to vomit.

The imprisoned thing sank into quiescence, not breathing, not moving, as silent as a corpse. Just looking at it made me feel filthy. Who would do this, to anyone? To *anything?*

I took a step forward, and it didn't move.

I walked back up to the cage. The creature was as physically devastated as a mummy. It was nearly impossible to determine sex—determining age was hopeless.

When I reached its side, the flesh the rat had fed upon had aged to match the other old sores that perforated its flesh. The motionlessness was so complete that it was hard to believe that I wasn't looking at an inert corpse.

"Raven?"

I jumped at the breathy whisper. It shocked me badly enough that I nearly put a bullet through the cage.

"I see your name." It slowly turned its head, eyes burning red in its deep sockets. The voice was weak, paper thin,

and it terrified me. I leveled the Eagle, aiming between those red eyes, but I didn't fire.

My hands shook.

"Let us sup, you and I," it said. I felt gore-spotted talons clawing into my mind. I could feel its will pulling me down toward it.

Strength, I thought.

"No," I whispered, raising my gun and tearing my eyes away from the gaze of that thing.

"Sate my hunger and I will be yours," it whispered. I kept backing away, into the kitchen. I was relieved when I finally slipped away from that thing. There was something very special about that creature in the cage—

Before I had enough distance to think, I was interrupted by the sound of voices outside, behind the house. The thing in the cage must have heard them, too, because I heard something that might have been a laugh. The sound it made was little more than a whispery cough, but there was a malignant humor woven into it, a weight of malicious unreason.

It was hard to retreat into the stairwell. The corpse-thing pulled attention to itself, even when it had receded from view. It was hard to concentrate on anything else, knowing it was there.

The voices behind the house were close enough to be intelligible over the music blaring next door. It was the hard rhythm of gangster rap more than the voices that pulled me back into the present.

"—the fuck's the matter with Joey, man?" The voice was fast, high-pitched. It came from almost directly under my feet and I edged up next to the window across the landing from the kitchen door.

"Wake up, Joey. Say something!" Female voice, deeper, rougher than the first. When I was next to the window, I peeled some yellowing newsprint away from the window, so I could see down into the yard. The paper came away in a shower of dead flies.

I saw six figures, struggling along the path between the back door and the cemetery. They were half-dragging a bald man with staring eyes.

"What, Hel? Like Joey said anything before? We had to

lock him up, remember?" This was another woman, back to me, who was leading the bald guy by the arm.

"Shut up!" said the first female voice. There was a paleness to that woman, to all of them except the bald guy, more than makeup could account for. Their skin was near-translucent. Hel's skin was white enough to make her lips appear black by contrast.

Everyone's hair was black as well, again, except for the bald guy. The bald one was dressed in the same Goth-punk outfit as the rest of them, but rattier, mud-spattered.

It wasn't until they were close enough for me to see the hole blown in his shirt that I realized that I was looking at zombie-boy. That shocked the hell out of me, because there wasn't any of the leprous rot on him anymore. He wasn't even pale, like his escorts. Joey's skin was now smooth, pink, and as blemish-free as a baby's. I didn't see a speck of hair, or a sign of the bullet holes I had put into him.

However, his eyes were as blank as a dead television set. He stared straight ahead, being led by his fellows, showing no sign of anyone at home.

"We *are* vulnerable," I whispered. I had shot this guy in the head and all the mechanical damage, even to the brain tissue, had regencrated. The mind, it seemed, had not.

I swallowed, thinking about what would have happened to me had the late detective fired an inch or two higher into my face. I'd be dealing with more than a little amnesia.

However, the fact that the body had returned to a state healthier than when I had shot him, that I had trouble figuring.

I had two choices—run for it, or force a confrontation.

With Gail missing, I had one choice. The Eagle didn't counterbalance being outnumbered like this, but these were the beings responsible for the disappearance of my daughter, more so than Childe—whose fate I was only now beginning to comprehend.

I didn't want to meet with the cage-thing again, so I started down the stairs for the first-floor apartment. I listened to the two women argue over Joey as I ran down two flights of stairs. "Joey's nuts, Hel."

"Shut up. We'll get him better—we're promised that much."

"Yeah, for sitting on the missing newbie. Did you forg—"

"Shut up!"

I had reached the landing behind the kitchen door on the first floor when I heard a new male voice say. "Girls, we've got a problem." With the voice, I heard the rear door creak open. It was a voice I had heard before, from the rear of Sam's car, and Childe's answering machine tape.

I braced the Eagle in both hands as I approached the landing.

I heard one whisper from the woman who wasn't Hel. "Stace, stay with the geek." Then the voices silenced themselves.

The shadow from the door below slid by the wall next to me. I backed to the far corner from the door and tried to become part of the shadows. My Eagle was focused down the flight, toward the back door. Next door, amplification distorted a voice rapping about natural-born killers.

Three figures slipped into the stairwell. Even in the dark, the albino skin on the trio lifted their images out of the shadows. The clothing they wore faded into the blackness, making their heads and hands gray and disembodied.

The one in the lead, the male, looked directly toward me and said, "So what the fuck's this?" It was eerie to see this guy close up. He looked like someone playing at being undead, someone who could blend in with all the other teenagers who'd read Anne Rice once too many times. However, at this distance it was obvious that the pale skin wasn't makeup. I could see the shadow of his veins weaving under the surface. The vivid mouth could have been lipstick, but I suspected a play-actor would have chosen pure black or red, and not a shade exactly the color of clotted blood.

"Where is my daughter," I said to him.

The guy laughed. "You don't know what the fuck you're doing, do you?"

I kept my gun leveled at him. "Neither do you. I'm supposed to be dead, remember? *Where is she?*"

I looked past him at the two women. One, with hair long and black, was wearing a floor-length dress that looked extremely impractical for anything other than hiding bloodstains. The woman next to her was more punk than Goth. She had shaved the sides of her head, and wore about a pound of jewelry through various holes in her face. Like the lead guy, she wore a studded motorcycle jacket, self-consciously abused black denim, and a pair of Doc Martens.

Thirty years ago, Childe's disciples probably wore tie-dyed peasant shirts, granny-glasses and love beads.

The guy took a step forward, up the center of the stairwell. The two women slid to the walls and followed, a foot or so behind him. The punked-out girl was giving me a hungry, long-toothed smile.

"I'd stay where you are," I said.

The guy shook his head. "That gun can't do anything to us."

It was my turn to smile. These kids were more ignorant than I was. "Joey would tell you different if he could still talk."

Hel screamed and leaped toward me, and I would have put a bullet through her if the guy hadn't blocked her. Punk-woman was no longer smiling.

"I don't believe you," he said, his words slurring a bit behind a long grimace.

I felt a shriveling in my gut as I realized I was watching them change. Their skulls were shifting, favoring an inhumanly long jawline and carnivorous teeth. Their nails were lengthening, turning into black claws. The punk one was turning into a pierced version of the vampire from that silent German film, *Nosferatu.*

The moment I noticed, I could feel the skin in my face tightening in sympathy.

"A slug through the brain," I said. "The nerve tissue might grow back, but I doubt it knits into anything really complex."

He took another step, and Hel was pushing to get by him. Her eyes had gone blood-red with fury. She snarled like an animal, her skin had gone gray and twisted, and her skull was forming a muzzle.

"Stop!" I put what will I could into the word. I tried to force down the trio with my stare, as I had tried with Joey. I pushed, but with the three of them it was barely enough

to force a pause in their advance. "I took third in marksmanship. I'll drop one of you, probably two, before you reach me."

They stopped advancing; even Hel stopped snarling for a moment.

"Where's my daughter?" I said.

"You know where she is, Kane." His voice had become high and hissing. Where Hel was changing into something animalistic, he was turning into something demonic. His forehead had distorted into a shape that suggested a crest and horns.

"Where's Gail?" I yelled at them. My own voice was slurring, my tongue was too thick in an oddly formed mouth.

There was something wrong. The demon laughed and I realized that it wasn't my will forcing them back. They were waiting for something.

It struck me all at once. There'd been six of them. Joey was guarded by someone out back. Werewolf, Demon and Nosferatu were in the stairwell with me—

Where was the last vampire?

I tensed, expecting it, and when the door to the kitchen exploded open, I fired the Eagle into the Demon's face before I began turning. I was tackled by a punk nightmare before I finished my movement. I had a visceral glimpse of chain and leather, then my back slammed into the wall, crushing plaster and splintering lathe. Claws pierced the wrist of my gun hand, pinning it to the frame of the window next to me.

More claws pierced my abdomen, just above the groin. I felt its hand slam against my spine in a white-hot explosion of pain.

My vision fogged red. I watched its face, which seemed small and distant through the pain, despite being an inch away from mine. He was somewhere between Nosferatu and the Demon, ugly, but still vaguely human. Even more jewelry hung off his face than the other punks. Rings and chains jingled, almost touching my face.

Its jaw levered open, revealing carnivore teeth in a waft of carrion breath. One gold tooth remained disturbingly human.

I forced myself to move through the shock. I reached up

to push its face away with my left hand, and found myself with my hands on a chain that dangled between its right ear and the bony ridge that used to be a nose. I yanked to the left, toward the wall next to me.

The chain came free of the ear instantly, it seemed, and its jaw snapped shut short of my neck. Its nose was more durable, especially with the cartilage that seemed to have grown around the end of the chain.

Its head snapped to the side, following the chain, slamming into the wall, going through the plaster. Its hands fell away from my gut and my wrist.

I stumbled back, away from everything, up the stairs toward the second floor. I faced down the stairs, leveling the Eagle two-handed as the flesh knitted on stomach and my wrist.

I heard Hel before I saw her—a feral growl to my right, behind the wall separating the stairwells. I'd stumbled halfway to the landing above when the growling thing rounded the wall into view. Whatever it was, it was no longer even vaguely human. It was wolflike, a wolf with sickle claws and sharklike teeth. It loped toward me, clumsily, on all fours.

The Eagle barked in my hand, drowning the thing's growls. The kick from the gun slammed spikes of pain into my still-healing wrist. The wolf-thing was close enough to the muzzle-flash that I smelled its coarse fur smolder.

The shot took out a chunk of its shoulder above the left foreleg. It tumbled backwards into the punk I'd slammed into the plaster, who was just now unwedging itself. They both tumbled into a heap under the window on the landing below me.

I scrambled up on the landing behind me, my gut leaking despite my body's efforts to repair itself.

My ears still rang from the gunfire as Nosferatu rounded the corner. She was still recognizable, even with the long clawed fingers and the vast forehead, and that made the transformation seem even worse.

I realized I was snarling as badly as the wolf, and my remade hands were making it difficult to keep the gun level. *What the hell have I turned into?*

Nosferatu looked up at me and held a hand back, gesturing her tangled comrades still. *"Everyone chill the fuck out!"*

Amazingly, her voice was unchanged, despite the radical dental work her front teeth had undergone. Everyone stopped moving. I was grateful for the pause, because I could feel parts of my stomach moving around by themselves.

"Now what?" I asked, keeping the gun leveled at her skull. I had to lean against the wall to keep my hands steady. It was a standoff, and they knew it. I was pretty sure they could take me, but only with a high cost. The trio gathered at the foot of the second stairwell; it was just wide enough for two of them to rush me.

No sign of the demon, or the one guarding Joey.

That one must have heard the shots, and I was worried about being blindsided again. I was next to another window on this landing, facing the driveway. I tried to keep an eye on it, as well as the half of the stairwell going up to the second floor. I was too exposed where I was, but I couldn't keep retreating upward without losing sight of the vampires below me.

"You better put the gun down, Kane," Nosferatu finally said. "You aren't getting out of here." I felt a dominating pressure behind the words, but it was almost perfunctory. It didn't even compare to the thing in the cage, much less the one glimpse of real power I had seen in Jaguar.

"My chosen name is Raven." I smiled, which felt odd with my altered jawline.

"You're outnumbered, in our domain. You belong to us—"

I shook my head. "It doesn't work like that. Your horned friend might have chewed on my neck, but I took nothing from him. I own my own blood." I shook my head. "Nothing here belongs to you. It all belongs to your master."

I felt a wave of contempt wash up the stairwell. I couldn't tell which of the three it was coming from, or if it was inner- or outer-directed.

"To our master, then—"

"No one's my master." I slurred my speech, but it was becoming easier to talk. I was getting used to the shape of my jaw, which was good, since no one seemed to be changing back. I hoped that it was related to stress, and I wasn't stuck as whatever I was now.

"That can change." Nosferatu had slipped easily into the

spokesman role. I suspected she wasn't that unhappy that demon-boy had taken a bullet in the face.

The thought reminded me of Joey and his keeper. Where were they? For that matter, what about Cecilia? If she had any brains, she'd run for it, or had swiped the Chevette.

"We can take you, Kane."

"The Covenant would frown on my death—"

She chuckled. "Let Childe bear that responsibility, as he's borne so much else."

"Would it frown on the destruction of thralls that go to such effort to flout it?" I leveled the gun. "Anyone who stands between me and my daughter is going to die."

Hel growled, and the punk fondled the loose end of his nose-chain and looked bloodthirsty. Nosferatu smiled up at me with her surreal teeth. The ring piercing her lip glinted red. "That would be painful for both sides, more so than you think." The glint vanished as she spoke. "Surrender to my master's authority and I think we can avoid the pain. Both to you, and your Gail."

"What master is that? Childe, if he is that thing upstairs, appears no master at all."

The red glint had moved to the ring through her eyebrow as she laughed. "Childe? He's no longer my master—"

The glint had drawn my gaze to the window on the landing below. Like most of the windows, it was covered with newspaper. Enough had torn away in the scuffle for someone to see in, if they were in the right spot. As she spoke, I saw a tiny dot of red laser light track across some of the newsprint—

"Get down!" I yelled, a fraction too late.

The window exploded inward as a gunshot blew the contents of Nosferatu's elongated skull out the left side of her face. I never heard the shot.

29

I ran for it. I dashed up the stairs, holding the hole in my gut to keep from tearing open the just-healed wound. I heard growling behind me, and the sound of breaking glass. From somewhere I heard someone kicking in a door.

I passed by the door to the second-floor kitchen and heard a whispery laughing from beyond it. I kept going because I had no desire to confront the thing in the cage.

I shouldered through the door to the attic, dodging past the window on the landing, giving the sniper as little profile as possible. I was lucky. The window exploded, throwing glass, newspaper tatters, and dead flies across the landing, but only after I'd passed.

I smelled something bad upstairs, but the sounds of chaos below continued to drive me upward.

I ran up into a huge peaked space running the length of the house. Above were naked, uninsulated rafters, covering a floor of loose gray planking. The space was lit by bluish moonlight from the rear window, and the yellow sodium streetlight from the front window. Neither window had glass or newspaper, and the wind blew wisps of snow through the attic.

Staring at me, from places in the eaves, between the beams supporting the roof, were small white faces. There were a dozen children up here, dirty-faced, pale, and looking at me with a feral stare that was becoming too familiar.

None of them looked older than thirteen, and half were naked and nearly as bony as the thing in the cage. The smell up here was appalling, and there was no incense to cover it.

Seeing kids up there filled me with a mixture of horror and pity. The force of the emotion slammed against the panic driving me, striking me still where I stood.

The children did not move, but they watched, and from their combined stares I felt a pressure akin to what I felt when that caged thing spoke to me. I heard the thing's laughter from behind me, and it finally pushed me forward.

I advanced, slowly, toward the front of the house, becoming aware of how most of the beams up here bore the scars of claw marks. Gunshots and screams came from below, and I no longer heard rap music in the background.

The whispery laugh followed me to the window.

I kept an eye on the children; the sight of them was a weight in my gut. I edged to the window in the front of the house. I took a quick look out, too quick for anyone to get a shot off at me.

What I saw, however, was enough. I saw four cars pulled up down there, and one was a familiar-looking Oldsmobile. I also saw my Chevette, empty, with the passenger door hanging open. Sebastian was as good as his word. He was taking his revenge on the people who had taken his daughter. On Childe. He was going to save his daughter's soul.

I felt the growing weight of my own guilt. Not only had I drawn my own daughter into this mess, I had led Sebastian to his daughter—and he was going to kill her, unless she had had the sense to run for it.

I had to get out of here and find Gail. She wasn't here with Childe's thralls. Where was she, then?

"You know where she is," he said.

What had he meant by that?

"You are not of the other?" I spun around at the voice, and found myself leveling my Eagle at a naked six-year-old girl. At least, she looked like a six-year-old girl, except for her eyes.

"The other?" I stammered, unsure where to point my gun.

"The one who keeps our master from us," said a scrawny ten-year-old.

I shook my head, unsure of what they were talking about. I was shaking from the enormity of everything. They were *children.*

"We are bound here twice," said another child's voice.

"Once to Master."

"Once to other."

There were more screams from the first floor. Diving out

the window was looking more and more attractive. These children frightened me worse than the chaos below me, almost as much as the caged thing. And there was the porch roof one floor below me. I'd made worse jumps. I rubbed the wound on my gut. The skin felt raw, but intact.

The kids were all talking at me, their words running together as if they were one person speaking.

"Are you here to free Master?"

"Or kill him?"

"Who do you bring?"

"Who do you serve?"

"Will you free us from Master?"

"Or other?"

"One must die now."

Their words pressed me against the wall, even though none of them took a step toward me. The assault was verbal, but there was a psychic pressure behind the words to the point where I wasn't even sure I was *hearing* their voices, in the normal sense of the word.

"Stop it!" I yelled, with all the force I could muster.

The babble ceased, and I heard movement below me. Someone was walking on the second floor. Dimly I heard a voice. "Shit, what the fuck is that?"

"Gimme that cross," said another voice. The whispery laughter below had ceased. In its place I heard that same paper-thin voice say, *"Come."*

That one word filled me with dread, despite the fact that it wasn't addressed to me.

"Come," the whisper repeated, an undeniable force behind the voice.

The children, all of them, turned away from me, toward the stairs at the rear of the attic. "Master," said the one nearest me. There was reverence in that voice.

Below me I heard a panicked voice saying, "Murphy, what the fuck are you—get the fuck away from—*SHIT!*"

There was an agonized liquid scream, and three rapid gunshots.

The children began slowly walking toward the stairwell. "He will come."

"Free us from the other."

The kids had begun another monotone babbling. I missed

most of it because someone downstairs was putting shots through the floor. Two boards too close to me exploded outward, exposing splintered bullet holes shafted with candlelight from below.

The laugh was back. It no longer sounded like the laugh from a corpse. It was loud, vulgar, unashamed. The man with the gun was screaming something incoherent. It took a moment, between the gunshots, to realize that it was the twenty-third psalm.

"Yea, though I walk through the valley of the shadow of death!—" *Blam!* "—fear no evil: for Thou *art* with—" *Blam!* "—rod and Thy staff they comfort me—"

His voice was choked off, and there were no further gunshots. The laughter ceased, and was replaced by a wet sucking sound.

I shuddered, and one of the children standing around the head of the stairs turned to face me. "He will wish to see you, Raven. He will come to free us from the other."

That monotone sentence still hung in the air when I heard the sound of fabric tearing, glass breaking, and wood cracking apart. I looked out the window, below me, in time to see a body tumble onto the porch's roof. The parts of the corpse I saw were completely dessicated, shriveled to the bone. Its neck hung open, and it left red tracks in the snow as it rolled off the roof to the right, into the driveway.

It had been thrown through the window below mine, and tatters of red velvet drapery and newspaper were still floating to the ground in the front yard. A gold cross glinted in the snow.

If I wanted to move, I had to do it now. I jumped though the glassless window, to the roof of the porch below. I bent my knees as I hit, keeping the gun away from me. The impact shuddered my body, but no bones broke, and my abdomen didn't split open—though it felt as if it wanted to.

I rolled twice, to the left, slowing. I was just about to jump to my feet when I ran out of roof. There was a sickening lurch as I went into free fall above the driveway of the next house. I fell five feet onto a car below me.

The car's roof caved in with the impact. Safety-glass exploded underneath me. I froze for a second or two, as the pain of the collision washed through my body and evaporated. The car's owners, occupants of the neighboring house, were nowhere to be seen. They had vanished with their music.

I forced myself up, out of the concave roof, and the hood below my feet dimpled with a bullet's impact. The sniper was still out there.

I rolled off of the roof, scrambling to my feet, and ran through the snow in front of the house. The sniper had to be behind the house, somewhere in the cemetery, and Childe's house offered the best cover I had—

As I ran, I almost collided with more of Sebastian's thugs, running out the front of the house. I raised my gun, but they barely paid attention to me as they beat a panicked retreat. There were four of them, and two were busy carrying a wounded comrade.

They piled into an illegally parked Dodge, which began accelerating away before the doors were shut.

I ran for the Chevette, thinking, *Did I black out for a moment? All the damn cars are gone.*

From the looks of it, every one of the cars had pulled away at top speed. Snow had been sprayed across the side of the Chevette.

"What the fuck did you do to her!" I yelled at the now empty street. The Chevette was empty; the passenger door hung open with a shattered window. I was filled with a futile rage at Sebastian and Childe, and I didn't know if I was screaming for Cecilia, Gail, or the six-year-old girl in the attic.

When did those bastards catch up with me?

I looked up, the car between me and Childe's house. Standing in the attic window was a naked man. He had a Van Dyke beard and shoulder-length hair that blew in the biting wind. He was soaked in blood from the neck down. The face he wore belonged to the pictures I had seen of Manuel Deité.

He saw me looking, and smiled. . . .

Small forms were darting about in the shadows around the house, larger than rats.

I dove into the Chevette, fear gripping my chest. I fumbled the ignition and accelerated away without looking at the house again.

*   *   *

I raced the Chevette through night-empty streets. I had blown it. I was furious with myself, mad enough that I was halfway to Shaker before my body reasserted its normal appearance. I had led Sebastian's people straight to Childe's house.

Hadn't I?

I had a gut suspicion that the whole scene was staged, from act one up to Sebastian's untimely arrival. I thought of Cecilia's story, her convenient imprisonment on the site of the sacrifice I had witnessed.

Where the fuck had Gabriel been? He had been *looking* for Childe, he had seen Cecilia before I had, and Cecilia had led me straight to the maniac. That whole house seemed designed to piss off Gabriel, the whole unsubtle setup. Childe had been starved in a box so he couldn't interfere with what was going on, letting his thralls go on a rampage, causing all sorts of havoc.

I now knew where Childe had disappeared to, and where Cecilia had disappeared to—and it didn't fit.

I could visualize the box trapping Childe. A strong vampire could break out of that thing, but if he'd undergone a massive injury, and was locked in there—I could picture his body feeding on its own resources in the absence of blood, the body wasting away to become the skeletal thing I had seen. From the actions of his thralls, Childe had been in that box since before I'd ever heard Cecilia's name.

Nothing fit, unless Cecilia was lying. If someone had set Childe up, shut him up in the box up there, that same person had staked out that ritual site for me to witness; that same person had shut Cecilia up in the mausoleum with Joey; that same person had control of Childe's thralls and had staged the house for Cecilia to lead someone to.

All the talk of two masters was beginning to sink in. I was dealing with another vampire. The person who had transformed Cecilia, who had infected her, *wasn't* Childe. She wasn't the kind of person who Childe would take. Her father was a powerful man who would believe the bloody clues left for him, and would react accordingly.

That was what my wife and I were, bloody clues left to ensure that Sebastian would act. The vampire who had taken Cecilia, who had staged the sacrifice, he was my enemy. He was the one in the cowled robe, not Childe. He was the one who had taken my daughter.

I knew two vampires who had some grudge against Childe. Who would want some summary justice delivered for his breaches of the Covenant. Gabriel was the first and the most obvious, but his world revolved around the Covenant. Would he stage all this to give himself an excuse to dispose of Childe? It seemed unlikely now. More than that, if he had set up this charade, why was Childe still alive?

Someone else had set up Childe for Gabriel's benefit. And at the last minute, after talking to Cecilia, Gabriel had not risen to the bait. Cecilia had told him what she had told me, but I could see Gabriel talking to her as he had me. I could see him asking who her master was. I could see her lying. I could see him taste her blood, as he had mine—and maybe he could taste who her master really was. The old ones seemed to see, to sense, more than I could.

If it wasn't Gabriel, that left me one other suspect. The person I'd seen with the thralls, the person who was free to follow Gail to Sam's apartment, the person who'd been feeding me information on Childe all along. . . .

Bowie.

Bowie had shown up too conveniently at the Arabica right after my run-in with the thralls, he had broken me out of Sebastian's in a way that was sure to inflame him, he had disappeared right after I had sent my daughter to so-called safety. The bastard had been using me all along, using me to lead everyone to suspect Childe, everyone from Sebastian and Gabriel to the cops.

The demon thrall had said that I *knew* where my daughter was. I thought of the first time I'd seen Bowie and Leia together. I slammed the brakes and skidded the car around to head toward Shaker Heights.

30

I pulled the Chevette to a halt angled across the tree-lawn of the Ryan house. I threw open the car door and rushed the front of the house. I shouldered my way into the house as Doctor Ryan ran down the hall toward me. He wore a blood-spattered lab coat.

"What's going on here—"

"Where is she?"

Ryan stopped short, about ten feet down the corridor from me. He eyed the splintered doorjamb behind me. "Who?"

"Don't bullshit me, Doc," I said. "I want my daughter, and I want the man responsible for all this."

"Look, perhaps you should calm down."

"Fuck calm!" I drew the Eagle and leveled it at the doctor. "I want my daughter or I'm emptying your skull into the wallpaper."

"Mr. Tyler. . . ." The doctor backed to the wall. I advanced until the barrel of the Eagle was pressed against the white stubble on his cheek.

"Hey, man, you really ought to calm down," came a familiar voice from behind me.

I whipped around, keeping the barrel of my gun pressed into Ryan's neck. Bowie emerged from the den behind us. He stopped and leaned against the doorframe at the foot of the stairs. He looked unconcerned about Ryan.

"Give me my daughter," I said through clenched teeth. "Give her back, or I swear I'll kill him."

Bowie shook his head and tsked at me. "It doesn't work like that."

I chambered around and said, "Fuck that, you bastard. You've used me to set up Childe, and it ends now—"

Bowie kept shaking his head. "No, it doesn't. That's why

we have her. With all the pieces out there, Sebastian, the cops . . . Childe will self-destruct if he hasn't been killed already."

"It's over. Childe's freed himself, and Gabriel's on to you."

Bowie laughed. "Sure he is. But do you see him here? He won't stick his neck out for Childe. He wants the status for Childe's head."

"But—"

"If Gabriel's the cavalry, where is he?"

I kept the gun pressed into Ryan's neck, and he muttered, "Please."

Bowie shook his head. "Put the gun down."

"Why, damn you?" I shouted. "Why take her?"

"What's she ever done to me, she's never hurt anyone, she wasn't a threat. . . ." Bowie straightened up and took a step toward me. "That's what you mean, ain't it? Christ, ain't it obvious? Sebastian held her over you, and pretty damn soon you'd twig to what was happening, and we couldn't have you talking to Sebastian or the cops when you figured it out."

"Who's 'we?' " I breathed. Anger was twisting a hole in my gut.

"Me and my master," Bowie said. "And you have her word that no harm will come to your precious Gail if you just subjugate yourself to her."

Her?

"Put down the gun," came a voice from up the stairs, between me and Bowie.

I turned so I could keep an eye on the stairs as well as Bowie. Leia stood at the head of the stairs, glaring down at me. She was as pale as ever, and deep in her eyes I felt a tug that could only come from one source.

"Put down the gun," she repeated. I felt her will, like a mental undertow on my arm. I resisted it, despite the weight my arm felt. My hand shook, and fear from the doctor washed away any emotion I might have felt from her.

"You?" I felt the anger again, the stress. I felt bones dislocating, muscle tearing and reknitting, skin splitting and flowing back together.

So obvious, so damn obvious. I suddenly knew what was

wrong with the pictures on the wall of Ryan's office. There hadn't been a single picture of Ryan's wife. There'd been him in England, him and his granddaughter Leia, but none of a wife. What had *really* sparked his interest in vampires?

What if Leia wasn't his granddaughter?

"Yes, me. I've waited half a century for Childe's humiliation. You aren't going to stop it."

"My daughter or he's dead!" came a half-animal yell. I glimpsed a shadow of myself on the wall, and saw a hunching back, lengthened arms, and a distorted skull evolving a muzzle. I could feel myself willing the changes now. Everything was tinted with blood-red anger. I snarled.

"No," she shook her head. "And you harm him, and you'll watch me tear out your daughter's heart."

I was fighting an internal urge to drop the gun and rip out the doctor's throat. My body was burning itself with the effort of the change, and it sensed the heat within the doctor's flesh. It wanted that flesh.

Leia kept staring at me, and it was becoming difficult for me to concentrate. The gun shook in a clawed, leathery hand. The world seemed to be twisting away from me, as if the scent of the doctor's blood, even through the skin, were making me high.

"Childe is evil; he has to be punished. Punished, then killed." Leia took a step down the riser.

I tried to say, "Gail." But all I produced was a breathy growl. My clothes split and shredded.

"You weaken yourself with your anger," she said, and I found my neck turning so I could stare into her eyes. She was halfway down the stairs now, her cloying perfume in advance of her. Now, however, my sense of smell had become infinitely more acute, and I could smell the corruption that perfume cloaked.

She kept descending until near the end, where her eyes were even with mine.

"Look at what Childe did to me," she said. She grabbed the collar of her turtleneck and yanked it down. The fabric tore as she uncovered her left shoulder, neck, and breast—

A gaping, festering wound sank into her flesh. I saw the outline of a collarbone, glistening red.

I felt something stab into my side, opposite the doctor. I turned to see Bowie plunging the contents of a hypodermic into my side. I yanked myself away, breaking the needle, but I was too late. The hypo was empty. I readied to lunge at Bowie, the doctor all but forgotten—

"Look at me," she said.

I could not avoid looking.

"That blood's just to soften your will." I was locked in place, unable to draw my attention away from her. Heat rippled out from where the needle had pierced my skin, and my body sucked in the heat, along with something else.

"Fetch his daughter," she said to Bowie. He ran up the stairs. She turned back to face me. "You will be harder than a thrall. You have to accept my blood willingly."

She took another step down the stairs. "You ask me why? Childe took my blood and left me with this—" her hand went to the wound that ate into her shoulder and chest "—he seduced me, used me, and then left me to die from a long, suppurating infection. I lived for a month."

I remembered Ryan's words: *In most humans this entity can't survive the first twenty-four hours in a living host. Though, if another infection weakens the immune system, the entity can survive much longer.*

The warmth in my side had spread to every part of my body. I shook with a feverish heat, sweating, dizzy, my body beginning to tear itself back into a human form. I tried to recapture the emotions I had been feeling, but they slipped through my mental fingers like so much air.

My back collapsed against the wall, and the gun tumbled from my fingers. Everything seemed very far away, even the pain of my bones reshaping themselves.

"Death wasn't the end," a far away voice was saying, "I was left cursed with this unhealable wound. Every night for fifty years I've woken up to this pain. Every night for fifty years I've been tied by this political contrivance they call a Covenant. Every night for fifty years I've been waiting for Childe to slip, to give an opening for those who hate him. Even his own race wish him gone, and will happily destroy him for a misstep. You know what Childe is, you know he had to be stopped. Punished. Crushed."

I shook; my body was fighting off an alien infection.

The master-slave relationship, and the control it created, flowed from the blood, blood linked to a specific mind. The blood in my veins, the vampiric infection throughout my body, gave me control to the point where I could heal gunshots and restructure my entire body. Allowing another vampire's blood into my body, allowing another infection, could give that "other" similar control, both body and mind.

That was how she had taken control of Childe's people.

That was happening to me now. With that flash of realization, I tried to push back the encroaching apathy and disorientation that blazed across the surface of my fever.

"Cross," I muttered through a mouth that was still animalistic.

Somewhere, far away, I saw her nod. "My maiden name. My brother, the chief inspector, was responsible for those police files your detective friend ordered from England. Detective Weinbaum is almost as useful against Childe as Sebastian is. Now either they will kill him, or Childe will kill them, bringing all the force of the Convenant down upon his own head."

I barely heard her as I tried to concentrate, tried to gather together the tatters of my will against the fever. My body stopped changing back.

"With my brother's death, I knew Childe would never stumble on his own. I had to take his thralls."

I felt her breath against my sweaty cheek. My half-human body was vibrating with fever, drenched in sweat. Inside myself, I fought to retain my own identity, my own perception of reality, against the force this woman was exerting.

The pressure of the fever, the blood, and her will, was becoming impossible to fight. Her mind was as strong as my own, maybe stronger, and she was aided by the traitor infection that Bowie had injected.

I saw Bowie descending the stairs, bringing Gail with him. Gail stared blankly, going where Bowie led her.

"You have a choice," Leia's face was within an inch of my own. I felt her words brush my ear, burning it. "Take my blood. Become one with my blood as your daughter has. Or your daughter dies. The Convenant protects no thralls."

Gail. She showed no reaction upon seeing me, as if she were in a trance.

Leia had taken her. She had forced my own daughter to become one of them. A sound, somewhere between a cry and a howl, emerged from my throat. A spark of rage ignited, my own fire, and I concentrated on it.

Her arm extended in front of me, the vein opening for me as Jaguar's had. There was a flood of fire, a pressure willing me to taste, to drink. I wanted the blood, and I knew that it was the desire that was the key. The second I stopped resisting the desire, the burning hunger that she was pulling out of me, I would be lost.

She had taken Gail.

I felt the knot of anger harden.

I was not a thrall. I was not a human any more. I was a vampire whose chosen name was Raven. I was this woman's peer. She had had half a century to focus her will, but my own wounds were fresh.

I felt myself bend over her arm, felt the bones begin again to rewrite the structure of my jaw. I could smell her blood, and it was the sweetest thing I had ever smelled. Below me it leaked from her arm, a warm ruby glow, radiating with life.

Under it all I could still smell the taint of corruption.

She had taken Gail.

The world stopped spinning around me, and my sense regained a sharper focus.

"Take of me, Mr. Tyler. Your daughter has an eternity before her, don't let it end."

She had taken Gail.

Focusing on Gail allowed me to retain myself. Doctor Ryan had found a weapon for her, but the weapon wasn't absolute. The tainted blood increased her power over me, but it did not make me her slave. I was the master of my blood, not a thrall who carried another's blood in his veins already.

I held her arm with both hands. My nails were talons in leathery skin, my jaw a savage muzzle, my nose wrinkling at the sweet smell of blood. I knew, instinctively, that to give up control, even for a moment, would make me her slave.

"Drink, Kane—"

Raven, it is Raven now.

"—you should not be fighting me—"

My name is Raven and I am master of my own blood.

A voice came from out of the darkness within me. I heard myself whisper.

"From childhood's hour I have not been / As others were—"

I raised my eyes to meet hers. Leia stopped talking. I slammed the tatters of my will against her own.

"I have not seen," I whispered, "As others saw—"

I dropped her arm. I could feel her try to turn away, but I held her gaze with my own.

"I could not bring / My passions from a common spring—" I could feel the fever burning itself out within me. "From the same source I have not taken / My sorrow—" The blood inside me burned like a magnesium flare, brief, intense, leaving nothing but ash in its wake.

"I could not awaken / My heart to joy at the same tone—/ And all I lov'd—I lov'd alone . . ."

I was still me. My mind felt tempered, all the impurities burned away. I felt all the anger, the fury, the endless rage and fear burning through my skull. All of it focused on Leia in front of me.

Leia began to scream.

Bowie began moving toward Gail, who still stared into space.

"No!" I growled. My hand slashed in front of me, at Leia. Every last trace of emotion within me powered that swing. My hand was not a hand anymore, it was a weapon.

My talons sank into Leia's neck, tearing across her throat. Her scream gurgled to a halt. She slammed into the wall next to me.

Bowie had grabbed Gail, and she seemed to wake up from her trance. Gail yelled, and I leaped at him. His hands were on her throat as he looked up at me.

I saw fear in his face.

He raised his arms too late to defend himself, and I sank my teeth into his throat. I tasted blood, but I didn't drink. I tore at him, shredding flesh, tearing at him tooth and claw, driving him away from my child. Gail scrambled, panicked, up the stairway.

Bowie pounded at me, and I felt his bones shift under

my assault. His spine separated under my teeth before he could transform into anything threatening. I threw Bowie's corpse into the den to shatter through the French doors. His head stayed in the doorway.

I heard a renewed scream behind me. I turned around in time for Leia to grab me with a pair of clawed hands. Where I had turned into something wolflike, she had turned demonic. She threw me high against the wall. My back cratered the plaster, and a picture shattered underneath me. I slid to the ground, Ryan diving out of my way.

Leia dove upon me and slashed with obscenely elongated hands. Her nails were a foot long and tapered like swords. I raised an arm to defend myself and I felt the claws sever the muscles down to the bone.

I grabbed her wounded neck with my other hand, holding her at bay. It didn't work as well as I intended. My gut exploded in pain as her other hand slashed into my abdomen, burying itself in my stomach.

I roared, and Leia hissed at me in a way that was too reminiscent of the way Childe had sounded in his box.

She pushed away my other arm, its muscles severed and immobile, and began slashing at my face and neck. I saw my own blood spray across the hallway, splashed by her blows. As I weakened, I felt my body rebel against the alien shape.

Each slash knocked more of the beast out of me, and more leaked out of the fiery hole in my gut. My hand on her throat did more to pin me than it did her. As I began regaining a human form, she started laughing at me.

Then the world exploded as someone fired my Desert Eagle. Leia's face exploded across me. She stopped laughing. However, her hand kept slashing at me, as if by reflex.

The gun fired again, numbing my ears. Leia's head caved in with the impact. Her arm still moved.

Again it fired.

Leia's arm dangled by her side.

I was frozen in that tableau for nearly a minute, as my body shifted, sucking all its resources to return me to my human form. Above me, Leia's head was nothing more than a chunk of rotten meat above her lower jaw, good as decapitated. As I watched, her oozing blood faded from livid red to a sick, dead, black.

I let go of her neck, and her body tumbled to the ground.

Gail stood there, in the center of the hall, holding my Desert Eagle in both hands.

Gail held the gun, trembling, tears streaming down her face. "Dad?" she whispered.

I slowly pushed my back up the wall. I looked down the hall to where Ryan stood, shaking, staring at Leia's corpse with wide eyes. He didn't move.

I looked back at my daughter and said, "It's all right, it's over."

"Over?" she repeated.

I walked up and took the gun from her hands.

She buried her face in my shredded shirt and cried. "I'm sorry, Dad. I didn't want to lie, but they made me."

"You're free now," I said. I looked down on Leia's body. All her blood was now the black of death. Ryan had knelt down next to the corpse and was whispering. "Come on, honey," he mumbled at her, "wake up, wake up—"

I looked at Gail.

"You are master of your own blood now," I said to her. "Let's leave this place."

I walked her out the front door, out into the snow, toward the Chevette on the lawn. I was limping, feeling as if most of my flesh had been torn from the bone. For my injuries I must have looked almost as bad as Joey had.

Gail was shaking her head, and I thought of all she had to go through. For what?

"So pointless . . ." I whispered to the night.

"Things usually are," replied a cultured voice with an English accent.

I turned to face the Ryan house, and leaning up against an ivy-covered wall was a well-groomed gentleman who appeared to be in his fifties. He had a slight touch of gray at the temples of his shoulder-length hair, and his chin sported a Van Dyke.

"Childe?" I said.

The man made a slight bow. "My reputation precedes me."

I glanced back up at the house. Gail turned to me and whispered, "Oh, God."

Childe shook his head. "He has little to do with it. No, we're discussing Jaguar, actually." He smiled grimly and followed my glance up at the house. I saw erratic shadows cross the windows, semi-human in form. Nearly a dozen of them. No sound came from the house.

"Jaguar?" I said.

"The English of an otherwise unpronounceable Mayan name. I would think you'd remember meeting him."

Jaguar, my raceless visitor. I nodded as the lights went out in the house. "He told me Doctor Ryan was buried in the flesh."

"Some of us more so than others." Childe held out his hand. "Perhaps you two should come with me."

"What is he doing in there?" I asked.

"Fixing things."

I stared at Childe and after a moment said, "That was you, in that box."

He started walking away from the house said, "I have made better impressions."

"I should have killed you."

He paused for a moment and looked back over his shoulder. "Yes, by your lights, perhaps you should have. But come."

He waved us after him.

"I could have," I whispered.

He kept nodding. It was difficult to picture this man as the thing within the box. But I'd had that glimpse of him in the window, and he was unquestionably the same being. The same person whose picture was faxed from England.

How many of Sebastian's men had it taken to bring him back?

"For God's sake, why?" Gail said.

He turned around, and I noticed that the suit he wore had to cost close to a grand. The scarf and gloves he wore spoke of the same expensive taste. "Why ask for nepenthe of some strange black bird crossing my threshold? Is there balm in Gilead?"

Childe addressed me, giving me an odd grin. "I know something of you now, and you shan't offer such balm."

"What do you mean?"

"Don't make the mistake Leia did. She was one of us, but she wasn't *of* us. Applying a human morality to us is akin to applying that bird's morality to a human."

He turned around and resumed walking. "What souls we have, what minds, are chained within this flesh. All resides close to the surface. We become what we are. Our thoughts mold ourselves, our flesh, our reality. Our choices bind us—"

I nodded, not understanding all I wished to. Though I began to see how vampiric psychology could affect the flesh; from Joey's zombie-rot to Leia's wound, self-image molded the body.

"What she did," Childe continued, "forcing herself on the bodies of my thralls, with her blood, that was a worse act than killing me would have been." He shook his head and wiped snow out of his hair.

"All of them chose to be *yours?*"

The corner of Childe's mouth twitched upward. "I do not force the worm within my breast upon anyone. They each had time to decide."

We turned a corner and approached a black car. "What happened with her?" Gail asked.

"At the end of the war, I offered something to a woman. She gave freely, but when it came time for her to *take,* she refused to deal any more with me. I am always clear about what a relationship with me costs."

We stopped at the car, a Rolls Royce, one of the earlier models, before they started looking like Lincolns. Childe shrugged. "Her husband was a doctor, but she hid the marks too long. They became septic. She died. She lived. Her mind kept the scar alive, and she blamed me." He shook his head. "She existed for half a century, and all must have seen that wound in her heart. None sponsored her, took her into the community, or gave her a name." He gave me a meaningful look. "You're very lucky. Rogues come to bad ends."

I felt a small flare of anger at the society I had thrust myself into. "She was such a loose cannon, why didn't Jaguar, Gabriel, or *somebody,* stop her before it came to this."

"Her husband was useful, I suppose. He had a good, if

incomplete, model of our existence. If she was removed, so was the motive for his work. Also, I am not loved. They may have waited to see what my fate would be."

"They let this happen?"

"To an extent. But, thanks to you, this conflict began attracting too much attention to ignore." Childe looked up the street, back toward the Ryan house.

"Jaguar will fix this, as I had to clean my own house." I looked up and I began to see a flickering glow through the trees.

"I owe you something," he said, interrupting the memory.

"What?"

He opened the door to the Rolls. "They were mine, those who did this to you. By our law, I *am* responsible for what happened to you. I may indulge you in something compensatory—"

Gail hugged herself closer to me, and I said, "You can't bring Kate back."

Childe shook his head. "Do you desire something more within my power than forgiving your violence against my own? That I have already done."

What could I want from this creature?

I looked up at the sky, remembering how the moon looked as it hung low over Lakeview. If there was only one thing I could ask from Childe, I knew then what it was.

"Cecilia," I said.

"What?"

"If she still lives, free her from her father. Free her and sponsor her."

Childe appeared interested. "This will not change what she is . . ."

"She does not deserve Sebastian killing her. Your protection should be worth something."

Childe looked at me a long while, then said, "This I'll do, to cancel our debt." He slipped behind the wheel and said, "Shall I give you two a lift somewhere?"

I shook my head and said, "No. We have our own car."

I took my daughter and began walking back.

"Indeed," Childe said. I heard the door shut behind me, "But perhaps, my dear Raven, you'll indulge me a moment more?"

I stopped walking, and without turning around, I asked, "What more is there to say?"

I heard the Rolls' quiet engine start, and I heard the tires grind snow as it advanced to pull even with us. The wheel was on the wrong side, so Childe was sitting just on the other side of the door from us. "A story," he said through the open window, "an old one."

"What—"

"Shh. This predates that American drunkard you're so fond of by two millennia, and it is just as much part of your soul now."

I turned to face him, and Childe looked off, out the windshield. It began sinking in, as he spoke, what Ryan said, about Childe being so old.

"This occurred in the east, in the mountains there. Perhaps India, perhaps China. I prefer to think of it as Tibet. The thirst came upon a young man in a monastery. There was no one to tell this man what had happened to him, and when it overpowered him, finally, he killed his teacher and drank of his blood. The young monk was horrified by his deed. He ran off into the night, hiding in a cave far away from any other person. He sat in that cave, and vowed to sit there until he died."

He paused and stroked his beard. He still didn't look at me.

"This monk had a strong will, perhaps as strong as any other man's had ever been. Stronger when tempered by his horror at his teacher's fate. He did not move from his spot in the cave. Days came and went, the sunlight never reaching his flesh. He did not feed, nor did he move. Within a month, the monks found him there, after half his flesh had withered. They demanded answers from the young monk, for the death of his teacher."

Childe finally turned to look at me. When his eyes met mine, I could picture the scene. The cadaverous monk in a lotus position, and the robed elders, holding candles and shouting questions. I was unsure if the imagined scene was from my mind, or Childe's.

"The young man did not answer, and the only part of his body he moved was his eyes. The questioning went on for days, during which he did not move, or eat, or speak. He could smell the blood of the monks around him, but he held his hunger inside. The others saw this, and decided that the young man had achieved enlightenment."

Childe grinned as if this were his favorite part of the story. "They left him there, with his hunger. The young monk stayed unmoving for a year, then another. Word spread across the countryside about his enlightenment. Soon pilgrims visited the mountain, to ask their own questions, to which the young monk would offer no answer.

"The thirst gnawed away at him for a century, withering him away until he was barely a skeleton held complete by the force of his denial. As every day passed, his will strengthened along with the thirst. And the pilgrims still came, dozens, hundreds—all asking questions with no answers.

"The monks built a shrine around the cave, and the pilgrims began to worship at the young man's bones. They held him sacred now, though none knew that he still lived, and still kept his vow.

"A city grew up at the base of the mountain, below the monk's shrine. Eventually, the cave itself was walled up, for fear of anyone disturbing the young monk's remains.

"Slowly, though, the young monk was forgotten. The pilgrims ceased coming. Eventually, it was forgotten why the city was where it was. And, nine centuries after the young monk had walked into the cave, he moved.

"In the space of one night, every single person who lived within the walls of that great city died. A thousand, ten thousand. A quarter awoke the next night, with their own thirst, and found the shrine destroyed, and the young monk nowhere to be seen."

Childe turned back to face the windshield. "You can't deny yourself, much as you want to."

"That justifies all the killing?"

"It means what it means," Childe said. "There are hundreds of versions of that story. Will over thirst, thirst over will. Fate, destiny—" Childe shook his head. "There's just more there than I've said, and there's more here than you've seen."

He pulled the Rolls away from the curb, leaving us alone in the snow-dusted night.

"What did he mean?" Gail asked.

"I'm not sure," I said. "But we'll work it out, somehow."

We walked back to the Chevette. When we reached it, I could hear sirens in the distance, and the Ryan house was already engulfed by fire. I could picture another fire burning in East Cleveland, destroying Childe's house, burning away everything that might not be mundane.

I thought of Leia, and Bowie, and Ryan. I hugged Gail's shoulders and counted ourselves lucky. Leia had been right. Revenge is not a happy pursuit.

This book is dedicated to Michelle,
the love of my life—*Loads*.

THE FLESH,
THE BLOOD,
AND THE FIRE

ACKNOWLEDGMENTS

I'd like to thank everyone who went over this MS at the last minute; Sally Kohonoski, Geoff Landis, Charles Oberndorf, and Mary Turzillo. I's also like to thank the authors of a number of books that I found useful while writing this; especially Steven Nickel for *Torso: The Story of Eliot Ness and the Search for a Psychopathic Killer*, John Stark Bellamy III for *They Died Crawling and Other Tales of Cleveland Woe*, David D. Van Tassel and John J. Grabowski for *The Encyclopedia of Cleveland History*, and Ian S. Haberman for *The Van Sweringens of Cleveland: the Biography of an Empire*. As always, any errors within are stictly my own.

PROLOGUE

April 1934-September 1934
THE LADY IN THE LAKE

1934

1

Her name was Laila, and it had been over two weeks since she had fed. Death lingered in the shadows of the iron room where they kept her chained, naked, to a seat bolted to the floor. She could not remember another time when she had felt this vulnerable, and she had a very long memory.

The metal room, her prison, was a small chamber with slightly curving walls, ocher with rust stains. There was one light, the bulb wrapped in a hooded cage above her. The hood's shadow cloaked half the room in darkness. Oil and diesel fumes hung in the still air.

She was on a ship; the sound of the waves and the rocking of the room around her told her that. That was all she knew. She didn't know why she was here, or why her captors had not yet killed her. All she knew of her captors came from the few stray bits of German she'd overheard before hunger had completely dulled her senses.

They had known enough to take her in the day, while she slept. They had known enough not to confront her when she'd first awakened in this room.

It seemed an age ago, that first awakening. She had been able to escape the chains and attack the walls of this prison. But there were limits to her strength, even before the hunger had gnawed away at her. Her captors would wait for exhaustion to take her, then chain her again while she was unconscious.

For the first five days it had gone like that, until she had lost the strength to free herself from the bonds.

It made no sense to her. They had her trapped. If they meant to kill her, they could have done so a dozen times over. Why the torture? Why allow her to exist, allow the hunger consume her body? Why not simply cut out her heart during one of her lengthening periods of delirium?

She was coming out of an extended period of semiconsciousness when she sensed a familiar presence. At first she believed she was hallucinating, because the presence was from so long ago. Her senses were dulled. It couldn't be what she thought, no matter how familiar the scent of his blood might be.

He was dead—dead so long that she might have been the only one alive left to remember who he was and how his blood smelled.

She raised her head to face the darkness. Hunger had dimmed her once-sensitive vision until she could only make out a shadowy form beyond the pool of light centered on the seat she was chained to.

The presence did not recede. However impossible it seemed, the scent knifing into her mind was not a hallucination.

It was real.

He was real.

For the first time in two weeks she spoke, her voice a sandpaper whisper. Her lips cracked, weeping fluid as she mouthed the name . . .

"Melchior . . ."

"Such a long time," his voice came from the shadows. "Such a long, *long* time." The voice was slightly different, but she could feel him behind the words. His mind was like a choking fog filling the room, asphyxiating all that wasn't his.

"You . . . died . . ." The words came hard for her.

Melchior laughed. His laugh was condescending, someone laughing at a child, someone who hated children.

"You mean they were supposed to kill me."

She found her voice. She shouted at him. "You defied the only law we have!"

His voice was like a velvet garrote. "Your Covenant? It was an exercise in self-castration. I thought, once, that I had taught you better. Anyone who willingly cedes power deserves none."

Melchior walked into the pool of light so Laila could see him. He had changed his appearance. He was taller now, his hair was blond and longer than any man wore it nowadays. But his eyes had not changed. His irises were colored somewhere between violet and brown, a color close to that of clotted blood.

In his right hand, he carried a long knife.

"What has their precious Covenant done for those who condemned me? Who is left of them? Saul? Gildas? Kabir? All dust now, all but you—" He knelt and touched the tip of the blade to where a scar traversed her abdomen. "You still choose to bear the scar where they removed our child? You're overly sentimental."

"You will never understand, will you?" she hissed at him. "Without the Covenant we would *all* be as dead as Saul, Gildas, Kabir, *and* your son."

"We were kings once," he said. "I held more power when I was condemned than any one of you dreams of today."

She looked away from him and said, "What do you want?"

"What is mine. What was taken from me."

"They won't let you—"

"Who won't let me? Who, aside from you, knows who I am?"

Laila felt a knot of terror. There was no one else. Even out of those few that were as ancient, there were none left that would have felt his presence, known the scent of his blood. Only her, who had once called him master, and had spit on what she thought were his ashes.

He drew away from her, as if he knew her thoughts. He probably did. Laila steadied herself and gathered as much of her will as she could, her own presence, together in the face of her old master. "You care nothing for the Covenant. Why didn't you have your men kill me?"

Melchior smiled. If the Black Death could smile, its expression would resemble Melchior's. "Should I say I was sentimental? That I wished you to join me in my new kingdom as you were mine in the old?" He shook his head slowly. "No."

Laila watched his grip tighten on the handle of his knife. "No," he repeated. "You defied me, and this moment has been a long time coming." He bent so his breath brushed her cheek. "You were saved for me, Laila."

She barely had time to see what was coming before the blade swung.

2

It was still summer, but the dark clouds boiling off the lake seemed to carry the first knife-edge of winter. Detective Stefan Ryzard found himself looking up every few minutes as he walked through the park toward the beach. Occasionally he grabbed the brim of his hat to keep a particularly strong gust from blowing it away.

From the look of the sky in the direction of the lake, dark as a fresh bruise, they were in for one beaut of a storm. The threatening sky had done a lot to thin out the late-season crowd at Euclid Beach Park, and it was too easy for Stefan to believe he walked the broad avenues alone. The wind seemed to suck up every sound except for the rumble of a coaster, a noise that could easily be faraway thunder, and the insane laughter of the mannequin outside the funhouse.

The mannequin was a cartoonish female figure looming over passersby. As he passed, it rocked back and forth with an amplified laugh. Between the manic laugh and the cartoonish paint makeup, the thing reminded Stefan of a drunken prostitute, tragic and frightening.

He walked past it, and the rides, and the Humphry Popcorn stand, until he reached the pier and the walkway along Euclid Beach. Here it wasn't deserted. Kids, most younger than fourteen, lined the railing overlooking the beach. Half of them had climbed up on the rail and were craning their necks as if a baseball game were being played on the beach below. Standing behind the kids, adults milled around, watching over their heads. Most had the manner of waiting for a streetcar, a few whispered to each other, and a few— the ones with the least pretense, and coincidentally the

most shopworn clothes—wore expressions of undisguised
curiosity.

Stefan pushed his way through the crowd to the stairs
leading down to the beach. At the bottom a lone uniformed
policeman blocked his way.

"Sir, you have to watch from up there." He waved a
baton toward the spectators.

Stefan fished out his badge and said, "Detective Ryzard."

The uniformed cop looked at the badge and shifted the
direction of his baton. "Oh, everyone's up the beach over
there. And Inspector Cody wants everyone keeping an eye
on the shoreline, in case anything else washes up."

Stefan nodded. "Has the wagon shown up yet?"

The cop shook his head. "Nope, everything's still like
they found it."

Stefan stepped down, past the cop, and let his shoes sink
into the sand. The soles of his feet felt an anticipatory itch.
Grit was going to fill his shoes before he walked ten yards.

"Watch it," the cop said. "Ain't pretty down there."

Stefan said, "Thank you, officer," and walked down the
beach. He wasn't too worried about what he was going to
see. He had seen plenty of bodies in his career. He had
been a patrol officer in the Roaring Third before he made
Detective. Even today, that assignment was something out
of Dante, and during Prohibition it had been far worse.

The Third was poor, violent, and just this side of completely lawless. Stefan had started in a place cops usually
ended up. Coming from the Third made all the stand-up
cops wonder how bent you were, and it made the bent
cops—who assumed everyone else was bent—wonder what
kind of screwup got you assigned to the Third in the first
place.

In his stint there, he'd seen more bodies than most funeral directors. Corpses had lost their impact on him
through sheer repetition.

A knot of people were assembled a fair way down from
the Euclid Beach pier. About half were uniformed officers,
about half wore suits. They all seemed subdued, as if something about the crime scene or the oppressive weather
made everyone leery of raising their voices.

When he got within twenty yards, one of the suits waved
him over. "Detective Ryzard!" he called. Stefan recognized

Inspector Cody. He was holding the brim of his hat and shouting at Stefan through the wind. His tie had gotten loose, and every few seconds would flap toward shore.

Stefan waved acknowledgment without shouting back. The small crowd parted to let him walk up to the crime scene. He got there in time to see what was left of the victim bathed in the flash from a police photographer.

The flash dazzled him for a moment, and for a few seconds a part of his mind too primitive to know cameras waited for the rumble of thunder.

"Washed up sometime last night," Inspector Cody said, "during the last high tide."

Stefan nodded, and raised a hand toward his nose as the near subliminal smell began sinking in from the remains. It smelled of the lake, but there was an odor of corruption that turned his stomach.

He bent to look at what Lake Erie had disgorged onto Euclid Beach. It was discolored and wrapped in seaweed, so at first it was hard to make the mind perceive it for what it was. From a distance it could have been a twisted piece of driftwood. This close, the texture of the purpled flesh made it hard to make that mistake. Even this close—Stefan took out a handkerchief and raised it to his mouth, bending until he was barely a foot away from the surface of the skin—it was hard to tell what this had once been. The mind was used to seeing the human body as a whole; if it saw disjointed pieces, it was as functional units, arms, legs, head.

It took nearly a minute for Stefan to see the remains as part of a human body, even though he had some idea what to expect before he drove down here.

"Who found it?" he asked, unable to turn away. He could see it now, the curve of a thigh, the bend of a hip. His mind finally acknowledged that he was looking at the lower half of a woman's torso, severed at the abdomen and at mid thigh. He could now mentally place the bones and muscles in their proper relationships.

It was the most appalling mutilation he'd ever seen.

"A gentleman named Frank La Grossie," someone answered his question. "He was out for a walk this morning and almost tripped over it."

Stefan slowly unbent and turned to Cody. "How often do things wash up from the lake like this?"

Cody shrugged. "More often than I'd like. Who knows, it could be some med school's cadaver."

Stefan looked up at him and said, "Half a cadaver?"

He shrugged. "The cuts struck me as awful neat."

Stefan looked at the body again, at the wounds where it had been separated from the rest of itself. It did seem that the wounds were too neat.

This body had not been torn. The separation had been done deliberately with some sort of blade. That much was obvious, even as corrupted as the corpse was. "No idea how old it is?"

"We have to wait for the coroner to look at it."

Stefan nodded and walked around the remains, stepping aside occasionally for the photographer. After a while, Stefan asked, "Have you noticed it?"

"Noticed what?"

"Fish, something, should have eaten pieces of this while it was in the water. And it looks to've been in the water a long time."

A uniformed cop spoke up, "Maybe it's burned? The color looks like someone messed up burning the body."

Yes, if the color's charring instead of decay, that'd explain that. But it didn't *smell* like someone's fresh attempt to dispose of a body.

"There's another thing," Stefan added. He waved a hand over the corpse. "No flies."

Cody shook his head and muttered something that sounded like, "Christ."

The flash of a bulb came from behind him, and Stefan turned to look at the photographer. "What's over there?" he asked.

The photographer took the stub of an unlit cigar out of the corner of his mouth and pointed at the sand midway between him and Stefan. "Dead bird," he said, "probably nothing."

It was a seagull, partly buried in sand the lake had washed in. There was no indication of what had killed it. Stefan looked up and saw the seagull's fellows massed far down the beach, awaiting the coming storm. For a moment, Stefan had the oddest sensation that every gull's back was turned to their fallen comrade, as if the dead one had committed some unpardonable sin that even death could not forgive.

Stefan turned back to the thing that used to be part of a human body and wondered if its presence seemed as ominous to the others as it did to him.

He had seen lots of bodies. He had thought that such scenes had lost the ability to disturb him. They hadn't.

Looking at the body, Stefan felt threatened. His faith had been shaken in a way he hadn't felt before. For a moment it seemed that the light of God had abandoned this stretch of Euclid Beach, and his own presence made him a participant in some unholy sacrament.

"Who would do this to someone?" he whispered to himself.

Cody waved at the lake, a slightly darker shade than the sky, and said, "Like I said, most likely something a medical school disposed of. Second most likely, some Capone type chopping up the victim to make it hard to identify. Who knows how long it's been floating out there? It could have drifted all the way from Chicago."

Stefan nodded, though it seemed more likely that the body floated out of their own Cuyahoga River.

Eventually the coroner's wagon showed up for the body, and there was little left for them to do but walk up and down the beach and look for more pieces. No more showed up.

Not there.

3

The discovery of the lower part of a human torso on Euclid Beach was exceptional enough to be printed in one form or another in the *Plain Dealer,* the *Press,* and the *News.* Out in North Perry, halfway on the other side of Lake County from Cleveland, a gentleman named Joseph Hejduk came to the Central Station to tell them about some remains buried on his property.

On the drive out there, with a couple of uniformed cops, two detectives, and two shovels, Stefan listened to Hejduk explain how a nearly indescribable carcass had washed up on his property, how he had called the sheriff's office, and how a deputy had told him—on the phone, without ever seeing the remains—it was probably a dead animal and that Mr. Hejduk should bury it.

Mr. Hejduk wasn't someone to argue with the sheriff's department. But he'd been having nightmares about the thing he buried for the past two weeks. When he had read about what they'd found on Euclid Beach, he knew, he said, "That I bury no animal there."

Darkness and rain slammed into them as Mr. Hejduk drove his ten-year-old Studebaker to a stop next to his property. The uniformed cops grabbed the shovels as Mr. Hejduk led them out into the storm, and to the remains of a small mound of earth at the edge of a wooded area.

Stefan helped the uniformed police dig, trading places as people took breaks from digging in the cramped space. Inspector Cody continued to question Mr. Hejduk about what happened, making the occasional unkind observation about the Lake County Sheriff's Department.

The digging was hellish in the wind and rain. They only had the light from flashlights shining above them. The scant light seemed to do nothing but make the shadows even more impenetrable. Mud pulled at Stefan's feet, and water weighed his coat down on his shoulders. Everything smelled of damp earth, and after about an hour and a half of digging, a familiar decayed odor.

By the time they found what Mr. Hejduk had buried, Stefan had stopped breathing through his nose.

One of the uniformed cops called out, "I've found something."

He was standing in the far end of a hole that had taken on the proportions of a grave. Stefan was at the other end, and when the flashlight beams swept over to shine at that cop's feet, Stefan realized that end of the hole was a foot or two shallower than his.

The cop was scraping mud away from something with the blade of his shovel, and Stefan could tell that the remains couldn't be more than three feet long. If it had been a human-sized corpse, Stefan would've been standing on part of it.

He leaned over, hoping that the deputy had been right, but knowing, from the smell, that he hadn't.

The blade of the shovel scraped black clumps of earth off of something that looked even blacker. Like the thing on the beach, it took a while for Stefan to perceive the unearthed object for what it was.

The uniformed cop reached a point where he was satisfied, or had seen enough, and backed away, letting the rain wash the rest of the mud off the carcass. He tossed the shovel up on the ground next to the hole and climbed out, calling for the stretcher.

Stefan kept staring at what the cop had unearthed. He felt the same sense of unholiness here, a sense of God's abandonment.

In the hole was another piece of a woman's body, the upper torso this time, missing the head and the arms at the shoulders. It suffered the same discoloration, but looked oddly preserved for having spent the last two weeks or so in the earth.

Stefan pulled himself up out of the hole when they came

for the body. He emerged just in time to hear Mr. Hejduk tell Cody about the dead birds he'd found around the remains on the beach.

The next day Coroner Pearce fitted the remains together and declared them a match. He also ruled out the body coming from a medical lab. From the muscular contractions in the neck area, he concluded that decapitation was the cause of death. The discoloration wasn't from someone trying to burn the corpse; it seemed to be, in fact, the result of some sort of chemical preservative impregnating the victim's flesh. The coroner couldn't identify the chemical, but it explained the odd preservation of the body after what was estimated as six *months* in the lake and perhaps a month or two before that for the actual time of death.

The coroner described the woman as having been more or less average height and build, thirty-five years old or so, whose only unique distinguishing feature was having had her uterus surgically removed some years prior to death.

The lake was dredged, but no more pieces of the "Lady of the Lake" were found. Detective Stefan Ryzard spent much of his time over the next three months combing missing person's records for someone matching the Lady's remains. Despite following leads as far as Canada, the Lady was never officially identified, and it would be over two years before Stefan would know her name.

BOOK ONE

September 1935-June 1936
THE KINGDOM
OF HEAVEN

1935

1

Stefan Ryzard paced in an alley behind a drugstore in his old neighborhood around East Fifty-Fifth and St. Clair. He didn't like being here. It brought back too many memories. It had been years since he lost Mary and Jacob, and every time he came near the place where he'd spent the first thirty years of his life, he was reminded of the loss. Reminded of God's infinite indifference.

Being here with a body whose murder had little hope of being solved did little to relieve Stefan's sense of abandonment.

The body lay in the midst of half a dozen ashcans. He'd been finished off with a single high-caliber round in the forehead. The body had been dumped here, Ryzard suspected, as a warning to someone in the neighborhood— bumped off by one of the criminal mobs that had been running amok in this town since Prohibition. Stefan might find out who the triggerman was, might even discover why it happened, but as for evidence, or an arrest—

It wasn't going to happen.

So far, after sending uniforms out to canvass the area for three buildings in every direction, they hadn't a single witness who even thought they'd seen anything useful.

All he was doing here was marking time until the wagon showed up for the body. He hoped they'd get here soon; he wanted to get out of here. He didn't like the way the past seemed to stick to this place, sucking him in. In another few hours he might start walking back to St. John's, where he hadn't been since the funeral.

If they'd show up, he could get all of this out of his mind, get the report on this written up before lunch, and then maybe he could move on to some productive police work. If there was any such thing in this town.

"Detective Ryzard?"

Stefan turned to face the voice, which came from the entrance of the alley. A young man was there, giving him a quizzical look. Stefan's first thought was: *federal agent.* He looked like one of Hoover's boys, too damn neat.

Stefan nodded.

"Pleased to meet you." He walked over to Stefan and extended his hand, and for a moment Stefan thought: *lawyer.*

Stefan didn't take the offered hand. "Who in blazes are you?" Another thought crossed his mind, this one the most annoying: *reporter.*

"This is a crime scene, son. Are you supposed to be here?"

The young man looked crestfallen and lowered his hand. "I think so, sir. You are Detective Ryzard? They sent me here to meet you from the Central Station."

Last thought: *trainee. They've assigned me a goddamn trainee.* Stefan shook his head. "You have a name?"

"Nuri," he said after a moment of apparent confusion. "Nuri Lapidos. Sorry, I'm new here and—"

"They assigned you to me so I can show you the ropes, right?"

"I guess that's more or less it."

Stefan shook his head. "They could have warned me," he muttered to himself.

There was an oddly fatalistic sigh from Nuri, and he said, "If there's a problem, I can wait by the car."

"No, there's no problem."

Nuri Lapidos took a few steps around Stefan and looked down at the end of the alley where the corpse lay. "So what have you got here?"

"Why don't you tell me?"

Nuri looked up at him, then crouched by the body where it was sprawled. "He was dumped here, wasn't he?"

"Why do you say that?" Stefan prodded him.

"Position of the body, and no sign of blood from the wound on anything but his clothes." He kept staring at the body. "An execution. They had the poor bastard on his knees when they shot him—a garage or a parking lot from the oil stains." He pointed at the guy's pants where some dark stains peeked from beneath the blood.

He pushed back a sleeve and looked at the guy's right wrist. "He was tied or handcuffed. There's signs of abrasion."

Stefan nodded, "That's not bad."

Nuri stood up. "He was on his side long enough for lividity to set in, probably the trunk of a car." He stepped back next to Stefan. "He looks like a boxer. The fella's got heavy scarring on his hands, and on what's left of his face. You can see his nose's been broken more than once."

"Yeah," Stefan said with a touch of irony in his voice, "a boxer."

Nuri shrugged. "Well, someone who beat people up for a living."

Stefan nodded. The victim was some hood's pet gorilla, and someone had more than likely plugged him to get at his employer. Stefan looked Nuri up and down and revised his initial impression of the man. He was young, but not as young as he looked. The neat clothes and the overly open expression distracted from his gaze, which bore an intelligence that most of Stefan's colleagues lacked.

Stefan extended his hand and said, "When the wagon gets here, let me buy you lunch."

Sol's Diner was a little hole-in-the-wall place on East Ninth, a stone's throw from the nightclubs on Short Vincent. The proximity to all the glitz made the place seem that much darker, even in midday. Stefan didn't care; at times he preferred the dimness, and it was a small price to pay for Sol's corned-beef sandwiches.

He sat across from Nuri in one of the booths near the back. As they waited for their order, Stefan asked, "So what brings you to my little corner of Cleveland?"

Nuri gave him a quick grin. "I hitched a ride in a squad car."

"Yeah." Stefan leaned back and loosened his tie. "You know that's not what I mean. College educated, aren't you?"

"The damage shows?" Nuri chuckled. "Mama really

wanted a lawyer." He pinched his fingers and held them up. "Mrs. Lapidos' little boy came this close. Somehow I drifted from criminal law to criminology, and here I am, degree and all."

Stefan shook his head. "A cop with a Bachelors—"

"Masters."

"You know, when I first saw you, I had you pegged for a federal agent. Why aren't you one of Hoover's boys? It probably pays better."

Nuri chuckled. "Oh, yeah, I can see the newsreels now, 'Nuri Lapidos, the Jewish G-man.' No, I don't think I'm what J. Edgar is looking for."

"Oh, sorry."

Nuri shook his head. "Don't be. I wanted to be part of a real police department anyway."

The waitress came and slid plates in front of them.

"Well, the department's *real,* all right," Stefan said, picking up his sandwich and taking a bite out of it.

Nuri had only ordered toast and coffee. He took a triangular slice and dipped it in his cup. "That sounds a little bitter."

Stefan set down his sandwich. "It *is* bitter. Some days I just pray for a little shame in this city. I swear, sometimes it seems that half the department is taking payoffs from someone."

"You're exaggerating."

Stefan shook his head. "Just wait until you collar someone with connections and see him walk out of the building before you finish the paperwork. Officers, detectives, judges—"

"You weren't kidding when you said the investigation on the guy in the alley wasn't going to go anywhere?"

Stefan nodded. "There's no way we're ever going to get something like that prosecuted in this county, maybe nowhere in the whole state. Assuming we even find out who killed him." Stefan took a sip of his own coffee. It went down like molten lead, solidifying into a weight in his stomach. "Whatever happens in this town, someone in the department is being paid to look the other way. Hard to believe, but I think it's gotten worse since they repealed Prohibition."

Nuri shook his head.

"You think I'm kidding? When we were dry, a hell of a lot of people made a lot of money in liquor. A *lot*. Regular cops got used to looking the other way. One bad law corrupted this whole city, decivilized us until law itself became devalued. Now we don't even have the excuse of a bad law."

Nuri shrugged. "So Prohibition was a bad idea. I doubt anyone'd argue with you there. You make it sound as if Cleveland was the reincarnation of Gomorrah."

Stefan sipped his coffee. "Sometimes I wonder."

2

Saturday, September 21

Edward Andrassy sat in a bar as night descended, waiting for an old man. It was ironic. He had spent most of his adult life waiting for old men of one sort or another. If not for himself, then for the women or the boys who occasionally worked for him. It was a life few would envy, and he had spent the last few months trying to get out of it. He had been offered something that was pretty much unbelievable, and priceless if it were true.

Eternal life, he thought, sipping beer that was strangely tasteless now.

Listening to Him the first few times, it seemed so simple. It was impossible to say no, even when He started feeding them His blood. It wasn't even hard to call Him Master after that. What bothered Andrassy was when it came to others' blood.

He was still human, apparently, bound to Him, but not close enough to ignore the taste of someone else's blood in his mouth.

Now he waited for an old man, someone an age older than anyone he had ever met save his Master, Melchior. He hoped that this old man would be able to tell him a way through to where he was going, a way that wasn't lined with so much death.

The man he was meeting was his Master's enemy, but Andrassy was past caring. He had seen all the people who had come under Melchior's control become less and less human, more and more extensions of Melchior. Even Flo, who had started off the most human, even she was less moved at the carnage that Melchior fed them upon.

Andrassy set aside the beer, unfinished. He watched the

sky darken outside and wondered how many sunsets he would see.

Eventually a presence filled the crowded bar, a pressure at the back of his neck that told Andrassy that the man he'd been waiting for was here. One of the blood who didn't belong to Melchior. It was reassuring to think that there were others that weren't of his master; it meant that the Master's way wasn't the only way.

A hand touched his shoulder, and a voice said, "Let us walk away from here."

At the touch, it seemed that Andrassy had entered a world that only contained him and the old man. The bar and the crowd inside it seemed to fade away, and no one noticed their exit. The old man he left with was named Anacreon, and Andrassy suspected that he was one of the most powerful ones of the blood in this city. Physically, he didn't look like much. He was short, dumpy, middle-aged.

The old man was nearly six hundred years old.

Andrassy didn't believe that just because the old man said so. He believed it because he could feel the centuries in the old man's presence. He believed it in the sense of power he had next to him. He believed it because in Anacreon's presence was the only time he didn't fear his Master. In Anacreon, he saw someone who could protect him, someone who might be on a par with Melchior.

They walked through the streets of the Roaring Third, past the bars and tenements, past the hustlers and the prostitutes. None paid them attention, as if they weren't quite real.

As they walked, the old man spoke, "You must tell me everything you can now." The old man was insistent, and waves of the old man's will pushed against Andrassy's.

But Andrassy wasn't stupid, and he wasn't going to cave immediately. He had enough of his own will to act against his Master; he wasn't going to give anything to the old man without something in return. The old man wanted Melchior, and information was all Andrassy had to bargain with.

"You know what I want," Andrassy said.

"You don't realize what you ask."

"I want what He'd give me, without the strings. You want me to roll over on someone without getting something in return?"

The old man shook his head, "You ask me to warn your Master before I have anything to convince the Council to move against him."

"I gave you the corpse. Ain't that enough?"

"For me," he said, "Laila's death is enough. Your Master has violated the Covenant in a grievous manner. But for me to act without first convincing the Council would be little more than another violation of the Covenant. Taking you over the threshold now would warn him of what is to come."

"So why am I talking to you, old man?"

Anacreon turned and placed his hands on Andrassy's shoulders. The touch was like a lightning bolt through his body. Andrassy's mouth snapped shut as he felt the strength behind Anacreon's withering gaze. Under that stare, Andrassy felt as if his shoulders were being peeled apart.

Despite a gaze that struck Andrassy like a blow, Anacreon did not raise his voice. "Listen. You are thrall to this killer. You will not be free until he is dead. As for what you ask, you have it already. Enough of the blood runs through your veins that were you to fall now to mortal death, you would be reborn. Reborn a thrall. All I need is the Council to act against him, and when he is gone you would be born of your own blood. *Give me what I need.*"

They stood like that, and it seemed hours before Andrassy realized that the street life had abandoned them. The streets were empty of people now. They stood between a deserted warehouse and a vacant lot. Andrassy had never felt more alone.

"What do you want?"

"Very first— Your Master. In his secret heart, what has he named himself?"

Andrassy's lips moved to form the word, but he never had a chance to speak it. From the darkness around them, the wind carried a whispered name, "Melchior."

The old man let go, and Andrassy fell to the ground as if those hands were all that had been holding him upright. Anacreon turned around, facing down the street so fast that Andrassy barely saw him move. He faced an area of deepening shadow at the end of the street.

"You think to surprise me?" The words floated on the

wind, sinking so deep into Andrassy's brain it hurt. He felt it in the pit of his stomach, in the way his heart tried to tear free of his chest. His Master was here, and Andrassy had led Him here.

Anacreon faced the darkness, and his body radiated strength, a bright flare of unseen light. His body twisted like water, muscles rippling, bones shifting. "Melchior," the thing that was Anacreon said. "An old name."

"Yes," replied the wind.

"An arrogant name," Anacreon said. The old man was no more. What stood in his place was a form that was somewhere between an angel and a demon. Its skin seemed to glow with an inner light, and its claws seemed metallic in the streetlight. The perfection of form was painful for Andrassy to look at.

"The last name you will hear."

Anacreon spread its wings, and the darkness descended upon him.

The light and darkness tore at each other. Andrassy, on the ground, felt every blow as if it was falling on his own body. He should have moved, run, done anything to get away from what was happening. But he stayed there, frozen.

Melchior seemed little more than a shadow. But Anacreon's metal claws tore into it and tore pieces away. For a few eternal moments, it seemed that his Master was no match for the angelic thing wrestling him. Then something changed. The shadow seemed to wrap itself around Anacreon's head, and there was a gleam of metal that wasn't from any claw.

Something tore through flesh and Andrassy closed his eyes.

In the darkness he heard something drink.

Andrassy didn't run. There was nowhere he could have gone. When he opened his eyes, his Master stood there, over a body that was just the old man again. In his hands Melchior held Anacreon's head. Scars raked across Melchior's body, flesh torn so badly that it was a miracle that he still stood. As Andrassy watched, the wounds closed up.

"That was . . . inconvenient," Melchior said. "You brought me to this too soon, Andrassy. I'm still gathering myself. You will have to pay." He walked up to Andrassy, and his will clamped down on him. In the man's mind there were no longer any thoughts but those of his Master.

He would be punished, and the Master's children would feed.

3

Sunday, September 22

On Sunday, the Church descended on Stefan's Gomorrah. Cleveland, one of the midwestern strongholds of Catholicism, was host to the Seventh National Eucharist Congress. A religious fervor gripped the city in a mood that was more appropriate to a Rome or a Jerusalem.

Few were immune from the force of the event, whatever their faith. Tens of thousands of onlookers crowded Euclid Avenue, lining the streets to watch the procession. They packed the sidewalks, in some cases spilling onto the lawns of the remaining handful of old mansions on Millionaire's Row.

No one objected to the tide of immigrant labor trampling once-luxurious lawns. The mansions that didn't stand vacant were mostly occupied by some charitable institution that closed on Sunday.

As the procession marched past the remnants of nineteenth-century aristocracy, only one of the grand old houses turned other than a blind eye toward it. A massive stone structure, isolated from its cousins on the avenue, a building that seemed to resist the oncoming century by a combination of inertia and force of will.

High in one of the third-floor windows, a man who called himself Eric Dietrich, one of the first millionaires to occupy Millionaire's Row since the end of the Great War, stared down at the procession.

"All they need is a wounded Christ dragging his cross in front of them," he said.

The man seated in the room behind Dietrich winced and said, "Please, can we do without the blasphemy?"

Dietrich turned and faced the man, smiling slightly. "You

are in my house, Mr. Van Sweringen. If I say they should nail a Christ up in Public Square in front of that Tower of yours, what right have you to complain?"

Oris Paxton Van Sweringen sat in the dusty wing-backed chair and glared at Dietrich. It had been a long, long, time since he had to endure people talking to him like that. He and his brother were two of the most powerful men in the United States.

Except, for the moment, they weren't. All Oris Van Sweringen could do was nod politely and agree, "Yes, this is your house. But you could be more accommodating to a guest."

Dietrich let loose a humiliating laugh. Oris shrank under the weight of it. It was as if this man, this evil bastard, had seen into his mind and had taken all the laughter, all the derision that had ever been heaped upon the odd pair of brothers and had focused it into a single sound.

Oris couldn't take it any longer. He stood. "I think this will be all, Mr. Dietrich."

Dietrich walked away from the window, shaking his head. "Are you in a position to walk away from me, Mr. Van Sweringen?"

Oris stayed silent, his face burning. He knew he should be talking through a lawyer. He knew he wasn't at his best one-on-one, especially without his brother's support. "You can talk to our lawyers," he said, trying to force some iron into his voice.

Mr. Dietrich kept walking around the room, forcing Oris to turn to remain facing him. Framed by furnishings out of the last century, Mr. Dietrich seemed almost spectral. He was six inches taller than Oris, with pale skin that, by contrast to the muddy colors of the old furniture, almost appeared bleached. His face was framed by hair of near-invisible blondness.

Dietrich stopped walking and tapped his fingers on an oak sideboard. His fingers smeared arcane patterns in the dust. "Why would I wish to talk to an intermediary?"

"You've made a rather complex offer, Mr. Dietrich," Oris said, regaining some of his composure. "We need some time to evaluate it. It needs to be handled by our lawyers and accountants. We're talking about the control of a three-billion-dollar—"

"I know exactly what we're talking about." Dietrich's voice was as cold and characterless as the skin of a corpse. He ran his hand across the sideboard, erasing the marks he'd made in the dust. "I know how adept you and Mantis are at manipulating the illusion of money. You stand upon a mountain of paper." Dietrich slowly turned to face Oris. "No lawyers. No accountants."

Oris shook his head. "This is different than the license we granted you. That was just space in the terminal, right-of-way on some track. That was something a handshake could settle. This is so far beyond that it is beyond comprehension."

Dietrich spun around and stared at Oris. His eyes were purple-red, which Oris had always taken as a sign of albinism. Right now those eyes seemed to burn. The feeling was so intense that Oris felt his skin heat up. He reached up and loosened his tie.

"Enough," Dietrich said. He didn't raise his voice, but the word felt like a blow.

He took a step toward Oris.

"What will happen in New York if you do not have the capital? If your backers fall through?" Dietrich made a dismissive gesture with his hand, spreading a cloud of dust that settled slowly to the ground.

"They'll come through. We've drawn up contracts—"

"More paper," Dietrich said. "If I say so, you will go to New York naked."

"You have no right to interfere—"

Dietrich laughed. The sound burned into Oris' skull. "You have two choices. Agree to my terms, and you will go to the auction seven days from now, make your bid, and walk away with most of your empire intact. Or walk away from me, find your backers changing heart, and go to New York penniless." He took a step closer. Oris wanted to back away, but he couldn't move. "I am leaving for New York tonight. You will answer me now."

Oris felt the world crumbling away beneath him. Everything he and Mantis had built was teetering on a precipice. The whole empire—railroads, real estate, the corporate glue that held it all together—was being torn from his grasp again. It was humiliating enough to admit to J. P. Morgan that they couldn't meet the debt that bloomed in May, to watch as the bankers organized their public auction of everything the Van Sweringens had struggled to build. But the brothers had consented, after organizing a plan to retain what they had built.

Oris was supposed to go to New York on the 30th on behalf of a newly incorporated entity under the Van Sweringens' control. They already had the financial backing necessary to bid on the collateral being auctioned. It was a deal that had taken months to put together.

And now this shadow investor, a man who dealt in cash and handshake deals, was telling Oris that all that preparation was for nothing.

He wished Mantis was here. Facing this man without his brother for support was more than he could take. "We spent months putting the deal together. How could you undo it?"

Dietrich stared into Oris' eyes, and Oris couldn't turn away. There was a searing heat deep inside them, an intensity that terrified him and held him spellbound. "You are going to incorporate Midamerica with money from Mr. Ball and Mr. Tomlinson. How accommodating do you think their heirs would be?"

Oris wanted to back away. He wanted to *run*. He wanted anything other than to be here facing this man. But no matter what he wanted, he couldn't move. He couldn't even turn away or lower his gaze from Dietrich's burning stare. Every shred of doubt he had about Dietrich's will, his intent, his ability to carry out on his threats—all of it was torn away from him. Oris believed.

"You shall accept me as the unwritten part of Midamerica, won't you?"

Oris nodded, unable to speak.

As if the gesture broke a magic spell, Oris was suddenly able to move and break eye contact. He stumbled away toward the sideboard, leaning on it with one hand and rubbing his neck with the other. He was out of breath and felt as if someone had been trying to strangle him.

"Why?" he asked in a hoarse voice. A crystal decanter sat on a tray on the sideboard. He grabbed it with a shaking hand and filled a glass. It was water. Oris drank it, wishing for something stronger. "Why torment us like this? You have the resources to take it whole yourself. . . ."

Dietrich laughed. "You hired a man whose sole job is to keep your name out of the papers. You should understand when someone wishes to keep his privacy. That mountain of paper you built your empire upon, it provides me with shade from unwanted eyes."

Oris put down the glass and nodded. "Send me whatever arrangements you want, Mr. Dietrich. I'll be going now." He picked up his jacket from a chair by the door. It came away gray with dust.

"One last thing," Dietrich called after him. It was the cold conversational tone again, the corpselike voice that made Oris' skin crawl.

Oris stopped in the doorway and said, "What is it?"

"Never assume that I will take secrecy over power."

Oris shuddered as he left.

Stefan Ryzard was driving home to Lakewood after a long day of public service. All the talk at the Central Station was about how the Catholics were taking over the city, and Stefan was glad to escape. It wasn't the talk about the Eucharist Congress that bothered him, so much as the event itself. It was as if the descent of faith upon the city somehow brought his own deficits into greater relief.

It was after eleven now, and darkness had claimed the city for its own. Nothing seemed to stir this late on a Sunday. The stillness was probably why, as his car approached the Detroit-Superior Bridge, he noticed something out of the corner of his eye. There was ominous movement down Huron, toward the Flats of the Cuyahoga.

He rolled to a stop where Huron descended from Superior. Below, where Huron bottomed out on the shores of the river, Stefan saw a congregation of the derelicts and vagabonds who populated Cleveland's industrial bottomland. Normally it wouldn't rate any attention, it was a sign of the times, like a peeling NRA poster.

But there was something definitely wrong about the collection of tramps down there.

Stefan stopped the car and checked his revolver before he got out. He stood at the top of Huron, looking down, trying to interpret what he saw. Half a dozen men formed a semicircle around a lone figure. Some of the men carried boards, bottles, and one carried a length of pipe. The focus of their attention was a colored man who had backed up against a wall facing them.

Stefan descended, at first thinking he was about to break up a nasty lynching. But as he closed on the scene, he realized that whatever was going on here, it wasn't that simple.

The men in the circle, while they gripped their makeshift weapons as if they had murder in their hearts, had fear in their eyes, and were backing away. The man at their focus seemed terrified, whipping his head around, staring wild-eyed at his potential attackers. But as Stefan approached, it seemed almost as if he was looking *beyond* the men with the weapons.

Stefan walked down the center of the street, constantly shifting his attention, looking for any additional people. He could feel the tension in the air. Whatever was going on was near to exploding. He stopped a few dozen yards from the scene, his revolver out but pointed at the ground.

"What's going on here?" he called out, in a steady tone that he hoped wouldn't startle someone into a regrettable action.

The circle of men kept backing away from the colored man. A few of them glanced toward him, but quickly returned their attention to the man huddled against the wall.

"Don't get too close to him," said the man with the pipe, "That's one crazy jig—he fractured Larry's skull!"

Stefan scanned the semicircle and saw that one of the men did have blood splattered around the side of his head, apparently a chunk torn out of his ear. Stefan looked at the Negro and saw that the man was unarmed, and looked on the verge of panic.

"He's out there!" the Negro said, pointing a steady finger somewhere beyond the men encircling him. The arm he raised was splattered with blood.

One of the men raised a two-by-four as if to club away the pointing arm. Stefan raised his revolver and said, "Everyone calm down and drop the weapons."

The one with the busted ear turned and said, "Who the hell do you think you . . ." His words trailed off when he saw the revolver. The bottle he carried slipped from his hand to shatter at his feet, spattering his pants leg with the dregs it'd contained.

"The name's Ryzard, *Detective* Ryzard. Now drop all the weapons."

"Look," said the first one who'd spoken, gesturing with his makeshift club, "This nigger—"

Stefan leveled the gun at the man. *"Drop it."*

He backed away and dropped the pipe he carried. The others followed quickly, scattering their improvised weapons.

"I don't care what happened," Stefan said, "but I want all of you to beat it. *Now.*"

"But he—" the one with the ear motioned at the man they'd surrounded.

Stefan gestured with his head, keeping the gun steady. Slowly, way too slowly for Stefan's taste, they started moving away. All of them kept watching the terrified man, as if he were suddenly going to erupt into some sort of life-threatening attack.

Within a few minutes he was alone with the man, who looked as crazed as ever. He was still whipping his head around, staring wild-eyed into the darkness. As if the fellas who'd encircled him weren't even relevant.

Stefan took a deep breath and said, "Okay, now what's the problem?"

The man turned his face toward him, the wild eyes staring into his own. It was as if this was the first time the man had noticed him. It was also the first time that Stefan had gotten a good look at the man. The look wasn't encouraging. His face, from the cheekbones down, was shiny and wet. His teeth were stained dark red, as if he was coughing up blood.

"The devil is out here," he said. "His bulls are walking the tracks." He slid back along the brick wall, and with every step he seemed to shudder a little, as if he were in pain.

"Sure, sure." Stefan smiled in a way he hoped was reassuring. He put away the revolver. This fella did seem to be half out of his mind. Stefan raised his hands, "But the tracks are down there. You're up here."

The man kept edging away, but his movements lost a little of their jerky, panicked edge.

"Those men I chased off, were they beating on you?"

The man shook his head as if he didn't quite understand. "Get thee behind me, Satan."

Stefan kept inching toward the man, trying to keep from spooking him into running. "I work for the Cleveland Police Department, but I'm no devil. I was an altar boy."

The man started crouching, as if he thought Stefan meant to attack him. Stefan stopped approaching. The man shook his head and said, "Wicked, wicked."

This close, the man looked really bad off. He was bleeding out of his mouth, his nose, and his ears, and his overalls were spattered with blood in a way that Stefan found particularly disturbing. He had the feeling that the man was leaking his life away in front of him.

He began cursing himself for chasing away this man's attackers. If they were responsible for what happened, Stefan would never forgive himself.

"I have to get you to a hospital," he said softly, and took another step. The man scrambled away and made a sound that was more a keening than anything else.

After a moment, Stefan said, "Our Lord, who art in heaven . . ."

It worked. Some of the wildness leaked out of the man's eyes, and he seemed, for the first time, to be able to really see Stefan. Stefan kept talking, "Hallowed be thy name. Thy Kingdom come . . ."

Through the prayer, he managed to walk up to the man without him scrambling away. When he reached him, and put a hand on his shoulder, the panic had been replaced by an expression of extreme weariness. The fear had been all that was holding him up. By the time Stefan reached him, he was collapsing to the ground, and it was all Stefan could do to get an arm around him.

The last coherent thing the man said was, "Pray for me."

By the time Stefan got him to the car he was unconscious and barely breathing.

Hours later, in a hallway at St. Vincent's Charity, Stefan leaned back in a chair and waited. He didn't realize he had fallen asleep until he heard a doctor calling his name.

"Detective Ryzard "

Stefan jerked his head upright, and the chair—which had

been leaning back against the wall—obliged him by tilting forward, the forward legs hitting the linoleum with a crash.

"Yes, yes." Stefan emerged from the chair, which seemed intent on pitching him onto the floor. One hand reached out to shake hands with the doctor, the other grabbed his hat which was spilling out of his lap.

The doctor took his hand and said, "I understand you brought the man in."

Stefan nodded.

"You don't know the man's name? Have any idea who he is?"

"No, I don't." Stefan smoothed his hair and replaced his hat. "How's he doing?"

"I'm sorry, he didn't make it." The doctor looked back down the hallway from where he'd come. Stefan looked at him and realized how young the guy seemed. Dark hair, Errol Flynn mustache, he looked like some actor pretending to be a doctor.

"Didn't make it," Stefan thought. *Weak set of words, right up there with "passed away."*

"How did he die?" Stefan asked, feeling a growing anger at the men he'd chased away earlier in the night. Also anger at himself for letting it happen.

"Well, it isn't going to be a police matter, if that's what you're asking."

"What?"

"Natural causes. He died because we couldn't get his internal hemorrhaging under control in time before he bled to death."

"I grabbed this fella from a circle of club-wielding nuts, and it's *natural causes*?"

The doctor nodded. His eyes held a grave expression that seemed older than his features. "No one laid a hand on him as far as I can tell. No external trauma at all, no bruising, abrasions, broken bones— The man was sick, and suffered severe bleeding into the lungs, stomach, intestines—"

Stefan took a step back and said, "Good lord, what did he have?"

"I don't know, which is why the patient's history is important." He shook his head and sighed. "But you just picked him up off the street, right?"

"Screaming about how the devil was after him."

"He was delirious? Delusional?"

"That's a word for it."

The doctor shook his head again. "Maybe that might give me a lead on what was really wrong with him, before someone decides it was all TB and I shouldn't be wasting my time on it." He patted Stefan on the shoulder and said, "Go home, get some sleep."

"Okay. You're *sure* it's natural causes?"

The doctor nodded. "Believe it or not, people do die of that in this town."

Stefan turned to leave and the doctor said, "One more thing. If you see anyone with similar symptoms, or find out anything about his history, could you contact me. Doctor McCutcheon."

Stefan nodded. "Is whatever this is contagious?"

"I don't know."

Stefan shook his head and said, "I'll give you a call if the Devil starts chasing me."

As he left, he wondered if, in this town and with his job, he would be able to tell.

4

Edward Mullen worked long hours as a security guard at St. Vincent's. It wasn't a great job, but it was a job, and deep into the night it was peaceful. He sat behind a desk by the morgue, leaning his head on his hand and waiting for his shift to end.

The area was brightly lit and chilly, the tile walls reflecting light without heat. Mullen was used to it. Occasionally he would look up at the clock on the wall behind the desk and find that it was only another five minutes toward the end of his shift.

Nothing ever happened down here. The most exciting thing to happen this night was when they'd rolled down a fresh body.

Mullen was yawning, at about four in the morning, when he caught a shadow out of the corner of his eye. It was the size of a man, and was moving through the hallway.

Mullen stood up to greet the visitor. He was about to say something, but he was suddenly wrapped in an unaccountable feeling of dread.

The shadow strode through the hallway, shedding the bright light as if it never actually touched him. Mullen only had the impression of a tall man with long hair.

The man stopped in front of Mullen's desk and looked down at him. It was as if the man had carried his own darkness with him, wrapping himself in it. Mullen had a sense of pale skin and blond hair, but he didn't really see it. What he did see was the figure's eyes. The eyes, colored red-violet that faded almost to black, seized Mullen's attention. He couldn't look away.

"You have something that belongs to me," the figure said.

The words settled across Mullen's brain like a brand. He knew that he stood in the presence of something evil. All he could do was nod.

The figure waved a hand at the doors which led to the morgue. The room beyond was empty of people, but Mullen heard movement inside. He heard the scraping of metal, and then suddenly the doors swung open.

Walking through them was the Negro, naked, blood still caked around his mouth and chest. Mullen recognized the corpse that had been wheeled in earlier in the evening. The body moved like an automaton, and Mullen wanted to shrink away.

Edward Mullen was frozen to the spot.

The shadow reached out a hand with long fingers and touched Mullen's face. The touch burned like ice.

"You will tell everybody a story. You will not mention me."

Edward Mullen looked deep into those blood-colored eyes and couldn't conceive of refusing. At that point Mullen believed he was in the presence of the Devil himself.

At around six in the afternoon, Nuri Lapidos rode the Shaker Rapid home. He was just getting comfortable with the routine, a new city, a new job. Detective Ryzard was proving an able, if somewhat somber, introduction to the city and the department. Though the more he saw of the city, the more grateful he was for managing to find an apartment in the suburbs.

He was riding home, sometime between five-thirty and six, when the train began slowing down. Nuri looked up from the paper, slightly relieved to be distracted from the depressing stories coming out of Germany, and looked out the window. It wasn't easy, he was on the aisle, and the man next to him was already craning his neck to see the commotion ahead that was causing the train to slow.

His seatmate wasn't the only spectator. The train was passing through a valley, and before Nuri saw anything of the commotion on the tracks, he could see spectators lined up on the tops of the cliffs overlooking the tracks.

Nuri stood up, and finally could see the ground ahead of the train. He expected some sort of workmen fixing the tracks, but instead, he saw police. Three or four uniformed officers, and at least two detectives wandering around the underbrush at the side of the tracks, beneath a brush-covered hillside.

Curiosity had always been Nuri's curse. He got up and made his way down to the conductor.

He pulled out his badge, "Can you stop the train and let me out here?"

The man scowled and looked at the badge. "You want out, here, now?"

Nuri nodded.

"Sheesh, well, I guess you paid your dime." He pulled on a lever and the train started to slow even more. Before it'd rolled to a complete stop, the doors opened. "There you are, beat it."

Nuri had to take a jump that almost cost him an ankle on the gravel. He stumbled away from the train as it began speeding up. Through the still-open door he could hear the conductor. "Give people a badge, and they think they own the damn railroad."

Nuri watched the train slide by the scene ahead of him. He edged away from the tracks and started walking up to the two detectives. One was already starting toward him, apparently to see what the Rapid had disgorged.

They met about a hundred yards from the center of attention. "Can I help you?" the man asked. He was a tall man with a mustache, and he looked as if he was already irritated by the massing spectators.

"Hello," Nuri held out the badge which was still in his hand, "Detective Lapidos, I was wondering if I could help you?"

The man extended a hand. "Orly May, and I guess you can. Me and Emil just got here about ten, fifteen minutes ago—well, let me show you."

Detective May led Nuri to the focus of all the attention. Two men May said were Erie Railroad police were talking with the other detective, Emil. It was obvious what they were talking about before May led him into earshot. About ten feet from the policemen lay a man's body, naked except for a pair of black socks.

At first he thought that brush was concealing part of the body, but as he closed on the scene he could see that the head wasn't hidden by brush. It wasn't there. As if to add insult to injury, the corpse had also been emasculated.

Nuri shook his head at the sight. Bodies he had seen before, but the mutilation made it more disturbing than it should have been. He felt light in the stomach. "That's the first one," May said to him. "What's really creepy about all this is the lack of blood."

Nuri nodded. The corpse was remarkably clean of all the violence done to it. "Almost as if the killer washed the body off before dumping it here." As May nodded, the rest of what he said sank in. "You said 'the first one'?"

"Over here," May said, waving him over to a patch of thick scrub about thirty feet away from the corpse.

Nuri could smell it before he saw it, an acrid tinny odor that made his nose itch. Rounding the bush, Nuri saw the body of a shorter, older man. Laid out as carefully as the other body, arms at the sides, feet together. Just like the other, this man had been beheaded and castrated. Unlike the other, it looked as if the man had been dead for a much longer time. He mentioned it, and May nodded. "Both killed somewhere else, at different times. Which means the killer kept this one around for a while."

Nuri suppressed a shudder and asked, "You ever see a body decompose like this?"

The body did seem oddly discolored, reddish, as if severely sunburned. The skin had become almost leathery. "Maybe some sort of preservative chemical," May said, "so he could keep the body longer."

Nuri took a step back and felt something crunch under his foot. He jerked, afraid he had stepped on some part of the body. He lifted his foot and breathed a sigh of relief.

"What is it?" May asked.

"Nothing, just a dead sparrow." He kicked the thing, and its wings splayed like a fallen angel's.

"Watch it," May said, "We want to be careful we don't miss any evidence—"

May was interrupted when one of the railroad police called out, "I've found a head!"

The valley was called Kingsbury Run, and it cut through the east side of Cleveland like a knife scar between downtown and East Fifty-Fifth. It held the tracks that carried the Shaker Rapid lines, and all the passenger trains that passed through the Union Terminal, from the Chesapeake and Ohio to the Nickel Plate. At night it was an unlit haven for those transients with enough fortitude to risk the darkness and dangers of jumping a moving freight car in the gloom. During the day it was populated by strays, children, and dogs.

After five-thirty on September 23, 1935, a new population came to Kingsbury Run. Dozens of Cleveland police, detectives, and railroad police, began walking the tracks to discover anything related to the two headless bodies. The unrealized fear was that another corpse might turn up; the unrealized hope was that they might find some clue to the identity of the murderer.

They found the rest of the murdered men, the heads buried close to the bodies, and the genitalia had been tossed casually to the side, as if an afterthought by the murderer.

By evening, the police search up and down the Run had attracted an endless crowd of spectators lining the crest overlooking the murder scene. The ritual of the murder investigation was observed as intently as the procession of Catholic faith had been the night before.

Stefan Ryzard was one of the detectives who were not converging on Kingsbury Run. He had other business.

He stood leaning against the wall of an interview room while, sitting, handcuffed in a chair, was a man named Larry Alessandro. On the side of Larry's head was a white bandage covering his ear, the center darkened slightly with blood.

"You ain't got no right to hold me here!" he said for the dozenth time or so. Stefan simply nodded and said, "So you've told me. But you are here, Mr. Alessandro, so why don't you just tell me what happened."

"Look, the nigger bastard attacked me, look!" He jerked his hands and ended up shrugging his shoulder at the bandage on the side of his head.

"The man's dead, Mr. Alessandro. Show him some respect."

Larry Alessandro spat at Stefan's feet. "I ain't got to show respect for no nigger living or dead."

Stefan looked at the spot of moisture on the floor. "Spitting in public is a misdemeanor, Mr. Alessandro." He looked up and said, "It spreads TB."

Larry opened his mouth and Stefan said, "Shut that trap for a moment and let me explain something to you. We have a dead body, and as long as I have someone to hang for it, all the paperwork comes out nice and tidy. I like nice and tidy paperwork."

"But—"

"You have to give me a reason not to shove you into a hole where everyone can forget your ugly mug ever existed." Stefan walked up and leaned over Larry and said, "Like what happened. Tell me."

"He attacked me—"

"You keep saying that. I want details, Larry. I want your life story from the point you first saw this man."

"Goddamn it," Larry muttered. "You want to know what happened? I'll tell you what the fuck happened. Me and a bunch of other guys were minding our own business down in the flats. Under the bridge, passing the bottle around, and something starts screaming at us—"

"Who was screaming?"

Larry ignored the question. He had started the story, and the words were tumbling out. "It was the worst noise I'd ever heard. The sound of an animal in pain, like a dog that'd had its back broke. But you could tell a man was making the sound. Didn't end, it just kept getting closer and closer. Before we could tell what direction that sound was coming from, this blood-soaked jig jumps out of the darkness at me."

"He was already covered with blood?"

"He screamed something about the devil in me, or the devil in him. How he had to get it out. Then he proceeds to bite my fucking ear off. That boy just wasn't right in the head. The others pushed him off of me, and if you saw the way he was looking at all of us, you'd have started picking up pipes and bricks yourself. But we never touched him. We circled around each other, none of us wanted close to the bastard, the way he looked."

Stefan looked at Larry and decided he believed him. What he said matched the scene he had come upon last night, and it matched up with what the doctor had said about the death of his John Doe.

"Had you ever seen this man before last night?"

"No."

"Where did he come from, what direction?"

"What the fuck does that matter?"

"It matters to me, and I think that's all you have to worry about right now."

Larry shook his head and shrugged. "From the south I think, back toward where the tracks feed into the tower."

Stefan went over the story a few more times with Larry, then he had an ambulance come to the Central Station and pick him up. Larry wasn't too enthusiastic about going. He was even less enthusiastic when Stefan told him that the man who had bitten him had been deathly sick. But Stefan managed to package him for the trip to St. Vincent's despite his objections. Even if what John Doe had wasn't something as contagious as TB, Larry needed his ear fixed.

Stefan found himself hoping it was TB, even though he'd been exposed to all that blood. TB or some other unexceptional, earthly sickness. John Doe's pronouncements about the Devil made Stefan uneasy.

When he went back up to his desk, he saw Nuri Lapidos there, talking on the phone.

"I thought you went home already—"

Nuri held up a hand and spoke into the phone, "Yes. Yes. I'm sorry, honey. Something came up, on the trip home in fact. Well, it's sort of gruesome. These two bodies—okay, I won't tell you any more." Nuri looked up at Stefan and shrugged. "Maybe another time. Love you, too, bye." Nuri hung up the phone, and looked up at Stefan. "I *did* start home. Missed a date, too."

Stefan looked and saw that Nuri's normally impeccable suit was splattered with mud, and his trouser legs were covered with burrs. "Where've you been?"

"I've had a thorough introduction to a new part of town, Kingsbury Run, searching for body parts."

"What?"

"You haven't heard? I thought the story'd be all over the station by now."

"I've been busy," Stefan said, "questioning a witness about a death last night."

"Well, we have two pretty mysterious deaths down by

the railroad tracks. Two men, heads and privates cut off, the bodies cleaned of blood and laid out neatly as you please by the tracks."

"Lord save us." Stefan sat down at his desk.

"The coroner has the bodies now." Nuri shook his head and pulled a package of cigarettes out of his pocket. He offered one to Stefan.

Stefan shook his head, and Nuri took out a cigarette for himself. He lit it, and took a deep drag. "Why do that to someone?" Nuri muttered, more to himself than to Stefan. "Why mutilate a corpse?"

"There is evil in the world." Stefan looked down at his desk. There was a note slipped in at the corner of his blotter. Stefan pulled it out.

"Yes, I know," Nuri said. "But evil usually has some rationale behind it. Someone has a reason."

Stefan nodded, reading the note. There'd been a phone message for him while he was questioning Alessandro. It took him a second to place the name, "Sean McCutcheon." Fatigue had eroded some of his memory. Then it came to him, the youngish doctor last night, Errol Flynn mustache. It hadn't registered at first because the note omitted the "Doctor." The note was vague, just a name and phone number. Stefan wondered if it meant that Doctor McCutcheon had identified the cause of death.

Nuri was still talking, watching the smoke collect above his head. "It's the work of a crazy man. That's the obvious conclusion."

Stefan picked up the phone and started dialing. "You don't think it is?"

Nuri shook his head. "When it comes down to it, it ain't my case. It's just that I have an eerie feeling. There was a methodical, almost ritualistic feeling to the scene, like it was some sort of warning."

The phone started ringing, and after a few moments Stefan heard a muffled, "Hello?"

"Doctor McCutcheon?" Stefan said.

There was a mumble and a rustling on the other end, and Stefan could picture the doctor crawling out of bed. What time was it anyway?

After a few minutes the doctor spoke, "Yes, yes. Detective Ryzard?"

"Yes." Obviously he'd been expecting the call. "I'm sorry if I woke you up."

"No matter. Just came off of a long shift, that's all." He yawned, "But I thought you should know what happened."

Something in the way the doctor phrased that made Stefan uneasy. It must have shown on his face because Nuri sat up and looked at him. "What's the matter?"

Stefan waited a few moments before he said, "What happened, Doctor?"

"The man you brought in last night. His body is gone."

There was a minute or so of silence before the doctor said, "Detective? Are you still there?"

"Yes," Stefan took a few more moments to let the words sink in. "What do you mean *gone?*"

"The body's gone missing. Somehow the hospital lost it."

"How do you *lose* a body?"

Nuri leaned over and asked, "Who lost a body?"

"I'm as mad as you are," Doctor McCutcheon said. "I don't know. But the fact is, the body is gone. The guard down in the morgue swears that someone from the coroner's office came by with all the right paperwork and signed out the cadaver. But the coroner's office says they didn't, and no one can find the paperwork."

"So someone stole it?" Stefan asked. *Who would* steal *a body?*

"Someone *stole* a body?" Nuri asked, his voice taking on a layer of incredulity.

"I don't know," the doctor said. "Who knows if the guard's telling the truth? He's lying about the paperwork; he could be trying to cover up some sort of administrative incompetence. The hospital's put him on leave until they straighten this out."

"What's the guard's name?" Stefan asked.

"Mullen, Edward Mullen. You can contact him through the hospital if you need to." The doctor yawned. "That's all I have for you. Sorry about the mess up."

"Thank you, Doctor." Stefan slowly hung up the telephone.

5

Stefan Ryzard sat in the upper deck of Municipal Stadium, among a crowd of 150,000 people, trying not to think of death or Edward Mullen. The crowd was a strange mix, men in suits and hats next to men in overalls, young women in flowery hats, old women with beaded veils and black dresses. It was a random mix of everyone in the city, everyone linked only by the common gestures, the common responses, standing and sitting as one.

Below him, lit by electric arcs, sat the altar, tiny with distance.

The words of the mass echoed throughout the stadium, the priest's Latin distorted by the public address system. Midnight mass was supposed to be the culminating religious event of the Seventh National Eucharist Congress.

Stefan had wanted to reaffirm part of his crumbling faith. He had thought of going to St. John's, seeing his old pastor, Piotr Gerwazek, but he had never managed it. He hadn't been to a mass since Mary's funeral, and it had been so long now that he was afraid to see people he knew, afraid of the questions that Father Gerwazek might ask.

When he heard of the great mass here, he thought he might slip back into his faith anonymously, in the midst of a crowd of strangers. Somehow it didn't work like that.

He sat with thousands of people, here for the mass, and couldn't help thinking of them as spectators rather than worshipers. The setting was dissonant, too. This wasn't God's house, at least not the God to whom the wine below was being raised. The religion practiced here had Mel Harder pitching, and Earl Averill playing center field.

He sat and watched the ceremony, trying and failing to

gain any sort of connection with what was going on down on the field. The effort left him feeling, more than ever, that God had walked away from him, and from everything around him.

He left before they began communion.

Absent the thronging crowd, the parking lot was desolate. As Stefan walked away, he could still hear the words of God, amplified and reechoing, with no one out here to listen.

Stefan got into his blue Ford V-8, shutting the door on the sound. He drove slowly, as if he were sneaking away.

Almost inevitably his thoughts turned to death. The bodies that had been found in Kingsbury Run had distracted the city from thoughts of faith. The day the Congress had opened, people talked about how close the city had seemed to come toward God. It had taken a mere twenty-four hours for the mood to shift. The *Plain Dealer* was calling it the most bizarre double murder in Cleveland's history.

It was almost as if the bodies had been left as a warning against the arrogance of believing oneself so close to God.

Stefan turned east, away from home. He wasn't quite ready to face his empty apartment yet. His thoughts were too dark. He wove through the east side of downtown, passing the nightclubs and the lights of Short Vincent. He thought of stopping, but he didn't. Someone would recognize him, and because he was a cop, they would ask him about the murders in the Run.

He had no answers for them.

And no one cares about the man who died in the back of my car.

It was an evil irony that the man he had taken to the hospital had died the same evening as the headless men in the Run. The more spectacular murders had stolen any eulogy that the anonymous man might have had. Despite the disappearance of the body, it wasn't even an official police investigation. He was a nameless colored tramp—none thought him worth the trouble.

Even Edward Mullen the guard that had lost the corpse, seemed incredulous that Stefan was making such a fuss about the missing corpse. Stefan had taken him to the Central Station, and questioned him, and got nothing more than the repeated story that the coroner's office had picked the body up. In the end, he'd gotten nowhere and had let the man go.

Even so, Stefan had felt something dark had touched the man, something he was hiding. But it wasn't something Stefan could put a finger on, much less prove.

It was another fragment of evil that Stefan couldn't do anything about. Another empty case that would go nowhere. Another mystery ignored and filed away. Another victim who would be forever mute—

Almost out of some sense of predestination, Stefan found himself driving toward the dead end of East Forty-Ninth. Up ahead, beyond the end of the street, was the gully of Kingsbury Run.

He parked the car and stepped out into the cool night air.

He stepped over the barrier at the end of the street and began walking along the top of the bluffs on the southern side of the run. After a while he stopped. He stood on top of a hill overlooking the bottom of the Run, sixty feet or so below him. The scene below was inky black, except for where a lone railroad signal tower cast an eerie glow around the tracks below him.

Stefan had lived in Cleveland all his life, but he'd never known that this plot of ground overlooking the waste of Kingsbury Run was worthy of a name. However, in the last three days, Jackass Hill had attained a measure of fame. The bodies had been uncovered just below where he stood, discovered by a pair of teenage boys playing in the rugged terrain.

Stefan stood there a long time, letting thoughts of futility drain from him. He stared into the impenetrable darkness, as if there were some insight to be found there, some relief. If he had been younger, he might have prayed.

Clouds above him erased every feature of the sky, the only light in heaven the reflection of the city's electric glow.

A voice emerged from the darkness. "Troubled, aren't you?"

The sudden break of the stillness startled Stefan. He whirled upon the voice, his hand darting toward the holster at his shoulder. "Who's there?" he called out. His voice, at least, was firm, not revealing his sudden startlement.

A figure stepped from the shadow of a twisted elm, so

close that Stefan found it unbelievable that the man could have approached him without being heard.

"A fellow wanderer in the darkness," the man said, spreading his hands. "Nothing more."

In the distance a train whistle screamed into the night.

Seeing the man, Stefan stopped reaching for his holster and changed the movement of his hand into a brushing of his jacket. "This isn't the safest place to wander," Stefan said. At first, Stefan thought the man might be a tramp, here to catch a ride on the passing freight. But there was something in the man's manner that seemed to run counter to that impression.

It wasn't his clothes. He had the overalls of a laborer, and a dark porkpie set far back on his brow. But there was something in his bearing that set him apart from any of the unemployed army that the times had loosed upon the city. Hard times had beaten itself into the posture of such men, but the man facing him had a confident stance that bordered on arrogance.

"Then why do you wander here?" the man asked him. He spoke with a sly smile that Stefan didn't trust. It was a smile that changed into something else by the time it reached his eyes, eyes that were cold, remote, nearly colorless in the dimness.

"Unease," Stefan said, more of an answer than the stranger merited. He turned around, finding the stranger's gaze uncomfortable.

The man placed his hands in his pockets and stepped up next to Stefan. "This is an uneasy place."

Below them, the sound of a train grew louder, a screech and a roar in the darkness. Its light began to wash the eastern distance, preceding it.

Stefan doubted many tramps would try and hop this train here. This *was* an uneasy place now. "What do you know of what happened here?"

"Murder," the man said. "Murder most foul, as in the best it is, but this most foul, strange, and unnatural."

Stefan looked across at the man.

He shook his head, "I was an actor once, a long time ago. Ah, that things have come to this."

"What things?" Stefan asked. He had a feeling that he

had run across someone who knew about the murders. Instinct tensed him, readying him for a fight, or a chase.

The train's whistle screamed again, close enough that Stefan could hear motion in the sound. He turned to face his companion again, memorizing the profile as the other spoke.

"Things I cannot discuss with you." There was an ironic smile on the man's face. As the train shuddered by below them, its lamps washed them in a white light. For a moment Stefan had a complete unobscured view of his companion.

His brows, and small pointed beard were black, like holes cut into his face. His mustache was fading to gray at the sides. His flesh was a perfect, even white, no marks, no scars, not even a shadow of a beard beyond the edges of his goatee. His eyes were a deep gray.

"If you know anything about the murders, I think you should tell me." Stefan had to raise his voice above the sound of the train passing below them. Boxcar after boxcar rolled by, each of them mute and remote.

The man was laughing, a soft chuckle that somehow cut through the rumble of the passing train. "So typical of the police, so little subtlety, so little heed of the consequences the truth might bring."

"If you . . ." Stefan's words stopped in his throat when he realized that he had not told this man he was a detective. His hand began reaching for his gun again. The train below seemed to have found the rhythm of his heart, the rachet of the rails marking the time of his pulse. "You'd better explain yourself, or we're going to take a trip to the station."

Something akin to panic gripped Stefan. He felt sweat in the small of his back, and he tasted fear, like blood, in the back of his throat. There was no accounting for it; the man he faced had made no threatening moves.

The man turned to Stefan as the whistle screamed again.

Stefan's hand found the butt of his gun and froze there, the metal ice-cold against his sweating palm.

"What would you do if you knew? What could you do?" He took a step forward, and Stefan tried to draw his gun. "The truth would destroy you." He took another step, and Stefan was paralyzed. The fear fed upon itself, so unnatural that the fear itself became a fuel for panic. The man placed a finger upon Stefan's lips. "Shush, my dear policeman."

It may have been the touch, or it might have been that the fear—like a dike—could only hold back so much potential action before it broke. In either event, Stefan's paralysis broke, and he stumbled backward, drawing his gun and leveling it at the man before him.

"Don't you move!" Stefan called out, little caring that the strains of fear cracked his voice.

The man shook his head. "Oh, dear me." He lowered his finger, which had been left in midair. "You would be a strong-willed one, wouldn't you?"

"Keep your hands in view," Stefan shouted over the noise of the passing train.

The man spread his hands and said, "Now that you have me, what will you do with me?"

"Who are you?"

"I could tell you anything, so call me Iago."

Stefan kept backing away from the man, Iago, and tried to keep his gun arm steady. "What do you have to do with the murders?"

"Your imagination fails you if that is all you can think to ask." Iago's hands still were spread before him, but his posture, his *presence,* seemed threatening. "The deaths we speak of break a Covenant that I may not violate by telling you any of me or mine. But I can tell you that these are not the first or last, a thing you already know, Stefan Ryzard."

"How do you know my name?"

"It is written in the air before you," Iago said. "Mark me well, policeman. Hell is coming. Find Andrassy's whore; she is not yet bound to my vows."

Stefan shook his head. The panic seemed to recede, and his judgment was returning. "Come on," he waved the barrel of the gun slightly, back in the direction the car was parked. "I'm taking you down to the station, you can talk there all you like."

The train still passed below them, boxcar after boxcar—

Iago lowered his hands and said, "I am afraid you aren't going to do that." He moved too swiftly for Stefan to credit. One moment he was standing immobile before him, the next he had leaped out over the hillside.

Stefan followed his motion with the gun, yelling, "Stop or I'll shoot!" A wild bullet chased his words, aimed nowhere near Iago, who had already landed at the foot of the hillside where the bodies had been found. Stefan was scrambling down the dark hillside before the gunshot's echoes had been swallowed by the train's passage.

Scrub tore at his legs as Stefan struggled to keep upright in the mad scramble down the hillside. He could barely watch his footing, much less the retreating Iago.

When he reached the foot of the hill, he looked along the moving body of the train. Iago was ahead of him, a hundred yards away or more, running alongside the train, matching its speed.

Stefan started running after him.

"Stop!" he yelled again. This time, his shot was well enough placed. Iago fell next to the tracks with the impact. Stefan halved the distance between them as the last car passed him on the tracks.

The moment that car had passed Stefan, Iago got up. Surprise made Stefan fire two more shots, and despite the distance now quartered between them, neither had any effect on Iago.

Iago ran, pacing the train, and leaped at the second-to-last car. By then the train had outdistanced Stefan, making it impossible for him to follow. Stefan slowed until he reached the spot where Iago had fallen. The train was already small in the distance, only visible by its lights. The sound of its passage faded into the night.

"He timed it just right," Stefan muttered. "Probably never was hit."

He shook his head. The speed of Iago's movement still seemed incredible, but less so in retrospect. Stefan felt more and more that it was himself who wasn't acting up to par.

He turned to walk back to the hill, and his car, when he stepped on something next to the tracks. He had to crouch down to see what it was in the darkness.

It was Iago's porkpie hat.

Next to it, a small pool of blood stained the gravel.

Stefan picked up the hat and turned to face where the train had gone. He could still hear it in the distance.

6

Monday, September 30

The auction rooms of Adrian H. Muller & Son was known as the securities graveyard. It was here that creditors tried to dispose of the assets of their defaulted debtors. It was where old corporations went to die.

It was here that J. P. Morgan & Company would put on the block the life's work of the Van Sweringens. At 3:30 PM, the collected assets of the Van Sweringen railroad empire would cease to exist as an entity unto itself. By five it would have transformed into something else.

Oris Van Sweringen straightened his tie in the mirror and prayed that it wouldn't be Midamerica that it transformed into. It was a sick thought, abandoning the careful structure that he and his brother had put together. Abandoning Midamerica was one of the hardest things that he had ever done. It had to be done, though. He had to get himself, his brother, and their railroads away from the shadowy Dietrich. The man wasn't to be trusted; even if his money had helped keep the Van Sweringens afloat through the depths of financial crisis, it was at a cost he doubted they could pay any longer. . . .

J.D. Rockefeller might be, in his way, as much a demon as Dietrich, but Oris knew the costs of dealing with the old oil man—and he doubted they were nearly as dear as the costs of dealing with Dietrich.

Even though all the arrangements were at the last minute. Even though he was walking into the auction only with an oral agreement that the Rockefeller interests would outbid Midamerica, he should have had some measure of confidence. He and Mantis had worked financial miracles on less firm a footing.

Somehow, though, the confidence that had been with him—*them,* both him and Mantis; lord, how he wished his brother was here with him—that confidence had abandoned him.

The Wall Street Journal was positive that Midamerica would win the day. In their eyes that meant that the Van Sweringens would again be in control of their empire. Oris had read the article several times. "They have weathered earlier storms," it said, "and had come through them seemingly none the worse off."

The praise and confidence of the *Journal* would have cheered him if it wasn't for the fact that Midamerica had become a sham, a puppet where it wasn't the Van Sweringens, but Dietrich, who was pulling the strings. The papers would have his name on them, but Oris knew who would triumph if Midamerica won the day. It wouldn't be them.

He paced the hotel room, and his mind kept fixating on the article as if it were some premonition of doom. It went beyond his usual unease about the press.

It was the word, "seemingly."

As if the *Journal* knew of the secret deals that had formed the unseen heart of what was to be Midamerica. As if it knew about a devil calling himself Eric Dietrich. As if the *Journal* knew that their survival would be only appearance.

As he paced the hotel room, waiting to depart for the auction, the phone rang.

Oris turned on the black device as if it were a viper coiled to strike him. He let it ring twice more before he was able to move and pick up the receiver. He knew who it was, could *feel* who it was, even before the connection was made.

Oris held the receiver to his ear a long time before he said anything. The line was unearthly silent, no sound, no breathing, only the static hum of the phone wires nearly too quiet to notice. Oris was tempted to hang up, at the very least let the other be the first to speak. To do either would be a meaningless victory, something that wouldn't mean anything, even to his own self-respect. His self-image was too much constructed around the gentlemanly forms. Rudeness was as foreign to him as a desire for fame.

He finally said, "Hello, this is Mr. Van Sweringen."

It was with a dull dread that he finally heard Mr. Dietrich's voice on the other end of the line. "Good day to you, Oris." Oris sank inwardly at the familiarity. It made him feel unclean.

"What can I do for you, Mr. Dietrich?"

"I have just concluded some business, and I thought you would be relieved to know that your representative—excuse me, *Midamerica's* representative—arrived safely."

Oris gripped the phone and realized that the receiver was shaking in his ear. "Why would I have doubted it?" *Why does he play with me like this. Midamerica is* his *now.*

"Oh, I suspect that you might have had some concern over Colonel Ayres' safety. I made a point of meeting his train, and I assure you that he is unharmed."

Oris felt his blood go to ice. What kind of devil was it that he was dealing with? He had never felt such an absolute implication of violence, even when he saw union agitators. Until he had met Dietrich, he had thought die-hard unionists were the most dangerous men he had ever seen.

"I also hear that your brother's health is stable."

"Thank you, Mr. Dietrich," Oris said quickly and slammed the phone down on its cradle. The mention of his brother had so chilled him that it felt as if the perspiration on his brow would freeze his skin down to the bone.

Does he know?

The unbidden question ran through Oris' head and would not leave. There was no way that Dietrich could know. The only people who had any inkling of Oris' renegotiation to have the Rockefellers shut out Midamerica was him, Mantis, John D. Rockefeller, and the Rockefeller lawyer. Everyone else should believe, with *The Wall Street Journal* that the Vans had thrown their lot in with Midamerica.

It was barely seconds before the phone rang again. Oris let it ring a half-dozen times before he dared touch it again. When he picked it up, the voice on the other end was, thankfully, not Dietrich's.

"Mr. Van Sweringen? Your car has arrived downstairs."

"Thank you," he said, hanging up.

Oris arrived at the offices of Adrian H. Muller & Son at around three, and the dingy yellow rooms were already filled with people. Of the mass of humanity, perhaps four-hundred strong, Oris could only identify a few others that mattered.

He saw the tall figure of George M. Whitney, the partner from J. P. Morgan. He wasn't here to bid, and he looked as if this whole transaction were beneath his notice, and that he wished to be elsewhere. The person who was actually here to bid for the Morgan interests was a tense look-ing lawyer from Davis, Polk, Wardwell—Oris felt slightly embarrassed when he realized he couldn't remember the list of names that went with the practice. Not that it mat-tered. The lawyer wasn't important for himself; he was important because he was the voice of the Morgan inter-ests, the interests that forced this auction.

If things went as originally planned, that lawyer would make a single prophylactic bid, and allow Midamerica's representative, Colonel Ayres, to outbid and walk away with the lot. Oris walked up and talked to the Colonel for a few moments, but his mind was far away. He was watch-ing the room for the Rockefellers' lawyer.

The Rockefellers were going to outbid Ayres, and it would be enough of a surprise to generate the headlines that Oris detested. The last-minute plan was calculated to drive the price up just enough that the resources at Ayers' command wouldn't be able to outbid it. Oris' only worry at this point was that Dietrich himself might arrive to make a bid—Dietrich might be able to outbid everyone directly. Oris had no idea of the funds at Dietrich's command, but he knew they were considerable.

Oris slipped into an out-of-the way corner before the auction began, without seeing any sign of Dietrich or the Rockefellers. Dietrich's absence did little to calm Oris, be-cause occasionally his gaze would light on the Morgan law-yer. The man appeared so nervous that Oris suspected he had been talking to Dietrich.

At 3:30 the room was packed. In Oris' view, it was packed with people who had no business being here. It felt as if the crowd of strangers were invading something deeply personal. He put on his reading glasses and stared at some legal papers, but he was really staring through the page.

The auctioneer cleared his throat, silenced the room, and began reading what was for sale: Allegheny Corporation common stock; Cleveland Railway Company common stock; Cleveland Terminals Building Company second mortgage bonds; Higbee Company common stock. . . . It went on and on and on; it seemed forever to Oris. It felt as painful and degrading as having a public viewing of some intimate surgery.

The auctioneer rattled off numbers of common and preferred stock, gave values for notes and bonds in the millions of dollars, all in an antiseptic monotone that reminded Oris of Mr. Dietrich's dead voice. Alphabetically, he came to the most painful issues last.

122,000 shares of Van Sweringen Company common stock, 1.2 million shares Van Sweringen Corporation common stock—those, with the associated notes, made Oris' own name a repeated hammer blow into his skull. Six times the words "Van Sweringen" passed the auctioneer's lips, and each time felt like a violation.

Then came the bids.

The first bid came from the nervous Morgan lawyer. Somewhat shakily he called out, "Two million, eight hundred and two thousand, one hundred and one."

Colonel Ayers responded immediately to the auctioneer's call for higher bids. On behalf of Midamerica he placed a bid for two million, eight hundred and three thousand dollars.

Oris waited for the Rockefeller bid for three million.

It didn't come.

"Going once . . . Going twice . . ."

Oris stood up, the papers slipping through his fingers. Where were the Rockefellers? Where was the bid?

"Last call . . ."

He couldn't breathe while the auctioneer spoke. It was as if the universe was in abeyance, waiting.

But there were no other bids. Midamerica had won the auction.

Later, when crowds of people he didn't really know pressed too close to congratulate him, he began feeling as if he had crossed an impassable threshold. He was now tied to Dietrich, and there was nothing left for him to do but shake hands on Midamerica's behalf.

Oris was never able to talk to J. D. Rockefeller again. The man refused to talk to him, and his intermediaries refused to admit that there had ever been any deal between the Vans and the Rockefellers over the auction.

The New York Times would later call it the greatest auction of securities in Wall Street history, and an object lesson in what happens to such pyramidal financial empires. The *Plain Dealer* saw it as a net gain for Cleveland, that with the Van Sweringens retaining control, they would continue to bring the kind of economic development to Cleveland that they had in the past.

After the auction results were final, neither brother had more than fourteen months to live.

7

Stefan stood across the desk from Detective Inspector Cody, head of the Detective Bureau, and said, "I don't believe you're doing this to me."

Cody shook his head and looked over his glasses at Stefan. "It's not like you're being suspended. You aren't even being reprimanded."

"That's not what this feels like."

Cody took a smoldering cigar out of an ashtray on his desk and used it to point at Stefan. "I really don't care how it feels. You've been working nonstop almost since you joined the Homicide Squad, and I'm not the only one who thinks your judgment is starting to suffer."

"This is about the tramp, isn't it?"

Cody sighed and leaned back in his chair to the protest of springs and old wood. He puffed on the cigar and said finally, "Do you have to ask that?"

"I didn't do anything . . ."

Cody held up his hand, cigar clamped between two fingers. "This is just a vacation, Stefan. A rest. Take it."

"I don't need—"

"You don't? You're a good cop. Until recently you've had great instincts about what to pursue and what to leave alone. Now you're using up police time on a missing body that rightfully isn't even in the jurisdiction of the Homicide Squad. You're chasing suspects off-duty when you're one of a few cops that haven't had a part in the Kingsbury Run business. It's like you've started looking for trouble in your spare time. We don't need this. Starting Friday, you have a month off. Find a woman, have some fun."

"What about what he said, he knew Andrassy?"

"Stefan, have faith in the rest of the force. They have your report on this 'Iago.' What we *don't* need is yet another person working on one double murder."

Stefan nodded slowly.

"Starting Friday, you have four weeks off. Enjoy it."

Stefan left Inspector Cody's office, making an effort not to slam the door on the way out.

He stopped at his desk and picked up a stack of files. Nuri looked up just in time to see the pile of paperwork land in front of him.

"Hey, what are you doing?"

"Knock yourself out," Stefan said. "I'm going out for a drink." He picked up his hat and jacket from next to his desk and said, "See you in November."

"What?" Nuri asked.

Stefan didn't answer him as he left.

It was going to be a cold winter. Florence Polillo could feel it in the draft rattling the windows of her little flat. She sat in a rickety chair by the window and tried to remember what it was like to feel warm. Occasionally she would drink from the bottle she rested between her knees, but it didn't help.

She felt cold, and very, very old.

Eddie was dead.

The thought kept tumbling through her head, unwanted but irresistible. How could she go on with it all now . . . ?

She stood with the slow deliberateness of someone used to her own drunkenness. She rested the bottle on the table next to the paper. The story in the *Press* was about the identity of one of the decapitated bodies they had found in Kingsbury Run. One of them had been Edward Andrassy. The police had identified him by his fingerprints.

Eddie.

Of all the evil things to come home to after her mother's funeral. To find out that not only had Eddie been killed, but that someone had severed his head. Flo rubbed her own neck thinking, *That's how you kill* them. . . .

Flo tried to chide herself for caring. How many other men had left her for one reason or another? Men left her every goddamn night.

Somehow Eddie was different. Eddie was the only one

of the whole damned group that seemed to care beyond himself. Eddie had been the only one to question what was going on. He wanted out of this world as much as any of them. But he shared with Flo some questions about the cost, and more courage to voice them.

Flo wondered if that was what got him killed. She felt colder than ever.

The shades were drawn, but the sunset cut a molten line across the wall opposite the window. The line fell across the shelf holding her dolls. She turned to them and felt her eyes moisten. They stared back with eyes glassy and dead.

Flo loved the dolls. They were the one thing that followed her everywhere she moved. They were the only children she would ever have. But right now it seemed as if she shared her room with a dozen tiny corpses.

She sat at the table and watched the blind-carved sunlight cut molten-red stripes across the room. Everything was gray except the light. The room was colorless, emotionless, like every other room she'd rented by herself. She spent her life moving from place to place, wallowing in the ugliness. She liked to think that someday she would find someone or something that would make it better, lift her away from this endless numb grayness.

Melchior promised an escape from this dead world, and for a while she had believed him. But the grays were still gray, and the only promise of color was the sunlight washing her walls with the tint of blood.

If it was all true, she would even lose that, the smoky-red sunlight that sometimes refused to warm her. She would be trading the sun for what might be grayness without end.

The sunlight faded, plunging her room into darkness. She lifted the bottle to her lips with a shaking hand, and another ice-cold hand touched her wrist. She froze at the touch, unable to move.

"Hello, Florence," the familiar whispery voice said from behind her. "You were missed." The cold hand traveled up her arm, and the only movement that Flo was capable of was an involuntary shudder.

She opened her mouth to explain, but fear and liquor choked off her words leaving her stuttering, ". . . I . . . I . . . I . . ."

Another hand found her free hand, placing her in a cold embrace from behind. So cold, but in two places it was becoming very warm. Not the places a man usually became warm. His wrists, where they touched her skin, began pulsing with a warmth that throbbed deep within the vein.

Her visitor kept talking. "I know where you were, Florence. Your landlady, Mrs. Ford, drove you to Pierpont for your mother's funeral."

"H-h-how?" His wrists were like brands on her skin. A warm sensation spread beneath her skin, a feeling like the liquor, or like the first brush of sex before it became disappointing.

Lips brushed the back of her neck like the touch of a flame. She shuddered again and squeezed her legs together. "You are all a part of me now," he said. "Never forget that." His teeth lightly bit the back of her neck, drawing blood. A violent shudder shook her, and the bottle slipped out of her fingers.

She was no longer cold.

"I feel what any of you do." He licked the trickle of blood from her neck. "That was why Andrassy had to die with my enemy."

Flo was breathing hard now. Her body was filled with the warmth, the hunger, the need. Her world wasn't gray any longer, it was burning with reds and yellows. It was hard for her to speak. She wanted it so badly. But she managed to ask, "Why Eddie? Why that way?" Every word hung upon a shuddering breath.

"There are others like me, my enemies. Eddie betrayed me to them." He drew his tongue across the back of her neck. "All of you are too close to coming over to me now. A normal death might produce a crippled thrall. He had to die like one of us."

Flo was beyond speech now. She could smell the pulsing warmth in his wrists, his heart beating so slow it was agony. He released her hand and turned his wrist toward her. It felt like the sun shining on her face. He raised it to just below her mouth.

"You are leaving your world. Sever what ties you have left to it. When you join me, nothing and no one will follow you where you go." Below her, the skin slit itself along the vein. The long wound wept blood that seemed to glow with

an inner light. It was impossible to refuse, even had she
wanted to.

What was Eddie compared to this?

Flo descended on the offered arm and fed.

8

Stefan was at home, staring at a newspaper, but not really reading it, when the phone rang. He let it go a few times before he answered it. He was frustrated and didn't really want to talk to anybody.

When he answered the phone, it was Nuri's voice on the other end. "Hello, Stefan?"

"Yeah, what is it, Nuri?"

"I just called to see how you're doing."

Stefan shook his head. "I appreciate the concern, but how do you think I'm doing?"

"The vacation's got you out of joint, doesn't it?"

Stefan sighed into the receiver. "I just need to figure out what to do with myself."

"What are you going to do when you retire?"

"Let's change the subject. Are you calling from work? Is there a problem?"

"Yes," Nuri said. "It's not a problem, just something I thought you'd like to know."

"What?"

"Have you been following the Kingsbury Run murders?"

"I'm on vacation, remember?"

Nuri chuckled a little. "Well it's not like I'm doing any real investigating, but they need loads of people to tote that barge and lift that bale. They have me going through missing persons' records."

"So?"

"I'm looking at people who disappeared on or before September twenty-third, and while I've yet to find a match for our headless body, I did find someone you might be interested in."

Nuri paused and Stefan said, "Come on, spit it out."

"Apparently a colored woman lost her husband on September twenty-second, after a fight, last seen wearing overalls and walking in the direction of the railroad tracks around dusk."

Nuri was right, Stefan was interested. "Where, what tracks?"

"Would you believe East Forty-Ninth?"

"The Run?"

"The Run."

Stefan shook his head, "That has got to be the man I found—"

"Way ahead of you," Nuri said, "Get a piece of paper, I have her address."

Stefan quickly copied the name "Wilma Fairfax" and an address not too far away from the Run.

"If you're lucky," Nuri said, "the wife has a photograph of him, and you can put that case to bed."

"Thanks," Stefan said, shaking his head. He felt the return of some of the unease he'd felt when talking to Iago. Mrs. Fairfax's husband had been heading toward the Run at dusk. Hours later he'd been bleeding and screaming about the Devil.

Stefan wondered if the man had seen something.

He was quiet long enough for Nuri to ask, "Are you all right?"

Stefan nodded. "Yeah. I'm just wondering how I'm going to explain that the hospital lost her husband's body."

It was getting close on to nine o'clock when Stefan drove his car down the little brick dead-end street that Mr. and Mrs. Fairfax called home. The street was lined with apartment buildings that felt too large for such a narrow street. The bricks glittered, the street lights reflecting over broken glass.

As he rolled to a stop in front of the Fairfaxes' building, he thought he heard gunshots. He tensed and scrambled out of the car before he realized that the shots were from a radio, just someone playing the climax of "Death Valley Days" too loud. He straightened up, feeling somewhat embarrassed as the show drifted into a cigarette commercial.

He chided himself. There was an echo that made the radio program sound deeper, and made the sound a little more realistic, but the error had to be mostly his own nerves. Something about this was making him uneasy, far more uneasy than the typical notification of the next of kin.

The Fairfaxes' building was a tired pile of brick that waved laundry out a few windows, but otherwise drew blinds against the neighborhood it found itself in. He walked up the front steps, trying to ignore the radio in the background. He could feel glass crunching under his feet all the way to the front door.

The halls inside the apartment were dark and narrow. They smelled of cooking and rusty plumbing. From behind the doors he could hear more radios, at a more decent volume, children playing, couples talking or arguing, and he passed one door that closed in the sounds of two people being very passionate with each other.

He stopped in front of the door to the Fairfaxes' rooms, and heard nothing beyond it. His unease increased.

Stefan rang the doorbell, and he could imagine the bell echoing in an empty apartment. There was no response. He rang again and called, "Mrs. Fairfax? Police. I need to talk to you."

Still no response.

He knocked and rang again. "It's about your husband."

With that, the door swung open into a spartan apartment. The person opening the door wasn't Mrs. Fairfax. Stefan stared dumbly at the man for a few minutes. For a few long moments Stefan was convinced he had gotten the address wrong.

But when the man said, "Detective Ryzard, fancy meeting you again," it began to sink in who this man was. Stefan wouldn't need any pictures to identify Mr. Fairfax. He was standing in front of him, the same man he had driven out of the Flats, the same man who had supposedly died at St. Vincent's Charity.

At least now he knew why the hospital had lost the body.

"Mr. Fairfax?" Stefan said. He tried to keep the shock out of his voice, but he couldn't help staring. It was the same man, the same face, clean of blood now. The same hair, graying at the temples. The same crazed eyes that seemed to be looking beyond everything.

"Yes, yes," Fairfax said, nodding. His eyes belied the calmness of his voice, which was almost dead of emotion. His voice was a cold monotone, but his eyes were ablaze with something—anger, fear, hate, lust . . . Stefan couldn't tell, but it fed his own growing unease.

"Can I come in?" Stefan asked. "I think we need to talk."

"Of course," Fairfax said. "I apologize for any trouble we've caused you."

He opened the door on the little two-room apartment. The first thing that struck Stefan was the smell of burning wax. The main room was dim, lit only by a half-dozen candles. It took a moment for Stefan's eyes to adjust to the dimness enough for him to enter.

Fairfax walked over to a threadbare couch and sat next to an old woman that Stefan guessed was Wilma Fairfax. Now that the initial shock of seeing the man was receding, he noticed that the man was dressed differently. He wore a pinstripe suit that was tailored for him. It wasn't the height of luxury, but it was out of line for the apartment he lived in, as well as for the clothes Stefan had seen him in before.

"Mr. Fairfax—" Stefan began.

"You can call me Samson," he said, placing his hand on Wilma Fairfax's. Stefan noticed that she didn't move at the contact. She remained sitting, hands on her knees, staring at her lap. The woman didn't even look up to see the stranger enter her house. The posture worried him.

"Samson then. Just to reassure myself, you are the same Samson Fairfax that your wife reported missing? The same man I drove to St. Vincent's?"

Samson Fairfax nodded, much of his expression outside of his eyes invisible in the candlelight. "Isn't it obvious?" Stefan saw a hint of a smile that instantly vanished.

"Not if you believe the doctor at St. Vincent's."

Samson shrugged. "The doctor made a mistake, that's all. I have a sickness, gives me 'spells,' as my mother used to call them. I woke up on a cart with all these dead people, I got out of there fast."

Stefan nodded. "So why didn't you tell any doctors, or the police, when you recovered?"

"My family was more important. I had to take care of Wilma." Stefan noticed Samson squeeze Wilma's hand. The gesture looked less than tender. "You can understand that, can't you?"

Stefan nodded. Wilma's silence was beginning to disturb him. He turned to address his next question to her. "Why didn't you call us to tell us your husband had returned?"

"Why should she?" Samson said.

"She filed a missing person's report that's still open. That's how I found you."

"Oh," Samson said in a voice that seemed to grow even colder. "I did not know that." He turned to face his wife, and Stefan could almost see her wince. "I'm certain that it was just an oversight on her part. Wasn't it?"

Samson rubbed her knee, and Wilma gave a weak nod. She seemed to shrink in place. Stefan could almost feel what she was shrinking from. There was something present here, a weight behind Samson's eyes, steel in his voice, a hardness in his posture. None of it had been present the last time Stefan had seen the man.

Samson had been the same man who'd been crazed and near death in the Flats, but he wasn't. Stefan couldn't rationalize the feeling, but it felt as if the core of this man had been hollowed out and something ominous had been poured in to fill the empty space.

"Forgive my wife," said the man who looked so much like Samson Fairfax. "When I returned, she was quite ill. I've been doing what I can to tend to her."

He commanded attention away from his wife, as if she were mere furniture. Stefan felt the pull of his words and resented it. It was disquieting to realize that he disliked the man whose life he had saved.

"Are you a religious man, Mr. Fairfax?"

Samson responded with an iron stare. Stefan could feel the offense carried in the gaze. It wasn't the offense of a man whose faith was questioned.

"I'm asking," Stefan continued, "because of some of the things you said to me when I took you to the hospital. You talked about the Devil walking the tracks. You asked me to pray for you—"

"I do not need your prayers, Detective Ryzard."

"I just wondered what you had been referring to—"

"I was referring to nothing. It was deranged babble. There is no devil."

"Perhaps you saw something farther up the tracks. You've heard about the murders that happened in the Run the same night?"

Samson stood. "I think you should go. You are upsetting my wife."

Stephan stood, maintaining an uncomfortable eye contact with Samson. Something made him start to repeat the Twenty-third Psalm in his head. *I shall fear no evil,* Stefan thought as he asked, "Did you see anything on the tracks that night?"

"I was not in my mind then. I remember nothing of that evening."

Thy rod and thy staff, they comfort me. Stefan stared into Samson's eyes. "Then how is it that you know who I am?"

An ugly expression, near to hatred, broke across Samson's face like a wave cresting an insufficient breakwater. In his eyes, Stefan saw a fury that made him start reaching for a gun that wasn't there. He was off-duty. He shouldn't even be here.

I will dwell in the house of the Lord forever.

It was Samson who broke eye contact. "Get out of my house," he said. Stefan backed toward the door. He could hear the threat in Samson's voice, and he was in no position to test it. Maybe if he was here officially, he would have. Not now.

As he backed over the threshold, he could catch a glimpse of Wilma's eyes as she finally lifted her head to regard him. That glance frightened him, a glance from eyes that were as dull as those of a corpse.

"I did pray for you," Stefan whispered as Samson slammed the door on him.

Stefan stood before the door for a long time, but no noise emerged from the apartment beyond. Eventually he turned and walked away. As he left, his mind drifted back to Iago. There was no logic to the connection Stefan began making between the men. Nothing to link them but a similarity of presence.

And the murders in Kingsbury Run.

As Stefan walked to his car, his feet crunched across glass again. This time he looked more closely and saw fragments of a broken mirror.

9

Carlo Pasquale drove. That's all he did. There was more to what was going on, but he was involved in the Mayfield Road Mob through relatives, not through ambition. He had no desire to know. When Papa said drive, he drove, no questions.

As Carlo drove the long black V-12 Lincoln toward the docks, he thought he wasn't quite as ignorant as he wished to be. His passenger was going to a meeting with a man named Dietrich, and from the shotgun his passenger carried, it wasn't to shake hands. Carlo didn't want to know what Dietrich had done to anger Papa.

The Lincoln slid into fog coming off of the lake. The world turned gray outside. Carlo felt that the night had turned very cold, even though he was safely buttoned up in the car.

They were passing warehouses, and his passenger, till then mute, started giving him directions. In the fog, the car traced a maze that Carlo barely felt able to retrace, only from memorizing his passenger's directions, not from any visible landmarks.

Eventually Carlo heard the instruction, "Kill the lights and turn right into the next open bay."

Carlo did as instructed, turning the darkened Lincoln through a doorway already open to accommodate a large panel truck. Carlo pulled the Lincoln up next to the truck. The way into the vast darkened space was blocked by a concrete dock that rose to the level of the Lincoln's hood ornament. Carlo noticed that there weren't any men by the truck.

"Keep the engine running," his passenger said. "Be ready to pull out of here."

Carlo nodded. He knew his job. He wished it was all he knew.

As his passenger slipped out of the car, Carlo wondered if they would take the body or leave it here. He hoped they'd leave it here. He hated it when his passengers would ask him to help lug a newly dead corpse. Carlo wasn't particularly squeamish, but the idea of chauffeuring a dead man made him uneasy.

From the looks of things, it wouldn't come to that. The man with the shotgun would do his job and run. There would be other people here, and they wouldn't have the time to remove Dietrich.

Papa would be appalled at the thought, but Carlo hoped that whatever bodyguards Dietrich had would finish off his passenger as he shotgunned his target. It would make Carlo's job easier, give him a chance to stop for a drink on the way back.

Carlo's passenger was now just a shape slipping over the loading dock into the darkness. As Carlo's eyes adjusted he could see that the warehouse beyond wasn't completely dark. None of the lights inside the giant space were lit, but blue arcs from outside filtered through the fog and dirty windows to cast dim illumination across the floor in front of the loading area.

Carlo watched his passenger melt into the blackness edging the one irregular aisle of light. Then there was no sign of him anymore, his shadow inseparable from the vague mass of crates filling the void beyond Carlo's vision.

Carlo swallowed. His throat was dry, his palms slick against the steering wheel. The vibration from the Lincoln's idle didn't quite mask the fact that he was shaking. He felt his breath catch as if his throat were filled with broken glass.

Christ almighty, what's there to be scared of?

The terror made him want to cut out of there, cut out and keep driving until he'd put at least one state line between himself and this place. His hand even moved to shift the Lincoln into reverse.

Wherever the impulse came from, it came too late. Carlo saw something move in the aisle, and the sight transfixed him. The figure was a man, blond hair and pale skin cutting a shape in the darkness. When Carlo saw the figure walking in the dim blue light, he knew that he was looking at the source of his fear. There was nothing inherent in the sight of the blond man that should terrify Carlo, but Carlo froze, as if any movement at all would draw attention toward him.

Carlo was so focused on the figure of the man that when the shotgun went off, it caught him completely by surprise. A flash briefly tore through the darkness, silhouetting the blond man. The sound echoed through the empty space reverberating around the towering stacks of briefly-illuminated boxes.

On the boxes so briefly lit, Carlo thought he saw lettering in German gothic.

As the pale man collapsed, Carlo could move again. He began shifting, preparing to back out as soon as his passenger made it to the car. Carlo could see him running past the corpse, no tries at stealth now. The assassin's trenchcoat billowed behind him like a cape, and he held the shotgun before him as if warning the darkness out of his way.

Carlo revved the engine. He wanted out of here *now*.

The gunman made it nearly all the way back to the loading dock. Then, in response to something Carlo couldn't see, he turned around, raising his shotgun to bear on something behind him. There was no flash this time, but Carlo heard something snap as the shotgun flew away, thrown tumbling and broken into the darkness.

Carlo slammed the gas, backing the Lincoln out of there as fast as it could accelerate. Before he had made it halfway out of the loading bay, the gunman's back slammed into the windshield. Glass blew into the car, slicing at Carlo's face. The gunman fell all the way into the Lincoln, his head landing in Carlo's lap, bouncing on a neck too loose to be in one piece.

Carlo screamed obscenities at the dead gunman's face as he tried to keep the Lincoln from swerving out of control.

He looked up and saw, standing on the edge of the loading dock in front of the Lincoln, the pale man, Dietrich, the man who was supposed to be hit tonight. He stood impassively, arms extended in a Christlike gesture. Carlo could still see the ragged edges of the exit wound through the hole torn in his shirt. Carlo thought he could see the flesh moving.

In trying to maneuver the car back out on the street, the

front fender clipped something as he attempted to turn. His hand slipped while trying to shift across the gunman's body, and he couldn't straighten out on the road. The back of the Lincoln slammed into the rear of a parked truck. The impact threw Carlo against the steering wheel, stunning him.

Carlo pushed himself away from the wheel and glanced behind him to see the damage. The Lincoln wasn't going to move again. The rear corner of the truck had crushed the back of the car past the rear axle. The back seat had buckled, and the metal of the truck had twisted to obscure his view out the rear. The inside of the car was filling with the smell of gas.

He pushed the body off of him and began forcing the driver's door open. He could only move it a few inches against the twisted frame, but it was enough for him to scramble out of the car. He fell on damp pavement, the spreading gas stinging the cuts in his hands. He forced himself up, fighting a throbbing dizziness that made him unsteady on his feet.

He stumbled away from the wreck in a direction that he hoped was away from the warehouse. Between the fog and the stinging in his eyes, he couldn't see where he was going. He tried to wipe the blood off of his face, but it only made things worse.

He almost stumbled into the pale man before he saw him. Carlo stopped when he could see the figure a few feet away, facing him. Carlo's throat was clogged by fear. He tried to reach out to steady himself, and his hand found nothing. He collapsed onto one knee in front of the man.

He felt his pulse in his neck, and in his temples. His breath was shallow and ragged, sounds muted under the rushing of his own heart. Before him, Dietrich stood, arms extended.

Carlo could see clearly now where the shotgun blast had torn away Dietrich's clothes. Underneath, Carlo could see the torn flesh in his chest and side. The edges of the massive wound seemed to knit together as he watched.

Carlo wanted to move, to run. He wanted to die, if that was the only escape offered him. He looked up and couldn't tear his gaze away from Dietrich's eyes.

"The lords of this city will acknowledge me," Dietrich

said. The voice was like a solid lump of ice lodged in Carlo's heart. "You shall become a vassal of my blood."

Carlo couldn't move, couldn't nod or shake his head. Speech was lost to him. Even if his throat could have formed words, language seemed stripped from him. The only words he could understand were those Dietrich spoke. The only meaning was in those words.

Dietrich's pale form was suddenly illuminated by a flickering orange light. A warm acrid wind blew by them, but Carlo was too far away from himself and the Lincoln to notice. His attention was focused in front of him.

Dietrich lowered his gaze, and Carlo's gaze followed as if he was looking with the same set of eyes.

Dietrich had begun to bleed. Until then, no blood had spread to stain his tattered clothes. But now a violent red began to seep from the closing lips of the wound. It almost seemed to glow in the flickering light, holding a warmth beyond anything that Carlo had ever experienced.

Even though Dietrich no longer spoke words, Carlo could feel his voice in his head. *Take of my blood. Take of my flesh.* It ran through his head, an obscene parody of the sacrament.

You've never held any power, Carlo. You've always lived in fear of those around you. You've always been an instrument of someone else's will. Take of me, and you will see those who have owned you bound to you in servitude. Or dead.

Carlo shuddered. Panic still raged in his body, but now other emotions raged alongside it. Anger led them. Carlo felt a burning rage at a family that thought so little of him that all they could see him as was a chauffeur for their hired assassins. Assassins they treated better than their own flesh and blood. The only respect he had belonged to Papa, and Papa had none for him. Carlo hadn't seen it until now, but all the talk of sending him away to college was simply an excuse to get rid of him.

With the anger came another emotion. A feeling even hotter against the growing coldness in his chest.

Grant me your fealty, bind yourself to me, and you will feast within my kingdom.

The feeling was hunger.

Carlo reached for the pale man, and the long arms embraced him as Carlo buried his face in the still-bleeding wound.

In the *Cleveland Press* the next day, the burned out Lincoln was mentioned alongside two other traffic fatalities. No one paid much attention to the accident, everyone knew how dangerous Cleveland traffic was. The only remarkable thing about it was the fact that the supposed driver was the only fatality.

10

Doctor McCutcheon led Stefan through a file room at St. Vincent's Charity. All the while the doctor shook his head and kept saying, "I don't know what to tell you, Detective Ryzard. The man was dead."

Each time, Stefan would nod and remain quiet. As far as he was concerned, he had seen Samson Fairfax alive and well, and he only had this doctor's word that he had ever been anywhere near death. He followed the doctor through narrow aisles of wood and paper. The single low-wattage bulb cast a yellow pall on the file room, drawing the brown rust stains on the walls, and some of the cabinets, into relief. The place smelled of steam heat and old paper.

"Here we are," said the doctor, stopping in front of a cabinet and smoothing his Errol Flynn mustache. He drew open a file drawer, which came free with a squeak of pained wood. The doctor began rummaging in the files.

"He claimed to have 'spells' that someone might take for death."

Doctor McCutcheon snorted. "A layman maybe. Sure, there are conditions that could produce a temporary comatose state. But the John Doe you brought me wasn't suffering a fit, a trance, a fugue, a coma, or anything else—here we are." He drew out a slim folder that was labeled, "John Doe, September 23, 1935."

The doctor opened it. "Here are my notes. Respiration stopped at 2:30 AM. Despite efforts to revive him, we lost his pulse for ten minutes later. He never started breathing again. By 3:00 AM I declared him dead. It's all here if you want it—down to the names of the attending nurses."

Stefan took the folder and glanced at Doctor McCutcheon's notes. They told the story the doctor said they did. Stefan shook his head. "I'm sorry to lean on you, Doctor. I'm just trying to understand how I could see this man again, alive and well, weeks after you declared him dead."

The doctor shook his head, "You couldn't have. There's no way it could be the same man, no matter what he said."

Stefan sighed. "You don't think there might just be a possibility—"

The doctor slammed the file cabinet shut. "The man I tended died. Period. You have the file right in front of you."

"If it weren't for the missing body—"

The doctor shook his head. "Talk to the guard who lost the damn body. All I can tell you is that if the man you saw was Samson Fairfax, the John Doe I treated was not."

Stefan learned from the hospital administration that Edward Mullen had been let go because of the incident. From the sound of it, he had maintained throughout that someone from the coroner's office had picked up the body, despite the denials of Coroner Pearse and the absence of any paperwork. It also sounded as if Mullen had been sacked less for losing a body than for insisting on his own innocence.

Mullen lived above a bar northeast of the intersection of Euclid and East Fifty-Fifth. The building looked as if it were a refugee from the other side of that intersection, a refugee from its poverty-stricken and ill-kept peers in the Third. It squatted on the corner of two unremarkable streets, seeming to shrink from the working-class homes surrounding it.

Evening was coming as Stefan pulled up in front of Mullen's building. The bar was open and getting a start on the after-work crowd. The sky was a darkening pall above him, and the folks on the street had to hunch themselves against the wind.

Stefan checked the address twice before he got out of his car. The only lights were from the bar, the small curtained windows glowing out into the dusk, a small globe of light carving out the doorway of the establishment, another lamp picking out the name "Armand's" above the door.

The windows above the bar were dark. Half-height

wrought-iron fences tied themselves to the brick in front of the darkened windows, forming a faux balcony barely a foot wide beyond the sills of the windows. The one to the right had a window box that had bloomed once, sprouting flowering vines to wrap the iron rail. The plants' season was long gone, and the vines gripping the iron were brown and dead.

Stefan found the door to the upstairs hidden in the darkness along one of the side walls. The stairs and the hallway were lit only by two incandescent bulbs, and Stefan had to pick his way carefully up the stairs, half-wrapped in gloom.

Upstairs, from the sound, he might have been inside the bar itself. The sounds of clinking glasses, music, and loud conversation filtered through the black-and-white-checked linoleum. The sound carried so well that Stefan was worried about the strength of a floor that was thin enough to transmit sound so freely.

As if designed to capitalize on the fear, the floor of the hallway sagged in the center, a dip that followed the hallway along its short length across the building.

There were four apartments. Two doors on the right, toward the front of the building. Two on the left, toward the rear. Mullen lived in number four, the second door on the left.

Stefan walked up the hallway, away from the lights. The only thing that prevented Mullen's end of the hallway from being completely dark was the dim light filtering through the window here.

Stefan snorted. It smelled up here, of alcohol, urine, and food gone bad. He could hear flies tapping on the inside of the window, and on the sill was a strip of fly-paper that had fallen from the ceiling. The amber cellophane was almost completely covered by black insect corpses.

He pounded on the door. He heard nothing except the sounds of the bar below him, and renewed activity from the flies. The sluggish buzzing was just loud and close enough for him to hear above the noise downstairs.

Mullen, if he was home, didn't respond.

"Mullen, Edward Mullen! This is Detective Ryzard from the Cleveland Police Department. I want to talk to you!"

As he called out, a fly landed on the back of his hand. He had to shake his hand twice to get it off. He pounded the door again, and as his eyes adjusted to the dim light, he was beginning to see that a host of flies had settled on Edward Mullen's door. They were sluggish in the cold, and didn't fly away when he pounded on the door.

No one answered.

Stefan tried the door. It wasn't locked. He pushed it gently into an apartment that was shrouded in even deeper gloom than the hallway. The smell became much worse, the smell of something rotting. He gritted his teeth while pushing the door open with his foot.

He felt flies batter against his face and his arms, causing his skin to twitch.

It was still dark beyond. He couldn't see a foot beyond the doorway. All the shades in Mullen's apartment were drawn against the windows. The only light was what managed to leak past Stefan.

He already knew what he would see. He hoped differently. He prayed to God that he was wrong. But he knew he wasn't wrong. He reached inside the apartment, next to the door, fumbling for a light. When he found a switch, he hesitated for a few long moments.

For a little while he fantasized that he could just walk away.

He stood in the door, sensing—half imagining—that it was too warm. The smell of decay was a humid smell, making the air too fetid to breathe through his nose. Between the warmth, the dark, and the smell, he felt as if he'd been buried in a gangrenous wound.

Stefan turned on the lights.

It was as bad as he had feared. Flies were everywhere, dotting the walls, the ceiling, the couch against the wall.

Mostly, the flies covered Edward Mullen.

He was seated at a desk directly across from the door to the apartment. His back was to Stefan. He had collapsed across the desk, his head face-down on a stained blotter that was writhing with insect life. His right hand lay on the desk next to his head. It clutched a large revolver.

Automatically, Stefan's gaze followed the path of the phantom shot, to the wall left of the desk. The wall was alive with flies, almost a solid sheet covering the area where the contents of Mullen's skull had sprayed the wall.

Stefan's stomach tightened as he walked into the apartment, but he didn't let his mind dwell on it. He stepped up next to the corpse. Mullen had to have been dead, rotting up here, since he'd been fired from St. Vincent's. Stefan did as thorough an examination as he could without touching anything.

Mullen had written a note and weighted it down with the penholder in front of him. Gore had spotted the page, and old blood had spread beneath it, sticking the page to the desk, but Stefan could read what it said.

I cannot lie for the Devil, the only explanation that Mullen gave for taking his own life. Stefan looked up from the page, and noticed the crucifix hanging on the wall above the desk. The figure of Christ seemed to be looking down at Mullen with a grieving expression. The blood on the cross wasn't from the Savior.

Stefan left the apartment to call the scene in to the Central Station.

"What am I going to do with you, Stefan?" Inspector Cody asked. He had come, with a few more cops and the coroner's wagon, in response to Stefan's call. He stood next to Stefan's car, shaking his head at the spectacle of the body's removal. "What was it you were doing here?"

"I was trying to find out what happened to a body that disappeared from the morgue at St. Vincent's."

Cody sighed and looked up at the darkened apartments above the bar. "What did our suicide have to with it?"

"He was security when the body disappeared."

"And this body, it's part of a case you're working on?" The silence stretched until Inspector Cody said, "Well?"

A wind came down the street, off the lake. It got under Stefan's overcoat and chilled him. Eventually he shook his head and said, "No, it isn't part of any official investigation."

Stefan could see his superior shake his head, as if in disappointment. "God, don't you have better things to do with your free time? Was the body a murder victim?"

"No—" Stefan said, then hesitated.

"What else?"

"—he may not even be dead, sir."

Detective Inspector Cody lowered his gaze to look into Stefan's eyes. "You'd better tell me the whole story here."

Stefan gave as complete an accounting as he could. Cody stayed silent through it, only moving to pull out a cigarette and light it. When it was over, he blew smoke toward the bar, as if trying to erase what was happening.

"Okay," he said finally, "I'm not going to reprimand you. It's just too much trouble when I'm retiring tomorrow." He looked up at the bar, "This and the Kingsbury Run business—what a note to leave on."

Cody shook his head, looked at Stefan, and said, "This isn't as your superior, it's just some advice from an old cop. Don't muddy the waters any further with extracurricular activities. What you have is a John Doe who didn't die, a doctor who couldn't admit his mistake, and a guard who lied to cover his own oversights and couldn't live with it when he lost his job. You try and read any more into it, my successors may not be as forgiving."

"But—" Stefan began. In his mind he saw the connection between Samson Fairfax and Edward Mullen. They had both seen the Devil, in some form or other. But as the thought formed, Stefan knew it bore little weight, no matter how certain it seemed to him. He was chasing a shadow that no one else could see.

"If you keep investigating anything off duty, beyond what's assigned to you, you risk getting canned. Do you understand that? I'd hate to see the department lose you."

Stefan nodded.

The doors slammed shut on the coroner's wagon. As it drove away, Stefan wondered what other lies Mullen might have told for the Devil.

11

Eliot Ness stood by the bar, martini in hand, and watched the powerful people mingle. He was here because someone in the Burton campaign invited him. Ness was a loyal party man and the invitation intrigued him, so he attended. He also attended the victory celebration because it was one of those high-profile parties where attendance could be a career move. Filling the ballroom around Ness were the most important and influential people in the city and, in a few cases, the whole country.

Ness sipped his martini and wondered who had invited him and why. There had been hints about openings in the incoming administration, but no one from the campaign staff had approached him. He certainly hadn't any opportunity to see the mayor-elect yet, much less talk to him. Burton was probably only going to show up to give a climactic, and boring, speech to the mass of high and mighty gathered in his honor.

Most of the guests were party officials and big donors. Ness was neither. He wasn't even local. The government he worked for was the Federal one. He lived in Bay Village, two suburbs west of the city, which meant that he hadn't even voted in the Cleveland mayoral election.

The explanation he'd come up with was the suspicion that someone invited him as part of the decor. The mayor had been elected in large part due to his platform of reform, law and order. Since the local police were as corrupt as anything Ness had seen outside Chicago, if the new mayor wanted law enforcement represented at his victory party, he probably wanted to go a little farther afield for those representatives.

"Mr. Ness? Mr. Eliot Ness?"

Ness turned to face the man calling his name. He was the one person in the ballroom younger than Ness. The man was in his late twenties and looked a little uncomfortable in black tie and tails. His hair was slicked back, not quite hiding its flaming red color.

"Yes?" Ness said, as he began to sense a familiarity. "You work for the *Press,* don't you?"

"The *News* now. Peter Napier." Napier extended his hand, and Ness was able to picture him in a rumpled suit and hat.

Ness shook the man's hand and said, "I never forget a reporter's face."

Napier chuckled. Ness' love for the press was no secret, and the press usually did its best to return the favor. "So, are you on some big case right now?"

Ness shook his head, "Not unless the Canadian whiskey stocking the bar missed passing through customs." Ness looked across the bar, and the bartender, an elderly man in a white jacket, shrank back a bit at Ness' glance. Ness sighed and said, "It's a *joke.*" The bartender smiled and laughed nervously. He returned to face Napier. "No big case. I'm just a guest here."

Napier nodded. "Well, I'm on duty here. Care to spare a few minutes?"

"Always," Ness said, draining the remainder of his martini.

"You were invited here— Were you involved in the Burton campaign at all?"

Ness chuckled. "If I'd been, you'd know, wouldn't you? No, I'm here as a private citizen to offer my congratulations to Mr. Burton."

Napier whipped out a notepad and jotted down a few words. "Do you think that inviting you here is intended to send a message to local gangs?"

"I can't speak for Mr. Burton, but I would like to think that it means that the new administration will have a cordial relationship with the Federal law enforcement agencies."

"Are you saying that Mayor Davis didn't have that kind of relationship?"

Ness shook his head, "Not at all. I simply think it is a

positive note that Mayor-elect Burton has shown signs that he fully intends to carry out the spirit of reform that his campaign promised."

"Would you consider an appointment within the new administration?"

The question took Ness aback somewhat. He was answering before it fully sank in, mostly because he had long ago trained himself never to fumble for words in front of the press. "Now that is a novel question. It would mean a big change. I've always worked for the Federal Government. Playing any role in a municipal administration would be a much different thing than anything I've done before."

"Does that mean that you wouldn't want the job?"

"Now that would depend on the job, wouldn't it? I've never been averse to a challenge, but the answer would have to depend on the exact situation. Right now it's all hypothetical." Ness looked around at the ballroom and finally whispered to Napier. "Off the record, where did that question come from?"

Napier smiled, "Off the record?"

Ness nodded.

"Friend of a friend who works for Burton. Someone close to the new mayor is going to suggest you for a job, a someone who's in love with the reputation you got in Chicago."

"No kidding?"

"Honest." Napier scribbled something on his notepad and looked up. "Now let me ask you about—" His expression changed. "Holy Mary, you must be pulling my leg."

"What?" Ness said, nonplussed.

Napier was looking over Ness' shoulder now, his eyes following something near the entrance of the ballroom. "I don't believe it."

"Believe what?" Ness turned to see what it was that was attracting Napier's attention. He saw people mingling, talking to each other. It took a moment before he recognized what it was that was attracting Napier's attention. A man was working his way toward a set of tables to the right of the main entrance. He wasn't dressed for the event, and what would normally be an impeccably cut three-piece suit stood out in the midst of the tuxedos.

Napier started moving to intercept the man, and Ness

followed. "Who is that?" he asked, managing to suppress a little irritation at having the interview interrupted.

"That's Van number one," Napier said. The comment did nothing to enlighten Ness. The man was obviously someone of some importance, otherwise someone would have stopped him before he had reached the party itself. Ness had the feeling that the man should be familiar to him, but his face held nothing that really distinguished him.

Meanwhile Napier was nodding, "Yes, it is. Oris Paxton Van Sweringen, by God. Someone left his ivory tower unlocked—"

The baroque name finally triggered Ness' memory, though the result was something less than concrete. He remembered a number of articles about the Van Sweringen brothers, all about trains, real estate, and financial pyramids.

"Didn't he just go bankrupt or something?" Ness asked. They were slipping through the high and the mighty, converging on the Van Sweringen brother. Ness could see where the man was heading, a table at the far corner of the ballroom, at which sat an ominous-looking blond man flanked by a pair of gentlemen whose type was all too familiar to Ness.

"Their corporate assets were auctioned off in the sweetheart deal of all time. They never lost control, despite all the lost and misinvested money." Napier shook his head. "The Vans almost never come out in public. They weren't even at the dedication of their Union Terminal Building. God only knows what Oris is doing here."

The two of them reached the table at the same time as Van Sweringen. Napier called to him as he had to Ness. "Mr. Van Sweringen?"

Once Napier spoke, drawing attention to himself, it seemed as if the world around the table slowed to a near stop. Van Sweringen and the blond man at the table turned their attention to Napier, while the other two turned their attention to Ness. Ness returned the attention.

"Yes, can I help you with something?" Van Sweringen's voice sounded strained. He kept glancing back to the table even as he spoke to Napier. Ness was unsure if it was the blond man, or his hoodlum bodyguards, that was making Van Sweringen so nervous.

"Peter Napier of the *News*," Napier said, holding out his hand. "If I could have a minute of your time?"

Van Sweringen left Napier's hand hanging in midair. "No." He shook his head. "I'm here to talk to Mr. Dietrich, not the press."

Napier wasn't put off that easily, "Perhaps I should introduce both of you to Mr. Eliot Ness?"

Ness stepped forward, saving most of his attention for Mr. Dietrich. All three of the table's occupants stood up, and Ness noticed that the bodyguard on the left looked a little uncomfortable at Napier's mention of his name.

Napier continued, "You might be familiar with his crime-fighting career back in Chicago."

"Mr. Van Sweringen." Ness gave his most disarming smile to the man as he took his hand. He noticed that the mention of law enforcement seemed to make everyone but Dietrich nervous. Van Sweringen's hand felt like a dead fish. He held out his hand for Dietrich, and it was taken in a much firmer grasp. "Mr. Dietrich."

Dietrich nodded and looked at Ness as if he was seeing much too deeply into him. Ness felt the man was measuring him for something. The man had more *presence* than anyone that Ness had ever met. There was a charisma there, a confidence that informed every movement Dietrich made. Looking into Dietrich's eyes, Ness could sense a will that had rarely been thwarted.

"Mr. Ness," Dietrich said in a richly accented voice. Even the European flavor to his voice added to the impression, as if Ness was in the presence of a peer of Stalin, or Mussolini. Ness kept eye contact, despite every impression that told him to defer to the man. Ness was proud, and he wasn't about to back down from anyone out of nervousness. If anything, nervousness made Ness more apt to stand his ground.

Ness smiled and let Dietrich let go first, even though it was a relief when the physical contact ended. "You are an uncommon man, Mr. Ness," Dietrich said with a small smile.

"You know me, then?" Ness asked.

"No, I do not." The smile became a little wider. "I am a recent immigrant to this country. All I know of you is what I see in your face. Iron overlaid by the appearance of youth. I am certain your opponents often underestimate you."

"He's the man who broke up the Capone gang in Chicago," Napier said. He was still watching Van Sweringen. Dietrich didn't seem to interest the reporter.

Van Sweringen seemed flustered by the attention and protested, "I'm here on private business with—"

Dietrich raised a hand, and Van Sweringen stilled his voice. "Just a moment," he said in a level voice. Ness was still trying to identify the accent. It seemed Central European, which was common enough in this city. "I am talking with Mr. Ness."

Dietrich seemed to take an interest in him. That was fine with Ness, the feeling was mutual. He should be aware of someone who flanked himself with Sicilian thugs and wore his own power like a tailored suit. "You're a recent immigrant, might I ask where from?"

"Recently I come from Budapest. Originally from some small country that you never heard of, which no longer exists."

Ness nodded. "Europe is an unfortunate place lately."

Dietrich laughed. "It has always been unfortunate, Mr. Ness. That is the nature of Europe." The two hoods didn't laugh. From the way they and Van Sweringen looked, he and Dietrich could have been holding each other at gunpoint, rather than making small talk. "But I see your next question, the current environment—especially around Germany—made it more reasonable to take my business here, to America."

"What is your business, Mr. Dietrich?"

"Investments," he said. "I took my capital out of Europe, and I am investing in this country's future."

"Ah," Ness looked around at the ballroom. "I assume one of your investments was supporting Burton's campaign."

"You are perceptive. I am a supporter of law and order."

Napier spoke up, sounding a little irritated at having been left out of the conversation. "I'm sure Van Sweringen can appreciate that, what with dismembered corpses being found on his rail line—"

Van Sweringen's face reddened. "How dare you connect that atrocity with me! That is no more related to me than—

than—corpses washing up on the beach are related to the Humphry Popcorn Company! One more statement like that and I'll have you brought in for slander! Leave—both of you—before I have you removed!" Van Sweringen's voice was steadily rising, and people were turning to look at them now. Ness suspected that if he continued shouting like that, it would be Van Sweringen they'd remove—on a stretcher after a heart attack.

Van Sweringen took a step forward to confront Napier physically, but Dietrich stopped him by placing a hand on his shoulder. Van Sweringen turned to face Dietrich, and they stared at each other.

For the first time, Ness could see anger in Dietrich's expression. Deep in his eyes was a consuming rage that focused on Van Sweringen. "That is enough, Oris," Dietrich hissed quietly. Ness would have expected Van Sweringen to start raging at Dietrich next, but instead he seemed to deflate under Dietrich's gaze. Without turning to face them, Dietrich said, "I'm sorry, Mr. Ness. Perhaps you and your friend should go now. Perhaps I will see you again."

Ness nodded, looking at the two thugs staring at him. "Perhaps," he said. Then he took Napier's arm and led him back toward the bar. They withdrew slowly enough for Ness to hear the start of a whispered argument between Dietrich and Van Sweringen. All he made out was Van Sweringen's voice saying something about his brother, and Dietrich saying, "How dare you talk so loosely—"

Ness wanted another drink.

Back at the bar he ordered a martini and asked Napier, "What was it you were taking about, that made Van Sweringen so furious?"

Napier ordered whiskey. "It wasn't like I was implying anything, Christ."

"What was it, though, 'dismembered corpses?' "

"Oh, well, there's this place, Kingsbury Run, where the trains cut through to the Union Terminal . . ."

Napier told Ness about the Kingsbury Run murders in all their gory detail. It only took a little while for the case to spark some familiarity. Ness had heard about it two months ago. Some paper had called it, "the most bizarre double murder in Cleveland history." He hadn't heard much about it since.

When Napier was done, Ness finished off the martini and asked, "So what was his comment about the Humphry Popcorn Company supposed to mean?"

"God knows; I don't. Something about Euclid Beach Park, I guess."

"Know anything about Mr. Dietrich?"

Napier shook his head. "First time I ever met him."

"I thought the high and mighty was supposed to be your beat?"

Napier shrugged and swirled the Scotch in his glass. "Hey, I don't know the guy. Maybe he's new in town, maybe he isn't all that important. Either way he's low-enough profile that I haven't seen anything about the guy. Maybe 'Dietrich' is an alias?"

Ness nodded. "That would make sense."

Napier looked askance at him and said, "Why do you say that?"

"Did you see the goons with him?"

Napier nodded.

"Well, I think one of them is Carlo Pasquale, from the Mayfield Road Mob."

"Oh." Napier nodded sagely and drank his scotch.

Meanwhile, the lights dimmed and the mayor-elect began to speak. By the time the lights came back on, Dietrich, Van Sweringen, and Carlo Pasquale were all gone.

12

Florence Polillo waited until nightfall before she walked out of her flat. Sunlight was painful to her now, and she wouldn't face the day unless she had to. Shortly, the day would be lost to her forever. The bars were coming to life around her, and people she once knew occasionally shouted a greeting, or made a proposition. She ignored them all. She strode the sidewalk like a ghost. This world had been taken from her, and no one had yet given her one to replace it.

She didn't even feel that she belonged with Rose and the others. They, all but Rose, had been brought over already. She was the only other one left who hadn't. She and Rose were still human.

Still human, but with His blood in her veins, pressing His will into her own, opening every wrinkle of her mind to Him. She wanted Him, and she was terrified of Him. She wanted to join them in their eternity, but the necessary death scared her.

She had seen the death. The ceremony He underwent with His inner circle. They all had to see, and had to share the blood as it was all drained from the disciple from slashes in the neck, the arms, the legs. Only when it was completely gone would He replace it with his own.

Flo had seen it ten times now, and every time it seemed that more than blood was replaced. It was as if He filled the bodies with his own soul.

She shuddered at the memory and slid into a familiar tavern, a place where she had once spent time with poor Eddie.

The bartender recognized her when she pushed her way

through the crowd. "Hey, Flo," he said over the head of a patron, "long time no see."

Flo nodded and squeezed next to the bar. Before, she had been growing to hate these places—smoky, crowded, loud. Now it almost filled her with a painful nostalgia for a time before the blood, before the ache, before the death—

She gave the bartender a fiver and said, "Whatever that will buy me."

The bartender looked at her, looked at the five, and swapped a bottle of amber liquid for the money. He handed her a glass and she pushed away from the bar before he could say anything more.

She found a dark corner with a table all to herself and proceeded to get quietly drunk.

When she got to her third glass, an unfamiliar voice said, "Florence? Florence Polillo?"

She slowly looked up from the glass. She resented the speaker before she ever saw him. The liquor had barely had a chance to warm the December chill away, and when she saw him, the chill deepened, evaporating the grip of the booze.

The man wore overalls, clothing that was almost anonymous. His hair was black, except where his mustache met his goatee, where it had begun to gray. But what chilled Flo were his eyes, eyes as gray and hard as slate. For a moment, Flo thought He had finally come for her.

It wasn't Him, and that frightened her all the more.

He stood opposite the table and said, "Don't deny it. I can see who you are, what you are."

Flo finally spoke. "I don't know what you're talking about." She set down the glass because her hand was shaking.

The stranger shook his head and sat down opposite her. "You know Andrassy. You have the same master."

"I don't know—"

Her friend the bartender stepped up behind the stranger and placed a hand on the man's shoulders. *Not a man,* Flo thought.

"I think the lady wants to be alone, Mister." Flo was grateful for the interruption, and was simultaneously frightened for the bartender. He had no idea what he was interfering with.

The stranger turned to face the bartender, and Flo had a horrible fantasy of the stranger striking him down right there, tearing out his throat, of blood pooling on the stained barroom floor. But the stranger didn't attack. He stared at the bartender and said quietly, "I am bothering no one. I am not even here."

All the color drained out of the bartender's face as he nodded. The expression he wore was one of extreme terror, as if he had also seen Flo's gory fantasy and for a moment believed it might happen. He quickly slipped away, and once he was back behind the bar the stranger turned back around to regard her.

"Who are you?" Flo whispered.

"Call me Iago," the stranger said.

"What do you want?"

Iago's gaze bore into her skull. She felt as if her forehead was made of glass, and that those gray eyes could see every working of the mind underneath it. "I want you to name your master to me."

She felt as if her heart had stopped beating in her chest.

"One of the blood has thrown aside the Covenant, one of enough power that he threatens the Covenant itself."

Flo just shook her head.

"Do you think you and yours are the only ones of the blood? There is a society here, one your master could destroy. He has already killed one of us in addition to your friend; do you know how grievous an act that is?"

"I can't talk to you!" Flo said in a harsh whisper. Running through her mind was what He had done to Eddie. He had severed his head while he was still alive. He had mutilated the body . . . "Leave me alone."

"Unlike your master, I respect the Covenant. I shall not force you against your owner's will." Iago stood. "But I see your master's blood in you as I saw it in Andrassy. You and your master are part of the Covenant whether he holds it or not."

Flo felt a shudder inside herself. She knew that she had to let Iago leave. She knew that it would mean her life, and her chance at something beyond life, if she opened her mouth.

Her hand shook as she whispered, "You knew Eddie?"

Iago stopped. "I knew the person your master slaugh-

tered with Andrassy. I saw them both a few days before
they were killed." He stepped back and returned to the
chair. The crowd in the barroom seemed to recede from
them, as if they'd been abandoned in a small corner of the
world that no one could quite see. No one faced them, no
one paid them any attention. Even the sound of their voices
seemed to fade under Iago's, as if it came from a different reality.

"His name was Anacreon, and he was the oldest and
wisest of the blood that I have known." He must have seen
her expression, because he said, "No, not as old as the
name. He was a scholar. He was my friend, he was once
my master."

Flo shook her head, "But Eddie—"

Iago raised his hand, silencing her. "Anacreon took me
long ago, initiated me into his circle, taught me the Covenant that has held our society together for nearly a millennium. That we do not slay those of the blood, allow those
of the blood to be exposed, and take responsibility for
those we bring into the blood. Without that law between
us, all those of the blood would be slain—at our own hands
or the hands of others."

"You told Eddie this?" This was not what He said. He
said law belonged to the powerful, and that all those of His
kind were His subjects or His enemy. He was the true lord
of this world, and eventually all humanity would bow down
to Him and His kind, and all of His kind would bow to
Him. Anyone who opposed Him forfeited their lives.

All He had given the thirst thought His rule was a small
price for the power, and the life, that He offered.

"Anacreon told Eddie this. I know that Anacreon had
spent a year investigating something. An ancient who did
not observe the Covenant. The last I saw him, he was with
Andrassy, and Anacreon thought he knew who this ancient
was. He did not tell me who, and within days they both had
died." Iago leaned forward. "At the hands of your master."

Flo couldn't move, but she could feel Iago reading the
agreement in her eyes. She wanted to tell him, scream everything, punish Him for taking Eddie. She couldn't. The
price was too high. She could feel what He offered slipping
away from her just for being in Iago's presence, and some-

thing inside her wanted desperately to hang on to what she had. All she had. The only thing she had.

"Anacreon was one of the great ones in this city. His loss, in this way, has panicked and confused those of the blood. My circle is devastated, nearly powerless without him. Without the information you can give me, I have no voice for the others. I need a name."

Flo felt the force of Iago's will pushing her, pulling the information. Even though He controlled her, body and soul, He wasn't here. Somewhere under Iago's gaze, her internal struggle transformed from her attempt to resist Iago to His influence trying to keep her from speaking.

"I found you," Iago said, his words pushing away everything but them and the table. She was alone, utterly alone with herself and Iago. Nothing could reach her here. "Others can find you," he said.

Flo felt she was falling into his gray eyes, losing herself. It was like giving herself up to Him, but without the pain.

"A name," Iago said.

Slowly, as if in a dream, Flo said, "He calls himself Eric Dietrich." Then, through the evening, Florence Polillo committed suicide with her words.

13

When Eliot Ness saw the reporters, he knew he was going to take the job the new Cleveland administration was offering him. He had only talked once on the phone with Mayor Burton, and since then he'd been wondering if the job of Safety Director was for him. Until now, his entire career in law enforcement had been within the Federal Government, and he'd always been on the front lines, not an administrator.

He came to City Hall to talk to the mayor, still a little unsure. Unsure until the press began to crowd around him. The third time a reporter asked, "Is it true you're going to be the chief lawman in this city?" he knew he'd take the job. It wasn't even lunchtime yet.

Ness was one of a crowd of people here to see the mayor, most probably here to see about jobs in the new reform-minded administration. Even so, he didn't have time to shuck his overcoat before he was ushered into the mayor's office.

The door shut, leaving him facing Mayor Burton. The politician stood behind his desk, leafing through papers as he talked to another man. His eyes glanced up at Ness once the door closed. "Thank you for coming, Mr. Ness. I'd like to introduce you to Joe Crowley, Assistant Law Director for the city."

Ness stepped up and shook hands with Crowley, then the mayor. "Thank you for inviting me. I was somewhat surprised at your phone call."

The mayor nodded. "I was surprised at how well-recommended you were. I'm afraid I did not know you beforehand," he glanced down at the pages in his hand, "though it seems I should have."

Ness felt irritated at the admission, but he didn't let it show in his face. He just nodded politely.

"Seems you were hell on bootleggers, and you helped put Al Capone away. Is that right?"

Ness nodded again.

The mayor put the papers on his desk and looked into Ness' eyes. "They tried to bribe you, and you threw them out. That's what impressed me the most. I need someone like you. The city's in a hell of a mess, and my predecessor practically abdicated while in office. I told the people that I was going to do something about crime, and the only way that's going to happen is if we clean up the police department. I need someone with an incorruptible reputation. If you're willing to take on the job, Joe here can swear you in right now."

Ness said he was willing.

Within moments he was holding up his right hand as Joseph Crowley swore him in before a crowd of reporters and city employees.

14

Oris Paxton Van Sweringen sat next to his brother's bed and tried to comfort him. Mantis James, normally light-complexioned, was even paler. His brow glistened under the single light in the private room, and his breathing was shallow and wracked with congestion. He had lost too much weight. His wrist was too bony under Oris' hand, and underneath the burning skin Mantis' pulse was much too fast.

The disease was in his heart, in his blood, and it had been made much worse by the influenza. Oris spent his time trying to think of some way out of this, some solution, better doctors, something. As usual, he was left empty, watching his brother, his companion, his best friend, being torn apart from the inside.

Tonight was another night that the doctors doubted Mantis would survive. His fever was too great, his blood pressure too high, his damaged heart working too hard to maintain a traitorous body. Oris tried to convince himself that he would rally again, as he had after the auction. But he hadn't been this bad off then.

There was a sour smell in the room, under the smell of fever and sweat. Oris tried to ignore it.

It was after midnight, early Friday morning, when Mantis opened his eyes and looked up at his brother. Quietly, he asked, "How goes the business, O. P.?"

Oris shook his head. "You were right about him."

His brother grasped Oris' hand. His grip felt hot, as if his skin was drawn tight over a boiler. "You did what we needed," he said.

"What we needed?" His own voice had weakened. "Is the business all we had? Is that all we ever had . . . ?"

"We have each other," Mantis said weakly. His eyelids drooped.

It shouldn't be you, Oris thought. He might have spoken, but if so, the words were too soft for Mantis to hear. *He put you here, because of me, to control me.*

"We have each other," Oris said so his brother could hear. Mantis' eyes remained closed.

Oris gripped his brother's hand tighter and realized that he was no longer feeling the flutter of Mantis' erratic pulse. "No," Oris whispered, "we have each other. We have to have each other."

He shook his brother with his other hand. His brother was so much dead weight. Still holding his hand, Oris called for the doctors, the nurses, someone to help. When the help came, Oris' throat was sore and the doctors had to pry his hand away from his brother's.

When they pulled his hand away, it was as if they were prying the heart out of his chest. He was pushed slowly away from the bedside as doctors and nurses crowded around. From their faces, Oris knew that there was nothing to be done.

"Why?" Oris asked. The question was silent, his voice had no breath to make a sound. The word stayed trapped in the hollowness inside him.

It was the devil Dietrich. He had taken away the two things that mattered most to Oris. And as he stood in the doorway, shaken and grieving, he thought of ways he could take revenge on the devil.

Two days into the job, Ness carried the last box of personal effects into his new office. The transition was going cleaner than he'd expected. He hadn't even had to miss his traditional handball game. Things were going well.

There was a paper lying on his desk telling him of all the meetings he had today, and the interviews he'd agreed to give. Next to that was a stack of file folders, personal histories he'd requested yesterday. By next week he expected to have a list of people within the department he'd be able to trust. He doubted that the majority of the cops in this city would appreciate him once he started in on his number one priority, cleaning up the corruption in the department.

It was about ten in the morning, the box put away, and he was halfway into the pile of folders when the intercom buzzed. Ness sighed.

"What is it?" he asked the box on the desk.

"Call for you, Mr. Ness," the secretary on the other end responded.

"Who?"

"The man won't give his name. He says he knows about a murder."

"Can you transfer that to a Homicide detective? I'm busy here."

"I tried. He says he'll only talk to you."

Ness looked at the folder in his hand and laid it on the desk in front of him, shaking his head. "Put the call through."

He picked up the phone with one hand, while saving his place in the folder with the other. "Hello, Eliot Ness here. What can I do for you?"

"Eliot Ness?" The caller was obviously trying to disguise his voice. It sounded as if he were at the bottom of a well.

"Yes, and you are?"

"Listen," the voice said. Ness could hear terror in the voice. The terror made him pay attention. Cranks aren't afraid. They don't sound as if they'll hang up if you do something unexpected.

"I'm listening," Ness said trying to sound authoritative. He was suddenly interested in the call.

"September fifth, last year, half a body washed up on Euclid Beach. A woman, killed by decapitation. Last September, two bodies were found by the tracks."

Ness had grabbed a pen and began taking notes on the cover of the file he'd been reading. *9/5/34, female, decapitated, Euclid Beach; 9/??/35, two men, tracks.* He was instantly reminded of the odd conversation he'd had at Mayor Burton's celebration.

"Yes, those were in the paper. What about them?"

"The same man is responsible for all the killings. He is a Hungarian named Eric Dietrich."

The blond man who'd been guarded by Carlo Pasquale. *Eric Dietrich, Mayfield Road Mob,* Ness wrote, then he added, *Van Sweringen?* Ness gripped the phone tighter as he wrote. "How do you know this?"

"I know Dietrich. You need to stop him. He's becoming more powerful."

Ness could hear the stress in the voice. There was something there, and he needed to draw it out. "I can't involve anyone in a murder investigation just on the basis of a phone call. You need to give me more."

"You have enough already. There will be more murders if you don't stop him. Murders and worse."

"Can you at least give me your name?"

"Good-bye, Mr. Ness." The line went dead as the caller hung up the phone. Ness held the phone for a moment, then hung it up, shaking his head.

In his brother's office in the Union Terminal Tower, Oris Paxton Van Sweringen hung up his brother's telephone and removed the handkerchief from the receiver. When he walked away, he left his brother's desk lamp on, leaving the desk as if Mantis James were just about to return to work.

As Oris left his brother's office, Eliot Ness was already ordering the immigration records for an expatriate Hungarian calling himself Eric Dietrich.

1936

15

Friday, January 24

The city was cold, the night air biting into Florence Polillo's face. It felt worse because it was after nightfall, and she had been avoiding the sun for so long. Her coat was too thin for the weather, and the cold she felt in her veins made her feel like she was a moving pillar of ice.

She had been meeting with Iago, and he'd been telling her of the society that existed in the night, beyond the control of the creature that would be her master. Iago had taught her a valuable lesson, even though His blood was in her veins now, even though His domination was irresistible in His presence, her mind was still bound more by fear than by Eric Dietrich's will.

She was able to shut him out, keep the Master from her own private thoughts. Enough will and she could become her own . . . She had a chance to escape His notice, maybe slip into that other world Iago was showing her. Slip into a world without Him.

She maneuvered through dark, snowbound streets toward the bar where she was to meet with Iago. For once she was focused on the future with some optimism. For once it felt as if the path she had chosen wasn't irrevocable. For once it felt as if the ice inside her might melt.

She cut through an alley between two tenements, and she didn't see the shadow before it was upon her. A pall dropped over her vision, turning the world black and empty. Before she felt consciousness slip away, she heard His voice say, "Florence."

His manner was that of a chastising parent, and it became even colder before Flo lost her sense of the world.

Iago looked up from his drink. Nothing visible had changed in the bar, and until a few seconds ago, Flo had just been late. But he was aware enough to feel a shift. It was almost as if some of his blood rode in Florence Polillo now. She was close enough for him to feel something through it. Close enough to know that the worst had happened.

Iago stood up and left. No one stood in his way, or noticed him leave. He walked as if he had partially left the world. He walked as if the Devil himself was after him.

When Florence Polillo regained her consciousness, she was chained to a metal table in a long narrow room. Her mind was fogged, blurring her vision, turning the faces in her view into distorted monstrosities. She saw Him. He spoke to the assembly, those He had already brought over.

Most of the audience Flo had known for nearly a year. At the moment she couldn't recognize any of them. The speech He made was all about her betrayal, her unfitness for the new order, her ungratefulness, her rejection. . . .

She could feel the sense, even though the words were lost to her in the fog clouding her mind.

The ruddy light was dim, only revealing herself and those immediately next to her. She couldn't see to the end of the narrow room, and she could barely see to the ceiling.

They had stripped her, and the iron holding her was cold against her skin, almost as if her flesh had bound fast to the metal. Then He touched her, and what warmth she still felt inside her was drained away at His touch. The hand rested on her shoulder, and through the contact she could feel all the contempt, and the anger.

She could also feel the prod of His mind, trying to unfold hers. She resisted it. It would have been a final violation. In His touch she felt the frustration and the anger, and she knew she had managed to keep Iago's identity, if not her betrayal, to herself.

You will never be with us now.

He spoke, but she felt the words rather than heard them.

She could feel Him withdrawing His influence, taking back all His blood had given her. The isolation was devastating. When He finally drew the blade, she welcomed its bite into her neck.

16

Wind carved through the alleys around East Twentieth, slicing away any heat it found. As the morning dawned, little moved outside except that wind. Zero temperatures for a second week kept everyone inside, near some source of heat. Some never even left their beds. Many churches stood empty.

As dawn broke, a dog began howling over the wind. The howls were almost painful, as if the cold were killing it. It howled, straining at its leash as if to break it. Its claws scraped for purchase on the ice-covered ground, and it would occasionally leap, to have its lunge snapped short by the chain that held it captive.

The dog's tongue lolled, and occasionally only the whites of its eyes would show. Where the collar bit into its neck, there were flecks of frozen blood marring its black coat. It appeared as if the cold had driven it mad.

It hadn't.

The animal's straining, its howls, its abortive lunges, all had the same object at their focus. A few yards away from the extent of the leash, across the alley, a bushel basket lay against a factory wall. Across the top of the basket was a burlap sack, its weave slowly turning white with frost. Slightly visible underneath the burlap sack was part of a human hand.

Stefan and Nuri were one of the first homicide teams to visit the scene. The call had been put in by a local butcher who thought the basket had been filled with hams stolen from his shop, at least until he had a decent look at its contents.

When he and Nuri arrived, Stefan thought that the scene was more appropriate to a Hieronymus Bosch depiction of Hell than of a police investigation. A man held a howling dog back from the police clustered in the alley. A photographer was taking pictures while the detectives and the coroner's people took an inventory of the basket's contents.

Stefan watched the inventory as if in a dream; right arm, both thighs, the lower half of a female torso. All were neatly dismembered, the cuts too clean to seem real. It was as if the victim were little more than a disassembled mannequin.

Stefan couldn't help but remember the time on Euclid Beach, finding the body that had been so insulted that it ceased to be perceived as a body. The feeling was reinforced when the police spread out to search for more remains.

He, Nuri, and the other detectives questioned the local residents, but the bitter cold had kept them all inside. The most anyone had heard was the dog. As the Sunday progressed, Stefan felt more and more that something evil had fallen over the city.

The cold continued as the police tried to reconstruct the life of the victim. Her identity was quickly discovered through the fingerprints of the one arm. Florence Polillo had a six-year-old record in Cleveland for soliciting and occupying rooms for immoral purposes.

Stefan and Nuri were part of the investigation, questioning Flo's associates, acquaintances, visiting the bars she frequented in the Third Precinct. Little clearly emerged about her past. She wasn't someone that people *knew*.

They found three possible marriages, but only one of the husbands was found. They found no trace of the first. Andrew Polillo was her second husband, but he'd been abandoned by Flo six years ago, and hadn't even known where she'd been staying. The third called himself Harry Martin, a tall blond man she had apparently brought back from Washington, D.C. The most solid sign of Mr. Martin was a hotel manager who said he'd given rooms to Flo and her husband, and that her husband seemed to be rough on her. Harry Martin himself, couldn't be found.

Added to that was a rat's nest of tangled lovers, aliases,

jobs, and arrest records out of which nothing concrete emerged.

A week into the murder investigation, Stefan heard of another ephemeral lead, but one that disturbed him. It disturbed him all the more because there was nothing he could do to follow up on it.

There were literally dozens of people that the detectives wanted to find; old madams who had employed Flo, people who provided her with drugs, a long list of Italians who had associated with her, a seaman who had visited her, a black woman who had visited her in jail, a gambler, several black men who might have been her lovers—and one gentleman, possibly Italian, who matched the description of someone who had been seen with Edward Andrassy.

It was the last that disturbed Stefan, because the description of this man also matched that of Iago.

By Thursday the seventh, more of Flo's body was found, preserved by the cold, close by to where the basket had been found. The new pieces included Flo's upper torso, which was enough for the coroner to pronounce decapitation as the cause of death.

Despite this, and a possible link to Andrassy, the newly appointed head of Homicide, Detective Sergeant James T. Hogan, told the press that the Flo Polillo murder was to be treated as totally unrelated to the Andrassy case.

Stefan wasn't the only one who didn't believe Detective Hogan's pronouncement.

17

Stefan and Nuri left the Central Station at eleven in the morning. The day was as cold as any yet. Their breath fogged in the car, even with the heater going.

"What a day," Nuri said in a puff of fog. He rubbed his hands together. "Do we have to go out in this?"

Stefan pumped the brakes to stop his Ford at the corner, allowing some of the insane Cleveland drivers to barrel past the intersection in front of him. He looked at Nuri. "We're supposed to follow up this call."

"Another anonymous call— Am I the only one who thinks the Polillo case isn't going anywhere?"

Stefan shook his head as he watched a Lincoln shoot by in front of him. Watching it, he thought that Clevelanders drove as if their cars were weapons. The light changed, and Stefan paused to make sure that the cross traffic had actually stopped.

During that pause, the rear passenger-side door opened, letting in howling wind and snow. Stefan turned with Nuri to see what had happened. Behind them, someone's horn blared at them.

A young man pulled himself into the back seat of Stefan's Ford, pulling the door shut behind him. Stefan reached for his gun and began to ask, "What the hell do you—"

"What the—" Nuri said, apparently achieving recognition about the same time that Stefan did.

The horn blared again, as Eliot Ness shook snow out of his hair.

Ness looked at both of them from the back seat and said, "I think you better start moving again."

Stefan turned away from the chief law enforcement officer in the city, and pumped the gas. The V-8 sprang through the intersection, tires squealing.

"Detectives Ryzard, Lapidos," Ness said.

"Yes," Nuri responded. "Sir, what are you doing here?" Nuri echoed Stefan's thought.

"I'm not here," Ness said. "And you can forget the tip, it won't pan out."

"You know that?" Stefan asked.

"Yes. I made the call."

Stefan squeezed the wheel and felt his knuckles pop. "What the hell are you doing, meddling in a murder investigation?" Stefan looked at Ness in the rearview mirror. He looked younger than Nuri, with a face that belonged on a college campus, not a police force. This was the man the papers made such a fuss about, the man who was going to clean up this city. Stefan didn't like him.

"I want you to drive to City Hall—"

"Am I a chauffeur now?" Stefan said.

Stefan saw Ness frown in the rear-view mirror. He didn't care. He'd never liked what he'd seen of the Safety Director's grandstanding, and his first meeting with the man wasn't improving the impression.

"What are you doing here, sir?" Nuri repeated. His voice carried the tone of someone stepping between two men throwing punches at each other, carrying equal parts reassurance and fear at being drawn into the melee.

"I'm here because you two are being assigned to something that can't be dealt with through normal channels." He stared at Stefan through the mirror. "I need an investigation that won't ripple the political waters."

Timid attitude for the centurion who's supposed to deliver the city from the barbarians.

"What investigation?" Nuri asked.

"The same one you're on now, the Polillo murder—"

"Everyone and their brother is on that already," Stefan said.

Ness nodded and began pulling folders from a briefcase he carried, leaving them on the seat next to him. "You two are no longer on the official list of investigators. You're now reporting directly to me." He patted the folders next to him. "No one else is to know about your investigation."

Stefan started to say something, but a burning feeling in his gut stopped him.

"Why?" Nuri asked.

"Your investigation will include powerful men that the rest of the force don't even know are part of the investigation. The evidence is too slim to make this public even inside the administration—"

"There's a connection," Stefan said. "Hogan's denying it, but there's a connection to the Andrassy murder."

Ness nodded. "I've ordered that there be no official connection between those murders. That's what you're going to do. Connect them, Polillo, Andrassy and his John Doe companion, and the Jane Doe that washed up on Euclid Beach in September '34."

They were pulling up on City Hall. "Why the secrecy?" Stefan asked.

"I've left you some notes on it. There're also some numbers that you'll report to. Go back to the station and type out a report about how this lead never panned out. You'll find orders reassigning you. I have to go now, I'm meeting the press upstairs."

Ness left the rear of the car, slipping up the snowbound steps of City Hall. "I'll bet," Stefan muttered.

In the rear seat were a pile of papers. Stefan looked at Nuri as he turned back to the road. "Get those, would you?"

Nuri pulled the stack of folders on to his lap. He opened the top folder. "It seems to be the immigration records for someone named Eric Dietrich."

Stefan led Nuri up to his apartment. Nuri followed him up the stairs, carrying the pile of folders Ness had left them. Stefan had decided that, with the secrecy involved, it would be better to go over everything somewhere private. He distrusted the publicity-minded Ness, but he was also drawn to the assignment, the same way he'd been drawn to the nondeath of Samson Fairfax.

Behind him on the stairs, Nuri said, "I keep wondering, why us two? Wouldn't Musil and May make more sense?"

Stefan shook his head, "Not if there's supposed to be a secret investigation." He stopped in front of his door and pulled out his keys. "Whatever Detective Sergeant Hogan says is 'official,' everyone is making a connection between Andrassy and Polillo. If Musil and May were suddenly reassigned off of both cases, someone would notice. You and me, we're only part of the Polillo case."

The door swung open into Stefan's sparse apartment. A sense of social unease struck him. Stefan couldn't remember the last time he had invited someone into his apartment. He was suddenly conscious of how empty it seemed.

Blinds cut off the rest of the world, and as Stefan turned the switch, the living room seemed to shrink under the light. The only furniture here were a few cane-backed chairs and a table. There wasn't even a carpet to moderate the sound of their footsteps.

Nuri walked in and unloaded his burden on the table as Stefan took away a coffee cup and plate left over from breakfast. Thankfully, Nuri made no comments about his apartment. Though he did glance up at a crucifix, the only decoration on the wall.

"What is this about a Jane Doe?" Nuri called to him as Stefan put the dishes in the sink.

"Two years ago, part of a body washed up on Euclid Beach. I was there."

"Part of a body?"

Stefan started putting a coffeepot together. "Yes, the lower part of a female torso. We found the upper part later on. Cause of death was probably decapitation."

Nuri whistled. "That makes all of them, then," he rustled through the files, "All killed by decapitation. Something of a signature."

Stefan made coffee while Nuri perused the files. When Stefan returned with two cups, Nuri said, "I don't see any connection to this Eric Dietrich, other than that he seems to have arrived in the country the April before Jane Doe washed up."

Stefan took the other chair. "As far as I'm concerned, we're investigating the murders, not Dietrich—"

"But—"

"Eric Dietrich is just a hunch on Ness' part," Stefan sipped his coffee. "First, I want to look at all four of these deaths and see everything that ties them together."

Outside, the winter wind rattled the windows. A radiator hissed in the corner. Nuri cradled the mug as if using the coffee to warm his hands. "Other than the decapitation?"

"What else?"

The folders for four murders were spread on the table. "They were all moved. None were killed where they were found. All the blood ended up somewhere else." He tapped on the file for Andrassy and his John Doe companion. "These bodies were actually cleaned off."

"Think there's any question that we're dealing with a maniac?"

Nuri nodded. "It looks like that, though . . ."

"Though what?"

"I get an odd feeling looking at these bodies." He picked up a picture of the basket where Polillo's remains were found. "Don't you get the sense that there's some ritual involved?"

"Doesn't mean we're not dealing with someone's private madness."

"I guess not."

Stefan looked at Nuri, whose expression was cast down at the files before them. "But you think differently?"

"What if we're dealing with a group here?"

The idea made Stefan shudder. "Let's concentrate on what we have, what we know. We can speculate later."

Nuri nodded and added, "Have you noticed the really odd thing?"

"This whole case is odd."

"No, I mean it might be coincidence, but according to this, both unidentified bodies were preserved in some sort of chemical. The body that washed up on Euclid Beach, and the body next to Andrassy, both had some odd chemical reaction with the skin."

Stefan nodded, "Okay, so our killer stores the bodies somewhere. He probably is a madman—"

"But why not Andrassy and Polillo? The only real difference is that we've identified them."

18

Iago stood before a long table. The table had chairs for twelve, but only ten elders faced him. Deaths had emptied the last two seats. Despite that present evidence of danger, the audience was both the most impassive and the most hostile he had ever performed before. Out the windows beyond them, the gray-black skyline—night-dark and wrapped in smoke from the Flats—was more attentive, and more welcoming.

He had come here to warn them, the greatest in each circle that ruled Cleveland and the surrounding state. None wanted to hear what he had come to know; about the being calling himself Eric Dietrich; about the humans Polillo and Andrassy; or about the deaths that had emptied the chairs at this high table.

When Iago had finished, the room fell silent. For a while the only sound in the boardroom was the soft moan of the waning winter wind outside. Inside, under stares from the soft-lit portraits on the wood-paneled walls, Iago waited for a response.

Lucian, first among all that were here, was first to talk, as always. "Iago, your information serves you and those of the blood well." Lucian leaned back, narrowing his ebony eyes, taking away half of what he had given, "But I do not hold such a high regard for your *opinions*."

That was it, Iago felt. He faced the most senior and powerful of their kind that were in the region. Lucian had known Moses Cleaveland when he'd stepped off at settler's landing in 1796, the two women here had been in the Indian communities here before then. Every one of the faces looking at Iago were of the blood before the Civil War—

when he was still a human actor drafted into the Union Army.

They were old enough to be too conservative. To be too blind.

Byron, second to Lucian, but a power in his own right, spoke, echoing the elder's words. "The two humans, as you say, may have been in the process of coming over to the blood. Their deaths, so entwined with our peers Laila and Anacreon, speak to that. And, what that loss has meant to your circle has not escaped us." Byron shook his head. "But to accept the word of a human prostitute that her master is *Melchior*? That creature was destroyed long before any here was born."

Not before Laila, Iago thought. *She would have been the only one of you to know him for what he was.* He did not speak. He could not interrupt the elders. If he did, the impropriety would prevent any of them from hearing what he said.

Byron continued. "Again, while there may be a grave violation of the Covenant here, and the humans' master is likely responsible, there is little evidence that that master is, in fact, the man Eric Dietrich. That man has been photographed abroad in the daylight, and none here or abroad claims him as one of the blood."

To do both would be too powerful for you to credit, Iago thought. If they couldn't accept that Dietrich was the ancient Melchior, then of course they couldn't accept him abroad in daylight. The chief vulnerability they had, aside from the thirst, was the light from the sun. In all of history, there had been only half a dozen of the blood who had achieved enough of a level of power and self-control to walk under the sun without turning into so much dead flesh.

Believing Iago was wrong was much easier than accepting that there might be a hostile presence here, millennia old, and more powerful than any who sat in this room.

Raphael, several seats down from Byron and Lucian, looked at Iago with what might have been sympathy. "The Covenant has been broken, even if not by whom Iago suspects."

One of the women, Jana, asked, "Has that ever been established?"

"It would be wise to treat it so," said someone else.

"That means that someone is attacking the Council directly," said another.

Iago noticed Raphael looking across at Byron and Lucian as he said, "That's not necessarily so. There were the two humans who had nothing to do with us." That seemed to head off the scent of panic that the question had begun to spread through the room. Iago frowned. He thought that these old fools could use a little panic. At this point, some more fear would be constructive.

It seemed wrong. He remembered the panic through his own circle. Centered around Anacreon the circle had been chaotic, but powerful. If Anacreon had still lived, it would have been him to speak after Lucian, not that smarmy Byron. And from what Iago saw, Byron was little better than a thrall to Lucian. Byron led a circle which seemed little more than an extension of Lucian's own power.

Iago didn't listen to much of the debate, after it began. Debate was a kind word. It was little more than a war of assertions, each gaining weight with the seniority of the proposer. None contradicted the root assertions by Lucian and Byron, that Iago was wrong, and that Melchior was so much ash scattered on the hills of Bavaria.

Iago left the building lost in disappointment. The leaders of his kind would treat this as a simple matter of murder, not as the threat it was. He slogged along the sidewalk downtown, wondering what was going to happen to his people.

He kept walking until he felt a tap on his shoulder. He turned to see Raphael standing behind him. He hadn't sensed him approach. That made Iago even more nervous. Raphael came from an era of ships and whaling a hundred years before Iago lived. If Raphael hid himself so well from Iago, what hope did any of the elders have against a being that was millennia old?

"Iago," Raphael said.

Iago nodded. "Sir." The word tasted sour in his mouth.

"Eric Dietrich is doing too much good for many of the Council to move against him."

It wasn't what he was expecting to hear, so Iago didn't respond for a moment. He just stood, staring at Raphael's face, wondering what the other was thinking.

"Whoever he is," Raphael continued, "he is warring with human forces that some of our own would like to see diminished. As long as Dietrich is an enemy to certain criminal elements in this city, parts of our Council will not move against him."

Iago nodded. "I see."

"There is worse," Raphael said. He reached out his hand. "But I need a pledge of fealty from you before we talk further."

Iago looked at the hand. "Why?"

"Because otherwise I cannot say what I need to say. Because you have no friends on the other side of the table. Because Anacreon's circle is disintegrating without him."

Iago looked at Raphael and said, "What about my loyalty?"

"To Anacreon? He is no more. Your only loyalty is to help avenge him."

After a long time, Iago took Raphael's hand and said, "By the name I've chosen between us, I so pledge." In his heart he apologized to Anacreon.

The event was small in ceremony, but it hung heavy with power. It felt as if the center of gravity shifted between them.

After their hands separated, Raphael said, "Perhaps you know that there are those who are not grieving for the loss of either Laila or Anacreon. . . ."

19

A month into the Safety Director's special assignment, Stefan's apartment was papered with notes, charts, and copies of police photographs. His spartan apartment had become a shrine to the murders. The investigation was the last thing he saw when he went to bed, the first thing he saw when he woke up in the morning.

He and Nuri would spend hours poring over the papers, looking for common threads binding the murders together. They also reinterviewed dozens of people the initial investigation had talked to. Stefan managed to confirm to his own satisfaction that the man who called himself Iago was seen in the company of both Andrassy and Polillo, but little else new surfaced.

The only connection between Andrassy and Polillo seemed to be their sordid pasts. Both frequented the Roaring Third Precinct, a morass of tenements, bars, flophouses, and pool halls. Polillo was a prostitute, and Andrassy had been involved in pimping men and women.

It seemed likely that they met, might have even known each other, but there was nothing to confirm it. Stefan, however, was growing convinced that when Iago had said, "Andrassy's whore," he was referring to Polillo.

Because they were covering so much ground, on four murders, by themselves, it wasn't until a month into it that Stefan drove his Ford up Walnut Street and pulled in front of a run-down hotel. "Here we are."

"This is it?" Nuri asked.

The building was in sad shape. Most of the windows were gray, except where yellowed newspaper covered a break in a pane. The brick walls were black with grime. On the stoop, under the rusted sign, two old men were sharing a bottle between them.

Stefan opened the door and stepped out. "Time to check out Polillo's last known husband."

Nuri got out of the car and lit a cigarette. He shook his head. And said a phrase that he'd started chanting before every one of the past dozen interviews, "This is not going to be another vanishing lead."

Stefan walked around the car and patted Nuri on the back. "Come on."

The manager had a little fly-specked office off of the lobby. There was barely enough room for him to sit, so Nuri and Stefan were left to crowd the doorway. After the man had made the obligatory noises about already telling the police everything, they got down to questioning about Polillo's past.

"She came back from Washington, D.C., with a new husband?" Stefan asked.

"Don't know where she been," the manager said, "but she called the guy her husband."

"Harry Martin," Nuri prompted.

The manager nodded. "That's the name he gave. Queer, that guy. Didn't like him. Misused her, I think."

"Misused her?" Stefan asked. "How?"

"She got too damn pale." The manager tapped under his eye. "Shadows like bruises. Seemed hurt a lot. Then there was screaming from the room." The manager looked up at both of them. "Don't look at me like that. I don't mess with my tenants' business."

"This was through the end of 1934?" Nuri asked.

The manager nodded.

"Can you describe the Harry Martin gentleman?" Stefan asked. From the files, the police had yet to find the man.

"Yeah, sure. Hard to forget. Tall, blond, hair too long. Foreign-like. Gave me the willies just by hanging around—"

Nuri surprised Stefan by pulling out a photograph and handing it to the man. "Is this him?" Nuri asked.

The manager took the picture, his eyes widened. He began nodding vigorously, "Yeah, yeah. That's the guy right there. Never forget those eyes."

The manager handed the picture back to Nuri, and Nuri handed the picture to Stefan. Stefan looked at it.

It was the picture of Eric Dietrich from the immigration record.

Back in the car Stefan said, "I guess Ness is on to something." He didn't want to admit it. The crowded morass of the Roaring Third slid by the Ford. For a while they both sat in silence. Eventually Nuri said, "You really don't like Ness, do you?"

Stefan snorted. "He's a glory hound, in it for the press coverage."

"Come on," Nuri said, "He strikes me as one of the most honest cops in this town. The force could certainly be cleaned up. You told me that yourself."

"Maybe I'm wrong," Stefan said, "But I think he's too in love with his own image. The gangbuster from Chicago."

Nuri shrugged. "Well, we have a connection with Dietrich now."

Stefan nodded. The car slid past a pawnshop, the window was crowded with misplaced objects. One of the objects was a golden crucifix that reflected sun into Stefan's eyes as they passed. "We can't question him directly," Stefan said. "Not if we're to maintain this secrecy."

"What should we do next?"

"The obvious thing is to get missing persons records from Washington, D.C. If that was where Polillo met 'Harry Martin,' there's a chance that's where 'Martin' met the other victims, if he's involved. And since Dietrich is a businessman, we should uncover any business he had in D.C." Stefan shook his head. "What do we know about this fella anyway?"

"He's an immigrant from Hungary, he's wealthy. We don't have a lot else."

"Is he a Nazi?"

Nuri shrugged.

"The Nazis are into rituals. Think that may have something to do with what's going on?"

Nuri shook his head. "From what I've heard about the Nazi Party, I wouldn't be surprised."

"That's worth following up. His political affiliations. How

he arrived in the country . . . Do we know how he arrived in the country?"

Nuri nodded, "He had his own ship. The *Ragnarok*, a small freighter, German registry. From the information I have, it's in port here."

"You don't say?"

Night was falling as Stefan drove the Ford toward the docks. He pulled to a stop a few blocks short of the warehouse they were interested in. Beyond, the lake was visible. On it, the bulk of the cargo ships nearly dwarfed the small form of the *Ragnarok*. The small freighter that Dietrich owned was marked by the red and black German flag. People moved over the docks, and lights blazed through the night. Except on the *Ragnarok* and the warehouse.

"Doesn't seem to be a lot of activity around Dietrich's property," Stefan said. "Are you sure that he's still using it?"

"According to the shipping records," Nuri said while shuffling a stack of all the papers that the two of them were able to liberate without a warrant. "This warehouse and the ship have been seeing constant activity back and forth from Europe ever since Dietrich emigrated."

"Does it say where in Europe?"

"Spain."

"Figures." Stefan opened the door and looked toward the darkened warehouse. "Shall we go take a look?"

"Without a warrant?"

Stefan shrugged. "I don't think we'd be able to get one and maintain Mr. Ness' secrecy." He shut the door behind him. The wind off the lake carried the smell of rotting fish and diesel fumes. It chilled his skin. "Besides, whatever connection we have between him and Polillo, this is still a fishing expedition." He walked around to the rear of the car, opened the trunk and removed a flashlight.

Nuri got out of the car as Stefan slammed the trunk shut. "Let's see what Mr. Dietrich is bringing into the country."

"Who says he's bringing stuff *into* the country?" Stefan asked.

Nuri shrugged.

The two of them walked down the darkening aisle between the waterfront buildings. The temperature dropped, and a light dusting of snow drifted past the lights around them, a swirl of pallid motes against the darkling sky. The noise of the docks, the sound of engines and of foremen shouting orders, all seemed muted the closer they came to the darkened warehouse.

They stopped in front of the massive double doors closing the loading dock. Low and to the right was a more human-sized door, dwarfed by its neighbor. The building carried no markings identifying it, the entrances plain and whitewashed. Stefan tried the knob on the smaller door, and found it locked.

He stepped back. "Are you sure this is Dietrich's warehouse?"

Nuri nodded. "I did some work on Dietrich's background. I unearthed as much of his business holdings as I could without drawing attention to myself."

Stefan looked at Nuri, "You were doing this in your spare time?"

"You didn't like him as a suspect, but I had the feeling he was going to turn up." Nuri turned to face Stefan. "I hope you don't think I was going behind your back."

"No. No." Stefan shook his head. He felt uneasy again. He hoped that it wasn't his distaste for Ness that kept him from following up on Dietrich sooner. "So this is it?" He looked back at the massive locked portal. "It looks abandoned."

"Dietrich owns it."

"Does he use it, I wonder." Stefan edged around the side of the building. There were windows on ground-level, but they'd been whitewashed, too. Stefan's unease heightened. Something was being hidden in here. For a moment he wondered if it would be a good thing to know what it was.

He kept edging down the alley between this warehouse and the next, the only light filtering through the frosted windows of Dietrich's neighbor.

Halfway down the alley, the way was blocked by a new fence, about eight feet high. Stefan could see, through the boards of the fence, a metal ladder bolted to the side of Dietrich's warehouse. He looked back at Nuri, who was following, and pointed above the fence with the end of the flashlight. There the ladder was visible, hugging the wall all the way to the roof. Then he handed the flashlight to Nuri, grabbed the damp wood of the fence, and began climbing.

His body protested the exertion. His joints were too old to take these kind of athletics with good grace. However, he managed to reach the top of the fence. Straddling it he could see into the fenced-off alley beyond. Another fence blocked off the other side of the alley from the ladder. Next to the ladder, a side door led back into Dietrich's warehouse.

Stefan looked down and waved Nuri up. Then he dropped down on the other side. He heard a ripping sound and felt a sharp pain as a nail caught his pants leg. He fell to the ground and stumbled, trying to keep his balance.

Nuri dropped down afterward. "Are you all right?"

Stefan nodded as he looked at his left leg. The pants were torn up to the knee, and a narrow gash followed the line of the tear up his leg. It bled badly, but Stefan could feel that the wound was shallow. "Not bad, just a scrape."

Nuri pulled the flashlight from his belt, where he had shoved it. He walked up to the side entrance and tried the door. "Locked here, too."

"Let's go up and take a look around." Stefan walked up to the ladder and started pulling himself up.

"Are you sure you're up to that?" Nuri was staring at his leg.

"I'm fine," Stefan said. He tried not to wince when he put weight on his injured leg. "Come on."

After he pulled himself up a few feet, Nuri followed.

The roof was a treacherous slope of corrugated steel. The troughs were slick with ice, and parts were buried under a foot of snow. The roof angled up to a wall where Stefan could see windows, windows that weren't whitewashed.

There was a narrow wooden catwalk laid on the roof. It led from the ladder to where another catwalk hugged the wall ahead of them. It was snowless, and the only place on the roof where he could step without being certain of breaking his neck.

Stefan walked nervously onto the narrow strip of wood. Even though it was covered with tar to help traction, it was as icy as the roof around it, and it had no guardrail.

"Be careful," Stefan said to Nuri as his partner cleared

the edge of the roof. Slowly he began ascending the slope to the wall ahead of them.

Nuri joined him on the roof, his breath coming out in an even fog. "What are we doing here, Stefan?"

Stefan edged up on the wall. The wind was sharper up here; the cold cut into the skin of his face, his hand, and especially his wounded leg. He looked back at Nuri, who was edging gingerly to follow him. "Anything more concrete than we have," Stefan answered him. "A connection to Andrassy. Some indication of who the other victims are. Maybe the killing ground."

Nuri lurched up to the wall and hugged it. "Killing ground?"

"Our killer has someplace private he can do his work. Where he kills, mutilates the bodies, drains them, cleans them off, stores them."

Nuri looked around and nodded. "He could do it here. It's private enough."

Stefan nodded. "I'm wondering why the windows downstairs were whitewashed." He edged along the wall until he found a window that had been damaged by the ice. It sat crooked in its frame, and after he'd kicked the ice and snow away from it, it opened freely.

He peeked through the window, into the darkened warehouse. He saw no sign of movement. The floor was a mass of darkness marked only by the blocky shadows of shipping crates. Below the window, Stefan could see a catwalk following the length of the warehouse. He looked over at Nuri and waved him forward. "Looks like no one's home," he whispered. "Give me the flashlight."

Nuri handed it to him, and Stefan slipped in through the window, dangled a moment, and dropped onto the catwalk. He listened for a moment for any movement in the warehouse, and all he heard was the echo of his own steps. He waited until he was certain that no one was walking around in the warehouse before he turned on the flashlight.

He shone it down the catwalk toward the front of the building. A ladder led down from that end.

Stefan inched away from under the open window and waved Nuri through. After a moment there was a grunt, then a loud crash as Nuri dropped onto the catwalk. The sound seemed to echo forever in the open space of the warehouse.

"Could you try to be a little more quiet?" Stefan whispered.

"Sorry, it's icy up there. Lost my grip." Nuri wiped his hands off on his jacket, then pulled out his gun.

Stefan waited until they'd both reached the floor of the warehouse to pull his. The longer he was in this place, the more dead it seemed. The air hung still, musty and cold. Nothing moved in the darkness as Stefan shone his flashlight around. Even the rats seemed to have abandoned this place.

Nuri walked up beside him as Stefan shone the light on the crates stacked on the floor of the warehouse. There were dozens of them, oblong crates eight feet long, stacked like bricks. Black German Gothic was painted on the sides of the crates.

"Coming or going?" Stefan wondered aloud.

"Coming," Nuri said, placing his hand on top of the flashlight so the beam moved down a few inches. It now illuminated more writing on the side of one crate, this time in Spanish.

Stefan moved down an aisle between the crates, sweeping the flashlight over them. "Any sign what's in these?"

"Nothing in English."

Stefan looked over the crates, dozens of them, all the same size, the same proportions. He felt the unease attack him again. The subliminal wrongness striking him full force.

"We have to open one of these," Stefan said.

Nuri stepped in front of the flashlight. "Are you sure?"

"Look at the crates, look at the proportions. We're looking for a killing ground."

Nuri looked around. For a moment he didn't seem to know what Stefan was talking about. Then recognition seemed to strike him. "My God. They're just like coffins."

"Slightly bigger," Stefan said. "We should check this out." He stepped up to a lone box near the edge of the main piles. It lay by itself on a wooden pallet, the top coming up to a little less than waist height. "See anything we can pry this open with?"

"There's a fire ax on the wall over there." Nuri pointed

at the near wall. Stefan swung the flashlight over to illuminate an ax and a fire bucket hanging on the wall. He handed the flashlight to Nuri and walked over to retrieve the ax. Freed from the hooks holding it to the wall, the ax was heavy, handle cold and damp to the touch.

He stepped up next to Nuri. Stefan wondered how close he came, at that moment, to feeling like the murderer—weapon in hand, the burning feeling of fear in his gut, the tension.

Nuri swept the flashlight so the beam illuminated the crate. The wooden lid was nailed shut and held fast by two thin metal bands. The edges were splintered and chipped. The surface was stained by oil and grease. The crate had been on a long journey.

Stefan hefted the ax, and brought it down on the side, where the top met the rest of the crate, over one of the thin bands. The band snapped and whipped away from the ax with an eerie vibrating sound. It echoed through the warehouse long after the sound of the ax's impact had died. When the band stopped moving, Stefan took the ax to the remaining one. That one snapped just as easily.

Stefan then wedged the blade in under the lid of the crate and began prying it open. The nails slid free with a screech of the damned. He had to move around, prying at every edge. When he'd opened it an inch or so, he had to adjust his grip on the ax and open it with the flat of the blade.

Eventually the lid was free, and he could slide it off the edge.

Nuri stepped up to the box and shone the flashlight in. All that was visible at first was a layer of straw packing. Stefan reached in with the ax and pushed the straw aside with the flat. Underneath was a polished wood surface, slightly curved, dark, reflecting the flashlight.

"My God," Nuri whispered as Stefan reached in with his hand, scooping the packing away from the object buried inside the crate. "It *is* a coffin."

Stefan stared at the head of the coffin. It was relatively plain, dark wood with little embellishment. But there was no mistaking what it was. He told himself that this was beyond what he expected, but somehow it wasn't. The fear and unease were growing in his stomach. He wanted nothing more than to leave now, have his questions safely unanswered.

Instead, he looked across the coffin at Nuri and said, "We have to open it."

"This is macabre," Nuri said. But he nodded.

Stefan cleared all the packing off of the top of the coffin. He walked around to Nuri's side, the side that opened. There, he saw something that his knotted fears didn't expect.

Centered in the flashlight beam was a latch and a padlock. "Who locks a coffin?" Nuri asked.

Stefan didn't know. But now they had to know what Dietrich was shipping inside this box. Stefan brought the ax down on the padlock. He had to do it three times before the lock gave, springing open, falling into the packing around the side of the coffin.

The two of them stood there for a long time, making no more moves toward the coffin. Stefan told himself that he was just waiting to hear if all the noise they'd made had alerted anyone else in the warehouse. The warehouse was silent as ever—the air heavy, cold, and unmoving.

Again, he felt the impulse to abandon the coffin unopened. There was a feeling he didn't want to know what was going on here.

Stefan leaned the ax against the crate and wiped his palms against his legs. Despite the cold, a drop of sweat stung the cut on his leg like a bee sting. He looked at Nuri, who held the flashlight and his gun.

"Here goes," he told Nuri. As he leaned over the coffin, he said, "Cover me."

Stefan was glad that Nuri didn't ask, "From what?" Stefan didn't have a ready answer for that question.

Stefan took hold of the lid, expecting resistance from fused hinges, expecting the sound of protesting metal. Instead, the lid flew up silently, as if the coffin had been made the day before.

The smell hit him first, making his eyes water, obscuring his view of the occupant. There was a heavy perfume that almost burned, and underneath a festering corruption that matched any corpse he had ever come across. He had to back away from the coffin.

"This is incredible," Nuri said. He held the flashlight trained inside the coffin. His gun was pointed at its tenant as if it might suddenly start moving.

Stefan blinked his eyes clear. The body inside the coffin was an old man. He was bald and had a long white beard and mustache. The flesh had sunken on his face and the hands folded on his chest. The skin on the skeletal body was white and papery. The funeral suit he wore was loose and baggy. The satin on which the corpse lay was marred by dark stains.

Nuri raised the flashlight to point at the rest of the warehouse. "Dozens," he whispered. They had found evidence, beyond what Stefan had ever expected.

"Why ship corpses into the country?" Stefan asked.

"Maybe he is a maniac," Nuri said. "This is insane."

Stefan nodded. "But we have something now. We can box this body back up, call in Ness, and get everything cleaned u . . ."

Stefan trailed off, because a sound had intruded into the silent warehouse. A rustling noise, very close by. Then a voice, barely above a whisper—

"Du bist nicht der Meister."

Nuri swung the flashlight back to the coffin. The corpse was gone. He kept swinging until the light landed on the dead old man, standing next to the coffin.

"God save us all," Stefan whispered.

"Es war schon so lange . . . Ich kann das Leben riechen." The thing spoke, grimacing. Its face distorted, the jaw shifting, the teeth growing longer. Its nostrils flared as it stared at Stefan. Stefan wanted to move, but his gaze was locked on the thing's cloudy gray eyes. Despite the core of panic that raced through him, igniting every nerve in his body, he was unable to move.

The thing had become bestial, the face twisted almost into a canine form. Nuri shouted something at it, but Stefan couldn't hear it through the blood pulsing in his ears.

It leaped at him.

In the moment eye contact was severed, Stefan could move. He only had time to stumble backward, away from the thing. It wasn't enough. Clawed hands, smelling of perfume and decay, seized his legs, toppling him.

It sank its teeth into his left leg, above the wound. Its

teeth were like a brand searing his flesh. He might have yelled in pain, but he didn't hear himself over the gunshots.

Nuri fired at the thing as soon as it had leaped, and he kept firing until the gun was empty. Stefan saw the shots hit. He saw blood splatter from the thing's chest. He saw the thing lurch with the impact. He saw tattered flesh hanging from the exit wounds.

It remained on his leg. Stefan was starting to feel cold and fatigue. As if all the warmth in his body, all the life, was draining out the wound.

Stefan grabbed the thing's head. He tried to pry it away. His fingers tore at the thing's flesh, digging long bloody grooves in the sides of its face, but Stefan couldn't move it.

"Stefan, move!" Nuri's voice shouted from above him.

Stefan let go and collapsed. He felt as if all the solid matter in his body had liquefied. He was losing the feeling in his hands and feet. He looked up with a darkening vision and saw Nuri, partially illuminated by a flashlight that had fallen somewhere, facing the three of them. Nuri was raising the fire ax.

Nuri brought the ax down on the back of the thing's neck.

It did more than every gunshot, and all of Stefan's struggles put together. Its back arched, tearing away part of Stefan's flesh as its face pulled away. Stefan used the last of his strength to pull away from the thing. He pushed away with his arms, sliding on a slick of his own blood.

The thing made a sound, a screech that tore through Stefan's chest as if one of its putrescent claws was wrapped around his heart. It tried to turn to face Nuri, but Nuri pulled the ax free and brought it down again. Its body stopped moving as its head was turned on a half-severed neck at an impossible angle.

A final blow separated the head completely from the body.

Stefan tried to push himself upright, even though he felt consciousness slipping from him. Nuri dropped the ax. He was shaking his head, looking at the thing that was a corpse again. Not only had it stopped moving, it had returned to being the same skeletal old man that had lain in the coffin. The hands were just hands. The face was human again. If not for the blood covering the thing's lower face, it looked as if they had just removed a body from the coffin to mutilate it.

Nuri grabbed the flashlight from the ground and walked over to Stefan, shining it at his leg. Stefan wished he hadn't. His lower leg looked like a piece of raw hamburger. It was still bleeding, and Stefan felt as if all the heat in his body was spilling out the wound.

"We have to get you to a hospital." Nuri set down the flashlight, stripped his jacket and tie, and tore off his shirt to wrap up his wounded leg. The white shirt turned red instantly.

"Call in," Stefan said, his voice coming out in a hoarse whisper. "Ness was right."

"Yeah," Nuri said. "After we get you to—" He looked up from the makeshift bandage. "What's that?"

A sound filled the empty air of the warehouse. It was soft, almost subliminal. It wouldn't have been noticeable if it wasn't for the silence that had greeted them here. The sound was a scratching, almost ratlike.

Nuri picked up the flashlight and swept the beam around, searching for the source of the sound. It illuminated nothing that wasn't there before. Meanwhile, the sound grew louder. It grew louder until Stefan could tell where it was coming from.

"God save us," Stefan whispered. "The crates . . ."

Even in the dark, behind the flashlight beam, Stefan could see the color drain out of Nuri's face. There were dozens of crates, and the sounds were coming from inside, as if in each one, something had awakened.

Nuri got on Stefan's left side and slipped an arm under him. Nuri was only in an undershirt now, and where his skin touched him, it felt hot where his own was cold and clammy. Nuri pulled him upright fast enough to make him dizzy.

They stumbled together, as around them the scraping turned into pounding. They were accompanied by mumbled voices. Incomprehensible whispers. Stefan could feel the things in the crates now. More horrors like the old man thing. All half-dead, but animate. Animate and hungry.

Their progress toward the front was too slow. The noises

increased in volume the closer they got to the entrance. Stefan felt panic that one of the crates might explode open, and that one of these things would look upon him.

Stefan feared that if he fell under that stare he wouldn't be able to move.

Nuri managed to drag him all the way to the front door. Stefan leaned against the doorframe as Nuri fumbled with the latches holding the human-sized door shut. "What *is* this?" he said as he pulled at the bolt locking the door.

Behind him, the warehouse was dark without the flashlight. But the silence was only a distant memory. The scraping and pounding had stopped, but now the warehouse was filled with the sound of dozens of voices whispering to each other in several languages.

Stefan clutched his wounded leg, but blood still spilled from between his fingers. His awareness of everything other than the voices was fading. He seemed to be falling into a dark, whispering void. When Nuri pulled him through the door, Stefan fell into darkness.

20

Stefan woke up in a hospital bed. He knew it from the smells and sounds before he had opened his eyes. When he did open his eyes, and saw the face of the public safety director, he immediately wanted to close them again.

"How do you feel?" Ness asked him.

Stefan almost responded by asking, *Where are the reporters?* But, instead, he told Ness, "I feel like my leg's been torn open."

There was a ghost of a smile on a face that looked younger than Nuri. "I suppose so. You lost a lot of blood. You've been unconscious for nearly forty-eight hours."

Stefan leaned back and groaned. After a few minutes he said, "Did you get him, at least?"

"Who?"

"Dietrich. Who else? We connected him to Polillo and his warehouse is filled with—"

"No, we don't have him." Ness turned away. "Your partner's crazy story aside, by the time he got you to the hospital and called in this whole mess, the warehouse was empty."

"But the connection to Polillo?"

Ness nodded. "Hotel manager's gone missing, too."

Stefan closed his eyes. It was almost as if he could still hear the polyglot babble from the crates in Dietrich's warehouse.

"—until I could talk to you."

"What?" Stefan asked, opening his eyes.

"I said I've put Detective Lapidos on leave. I need to talk to you about what happened in the warehouse."

Stefan shook his head. "I'm not sure I believe it."

"Whatever happened put one of my men in the hospital, and I want to hear it."

Stefan looked at his boss and wondered if it was a good idea to tell everything. He decided it wasn't, but he told Ness everything anyway. He retraced their steps from the hotel manager's office until the point where he'd lost consciousness.

When he was done, Ness was wearing an incredulous expression. "Well, it matches your partner's story."

"But?"

"But *what*?" Ness looked at Stefan with a penetrating stare. "Do you need to be told that it's so much bushwa? Have you been listening to yourself?"

"It's what happened."

"I don't know what happened, but it didn't involve animate corpses." Ness shook his head. "If it weren't for some witnesses, I'd have trouble believing you were there at all."

"What?" Stefan sat up. He didn't expect any part of the story to be believed. He would have expected Ness to assume that he and Nuri were just two more dirty cops who'd conspired on a crazy story to cover something up. That's what he'd think in Ness' position.

Ness pulled a chair up to the side of the bed and sat down. "A longshoreman saw some men empty out the warehouse. They were the crates you describe." Ness shook his head slowly. "You and Nuri spooked somebody."

"But you don't believe what we saw?"

"What do you think?" Ness looked down at Stefan's leg. "The doctor confirmed that's a bite wound. But in his words, 'probably from a large dog.' " Ness looked up into Stefan's eyes. "I would never abide my people lying to me. If not for your record, I'd fire you right now. As it is, I'm sure you told me things as you remember them."

"What about Nuri?"

"He's new to the department. I hoped that the corruption hadn't gotten to him yet." Ness looked thoughtful for a moment. "You two stumbled onto *something*. It was dark and confused . . ."

"But what *happened* in there?" Stefan asked, mostly to himself.

Ness stood up. "I don't know." He walked toward the door and turned. "I'm spread thin with the department investigation, so I'm keeping you two on Dietrich, for now. Despite all this."

"Yes sir," Stefan whispered. He closed his eyes and tried to forget the voices.

"But I don't want to hear another thing about walking corpses."

Even after two days, the smell was rank to Iago. It hung in the air around the docks, over the smells of the lake and industry. Iago squatted across the street from the unmarked warehouse, sensing the smell of death, like old smoke around a dead bonfire. The smell was little more than the psychic vapors of one of the blood, the remnants of the emotion as the spirit was torn from the flesh.

Iago crouched on the roof across the street and watched the warehouse. He knew it was empty now. He had come here two nights ago, when he had first sensed the death within. He had arrived in time to see the trucks loading their cargo. He had felt the presence of the others within, agitated inside their boxes, death fresh in their senses as it had been in Iago's.

He had followed the thrall convoy as far as he could into the city, but he had been on foot. That plus caution had made him lose them within the city.

Now all that was left was the scene of death here, and the sense of blood. Iago contemplated the blood-smell for a long time. He was not as good at reading as some, but he could tell that it was a thrall's blood, someone bound to Melchior—someone bound to the same being that had been binding Florence Polillo—another of Melchior's followers, purged for betrayal.

What worried Iago more than the death was the presence of all those crates. Melchior wasn't just collecting thralls here, he was bringing them over from wherever he had been hiding the past millennia. A single vampire as old as Melchior flouting the Covenant was frightening. The possibility of him having a whole circle of followers, all raised outside the Covenant, made Iago's heart cold with terror. There might not be enough of the blood within the Covenant here to stop him.

After a long time of watching, Iago felt the warehouse was truly empty. He jumped off the roof and darted across to the entrance next to the loading bays. The door hung open on its hinges, the doorjamb splintered. He paused to examine the door. It had not been like this when the thralls left with their cargo. Someone had broken the door in.

Iago slipped through the damaged entrance and paused.

Who had broken in? Not Melchior's thralls, nor anyone in a circle known to him. That left the humans. If so, it wasn't thievery. The break-in was too blatant for the docks, which never truly slept. Also who would steal what had been contained within?

No, Iago thought as he ran a finger along the edge of the splintered wood, where the lock had gone. *Police or the Mafia . . .*

Iago shook his head. He suspected that if it had been the Mafia that had struck this place, it would no longer be standing. It had been the police. Fortunately for those officers, they had arrived after the thralls had left.

There would be nothing inside now, Iago knew. However Melchior flouted the Covenant, Iago knew he would leave nothing of importance for the humans to uncover.

Even so, to come this close to having human law enforcement discover the nature of those of the blood, that was itself an egregious violation that demanded punishment, if not execution—if the council could ever admit it had happened.

Iago's hand tightened into a fist. He was tired of being powerless. He was tired of the blindness of those more powerful than he. All of them, everyone who sat on that council, had been created by the Covenant, were protected by it. The threat was aimed at their own hearts, and they would not see it.

Laila would have seen it. Anacreon had been about to.

Raphael was the one left who might . . .

Iago stepped into the warehouse. His footsteps echoed through a space that was large and completely empty. The thralls had taken everything but the smell of blood and death.

He walked to the center of the floor, under the high ceiling, and stood under a shaft of blue moonlight that filtered from the unpainted windows far above him. He closed his eyes, spread his arms, and took a deep breath.

The impression slammed into him: a hideous hunger; the smell of fresh blood; hammer-blows to the chest; still moving toward the blood; the taste of it fills his mouth as the final blow slams into his neck. The vision, the sensation, slammed into Iago like an ice pick to the brain. He dropped to his knees.

The dead one. He'd been feeding.

Iago shook off the remnants of the dead soul, and pushed himself shaking to his feet. It hadn't been ritual. It hadn't been retribution. It hadn't been Melchior at all. It was the first time that Iago had considered that the death inside the warehouse might not have been like that of Andrassy, or Polillo. He had assumed that Melchior had disposed of another of his chosen.

He'd been wrong. It was in the ghost-taste on his lips, and the phantom ache of bullet holes in his chest. Humans had killed one of Melchior's thralls.

Humans.

That explained why the cops had broken in, and why Melchior had abandoned this place. Iago had been wrong. He had thought Melchior had avoided revealing those of the blood.

Humans had seen, had felt, and had lived to tell others. Human policemen.

As the blood-taste faded from his tongue, Iago realized that the taste-smell was familiar. He knew at least one of the policemen who had been here.

What remained for him was to decide what to do about it.

"Wake up, policeman."

Stefan was pulled out of a drugged slumber by a cold presence. He felt it in a paralyzing panic that gripped him— a panic, like drowning in quicksand, leaving him unable to move.

A familiar panic.

"Wake up, policeman." The voice came from outside, but Stefan could feel an echo that seemed to come from the depths of his chest, as if he was hearing half the voice from inside himself.

A familiar voice. It took all of Stefan's willpower to open his eyes and look at the speaker.

It was the man he remembered: Iago of the train tracks. He wore the same overalls, the same pointed beard, the same cold gray eyes. He wore a different porkpie hat, but otherwise he was the same anonymous figure he'd been before. There was still nothing in his appearance that could account for the racing of Stefan's heart.

"What are you doing here?"

"You ask a troubling question." Iago paced around the foot of Stefan's bed. His dull clothing seemed to fade into the shadows, emphasizing his pale face and hands. Iago seemed ghostly, almost insubstantial. "I came here before I knew myself what I would do with you."

Stefan struggled to sit up, against his injury, and against the weight of his fear. He wished he had his gun, even if he was unsure what good it would do him. He was beginning to recognize the cold presence that Iago had in common with the thing in the box, especially in the eyes.

Especially in the eyes.

"God help us all," Stefan whispered.

Iago took a step back and smiled. "Hold on to your faith, my dear policeman. It may be the only thing you have that is worth anything."

For some reason that comment wounded Stefan more than the fear. His memory locked on to his wife and still-born son.

Faith? What Faith?

"What are you—"

Stefan's question was interrupted when Iago made an inhuman leap, landing on the bed as lightly as a cat, feet to either side of Stefan's torso. Iago squatted above him, laying a finger on Stefan's lips. "Shh, be quiet. Ask no questions I cannot answer, policeman."

Iago looked into Stefan's eyes, and Stefan felt as if his soul was under assault by the stare. "We have a common enemy. I know you were in his storehouse. I know what you found there."

"What?" The question forced itself through Stefan's lips.

"I shall not tell you what you already know. Prepare yourself, policeman. Polillo and Andrassy are incidental to what's going on. Dietrich must be stopped."

Iago leaped off the bed.

"I will help you if I can, policeman."

Stefan tried to ask a question, but his visitor had already slipped back into the shadows, disappearing. All that remained was the sense of anxiety he left behind him.

21

Somehow, Stefan's wound began healing without becoming septic. The hospital sent him home with a pair of crutches. It would be weeks before he'd be fully healed, so he stayed at his apartment while Nuri kept an eye on Dietrich.

All though the warming days of April, Stefan's apartment became a repository of information on Dietrich. Nuri would take photographs, research, bring documents, and Stefan would spend the days studying them.

Dietrich wasn't the only thing Stefan investigated. Every few days Stefan would send Nuri afield to a number of university libraries to find books on the occult, demonology, and finally—almost reluctantly—vampirism.

Nuri had seen the same things that Stefan had, but he had the same reaction as Ness—the "Dracula stuff" was so much bushwa.

Stefan was less sure, and he carried on his house-bound investigation on two parallel tracks; Dietrich—and the creatures of the night.

Dietrich was nominally in the import-export business. The most specific record anywhere about what he actually handled was from customs, and all that said was "European antiquities." The customs officers who had signed off on the paperwork, clearing a half dozen loads of "antiquities" into the country, all had the ominous characteristic of no longer working at customs. None of the officers were reachable by the time Nuri traced the paperwork. They were gone, and the hotel manager was gone—it was too reminiscent of Edward Mullen, the suicide.

After the confrontation in the warehouse, Stefan had some idea of what those "European antiquities" might be.

There had been six loads of them since April, 1934.

The first arrival of the *Ragnarok,* five months before part of a human torso washed up on Euclid Beach, seemed now more than a coincidence. The victim could have easily been thrown overboard, floating for months before the current let the pieces drift ashore.

Other records, from the State Department, confirmed the fact that Florence Polillo could have met Eric Dietrich in Washington, D.C., that same year. Dietrich went there shortly after first coming to this country, demanding and receiving political asylum.

If he was a Nazi, he was an out-of-favor one. The German government wanted his deportation. Dietrich was wanted by the SS for crimes of vague and unspecified nature. Apparently, someone in the State Department thought Dietrich enough of an asset to the United States for it to thumb its nose at the Germans and allow Dietrich to stay in this country.

It was about the time Dietrich cleared his way through the State Department when Florence Polillo returned from D.C. with her new "husband," the one the missing hotel manager had identified as Dietrich.

After that point, around the end of 1934, the paper trail began to vanish. Dietrich had formed a corporation around himself, but little of that corporation's transactions made it into the public record. The warehouse, the *Ragnarok,* and the dusty old mansion on Euclid were all the concrete assets that could be traced to Dietrich's corporation.

But there was little question that Dietrich's corporation was something major. He'd been seen with the likes of the Rockefellers, the Morgans, the Van Sweringens. Aside from a handful of political donations, Dietrich's business dealings were invisible.

Dietrich, fortunately, wasn't. Only a few days into the investigation, Nuri had managed to compile an extensive photo album on their quarry. One of the first things that Stefan picked up on was the driver of Dietrich's limousine. He recognized the man as Carlo Pasquale, a small-time member of the Mayfield Road Mob. At first it seemed that Dietrich might be working with the local Mafia.

One of the pictures changed that assumption. Nuri had caught Dietrich visiting the scene of a warehouse fire. The fire was long over, and Dietrich looked over the ruins with an ugly expression. Nuri explained that the warehouse was apparently one of Dietrich's holdings, two or three companies removed from him. The fire was apparently arson.

Dietrich was at odds with the local mob, perhaps even at war.

Other photographs seemed to suggest the range of Dietrich's interests. He was at the Union Terminal downtown. He was at the East Ohio Gas Company. He showed up at banks and at factories. Nuri could follow him all the way across town in a single day.

Stefan's research on vampires was just as earnest, if less informative. All the traditional folktales were different and, in some cases, contradictory. The only common theme seemed to be a dead thing that fed on the blood of the living. There wasn't even any common thread that agreed on how a vampire was created. The folk causes ranged from being born with a caul, to having a cat jump over the grave.

However, most accounts agreed that decapitation was an element in the destruction of a vampire. That made Stefan think about the unknown victims again. Decapitated, mutilated, and drained of blood. In both cases, the flesh had undergone some chemical process. It had possibly been a preservative, but what if it had been something else?

That didn't explain why Andrassy and Polillo suffered the same fate. As far as Stefan could tell, they'd only been creatures of the night in the mundane sense.

Then there was Iago, who might be the unknown Italian that had been seen with both Andrassy and Polillo. Someone who spoke of a Covenant that the deaths broke, who spoke as if some Sicilian *omerta* was at stake. Someone who knew what happened at the warehouse, and who believed Dietrich was involved in the murders. It was as if Dietrich and Iago were on opposite sides of a gang war.

Was Iago an undead thing, like the creature in the warehouse? Stefan thought he could feel it in Iago's eyes, in the way his psyche seemed to press against his own.

What foiled all his wild speculations about Eric Dietrich was the fact that almost all the pictures Nuri brought him were of Dietrich abroad in daylight. That seemed to argue against such thoughts.

Near the end of Stefan's convalescence, Nuri brought in

a picture that Stefan hadn't expected. In retrospect, though, it made a perverse sort of sense. It was a nighttime picture of Dietrich walking with a Negro. Stefan recognized the man. He was Samson Fairfax, the man he had found bloody and crazed the night Andrassy's body had been dumped. The man who had been declared dead.

The memory came back, the last time he had seen him. The feeling of an evil presence, and the fragments of a shattered mirror outside his tenement building. Samson Fairfax *had* seen the devil on the tracks that night. Stefan wondered if it had been Dietrich.

Edward Mullen, who had allowed Samson's body to escape, had lied for the devil, according to his suicide note.

They needed to talk to Samson Fairfax.

Stefan still limped as the two of them stepped out into the tenement-lined brick dead-end where the Fairfaxes lived. They stepped out of the car in broad daylight. People watched them suspiciously from the stoops, and from a few open windows. Children yelled at each other across the street.

Nuri looked at their destination and said, "You know, you're making me nervous with this supernatural crap."

Stefan fingered a rosary he held in his pocket and said, "If you forget about all that, Samson Fairfax is the best bet for a witness we have."

Nuri nodded, but his expression showed that he was still uncomfortable with Stefan's thinking about the undead. Stefan couldn't understand it. Nuri had been at the warehouse, too. He had killed the thing.

They both entered the building, which had stayed just as Stefan remembered it. It was as dark in the narrow hallways as it had been the night he had first come here. They passed a few open doors, and occasionally a face would look out from the crack in the door and ease it shut as they passed.

When they reached the door to the Fairfaxes' apartment, Stefan knocked. Nuri stood next to the door, hand on the butt of his revolver.

There was no answer. Stefan hadn't expected any, not at this time of day. He knocked again, as his other hand fingered the rosary.

"Police, open up."

Again, there was no answer. Stefan looked across at Nuri, and tried the door. It came open, unlocked. He felt a strange sense of déjà vu as the door opened on a darkened apartment. It was the sound of the flies, and the smell of sour meat, long gone bad.

The light didn't work, and Stefan was forced to walk across the room and open the shade on the window. The shade was fastened so securely that Stefan had to tear it in half to let light into the apartment.

Behind him he heard Nuri say, "Good Lord."

Stefan slowly turned to face the room behind him. It was the same as he'd seen it before, peeling wallpaper, candles long ago guttered out. The threadbare couch.

Wilma Fairfax.

Stefan identified her because she still sat in the place where he had left her, slumped slightly against the arm of the couch. Otherwise, she was unidentifiable. She had been here long enough for the flesh to recede, for the soft tissues to shrink away. She sat, nearly mummified, just as Stefan had left her six months ago.

Nuri shook his head as Stefan hobbled to the couch.

"He's not coming back here," Nuri said.

Stefan nodded, wondering if he'd been responsible for her death, leaving her with her husband back then.

"You'd think someone would have called this in before," Nuri said. "At least complain to the landlord about the smell."

Stefan turned to look at Nuri, "We'd better call this in."

"Do we bring up the connection to Mr. Dietrich?"

Stefan shook his head, "Leave that to Mr. Ness. Right now it's just a suspicious death, and we want Mr. Fairfax for questioning."

22

Iago stood outside the Union Terminal and stared off at the Soldiers and Sailors Monument. The monument took over a quarter of Public Square, its lone eagle-topped pillar reaching toward a dark, starless sky. It was a concrete memoir of the Civil War, and Iago was drawn to it, to the bronze statues at its base, the men trapped eternally in the throes of death.

Sometimes that was how he felt, a being trapped eternally at the precipice of death, suspended over the abyss, never to fall.

He was waiting for a disreputable man.

The night-life crowds had thinned, leaving the area dark and lonely. It also made Angelo's approach all the more obvious. He tried to appear subtle, but there was no doubt where the dark hulking figure was walking, even though he didn't make eye contact with Iago. He stopped on the sidewalk about four feet from him, facing the terminal, looking over the facade as if his stopping next to the lone figure of Iago was a coincidence.

Iago didn't care. It was Angelo who should be worried if their conversation was seen. Iago handed the man a fat envelope, and Angelo took it.

"It's like this," Angelo said, as he slipped the envelope into his pocket. "I ain't seen these guys so twitchy since before the last Porrello brother was hit. The guy's racket is moving stuff into the country, moving it all over the place. But he don't act like he knows who runs this town. You get it?"

"What kind of stuff?" Iago asked.

"Who the fuck knows other than he jimmied Customs to

get it in? Even if you're legit you gotta pay us respect, right? This guy ain't legit. He's gotten warnings. Big Al is pissed."

Iago nodded.

"More pissed since his people turn up dead, and no one can get a finger on this Dietrich's people. It's like they're all ghosts, no one sees them."

"They've tried to take him out?"

"Hell, of course. Big Al sends his best guns up against this guy. They don't come back. Worse, Carlo—like a son to him—ends up this Dietrich's driver. Six months, five hits, all balls-up—and on top of everything there's this Ness guy . . ."

"Listen, Angelo," Iago said. "Fire's your only chance against Dietrich."

"Don't worry, we'll get the bastard. People don't get away with this shit with us."

"You don't know what you're dealing with."

"Like I said, don't worry. Big Al's collected more hard-ware than Mussolini took into Ethiopia. Dietrich's going to come down *hard*." Angelo made a point of looking at the clock above the Union Terminal entrance and said, "Got go now." He patted the breast pocket where he had stashed Iago's envelope. "Nice talking to you."

He walked away, leaving Iago with a hollow feeling. How could he warn him, warn *anyone,* without breaking the Covenant?

23

Sunday, May 10

At three in the morning, a quartet of dark sedans drove down Euclid, heading west. Each sedan carried five heavily-armed men and a driver. They drove past all but one of the remaining decayed mansions of Euclid Avenue. At the last one, a sandstone structure out of the last century, the cars pulled onto the lawn and began disgorging gunmen.

Stefan Ryzard saw the assassins approach from his station overlooking the Dietrich house. He was on the roof of a neighboring warehouse where he could watch the whole grounds of the black sandstone mansion. When he saw the first sedan drive up, he had some idea what was happening. He dropped his field glasses and began running down to his car, and the radio.

As Stefan ran, dark-suited men ran around the house, covering every entrance. Half carried shotguns, the other half carried Thomson submachine guns. The small army coordinated their activity, all of them kicking in doors at the same time.

There'd been lights on in the Dietrich house. When the doors splintered open, they all went out. The gunmen rushed the mansion, and shortly afterward, the gunfire began, flashing light across the narrow windows.

Stefan reached his car and called in what was happening. As he did, he heard the first scream. It was high-pitched, more like a dog's yelp than a human voice. The sound tore into Stefan. He dropped the microphone and drew his revolver.

He still limped on his barely-healed leg as he ran across the street. He took the long way around, crossing far enough down Euclid that the drivers wouldn't notice him. Fortunately for him, the drivers' attention was riveted on the mansion.

It sounded like a war zone inside there. The rapid fire hammer-blows of the Thomsons occasionally punctuated by the sledgehammer of a shotgun blast. In the few lulls in the gunfire, Stefan heard breaking wood and glass.

He circled around a small neighboring office building, so he could approach the property from the rear. Even as he was doing so, he was thinking of how insane this was. He was closing on a mob of over a dozen gunmen without any backup. He was trying to get himself killed.

As he crossed the property line, emerging into underbrush that used to be a formal garden, he heard more screams. For a moment it sounded as if, somewhere inside the dark Victorian manse, the gates of hell had been opened up and Stefan could hear the damned.

Despite the death that certainly awaited him, Stefan was pulled forward. Something in there drew him and wouldn't let him go. He pushed his way through the overgrown garden, toward the gunfire, toward the screams.

As the noise reached its apex, Stefan was almost at the edge of the undergrowth. As he pushed forward the final few yards, he tripped on a small ivy-covered statue. He fell on the ground, face-to-face with a stone cherub with a broken arm. It took him a few frantic moments to catch his breath before he pushed himself upright.

When he got to his feet, there were no more screams, no more gunfire. The dark edifice was mute.

Stefan slowly approached the rear porch where the gunmen had kicked in the door. The only sound now was the wind through the wild garden behind him. He held his revolver before him as he climbed the stone steps before the entrance. He could see little beyond, the door had swung mostly shut behind the gunmen.

He reached the door and pushed it in, slowly, with his foot, bracing his gun to follow the transit of the door. The air was thick with the smell of gunfire.

Once the door was open, Stefan stood in the doorway, allowing his eyes to adjust to the gloom. He looked beyond a short hall, into a sitting room that had served as a battlefield. An antique table had been splintered, garish nineteenth-century wallpaper was torn through with bullet holes, chairs were overturned, and broken glass glittered in the moonlight that filtered past the torn drapery.

In the middle of the floor, on an Oriental carpet, was a Thomson amidst its scattered cartridges. The only sign of the man who had carried the weapon was a crushed fedora pinned to the ground under the remains of a Tiffany lamp.

Stefan inched into the mansion, feeling the pull combined with a growing anxiety bordering on panic. What was he doing here? Patrol cars should be arriving any minute. . . .

He pushed through a doorway into a main hall dominated by a curving staircase. Like the sitting room, the walls were marred by gunfire, and the air was thick with smoke. Two more weapons lay scattered on the ground at the base of the stairs, about thirty feet from the broken front door.

As Stefan stood in the empty hall, he heard a noise. It was the thump-thump-thump of something solid hitting the floor repeatedly. It took him a moment to realize what the sound was. When he did, he ran to the foot of the stairs and brought his gun to bear on the grand staircase.

He did it just in time to see the source of the noise before it disappeared. Someone had dragged a body up the stairs, and Stefan had turned just in time to see the feet of the corpse disappear around a corner.

Stefan ran up the stairs, but the pain in his leg delayed him long enough so that when he reached the head of the stairs, there was no sign of his quarry. He stood there, in the darkness, listening. What he heard was the faint sound of something ripping, as if something was being torn apart in some remote part of the mansion.

He slowly walked down the corridor. His pulse was in his throat, and he felt the acid sensation of near-panic in his gut. He was too aware of his own breathing and heartbeat. Again, he asked himself what he was doing here.

However, he continued to follow the sound. It was nearer than it first appeared. A door stood closed at the end of the hallway. From beyond it came the sounds, and a ferric smell. Eventually the tearing sound was replaced by a wet sucking.

When Stefan reached the door, he found himself unable to move. His hand froze on the doorknob, and he couldn't force himself to open it.

In the distance, he heard the engines of several cars rev up and retreat, accompanied by a squeal of tires. His grip tightened on the knob, and he slowly began turning.

In response, the sound from beyond the door ceased. Stefan sucked in a breath and began pushing the door open.

He felt a hand on his shoulder. It was as cold as a block of ice.

Stefan whipped around, bringing his gun to bear on the tall pale form of Eric Dietrich. The man was unarmed, but Stefan felt such a wave of unmistakable menace that his first impulse was to fire his revolver, and continue firing. But his hand was frozen, unable to pull the trigger.

"Detective Ryzard," Dietrich said. He barely spoke above a whisper, but the words throbbed in Stefan's ears. His hand still rested on his shoulder, and the touch seemed to suck all the heat, all the will, out of Stefan's body. Dietrich's eyes were holes of deep black, portals to something invisible and terrifying, something that wouldn't let Stefan turn away.

"Put down the gun, Detective. The assassins are gone." There was a smile on Dietrich's pale face. His expression was condescending, as if finding amusement at a crippled man.

Stefan didn't want to lower his gun, but his arm acted on its own, obeying Dietrich's words.

"They've escaped, Detective. I suspect your job is elsewhere now." Dietrich released his hand, and Stefan said a silent prayer of thanks. Stefan moved his head slightly in the direction of the door behind him.

Dietrich's expression darkened. The change in Dietrich's manner froze Stefan with a force as if Dietrich had reached into his chest and squeezed shut his heart.

"You wish to *see*?" he said. Anger thickened Dietrich's accent. He grabbed Stefan's shoulder again. The force let Stefan know that Dietrich could snap his collarbone if he wanted to. Dietrich spun him around to face the massive oak door. The wood was black in the darkness, and Stefan felt as if he was about to be cast into the abyss.

"Open the door," Dietrich said from behind him. Stefan could feel Dietrich's breath on his neck. It wasn't warm. It was dry and cool and smelled of carrion. Stefan understood now, in his gut, the devil that Samson Fairfax had met on the tracks.

Again, his arm, unbidden by him, reached for the doorknob. Stefan tried to lower his arm, pull it away. His will crashed against Dietrich's words like the lake before a breakwater.

Stefan's hand, almost alien to him now, grasped the doorknob and began to turn.

With all his will, Stefan tried to keep himself from opening the door. Sweat blurred his vision, and his pulse hammered at his temples. He pushed against his arm, but he couldn't even slow the movement.

The door opened.

Dietrich pushed him forward, into an empty room. Stefan stood, dumbstruck for a few moments. There was no sign of the things he thought he had heard. The windowless room was bare of anything but a dusty, threadbare carpet. There was only the one door.

"Here is what you wished to see," Dietrich told him, the accent receding. "An empty room. Those rooms here I don't yet use are equally empty."

Stefan asked God for the strength to speak, and somehow he found it. "Where are the others? Servants, bodyguards . . ." He trailed off before he said *undead.*

"There is no one else here," Dietrich said.

There was an arrogance to the lie, as if Dietrich didn't care if Stefan believed it or not. Standing in the empty room, Stefan believed if any others were here, he wouldn't find them—nor would he find any bodies.

He turned to face Dietrich. He put his free hand into his pocket and found a rosary. It comforted him more than the revolver that he still held limply in his right hand. He looked at Dietrich and tried to fathom where the sense of menace originated. Dietrich didn't look menacing; the only truly unusual aspects of his appearance were his overlong, feminine hair and the depth of his eyes.

The eyes . . .

That gaze was like hell staring into him. Stefan gripped the shreds of his faith together and asked, "What happened here, Mr. Dietrich?" He didn't even expect an answer, but the questions gave him a feeling of being afloat in a situation that was out of his depth.

Dietrich did answer him. "A number of gunmen stormed my house, destroying furniture, shooting holes in the walls. They are gone now."

"You survived." Stefan squeezed the rosary. To ask anything, to act at all, took a supreme effort. He was suddenly convinced that the questioning was a test of his faith, and if he stopped his questioning he would be damned forever.

"They never shot me."

"Never shot you," Stefan repeated involuntarily. He felt his will slipping and he forced out, "What were they doing here, then?"

"A warning," Dietrich said, "from people whose protection my company has refused to pay."

"Who?" Stefan asked. The air seemed thicker, making it hard for him to breathe.

"That is your job to find out. I have no further interest in the matter."

In the distance, Stefan heard sirens. The backup he called for was finally arriving. Dietrich cocked his head slightly at the sound. To Stefan, it felt like the sound of salvation. It became easier for him to think, to talk, to act.

"Why did the gunmen drop their weapons everywhere?"

"I think you are mistaken," Dietrich said. "If you look again, I believe that you'll see that they left nothing behind."

The missing servants probably cleaned that part up.

"We're going to have to search this house," Stefan said.

"Of course you are." The assertion was followed by the same condescending smile. "And you will find nothing."

The sirens closed and Stefan slipped out from under Dietrich's hand.

"We should meet them," Dietrich said, motioning Stefan back down the hall. Stefan walked ahead of him, feeling as if he had just avoided damnation.

He walked outside, down the great stone steps at the entrance of the old Victorian house. Ugly-colored police cars, their lights ablaze, were there to meet him. He walked across the lawn as if in a dream. Somewhere along the way he had holstered his gun and pulled out his badge.

When he approached the first officer, he told him what had happened. Or, more exactly, what Eric Dietrich said had happened. He wanted to say something of the menace he felt in that house, of the things he'd heard, perhaps almost seen—but the words wouldn't form.

All that was left of what happened was the gunmen, attacking and then disappearing.

With some trepidation he assigned officers to guard the site while more patrols and detectives arrived. As he waved the men toward the house, he saw Eric Dietrich standing in an elaborately arched doorway. In the doorway he seemed taller and more pale. The wind tore at his long blond hair; that and his evil smile gave him the aspect of an angel of destruction.

After giving the officers their orders, he walked back to where his own car was parked. When he'd turned the corner, out of sight of the old house, he became aware of how his left hand ached. He pulled it out of his pocket, and found his fist still clenched around his rosary.

He eased his hand open. When he did, a few drops of blood fell to stain the ground. The crucifix was embedded in his flesh, its bloody imprint now carved into his palm.

Stefan repeated Our Fathers until he reached his car.

24

S t. John's was a small whitewashed box of a church hidden in the midst of the working-class homes and shops
in Stefan's old neighborhood. It was wrapped inside a
wrought-iron fence. Flowers grew in small plots behind the
fence, taking up most of the tiny yard that served the
church. The sky was overcast, and the splash of blues and
yellows seemed the only color to a monochrome scene. Stefan stared at the building for a long time before he stepped
through the gate.

He thought it would mark some transition when he
walked back here. He feared it wouldn't.

Stefan walked the slate walkway, past the subdued
statue of Mary, past the sign naming the place. Father
Gerwazek was still pastor here, like he'd been all of Stefan's life. He stopped and wondered how close Gerwazek
might be to retirement; the man had to be nearing seventy. They'd probably close the church down then. St.
John's was a small, redundant parish. Too close to St.
Vitus. The congregation was never very large, mostly
eastern European immigrants that weren't of Slovenian
descent like the rest of the community around Fifty-Fifth
and St. Clair.

He quietly slipped through the doors in the front of the
church, where Mass was already in progress. He did his
best to be unobtrusive as he took off his hat and crossed
himself and faded to one of the back pews. Gerwazek was
in the middle of a Latin prayer, but Stefan couldn't help
but think he noticed his arrival.

Stefan sat through Communion this time, but he didn't
walk up to take the host. He hadn't taken confession in

years. In a way, that, not the Mass, was what he was here for.

"What brings you here, son?" Father Gerwazek sat behind the desk in his little office and looked Stefan up and down.

Stefan wished he could tell if the look was disapproving or not. He had an urge to leave right then, to forget about it all. None of this, none of his past was going to help him. He wasn't even sure what kind of help he needed.

He sat down and shook his head. "I don't know, Father. I think I'm trying to find my faith again."

"You haven't been here for a long time, have you, Stefan?"

Long enough that Stefan was surprised that Gerwazek remembered his name. "Not since I buried Mary, and our son."

"I remember." The sympathy in Piotr Gerwazek's eyes was difficult to look at.

Stefan waited for the trite words that usually followed, about how tragic to lose his wife in childbirth. Tragic to lose his only son as well. How hard it must be. Must have been. Stefan waited, but Gerwazek said nothing more. None of the phony words of comfort that Stefan heard so much of whenever someone learned of his past.

Just *I remember.*

Somehow Gerwazek knew that was enough.

Stefan felt his eyes burn as if the loss was still fresh. "I know I shouldn't," Stefan said. "But I feel abandoned, as if my beliefs counted for nothing."

"You still grieve," Gerwazek said. "He grieves with you."

Stefan stared at his hands. "Everything around me, everything since, is so corrupt, so base— What if He had abandoned us? What if this is all there is?"

Gerwazek stood and walked around the desk. He placed a hand on Stefan's shoulder. "We all feel abandoned at times. It's our faith that draws us through those times whole. You're here because of that. You know."

"I don't want to be lost, Father."

"You aren't, my son." Piotr Gerwazek squeezed his shoulder. "You aren't."

25

Every circle had its meeting place, and the place Raphael chose for his befit his past as a seaman. To Iago, little distinguished the *Janus* from any of the other vessels docked at the marina. As yachts went, it was of average size, smaller than many. It was outshone by those representing ostentatious wealth that survived the Depression.

Iago had a membership card, given to him by Raphael. But it was deep night, and he had to use the keys Raphael had presented him. He had to pass two gates before he even stepped onto the pier where the *Janus* was docked.

It appeared that he was one of the last to arrive. The *Janus* was lit in a subdued manner, and he could feel the presence of others. As he walked up, a guard slipped out of the shadows to confront him. He wore a tuxedo, but he carried a tommy gun loosely in his hands.

The guard represented fear, and Iago didn't like it. The guard wasn't even one of the blood, just a human servant—perhaps bound, maybe only an employee.

Iago shook his head and said, "I am a guest of Raphael."

"Why are you here?"

"To take in the night air."

The guard nodded at the correct responses and stepped aside, back into the shadow from which he'd emerged. Iago walked up the gangplank, around the deck, and stepped down, through a door, and into the meeting room.

Raphael stood at the far corner of the room, arms folded. Everyone else, about a dozen, were seated on couches, facing him. Raphael was in the middle of a speech.

". . . members of the Council have interests in direct

opposition to the Mayfield gang, and will not act while Dietrich is diminishing them. Other members might take the threat seriously, but are afraid to act. Worse are those members who see this as an opportunity to advance themselves among us, those who'd use Melchior's own methods if the Covenant did not bind them—" Raphael paused as he saw Iago enter the room. "News?" He directed the question at Iago.

Iago shook his head. "The Mayfield gang isn't going to risk anything more on Dietrich. They've lost too much already." Iago had spoken to Angelo several times, and each time the local gang seemed less eager to confront Dietrich. Every time they had tried to "teach him a lesson," they lost more men.

Raphael shook his head. "It is time for us to act," he said.

"Without the Council?" asked one of the younger ones.

"What about the Covenant?" asked another.

Raphael looked over all of them and said, "The Council will not defend the Covenant. The duty of protecting it falls to those willing to do so. It is either that, and slip the balance of power toward us, or bring in outside forces and cede our heritage here to them." Raphael looked at each of them in turn. "We will fight this invader."

"What about the thralls he has brought into the country?" Iago asked. "His force may already outnumber our circle."

Raphael shook his head and paced in front of the cabin's bar. "Numbers should not worry us. Our target is the master, not his blood-bound slaves. What are they without him? A loose collection of rogues, easily dealt with."

Iago didn't feel as optimistic, but he kept his mouth shut about it. He was still the newest member of this circle, little better than a thrall himself. His connection with the underworld, the information he brought, that gave him a seat here—little more than that.

It was galling, after being Anacreon's right hand. That was, unfortunately, how it worked. One's status rose and fell with those above. When Anacreon met his death, most of Iago's voice in the community died with him. Joining with Raphael at least gave him back something, even if

Raphael seemed to be after Dietrich-Melchior for the status it would bring him and his circle more than protecting the Covenant, or even avenging Anacreon.

Iago didn't care; at least Raphael was doing something. Those who moved the Council were paralyzed by fear or the thought of gaining power.

Raphael talked on about his plan to destroy Melchior. The options were limited because of Melchior's age and power. He had enough control of the flesh to go out in sunlight. It was possible that even decapitation and removal of the heart might not bring the true death. Then there was the problem of the dozens of thralls under his command. Avoiding them would be difficult, and dealing with them after their master's death would be more so.

Raphael went over all of that and came to the conclusion that Iago had tried to impress on Angelo—as far as he could without breaking the Covenant. "To be certain of Melchior's destruction, he must be trapped in a conflagration. No ordinary fire that he might escape, but a thing intense enough to consume the flesh before he has the time to react. If this happened where a number of his thralls are, so much the better." Raphael smiled. "Fortunately, I see a simple way through to this."

Iago sat up, suddenly more attentive. He thought that any trap involving Melchior would be terribly elaborate.

"I have some of my own contacts," Raphael said, "And I've learned where he is keeping many of his thralls. Melchior has hidden them among the immigrant population of this city. Much of this city is of the same European descent as his thralls, and they find comfort with the Slavs, the Poles, the Czechs—the neighborhood that he has chosen is perfect for our purpose. In the midst of this neighborhood is the device of his own destruction. He has even visited there already. Melchior may not yet be enough of this century to realize . . ." Raphael trailed off.

Iago sensed it, too. Something was wrong. There was a sudden deep tension in the air, and something that could have been fear. Everyone in the cabin stood at the same time, all sensing the same thing.

"All of you, get out of here," Raphael shouted. His head was cocked as if he were seeing something other than the cabin around him. His smile was gone, replaced by a stony expression. "This place is no longer secure."

Iago backed toward the door he had just entered. As he did, he heard something thump onto the deck. He pushed his way through the door and was swamped by the smells of blood and petroleum. He was the first to reach the head of the stairs.

Someone stepped out in front of the stairway, leveling a machine gun down toward the cabin. Iago didn't have time to think. He dove as the man began firing down the stairs. Iago felt two or three shots slam into his chest and abdomen as he hit the deck by the gunman's feet. He could feel the pull of his flesh as his skin tore apart and reknit around the wounds. It felt as if the muscles tore free of the bone.

A wave of heat and orange light washed over the end of the yacht in front of him. He ignored it for the moment as he pushed himself upright next to the gunman. The man was ignoring him, firing down the stairway, emptying his Thomson.

Iago grabbed his neck from the side and pulled him back like a rag doll. He could tell by touch and smell that this one was just a bound human, which meant he didn't hesitate when he tore open the gunman's throat.

He tossed the body aside, and it landed next to another. Iago saw the broken corpse of one of Raphael's guards. Iago turned back toward the stairway. He had just barely formed a thought of helping the others . . .

The other end of the boat was an inferno. Orange flames rippled across the deck, in his direction. Before Iago had taken a step, he heard glass shatter at his feet. The gasoline wiped out any other odor. He felt it on his skin.

He only had one choice. He raced the fire to the edge of the boat and dived over the railing. He hit the water like a rock, flames already tearing at his legs. The black water grabbed him and pulled him under.

The sense of death followed him into the water. He could feel the life being torn away from those on the boat. He sank, unbreathing, to the bottom.

26

Stefan was at the Central Station, sifting through files he'd amassed on Dietrich, when he heard the news. All morning, like the whole week before, talk had been on the upcoming Republican National Convention. It would open on the eighth, and a good proportion of the police force, including Ness, was involved with the security.

Stefan wasn't. He sat behind his desk and tried to make sense of the information they'd gathered on Dietrich. Occasionally he would tell Nuri about his speculations, but for the most part, he kept them to himself. There was still little direct connection between Dietrich and the bodies.

But late on Friday, the conversation slipped away from Republicans and began to dwell on murder. Stefan was poring through a typed list of Dietrich's known business associates when he overheard Detective Orly May saying to someone, "They found another one."

The way he said it prompted Stefan to get up and walk over to him. "Another what?" Stefan asked. He suspected what the answer would be, since May had been on both the Andrassy and Polillo murders.

He turned around, and the answer wasn't a surprise. "Two kids found a head by the railroad tracks, wrapped in a pair of trousers."

"Which tracks?"

"A little west of the Kinsman Road Bridge, by the rapid-transit."

That was less than a mile from where they found Andrassy in the Run. Trains again . . .

* * *

Stefan drove out to where Nuri was supposed to be staking out Dietrich. He found him at the same warehouse overlooking the Dietrich mansion. When he walked up, Nuri turned around and said, "You're early. I thought you weren't going to be here until eight."

"Change of plans; we have a meeting."

Nuri looked back in the direction of the mansion. "But he hasn't left the mansion. If we're supposed to keep an eye—"

"We've missed it." Stefan walked to the edge of the roof and leaned against the wall overlooking the mansion. The clay tile was warm under his hands. "There was another murder. We missed it. We were watching him, and we missed it."

"Is it connected to—"

"A severed head, found by the Kinsman Bridge over the Run. I'd think so."

He looked down at Dietrich's residence. In the light it seemed out of place, a chimera of the prior century. "Hard to believe," Stefan muttered, "that thirty years ago all of Euclid was like that. . . ."

"Where'd he slip by?" Nuri asked.

Stefan kept staring at the building. Looking at the blackened sandstone for signs of life. "He knew," he said finally. "He knew we were watching him. He probably knew from before we started." He turned to Nuri. "Somehow we have to get ahead of him."

"So what's this meeting? How do we get ahead?"

"We're going to talk to someone about Dietrich."

A half hour later, the two of them were walking into the Union Terminal downtown. When they entered the lobby, the last of the commuters were being replaced by the first of those coming into town for the nightlife.

"I've seen Dietrich coming here often enough," Nuri said as they pushed their way through to the elevators.

Stefan nodded. "Something about trains. And we're standing at the heart of the largest rail empire in the country."

The elevator doors slid open and the two of them slipped inside.

"Do you really think Van Sweringen is involved?"

"I'm not sure, but Dietrich has been seen with him, and the bodies are collecting on the rapid-transit property."

They rode the rest of the way up in silence.

There was a sense of foreboding as they left the car and walked to the offices of the Van Sweringen Company. Stefan tried the door and found it unlocked. When they entered the offices, though they were lighted reasonably well, the sense Stefan felt was of an empty darkness, a sense of void.

There was a desk for a secretary, but no one was manning it.

"Now what?" Nuri asked.

"We see if Mr. Van Sweringen is in." Stefan led Nuri down a hallway past rows of empty offices. The sense of emptiness became oppressive. Near the end of the hallway, close to the corner of the tower, they passed an open office whose door read, "Mantis James Van Sweringen."

Nuri stopped at the door and whispered. "Do I remember wrong, or did the papers say this one died?"

Stefan nodded without saying anything. The office of Mantis James was eerie. The desk lamp was on, illuminating a neatly kept desk. A small stack of papers rested on one side of the desk, as if waiting for someone to return and read them. Everything was clean and dusted, as if the occupant was just about to return. The only sign of how long it had been since Mantis James had been here was a Christmas card peeking out from the stack of papers.

Stefan pulled Nuri away, feeling as if they had just desecrated a tomb.

Oris Paxton, the surviving Van Sweringen, kept an office a little farther down. It was the only one that was occupied. Stefan stopped in front of the half-open door and pushed it open with one hand. The office was a mirror of Mantis James'. Sitting behind the desk was an average-looking man in his late fifties. He was dressed plainly, and the clothing contributed to the subdued impression the man gave.

He was shaking his head at the papers in front of him, the expression on his face grave. He didn't look in their direction when he said, "William? I thought I told you to go home. . . ."

"Mr. Van Sweringen?" Stefan said.

Oris Van Sweringen turned to face them with a bit of a start. "Who are you?" There was a challenge to the words, but Stefan thought he could hear a little fear in his voice.

"My name is Detective Ryzard, and this is Detective Lapidos. We would like to ask you some questions about a business associate of yours."

The fear left, replaced by an expression somewhere between disgust and contempt. "The ICC just can't leave a businessman alone, can it? We almost tottered over the edge, and you won't be happy until you push us over, will you? At this rate," he tossed the papers he'd been reading down on the desk. They scattered in a fan across his blotter. "At this rate, everything will go bankrupt in four months. You can talk to our council—"

"We aren't from the Interstate Commerce Commission," Nuri said.

Oris Van Sweringen stood and looked at both of them again. His eyes narrowed. "Who are you from, then?"

Stefan pulled out his badge and showed it to him. "Cleveland Police. We want to ask you about a gentleman named Eric Dietrich. We believe you may have had business dealings with him."

He looked from the badge to Stefan's face, and Stefan could tell that the fear was back. The man had some self-control, since it only showed in his eyes and in a twitch at the corner of his mouth. It took him a long time to say anything. He eased himself back into his seat and said quietly, "I have had informal dealings with the man. I know nothing about him except that he came from Europe, escaping the Nazis."

"What kind of informal dealings?" Stefan asked.

"I don't think I have to answer that."

Nuri stepped forward. "This *is* a murder investigation, Mr. Van Sweringen. We would appreciate your cooperation."

Oris Van Sweringen glared at Nuri, but as he did so, the color drained from his face, and his knuckles whitened where he gripped the desk, but his voice was clear and steady. "I would appreciate it if you would talk to my lawyer."

"If—" Stefan began.

"Would you gentlemen please leave my offices?"

Nuri looked across at Stefan. Stefan nodded and took a step back. "I'm sorry you don't want to talk to us, Mr. Van Sweringen."

As the two of them backed out, Oris Van Sweringen said quietly after them, "Is this Ness' doing?" It sounded less like an accusation than a genuinely worried question.

They didn't answer him.

On the way to the elevator, Nuri said, "We're on to something here."

Stefan nodded. At the moment he was thinking less about the connection between Dietrich and Van Sweringen than about his final question about Eliot Ness. There was no way that he should know that the two of them were working directly for Ness. There was no way for him to know that this was nothing other than a normal investigation. Ness wasn't even publicly involved in the murders, much less Dietrich.

Either something had leaked—or Oris Van Sweringen had some reason to think that Eliot Ness might be interested in him. As they walked to the elevator, he asked Nuri, "If you were going to keep an eye on Mr. Van Sweringen, where would you camp out?"

Nuri stopped walking and turned to face him. "What are you thinking?"

"Maybe Dietrich isn't the only man Ness has staked out."

Nuri looked thoughtful. "I'd want some place in this building. There's nothing overlooking it. Maybe on this floor, or a floor above or below." Nuri looked up and down the hallway. "Rented under some sort of front, since Van Sweringen's company owns this place, doesn't it?"

"One of his companies." Stefan said. "And you'd probably want to tail him as he left."

"What do you want to do?"

Stefan walked back toward the elevators. "We're going to tail Mr. Van Sweringen ourselves and see who turns up."

Saturday, the papers all reported the discovery of the body. As the coroner was matching the head with the body, Eliot Ness was working—nominally—on security arrangements for the Republican National Convention.

At ten-thirty in the morning, Detective Stefan Ryzard, disheveled and sleepless, burst in on the Safety Director and demanded, "What do you think you're doing with this investigation?"

Ness looked up from the desk. In contrast to how Stefan looked, he was neat, eyes clear, hair combed back. To Stefan however, he still looked like a college student. "Detective Ryzard?" he said.

Stefan leaned forward on the desk and said, "Why weren't we told about the surveillance on Van Sweringen?"

Ness put down the files he was working on. "What are you talking about?"

"I'm talking about the two boys you had attached to him from the Union Terminal all the way back to Hunting Valley." Stefan glared at Ness. "We're supposed to be investigating Dietrich and his connection to these murders. Another one shows up yesterday, and I find out now that we're operating on incomplete information."

Ness shook his head. "You have all the information on Dietrich we have."

"Do we? Why weren't we told of the surveillance on Van Sweringen? What has *that* turned up?"

Ness leaned back in his chair. "If there is such an operation, you wouldn't be told for the same reason they couldn't be told of yours. We're dealing with powerful people, people who could interfere with the investigation. The less exposure the elements have with each other, the less likely the entire operation will be exposed—"

Stefan made a disgusted noise and turned around. "We're policemen, not spies."

"Right now you're both."

There was a long pause before Stefan said, "Do you want my badge?"

From behind him he heard Ness say, "What?"

Stefan studied a corner of the frosted glass window on the door. It was like peering into a depthless gray fog. He swallowed and said, "If I can't have all the information on this investigation, I'm resigning."

Stefan heard Ness stand. "You can be reassigned."

Stefan spun around, looking into Ness' eyes. The contact gave him uneasy memories of looking into the eyes of the undead thing in the warehouse. But behind Ness' eyes there was life, and a soul. "You don't understand. I've lived and breathed this investigation for too long. I have a hunk missing from my leg. You gave me the assignment because you said I could be trusted. If I can't have full information after what I've been through, I want no more part of this department."

They looked at each other. Ness glanced down at the files on his desk and said, finally, "I don't want to lose you. Not now." He glanced up and his eyes were hard. "I take threats as badly as I do bribery. If you had given your ultimatum at any other time, I would have shown you the door myself. Remember that."

Stefan wondered what was so special about this particular moment.

"What do you want?" Ness continued.

"I want to know why you're watching Van Sweringen, how long you've been watching, and anything substantial you've found out."

"Sit down," Ness said, motioning to a chair. When Stefan sat, Ness began, "It started with two events. First, I overheard a conversation between Dietrich and Van Sweringen. Then there was an anonymous phone call I received last December thirteenth. Does that date recall anything to you?"

At first Stefan tried to connect it with one of the murders, but after a moment it came to him. "That's when Van Sweringen's brother died . . ."

"That call began this investigation." Ness stood up, walked to a filing cabinet and took a key out of his pocket. "That call connected Dietrich to the Andrassy murders, and with the body that washed up on Euclid Beach in September '34." He opened the cabinet and withdrew a thick file. "From what I overheard months earlier, I had a strong immediate suspicion that Oris Van Sweringen made that call. Maybe prompted by the death of his brother."

Ness handed the file to Stefan, "That is the accumulated information gathered by the detectives watching Van Sweringen. Take notes, but the file isn't leaving this room."

Stefan nodded.

"You're the only one other than myself that knows this." Ness sat down and looked at Stefan deeply. "If I'm right, if Van Sweringen made that call and his accusations were right, then it has to stay that way or Van Sweringen is in danger."

Stefan leafed through the file. "What about this conversation you overheard. What was it about?"

"It was at a victory party for the Burton campaign—"

Carlo Pasquale could barely remember his previous life. So much had changed within him that he felt like another person. He no longer even thought of Papa, or his family, or his former job, in anything but the most abstract sense. He was part of the Master now, an extension of the Master's will, and his body.

The pain and blood of that conversion was so distant it was no longer even a memory. In the parts of his mind that still moved freely, Carlo thought of himself as a machine wound by the Master. A human machine that would eventually cease being human.

But Carlo Pasquale still drove.

This Monday it was a limousine owned by Eric Dietrich, and it stopped at several hotels to receive the Master's guests. He stopped to pick up half a dozen men, all in Cleveland for the convention. Three were senators, three were congressmen, all held seats on important committees. All were invited to dine with Mr. Dietrich, who had become a very important contributor in the past three years.

Carlo Pasquale listened to them talk among themselves. They talked about the growing crisis in Europe, about the economy at home, about their fears about FDR's executive power. Carlo was still human, but his thoughts and concerns had drifted so far from humanity that the conversation was little more than an alien language to him.

He drove the party down Euclid as the sun set. He knew that these six men would have the Master's blood forced upon them, that they would become as much a human machine as Carlo was. Carlo still had enough of himself left to realize that he should feel some emotion at that fact, but the only thing he felt was a detached sense of irony that the most powerful would be brought to slavery.

Like Carlo.

And Carlo Pasquale drove.

BOOK TWO

July 1936—February 1937
THE PHANTOM OF KINGSBURY RUN

1

Iago stood in one of the darkened exhibition halls of the Great Lakes Exposition. It had taken him a long time to recover from his injuries. Even when he fed three times as much—which meant four or five people if he wished to stay short of killing—it had taken weeks for the burns on his legs to heal.

Even so, he was lucky.

He stood in the long echoing hall, alone. He stared at the glass case in front of him. It was unlit, the Exposition was long past closing this evening, but Iago's sensitive eyes could focus the dim light enough to see by.

Behind the glass, behind the ghost of his own reflection, was a display that wasn't part of the planned exhibits. This one was more makeshift. Room for it had been made at the last minute.

Resting behind the glass was a death-mask, along with a small placard asking if anyone could identify the man. Iago could. In the dark, Raphael's face hung, almost floating in the darkness behind the glass. His expression was peaceful, almost one of sleep—not the slack inactivity that plagued his kind in the daytime, but a true mortal sleep.

For Raphael, the long endless hunt was over.

His head and body had been found by the railroad tracks, like Polillo, Andrassy, and Anacreon. . . .

Anacreon, and now Raphael. Iago had known two communities, two homes, since he had walked into the night. Melchior had destroyed both of them.

"What use is a Covenant that only I keep?" Iago whispered, placing his fingers on the glass above Raphael's face. The glass was cold. Iago felt as if Melchior had torn out a

piece of his soul. Anacreon was one thing; he had lost his mentor, his friend, and the master of his circle—but there was still a community out there. His world still had rules, and he still had a place within it.

Now it seemed as if that had crumbled, leaving him adrift.

What use is a Covenant that only I keep?

The thought itself was self-destructive heresy. Simply questioning the Covenant was a dangerous thing to do. It was supposed to protect those of the blood, fashioned at a time of their near-extinction. But if one as powerful as Melchior flouted the Covenant, what point was there to it? Especially if those who were supposed to be first among those of the blood enforced nothing. . . .

Now Iago suspected that it was beyond enforcement. He had tried to contact members on the Council, but he had not found them. He suspected that those who had not suffered Raphael's fate had fled.

Once he had pictured his kind as having a certain dark nobility, a dignity granted by a centuries-old culture. It was a fraud. They were all little more than brute animals, savage and cowardly at the same time.

What use is a Covenant that only I keep?

The answer was, no use at all.

Melchior had to be stopped at any cost, and if Iago stood by and obeyed his own Covenant, he would soon be fighting alone. And there wasn't any way he could defeat Melchior alone. To someone that ancient, his own blood would betray him. Melchior would sense him long before he was able to do any good.

"What was your plan, Raphael?" he asked the glass. "What conflagration? What is it that Melchior is not enough of this century to realize?"

Iago had tried in vain to uncover some evidence of Raphael's plan, some sign that might tell him. But Raphael had been too smart for that. He had left no evidence that could be uncovered. Nothing had been left behind him. All Iago knew was that it had to do with the location where Melchior had placed his thralls. Somewhere in the Slovak community.

Once he knew where, he would know how.

2

He called himself Byron. He had been the second most powerful member of the Council that ruled the night in his city. Now he was dressed in rags and bound inside a wooden box. His mind reeled with the hunger. He hadn't fed in days. The only sensation he had, aside from the hunger, was a rhythmic rattling sensation, and the maddening smell of blood.

He had tried to escape what was happening. He and his circle had abandoned Cleveland when he saw that the power games he had fallen into with Lucian were wildly unbalanced. The Council might have been moved to act with the death of Raphael, but Byron had known it was already too late.

He had made it all the way to Chicago, and had begun talking to others of the blood, trying to find someone with the power or inclination to intervene. But before he had gotten anywhere, he had been taken.

Through the darkness he heard a screech of metal, and the rattling rhythm stopped. It had happened before, and like the prior times, the sudden change in his environment cut through the haze of his hunger, and he began fighting his imprisonment.

The aching lack inside him had yet to eat away all of his strength, or all of his mind. In his manic kicking and pulling, he focused his mind upon the smell of blood outside. His feet slammed the inside walls of the box containing him, his hands struggled with his bonds.

This time, after days of motion and stillness, dazed hunger and manic rage, something gave. His foot broke through one of the sides of the crate. The smell of blood was intense now, overwhelming. He scrambled for the hole like a madman. The force of the smell gave him the strength to break his bonds and push apart the crate around the hole his foot had made.

Driving him was a hunger frozen deep in the core of his body, a void inside him that could only be filled by the essence of the living. The drive was primal, and almost absolute. It was powerful enough for him to take two steps away from the crate that had been his prison before he realized exactly what he saw.

He stood inside a long rectangular chamber. The wooden walls had gaps between the boards that allowed moonlight to slice the interior into strips of narrow light alternating with wide bands of darkness. The smell of blood was rank within the car, as was the smell of overripe meat. Outside was the sound of chirping insects, but in here was only the buzz of flies.

Near his feet was a head, severed from its body. Moonlight slashed across it, revealing an eye and a swath of skin that had already begun to discolor. A fly walked across its cheek as Byron watched. He knew the face.

It had been one of his circle, one of the trusted ones he had taken to Chicago with him. He raised his eyes, and, for once, the hunger was forgotten.

They were everywhere, the bodies of his chosen. A dozen souls who had pledged fealty to him lay in this car, mutilated, their essence staining the straw bedding their corpses sprawled upon. Heads, their staring eyes accusing him.

Fear had completely replaced hunger.

There were giant sliding doors on either side of him. He dove to the right and began pulling madly at the latch. The door had been secured from the outside, but that hardly mattered to him. He pulled, and eventually the latch snapped. He spilled out over the moonlit railroad tracks.

Byron pushed himself upright and moved with a terror that he had not felt for over a century, not since he was human. He stumbled, running, through the weeds by the tracks. He had no idea where he was; all he wanted was to get away from the massacre behind him.

He had not gotten far before he heard a voice say, "Do you think you can escape *me* so easily?" It was as much in his head as in his ears. He knew then, felt in his core, that it was the ancient Melchior bringing this evil.

Byron spun around to find the source of the voice. Melchior was not that simply found. He saw the tracks, the woods bordering them, and a motionless boxcar, alone on a siding.

Byron screamed at the sky, "Why?"

"You are weak," came the shuddering reply. It slammed into his brain like a hot iron, dropping him to his knees.

"You hide from yourselves and the cattle that should serve us."

Byron looked around wildly, but his gaze could not find the speaker. The area felt abandoned, far from any artificial lights. The long grass rustled around him as he tried to gather his courage in the face of the thing threatening him. He spoke, his words sounded small and hollow on the wind. "*We* follow the Covenant."

"Empty words." The voice slammed into his head. "You knew me, what I did. If you loved those chains of the Covenant so much, you would have moved against me. But you did nothing, and when that no longer served you, you tried to flee." A shadow moved in the long grass in front of Byron. "Your kind disgusts me. A member of my proud race, nothing more than a scared animal."

Byron tried to stand, to move, but his body was still locked in the grip of his fear. That and the force of the being talking to him held him fast to the spot. As he tried to move, the shadow before him unfolded itself, became a dark figure emerging from the grass.

Facing him was Melchior, the ancient one. The first vampire ever to be punished under the Covenant, his corpse supposedly reduced to ashes. "What do you want?" he whispered.

The shadow stepped closer, parts of it resolving into pale skin and hair. "I want to take back everything that was lost to us with that blasphemous Covenant. I want us to rule again. I want the heads of my enemies on pikes in front of my palace. I want the cattle to worship my name."

Melchior reached out and touched him. Byron felt the touch like a brand that seared his flesh down to the bone, bone that felt frozen. "You were to be honored, like the others. Their blood fed my power, my service. Their essence will be part of my reign." Melchior shook his head slowly as he looked down at Byron. Byron could feel a wave of emotion that was too much like pity. "Not now. Your coward's blood will soak useless into the ground."

Byron heard the slide of metal, and managed to turn just in time to see the blade descending.

3

It had gotten to the point where the investigators began numbering the bodies. The newest one, decapitated and left by the B&O tracks in Brooklyn Township on the West Side, was labeled Number Five. It was Five because there was still no official connection to the corpse that washed up on Euclid Beach back in 1934. Officially, Andrassy and his still-unidentified companion were the first two of these murders.

Number Five was different because it was obvious that the man had met his death on the spot where the body was found. Unlike the others, he lay in the blood spilled by his death. To most everyone in the department, the recurring theme of the railroad tracks made it certain that the murderer was preying on transients that rode the rails. It seemed an obvious conclusion.

Stefan Ryzard felt it meant something else.

"As far as I can tell, he hasn't left his hotel room," Nuri said. His voice was thin and rattled at the other end of the phone.

Stefan shook his head. Nuri had followed their quarry to his business meeting in Chicago. He had watched him for nearly a week, reporting back nothing more sinister than meetings with a few congressmen—

That was sinister enough when Stefan thought about it.

"Something's rotten here." Stefan massaged the part of his leg that still ached.

"Yes," Nuri said, "but we've been watching him for months. We've yet to catch him doing anything."

Something rotten. "Are you certain he hasn't left?"

"I've been watching the room—"

"Dietrich knows he's being watched. Maybe he slipped out unobserved."

There was a pause, and then Nuri said, "You don't think I'm doing my job?"

Stefan tapped the desk with his fingers. "No, that's not it. But can you get a look inside his hotel room?"

"Yes, but wouldn't that be tipping our hand? You know he could order what's going on from anywhere."

Stefan nodded. "I want to know for sure that he's there. Otherwise I don't think we have a hand to tip." Stefan stared at his desk. On the blotter were fountain-pen doodles of fangs and crosses, the words "vampire" and "blood" heavily embellished. "One thing, though," Stefan added.

"What?"

"Go in during daylight."

"You want me to break into a hotel room in broad daylight?"

"It's safer."

Stefan could hear Nuri sigh. "This is more vampire stuff, isn't it."

Damn it, you were there, Stefan thought. *You saw everything I did.* He wanted to say it, but instead he said, "Just do it that way."

"If you say so."

"I do."

Nuri hung up the phone and wondered what he was getting into. The Chicago cops didn't know he was here, and if he got caught breaking into someone's hotel room, especially someone as wealthy as Eric Dietrich, there would be a lot of explanations to go through.

Nuri didn't know how Dietrich could have gotten past him. He had a room on the same floor, positioned where he could watch the exits downstairs, and the door to Dietrich's room. There were windows, but they were fifteen stories up.

Nuri checked his gun and slipped out into the hallway.

He felt oddly out of place here, disconnected from the rest of the world. He walked through a hall emblazoned with garish wallpaper, over deep red carpeting. It was a hallway into another era.

Dietrich's door was at the end of the hallway, with the most expensive suites. When Nuri reached it, he knocked just below the gilded numbers. He wanted to be sure that no one was home before he blithely popped the lock. A long minute passed without an answer. Nuri knocked again.

Again, no answer.

Maybe Stefan was right, and Dietrich managed to slip out from under him. That worried Nuri. If this time he missed him, how many other times? How long had he thought he'd been watching Dietrich, when he wasn't?

He knocked for a third time, and when he received no answer, he began working on the lock. In a few moments, the door swung open on a darkened room. The smell was musty for a hotel room, and it took him a few minutes for his eyes to adjust to the gloom beyond.

It was a huge suite, and Nuri faced the living area. Two large windows would have looked out over Chicago and to Lake Michigan beyond, but the drapes were closed on them. It even looked as if additional drapes had been added over the hotel's own, so not even a glimmer of the late evening sun leaked through.

Nuri had been trying to ignore Stefan's superstitious fears. Vampires were creatures of myth. But alone, facing these windows, shut against the day, it was hard to deny Stefan his myths. . . .

Which made no sense, since Nuri himself had seen Dietrich walking abroad in daylight.

Whatever the case, he didn't hear or see signs of anyone present. He let the door close behind him as he fumbled for the light switch. The lights came on, but feebly, half the bulbs dead or removed. They gave a weak illumination that was thick with shadows.

Something was disturbing about this room, something that Nuri couldn't quite identify. After standing by the door a long time, Nuri thought it could be something in the smell. It was rusty and didn't belong in a hotel room.

Nuri slowly walked into the living area, looking over the furniture, the end tables, the additional curtains on the windows. He could see signs that the room had been used; no maid had been here to clean up after the visiting congress-men. The ashtray was dirty and held the stubs of two cigars, and a few crystal glasses sat here and there on the tables.

Nuri bent over and took a whiff of one of the glasses. There was a strong smell of whiskey, but it wasn't the odor he was looking for.

He moved around toward a short hall that led to the bedroom, and across from it, the bathroom. As he stepped into the hall, the smell was worse. He identified it now.

Blood.

Nuri swallowed and drew his gun. The smell was stronger near the bathroom, so he slowly opened the door, using the jamb for cover. The smell of blood became more intense as he swept his revolver to cover the small darkened room. The smell was becoming sickening, so Nuri tried to breathe through his mouth as he fumbled for the light switch.

Above the sink, a light came on.

There was a mirror above the sink, but it had been cov-ered with a layer of butcher paper. As Nuri's gaze traveled down it, he saw a few red-brown dots sprinkled across its lower surface. Then he looked at the sink itself.

The porcelain was covered in blood. From the looks of it, it had once filled the sink. It had dried in patches, but a thick blackish-red liquid still filled the bottom about half an inch deep. On the counter, next to the sink, sat a crystal glass, twin to the whiskey glasses the congressmen had drunk from.

The inside of the glass was also coated in gore. One side of the rim was smeared with it, inside and outside, as if someone had drunk from it.

The sight made Nuri ill.

Nuri pulled out a handkerchief and held it over his nose. He had seen dead bodies before. Most were bloody to one extent or another. This was somehow different. It wasn't the sight, or even the smell that sickened—it was the thought of what had been done here.

Nuri stood a long time in the otherwise empty bathroom, staring at the sink. What *had* happened here?

Nuri had little chance to reflect, because the door oppo-site the bathroom flew open. Nuri turned in time to see a shadow fly out of the darkened room beyond. It came straight at him, and he barely had a chance to dive out of its way through the bathroom door.

He rolled onto his back in the hallway to the living area. The shadow dove on him, and Nuri fired. In the dim light he saw the bullet slam into the gut of Samson Fairfax. The bullet tore through the expensive suite he wore, spattering it with flecks of gore. The wound didn't bleed.

Fairfax dove on top of him, his face distorting as fangs seemed to grow from his jaw. Fairfax grabbed his gun hand in a grip like an iron band, and Nuri could feel the bones in the hand shifting and each finger became a clawed talon.

Nuri struggled under Fairfax, trying to break free, but all he accomplished was to inch the fight deeper into the room. Fairfax straddled him, his face turning into something demonic, taloned hands drawing blood from Nuri's wrists.

It opened its mouth and began leaning its face toward him. The breath was fetid, stinking of carrion. But worse than the smell was the fact that it was cold. Fairfax's breath held nothing of the heat of life in it.

Nuri whipped his head around in a panic, but he couldn't move. He was pinned to the ground. The thing held his wrists so he couldn't turn his gun—

His gun.

Nuri was panicked beyond his disbelief, and he was ready to try anything. His gun was pointing toward the overdraped windows. It was the only chance he had.

As he felt Fairfax's lips on his neck, Nuri struggled to aim his revolver, and fired. Four times he shot at the upper-right of the window, where the curtain was anchored. The fourth shot hit something.

With the crashing of glass, the curtains fell away as their weight tore the rod from the wall. Suddenly, the whole room was washed in the rose light of sunset. The light washed Fairfax and Nuri.

Fairfax pulled away, and Nuri could see the muscles trying to tear themselves back into human form. He moved fast, faster than Nuri could credit, but he didn't see where he was going. His eyes were squeezed shut, as if the light was too painful to see.

Nuri scrambled away, backing toward the center of the

light. He stopped and held a gun on Fairfax. It wasn't necessary. Fairfax was paying little attention to him right now.

Fairfax had stumbled backward quickly, seeming to attempt a retreat into the safety of the darkened bedroom. But, with his eyes closed, he had slammed into a wall instead. He staggered, as if numb or disoriented, each step seemed more unsteady than the last. All expression was gone from his face, the skin a slack mask, the eyelids no longer bunched up, but drooping over half closed eyes. He waved his hands as if blind, but his arms hit furniture and lamps without his notice.

The spectacle was even worse than the demonic transformation when he had tried to kill Nuri. In less than a few seconds he seemed to have become little more than an animate corpse, stumbling around blindly.

Nuri slowly pushed himself to his feet.

Fairfax stumbled into the room, like an exaggerated silent movie drunk. That was the most disturbing, the silence. Fairfax said nothing, didn't even seem to breathe. The only sound was from the furniture he toppled. Every step now, he seemed on the verge of falling.

Nuri was over the panic now. He knew he had to get this man out of the light, somehow the sunlight was killing him. Nuri needed a witness, someone who had seen what was going on.

Nuri ran up into the center of the room. He held his gun level, and reached out with the other hand. "You need to come with me, Mr. Fairfax."

Fairfax didn't seem to hear him, and he stumbled blindly into his arm. Nuri tried to grab him, but as soon as Fairfax seemed to notice the resistance to his forward movement, he stumbled backward—straight into the window.

Nuri tried to grab him again, but he was moving too fast, and bullet holes and the wreck of the draperies had weakened the windows already. When Fairfax's weight fell on it, the windows gave way, spilling Fairfax into the sky.

Nuri saw him fall the fifteen stories to the street below. The body slammed into a parked sedan with an explosion of glass. He seemed to stop moving long before he hit.

Nuri watched as a crowd began to circle the car, a few looking up toward him.

Nuri was certain that this time Samson Fairfax was dead.

Now all he had to do was figure out how to explain this to the Chicago cops.

4

Stefan stood in the corner of Ness' office. "We're getting Detective Lapidos back," Ness told him as he hung up the phone on his desk. "We're lucky that they weren't too ornery about it."

Stefan exhaled a little in relief. He'd been worried that the Chicago DA might make a stink over Nuri's presence there.

"What were you thinking, telling Nuri to break in there?"

Stefan looked at Ness. Staring at his young boss made him feel that much older. "Another body turned up, and I wanted to be sure that Dietrich was there."

"And he wasn't," Ness pointed out. "I let you get away with the warehouse, but this is completely out of our jurisdiction. We're both lucky I know people in Chicago that could smooth over this mess."

"But we have him now," Stefan said. "The blood, the attack on Nuri—"

"What we have—more precisely, what the Chicago Police have—is Samson Fairfax, already wanted in connection with his wife's death."

"Aren't they even going to talk to Dietrich?"

Ness nodded. "Of course they are. But Dietrich wasn't there, and Fairfax was. Without a witness tying him to anything illegal, the DA won't lift a finger when he's got a corpse to hang everything on."

Stefan balled his hands into fists and muttered, "How many bodies is it going to take?"

Ness narrowed his eyes and said, "That's quite enough. Don't push things." He leaned back in his chair. "I know that ever since the warehouse, you've had some odd ideas about Dietrich, and I've let them by because it'd be hard to replace you." He glanced at a stack of files piled on the corner of his desk. "But I'm beginning to wonder about your judgment."

Stefan had unpleasant memories of Inspector Cody telling him the same thing.

"I'm thinking about putting you and Nuri back on regular duty."

"But what about the Dietrich investigation?"

"I can put a pair of fresh eyes on it," Ness said.

Stefan felt himself sinking. How could he explain Dietrich in a sane manner? How could he tell Ness that no one that replaced him would understand the evil? Stefan tried. "No one else is going to understand what they're dealing with."

"And you do, Stefan? You know everything?" Ness shook his head. "That's just what I mean. You're too close to this investigation. Your reports come close to being hysterical. Sometimes they read as if you believe something supernatural is going on here."

Stefan swallowed. Something supernatural *was* going on here, something demonic. What he said was, "I've kept myself to what I've seen, and what I've gotten from witnesses . . ."

"Maybe new eyes will see something else." He reached over and began shuffling through the files on his desk. "Anyway, I need to do something about this Chicago business. I've been trying to deal discipline to the whole department, so I can't just let it by. You and Detective Lapidos are going on two week's leave, then you're being reassigned."

"But—"

"This may only be temporary. But I want you getting some distance from your work. You can't fly off the handle every time a body shows up."

Stefan nodded, "Yes, sir." His stomach was tied up into a knot of bile; he needed to leave. "Can I go now?"

Ness nodded, his face already turning toward a file he had pulled off of his desk.

Stefan really began to hate him. The only reason he saw for being removed from the case was he had come too close to breaking Ness' precious secrecy. With Nuri's conflict in the hotel, there was almost certainly some press attention. Press that Ness didn't orchestrate.

God forbid that the press might say something unpleasant about Ness and his department. Stefan felt cynical enough as he left that for a while he believed that Ness' whole departmental cleanup was a public relations gag.

Stefan was back at his desk putting things away when Nuri called. Stefan picked up the phone, and the first words he heard were, "Stefan, I've talked to the coroner, something strange—"

"Nuri, you better get back here," Stefan said. "Ness pulled us off the case."

"What? Why?"

"I guess he didn't like how we were handling it."

There was a long pause and Stefan could almost hear Nuri thinking, *you mean how you were handling it.*

"Does he know about this?" Nuri asked, finally.

"Know about what?"

"The autopsy on Samson Fairfax."

Stefan shook his head, "I thought he fell out a window after you shot him."

Nuri sucked in a breath and said, "That's what I thought, too. But the coroner insists he's been dead at least a couple of weeks, and that the gunshot and the fall occurred afterwards."

Stefan held the phone, unable to say anything.

"He says there seems to be some sort of chemical preservative contaminating the body. Just like Andrassy's friend." Nuri waited for a response, and after a few moments said, "Stefan, are you there?"

Stefan nodded, as if Nuri could see him. "I'm here, come back. I said we're off this case."

"Okay. Are you sure that you don't want this followed up? I'd hate to think I've gone through all this grilling for nothing. I can probably get a copy of the coroner's report."

"It's over, Nuri," Stefan said, his voice heavy.

"If you say so. I'll get on the first train back."

Stefan was about to say good-bye, but instead he told Nuri, "But get a copy of that report before you go. Just in case."

"Like I said, if you say so."

"Godspeed, Nuri."

"Are you all right?" Nuri asked.

No. "Yes, I'm fine."

"See you tomorrow, then," Nuri said. The line died as he hung up.

Stefan slowly rested the handset back into the cradle and resumed cleaning his desk. There were notes and speculations he didn't wish to leave in the office while he was gone.

5

FDR was in town to visit the Great Lakes Exposition. As usual, the president was followed into town by dozens of aides, officials, and other political types. As usual, when such people came to town, Carlo Pasquale waited in a limousine. A few of FDR's entourage would be meeting the Master tonight.

Despite accusations of being a class traitor, members of FDR's administration weren't averse to meeting with wealthy businessmen. Carlo thought it was almost amusing.

He waited outside the Exposition, far back from the rear of the motorcade. He watched the uniformed police controlling the swelling crowds and waited for his guests. Cops used to make him nervous. Even before, when he was working for the Mayfield Road Gang and two-thirds of the cops were bought off, cops had made him nervous.

Not since he started serving the Master. The Master's protection went far beyond anything his old bosses could manage. No one could mess with him; he was invulnerable. The Master saw what he saw, and those who saw Carlo saw a piece of the Master. Carlo saw it in the way people turned away when he looked at them.

His old employer had tried to bump him off several times. Each time the Master had seen it, and the assassins were as dead as those who tried to kill the Master—except for those the Master chose to serve Him, as Carlo did. The Master was very persuasive.

Carlo watched the evening sky and wondered how many more sunsets he would see.

Carlo pushed away the thought. The Master needed service in the daylight as well as at night. It was his honor to remain human. If the Master would grant him eternal life, He would in his own time. It was best for him not to think about that.

Carlo turned and studied a sign for the Aquacade at the exposition.

It was after dark when Carlo Pasquale delivered his passengers to the Union Terminal Tower. They were going to meet the Master in one of the offices he held in the building. The Master had just come from Chicago. Carlo heard that He had dealt with a legal problem.

Carlo smiled. He knew that all the Master needed to solve any legal problem was talk to the DA. Money didn't even have to change hands. The Master could *convince*.

Carlo waited outside, leaning against the fender of the limo, taking drags on a cigarette. He felt good, as if he had found his purpose in life.

Behind him, through Public Square, transit cars rattled by. Carlo listened to the sound of the electric trolleys as he watched his smoke curl up into the darkened sky. He was watching the smoke spread in the windless air when he felt something stab him in the back of his neck.

He tensed up and dropped the cigarette, more in surprise than in pain. It fell against his leg, burning a hole in his trousers and searing his leg. He sprang away from the car, slapping at his burned leg and simultaneously turning to see what had stabbed him.

His move was way too awkward, and as he turned, his leg slipped from under him. He slammed into the sidewalk, but he didn't really feel it. His body felt wrapped in cotton. His vision blurred as he tried to look up. All he could make out was a darkened shadow leaning over him.

His last thought, as he lost consciousness was, *Master . . .*

Carlo Pasquale woke up hearing a babbling chorus of shrieks and smelling the rankest odor he had ever encountered. The sound was like the entrance to the gates of hell. The smell was old blood that had gone sour. He had smelled it before, and for a few panicked moments he thought that he had offended the Master and was to be executed like an enemy.

Then he opened his eyes and faced a light shining down

on him. It was too bright for him to see anything except what was immediately next to him. He was on a concrete floor, stained and tacky with blood. Also, Carlo noticed with a sense of disorientation, the floor was dotted with feathers. After blinking a few times, he noticed cages just outside his field of vision. Tiny cages, coated with feathers and manure.

The horrid sound was the cackling of chickens, thousands of them outside the area he could see.

He tried to sit up, but he couldn't move. He was weighted and bound with chains, too much for him even to lift, much less escape.

Beyond the light, a voice spoke above the sound of the imprisoned birds. "Are you awake, Carlo Pasquale?"

Carlo yelled at the voice, "You're making a hell of a mistake. I got protection."

"I know. That is why you're here."

"Mr. Dietrich is going to find you—"

"No, he isn't." The voice was much too calm. "Your master can't save you."

Carlo was about to shout something more, but he stopped when he realized that the voice had said "master." That was a secret. No one was supposed to know that he had fed from the Master. No one should know that He was the Master.

The voice moved in a circle around him, but he couldn't see the speaker, or hear the footsteps over the din. "Your master is bound through you, can see what you see, but what do you see? What do you hear? What do you smell? This place is so rank with sensation that even someone as powerful as Melchior will not be able to pick you out of it before I've had what I want."

When the voice said "Melchior," Carlo shuddered. Others weren't supposed to know the Master's true name. He struggled and began to feel the first stirrings of fear, the first sense that he might not be fully protected.

"You can't do this," Carlo yelled. "He won't permit it."

The voice laughed. "I'd admire your faith, if it wasn't Melchior's blood talking through you. You're less than a thrall, less than human even, a debased thing, a perversion."

"I work for Dietrich, and he'll—"

Something splashed across his legs from the shadows. The smell of gasoline watered his eyes. His voice caught in his throat, choking on the fumes. The cacophony of poultry redoubled in volume. Carlo began a renewed struggle against his bonds.

The voice spoke again, as another splash of liquid fell against Carlo's chest.

"Melchior fed you just enough of his blood to bind your will to his. Not even enough to pull you into our world had you died."

"I don't know what you're talking about."

More gasoline splashed into his face, burning his eyes and searing his lips. He maniacally shook his head from side to side, fighting the pain. He had to hold his breath against the smell.

"Melchior is one of the blood, Carlo. A demon out of your mythology. A vampire. His blood contains the seed of his nature, his will. A little, and you become a willing extension of his will. Enough will pull you across the threshold of death, make you a thrall, an extension of his body, of his unlife, bound to him until his destruction." The voice stopped circling, stopping at Carlo's head. The speaker bent forward. Carlo strained to see the man's face, but even when he leaned into the light, Carlo's burning eyes couldn't make out more than a blur.

He wanted to call out, deny what the man was saying, but something held him silent—more than the choking fumes that kept his breath from him. Something in the core of his being was frozen at the presence of this anonymous being. Something fearful that bound his will like a vise. It was terrifyingly similar to what he felt in the presence of his Master. . . .

"Those of the blood have few weaknesses, Carlo. Sunlight can kill the flesh of all but the most powerful. Dismemberment is Melchior's favored method of assassination. Then there's immolation of the flesh." Carlo felt a hand brush his cheek. He felt a leather glove leave a trail on his wet cheek. The touch felt like a brand against icelike skin. Carlo began shivering. Inside, his body felt frozen. It had been several long minutes, and he still wasn't breathing.

What's happened to me?

"Your master promised you life after death. . . ."

Somehow his voice managed to find itself. "No," he whispered, tasting gasoline along with his own stale breath. Even through the fumes, Carlo began to realize that the smell of blood came from him as much as anywhere else. His breath was like cold carrion, and tasted like sour iron through the gasoline.

"I needed you to talk, Carlo. To talk against the creature that bound you. The only way to do that was to take you as my own. You're mine as much as his now. My thrall. My flesh."

"But what . . ."

"Look at me!"

Carlo could do nothing but obey the command. His eyes opened, despite the burning. Despite the streaming tears. He looked up into a golden mask. The mask was twisted and frowning, covering the whole face except for the eyes. Those eyes stared into his own with a burning pressure that made him forget the sting of gasoline.

The other gloved hand laid itself on Carlo's other cheek. Both hands clamped down with a pressure as heavy as the chains across his chest and legs. His head was held immobile.

"I see into you, Carlo Pasquale. You will remember everything of Melchior that you saw or heard. His actions, his plans, where he keeps his allies. You will remember, and you will speak them to me."

Carlo felt Melchior draining away inside him in the presence of this new Master. He opened his mouth and spoke, despite the part of him that was terrified of doing so. He spoke, and he couldn't tell if he used more his voice or his mind. It seemed days he spoke, everything falling up into that frowning golden mask.

After he had said everything, the hands let go, and his head fell exhausted to the ground. It was over. Carlo began to recover a little. It was just another change of bosses, after all. He had gone through it once, he could go through it again. Hell, this guy, mister anonymous, had pulled him all the way over. Which was more than Melchior did.

He really was invulnerable now, he couldn't die. . . .

Carlo screwed up his courage and said, "Okay, you've got everything, boss. Can you let me go now?"

Carlo realized that he could sense, somewhat, what his

boss was feeling. The emotion seemed to roll off of him like an invisible cloud-bank. The feeling Carlo got wasn't reassuring. It seemed like pity.

The masked man stood and reached into the pocket of his dark overalls. "You don't understand," he said. "I cannot allow Melchior to discover my blood within you. If he finds that, he can find me."

"Look, I won't roll over on you," Carlo's voice took on a pleading tone. "Hell I don't even know who you are."

"I'm afraid you never will." The masked man pulled out a book of matches.

Carlo Pasquale burned.

When Carlo's burning corpse stopped trying to move, Iago removed the mask of Tragedy and tossed it into the fire, followed by his gloves. The air was rank, with thick tarlike smoke, and the surrounding poultry were deafening with their objections.

Iago couldn't breathe comfortably, but he stayed to watch Carlo reduced to ash. He didn't watch with any enjoyment. If it had been possible for Carlo to live, as thrall or as owner of his own blood, Iago would have preferred it.

But Melchior had claimed this one as his own, and that meant that Melchior would find him, eventually. It would be simple for Melchior to sense an elder's blood in another, and sense whose. It would be simple even if Carlo had been slain in a less complete manner. Iago could not leave any trace of himself behind, otherwise there would be little chance for him. The fate of the Council told him that much.

All Iago had was anonymity. Even if Melchior sensed what happened to his puppet, all he would have was a forest of impressions impossible to pin down, a masked figure draining Carlo of his secrets.

Iago stared at the charred black flesh as the flames died down. He wished Carlo had known more for the price he paid. For the price Iago paid. The slaughter he had just committed, taking what another had claimed, and bringing him over only to kill him. It savaged the Covenant as badly as Melchior did.

Those of the blood do not kill those of the blood. . . .

6

Stefan Ryzard stared at the ceiling of his apartment, trying to sleep. Moonlight washed through the bedroom, giving everything a pale blue glow. In the shadows, barely visible, pictures still clung to the walls. Stefan had not taken down any of the remnants of his long investigation into Dietrich. The walls were still covered by papers, surveillance photos, and forensic details of the mutilated corpses.

His part was over. It was no longer his problem. He kept telling himself that. Despite that, he didn't take the papers off of his wall. He couldn't stop thinking of Dietrich.

The fact that Dietrich existed was an ache inside him. The more Stefan thought about him, the more he became convinced that Dietrich was the devil that Samson Fairfax had told him about, the devil that Edward Mullen couldn't lie for anymore.

Whoever investigated Dietrich, Stefan knew that they'd find little more than he had. No direct connection to the murders. Perhaps they'd see signs of the supernatural that no one else would credit. Surveillance would be useless, and Stefan expected anyone who got too close to Dietrich would disappear like those mob assassins.

He lay naked on sweat-stained sheets, trying not to think of what was happening out there. It wasn't his business anymore. . . .

A shadow passed over his bedroom window, wiping away the moonlight, plunging the room into darkness. Stefan bolted upright, his heart racing. Before he could make out what had passed in front of his window, it was gone.

Still, Stefan sat up on his bed, the copper taste of fear searing his mouth. The window was open to the night air, and next to the window a picture of Edward Andrassy's decapitated body fluttered in the breeze.

In a few minutes, his breathing and his pulse returned to normal. He slipped off the bed and walked over to the window. He closed it, throwing the latch.

Even with the window closed, there was still a chill in the room.

"Greetings, Detective Ryzard."

The voice came from behind him, and Stefan spun around to face it. Standing in his bedroom, in front of the only door, stood Iago. His overalls were black in the moonlight. He looked paler, gaunter than he had seemed the last time Stefan had seen him.

"What do you want?" Stefan whispered. He didn't ask how he had gotten in. If Iago was the same kind of being as Dietrich, it seemed that they had a talent for not being seen when they didn't want to be seen.

"I want an end to Eric Dietrich."

Stefan shook his head. "You're too late, I'm off that case."

"Look at your own walls," Iago said, his eyes boring into him.

Stefan couldn't answer that. He wasn't actively investigating Dietrich, or the murders. He didn't interview anyone. He didn't watch the suspects. . . .

But the case still obsessed him. Dietrich still gripped his thoughts. Stefan still felt the cold overpowering presence of the devil named Eric Dietrich. It was as if, having touched him, Stefan had tainted his own soul.

"Why are you here?" Stefan said. His breath was dry and tasted like copper.

"I need an ally, policeman."

Stefan felt the force of Iago's will spilling over, overwhelming his own. He prayed to God for strength, and found enough to take a step backward. "Why should I help you?" his voice came out in a hoarse whisper. "Why should I help any of your kind?"

Iago took a step forward. The moonlight splashed across his face, carving shadows across his pale skin, making him look like a marble bust of the Devil himself. He ran his hand over his beard. "You know me so well that you know what I am?"

Stefan backed to the wall, the wall that bore a crucifix. "An undead thing," Stefan said. "A damned soul. A creature of Satan."

Iago laughed, but he stopped advancing. "You've decided, then, haven't you? We're Vampyr, Nosferatu, Dwellers of the Darkness." Iago released his beard and bowed with a flourish. His eyes, however, remained on Stefan's own.

"I won't help any servant of evil," Stefan said. He wanted to cower, he felt his knees wanting to bend, but he held his back straight to the wall. Thumbtacks dug into his backside, where he had posted pages on Dietrich and the murders. He didn't move. He held his spot under the cross, fearing that any more movement might lead to collapse.

"Am I evil, then?" Iago said. "This your Bible says?"

"You feast on the living."

"Didn't your savior say to drink of his blood? Eat of his flesh?"

Stefan's stomach tightened at the blasphemy. He straightened and said, "In the name of God and Jesus Christ, I command you to leave me."

Iago actually took a step back. "You should listen to me, policeman."

The retreat emboldened Stefan. He stepped away from the wall and reached for the crucifix. "In the name of the Lord—"

Iago hissed at him. His face retreated into shadow, but Stefan thought he could see parts of it, bone and skin, move and distort. Iago's voice lowered from the cultured tone it usually took, and became closer to a growl. "What Christian charity is this?"

Stefan took a step forward, holding the crucifix.

Iago slunk backward. He spat like a cat, his body hunched over and twisted, completely in shadow now. He pointed at Stefan, his finger reached into the moonlight. It had changed, becoming a twisted thing that was almost a talon. "You make a mistake." The voice was harsh now, barely human. "You might pain me, but your faith in that stick will be as nothing to Melchior. He is your enemy."

"Begone, fiend of Satan, in the name of the Lord, Jesus Christ." Stefan took another step forward.

Iago shrieked and leaped. Stefan stumbled backward, but

the leap didn't carry Iago toward him. Instead, Iago leaped at the bedroom window. The manic dive carried him back into the moonlight, and gave Stefan a single terrified glimpse of what he'd become before he slammed through the window.

The window shattered, the frame exploding outward, as Iago sailed out into the night— If what Stefan saw was still Iago. He had only a glimpse as it had sprung by him, but what Stefan had seen resembled a twisted bat-winged gargoyle, skin like horn, and a mouth with pointed jaws and teeth longer than its clawed fingers. It had crashed naked through the window, tearing most of it away from the wall. He heard the wreckage crash onto the ground below before he stepped up to the window.

A chill wind blew in, rocking pieces of the window frame back and forth. Around him. Pieces of wood now pointed out into the night, while below him, broken glass glittered on the street. The only sign that Stefan saw of Iago was a shadow moving, almost too quick to see, on the roof of the apartment across the street, three floors above him.

Stefan stepped back from the windows and saw, on the floor, the remnants of a pair of black overalls. The seams had burst open. Stefan crossed himself and prayed for his own soul.

An elder named Abraham began the last twenty-four hours of his three hundred years of existence in the Union Terminal Station. He had traveled from Chicago in a private car, and upon his arrival there was little of the night left. This didn't disturb him. He wasn't hurried. After three centuries, he was never hurried.

He walked out to the street, ignoring the humans around him, and because he wished it, the humans ignored him. None would remember seeing him pass.

Once he passed through the foot of the Terminal Tower, and faced Public Square, he stood in the middle of the night-empty street and breathed in the air.

Even here, far removed from everything that had happened, he could smell the corruption. Something ugly was at play here. For the first time, Abraham felt his confidence shaken. He knew that there was a slaughter going on here. The circles in Chicago knew that there were circles here

being devastated, their leaders being killed and left for
dead.

For years, those outside the demesne of Cleveland saw
it as an internal problem. A circle, however large, was loath
to interfere with the internal problems of another circle.

It wasn't until those outside lost all contact with the
Council in this city that they even considered sending one
of their own to investigate. Even then, the debate took
months, while the only contact with the community in
Cleveland were confused individuals escaping the collapse
of their society—some little more than thralls freed too
soon by the death of their master.

Until now, Abraham had theorized that the destruction
had been wrought by a member of the Council itself, someone whose ambition for control finally outstripped his loyalty to the Covenant. The other likely suspect was someone
in the society who had lost his mind. Though, when one of
the blood went mad, the madness rarely persisted this long
before the offender was disciplined.

Abraham now felt that both possibilities were wrong.
There was an oppressive psychic pall over the city. Some-
thing dark and powerful was in control of the city now.
Abraham could almost feel it become aware of him.

In the past century, nothing had been able to frighten
him. The emotion was so old and ill-used that it took a few
moments for Abraham to realize that fear was what he was
feeling right now. A cold hand gripped his chest, and for a
few long minutes he stopped breathing and his heart
stopped beating.

He had an impulse to walk back into the Union Terminal, reboard his velvet-curtained train car, and leave this
place. For moments he considered accepting the disgrace
of abandoning his job here, rather than stepping forward
and confronting what had taken this city.

Abraham only considered it, and the fear was only fleet-
ing. He was, after all, one of the oldest and most powerful
beings in this country. He walked off into the night, to find
the remnants left by those of the blood, and of the creature
that had slain them.

Abraham stepped into their meeting place, a long table
before a set of tall windows. From here he could see into

the seething industrial valley of the city. He stepped up to the table and placed a hand upon it. It disturbed a layer of dust.

Twelve chairs were behind the table, five were overturned.

Abraham looked at the chairs and spoke quietly to himself, "Laila, Anacreon, Raphael, Byron . . ." Abraham looked at the last chair, lying on its back on the floor. "Who?" he asked.

The being responsible had been in this room. Abraham could feel the presence. It had sunk into the walls like an evil smell, a spiritual rot. He could almost see the man walking into this private chamber, and methodically tipping over the chairs of his victims.

Like disposing of the bodies in public, it showed an almost incomprehensible arrogance.

The air changed. It became heavy, weighted with the darkness around him. He could smell, sense, one of the blood enter the room. Abraham should have noticed another's presence long before it was this close. As he turned to face the visitor, he had a disturbing thought—he was only perceiving the other because the other permitted it.

The darkness seemed to deepen near the doorway where the visitor stood, but Abraham could still see him clearly. His most notable feature was blond hair too long for this age. The spirit behind his eyes flared brighter than any Abraham had ever seen before. Behind most eyes Abraham saw a candle he could make dance or dim at his whim. Abraham knew that he could no more influence what was behind these eyes than an eyedropper could influence a bonfire.

The visitor leaned forward on a cane, and looked Abraham up and down. There was a half-smile on his face, as if he saw something amusing. "Are you looking for something here, my friend?"

Abraham didn't lie. His purpose was evident. "There's been a violation of the Covenant here. The local elders have failed to deal with it—"

The other laughed. When he did, whatever heat and light were left in the room seemed to drain away. "The elders are gone."

"Four, yes—"

"All." The visitor walked forward. His presence seemed to radiate cold, sucking the heat off of Abraham's skin. "All of them have left, one way or another."

Abraham couldn't look away from his eyes; the power there, the age, the infinitely cold arrogance wouldn't allow him to. "It is you," Abraham said. This was the creature he had been sent here to stop.

Abraham moved in a flash. Before he had even allowed his conscious mind to think, talons had extended from his hands and he was bringing them down on the visitor. Both hands aimed overhand, across the chest, toward the heart. Removal of that organ would be as fatal as decapitation.

Abraham's victim didn't move as his talons came down, slicing into the chest cavity. He tore through clothes, flesh, and bone too easily. It was almost as if the flesh gave way before he reached it. Then his hands jerked with an impact that almost dislocated his shoulders.

The cane clattered to the ground.

The visitor held each of Abraham's wrists. Abraham's hands were buried deep into holes in the visitor's chest, just below the pectorals. The visitor's suit was shredded, and Abraham's arms were spattered with tarlike blood up to his elbows. Light glinted off of the torn flesh, as if it were moving.

The visitor showed little sign of pain, or even discomfort. That was when the fear came back. Abraham could feel the lungs shredded beneath his hands. Such an injury would have taken Abraham to the ground at the very least. This thing before him barely noticed.

Abraham tried to remove his hands, but the visitor was stronger. Much stronger. He was held fast.

The laugh was worse this time, worse because he felt it in his hands more than heard it. It was nearly silent, and it was accompanied by blood dripping from the visitor's lips.

"This is your Covenant?" The voice was below a whisper, its breath sucked in through the holes in his chest. "Strike down any with the will, the power, to take what is due him? Hobble our race? Keep us silent and cowering in the shadows? That is your creed?"

Abraham tried to pull his hands away. His muscles tore

from bone and reknit themselves into more efficient patterns, but it was no use. And while he struggled, the flesh around the wounds began pulling together, the gore flowing into itself, fusing under new skin.

"So terrified of death, of discovery, that a handful of bodies can paralyze you. The fact I am here is proof enough that I am necessary."

Abraham struggled as the stranger's flesh wrapped itself around his hands. As he struggled, the tarlike blood that coated his arms began to flow upwards. He could feel it under his jacket advancing along his upper arms, toward his neck. Feeling that, the fear turned into panic.

The blood was everything to his kind. Mind, soul, and flesh were all one with the blood. In all of them the flesh shifted with the will, but it was near the apotheosis of power for the blood to act as an extension of the body, moving to its own will. Abraham had never seen it, and had never met anyone who had. It was something a millennial ancient might aspire to.

The blood tightened around his arms like a serpent. He felt his own skin tear and give way as the burning tendrils sank into his own flesh. When the blood seared down to the bone, he felt the flesh binding him give way. He was thrown backward, slamming up against the unused meeting table.

He slid to the ground, unable to move. A burning alien presence slid beneath the skin, traveling from his arms, to his neck, his head. While Abraham felt the presence burn into his mind, he felt something else. The blood carried a name, an old name.

"Melchior," he whispered, a last conscious act of his own will.

Melchior stepped forward, the tatters of his suit bloodstained and hanging over a naked, unblemished chest. "I can read you now," he said, standing over him. "I read you, Abraham, as easily as you could once read a witless thrall. I smelled your presence the moment you entered my demesne." He knelt down next to Abraham and cupped his chin. "It *is* mine now, no one left here to challenge my authority. I already own countless human puppets, and thralls beyond your own petty imagining. I see through all their eyes, as I see through yours now."

He stood up, pulling Abraham upright by the chin. Abraham's legs followed through with the motion against his will. He felt the complete domination of Melchior. He couldn't act now except as Melchior willed.

Abraham kept thinking, over and over, that Melchior had died centuries ago.

"You came to see," Melchior said. "See you shall. I shall take you to Lucian; you will bear witness to my kingdom." He passed his hand over Abraham's eyes and the world became a black void.

When Abraham was called awake, he had recovered some of his will. Enough to move, to turn his head, to think. All of it was too late to do him any good. Melchior had overwhelmed him for long enough to bring him into the heart of his new kingdom. Long enough for him to be chained.

The room was long and dimly lit. He was at one end, and a mass of pale faces filled the other end, spreading back into the darkness. Melchior stood between him and the crowd of spectators. The watchers were of many races, and wore the battered clothing of the unemployed, the drifters, the homeless. Their faces were worn and dirty, and all wore the same expression. They all looked upon Melchior with a beatific expression of faith.

Melchior held a golden cup in front of him, and gave it to the crowd. When he handed the cup to someone, he would say, "Drink of my blood," and they would drink. It was a dark mass, and it disgusted and horrified Abraham at the same time. The bond between master and thrall was personal, sacred. To spread one's own blood so widely was something close to pure evil. Melchior's kingdom was a megalomaniac's attempt to control as many beings as possible.

Abraham saw the cup pass from mouth to mouth, and he saw in those eyes a worship. These dregs saw Melchior as a god. Trash that no one of the blood would lower themselves to call their own, these Melchior took.

It sickened Abraham.

As the ceremony continued, he tried to free himself. He struggled, but while he normally would have the strength to part his chains, his confrontation with Melchior had drained him too deeply. Melchior's blood, the blood that bound the slaves in front of him, had burned too long within him. Abraham's body and spirit had exhausted itself just to fight free from those internal chains.

If only he could feed, himself, regain his strength.

After what seemed an eternity of struggle, Melchior turned with the cup in his hand.

"Welcome to my kingdom, Abraham," Melchior said. "These, and countless others like them, they call me Lord." Abraham strained against his chains and Melchior smiled at his struggles. "You're the pinnacle of what our race has become. Weak. Without even the strengths of your dubious Covenant." Melchior held up the golden chalice, the inside stained with red. It glittered in the candlelight, the odor powerful, seductive. The liquid pulled at him, tearing at the emptiness inside him.

"You want to take it," Melchior said. "Take it, partake in *my* Covenant." Abraham's soul was at such a low ebb, the weakness and the hunger so strong, that he wanted to take it. Abraham was close to pledging fealty to this dark lord if it meant to end to the burning void inside him.

Then disgust overwhelmed Abraham. He was of free blood. He took his own blood, untainted by any others of his kind. What had flowed through Melchior's veins wasn't blood, it was liquid slavery. If he partook willingly, he would become Melchior's, little more than the rabble worshiping him.

From somewhere, he found the strength to say, "Go to hell."

Melchior frowned and upturned the cup next to him. Blackish liquid spilled on the straw-covered floor. He dropped the cup and took a step toward Abraham. As he moved forward, his followers surged forward to fall on their knees before the spilled blood.

"This *is* hell," Melchior said, "and I am its lord and master."

Melchior walked close enough that Abraham felt his breath on his cheek. It was cold against his skin.

"Poor choice, my friend." Abraham heard the scrape of metal. "You will become part of my body one way or another." Abraham saw the shine of a blade in Melchior's hand. "If my blood does not flow in your veins, your blood shall flow in mine."

The last thing Abraham saw was the circle of Melchior's thralls sucking his blood off of the floor.

Then the world went dark for good.

7

"Something has to be done about these bodies that keep showing up," Mayor Burton said. Sweat sheened on his face as he looked across the court at Ness. They stood in a handball court at the Cleveland Athletic Club. Ness was holding his own against the older man. His matches with the mayor almost inevitably turned toward business. Ness suspected half the time it was to throw off his game.

"I wanted a crime-fighting administration," Burton gave the ball a savage return. "This is making it look bad."

Ness scrambled for the return and said, "Which bodies?" Ness suspected "which bodies;" he read the same papers that Mayor Burton did. What had been a deep, almost subliminal, unease about the decapitated corpses turning up in the Run and elsewhere seemed to have erupted into full-fledged panic. The papers were beginning to scream now.

This was the first time that the mayor had brought up the subject.

Burton made it to the ball, and in a breathless voice told him, "The Kingsbury Run murders, Ness."

Ness let the ball pass by him and turned to face Mayor Burton. "I have investigations ongoing—"

"I'm sure you do." Burton nodded and wiped sweat from his forehead. "That's not the point. I'm sure you're doing your job. You've done good work cleaning the graft from the police department, and in everything else from organized crime to traffic safety."

"But?"

Burton turned and looked at him, "*But* people are raving

that there's a maniac loose in the city and the police aren't doing anything to catch him."

Ness nodded. "Making public any suspects might sabotage the investigation."

"I need something public, Ness. Your greatest strength is making yourself look good in the press. I need you to do that. I need public demonstration of the department's will in this matter." Burton walked over to a bench, grabbed a towel, and flung it over his shoulders. "I want the public to know we're after this guy. I want every spare man on it. You understand me?"

"Yes, sir, I think I do."

The meeting was on a Monday. A month and a half after being taken off his secret investigation of Dietrich, he was called in with a lot of other cops into a briefing on what was being called the "Torso Murders." He was there, with the other detectives, under orders to behave as if everything was new to him.

He noticed some press on the way to the meeting, and he couldn't help thinking of it as some sort of publicity stunt. Stefan didn't know if he really wanted to be here, so he took a seat way in back of the room, far away from the blackboard, the tacked-up pictures, and the coroner.

Ness was here, as well as Emil Musil and Orly May, the detectives in charge of the public investigation. Nuri wasn't, but Stefan didn't think too much about that. Their partnership had ended when he was removed from the Dietrich assignment, and he hadn't seen much of his former partner since.

The room was cramped as more of the Homicide squad filed in. Eventually no seats were left and people began lining up in back. By then the room was filled with thirty or forty people. The air was stale and thick with cigarette smoke, and the crowd added a claustrophobic pressure to the room.

Ness spoke first. "We all want this madman caught. Every new body is cause for growing panic. We're here to go over what we have, to try and get a picture of the man, something concrete we can give to the press."

That confirmed Stefan's opinion that this was all a grand-stand play for the reporters. As Ness kept talking, Stefan scanned the room, reporters and policemen, sweating in the stifling heat of this enclosed room. No windows, or even a fan.

Even so, as the coroner and the county pathologist got up and began reviewing each individual murder, Stefan felt cold wash over his body. They explained the deaths by decapitation, the emasculation of three of the bodies, the locations they were found.

Every single one of the deaths had been by decapitation. Some were dismembered, some not, but that was the singular fact of all the murders.

As other detectives added details of their own investigation, Stefan remained silent. Every one of them told of leads that went nowhere, crank calls, and bogus confessions, but none of them came close to the land where Stefan had trod.

They all talked of homosexual madmen, sexual perversion, insanity, even Jack the Ripper. None came close to discussing Eric Dietrich; none, it seemed, had come near the man Ness had set him to investigate. Ness himself didn't add Dietrich's name to the mix. It was as if his whole investigation had meant nothing, had never happened.

They were all looking for a human madman. Even Ness, who had heard everything that Stefan had seen. Even when they mentioned the lack of blood in and around most of the corpses, they didn't see. Maybe they *couldn't* see.

They were looking for something darker than a sexual pervert.

One of the doctors present was talking about the hypothetical profile of their murderer, "He commits the murders in a private place. He has to be middle class or above—have his own house or a large apartment where he can dismember the bodies and clean them off."

"That," someone said, "or access to someplace private professionally. A warehouse, a storeroom . . ."

A train, Stefan thought.

He was here just as a member of the Homicide unit. But as the talk went on around him, he was back on the case again, and thinking of Dietrich's business dealings with Van Sweringen, and all those pictures of Dietrich at the Union Terminal Downtown.

8

Nuri Lapidos stood at the edge of a fetid swamp and watched the Pennsylvania authorities drag bodies from it. One of the New Castle cops was explaining to one of the Cleveland detectives that this swamp was a dumping spot for crime gangs, that there'd been half a dozen bodies found here over the years.

The latest one lay next to the shore waiting for the coroner's van. It was dark with slime, swollen by decomposition, and emitted a smell that was beyond Nuri's experience. The black midges that seemed to coat the surface of the swamp also coated the body like a second skin.

Nuri held a handkerchief over his face and tried to be unobtrusive. His, now solo, investigation of Dietrich was still secret, even if the murder investigation was becoming more high profile. This was the first time that any of the detectives tried to connect the murders in Cleveland with anything out of state.

There was one obvious connection. The corpse was missing a head.

How many more bodies have we missed because they weren't dropped somewhere obvious?

The question disturbed him. The corpse that washed up on Euclid Beach, how many others might be still in Lake Erie? How many more might be in this swamp?

The search for other bodies dragged on into the night. Nuri left the scene after it became too dark to see anything. He had seen enough, anyway. He had added the new bodies to the "torso killer's" tally. The body was far enough gone that Nuri doubted that it would be identified. Anonymous, like five others.

He waited by the one Cleveland police car and lit a cigarette, waiting for the other detectives. He took long drags on his smoke, trying to empty his lungs of the smell the corpse had left there.

Somehow it felt ominous that there were bodies this far afield. It gave the impression that the high-profile investigation only covered a small element of what was going on here.

Nuri watched the flashlights shining through the woods between him and the swamp. The beams were fragmented, seeming more to cast shadow than illuminate anything. The dark seemed to sink into Nuri, down to the bone.

"Nuri Lapidos," a voice called from the darkness.

The voice startled him. He dropped his cigarette; it tumbled off his clothing, throwing embers into the night. He turned to face the speaker, who stood on the other side of the dirt road, away from the police lights. "Who's there?" Nuri asked quietly, his hand drifting toward his holster.

The man stepped out of the darkness. He was dressed anonymously, his overalls and porkpie hat matching thousands of unemployed workmen who drifted from city to city. His face was different, pale skin, black goatee, and riveting eyes—all were more extraordinary.

"Good evening, Detective," he said.

"Who are you?" Nuri asked. "How do you know me?"

"I've seen who you are. You watch a creature calling himself Dietrich. You play your detective's games as if he were a mortal open to human forms of prosecution."

Nuri stepped back. His hand was on his gun now. "Who are you, one of Dietrich's men?"

The man laughed. "You fight an arrogance which sees you as less than a threat. Human authority can never touch him within your law." The man looked into Nuri's eyes, and he felt something deep within those eyes pressing down on him, preventing him from moving. He tried to draw his gun, but his hand refused to move. He tried to speak, but his mouth wouldn't move.

The man stepped up to him, close enough that the weight of his presence was like a pressure in Nuri's chest. "Say nothing," he said to Nuri. "An army of police, playing your police games, would not bring down the thing called Melchior. Melchior must be destroyed."

"Wh—" Nuri barely managed to choke out a word before the man reached out and grabbed his throat. It was barely a touch, but it crushed the breath from his voice.

"I said, do not speak." The man's voice lowered to a whisper. "I want only one thing from you. You will convince Detective Stefan Ryzard to meet with me."

Nuri tried to say something, but all he managed was a strangled breath.

"You will tell him to meet with Iago when he calls. Every passing day, Melchior increases his temporal power. His tendrils already reach to the farthest points of this country and beyond. Eric Dietrich must be destroyed before he becomes unassailable."

Iago lowered his hand from Nuri's throat. Nuri bent over, gasping for breath.

"You will tell your partner this, and he will meet me."

Nuri raised his head and drew his gun.

It was too late. Iago had retreated into the darkness from which he had emerged.

"He could have killed me!" Nuri yelled at Stefan. He stood in the center of Stefan's spartan living room, turning, staring through the papers that were still tacked up on the walls. Stefan stood by the entrance to the kitchen, two cups of coffee cooling in his hands.

"Calm down, Nuri." Stefan tried to sound reassuring, but even in his own ears he sounded condescending.

"*Calm down?*" Nuri stepped up to a wall and tore a page off of it. "What *is* this?" He tore off another sheet and waved the crumpled pages in front of him. "What the fuck is this? You're off this case."

Stefan nodded. He was. He kept telling himself that. But he had no ready explanation why these pages still collected on his walls—some of them added as recently as this morning.

"Why does he want *you*? Of anyone, why you—and why go through me to get you?" Nuri stared at him as if Stefan was the one threatening him.

Stefan walked over to the lone table and pushed a pile

of papers out of the way with the cups as he set them down. A few years of recently-acquired train schedules slid to the ground to scatter over the bare wood floor. Stefan didn't move to pick them up.

"Sit down," Stefan said.

Nuri dropped the documents he'd torn from the wall and walked up to the table. He leaned on it and stared into Stefan's eyes. "What's going on? Why you?"

"Maybe I'm the only one who believes."

"More vampire crap? With what I've seen, I almost believe it myself—at least we have some nut group that really makes an effort—"

Stefan shook his head. "No, Nuri. I am talking true evil, supernatural, blood-drinking demons walking upon the earth."

There was a long silence before Nuri said, "No, I don't buy spirits, seances, mediums, or supernatural beings. If there are such things, there's reason behind it, a disease or some sort of infection—"

Stefan's voice became grave. "Sit down."

This time Nuri did as he asked.

"Iago came here before he confronted you." Nuri looked surprised, but he stayed quiet. "He is one of these dark things. He cringed before the crucifix, and when I called on the Lord, he became a bat-winged demon and escaped."

Nuri stared at him, his expression told Stefan that his former partner thought he had cracked.

Stefan waved toward the bedroom door. "The window hasn't been fixed yet. You can see the wood covering the hole. And I still have the overalls that tore away when he changed."

The silence stretched a long time before Nuri reached for the coffee. He looked at the cup as if he wished it was something stronger. "I wish I had more trouble believing you. But I've seen bodies that soaked up bullets and kept moving." He drained the cup. After a while he said, "All we need is Boris Karloff."

"Bela Lugosi," Stefan said.

"What?"

"Lugosi. Karloff played Frankenstein's Monster."

"Oh." He kept sipping his coffee. "I suppose you've gotten holy water and all that other good Catholic stuff."

Stefan nodded.

"I want to know what a Jew is supposed to do with a vampire."

Neither of them laughed.

9

It was a couple of weeks before Iago made himself known. This time he called and specified a meeting place. Stefan agreed, and took Nuri with him. The place was on Short Vincent, in one of the smaller nightclubs vying for space in the narrow alley. The crowd was thick with Friday night partygoers. The area was noisy and garishly lit.

To Stefan the whole area seemed a manic attempt to frighten away the evil spirits of the night. Not far beyond a caveman chanting around a feeble campfire. The club they were meeting in was hidden between two other, more impressive, facades. The entrance was little more than a narrow doorway. It would have been easily missed if they hadn't known where they were going.

Stefan led Nuri inside, and immediately the character of the night changed. Outside, the bars of Short Vincent tried to push away the night. Here, inside, the club seemed to embrace the darkness. The lighting was dim enough that Stefan had to wait for his eyes to adjust before he could distinguish anything about his surroundings.

The windowless main room was several steps down into the ground. The decor was a decadent combination of brass and red velvet. Stefan noticed that the place had no windows, and no mirrors. As they stepped into the room, Stefan noticed a few faces among the patrons turn to look at them. The stares continued until a rail-thin waiter came to them and said, "Gentlemen, you are expected."

He extended an overlong arm toward the rear of the room, and began to lead them into the depths of the club. Stefan and Nuri followed through the unusually quiet crowd. Near the back stood a line of velvet curtains hiding individual private booths. Their guide led them to one and drew aside the curtain.

Iago sat on one side of the table. Stefan slid in on the other, followed by Nuri. The curtain slid shut, leaving them alone with the demon. Stefan felt in his pocket where he kept a rosary and a vial of holy water.

Iago's long hands cupped a glass in front of him. Stefan couldn't see what he was drinking, and he didn't want to. He still wore overalls, though they didn't make him seem as out of place as they should have. The aura of darkness he carried with him seemed to match this place.

"We're here," Nuri said. "Speak your piece." There was an edge of confrontation in Nuri's voice. More than Stefan would have liked. He let Nuri go on. His nerves had been frayed ever since Iago had confronted him.

Iago rotated the cup under his hand. The glass fractured the light from an electric candle that was the sole illumination in the booth. "I'm fighting a war, gentlemen."

"With Eric Dietrich," Nuri said.

"His name is Melchior, and he is older than you can imagine. He was near a myth among my own kind. Among yours he was forgotten entirely."

"Your kind . . ." Stefan whispered, letting the words hang in the air.

A small smile drifted across Iago's lips. "Ah, you still maintain that we're the incarnation of evil. Believe what you will. You will still help me. I have stepped too far beyond the bounds of my own Covenant to allow you not to."

"What Covenant?" Stefan asked.

"We shall be civil, then?" Iago's gaze drifted downward and back, almost as if he could see the holy items in Stefan's pocket. He looked from Stefan to Nuri and back again. "Believe me, I do not like using threats. I could have taken you, either of you, into the fold—you would have done all that I wished then, willingly. But that is counter to my purpose. My hope is that, hearing me out, you will see what the real evil is." He took a sip from the glass. "I am evil in your eyes solely because your mythology tells you so. Melchior's evil is much more tangible, much more threatening to both of us."

"We know he's killing people—" Nuri started to say. Iago held up a hand, silencing him.

"You know little or nothing," Iago said. "It all begins and ends with the Covenant, a Covenant that has crumbled around me until I've come this far. Respect the sacrifice I am making by enlisting your aid, respect it by hearing me out without interruption." There was a tangible force of will behind the statement, originating in his depthless eyes. Stefan felt as if he couldn't interrupt even if he wanted to.

"As long as there has been man, there have been those of the blood. Because we were ageless, lived in the night, and mostly because we fed on man, we've been hunted to near extinction countless times. Even as we chose humans to bring across into our own world, even as the rare human would rise to us on his own account, our numbers were always small. The last time we were brought that close to annihilation, those of the blood formed the Covenant." Iago leaned forward. "That was close to a millennium ago. The Covenant was a simple law, designed to preserve us from man, and from ourselves. We do not slay those of the blood. Any act by one in thrall to us is taken as an act of ourselves. And we never reveal those of the blood to those outside the blood. . . ."

Iago allowed the sentence to trail off, allowing its significance to sink in.

"My life would be forfeit for saying this much to you, if my society still existed here. However, in this demesne the Covenant now means as little as human law did a few years ago." Iago frowned, and Stefan could feel the aura of hate, anger, and perhaps fear emanating from the being sitting across from him. He fingered the rosary.

"There was, at the time of the Covenant, an old one. Melchior may have been thousands of years old by then. He ruled his own kingdom, safe from the purges mankind laid upon his own kind. He was ruthless in his rape of his people and his land, he amassed riches, and was unashamed in public displays of his nature. He would execute his rivals, human and vampire alike, beheading them, dismembering them, emasculating them."

Iago took another sip from his glass. "He slaughtered until the only ones of the blood under his rule were those under direct thrall to him. When the Covenant was made, he was the first one of us to be condemned by it. He was to be burned on a pyre of his own followers.

"Somehow, he survived."

Iago paused, and Stefan felt the hold on his tongue loosen. He let the question rise to his lips. "How? Doesn't fire kill your kind?"

"As well as any of you. It wasn't Melchior on the flames." Iago lifted his hand, and while Stefan and Nuri watched, the flesh began to flow like melted wax. The fingers lengthened, nails grew into black talons, the skin became thick and leathery. Stefan squeezed his rosary as the hand before him turned demonic.

"Our will," Iago said, flexing the transformed hand, "Our soul, everything within us is bound within the blood. Our blood controls the flesh, moving it to our will. Wounds are nothing to us unless they destroy flesh and blood, dismember us, or destroy the brain or the heart." He clenched the demon hand and the transformed flesh spilled back into itself, becoming nothing more than a hand again. "Melchior avoided the flames, by allowing another to be burned in his stead, a mere thrall."

Iago looked into Stefan's eyes, and Stefan felt as if those disturbing eyes were seeing too deeply. In his head, Stefan began to recite Our Fathers until Iago's gaze shifted to Nuri.

"Those fulfilling the then-new Covenant believed that they had taken Melchior. What they saw was a corpse with Melchior's face, and Melchior's blood in its veins. They didn't realize the extent of Melchior's power, even then."

Iago held out his hand. "The power of my blood ends at my skin. I could make of you thralls bound to my blood, have my blood run through your veins, and you would be mine, but only in that your will would become mine. Melchior's thralls not only become his will, but his flesh as well, his eyes, his ears." Iago balled his fist. "My will can change my flesh. Melchior's can change any of his thralls'."

The realization began to sink into Stefan. They never had a hope with the surveillance, not when Dietrich could change himself to appear as anything. He had probably walked by both of them, under their noses, countless times.

"His power is such that he can walk abroad in full daylight without the sun driving the spirit from his flesh. He might even be able to survive the kind of dismemberment he issues his victims. Total, complete destruction of the body is the only certain way to kill him before he becomes unapproachable."

There was a long pause. Stefan could feel that Iago was leaving it to be filled with questions. It was Nuri who asked, talking for the first time since Iago entered his monologue.

"You said we didn't know what is going on. What is going on?"

"Melchior wishes to reclaim his temporal kingdom. He believes that our race should rule, and that he should rule our race. He has begun with subtlety, binding humans to him, sometimes with money, sometimes with blood. He already has a secret hand in all the affairs of this city, and his influence extends across this continent."

Stefan shook his head. "Why are you talking to us? You have this Covenant, there should be others of your kind to help you—"

"You don't understand," Iago said. "The bodies you've been finding, headless, dismembered, they are the leaders of our race. Melchior has been systematically exterminating those of any power and influence that could be in his way. Those not yet executed are paralyzed by fear. We know, you see. He leaves the bodies to inspire terror, while our own Covenant prevents any from revealing what is going on."

"Except you," Nuri said.

"It is my survival," Iago said. "Carried to its limits, Melchior's plan will be the extermination of every one of us who is not of his own blood." He looked at Stefan, and again he felt the sensation of Iago seeing too much of him. "You I chose because I need untainted humans to aid me. Melchior would sense one of the blood if any approached. He would know me, because his thralls have tasted my blood. Humans would be a cipher to him. No human organization—not the police, not the crime mobs, not the FBI— can close on him, because he has ears in every corner of those groups. But individually you can act without his knowledge. He is not omniscient."

"Beyond your threats," Nuri said, "why should we help you?"

Iago looked at Nuri. His expression was grave. "Didn't you hear what I said? Melchior plans the extermination of everyone who is not of his own blood. Humans who enslave themselves to him will have the privilege of being the cattle for his empire. Those who don't . . ."

Iago didn't finish the statement, but Stefan could feel the implications in his gut. For all he believed this thing across from him to be evil, there wasn't any way he could walk away from this now.

10

Detective Simon Aristaeus stood in an unobtrusive corner of the Union Terminal Building, leaning against a bank of phone booths. He held a copy of the *Cleveland Press* in his hands, but his eyes weren't focused on the paper. With his head lowered, and the brim of his hat shading his eyes, he watched the crowds coming and going through to the train station. He was watching for one man in particular.

He wondered what Van Sweringen would make of the police surveillance of him in his own building. Detective Aristaeus didn't quite know what to make of it himself. He was reporting to Ness, not his supervisor, or even the Chief. That, with the vagueness of his orders, and the cover of secrecy, gave this the feeling of a fishing expedition. He knew he wasn't the first cop to be given this duty, and the way things were going, he wouldn't be the last.

He listened to footsteps echo off marble and wondered if he was ever going to see Van Sweringen. He was supposed to be making a business trip to New York, but there were a lot of ways down to the tracks, and one of the other cops down here could have already seen him and called it in. He wondered if anyone would have the courtesy to tell him if Van Sweringen had already left in his private passenger car, or if they'd just leave him here, forgotten, waiting.

It was late evening when he finally saw his quarry. Van Sweringen walked through the station with near anonymity. As he watched, Detective Aristaeus doubted any of the crowd realized that the man walking in their midst was the titular head of one of the largest railroad empires in the country, and the man responsible for the construction of the building they walked through.

Detective Aristaeus didn't move his head, but his gaze followed Van Sweringen, picking out the people accompanying him. He noted Wenneman, Van Sweringen's secretary. He also noted two others following the pair—

Detective Aristaeus was taken by surprise when he recognized one of the two men following Van Sweringen. He knew Detective Ryzard; he was part of the homicide unit. What was he doing here?

He didn't spend much time worrying about it. Once Van Sweringen passed him on the way to the trains, he casually folded his newspaper and slid into one of the phone booths. He called into the station and made a perfunctory report to one of Ness' secretaries. Ness himself probably wasn't even working on a Sunday.

Detective Aristaeus hung up the phone, hesitated a moment, then made another call. He made a report similar to the one he had just given, but this time he added the detail of Detective Ryzard's presence. After he had spoken, he listened for several minutes. Then he nodded and said, "I shall do as you will me to."

Detective Aristaeus hung up the phone, left the paper, and walked into the terminal, following Ryzard and Van Sweringen.

Stefan and Nuri boarded the train about three cars up from the private car carrying Oris Paxton Van Sweringen. Stefan was still wondering how they were going to confront Van Sweringen. The last time they hadn't gotten very far, and now they had to press it. Stefan needed to know which trains were running under Dietrich's—Melchior's—control.

They sat in the car, waiting for the train to begin moving. Next to him, Nuri muttered, "I don't believe we're going through with this." He was looking out at the platform.

"You've seen what Melchior is doing."

Nuri shook his head. "I've seen odd things, but nothing that convinces me Iago is telling us the truth."

Stefan frowned. That was one of his own fears. How could he trust a monster from the same race as the being they were charged to destroy? Evil was evil, and by merely listening to Iago, he felt that they were being ensnared in the darkness.

"We're just gathering information right now. We'll do nothing until we're sure of where we stand."

The words sounded empty even to Stefan. By boarding the train they had stepped outside their roles as policemen. Ness had warned them off of Van Sweringen, and being here would be grounds for a suspension or a transfer. If, as Stefan suspected, there was any strongarming to get what they needed to know, they could be very easily dismissed from the force.

What they were doing was very close to the edge, and their motives were completely beyond the pale. They were gathering information to help them target Melchior. They were engaged in conspiracy to murder.

"Just planning," Nuri whispered.

The underground platform of the Union Terminal slid by them and the train pulled itself along the tracks. Soon the motion fell into a rhythm as they slid out the east side of downtown. Behind them, the lights of the Terminal Tower cut a hole in the night the shape of a thin gravestone.

"Just planning," Stefan said. That's all they were doing. Planning the death of a man named Eric Dietrich, who was supposedly a thing named Melchior.

On one level, they were just marking time until they found a way to deal with Iago and his threats. On another, they were really going through with it.

Stefan had decided early that the worst place to attack Melchior would be his residence. He had seen an attempted hit by a score of assassins. He was too well defended there. No, the best place, in Stefan's mind, to attack Melchior would be in transit. Stefan knew that Melchior controlled trains somewhere, even if there was no official records of the fact. Stefan was almost certain that there was some private agreement with Van Sweringen, and that parts of their rail line were under Melchior's control.

If they discovered the lines that Melchior used, they'd have a better chance of isolating his movement. If Iago was right, he wouldn't be aware of surveillance originating outside of the police department. With only the two of them, there would be no spies to warn him.

Once they knew the cars Melchior used, it would just be a matter of planting some explosives.

Stefan shuddered at the thought. He still wasn't used to the idea, even if he'd been partly aware of the implications ever since he'd known what Dietrich-Melchior was. He had known that the presence of a vampire required it to be slain.

He just wished there was another way. Iago maintained there wasn't. Melchior was so powerful that only complete and instant destruction of the body would kill him.

"When do we go?" Nuri asked.

"After everyone's asleep. You might as well catch a nap yourself."

Nuri nodded, but didn't close his eyes. Instead he stared out the window at the darkened world.

Detective Aristaeus sat in first class, the only conscious person in the private cabin. Across from him, three people were crumpled in a heap on the seat. He paid no attention to them; once they had fallen unconscious they no longer mattered to his plans.

The shades were drawn on all the windows, and he sat illuminated only by a single weak electric lamp. The light made the world slightly jaundiced.

His revolver lay on the seat next to him. In his hands he held two bottles of liquid so red and thick that it was almost black. His hand shook as he set down one, opened the other, and drank.

They were into Pennsylvania before Stefan decided to move. It was nearly three-thirty in the morning, and the train had gone silent except for the rattle of its passage across the tracks. Most of their fellow passengers were asleep.

Stefan grabbed Nuri's arm and they made their way back through the car. Neither of them spoke. They passed through three cars before they reached the end of the passenger cars. They stood on the platform before Van Sweringen's private car.

The entrance was locked, but the lock was a simple one to jimmy, even with the motion of the train and the wind whistling between the cars. Nuri muttered something about feeling like a hit man. Stefan didn't comment. In a way that was exactly what they were.

They slipped into the car, which resembled one of the first class passenger cars, only with two cabins and richer decoration that Stefan could barely see in the darkness. All he could really notice was the brocade of the carpet.

The two of them slid along the darkened aisle to the rear, where Van Sweringen's room was. Again the door was locked and Stefan found himself forcing it. Behind him, Nuri had taken out his revolver and was watching back the way they had come.

In a few minutes he popped the door open.

The two of them slipped into the darkened chamber. The half of the cabin they entered had chairs and a table, and a window watching the darkened Pennsylvania wilderness pass by under an overcast sky. Half of the cabin was shut out by a heavy curtain that rippled gray and black in the darkness.

The curtain was moving.

Stefan and Nuri exchanged glances and looked again at the curtain. Stefan felt a wrongness here, almost as if he was in the presence of Iago, or another minion of darkness. With one hand he pulled out a rosary, and with the other he withdrew his revolver.

He motioned Nuri to one side of the curtain, and he stationed himself on the other. Once they were set on both sides, Stefan motioned for Nuri to pull back the curtain.

The curtain drew aside, revealing Oris Paxton Van Sweringen lying on his bed, and another man leaning over him. When the curtain drew aside, the man dropped something from his hand, something he'd been holding to Van Sweringen's mouth.

He turned, holding a revolver, but Stefan saw the man's face, and recognition made him hesitate. The man was Simon Aristaeus, a fellow detective in the Cleveland Police Department. The shock of seeing him gave Aristaeus enough time to turn fully around. Nuri had his gun leveled at Aristaeus and was shouting, "Drop it!"

For a moment the tableau held, the three of them unmoving, guns pointed at each other. The silence was filled with the rhythmic clatter of the rails. From the slowing of the car, and the shadows outside, they were entering a rail yard. It lasted until Van Sweringen stirred, groaned, and sat up. Stefan had just enough time to see that his mouth was dark with blood before hell broke loose.

Aristaeus used the distraction to move, and there were two gunshots in rapid succession, neither from Stefan's gun. Aristaeus kept moving to the side of the car, while Nuri folded over and fell against the wall. Van Sweringen yelled something incomprehensible as Stefan turned to cover Aristaeus.

This time he didn't hesitate firing. He couldn't tell if he'd hit him or not. Whatever happened, Aristaeus fell upon the emergency brake cord and everything shuddered against the sudden lack of motion. Stefan fell over and Van Sweringen tumbled out of his bed.

Aristaeus remained upright and scrambled out the front door in all the confusion.

Almost immediately, there was another jerk as something outside collided with the car. Then there was silence.

"What the blazes is going on here?" Van Sweringen said as he pushed himself off of the floor. Stefan ignored him and went to Nuri. Nuri was clutching his right shoulder; he looked up at Stefan and groaned a bit.

"We need to get you to a hospital—"

"No," Nuri said through gritted teeth, "This will keep. Get after that bastard."

Stefan hesitated a moment, then nodded and ran out the door. The door between cars was already swinging shut behind Aristaeus. In the distance, came the sounds of people roused by the sudden stop. Stefan ducked through the door, and had to duck back as a gunshot whistled past him.

Aristaeus was outside, and Stefan's few quick glances saw him running away across the tracks. When he was sure Aristaeus wasn't taking aim at the cars, Stefan dove out after him. He stumbled. The area between the cars was broken and uneven. Van Sweringen's car had been pushed up in a collision with its neighbor, buckling the space between cars.

Stefan fell out to the side, and pushed himself up as a bullet kicked up a divot of gravel near his hands. This time he had a chance to steady himself and return fire.

Aristaeus was about fifty yards off, and showed no sign of being hit. Stefan fired again, and Aristaeus dove behind a stationary boxcar. Stefan began running across the gravel, chasing him. He ran, following the tracks through the sparsely lit railyard.

Aristaeus was ducking behind lone boxcars parked on a siding at one edge of the yard. Stefan just reached the first in the series of cars when another shot splintered the wood about a foot from his shoulder.

He could hear Aristaeus moving out there, and Stefan suspected that if he moved from the cover of the boxcar the next shot would find its mark.

He holstered his gun and swung himself up on the rusty iron rungs set in the side of the car. He pulled himself up toward the roof of the boxcar. Once on top, it gave him a view of the other boxcars on this side of the railyard.

He knew that Aristaeus was behind one of the cars, so he waited for him to make a move. Aristaeus did—he ducked around a car about twenty yards away, at the edge of the tracks, and put another shot into the side of the boxcar Stefan was on top of. Then he began running into the long grass lining the rails.

Stefan yelled at him, "Stop, drop the gun!"

Aristaeus responded by beginning to turn back toward him. Stefan didn't wait, he fired two shots. Aristaeus buckled, the gun going off wildly. He dropped and disappeared into the grass.

Stefan stood there, on top of the boxcar, watching for more threatening movement. There wasn't any. It was as if Aristaeus had fallen through a hole in the earth. Stefan couldn't see where he had fallen, the dark grass had swallowed him up.

Behind him came the sounds of machinery, trains, and the babble of people. Stefan could also hear the voices and footsteps of three or four people—probably rail police—running toward him.

Around him and the boxcars, everything was suddenly silent. The only movement in his field of vision was the twisting fog from his breath, and the distant motes of campfires just outside the boundaries of the yard.

Stefan holstered his weapon and let himself down. He headed toward the edge of the tracks, where Aristaeus had run off into the grass. He had just reached the edge, spotting the barely visible signs where Aristaeus had torn up the grass in his scramble to escape, when behind him came a voice, "Hold it right there!" Stefan's shadow sprang up in front of him transfixed in the center of a flashlight beam.

He turned around, squinting in the light, to face three railroad policemen. "I'm the police," he called out to them, reaching slowly for his badge. "Detective Ryzard." He held out the badge so it glinted in the flashlight beam. He neglected to name the city, because, wherever in Pennsylvania they were, they were far out of his jurisdiction.

"The man out there just shot my partner," he added.

One of the railroad bulls edged up to see Stefan's badge, then he waved at the one with the flashlight. The beam left Stefan and began sweeping over the grass.

"Sorry, Detective," said the one next to him. "We have this accident on the Nickel Plate Line, and then all the gunshots . . ."

Stefan nodded. He wondered if the man knew how deferential he was sounding now. Stefan supposed when your job was predominantly rousting hobos off the tracks, you might get over-respectful for a "real" policeman.

Stefan ended up leading the three railroad cops into the grass, following Aristaeus' broken trail. At this point Stefan was glad for the backup, even though it seemed that Aristaeus had dropped like a rock. With what he was involved in, Stefan wasn't going to take anything at face value.

They made their way deeper into the grass, closing on where Aristaeus had dropped. Stefan noticed that they had gained a quiet audience off in the distance. The hobos and tramps had abandoned their fires for the moment and had closed in to watch the commotion. They were far away, too far to make out individuals, and apparently too far for the railroad cops to care, but they gave the whole scene the feeling of a performance, as if Stefan was an actor in some medieval morality play.

The four of them reached the place where Aristaeus had dropped. The place was marked by flattened grass and splatters of blood. To one side lay Aristaeus' revolver.

There was no body.

"What the hell?" said the railroad cop who'd checked Stefan's badge.

"Ain't no way he could've run off without us seeing

something," said the one with the flashlight. Even so, he panned his light across the edges of the grass, looking for signs of where Aristaeus might have retreated. The grass waved back, undisturbed.

Aristaeus was gone.

Nuri lay slumped against the wall, his hand clutching the hole just below the shoulder. He tried to keep pressure on the wound, but blood kept leaking through his fingers. His other arm lay useless at his side, warm and slick with blood. The wound, and the entire upper quarter of his chest throbbed with every beat of his pulse, as if a giant hand was squeezing the life out of him with every heartbeat.

"Good lord, what's happening here?" Oris Paxton Van Sweringen bent over him. The man was gathering up a bedsheet and bent over Nuri to press it to his wound.

Before Nuri had a chance to speak, the door burst open a man stepped into the car. Nuri recognized Van Sweringen's secretary. He looked as if he'd just fallen out of bed.

"Are you all right, sir—" The man stopped when his gaze landed on Nuri. The carpet had already soaked up a pool of blood that nearly reached his feet.

"I'm fine," Van Sweringen said, wiping blood off of his mouth with the back of his hand. "This man needs to get to a hospital. Get an ambulance, and for heaven's sake keep it out of the papers."

"Yes, sir." The man turned on his heels and left.

Van Sweringen shook his head as he tried to keep pressure on the wound. "Why are you here?" he whispered, half to himself.

"Dietrich," Nuri said. His voice was weak and tasted of blood.

Van Sweringen showed no sign of surprise. In fact, he nodded. "He's finished with me, isn't he? Just like he was finished with Mantis." His face took on a longing expression, and he shook his head a few times as if to clear it. "He was an assassin, wasn't he? The man who shot you."

"Need to know—" Nuri started to say, but he began coughing up blood.

"I know who you are. You walked into my office a few months ago. I chased you away." He shifted the sheet over the wound and Nuri groaned. "It was fear. It kept me from doing more than I did. Even when I lost Mantis, all I could do was call in secret. . . ."

"What—" Nuri tried to form a question, but the pain and the blood wouldn't let him. He felt as if he had started tumbling through empty space, and Van Sweringen's face seemed impossibly far away.

"I think you were too late," Van Sweringen said. "I can taste my own death coming. Nothing left to be afraid of." With his free hand he reached around his neck and removed a chain. Hanging from it was a large, plain cross. Van Sweringen dropped it over Nuri's head.

In his mind, Nuri tried to explain he was Jewish, but by then his brain seemed to have lost any connection with the rest of his body. He wondered if Van Sweringen was wrong about whose death he was probably tasting.

Van Sweringen leaned forward, as if to kiss his cheek, and Nuri distinctly heard the words, "Cleveland Trust."

Then, as the world began fading away into a dull gray void, Van Sweringen's secretary ran in saying help was coming. Van Sweringen nodded, and said, "Arrange for a new car to New York."

"Yes, sir," the man said, and vanished.

Van Sweringen said other things, but Nuri was past hearing them.

11

Nuri spent days in a drugged stupor, long enough for a dusting of snow to collect on the ledge of the window next to his bed. His arm was in a cast up past his collarbone, held upright by weights. Tubes entered and left his body, and the upper right quarter of his chest was home to an intolerable itching.

Becoming conscious of his surroundings seemed an interminable process. It seemed an eternity before he could even focus on Stefan's presence.

"What . . ." Nuri whispered when he finally managed to find the power to speak. It was as if he were trying to finish the question he had been asking Van Sweringen.

Stefan leaned over and touched his good shoulder. "Rest."

Nuri turned and tried to focus on Stefan's face. His memory was a feverish jumble of images. He knew he'd been here for a long time, and he knew that Stefan had been here at times, but the images and the memories never settled down into a coherent whole. It was frustrating, like trying to remember a dream as it slipped away.

"Rest," Stefan repeated. "You've been fighting an infection."

Nuri closed his eyes and rested.

Later on he woke up and asked, "How long have I been here?"

Stefan was still there, or he was there again. "Ten days."

Nuri looked sideways at Stefan, "What happened?"

"How are you doing?" he asked. Stefan looked ragged,

as if he hadn't showered or shaved in days. "The doctors say you'll be able to go home in a few days."

"What happened to Aristaeus? Van Sweringen?"

"Aristaeus got away." Stefan pulled his chair closer to the bed. "Van Sweringen's dead."

Something sick filled Nuri's chest as he heard that. "Dead?" he whispered. He kept thinking of the man saying he tasted death. . . .

"Heart attack on the way to New York," Stefan said. He ran both hands through his hair and said, "We were too late."

"You don't think it was a heart attack?"

"I'm sure it was. Didn't you see what Aristaeus was doing?" Stefan pulled a small bag out of his jacket pocket. It was wax paper, and Nuri could see brown stains inside of it. "He dropped this in Van Sweringen's car."

"What is it?"

"A vial of blood. Half empty. He was pouring it into Van Sweringen's mouth when we showed up." Stefan looked at it. "You listened to Iago, didn't you? Melchior's blood."

Nuri looked at the bag in Stefan's hand, and looked at Stefan. "You think Van Sweringen was killed. With that?"

Stefan nodded.

Nuri didn't know what to say. What Stefan was saying smacked of voodoo, of magic. Nuri had seen things were close to the supernatural, but he still clung to the belief that there had to be a rational explanation for what was going on.

"Did he say anything to you?" Stefan asked, putting the envelope and its vial back into his pocket.

"He said he tasted his own death." He reached up to his neck and felt under his hospital gown. The cross was still there. Clumsily, he lifted the chain up over his head and gave it to Stefan one-handed.

Stefan took it.

"He gave it to me. You can have it."

Stefan held the cross up to the light. "Did he say anything about it?" He seemed to be studying it, turning it on edge.

Nuri searched his memory and remembered the words. "Cleveland Trust," he said.

"Ah-hah," Stefan said as he pulled the oversized cross apart. The cross split apart into two separate crosses hinged at the base. Sandwiched between them, glinting in the light, was a key.

12

Downtown Cleveland was covered by a fresh dusting of snow. Christmas lights decorated the outsides of the department stores, and windows were draped with ribbons of red and green. As Stefan walked down Euclid, he heard carolers in the distance singing "Silent Night."

The season didn't move him. He walked with his head lowered, seeing mostly the gray slush that covered the sidewalk. He held his trenchcoat close to him, holding his hat against the cold. In one hand he clutched the key that Van Sweringen had passed on.

Stefan wished Nuri was with him. He felt isolated, alone. He walked past the holiday decorations and felt as if he was the only one who saw the darkness under the surface.

He stopped at East Ninth, and looked across at the Cleveland Trust Building. It squatted at the opposite corner of the street, a neoclassical building with a domed roof. Even this staid building had a few wreaths in deference to the season.

To Stefan, the way the late afternoon shadows had darkened every portal of the building, it resembled a massive tomb, the wreaths from some recent funeral.

Stefan crossed the street and entered the edifice. Once inside, the small decorations, a ribbon here, a bough there, did little to dismiss the somber character of the bank. Stefan swallowed and walked toward the manager's desk.

It took some convincing, and the flash of his badge—which meant little since he and Nuri had been suspended—but the manager eventually allowed him down to the deposit vault to use the key.

Stefan carried the box to a cubicle, wondering what Van

Sweringen saw fit to hide here. The account wasn't even in Van Sweringen's name, which meant that the lawyers handling the Van Sweringen estate, and the lawyers handling its creditors, didn't know this box existed.

Alone, in a stall, Stefan lifted the lid of the safety deposit box.

It finally felt a little like Christmas. On top was a copy of an agreement between the Van Sweringens and Eric Dietrich. It dated from September '35, but seemed to carry hints of an agreement several years back.

Stefan rifled through the other papers. There was documentation of European investment in the Van Sweringens' pyramid of corporations. Stefan wasn't an accountant, but the papers listed numbers that, to Stefan, seemed to have kept the whole Van Sweringen pyramid afloat much longer than it should have.

Stefan suspected that without Dietrich's money—the context made it clear who the money came from even if the benefactor was never named—the whole system of interlaced companies would have tumbled apart as early as '31.

By September 30, '35, Eric Dietrich had become a full-fledged silent partner. It went far beyond what Stefan had expected. From the papers that he held, it seemed possible that Dietrich was in control of the largest rail empire in the country.

Stefan had thought that, at the most, Dietrich had control of a few lines through his relationship to Van Sweringen. Stefan felt cold as he realized that the thing calling itself Dietrich had access, control of, lines from the Missouri Pacific to the Chesapeake & Ohio.

He had planned to find Dietrich's private car and use that as a point of attack. That target now seemed much more remote.

13

"Y ou're delaying," Iago said.

Stefan didn't look at him; he knew what he would see in those eyes. Instead, he looked out over the frozen lake, toward the breakwater. The night was cold and quiet, Lake Erie black as onyx, refusing to reflect the feeble stars. "I don't want any innocent bystanders caught in this."

"Do you know what we're dealing with?" Iago said. "We cannot afford to be gentle."

"What is the point in fighting an evil if we ourselves become evil in the process?"

Stefan could hear Iago pacing behind him. "You are quite clear in your belief that I am myself an evil worthy of damnation."

"I'll move when I am certain that I can destroy Melchior without harming anyone else."

"The point is destroying him before he becomes unapproachable, if he isn't already—"

Stefan shook his head. "We're dealing with explosives here. I won't set off a bomb in the middle of the city."

Iago made a disgusted noise. "A train, then," Iago said. "Which one?"

"I need you to find that out for me."

There was a silence. "Do you know what you're asking?"

"I don't want to know," Stefan said, staring out at the black horizon. "What I need to know is a train he'll be on, and when. One of the trains he's using for his own purposes."

"This is all you need?"

Stefan nodded, turning away from the darkness to face the lights of the city. "Yes," he said.

Iago was facing away from him, toward the city himself.

"I'll give you this. Stay by the phone the next three nights, be ready to act when I call."

Two nights later Iago wore the mask of Tragedy again. He carried the chained body of a person who in life was a prostitute named Rose Wallace. He had wanted one of Melchior's human thralls, the ones who had yet to turn and had less of a bond to their master, but time was too short to be picky.

He carried her into the darkness of another slaughter-house, awash with the smell of chickens and blood. It was a different place than where he'd talked to Carlo Pasquale, but it hardly mattered. The place was the same concrete darkness filled with animal shrieks and the smell of blood.

He dropped Rose Wallace on the ground and pulled out a hypodermic needle. In the darkness, the steel needle, twisted handle, its glass shaft, all seemed to be some obscure torture device.

Iago slid the needle into the flesh of his wrist, the gap between glove and sleeve where a small strip of skin was visible. The needle sank in to the base, and Iago withdrew the plunger, allowing the glass tube to fill with his own black-rose-colored blood.

Iago withdrew the needle and knelt next to Rose Wallace. He slid the needle into a vein in her neck. Her body jerked as he injected the blood into her system. He watched the blood push from the tube, knowing that it was now a matter of his survival or Rose's. Once his blood was taken into her body, he couldn't allow her to leave. Melchior could not be allowed to taste Iago's blood on one of his thralls.

Knowing that he would have to destroy Rose, whatever she managed to reveal to him, made him feel that Stefan Ryzard was right. His kind *was* evil.

He could feel the pull toward Rose as his blood sank into her system. He didn't hope to displace Melchior's influence as completely as he did with Carlo, but he hoped that he connected deeply enough to have Rose answer his few questions.

He knelt over her and watched as Rose Wallace's eyes opened. In them Iago saw a maelstrom of terror and betrayal. Iago began asking his questions.

*   *   *

The phone tore Stefan from sleep. He ran and grabbed the receiver.

"There's a special run of the Nickel Plate, February fifteenth. It leaves the Union Terminal at three in the morning. He will be on it, the last car."

"Iago?" Stefan asked. Something sounded odd about Iago's voice. It had always sounded diabolically confident, superior. Something had drained out of it.

"I must go. You won't hear from me until it's done."

Stefan opened his mouth to ask a question, but the line was already dead. His hand shook as he laid the receiver back in the cradle.

This was it. He had the information he wanted. Now he just had to go through with it.

That Sunday, Stefan saw Father Gerwazek before Mass.

He had been going more regularly since all this had started happening, trying to rebuild some relationship with God. He was unsure if it was working. He still felt as if the divine was impossible to reach from where he was. Yet, he went to the confessional, like he had when he was a child, like he had before his own wife and child had died.

He knelt in the booth, and for a time it was completely dark. He could feel a surge of claustrophobia. Then the door on the other side of the screen slid aside, letting in light and dappled shadow.

Before anything else was said, he asked, "Do you believe in the supernatural, Father?" The question came out of him in a rush. He had never talked to Gerwazek about the things he'd been experiencing, about Dietrich, about Iago's kind. His confessions had been about more mundane matters.

There was a pause, as if Gerwazek was gathering his thoughts after the break in form. "I believe in the supernatural," he said. "I believe in God. I believe that the host becomes the flesh of Christ. I believe in the possibility of divine intervention in worldly affairs."

"And Satan? Tangible physical evil?"

"That, too, is part of my faith." Gerwazek paused. "What troubles you?"

"I believe that I am fighting a supernatural evil."

There was a longer pause, then, slowly, Gerwazek told him, "You must pray, my son. There is only one good in the realm of the supernatural, and that is what comes from God. If what you fight is not worldly, then your only aid can come from Him."

Stefan opened his mouth to say more, but something inside him felt as if he had said enough. It was time to purge himself of his burdens. Slowly, Stefan began to tell Gerwazek of his sins.

Afterward, he took Mass.

14

Stefan waited in the darkness and prayed. He stood in a concrete alcove deep under the Union Terminal Tower. Beyond the track in front of him the darkness was subdivided into a forest of girders. There were a few lights, red and green and sodium yellow. None seemed to reach very far. The smell was damp and musty, heavy with soil and grease.

Stefan cupped a flashlight with his hand and shone it so it only illuminated the watch on his wrist. His train had ten minutes to arrive. His breath was short and burned the back of his throat with the taste of copper.

At his feet was a satchel, pushed far back against the concrete wall. It was heavy, and carried enough dynamite to reduce a railroad car to kindling. It also contained the blasting caps, wire, several rolls of cloth tape, a pair of wire cutters, and a small hand-held plunger.

Stefan had wanted a timer, but he was lucky he could get his hands on what he did. What it meant was that he was going to be on the train when Melchior's car detonated. He would just have to hope he was far enough away.

It was noisy down here, even at this time of the morning, with the trains coming and going through the underground passageways. So Stefan felt the oncoming train before he realized he heard it. It was early.

He pressed himself back into the protection of the alcove and extinguished his flashlight. The train screeched by him, a moving wall close enough to touch. It was already slowing to a stop. The air resonated with the screeching of its brakes.

The train was short, only a few passenger cars long, and

it passed from in front of him as quickly as it had appeared. As soon as the last car slid by Stefan grabbed the satchel and stepped out on the tracks. The train was receding down the tunnel, slowly coming to a stop. Stefan ran after the train.

He caught up with the rear car just before the train came to a complete stop. He grabbed a rung on the rear of the car, pulling himself up as he flung the satchel over his shoulder. When the train had stopped completely, Stefan was laying flat on the roof of the rear car.

Stefan buried his face into the roof, praying that his dark clothes helped him blend into the gloom in the top of the tunnel. The concrete ceiling of the tunnel lay flat above him, pressing down. Below him, he heard motion on the platform. People moved down there, oddly silent.

Carefully, Stefan turned his face to look down on the lighted platform. It was almost a shock to actually see him, Melchior, Eric Dietrich, standing on the platform. Melchior stood oddly still as others moved bags around him. He stood, hands wrapped around a long cane, long pale face framed by a mane of too-long blond hair, his shoulders covered by an ankle-length fur-lined coat that seemed more appropriate for a prior century.

He radiated power. Just standing there, Stefan could feel that he was the axis on which everything in his field of vision was turning. He could feel that, even though Melchior didn't move, didn't speak, didn't even turn his gaze away from the middle distance where he was staring. He didn't do a thing, but still, when Stefan saw him, he had an urge to turn and run, to abandon what he was doing, to leave the whole city and whatever else to Melchior.

He closed his eyes and prayed for himself, and for his actions. He hoped to God what he was doing was right. If the creature down there was merely a man, what he was going to do was no more than murder . . .

He told himself that Melchior, at best, was a murderer. And what Stefan had seen made him much darker.

As he prayed, he felt a burning awareness cross over the side of his body. He carefully looked back to the platform, and for a horrified moment he thought Melchior was looking directly at him.

The moment passed as Melchior's head kept moving. He

hadn't seen Stefan. Still, it was a few long moments before he was comfortable breathing.

He lay there for what seemed like hours before the train was loaded and began moving. It slowly pulled out, through the tunnels under the terminal. The car slid through the echoing darkness, slowly at first. Concrete passed over his head, much too close. Stefan hugged the roof of the car even closer.

Even though it couldn't be more than a few minutes, it seemed an eternity before the train left its underground warren, before the concrete ceiling opened up into a cold winter sky. All Stefan could think of was getting this done as quickly as possible, before someone discovered him.

Stefan pushed himself to his knees, icy wind searing his face. He had to turn his face to blink away the tears the wind burned into his eyes. He tied his satchel to the roof of the car and reached inside, taking out sticks of dynamite and the cloth tape.

Stefan crawled to the four corners of the car, anchoring the explosives, setting blasting caps, and wiring the deadly elements together.

As the darkened cliffs of Kingsbury Run slid by him, Stefan made a dangerous climb down the side of the moving car. He planted dynamite at the base of the car as he held on to the side one-handed. He scrambled up just as the train began reaching the lights of the East Fifty-Fifth railyard.

He'd been making good time. He had a lot of the car wired in just a few minutes. But as he pulled himself up onto the roof of the car, he had a sick realization.

The train was slowing down.

This wasn't in his plan. The train was supposed to leave the city limits. It was supposed to be on some tracks through some abandoned countryside when he pulled the switch—

But the train was going into the yard, not past it. He was losing his chance. Not only was the light enough that someone would see him up here, but there was no telling what would happen to Melchior when the train stopped. He could leave the car, change trains. . . .

He wasn't fully set up, but it was now or never.

Stefan maniacally connected the last two wires to a spool,

grabbed the hand-held plunger out of the satchel, and began moving, trailing wire, toward the front of the train. He stood upright and ran, the wind dying as the train slowed. He jumped the gap between cars twice before he lowered himself on a ladder between a pair of cars.

It might be too close, but he was out of time. They were in the yard, and the train was maneuvering itself into a siding. Stefan stood between cars and fumbled with the end of the spool, attaching wires to the plunger.

He only had one wire attached when the door between the cars opened.

In front of Stefan, caught in the cadaver glow of one of the yard's arc lights, was the face of Detective Simon Aristaeus. He saw Stefan and grinned. Stefan dropped the plunger, letting it dangle from one attached wire, and went for his gun.

His hand never reached it.

Aristaeus' arm shot out, faster than Stefan could fully react. He grabbed for Stefan's neck, and Stefan tried to dodge. It wasn't enough. Aristaeus grabbed hold of his shoulder with enough force that Stefan could feel his collarbone snap.

Aristaeus pulled him back through the half-open door. Stefan felt wood slam into his side, and he heard glass shattering. Then he was in the air, flying through the aisle between banks of empty seats. He landed on his wounded shoulder, and he felt the end of his collarbone tear through the skin. He shuddered with pain as the warmth of his blood spread across his chest.

"Detective Ryzard," Aristaeus said, walking slowly up the aisle. He shook his head, tsking.

He stopped to stand over him. "Aren't you a pain in the ass?" He laughed. "You think you can fight this? You think you can do anything to stop what is going on?"

He knelt and grabbed Stefan by the hair, pulling his head up to face him. Stefan groaned as the fractured bone in his shoulder withdrew.

"You killed me," Aristaeus said. "You know that? Stone dead, through the heart." He grinned, and the grin was predatory. Aristaeus' nostrils flared, and Stefan realized that the strongest smell in here was his own blood.

"Killed me, but there was enough of the Master in me

that it didn't even slow me down. You didn't save the old man, and now I'm stronger than ever. You're a sap if you think you can fight something like this."

Aristaeus' face was twisting. Stefan could hear the skin protest as his jaw distended and the skull began twisting into a muzzlelike form.

Stefan pulled the rosary out of his pocket and called on the name of the Lord.

God must have been with him, because Aristaeus backed up as if he had been struck. Even in the distorted face, Stefan could see signs of shock and surprise.

"Yea, though I walk through the valley of the shadow of death," Stefan said, holding the small crucifix out before Aristaeus. Aristaeus let go and Stefan fell to the ground, unable to break his fall with his bad arm. With the good arm he held up the rosary as he pushed himself past Aristaeus, toward the door, using only his legs.

"I will fear no evil: for thou *art* with me;"

He made it to the door, and he strained, his back to the door-frame, to push himself upright using only his legs. Aristaeus watched him, and Stefan kept the rosary between them.

"Thy rod and thy staff they comfort me— ugh"

He made it upright. He was standing next to the ladder, the plunger still dangled from its single wire. All it needed was for him to finish the connection.

He couldn't lower the crucifix.

"Thou preparest a table before me in the presence of mine enemies;"

As he spoke the words, he raised his right arm, feeling the broken bones dig inside his shoulder. His eyes watered with every movement, and his face had broken into a sweat in the winter air.

"Thou anointest my head with oil;"

His hand found the other wire, and with trembling fingers he managed to hook it over the unused terminal in the plunger.

"My cup runneth over."

He spun the wing-nut tight. But there was no way to activate the dangling switch one handed. He had to drop the crucifix. He looked at Aristaeus, who had become a slavering fiend, with a razor-toothed muzzle and claws dangling to his knees.

It was his only chance.

"Surely goodness and mercy shall follow me all the days of my life: and I will dwell in the house of the Lord for ever."

Stefan dropped the rosary and grabbed the plunger. Aristaeus began moving instantly, but this time Stefan managed to move faster. He clutched the plunger to his chest, shuddering with the pain of his wounded arm, and twisted the switch home.

Nothing happened.

Somehow, before Aristaeus descended on him, he managed to try it again. Nothing.

Stefan looked up, and Aristaeus was just standing there, in front of him. In the distance, down the car, Stefan heard someone clapping. Aristaeus stepped aside, and there, at the other end of the car, stood Melchior.

Standing next to him was a Negro woman holding in her hands two lengths of severed wire.

Stefan dropped the plunger, but Aristaeus grabbed him before he could make any move at escape. Stefan didn't even try.

Melchior looked at him with bottomless eyes that seemed to grab his soul and tear it from his body. Stefan prayed to himself as Aristaeus reached into his bloodied jacket and pulled his revolver from his holster. Then, with his foot, Aristaeus kicked the rosary off of the side of the train.

"You've done something impressive," Melchior said, ceasing his applause. His face was hawklike, more predatory in its human form than the distorted mask that Aristaeus' face had become. His mane of blond hair seemed to blow around his shoulders wildly, even though there was no wind inside the car. "You've attracted my attention."

He stepped next to the Negro woman who held the wires. She didn't move, even to breathe, as if she was a statue. Stefan wanted to run, to escape, but Aristaeus held him fast.

"You see, *I* decide who among the herd is important to my purpose. *I* pick those who will be in thrall to me. Of the countless, pointless millions, a handful are worthy of my touch, my direct control." Melchior drew a hand across the woman's shoulder. "Fewer come into my fold."

He nodded to Aristaeus, who pushed Stefan down to his knees. Stefan felt dizzy from blood loss and the pain in his shoulder.

"You're at the beginning of a new age, Stefan Ryzard. Soon the human trash will be burned from the face of the land. When the foundations of your civilization are stripped away, what's left of the cattle will call me Lord."

Stefan closed his eyes and shook his head. He felt as if he were in the train car with Satan himself.

"You think not?" Melchior's voice was soft, seductive. "The work you've seen was part of my plans before your ancestors decided to accept the middle-eastern cult you hold so dear. I knew when those of my own great race deposed me, nearly a millennia ago, that I would eventually reduce Europe to ashes. Within a decade, this land's troops will march from Paris to Moscow. I will follow that army, to rule those occupied lands."

He's insane. It was too much for Stefan to credit. Aristaeus grabbed Stefan's jaw and pulled his face upright. Stefan looked into Melchior's eyes, and his doubt dropped away.

Melchior nodded at him, still standing behind the woman. "My world is come. You cannot fight it. Those of my own race are impotent. Those such as you are less than nothing. And despite that, you interest me."

The train jerked, and Stefan heard the cars jostling against each other. Melchior waved to Aristaeus, and Stefan felt two inhuman hands clamp down on his shoulders.

"I've decided that I want you."

Stefan's heart shuddered and struggled against Aristaeus' grip. In response to his futile struggles, Aristaeus increased his grip, driving sharp daggers of pain into his broken shoulder. Stefan groaned. "God!"

Melchior shook his head. "Such misplaced faith."

Suddenly, and without warning, Melchior struck out at the woman before him. Stefan saw the flash of a silver blade reaching over the woman's shoulder. It slid through her neck without slowing. Stefan couldn't close his eyes or turn away, and watched horrified as the woman's head tumbled down the front of her body.

Blood didn't spray. It simply oozed weakly as the headless body dropped to its knees and fell forward, the mortal wound facing Stefan. Melchior stood over the corpse and stared at Stefan. "An act as simple as that is beyond your omnipotent God. Thousands have called upon Him to strike me down, and I still walk the earth."

Stefan stared at the body, lying in a small pool of thick blackish blood. He couldn't help thinking of the other bodies he had seen.

"You wonder why I killed her? My own thrall?" Melchior stepped over the body and began walking toward Stefan. "She had been corrupted by the blood of another. Not enough to displace my will within her, but enough to make her offensive to me. She suffered the fate of all those who offend me." He knelt down in front of Stefan, close enough that Stefan could feel his breath in his face. His breath was cold. "I offer immortality to all those who serve me by taking of my blood. I offer it, and I can take it away. I can give you more in this world than the empty promise of your tortured savior."

"Lord protect me," Stefan whispered.

He felt Aristaeus back away from him, but Melchior only smiled. "You think your lord intervenes? You think He causes those of the blood to shy away from you or your cross?" Melchior shook his head. "It is nothing more than you, Stefan Ryzard. Your faith is unpleasant for some, an annoying itch. They can see the devotion in your eyes and it drives the weak ones away."

"Hail Mary, full of grace, blessed art thou—"

Aristaeus let go of him, but Stefan never had a chance to react, because Melchior's left hand grabbed his shoulder. "Look at me, Stefan Ryzard. I am not weak."

Stefan's gaze fell into Melchior's eyes, pulling his soul after it. He fell into a void, surrounded on all sides by Melchior's irresistible presence. Melchior's will pushed against him like a tidal wave, swamping Stefan's feeble resistance. Every effort Stefan made to resist seemed to suck him deeper into Melchior's twisted soul.

With one set of eyes, Stefan was sinking into the depths of hell. With another, he could see Melchior before him, waving Aristaeus to the side. When Melchior raised his hand, Stefan was unrestrained, yet he couldn't move. It was as if his mind had been totally severed from his body. Even the pain of his injury seemed remote now.

Stefan tried to call for help, at least in his mind. But under the force of the mental undertow, he couldn't remember his prayers.

"Bare your chest to me," Melchior said.

Far away, Stefan felt his hands raise to tear open his clothes. It was hard to concentrate. It was becoming less clear to Stefan where he was, and what was happening to him. Even the basic knowledge of who he was seemed weak and eroded.

It would be very easy to forget, to give up. Somewhere inside his mind, that thought inspired a mortal terror. He couldn't give up his soul. What was left of Stefan didn't give up, it retreated. Everything he was, everything that trembled at Melchior's presence, drew back as far into his mind as it could. Stefan's identity shrank under the flood of Melchior's will and disappeared somewhere far from his conscious mind. Melchior's mind filled the spaces it left behind.

"Many give themselves to me willingly." Melchior raised his arm before the shell that had been Stefan Ryzard. He held his hand before him, and the skin split apart along the lines of the palm. Blood pooled in Melchior's cupped hand, spilling over the edges. "It pleases me to take from you."

With those words, Melchior took the blade in his other hand and brought it down across Stefan's chest. Even when the sword separated the rib cage, opening Stefan's heart to the air, his body didn't topple. Melchior's will was like a physical force holding the body immobile.

After the sword fell, before Stefan's blood had time to pool at his feet, Melchior's bloody hand entered the wound. The hand grabbed Stefan's still-beating heart, coating it with Melchior's own blood.

Melchior held him like that for an eon, Stefan's blood drenching the floor of the car below them. Stefan's heart slowed to a stop, and with it, the bleeding. Stefan's body never moved, and his eyes never closed. His gaze remained locked upon Melchior.

Eventually, Melchior smiled and withdrew his hand. It came out of the wound, soaked with gore, but as he held it in front of himself, the blood moved with a life of its own, drawing back into his palm, sinking into the raw meat of the palm before Melchior's skin pulled itself over the wounds in his hand.

As if an imperfect imitation of Melchior's hand, the edges of the massive wound in Stefan's chest began to pull themselves together. Now Stefan's body moved, collapsing to the floor, shuddering as the flesh and bones of his chest reformed themselves. Even the bone that pierced the flesh of his shoulder withdrew as the skin pulled itself over the wound.

In moments, Stefan lay on the floor, curled in a fetal position, eyes blankly staring. He lay in a pool of his own blood, but his body showed no sign of any injury. He breathed, and his heart beat, but both so shallowly that there was little sign of life. His clothes now hung upon him as if he had lost forty pounds.

"Rise up," Melchior said.

Stefan's face gave no sign of understanding the words, but his body obeyed. He got unsteadily to his feet. His eyes still stared blankly ahead.

"Accompany me," Melchior said, and Stefan did so, following Melchior and Aristaeus through the train. He didn't spare a look right or left, or even for the body of the woman that still lay across their path.

They passed through the length of two more empty cars. Past the one on which Stefan had planted his explosives, into a car that hadn't been on the train when Stefan had boarded. It appeared as a normal boxcar, misplaced at the end of a passenger train. And the trio of them had to step off of the unmoving train and walk to the side of the boxcar.

The door slid open on a dark empty space. A few candles flickered in one end of the car. Melchior led them up into the car, Stefan following, silent, staring and unaware.

Chained at the rear of the car was Iago.

Melchior looked upon him and said, "I wanted you to see your ally before you die. I wanted you to see how deeply you failed."

Iago looked up with a pale, wasted face. "You'll fail, Melchior. And destroy all of us with you."

Melchior laughed.

"The Covenant was to protect us. If humanity believes

in what you are, they'll do anything to destroy you and all like you."

"The voice of fear and weakness." Melchior walked up to Iago. As he did so, he gestured to Aristaeus to close the door. "Our noble race is meant to rule this mongrel cattle. Fear of them is a perversion that has poisoned our race since the inception of your Covenant."

Iago spat, carefully avoiding Melchior's gaze. "And you are meant to rule our noble race?"

"Who else of us remains unfettered by your perverted Covenant?"

"You are the perversion," Iago said.

Melchior took a hand and ran it along the side of Iago's face. "Take a look at what it is you fear." Melchior pointed his blade at Stefan, who stood, face blank, empty and staring. "Without your Covenant any of our race could have ruled, but you've preferred to cringe in the shadows."

"Your time was over a millennium ago."

Melchior shook his head. "No. Look across the ocean and see the rulers the cattle choose for themselves. Stalin, Hitler, Mussolini . . . The cattle beg to be controlled. If I only offer my hand, they will willingly wrap it around their own throats. My time is just beginning." He took the blade and brought it up to Iago's neck. "It is your time that is over."

Iago finally looked up into Melchior's eyes and said, "Because of you, the time of our race will be over."

Melchior raised the blade and sliced through Iago's neck. The body fell against its bonds as Iago's head toppled from his shoulders. The body twitched a few times, spraying the wall behind it with tarlike blood.

Melchior stepped back, shaking his head as if in disgust. He turned away from the corpse and faced Aristaeus. "Take another of my servants and dispose of the bodies."

Aristaeus' countenance had nearly returned to human form. "What about him, Master?" He nodded slightly at Stefan.

"Detective Ryzard is nothing but an empty shell now. Forget about him."

Aristaeus nodded and left to fetch another thrall to help him dispose of Iago and Rose Wallace.

15

Nuri Lapidos had come off of suspension only a day before someone found the body of "Number Seven," an unidentified woman. The tension in the rest of the city had filtered down into the squad-room. Everyone talked about "The Phantom of Kingsbury Run."

When he heard the talk around him, the bogus confessions, the innumerable tips and leads that went nowhere, the inability to identify the body, he could almost sense the presence of the unnatural. He could almost hear the superstition in the other detective's voices.

Nuri was still on probation, sitting behind a desk filling out paperwork, ignoring the ache of his barely-healed chest. He tried not to think about what was going on around him. He tried not to think of Iago. . . .

What could he do? Stefan had disappeared, presumably to act upon Iago's direction. Iago had disappeared, too. And yet another corpse turned up. Nuri couldn't help but think that it would be Iago and Stefan who would be turning up next.

No one was going to stop Eric Dietrich.

BOOK THREE

June 1937—August 1939
THE WAGES
OF SIN

1

Aristaeus disposed of the bodies in different places. It was months before the body of the woman was found, after it had been reduced to little more than a dismembered skeleton. It would be years before Iago's bones would be discovered in a Youngstown dump.

In one sense, Stefan was aware of this. His memory was still intact, and he was aware of what went on around him. In another sense Stefan wasn't even conscious. What thoughts crossed his conscious mind weren't his own.

Information from the outside world fell on his ears, as Dietrich's thralls talked around him. And while he heard the words, the ideas attached sank into his memory without a trace. Those words weren't commands by the Master, and therefore they weren't important.

But he heard and saw, even though his thoughts were a blank void.

He was in the basement of a house that stood somewhere in a Slovenian neighborhood around East Fifty-Fifth, near the St. Clair area where he had grown up. Down here with him, sitting around a card table, was Simon Aristaeus. Two others sat across from him, both former members of the Mayfield Road Mob.

"So that body was yours, eh?" said the one on the right. Aristaeus called him Dante. As he spoke, he tossed a few red chips into a pile in the center of the table.

"Nah," Aristaeus said, tossing a like number of chips into the pile. "Call." He looked at the other two and added, "Raise you five." He tossed in a blue chip.

The Italian on the left, who Aristaeus had called Tito,

shook his head and folded his cards on the table. "I thought you took the knife to her?"

"See you," Dante said, tossing in his own blue chip. "Isn't that what you said?"

"Aces over tens," Aristaeus said, spreading his cards on the table. Dante said "Fuck," dropping his hand, as Aristaeus pulled the pot over to his side of the table. "No, I just dropped off the body. I saw the Master Himself separate her neck. Anything I did was just to make it easy to move the dead bitch around."

Dante gathered the cards, shuffled, and began dealing. "Does that ever worry you?"

"What?" Aristaeus said, picking up his cards, one at a time.

"That He kills His own like that?" Dante said, finishing the deal and picking up his cards.

Aristaeus snorted, shaking his head and tossing a red chip into the pot. The others followed suit. "Two," he said, tossing a pair of cards in front of him. "Why should it worry me? I serve Him, that's what matters."

"Three," Tito said. "Didn't she also? She was the one who brought Iago to Him, wasn't she?"

"Dealer takes one," Dante said.

"She allowed herself to become contaminated with another's blood. She wasn't purely the Master's any more." Aristaeus glanced across at the dealer and tossed in a white chip. "Ten."

"Shit," Dante muttered.

"Here," Tito tossed in his own white chip and leaned over the table. "Now wait a minute. How many effing times have we watched Him take apart one of his rivals, and feed us the poor bastard's blood?"

"That's different," Aristaeus said. He looked across at Dante who was still looking at his cards. "Well?" he said.

"Give me a minute," Dante said.

"How the hell is it different?"

"First off, the bastard's dead when He offers us his blood. Second, He always takes first, it *becomes* his blood . . ."

"Okay, see you and raise ten," Dante said.

Aristaeus tossed in another white chip without comment.

"Then why don't it become *ours*—" Tito looked across at Dante. "What, you think I'm crazy? Fold."

Dante smiled, "Jacks over kings. There."

Aristaeus shook his head, "Four threes."

"Fuck," Dante said.

Aristaeus turned to Tito and said, "It don't become *ours* because we aren't a thousand years older and more powerful than anything we drink from, got it?" He pulled the pot in toward himself. "It's about power."

"So if we drank from the White Zombie over there," Tito pointed at Stefan, "we'd be all right?"

Aristaeus laughed as he took the cards. "You'd be in no danger of handing your soul over, but I'd still think you'd piss off the Master." He shuffled and said, "Change of pace, five card stud."

Dante sighed.

As Aristaeus dealt out the first two cards, Tito kept looking in Stefan's direction, as if he'd just noticed him standing in the corner of the basement. "What's the zombie's story?" Tito asked. "Don't he ever talk?"

"He's the Master's pet, and no, he don't ever talk. Now ante up, you got the king."

Chips flew into the center of the table.

"He was a cop, right?" Dante asked.

Aristaeus nodded. "And he tried to blow the Master up."

As the third card was dealt out, Tito looked over at Stefan and said, "Sometimes I don't understand our boss."

"King-ten bets," Aristaeus said.

Tito tossed in a chip. "Why's He kill one of His own, and bring over someone who tried to kill Him?"

"Don't ask questions like that," Dante said. "You were supposed to be in on a hit on Him, remember?"

Tito shrugged, "I'm entitled to wonder, ain't I?"

"You want to know why?" Aristaeus said as he dealt out another card. "Because it amuses Him." Aristaeus tilted his head toward Stefan. "That fella especially."

"Why him?" Tito asked, tossing his bet.

Dante looked at Tito's hand and said, "Fuck," again. He flipped his cards over and said, "Fold."

"I think because he was a Catholic." Aristaeus tossed in his bet and dealt out another card.

"So, *I'm* a Catholic." Tito tossed in a chip, "What's that got to do with anything?"

"I ain't fighting your pair of tens with this crap." Aristaeus folded his hand. Tito drew in the pot and Dante said, "Finally, someone else wins a hand."

"So?" Tito said.

"This guy here had some faith, Tito," Aristaeus said. "Enough so when he held up a cross, it was painful. He was the kind who think we're spawn of the devil, sold our souls."

Tito looked over at Stefan again and said, "No wonder he don't talk much."

Dante looked up at a clock on the wall and said, "I think it's time."

"What? Can't we go another hand now I'm finally winning?"

"Dante's right," Aristaeus said.

Tito dropped the cards and cursed.

"Let's get the zombie and go," Dante said. "I've lost enough here."

The trio, Tito somewhat reluctantly, walked over and led Stefan out of the basement and to a waiting car.

The summer night wrapped itself around the dark sedan as it slid through the empty dark streets of the east side. It drove south toward the train tracks. Their final destination was a warehouse that stood near the tracks a short distance from the East Fifty-Fifth railyard, also a short distance from the now-infamous Kingsbury Run.

The warehouse appeared dark and empty, but there was a lot next to it that was hidden from view by a twelve-foot fence plastered with old cryptic posters. They drove around through a large gate that slid aside for them at the last minute.

On the other side, the sedan found a space for itself in a crowd of similar cars. Dozens of people walked through the lot, between the cars, toward the gaping maw of the loading bays. In the back of Stefan's mind burned a memory of a different warehouse, a smaller one near the docks. But the memory didn't burn enough to make it to the front part of his mind.

He followed Dante, Tito, and Aristaeus through the pale

crush of people. Memory tried to assert itself whenever he passed a face that bore some familiarity, this one a reporter for the *News,* this other man a member of the city council, the third another detective, this fourth a local thug into the protection racket. Just passing them he could feel, in his gut, in the air he breathed, the difference between those who still wore a human form and those who had become damned completely, like him.

Somewhere he feared—not for the walking dead that accompanied him to the warehouse, gone already—a small piece of him feared for those that still lived. He feared for the ones who had not yet tumbled off the precipice into the abyss of the damned.

He feared, but he could not pray.

The maw of the loading bays took in the advancing crowd twelve abreast. The procession advanced in silence. The silence was out of reverence for, and fear of, the dark messiah they had come here to worship. They filled the darkened chamber, hundreds strong.

The only noise was a repetitive moaning that came, not from the silent throng, but from men and women who were chained to the support beams evenly spaced through the crowd. There were easily a dozen of these captives in place around Stefan, naked, heads covered by sacks, four to a post, facing each point of the compass, arms drawn back so far around the girder that the joints must be broken.

Stefan had been present, with the others, waiting, for fifteen minutes or so before he heard the doors behind them rattle shut. The faithful were all here.

For a few moments the warehouse was completely dark, the only sounds those of the moaning captives. Then a voice came from the darkness, a deep, instantly recognizable voice.

"Welcome, flesh of my flesh, blood of my blood."

A light shone upon a raised platform in front of the crowd. And there stood Melchior, arms outstretched as if in blessing. Even the moans seemed to cease in deference to the timbre of Melchior's voice.

"Welcome, those bound to my service." Melchoir lowered his arms. He was tall, and his hair hung loose around his shoulders. He wore a crimson robe that hung around him like a bishop's garb. On a small table before him was a long blade and a goblet. He took the goblet in one hand, and held the other over it. The skin of that hand split apart and blood wept from the wound into it.

"This is my blood, which has granted you eternal life. Drink it in my service."

Melchior held the cup aloft and lights came on, illuminating the pillars with the twisted, captive bodies chained upon them. Stefan could feel the edge of madness cut into the room, under Melchoir's bidding. In himself he felt the perverse hunger grow.

"This is my flesh," Melchoir said. "It is time to renew our communion. Feed, my children, and be sated."

At those words, it was as if someone had opened the gates of hell within that warehouse. The whole crowd descended upon the pillars as one. Stefan found himself within the horrid mob, tearing tooth and claw into the flesh of the chained captives, letting the bright, burning, living blood spill over his hands, his face, his mouth. Melchior's children climbed over themselves to reach the human victims, to sink their teeth into some yet-unmolested piece of flesh.

Even those who still lived, who didn't need the living blood to survive, joined the frenzy, tearing into the flesh with their bare hands.

Stefan fell away from the girder as soon as the gnawing hunger was no longer a force within him. Falling back he could see his victim. The frenzied crowd still undulated at the base of the pillar like some crimson multiheaded beast. Rising above it, where there had been a human being, was now just a bloody skeleton held together with strips of sinew.

Even through the empty, dead chambers of his mind, Stefan could feel the disgust and self-loathing coming from the small part of him that was still himself.

In front of the platform, a select group of Melchior's faithful had gathered to drink from his goblet. A dozen of the new and the favored were able to feed from the master himself.

As the frenzy faded, and the crowd withdrew from their feeding, Melchior again drew attention toward the platform. A light illuminated the back of the platform, an area that had been in darkness until now.

A body hung upside-down, dangling from a chain anchored in the ceiling. Melchior raised His knife and announced, "Here is a traitor to the blood. A keeper of a false Covenant."

The Master cataloged the multitude of sins committed by the creature chained behind Him. All amounted to being a vampire outside Melchior's fealty. Stefan saw the Master raise His blade and remove the creature's head. But by the time the head fell on the platform, and Melchior took the victim's blood, Stefan had withdrawn in himself past the point where the scene held any significance.

2

"No chance it could be Stefan Ryzard?" Nuri asked Sam Gerber, the coroner. Gerber had been elected successor to Pearse, and Nuri suspected it was because the small man looked at home in a morgue.

Nuri had come down here after hearing that they had found a number eight.

On the table before him Gerber had laid out an incomplete set of skeletal remains. His gloved hands touched the skull, briefly making him resemble a twisted Hamlet. He shook his head, looking at Nuri through thick glasses. "No. This was a woman, shorter, and a Negro."

"But she belongs on the list?"

"If you want, you can see the marks on the vertebrae where the knife—"

"No, thanks," Nuri said, turning away. "I should go."

Gerber continued to talk about when his final report would be ready. Nuri just nodded his head as he left, not really listening.

He had come down here expecting to find Stefan. He didn't know why he felt Stefan would end up on the list. It seemed that the decapitation was saved for special categories of Eric Dietrich's victims, and from his expedition to the swamp, Nuri knew that they weren't finding all of the bodies.

Still he expected the next headless corpse to be Stefan.

In a way he almost hoped so. The uncertainty of having his ex-partner missing, with no sign of his fate, was gnawing at him. Stefan had stepped into something dark, and what might have happened to him could be worse than a death by decapitation.

Nuri walked back from the morgue, returning to the mundane world of police work, unenlightened and fearful.

3

Tuesday, July 6

It was the summer that some of the worst parts of Europe came to visit the city. Striking workers mixing with Communists verged near to riot enough times that the National Guard had been called in to keep the peace. By the start of July the downtown area, especially around the Flats by the river, looked as if it was under martial law.

Carl Selig had never been to Cleveland before, and he felt out of his depth. He stood on a road overlooking some train tracks, feeling intolerably hot in his uniform, wondering what would happen if he got in a situation where he had to shoot somebody. He had his Springfield ready, as he was ordered to, but the thought of firing it made him weak in the knees.

Fortunately, today he had a quiet spot to observe. No demonstrators waving red-and-black flags, no one throwing stones or bricks, no hired thugs trying to club the workers into submission. Standing here, overlooking the quiet rails, Carl could try to believe that the presence of the guardsmen was quieting things down.

He could believe it if it wasn't for the rumors that found their way to him. He heard about shots being fired, of looting downtown, and one grotesque story about a human body, or parts of one, seen floating in the river.

Thinking of those things made him wish he was back in Oberlin.

At least he had a quiet spot to tend to. There was little here to watch but the occasional train passing by, and a small village of tin shacks where about half a dozen tramps made their home. The lack of anything else to draw his attention made him more aware of how hot he was, and how the sweat was gathering under his helmet. The tramps had a fire going, and the smell of it made the heat feel worse.

At least the sun was going down.

Night came, and though Carl was still a few hours short of relief, he began to feel a little easier about the riots. Nothing was going to happen in front of him today. He should have been able to relax a little.

Instead, he kept thinking of the body—or what the private telling him insisted, the *pieces* of it—found floating in the Cuyahoga. It was a gruesome idea, and Carl's mind had trouble letting go of it. Even more gruesome was the story that there was some maniac who had chopped up eight other people before this one. Every one killed by cutting off their head.

It would have been another stupid scare story if it wasn't for the fact that Carl had heard about the murders in Cleveland long before he ever came into the National Guard.

Carl decided that a maniac he could shoot. He had doubts about a striker or a Communist, but a full-fledged madman he figured he could shoot. Though as darkness fell across the tracks and the little shantytown, Carl hoped his theory wouldn't be tested.

Near the end of his watch, he heard a train. That wasn't unusual. What caught his ear was the sound of it, the odd lengthening note that made it seem as if the train was slowing down. The appearance of the castbound train bore that out. As the engine's lights swept across first him, then the hill below him, then the tramps' shanties, then the hills beyond, Carl could see that the train was screeching to a stop just below him.

There was no sense to it that he could see. There was no station, no siding, no landmark to speak of outside of the little collection of rough shacks below. The tramps themselves gave witness to the remarkable event. They made their lives on the tracks, and certainly knew more arcana of the rails than Carl, but they stood and stared at the slowing beast as if they, too, were dumbfounded as to the reason it was stopping.

The train came to a complete stop, the engine somewhat

distant now, and before the little tramp village sat a line of black boxcars. For a long time there was no sound but a soft hissing from the direction of the engine.

The tramps, out of curiosity, or out of a sudden wanderlust brought on by the proximity of transportation, began to approach the cars. The light was dim, only from the fire by the tramps' camp, but Carl counted seven of them.

Carl felt a sudden unease, a prickling at the back of his neck. Everything seemed suddenly so wrong, as if the normal world had just fallen away from him, leaving him naked in some netherworld. The scene below him was nearly a hundred yards away, but he still took a step back.

As if triggered by his evil thoughts, the doors on the dark boxcars slid open in front of the tramps. There was a sudden flurry of motion that Carl could barely make sense of. He had a brief impression of grasping hands from the darkness, some barely human. He thought some of the tramps tried to turn, perhaps even run. It seemed only a second before he saw the tramps' kicking feet retreat into the darkness of the boxcars and the doors slide shut.

Carl stood in stunned silence for the space of a heartbeat . . .

. . . and another . . .

When he heard a scream from below him, he broke from his paralysis and began running down the slope. He stumbled madly, brush tearing at his uniform, roots twisting his ankles, but somehow he remained upright even as he lost his helmet. He called out, "Stop," and the word was little more than an inarticulate bellow that seared his lungs.

The scream continued, merging with the sound of the engine firing up to move again.

Carl raised his Springfield in some vain hope to stop the train, and it was then that the brush finally caught his feet, sending him tumbling face-first into the ground. He lost the Springfield in the fall, but it didn't go off.

Carl pushed himself up to see the train moving past him, accelerating. As he watched, he was certain that he heard, under the sound of the screeching engine, the scream abruptly cease.

By the time Carl had reached his feet, the boxcars were long past him and the train was moving by as if it had never stopped. Cars slid by him, clattering along the tracks. There was no sign of what, if anything had happened.

Carl had no idea what to do. None of his standing orders covered this situation. He stood and watched the train pass by. Too soon, it seemed, the last car passed him. He was left in the darkness by the tracks, the only light the remains of the tramps' fire, the only sound the receding noise of the train's passage.

Slowly, Carl backed away from the tracks, climbing the hill, gathering his gun and his helmet. He began to wonder if what he had seen had actually happened.

1938

4

Monday, March 21

"Four of these in the past year," Mayor Burton said. He stood with Ness on the handball court, but neither of them were playing. "The last one floating down the Cuyahoga."

Ness nodded. There didn't seem to be much to say. With the press becoming less than supportive, Ness was hoping that the body in the river would be the last and that he'd hear no more of this madman. There had been a barrage of criticism after the last body, and the Democrats had used the failure of the Torso Murder investigation against Ness and Burton in the last election. During the campaign the Democrats said that they didn't need a "G-man from Chicago;" they needed a local lawman who wasn't more concerned about witch-hunts in the police department than he was dead Clevelanders.

"Something has got to be done to ease the public mind," Burton said.

Ness could only smile weakly at that. Every few months, the mayor would fixate on the one problem of the killer. Ness didn't have that luxury. He had to deal with problems as far-ranging as corruption in the department, to union racketeering, to traffic safety. Somehow, whenever anyone talked about these murders, they lost sight of all the progress Ness had made in these areas. It was annoying.

"Can't we do a dragnet, a house-to-house search—"

Ness shook his head. "You know what kind of resources that would take? We can't even be sure he's in the area. He hasn't left us any signs for nearly eight months."

THE FLESH, THE BLOOD AND THE FIRE   541

"You could find his butcher hall, the place he dismembers his victims."

"It's an extreme reaction, sir. I don't know if it·is warranted."

Mayor Burton leaned against the wall of the court and wiped a little sweat he had left over from the game. "Maybe. Have there been any leads in the case?"

"Too many." Ness waved over the hardwood floor of the court and said, "I could fill this court ten feet deep with transcripts of every tip we've gotten, every interview we've done, and every false confession we've received. Everyone from taxi drivers to National Guardsmen have seen something suspicious in the Run." He shook his head and said, "The publicity on this case makes people crawl out of the woodwork."

Burton gave him a look as if he couldn't believe Ness bad-mouthing publicity of any sort. "Well, I just want you to remember that a house-to-house is always an option."

"It's not even certain that our man's in the Roaring Third."

Mayor Burton shook his head. "The three victims you've identified were all from the area—"

"The identification of Rose Wallace was tentative, not official—the remains were skeletal."

Mayor Burton waved his hand as if it wasn't an important enough detail to be bothered with. "And you wouldn't get long odds that all these unidentified bodies weren't tramps and transients."

Ness nodded, Mayor Burton was just repeating the most popular theory, that this maniac was some homosexual predator, preying on the underbelly of Cleveland's population. Though the last one, in the river, had a manicure that was at odds with him being a tramp.

Ness would have felt better if one of the "tramp" victims had been invited. "We are investigating that angle. Every night now we have some detectives undercover in the shantytowns around the flats, and up toward the Run."

"*That* I'm glad to hear." Mayor Burton picked up a towel from a bench by the door and wiped the back of his neck. "Well, I have to get back to the office, I have meetings to attend to. I suppose you have work to get to."

Ness nodded.

As Mayor Burton left he turned to face Ness one last time, "Remember, it's always an option."

"I know," Ness said as the mayor left.

When Mayor Burton entered his office, Eric Dietrich was waiting for him. The man was seated across from his desk. Mayor Burton hung up his overcoat and said, "I've been expecting you."

Dietrich nodded, "I like to hear news of your administration from you. The newspapers can distort things." He twisted his cane in his hand so the handle spun in front of him.

"That's true," Mayor Burton said as he moved around behind his desk. He didn't extend his hand or make eye contact. He knew that Dietrich didn't mind; he seemed to be aware of how his touch, and his gaze, disturbed others. Dietrich remained seated at an angle, turning his cane, looking off into the corner of Mayor Burton's office.

"I do want to reassure myself that my recommendations for the next Republican administration reflect well on me."

"I understand." Mayor Burton did understand. Dietrich was very active behind the scenes in the Republican Party, and it seemed clear, ever since he'd become mayor, that Dietrich had some voice in the cabinet makeup of the next Republican president. Originally Burton's ambitions had never extended much beyond the cleaning up of his own city. But Dietrich represented opportunities he could neither refuse nor ignore.

"The mutilation killings, those still worry you. No progress?" Dietrich kept twirling the cane.

The mayor nodded. That seemed Dietrich's personal fixation. Rarely would the businessman ask him questions about taxes or how he managed to get the city coffers to pay deferred salaries of city workers. Always crime. Always the murders and how he planned to deal with them.

"Yes, but it's been months since we've had one. Maybe we've been lucky, and the monster died, moved, or was imprisoned for something else."

"And perhaps you just haven't found his latest."

Mayor Burton didn't like the way Dietrich said that. "I've talked to Ness about stepping up the investigation. We're already using every resource at our disposal."

"Not quite," Dietrich said, and he stopped twirling his cane. "If you wish to be sure to drive a dangerous wolf from the forest, drive away the deer. Perhaps even burn the forest."

Dietrich's voice sounded grave, and Burton leaned forward. "What, exactly, are you saying?"

"You know where he draws his victims. I've heard you say it often enough. The nameless tramps and hobos that line the tracks of this city."

"Drive the tramps away?" Mayor Burton asked. "How?"

5

Detective Nuri Lapidos was doing his turn in purgatory. He was dressed in old ragged clothes that itched and refused to fit right. The rain and mud weren't helping. He slogged along the tracks under the glare of the rail-yard lights, but more often in the darkness. The only things he carried that were at odds with the tramp outfit were a badge and a revolver, both well hidden.

The badge was for the railroad cops, the revolver was to be for the murderer that was supposed to prowl these rails. He doubted that the revolver would help if they met. He also doubted that they would meet down here by the train tracks.

Still, Nuri followed his assignment, slogging through the mud, stopping at the small temporary communities the rootless unemployed had thrown up around the flats. He would stop here and there, and try and dry himself by someone's fire.

Through the night he would try to talk to the people he met, talk about the stories they had formed about the predators in the darkness along the tracks. Between these talks he would walk along the tracks, looking like a potential victim for those predators.

Few of the stories he collected would be fit for the homicide squad. Even so, they made Nuri uneasy.

He heard stories about a pale man, or sometimes a woman, interrupted while drinking the blood of a sleeping man. Sometimes these nocturnal creatures would run, and sometimes they would turn demonic and attack the witness. The stories were always accompanied by nervous laughter—though whenever someone claimed to be that witness, they didn't join in the laughter.

It was late now, past midnight, and Nuri was slogging along to find a fourth group of tramps tonight. He pulled his ragged overcoat around him, more against the darkness than against the rain, which had already soaked him to the skin.

He stumbled forward, leaving the tracks, making for a blurry spot of light that seemed to hover underneath a drawbridge that extended over the Cuyahoga. He was halfway to it before he saw that the glow was more than a simple campfire. Some of the small makeshift buildings were burning.

Nuri started running. The night air in the river basin played games with sound. One moment he heard nothing but the rush of rain, and the next he was certain he could hear laughter. Under the laughter there could have been screams, inhuman screams, like an animal caught in the flames.

Nuri, still running, drew his gun.

Shadows ran out of the darkness toward him, faster than anything had a right to move. The shapes were only vaguely human as they loped by him. Nuri raised his gun, but the shadowy figures passed by him as if they didn't even see him, or didn't care.

Nuri had only the briefest impression of claws, leathery skin, and a loping stride. Then they were gone, and all that was left was an odd keening sound coming from between Nuri and the fire.

He didn't want to advance any further, but those things might have left people there, in the fire. Nuri looked back after the things, but the darkness had swallowed them. Then he advanced toward the fire.

The keening became louder.

The smell of things burning, flesh and hair, began to reach him through the rain. It became stronger as Nuri approached something that lay on the ground between him and the fire. The thing steamed in the rain, and Nuri was almost upon it before he could see what it was. When he did see it, he stopped.

Before him was a corpse burned across most of its body.

It was twisted, the flesh charred and black. Steam rose from it in the rain. The shape was only vaguely human, and not only because of the destruction wrought upon its flesh. Like the shapes that had passed him in the darkness, this thing's limbs were misproportioned, its back was arched, and its skull was twisted into a muzzle that had too many teeth.

Empty eye sockets stared at him from a face of blackened flesh.

Nuri looked up. The fire was dying away. He could still hear laughter, and a pair of voices. The voices weren't close enough to make anything out yet. Nuri started edging toward the fire again.

Something grabbed his ankle.

Nuri pitched forward, and his revolver went flying into the darkness. He sucked in a breath and got a mouthful of sour mud.

Something clung to his leg. Nuri scrambled to flip himself over to look at what was grabbing at him, and in a flash of lightning, saw the corpse clutching at him.

As he watched, the charred form moved. The flesh was burned enough that he could hear it rustle. The corpse made another sound, something like breaking bone, as it turned toward him.

Nuri sat up and tried frantically to pry the charred hand from his leg. The thing moved slowly, but it was advancing on him, pulling itself by the one arm. Fluid leaked from cracks in its black skin as it moved. The face had changed, the muzzle retreating, so what closed on him was a naked human skull covered with a few remnants of crumbling black flesh.

It was keening at him.

Nuri tore at the hand gripping him until his fingernails were bloody. Its grip was like an iron band on his ankle. He tore at the exposed tendons on the back of it, and in response, the grip briefly loosened. Nuri tore his foot away, leaving the thing with his shoe.

The thing opened its black jaw and keened at him. The sound was filled with an unnatural pain. Nuri could hear the hunger in the sound. He couldn't separate the noise into words; he suspected the thing had no tongue, but he could almost understand what it was saying.

Let me feed.

Nuri scrambled backward, away from the thing.

It tried to follow, but it moved slowly, pulling itself along the ground with the single arm. The other arm hung loose at its side, little more than blackened bone. Nuri outdistanced the thing and reached his gun. He kept backing into the darkness and kept the gun trained on the thing.

Nuri managed to get a dozen yards away, and the thing stopped moving. It began keening again, louder than ever. It seemed to have lost track of him.

Nuri was about to stand up, as soon as his heart stopped racing, when the voices approached. Nuri looked toward the dying fire, and saw four silhouettes walking toward the corpse through the rain. The one in the lead carried an ax.

Instead of standing up, Nuri lowered himself flush with the mud, hiding in the ditch where he found himself. He watched the quartet approach the still-keening corpse. Even though the thing still moved, splashing around itself with its single arm, none of the four showed any reaction. They walked on, businesslike, as if an animate corpse was no big deal for them.

In another flash of lightning, Nuri could see the face of the lead man, with the ax. It was Simon Aristaeus, the man who had shot him in Van Sweringen's train car. He led three other men whose faces he still couldn't make out in the darkness.

"What a frigging mess," he heard one of the anonymous ones say as they closed on the still-moving body. "We lost, what, four?"

Aristaeus shook his head and said, "And we got five. Six counting him." Aristaeus waved the ax in the direction of the corpse. "Not a bad night's work."

Another one of Aristaeus' followers said, "And at this rate we'll never get them all. And burning everything is damn messy. What if the cops see us?"

"Then we have to kill some cops," Aristaeus said, walking around so he was behind the thrashing creature. The thing had become even more animated, as if it knew what was coming. Unfortunately for it, the more frantic its movement, the less effective it was. It seemed to have lost not only its one arm, but most of its legs. It couldn't move more than a foot before Aristaeus stepped up behind it and placed his foot in the center of its back. The weight pushed the blackened skull into the mud, muffling the thing's cries.

"Besides," Aristaeus said, as he handed the ax to one of the others, took off his jacket, and rolled up his sleeves, "if the Master has his way, soon the cops will be emptying these hoovervilles for us." He traded the jacket for the ax.

"Why would the cops do that?" one of the others asked.

"They're looking for a maniac who's lopping off people's heads, don't you read the papers?" With that, Aristaeus swung the ax in a wide arc down toward the corpse. Nuri couldn't tear his gaze away as the blade descended on the pinned thing's neck. The ax came down with such force that the creature's neck barely slowed its progress, its momentum continuing its arc on the other side of the body.

Aristaeus rested the ax on his shoulder, and stepped forward to kick the head away from the body. It rolled a few feet before stopping, its eyeless sockets pointed at the sky.

The corpse was now only a corpse; it neither cried nor moved.

"So why would they roust the hobos around here?"

Aristaeus walked over to the head and crouched by it. "They can't identify any of the bodies, and the ones they could are from the Roaring Third. They're sure that their maniac takes his victims from the worthless garbage around here. If they don't find their maniac, and they panic enough, they'll end up rousting them. Incidentally rousting the last hiding place for the Master's enemies."

"Almost ironic," one of the ones in the dark said.

"Tito," Aristaeus said, "I didn't picture you as one for such big words."

"Fuck yourself," came the response.

"This is one less bloodsucker who's catching a train out of town." Aristaeus bent over and picked up the head. It was now completely inert and more skull-like than ever. He turned it so it faced the others. "Fire," Aristaeus said, "the great equalizer."

"I still think it's a frigging mess."

Aristaeus stood up and handed the skull to the speaker. "That might have belonged to someone over two centuries old. You think we could have taken him without torching everything?"

"*If* he was old and powerful," said the man now holding

the skull. "For all we know he could have been turned yesterday."

Aristaeus laughed and took back his jacket from the one he called Tito. "Well if he'd been turned yesterday, I doubt he'd be moving after we torched him. Besides, that's what an equalizer means; we don't have to care about things like age and power—now let the zombie get the body." Aristaeus craned his neck so he looked past his first two companions at the one who hadn't spoken. "Come over here."

The last member of the quartet walked forward, reached down, and grabbed the body by the shoulders. In another flash of lightning, Nuri saw his face.

It was Stefan.

Nuri sucked in a gasp and tried to push himself flatter into the mud. Pale and drawn, wearing a blank expression, but it was Stefan. Somehow they hadn't killed him, they had *taken* him. Nuri wanted to do something, to intervene, but fear rooted him to the spot. In his gut he knew he wasn't looking at a normal set of hoodlums. His gun would be useless against them.

He stayed motionless until they had carried the body away.

After giving them enough time to leave, Nuri stood up and walked back to where the fire had been. All that was left was smoldering ash. He looked for bodies, but they were gone, and any signs of blood or flesh had been washed away with the rain.

6

"**I** don't believe you," Ness said, "and I don't believe this."

Nuri stood there, in Ness' office, unable to say anything coherent in defense of his report.

"You sound less lucid than the tramps you're supposed to be taking stories from." Ness paced around his office, circling Nuri. "I don't know what went on back there, but it wasn't what you wrote down in this report."

"It's what I saw—" Nuri started.

Ness sighed, "And that's supposed to make this better? I expect stories like this when a witness walks off the street, or I talk to a drunk who's lived under a bridge and in a bottle for the past five years. Even Ryzard, after he started cracking, had a superstitious immigrant background." Ness stopped pacing and faced Nuri. "I expected more of you. You went to college, you're supposed to be smarter than this."

"Sir—"

Ness held up his hand. "I don't want to hear it. It was a shame that you were teamed with a man right before he went around the bend. It couldn't have been easy. But I expected you to straighten out. You're convincing me otherwise."

He picked up thin folder from his desk and waved it at Nuri. "You know what this says to me?" Ness said, "It says that you listened too well to the tramps' ghost stories, and probably drank something you shouldn't have."

Ness walked around and sat down behind his desk.

"The ashes are there, you can see where everything burned."

Ness nodded. "No doubt. Like I said, you might have seen something, but not this. At least I hope not, because I don't want to believe that one of my detectives, when seeing someone dismembering a body, would cower and hide. According to your own report, you had your gun drawn and they were armed only with an ax."

"It was Aristaeus and he was . . ." Nuri couldn't finish the sentence because it would have sounded absurd in the light of day.

Ness nodded, completing the unfinished sentence, "Undead? Do you know how ridiculous that sounds? I allowed Ryzard some slack because of seniority. He was an old hand and, unlike half the cops I found in this department, he was clean. I made a mistake. I won't repeat it. I will not have a detective who refuses to confront suspects because he thinks they might be the bogeyman."

Nuri felt his gut shrink inside him, but all he could do was nod. Ness was right.

"Aristaeus may have gone dirty, and he might have even shot you—though I have to say that when I heard about that debacle, I was half-convinced that Ryzard was the one who shot you—but that doesn't justify your behavior." Ness opened up the file and said, "If you strip away the eyewash about a moving corpse, what you have here is a report of two bent cops and a pair of Sicilian hoods chopping up a body—presumably killed by them—and carting away the evidence. While you sat by and watched."

Ness closed the file. He looked up at him with piercing eyes, and, for some reason, Nuri thought the Safety Director looked older now. "Do you realize that I have another victim of this maniac, a woman's leg floating down the river? And out of half a dozen officers I had in the field last night, you're the only one who saw anything—and it's all garbage."

Ness tossed the file back on the desk. "I'd transfer you to the traffic division if I wasn't trying to clean that department up." He folded his hands. "As it stands, you're going to be doing paperwork for a while, a *long* while, and maybe you should think about your choice of career."

Nuri didn't have an adequate response. Even though he thought he didn't have a choice at the time, somehow, in retrospect, he had screwed up.

Nuri turned to leave the office, and Ness added, "The only reason you're still on the force, Nuri, is because you're honest. For all my work, it still seems a rarity."

Nuri nodded and mumbled, "Thank you," as he left.

7

"So what were their names?"

The gentleman drinking across from Nuri hemmed and hawed until Nuri slid another few bills to his side of the table. The two of them sat in the back of a small bar a few blocks away from East One-Ten and Woodland, the Bloody Corner where so many of the Porrello family had been killed.

The gentlemen taking the money was part of a more recent, and more violent organization. An organization that seemed to have very tenuous ties back to Eric Dietrich.

Nuri sat back and waited, sipping his drink. He felt something like an outlaw himself, even if he wasn't doing anything illegal, yet. He was still officially desk-bound, but over the past two months he had been conducting his own private investigation, trying to track down Aristaeus and the goons who he'd seen with him. Eventually, he hoped to find Stefan.

He still didn't know what he'd do if he found any of them.

"Yeah," his dinner companion said, "Tito and Dante Marcello—Them the ones I saw with the Greek—"

"Aristaeus?"

"Whatever the fuck his name was."

Nuri nodded, "So you know where I can find these brothers?"

"They used to hang down on Mayfield, though as far as I know, they don't hang anywhere anymore."

"You know where they're likely to show up."

The man drank from his glass, and looked nervously

around himself. "You know that people who get in the way of these people tend to disappear or . . ."

"Or what?"

"Or they become these people." He polished off his glass. "I don't want to know what happens. Tito and Dante were supposed to hit Eric Dietrich. Now they work for him—though work for might be too weak a word for it."

"Where can I find them?"

"You might see Tito driving a sedan around St. Clair after dark." He pushed the glass away. "That's all I'm going to tell you. The stories I've heard about these guys make me sick and nervous, and I've blinded deadbeats with an icepick." He picked up his hat from the seat next him and put it on, casting shadow across his face. "If you fear the Devil, stay away from these people."

He left Nuri sitting there. After a while Nuri emptied his own glass.

8

It was a fetid day, and flies were alive all through the trash heaps along Shore Drive. The wind off the lake did little to mitigate the heat of the day. Men in ragged clothes poked through the rubbish looking for something salvageable.

One man waving away the flies from one section of trash stopped still for a long time. He stood still long enough to draw the attention of his anonymous fellows. A few walked up to where the man stood, staring, no longer waving the flies away. Some held their hands up to their mouths even though they were used to the smell of the garbage and the sour lake smell that covered the area like a blanket.

One turned away and vomited.

In front of them, covered by flies, laying in the detritus like just another piece of garbage, was a human torso, blackening with decay.

Some ran to get the police. Even as they did so, a crowd gathered like a storm. The news broke from the shoreline like a sour wave off the lake. When the police cars sped up to the scene, there was a waiting mass of spectators, and a few photographers still taking pictures.

The scene transformed. The men there were no longer the ragged scavengers, but uniformed police, detectives in cheap suits, and the mass of the public from the offices downtown. The police tried to keep the crowd back from the scene, clearing the rubbish for hundreds of feet in either direction.

It wasn't far enough. To one side, within the mass of the crowd that stood amidst the rubbish to watch the police's ghoulish work, came a disturbance. A ragged circle formed in its midst like an air-bubble on the surface of dirty water. The men on the edges of that circle wore suits and hats, but wore expressions not too distant from the sick faces of the scavengers. They held their hands to their mouths, holding handkerchiefs to their noses.

Police converged on the spot within minutes, hoping to find the missing pieces of the corpse. What they found was a new corpse entirely.

The bodies were number eleven and twelve before the coroner even looked at them. The story had flowed through the city flooding bar after bar, office after office, until the evening papers could only provide a footnote to the ocean of rumor.

The next day, Mayor Burton stood in front of Ness' desk and said, "This has got to stop."

He said it flatly, with little emotion. All the impact in his words came from the fact that he stood in Ness's office when he said it. Having the mayor stand there was unusual enough to emphasize everything he said.

Ness stood as well, out of deference, and motioned to a chair, "Why don't you have a seat?"

Mayor Burton didn't seem to hear. The door was still closing behind him as he dropped a copy of the *News* on the desk between them. The torso killings were front page news. *Fingerprint is Lone Torso Murder Clew,* though Ness knew they would be extremely lucky if they could line up a match for the victim's print.

"We've had to clear people out of the morgue," Burton fumed. "Over a hundred people today trying to get to see Gerber's autopsy. This is becoming a ghoulish circus act." He paced a few times in front of Ness's desk and repeated, "This has to be stopped."

"We're expending every effort—"

Mayor Burton shook his head. "Not *every* effort. I told you after the last victim how I wanted this handled. You're going to handle it now."

"Do you know what you're asking?"

Mayor Burton nodded. "I am asking for every single policeman, every single detective, I am asking you to raze his hunting ground and to do a house-to-house search of the

Third. You'll either find him, or put such a fear of God into this demon that he'll quit this city forever."

Ness glanced down at the paper, and wondered how the mayor's orders would be reported. He looked up at Mayor Burton and asked, "Are you sure you want this?"

"I was elected because I wanted to end the crime and corruption that's marred this city since Prohibition. This is the ultimate corruption, Ness. I'm thinking how the future is going to judge us over this case. You're young yet, you have a reputation and a future. Think of where you want to be after this, and think of how it would be if you had this—" Mayor Burton waved at the newspaper, "—as an unsolved albatross around your neck."

Ness looked down at the paper and nodded. At least this way the papers could point at something to say that there were things being done.

Judgment had fallen on Sodom.

That was the thought that kept running through Nuri's mind. Wagons of police, firefighters, and detectives drove down into the flats, followed by carloads of reporters. Everyone, it seemed, carried an ax, a sledgehammer or a crowbar. Nuri had no clear idea how many there were, but it felt like an army.

It didn't seem a modern army though, nothing like a scene from the war in Europe; this was more like a force contemporary with the pharaohs, a Judgment writ in wood and steel.

Nuri rode in the back of one of the open trucks, seated on a wooden bench at the head of a line of uniformed officers. There was an awful anticipation in the faces of the police. Some laughed and joked each other, but to Nuri it all seemed hollow.

They were anticipated. Even before the officers stepped out of the lead trucks with their megaphones, dirty men in ragged clothes had stepped out of their rough-built hovels to stare at them with clouded eyes.

Several officers with megaphones called out that everyone was under arrest, and there was to be an orderly file to the waiting wagons. There was little reaction at first. The ragged men stared at the new invaders to their realm as if they didn't quite believe they were there. Then the lead officers waved at the open trucks, and the policemen began to dismount off the rear.

That was when the chaos started. The sight of the ranks of police and firemen, all armed with clubs, pickaxes, sledgehammers, prybars ignited something in the spectating crowd. Some advanced on the waiting wagons, as they had been told. But many looked at the forming line of police, and fear filled their eyes.

Those ran.

The police descended.

The light seemed to fade from the sky as the world around Nuri seemed to erupt into anarchy. He followed the officers; his duty was to somehow note any suspects or leads as they passed through this little shantytown. Thrust into the midst of this riot his duty seemed laughable. The line of officers descended on the small army of transients and hobos, with a viciousness as if it was the fault of these that the torso killer had descended on Cleveland.

The police fell upon them with clubs, the handles of axes and sledgehammers. They pulled them down by the arms, the legs, by their hair. Following the police, the firemen brought the city's wrath down upon the little shacks that these people had made their homes.

Tarpaper shredded, wood snapped, and tin whined in agony as the firemen attacked the flimsy structures.

Then they burned.

Suitcases and trunks were trampled in the melee. The storm raged around and past Nuri, and as it passed him, it left little in its wake. Nuri stood on a trampled plain as the violence passed him by. There was nothing left that could be called a shelter. Broken wood and clothing littered the ground with no discernible pattern. Smoke rose from pyres that used to be people's homes.

Near Nuri's feet lay a small silver frame, broken in half, glass ground to powder by a fireman's boot. Torn and waterlogged with mud was a picture of a little girl, her face obliterated by the footprint.

Nuri looked away from the picture. It made him feel sick.

He looked upward and saw the sun about to set.

9

Thursday, August 18

While darkness fell over the city, a dark-paneled truck followed in the wake of the police. It drove slowly, two men in dark suits hanging off the sides, watching the remains of the shantytowns they passed.

Stefan sat in the cab with the driver, Aristaeus. He stared ahead at the road, a river of black. The truck's lights were out. Occasionally the truck would hit a bump and the weight in the back would shift. When that happened, Stefan winced, but not greatly enough for the driver to notice.

"There," called out either Tito or Dante, riding the sides in back.

Aristaeus slowed the truck to a stop, silent except for the crunch of gravel. He opened the door and stepped out, and he pulled Stefan after him. Stefan moved without resisting.

Tito and Dante had already dismounted. One carried a shovel, the other a pickax. Stefan could sense dimly what the others felt, the presence of one of the blood, somewhere near here. Aristaeus grinned and waved the two over into the debris-covered field that used to house a few dozen homeless men, and maybe one or two of the fugitive undead.

Tito and Dante walked straight to a pile of charred and splintered wood near the center of the flattened shantytown. Tito began moving the ashes aside with his shovel, and Dante stood aside with his pickax raised. Within minutes, Tito had uncovered a mound of loose dirt.

Aristaeus walked up to the scene. Stefan followed because it was expected of him. This wasn't the first time he had witnessed this tonight, and it wouldn't be the last. Not until the back of the truck they rode was filled. They were finishing off some of the last of the Master's enemies in this town. They were uncovering the few who were trying to hop a train unseen from the shanties along the tracks. The Master had choked off most of the other routes out of town.

Aristaeus nodded, and Dante let the pickax fall on the mound, the point of its blade sinking its full length into the soft earth. In response, the earth screamed. It was a sound torturous and brief, more felt than heard. It tore out a chunk of what was left of Stefan's soul.

Around where the pickax had fallen, a trickle of black tarlike blood emerged from the ground.

Tito began clearing away the earth, revealing the creature that had buried itself to protect itself from the sun. The face was revealed first, eyes staring, mouth packed with dirt. He was unremarkable, the face almost anonymous except for the contortion of pain left on it.

Tito cleared off all the dirt from around the body, revealing Dante's pickax embedded deep in the chest. While this was going on, Aristaeus had been staring at his watch. A little after all the dirt was gone, Aristaeus nodded at Dante and said, "Ten minutes, long enough. He won't get up again."

Dante pulled out the pickax, slowly and with difficulty. The body raised a few inches with the blade before it began sliding free from the wound. When the body let it go, finally, with a wet sound, it thudded back into the dead earth.

"Okay," Aristaeus said to Stefan.

Stefan had been here enough times that he didn't need elaboration. He reached down, grabbed the corpse by the shoulders, and began dragging it back toward the truck.

Meanwhile, the trio moved on to another mound of debris.

The process seemed endless. When it seemed that they had finally come upon the last transient village, there was another to be razed. Events seemed more and more detached from reality the deeper into the night it progressed. News of what was happening spread, and occasionally they would come to a collection of shacks that had been abandoned earlier in the evening. Even so, things progressed the same way. The officer with the megaphone would announce that everyone was under arrest, and then the police would descend on the empty shantytown, and the firemen would burn the place down to the ground.

It was one of those near-empty towns where Nuri was ambushed. He was in the lead, with a collection of officers, kicking open doors, checking for anyone hiding from the advance of the police. Not for the first time Nuri was feeling like an officer in the German SS, checking a village for undesirables.

Then, suddenly, the police were set upon by twice as many dirty men. The attack caught all of them off guard. One moment they were walking in the midst of a forest of empty tar-paper hovels, the next they were surrounded by angry hobos armed with bricks and broken planks of wood.

The two groups fell on each other as if they were both in the middle of a war. An officer fell by Nuri's feet, blood streaming from his temple, and Nuri reached for his gun.

Before he reached it, he felt something slam across the back of his head. The impact was blinding, and he stumbled forward. Even the sounds around him seemed blurred as the world turned to a dark mush around him.

By the time he recovered from the stunning blow, he was on his knees in the mud, retching. Nuri waited for the dizziness to pass before he opened his eyes and looked around.

There was no sign of the melee around him. He had the disorienting realization that he didn't know where he was. From his memory, he had only stumbled a few feet from where he'd been struck, but from a look around at the unfamiliar ground, and at how much darker the night was, he must have been wandering for much longer.

He pushed himself upright from the sour pool by his knees and tried not to collapse from the sudden wave of vertigo. After swaying a few moments, he checked himself out.

His hat and his jacket were both gone, but his gun still sat in its holster. The back of his head was a sore bloody mess, but his hair was matted. The blood had had time to clot.

When he took a few steps, he realized that he had lost one of his shoes in the mud. He cursed and took off the other one so he could walk.

As he made his way to the road, he could see signs of the war that Eliot Ness was waging on Cleveland's transient population. Beside him, he could see the remains of razed dwellings where he had passed earlier in the night. Both sides of the battle were gone. The police gone toward the next collection of hovels, the inhabitants fled or in police custody.

It was empty, and almost silent.

Almost.

Nuri walked, listening to noises that seemed to come from around a bend in the road. His stockinged feet slid silently on the bricks in the road as he made his way toward an area darker than the rest of the night. Around the bend, the road ran under one of the dozens of bridges that crossed the Cuyahoga. The bridge was a railroad trestle, and its girders were a dark spider-web against an overcast sky.

Coming from the darkness beyond, the source hidden by the corner of an abandoned warehouse, were the sounds of shoveling earth and shifting debris. Nuri also heard the sound of whispered voices, too low to make out individual words. When he reached the corner of the building he heard a soft, solid thud followed by a brief agonizing scream that abruptly cut off.

The sound seared through Nuri, causing him to close his eyes so tightly that color shot through his field of vision. The sound didn't even last half a second, but Nuri's head throbbed with it.

He drew his gun, already knowing what was around the corner from him. The darkness beyond was more than just the shadow of the bridge. His face and hands were slick with sweat, and his breath came in slow shuddering gasps. He wanted to run, to abandon this place. But he kept thinking of the time he had seen Stefan and had done nothing but hide.

He eased his way around the corner of the building, holding his gun before him. The first thing he saw was a dark silhouette of a panel truck, similar in size to the one he'd been riding. The back was covered, so he couldn't see what the truck carried.

Beyond the dark truck, he could see figures standing in the midst of one of the ruined shantytowns. He could see the edge of a shovel and the end of a pickax. As he watched, one of the figures drew the pickax out of the ground.

Nuri walked slowly to the side of the truck opposite the figures. Every step was an effort against a building well of fear. He knew what he faced. He could almost smell it. And he didn't have anything that could fight them. He had the gun, but he had seen the uselessness of it twice now. A bullet couldn't stop them. . . .

Nuri reached the other side of the cab and looked around the front of the vehicle. He saw another figure dragging what could only be a body from where the figures had congregated. The others walked away from the hole they had made.

They can die, Nuri told himself. He had seen them dead by fire, by sunlight, and by decapitation. He had no fire, and sunlight was hours away, but he dwelled on decapitation. These things still had brains, and they couldn't function without them. . . .

Nuri took a few deep breaths and began a crouched run from the front of the truck, around the debris, circling upon the three shadowy figures. The terrain tore at his feet, but he kept running, closing on them.

He was only a few dozens yards away when his foot slipped on a broken piece of wood. The three of them stopped and turned. Nuri could recognize Aristaeus immediately, even in the darkness.

Aristaeus held out a hand, as if to silence his two companions. The one carrying the pickax looked directly at Nuri with a stare that froze the blood in his veins.

Nuri swallowed his fear and braced his gun with both hands.

Aristaeus waved his hand, wearing an expression near a smile. Nuri was sure he saw him, and recognized him.

In response to Aristaeus' small wave, the other two ran for him. Nuri felt the impulse to flee, to run as fast as he could, get away even if there was no way to outrun them at the speed they were going.

Instead he brought the gun up to point at the face of the one with the pickax. As that one brought the pickax to bear against Nuri, Nuri fired, twice.

When Nuri fired they were only separated by about five yards. The shot was impossible to miss. The pickax fell to the ground as its bearer's head snapped back with two holes erupting in its face. The whole back of the skull seemed to have evaporated. The body dropped to the ground.

Before the body hit the ground, Nuri could see a shovel swinging at him. He dropped and rolled out of its way, barely fast enough. The blade grazed his head, hard enough that he almost blacked out.

Nuri rolled, pointing his revolver upward, toward his attacker. The shovel was coming downward as his gun fired. One shot missed, throwing sparks as it glanced off the blade of the shovel, the other shot found its home in his attacker's forehead.

The shovel still came down, but slowly enough for Nuri to dodge it. The blade buried itself into the ground next to Nuri's right shoulder. The body followed, face-first into the ground next to the shovel, the back of the skull a soft, dark mess.

Nuri pushed himself away from the body, scrambling upward to face the last of them, Aristaeus.

He turned on Aristaeus and saw a gun pointed at him. Aristaeus hadn't moved from where he stood, and he was much too far away for a sure head shot. Nuri saw all this in a moment and dived behind a pile of broken wood.

He dove just in time, because he heard Aristaeus' gun fire, and he could swear he felt the breeze as the bullet passed between his neck and his shoulder.

He landed on a pile of shredded tar paper, nails tearing into his legs and his left arm.

Aristaeus called out to him, "Good job, Lapidos. Those two will be out for a few minutes, at least. Probably never get their minds back, such as they were. But that's just an almost. What do you think your chances are now? I can see out here like it was full daylight, I can smell your blood now, and my reflexes are twice yours." Nuri could hear the crunch of Aristaeus' footsteps as he closed on his hiding place.

"I know exactly where you are," he kept talking. "If you move, I can put three bullets into you before you aim. But I'll make you an offer. Toss out your gun, offer me your blood, and you might have a new life."

Nuri swallowed. His throat felt dry.

"I've wanted both of you since the train, Lapidos. I didn't have to miss just then."

The gun in front of him was shaking. Blood was soaking into his clothes from the wounds tearing into his arms and legs, blood also dripped from his head, blurring his vision. Nuri's breaths were beginning to sear his throat.

He was going to have to dive out there and try to shoot Aristaeus. He didn't have a choice.

He tightened his grip on the revolver, and prepared to spring out from his limited cover. Then he heard something.

Aristaeus was still talking, but beneath the sound of his voice was something else, a rustling sound, as if the ground were shifting. At first Nuri thought it was Aristaeus, but as the sound became louder, Aristaeus stopped talking, as if he'd just noticed the sound.

Whatever the distraction was, Nuri took the opportunity to spring from his cover and level his gun at Aristaeus. But when he saw Aristaeus, he didn't fire.

Aristaeus was only ten feet away from him, but he had turned away from him. Aristaeus was facing something that was rising from the ground, clawing its way from a mound of earth. He wasn't talking to Nuri anymore.

As Nuri watched, Aristaeus fired four shots into the shadow clawing its way out of the earth. The thing showed no sign of being hit. It pulled itself upright in front of Aristaeus, dirt crumbling off of its shoulders. From the mid-chest up to its head, half of it was frozen. Half its face, and the right side of its chest was a twisted, pale representation of a human body, milk-white and frozen in a contortion of agony.

The other half was out of a nightmare, fanged like a demon, one arm as long as Aristaeus' body and ending in a taloned claw. It stared at Aristaeus with a face that was half a human corpse, and half a gargoyle. The human eye was pale and clouded, staring at nothing, the other eye was red, and as deep as hell itself, and stared directly at Aristaeus.

Aristaeus' gun shook and he pulled the trigger again.

The gun clicked home on an empty chamber.

The thing's arm swung up toward Aristaeus and clamped home on his neck. Aristaeus dropped the gun and his body began changing. Nuri could hear the sound of stressed bone, and the sound of flesh tearing like canvas. But whatever was happening to Aristaeus was happening too late to do him any good.

The demonic arm lifted Aristaeus off of the ground, and Nuri could see blood flowing from where the taloned fingers were crushing Aristaeus windpipe. Aristaeus clawed at the arm, kicked at the open air, and made strangled bloody noises. In a few moments he wasn't moving and the body had regained a semblance of humanity.

Nuri didn't move.

The half-thing drew Aristaeus' body toward itself and turned its monstrous face so its half-muzzle could smell the corpse. Its face wrinkled, and it tossed the body aside as if disgusted by it.

Then it turned its attention to Nuri. Nuri raised his gun to level on the animate half of the thing's face, but its one living eye held him in an iron grip impossible to break. Nuri fell into that one blood-red eye as if he was falling into a sea of fire.

Its taloned hand grabbed its opposite shoulder, the one that was human flesh, from which hung a dead human arm. It grumbled something, almost unintelligible through half of a nonhuman mouth.

In the grip of that thing's stare, Nuri could understand the words.

"Useless," it said. "Dead already."

It drew closer, and the smell of rot almost dropped Nuri to his knees. It looked down at Nuri, its body rearranging with the sound of breaking bone and tearing skin. Fangs and talons withdrew. As its arm came away from its shoulder Nuri saw that the dead human part of its body was pockmarked with sores that wept a fluid that smelled of rotting meat.

"Too far gone," it said as it grabbed Nuri's shoulder with the arm that had killed Aristaeus. The arm was human now, and the face that was within inches of Nuri's own was now fully human, half trapped in a putrefying death-agony, the other half twisted in a expression of frustration and despair.

"I cannot drink with half a mouth," it whispered, and closed its one demonic eye. When the stare left him, Nuri was able to move again. He backed quickly away, the thing releasing its grip on him.

It collapsed before him. "Too shallow," it whispered.

Nuri backed away from the thing that now was only a naked human corpse. He had only taken a few steps when he felt something grab his shoulder. He spun around and fired.

Nuri had a brief glimpse of his face as the bullet tore into Stefan's throat. He scrambled backward as Stefan grabbed the injury and fell to his knees. Blood spread from Stefan's mouth and from both sides of the wound. He swayed on his knees, and for a moment Nuri was certain that he had killed him.

Then he saw the edges of the exposed wound pulling together, as if the flesh was so much bleeding clay. He backed away from Stefan, and glanced back toward where the first two lay. The first one, the one who held a pickax, was still face down, but now his head was intact, and his limbs were beginning to vibrate as if he was having a seizure.

The wounded Stefan still knelt in front of him, but the wound was almost gone. He was hissing, and his face was distorting.

Nuri had one bullet left. He wanted to run, but he couldn't abandon Stefan again. Nuri looked into Stefan's face, and saw eyes that seemed a well of pain slicing into his mind. Nuri stepped to the side as Stefan lowered his lengthening hands from the wound in his neck. The only sign of the damage now was the blood. He reached a clawed hand toward Nuri as Nuri edged around him.

Nuri brought the butt of his gun down across the back of Stefan's skull. Stefan's eyes widened as a clawed hand grabbed Nuri's leg. Nuri brought the gun down again.

Stefan's eyes rolled and he fell forward.

Nuri looked at his friend's body and sucked in copper breaths as he looked for signs of life. The body didn't seem to breathe. Nuri was almost certain Stefan was dead, until he looked closely at the gash where his gun had landed.

Even in the dark he could see the edges of the wound knitting together.

Close by he heard moaning coming from the two he had shot in the head. The sound was mindless and chilling. He had to get out of here.

This time he wasn't going to leave Stefan.

He holstered his gun, grabbed Stefan by the shoulders, and began dragging him back toward the dark truck that was still parked by the road. The ground cut into his feet as he made his way backwards toward the road.

The moaning began to sound like an animal growl. He couldn't see any of the bodies any more. They had been lost in the darkness. Nuri's heart raced as the growls deepened, and seemed to move.

They seemed to come from all directions, echoing beneath the bridge, getting louder.

Nuri backed into the door of the truck, and he scrambled to get the door open and drag Stefan's unconscious body inside. Nuri was halfway across the seat, Stefan only half in the truck, when something leaped at the cab. Part of the roof caved inward, and the glass in the front window shattered, spraying shards across Nuri and Stefan.

Nuri was only half in the driver's seat, and he tried to run the clutch and the gas with one foot as he hit the starter. The engine made evil grinding noises as he shifted, but it lurched forward.

Nuri was driving and trying to pull Stefan all the way into the door when something else hit the truck hard enough to make it swerve slightly.

Nuri drove the truck as fast as he could push it, rocketing through the uneven roads of the Flats. As the truck shook across the broken pavement, something landed on top of the hood of the truck. It had jumped off of the top of the cab and it smashed the hood inward. The thing was wolflike, its face a naked slavering muzzle filled with dagger teeth. Across its leathery torso, it wore the bloody remnants of a cheap suit.

Nuri swerved the truck madly, trying to shake this thing off the front. It hung on tenaciously, talons piercing the truck's hood, twisting the metal into handholds for it.

It gibbered madly at him, nonsense syllables combined with an animal growling. It leaned into the driver's side, opening its jaws to tear at him. Nuri jerked the wheel to the left, trying to evade the creature's bite.

The truck jumped the curb and slammed head-on into a low brick wall. Nuri was thrown against the wheel with a force enough to crack his ribs. The thing on the hood tumbled backwards into the remains of the wall.

Nuri tried a few futile times to get the truck moving again, but the engine just whined at him. Something was moving in the back, and Nuri smelled gas. He reached over Stefan and tried to open the passenger door. When it didn't give, Nuri raised his foot and kicked it open. The door sprang open and Stefan fell out into the street.

Nuri scrambled out of the cab.

Even though the creature on the hood was buried under a pile of bricks, it still moved. Nuri heard the grinding sound of bricks rubbing together.

As he grabbed Stefan's collar and began dragging his unconscious form across the street, something began tearing at the canvas cover over the rear of the truck—tearing from the inside. Nuri could see the claws sticking out of the canvas as it shredded the cover.

Nuri allowed one hand for Stefan and pulled out his gun with the other. He hesitated, because the smell of gas was everywhere, even his stocking feet felt newly wet. Back by the truck, the ground glistened. Nuri kept backing away, saving his shot.

But he had little chance. In a moment the thing in the back had torn itself free of the canvas. It was even larger and more feral-looking than the one that had landed on the hood. And it still carried the pickax.

The other one had freed itself from the tumbled masonry, and it stood on the cab, turning toward Nuri.

Nuri fired.

The shot was wild, with him firing one-handed. It sparked off the brick street in front of the truck. As Nuri had feared, the glistening street erupted into a sheet of fire.

Nuri dropped the gun and grabbed Stefan with his other hand. He had dragged Stefan through the puddle of gasoline, and he was soaked with it. Nuri pulled him backward as fast as he could, as flames enveloped the broken truck.

He made it to the other side of the street, to a small ditch filled with stagnant water. He rolled Stefan into it and followed, more concerned with the fire than any demonic pursuit.

It wasn't until he was standing ankle-deep in the drainage ditch that he thought of the two creatures by the truck. He looked back.

In a few seconds the truck had become little more than shadow in a rolling sheet of fire. From the fire came a high breathless wail that Nuri knew didn't come from the flames. On either side of the truck were two humanoid figures, themselves little more than shadows wrapped in fire. They were moving away from the burning vehicle, but even as they stepped out of the radius of fire, the fire accompanied them. Neither made it more than ten feet before collapsing on the street.

On the street in front of Nuri, he could see his own footsteps blaze and gutter out.

10

The burning of Cleveland's shantytowns was only the
prelude. Police descended on the Roaring Third in a
house-to-house search for the murderer. Even as police
kicked in doors and crawled through every room in the
precinct, looking for signs of the killing ground, the papers
were beginning to sound sour notes about Ness.

The press couldn't stop what had become the largest
manhunt in the city's, and perhaps the nation's, history.
The house-to-house search found prostitutes and pimps,
gambling halls and numbers runners, conmen, thieves,
and hustlers . . .

But no killing ground.

The priest's office was crowded by bookshelves and files.
Papers towered over Nuri. The man behind the desk, Father Gerwazek, was older than Nuri expected, his hair
snow-white, his hands liver-spotted. Aside from that, the
man gave a reassuring impression of solidity.

The priest pushed his thick glasses back on his nose and
looked at Nuri, "But you won't tell me this man's name?"

Nuri shook his head. "I've told you all I can."

"But you want me to agree to come with you and retain
your confidence?" Gerwazek shook his head. "You're asking a lot from an old man."

"My friend needs a priest," Nuri felt odd saying that.

Nuri had already seen his own rabbi, for the first time in
years. While he never had the courage to explain fully what
had happened, Rabbi Schimmel had heard enough from
Nuri to realize that they'd been talking about a Catholic
man in some sort of spiritual crisis. "If this man was a

Jew," he'd said, "would you take him a priest? It's his faith, not yours." Nuri had still almost taken his friend to temple while he was still unconscious. In the end he had thought better, and followed Rabbi Schimmel's advice. It wasn't his belief that mattered, it was Stefan's, and the beliefs of those things in the darkness.

Nuri shook his head. "I've done what I can for him, and it isn't enough."

"And you won't tell me where he is?"

"It's better if you don't know."

Gerwazek seemed to debate with himself for a moment and then asked, "What made you decide to come to me?"

"I think my friend used to be part of your parish."

After a while Father Gerwazek sighed and said, "I won't turn away a request for aid, even if the secrecy makes me uncomfortable."

"Thank you," Nuri said, standing and offering his hand. "If it makes you feel better, think of this as a confession."

Nuri drove Gerwazek in a borrowed unmarked car. The priest made few comments as Nuri drove, aside from asking him once if he was Catholic. More than once Nuri wondered if he was doing the right thing. He was at the end of his rope. He couldn't think of anything else to do. Stefan needed help, and the help he needed seemed way beyond anything he could provide.

Eventually he drove through the Euclid entrance to Lakeview Cemetery.

"Here?" Gerwazek asked, voice uncertain.

Nuri nodded. "I needed a special place. I suppose a church would be better." Nuri maneuvered the car through twisting roads until he had passed a few hills into a quiet part of the cemetery. Behind them the sky was a flaming red beyond the imposing mass of the Garfield Monument.

When Nuri parked the car, Gerwazek put a hand on his arm. "Where is your friend?"

Nuri nodded up the hill, toward a large tomb set up on the hillside. "There's a small chapel in there."

"He's in there?" Gerwazek stared at him for a long time, his eyes distorted by his thick glasses. "Mr. Lapidos," he asked, "is your friend alive?"

Nuri let the silence stretch for a long time.

Gerwazek squeezed his arm and said, "Mr. Lapidos?"

"I don't know how to answer that question."

The priest just stared at him, and Nuri could almost feel his own foreboding rubbing off on the priest. Nuri turned and said, "We have to wait until sunset."

"I'm not sure this is a good idea," Gerwazek muttered, more to himself than to Nuri.

"I can take you back," Nuri said. He wasn't going to force anyone's involvement in this. There would be other priests—

"No, no," Gerwazek waved his hand, dismissing the thought. He was now staring up at the tomb on the hill. "Are you going to tell me now what is going on?"

"I think it'd be best to wait until you see him." Nuri turned to watch what of the sunset he could see behind the Garfield Monument. The color slowly drained out of the sky, the monument darkening until it was only a squat silhouette. He turned to the priest and said. "I should warn you though, I've had to restrain him."

Gerwazek didn't respond; he just continued to stare up at the tomb.

Nuri didn't let them leave the car until the last of the daylight had leaked from the sky. The place where they'd parked was in enough shadow that Nuri grabbed a flashlight so they could see their way to the tomb. Nuri went slowly, in deference to Gerwazek's age, but the priest seemed to take the climb better than he did.

"Why here?" Gerwazek asked as they reached the wrought-iron gate barring the door to the tomb.

"Because of the chapel," Nuri said. "A church would have been better, but I couldn't take him to one without too many questions." Nuri opened the gate; it was unlocked. "There are dark things connected to him now, things that are probably searching for him. I'm hoping that blessed ground might protect both of us."

Inside the tomb, there was a soft groaning. The sound was quiet, but it cut through the walls as if the stone was paper.

Gerwazek stared at the closed door.

"He's awake," Nuri told him. He could see the first signs of what might have been fear cross the priest's face.

Nuri pushed the inner door open on the darkened chamber, and took Gerwazek's arm. "Come on. He needs our help."

They took a few steps inside, and Nuri swept the flashlight until it landed on Stefan.

"Christ preserve us." Gerwazek crossed himself.

Stefan lay on the floor, under the flashlight beam. His clothes were filthy, torn, and covered with blood. The faint smell of gasoline still hung around him.

His arms and legs were tied, and he was cowering in a corner as if trying to escape the cross on the wall above him.

He turned to face Nuri and Gerwazek, his face sunken and pale, too close to the face of a corpse. "Let me return to Him," he said in a whispery voice that was little louder than the wind outside. Even so, the words cut into Nuri's ears as if they'd been shouted at him.

Nuri responded, "I brought you a priest."

"More torture," Stefan turned to look at Gerwazek. His eyes were dead, empty, black, though when Nuri looked into them, he thought something moved inside that darkness.

Gerwazek must have seen it, too, because he crossed himself again.

"I know you," Stefan said to Gerwazek.

Gerwazek nodded, staring at him. "What happened to you, Stefan?"

Stefan laughed. The sound was weak, almost silent. "Can't you smell it, Father? I've been damned. I've been dragged so far into the abyss that your presence is painful to me." Stefan turned away to face the wall. "Tell him to let me go, Father. Let me return to the darkness where I belong."

Gerwazek turned toward Nuri, "What have you done to him?"

"I had to restrain him, for his protection as well as mine—"

Gerwazek looked up toward the ceiling whose shroud of darkness wasn't pierced by the flashlight. "But here? He should be in a hospital."

Nuri shook his head. "Anywhere else, and he would die

with the morning light. Anywhere else, and I'm sure his master would come for him."

"His master?" Gerwazek said. He looked down at Stefan, who had withdrawn into a silent immobility. He walked toward Stefan, his shadow falling across Stefan's body. "Mr. Lapidos," he said as he knelt over Stefan's body, "you have to explain all this if you don't want me to report what's going on to the police."

Nuri walked up next to Gerwazek and said, "I am the police."

"Do your superiors know that you're keeping prisoners in a cemetery?"

Nuri shook his head.

Gerwazek reached out a hand and felt Stefan's neck. "He's cold as ice."

"Be careful—"

"He's *dead*."

"No, he isn't."

Gerwazek turned to face Nuri and said, "There's no pulse at all. You've killed him."

"Watch out," Nuri said. Gerwazek turned, but a bit too late. Stefan had already turned his head and sank suddenly-long teeth into the meat of Gerwazek's hand. Gerwazek gasped.

"Damn it," Nuri said. He raised his flashlight and brought it down across Stefan's face. The light went out momentarily. When the flashlight flickered on again, Nuri saw that it had been enough of a distraction for Gerwazek to pull his hand free.

Gerwazek held his bleeding hand and stared at Stefan. Nuri stared as well. As they watched, Stefan's nose, smashed by the flashlight, reordered itself, straightening, shrinking, healing itself. The fangs also withdrew. In a few moments all that was left of the incident was the smeared blood on Stefan's face.

"What is this?" Gerwazek said quietly.

"Do you believe in vampires, Father?"

11

Stefan wondered how long they could keep him like this. They had shut him up in a small room. Stefan suspected it was underneath Father Gerwazek's church, St. John's. He had not fed for days, and most of the time he was too weak to get off of the small cot in the room.

He wondered if it was possible for him to die of the hunger that gnawed inside him.

Most of the time he just lay on the cot, eyes shut, feeling the void eat away inside him, only noting the passage of the day by the crushing fatigue that tried to claim him. Despite that, he never truly slept, not even the non-sleep that normally claimed him in the daylight hours.

Worst of all, every night, Father Gerwazek would come in and talk to him. The man's faith was a burning presence, uncomfortable to be near, and the smell of his blood was an agony—an agony that was never sated since Father Gerwazek would always stay behind the door to the room, too wary to enter after Stefan's first taste of his blood.

This night was like every other night so far. Gerwazek was at the door, the smell of his blood permeated the room, igniting Stefan's painful thirst. He talked to Stefan, saying, "God has not abandoned you."

Stefan's voice didn't rise above a whisper. He stared at the ceiling as he said, "I was taken from God's sight."

"No one has that power, Stefan."

"You know nothing of what happened to me." Stefan's whisper became harsh with anger. Father Gerwazek should smell Satan within him, the same way Stefan could smell the priest's untainted blood. He should see Stefan with the loathing and fear that Stefan felt burn into him every time he saw that ember of faith burning behind Gerwazek's eyes.

"Our savior died for the wickedness of the world. That redemption is open to anyone who will take it. The only one who can deny that to you is yourself."

Stefan sprang at the door and screamed, "You know nothing of what happened to me." On the other side of the door, he could hear Gerwazek stumble backward.

"He ripped away any connection I had with your God when He damned me with His communion. I can't look upon your blessed icons without pain; if I mouth the words of your faith, my tongue cracks and bleeds. My presence here, in a place you deem holy, is a painful fire within me. My soul is destroyed, all your salvation offers me now is the destruction of my body." Stefan slammed the stone wall next to the door with his hand. The impact was hard enough to resonate the wooden door and splatter blood across his arm.

He pulled his hand away from the wall, the skin flayed over the knuckles. As Stefan watched, the skin pulled itself back over the wounds with a tearing sensation that was more painful than the impact.

"You cannot save me," Stefan said as he watched his hand restructure itself.

"You aren't dead—" Gerwazek said from the other side of the door.

"Yes, I am," Stefan said. "Yes, I am."

"You still walk the Earth," the priest said. "That means you are still open to Christ's redemption."

"I was killed, my soul damned, and my body cursed to walk the Earth. Don't you understand? Every legend casts me beyond the pale—"

"I know, I know. But you aren't dead, Stefan. You may have been infected with a dread affliction. But that cannot destroy your soul."

"But—"

"Those legends were propagated by people who believed that any disease was either a curse from Satan or a judgment for your sins."

"You don't know what you're talking about."

"Perhaps you don't know either," Gerwazek said. "What

I know is that, while your affliction is novel to my experience, the idea that God has abandoned you is all too common." Gerwazek paused before he finished. "Every time I've seen that, it has been the person who's abandoned God, not the reverse."

"Do you think I chose this?" Stefan screamed at the door. *"You think I wanted this to happen?"*

He heard Gerwazek move away from the door. "Perhaps I should go now."

"This was taken from me," Stefan said, collapsing against the door. The smell of blood, the hunger, was all forgotten. All Stefan felt was a deeper and even more painful void. "He took this all from me."

Gerwazek had left him, and all Stefan could do was lean against the door and weep.

12

Nuri came to Gerwazek's church regularly now. He never felt completely at ease there, but he needed to see Stefan. In an odd sort of way it was beginning to have an effect on his own faith. He was going to temple more, and beginning to pay a little more attention to the sabbath.

It was as if he was fighting off the visits to the church, trying to purge the Christian iconography that struck him every time he came here.

Each time he came, he told himself that Stefan might have improved. Each time he was disappointed. Nuri was coming close to giving up, even if Father Gerwazek wasn't.

He reached the church just when the day was dying. It was a small, unpretentious building in the middle of the Slovenian neighborhood near St. Clair and East Fifty-Fifth. It was an old wood-frame building that offered no competition to the stone cathedrals that congregated downtown, or even to the much closer St. Vitus, which served most of the surrounding community. This place predated the erection of St. Vitus by several decades, but looked as redundant as Nuri guessed it was.

The Civil War-era building was marked as Catholic only by a small sign and an unobtrusive statue of Mary standing next to the front stairs.

Nuri walked through a wrought-iron gate, and around to the side of the whitewashed building just as the last of the daylight was bleeding away from the sky.

The side entrance led to the basement. No one was there to greet him. He had passed this way often enough that no one paid much attention to him.

Nuri walked back into a rear chamber, inside which was

a small trapdoor that was barred with a padlock. Nuri had the key, and opened it.

As old as this structure was, it was built on the foundation of an even older structure. Gerwazek had explained that his building had once been a stop on the underground railroad during the Civil War. Under the basement was an old hiding place.

It was dark and damp down here. The walls were thick, and made of local stone. The floor was packed earth. The only signs of this century were the two bare light bulbs dangling from the wooden rafters holding up the floor above, and the stacks of wooden folding chairs.

Nuri wove his way through the narrow passages until he reached an old oak door blocking off one of the chambers. He was still a few paces from the door when he heard a whisper cut through the darkness.

"Nuri," it said. The quality of the word made Nuri shiver. Stefan had gained the odd ability to be perfectly understood even when his voice was just on the cusp of audibility.

"Yes," Nuri responded, even though it wasn't a question.

"When will you free me?" Stefan's whisper, and its echoes, seemed to fill the space underground.

Nuri stepped up to the door and slid aside the cover on its small inset window. The room beyond had the same stone walls, and a single incandescent bulb. A cot sat in the corner, the only real furniture in the room. The floor was scattered with dishes from the abortive attempts to feed Stefan—he was long past solid food.

"We're *trying* to free you," Nuri said.

Stefan laughed, a rattling whispery sound. Stefan turned his face toward Nuri. He was so emaciated now that it wasn't until he moved that Nuri could tell him from the rumpled blanket on the cot.

"Kill me, then," he whispered. His eyes stared into Nuri's, open pits that were much too large for his sunken face. They tried to suck Nuri in, but he had enough experience now to avert his gaze. There was something about eye contact that tried to impose Stefan's will on him.

"We're trying to save you—"

"*Save me?*" Stefan said. "I'm past saving. Melchior took that from me. . . ."

Nuri shook his head. "We're trying to save you from Melchior."

Stefan laughed, "You cannot save *yourself* from Melchior. I have His blood in my veins. I'm a part of Him. How can you undo that?"

"Tell me more about it," Nuri said. He'd taken out a notebook and a pencil. "About Melchior's blood."

He could hear Stefan lay back into his cot. "The blood is everything to us. Mind, body, soul, the blood contains it all, controls it all. Those of the blood, we call ourselves that because we're bound it, anchored to it. Because Melchior's blood flows in my veins, I have a piece of his damned soul within my own."

Nuri understood. Stefan was what Iago had once called a thrall. A slave to an older vampire. In some sense, that was what Nuri was hoping to free Stefan from. It had to be possible; otherwise there would be no such thing as a free vampire.

"Your own blood flows in your veins, too."

Stefan sighed. "What is my blood against Melchior's power? His will commands my flesh."

"Then why doesn't it command you here?"

"Perhaps he thinks I'm truly dead now," Stefan said. "Maybe I am, and in hell. I suspect that's what hell is, being trapped with this hunger."

"Maybe Melchior isn't omnipotent," Nuri said. "Somewhere you believe you're on holy ground. Maybe that belief holds him at bay. Maybe he can't control you through these walls." Nuri wasn't certain of that. He wasn't certain of anything. He hoped, and the hope now seemed to have basis in fact since Melchior had not shown up to claim his thrall. He was certain that it was Stefan's belief that was the only thing that could save him.

Stefan emitted a tired laugh that chilled Nuri. "Maybe I'm not important enough for Satan to care."

"Melchior isn't Satan," Nuri said.

"You don't know," Stefan said. "You haven't seen him in his glory, you haven't had him in your mind. He killed me, then he killed my soul. . . ."

The conversation spun again, full circle. Every time it led around again to the same point. The talks were a little longer each day, but they always began and ended the same way.

"He isn't Satan," Nuri said. "He's a monster, but he was a man once, just like you."

"Not like me, not like any of us."

Nuri slammed his fist against the door frame, "Why don't you even *try* to fight him?"

There was a long silence before Stefan said, "You think I haven't tried? When I see what he's done, what he's going to do? But even the *thoughts* sear me, like being in this cell, on this ground. Even though Melchior has forgotten me, his blood remembers."

"Fight his blood, then," Nuri said. "Melchior isn't here. It's just you and me. You have a mind, you have a will, *why can't you use it!*"

"Because . . ." Stefan's voice trailed off.

The silence was long and dark. After a few minutes, Nuri said, "Stefan?"

"Leave me," came Stefan's voice.

Nuri spoke again a few times, trying to entice Stefan—then trying to anger him—into talking. Stefan didn't break his silence. Nuri stood by the door for a long time hoping Stefan would change his mind, but he didn't speak again.

Eventually Nuri sighed and left him.

13

Fight his blood.

The thoughts echoed through Stefan's fevered brain. It was a statement that was pathetically simple, but it seared itself inside his mind like a revelation.

The blood was the life, the soul, the will, the flesh . . .

And the blood was the chain that bound him.

"Am I evil, then? This your Bible says?"

"You feast on the living."

"Didn't your savior say to drink of his blood? Eat of his flesh?"

Memories flew through his mind as he waited for the priest. What he wanted was insane, blasphemous, perhaps even suicidal—but he knew that Gerwazek wouldn't refuse him. Hunger burned in him as he waited, flaring brighter than it ever had. The aching lack inside him was worse than it ever had been. What was left of his pulse throbbed in his temples.

"Our will, our soul, everything within us is bound within the blood. Our blood controls the flesh, moving it to our will."

The wait seemed interminable. It seemed that he drowned in the hunger of his own decision for weeks before Gerwazek visited him. Every moment of that time was spent in a mental battle with the parts of himself that weren't himself. Every shred of his mind, every fragment of his will, spent every conscious moment holding on to the decision, keeping it from sliding under the pain of Melchior's will.

Stefan drew some strength from the desperation he felt

in that pain. It was as if the part of Melchior that lived inside him knew what he planned.

And he took bread, and gave thanks, and brake it, and gave unto them, saying, "This is my body which is given for you: this do in remembrance of me."

Likewise also the cup after supper, saying, "This cup is the new testament in my blood, which is shed for you . . ."

The words seared in his brain worse than the image of any cross, or his presence in the house of God. But somehow he held on to the verse in his mind, despite the pain.

When Gerwazek came, it was Stefan who spoke first.

"Father?" he whispered from his cot. He was almost too weak to move his lips, and his body was drenched in sweat from the mental effort he had been maintaining since Nuri had left him with his newfound determination.

"Yes, Stefan?" Gerwazek said. His voice was hesitant, as if Stefan had taken him off-guard. Perhaps he had heard something portentous in Stefan's voice.

"I want to take communion," Stefan said.

The resulting silence seemed to last an eternity.

Convincing Father Gerwazek took longer than Stefan expected. Apparently their meeting in the graveyard chapel had made a deep impression on the priest. It took all the strength Stefan could muster to convince Gerwazek that he wasn't going to lose control like that again.

Stefan also had to convince himself of that. The smell of Gerwazek on the other side of the door, the presence of that much living blood, ignited a hunger that rendered what Stefan had felt in the graveyard insignificant by comparison.

While every shred of Stefan's will was concentrated on the burning image of Communion, the well of hunger inside him tore at every fiber of his body. Every cell was pulled by the desire to feed, and the pull was only checked by the image in Stefan's mind, an image that pained him worse than the need for blood.

Eventually the talk ceased. The memory of the words fell away from Stefan's mind, which only had room for the image, the hunger, and the pain. Gerwazek left for a time, and for that time the hunger ebbed.

When Gerwazek returned, the hunger returned a hundredfold. When Gerwazek opened the door, the first time it had been opened while Stefan was conscious, the sensation, the *need,* slammed into his brain like a runaway train. The presence of Gerwazek, suddenly within reach, tore Stefan apart inside.

The tattered part of his will, holding onto the sacred image, was briefly torn apart by the screaming hunger from every part of his body. Stefan leaped to his feet, for the moment possessed only by a savage instinct to fill the burning void inside him with the pulsing life he felt moving just beneath Gerwazek's skin.

Stefan grabbed Gerwazek's robed wrist, and their eyes met. Stefan could in a brief moment see everything through the priest's eyes. He saw the fortress of the man's faith, he saw his pity for him, and he saw fear. . . .

Stefan saw the fear, and it gave him enough pause to draw the painful shreds of his will together. Somehow he looked at Gerwazek, at the life flowing through his veins, and feeling the demonic need tearing at every muscle, every nerve, he managed to fall to his knees.

Slowly he unclenched his hand from Gerwazek's wrist and said, "Thank you, Father."

Genuflecting in front of Gerwazek, naked, his bony knees scraping on the stone floor, the bonfire hunger raging inside him, that was the first moment he really believed he might not be completely lost.

That thought, a tiny kernel of faith, gave him the strength to reimagine Christ, reimagine the body and the blood. It gave him enough will to deny the physical hunger.

Gerwazek was visibly shaken as he took the gifts, the wine, the chalice, and the Communion wafer, and began the ritual. Before this moment, the presence of these icons of his lost faith would have been as painful as a brand.

He could look at them now without shrinking away. The pain was there, their presence seared themselves into his consciousness, but now it was as if it was something else inside of himself that was burning, something he could distance himself from.

Gerwazek broke the wafer and raised the chalice, and as he spoke in solemn Latin it was as if the entire room had become a kiln. The pain had progressed a thousand times beyond simple hunger. It was as if his flesh, each individual cell of his body, had burst into a slow fire that burned without consuming. Every muscle tensed and froze, as if it was tearing itself from the bone. Stefan felt as if his skin should blacken, crack and fall away in the presence of the glory. He had lost the ability to move voluntarily, and his body began to vibrate.

The vibration soon came close to a seizure. He swayed in place, kneeling on the floor, his upper body trying to shake itself apart.

Gerwazek held a part of the holy wafer in front of him. To Stefan, through blurred eyes, the wafer seemed to glow with an arc of light white enough to sear the back of his eyes with a purple afterimage.

Gerwazek hesitated.

Somehow Stefan managed to croak the word, "Please."

Gerwazek stepped forward until the only thing that Stefan could see, the only thing he could perceive, was the host. Then it touched him.

The sensation was falling into a molten cauldron of lead, swallowing the metal, having it sear every layer of his flesh from the inside out. Stefan could feel his flesh burn and crack. He could feel jets of flame shooting from deep inside the bone as it carbonized. He felt the consumption of his entire body except for the nerves that transmitted his pain. He felt his soul dragged screaming through every level of purgatory . . .

Then he opened his eyes and saw the light bulb dangling from the ceiling. He rose, every joint an agony to move, but the pain nothing compared to the immolation. He put his hands together in front of him. The skin was intact. Everything he had felt had been inside him, inside his mind.

He said, "Amen," in response to the priest's words he had never heard.

Gerwazek stared at him, and Stefan nodded.

Gerwazek picked up the chalice.

Fight his blood, Nuri had said. With God's help, that was what Stefan was trying to do. What better way to fight the blood of a devil than with the blood of Christ?

It didn't matter now what happened. Stefan had beaten Melchior. He could feel the part of Melchior inside him, screaming. For it, the pain had not yet ended.

Stefan took the wine. Again, it was a scalding heat inside him, but this time it was a light and a life far beyond what he could have taken from Gerwazek. It filled the void inside him, pushing aside the hunger. It kept filling, and spreading, pushing through him, displacing Melchior—

Gerwazek said something that wasn't part of the ceremony and crossed himself.

He repeated, "Christ preserve us."

In front of him, Stefan's hands, clasped in prayer, were bleeding. Stefan stood, slowly, feeling the glory burning within him. He separated his hands and saw the open wounds on them, spilling blood, Melchior's blood, pooling in his palms and spilling over onto the stone floor.

Other wounds had opened, on his feet, on his side, on his brow. . . .

He stood in front of Gerwazek, spilling blood from his own stigmata. He looked at his hands, said, "Amen," and collapsed.

14

Wednesday, October 4

When Nuri arrived at St. John's, it was nearly three in the morning. He burst into the priest's office.

"What happened?" he demanded before he was completely through the door.

Gerwazek nodded slowly. His skin looked waxy and pale, and he sat behind his desk dressed for Mass. Nuri slowed his approach when he saw that the satin robes were spotted with dirt and blood.

"What happened?" Nuri asked, softer this time. All Gerwazek had said on the phone, about fifteen minutes ago, was that he should come quickly.

Gerwazek looked at Nuri with eyes that were heavy and bloodshot. "Maybe a miracle?" Gerwazek looked down at his hands. Nuri saw a wound on his right wrist and shuddered.

"Did Stefan attack you?"

Gerwazek shook his head. "No, he asked—he begged. After what I had seen, could I deny him?"

Nuri walked around the desk, put his hand on Gerwazek's shoulder and knelt so he was at eye level with the priest. "What happened with Stefan? What did you see?"

"He took Communion." The statement lay heavy on the air. Nuri's mind raced through all the possibilities of what might have happened. A vampire was supposed to cringe from things holy—at least things Christian—what would Communion do to Stefan?

"He took the wafer, and I thought he was going to die. I never thought I'd see a demon possessing someone, but that's what it was. A demon throwing him to the ground, tearing at his own flesh. Then he came back, was rational, took the wine—" Gerwazek shook his head as if he couldn't believe it. "I saw him become the image of Christ. I saw him bleed from the wounds of the crucifixion—"

"He took your blood?"

"He collapsed and begged me for it. How could I refuse?"

"Where is he now?"

"I don't know. I slept, I don't know how long before I called you."

Nuri slammed his fist into the desk. "We lost him! After all this, he's going to fall back to Melchior!"

Gerwazek shook his head.

"He bit you and walked out? Where else is he going to go?"

"He won't return to evil. The Lord has touched him."

Nuri stood up. "How do you *know* that?"

Gerwazek held out his wrist in front of Nuri. "Because I am still alive."

Stefan walked the night-drenched streets of Cleveland, searching for a place to call home. In his wake he left five or six people sleeping, people who had looked into his eyes and couldn't refuse his request.

He was dressed in some of Gerwazek's clothes, old black trousers and a black shirt with a priest's collar. He wore nothing on his feet. Gerwazek's clothes hung loose on him, the cuffs of the trousers dragging on the ground.

Stefan looked out at the night and felt an uncanny sense of freedom. Melchior was a distant ghost to him, a dim memory of the purgatory he had crossed to reach this point.

For the first time since his death, since before his death, Stefan Ryzard felt whole.

As the night sky turned ruddy violet, he stopped. He had reached Public Square. On one side towered the Union Terminal Building, once the headquarters of the Van Sweringen empire. Across from the terminal stood a small sandstone church, walls black with age. The sign above the front of the building read, "Old Stone Church."

Before, when he'd felt himself damned for what Melchior

had done to him, being this close to a house of God would have put him in pain. Now, as Stefan looked up at the twin Gothic towers flanking the entrance, he saw it as a refuge.

He walked inside, and hid himself deep in the basement. He stayed there that day, knowing he was safe.

1939

15

"**W**ho the hell is *Frank Dolezal*?" Ness said. "Good Lord, was he ever a suspect?"

A collection of the highest ranking cops in Cleveland were crowded into Ness' office, and Ness stared at all of them in turn. A few looked abashed, a few stared blankly— the ones who hadn't heard about Dolezal yet. Someone said, "The name may have come up in the investigation—"

"Every name in the Roaring Third has come up in the investigation," a cynical voice answered.

Ness stared out at all of them, feeling a near-unbearable frustration. The case was like an albatross, dragging him down with it. When he had finally razed the shantytowns, he had hoped to take away the murderer's prey. Everyone agreed that he preyed on hobos and transients, and Ness had removed the population from Cleveland. The press and the public had blasted him for it, but in the time that had passed, he felt he might be vindicated. There'd been no more murders for nearly a year.

There had been one debatable case where someone found some human bones in a Youngstown dump, but it really looked as if Ness had faced the problem down. The press and the public might have begun to feel that way, too.

Now the damn county sheriff claimed to have gotten what Eliot Ness and the massed force of the biggest manhunt in Cleveland history had failed to get. Sheriff O'Donnell said he had the Torso Murderer, and he was some immigrant named Frank Dolezal.

That was bad enough—

"He went and told the press before he told *us*," Ness said to the assembled cops. He was fuming. "He's running a circus, and he's done everything to keep the city away from Dolezal."

Everything to make sure that Ness had no part of the credit. Worse, it made the effort of last summer look pointless. He had done so much else for this city, why did this keep haunting him?

"I want detectives going after Dolezal's background. Go over what we have, the interviews we've taken. If there's evidence either way, damning him or clearing him, I want us to get it before the county boys. Everyone understand? And I want some detectives up at the county jail. We're going to have a presence there, even if we don't get in to see Dolezal."

Ness clapped his hands and said, "Let's get moving."

Frank Dolezal sat in a chair while the sheriff and his deputies walked around and badgered him with questions. Every time O'Donnell said, "We know it was you, Frank," Dolezal felt a tremor of fear shoot through his body. He was afraid of the words, that his slurred answers weren't quite right, that in the end they wouldn't believe him.

The room was hot, stifling. They sat him in a hard chair, and refused to let him move. Occasionally one of the deputies would strike him, and the pain would make him forget the heat, the lack of sleep, and let him concentrate on the fear.

They had to believe him, or he would lose his chance at a golden eternity. He managed to keep the denials going. That was the worst part. Taking the beatings, the heat, the violent shouts in his face, and still give them denials that he knew he would recant.

He knew they had the knives in his apartment, he knew that they'd tracked down the stories he'd been told to propagate. But he knew that they wouldn't believe him unless he began with denial.

Time was all. He needed to deny everything for six hours at least, before he gave them a confession. And the confession needed to be convincing. The sheriff needed to believe he had the Torso Murderer.

If he didn't, Frank Dolezal would lose his chance at eternity.

So Dolezal sat, drenched in sweat, bruises turning livid on his body, until his Master's blood moved inside him and he felt that it was time.

"Okay," he said in a thick accent, "I did it. Just stop."

That got their attention. They began on him, asking for details, and Dolezal gave them, feeding them bits and pieces of the murders just as his Master had fed them to him. The confessions took hours more.

At the end Dolezal stared blankly ahead of him, the only emotion inside him a desire to fulfill his Master's will.

16

Nuri was given the unenviable job of being present when Sheriff O'Donnell unveiled his big catch. As soon as he got to the county jail and saw all the press, he knew it wasn't going to be good. He was glad he was plainclothes. If he wore a Cleveland uniform, the reporters might ask him some embarrassing questions.

A sense of futility hung in the air, though perhaps he was the only one to sense it. Nuri knew for a fact that Frank Dolezal was at best a fall guy for the murders, at worse he was just an innocent schmo who crossed Sheriff O'Donnell's path at the wrong time.

Nuri couldn't even get to talk to the sheriff on behalf of the department. The sheriff was too busy.

So Nuri was stuck in a room with all the reporters, waiting for the sheriff to throw them all the story he wanted to give.

Eventually Sheriff O'Donnell walked in, a pair of his deputies leading in a man who had to be Frank Dolezal. The room became alive with a chain lightning of flashbulbs. Dolezal stared into the flashes as if he didn't quite see the room of reporters.

Sheriff ODonnell spoke to them all, about how he had finally closed this five-year-old investigation, about how Dolezal had given him a detailed confession.

Nuri stared at Dolezal. The man was wide-eyed, staring ahead, looking like an empty husk. As Nuri stared, he thought he could see something in those staring eyes, a familiar depthlessness, as if he were looking into an abyss, an abyss which stared back.

The reporters began shouting questions. Nuri didn't lis-

ten to them. He kept looking at Dolezal. The man was
sweaty, unshaven, probably beaten by his captors, and he
just kept staring. Nuri moved around the back of the room
until he looked directly into the man's eyes.

He hadn't imagined it. Nuri could see it in the man's
eyes. A blackness that filled everything behind his eyes. A
cloud of darkness more felt than seen. Nuri saw that and
knew that the devil had touched this man.

Of course he confessed, Nuri thought. *He was told to
confess. Ordered to confess. Willed by the darkness flowing
through his veins.*

Seeing that, Nuri was consumed by the same helplessness
he had felt when he had lost Stefan. There was a man here,
still human, who had fallen so far in the darkness that Nuri
couldn't help him even if the sheriff would let him near
him. Everyone wanted the Torso Murderer, and Dolezal
and his owner had provided that.

All Nuri could do was say they were wrong.

Nuri watched as the legal road to Melchoir was shut
down.

17

Thursday, August 24

A deputy sheriff sat at a desk at the entrance to the holding area of the Cuyahoga County Jail. It was during visiting hours, a dull routine of ushering prisoners to the visiting area and back again. One of the prisoners was the Torso Killer, Frank Dolezal.

There was a pause, shortly after lunch, so the deputy's feet were up on his desk, and he was thumbing through the latest copy of *Weird Tales*.

A shadow fell across his magazine, and he looked up.

His eyes met the gaze of Melchior, and his face turned into a slack mask. No words were exchanged, but when Melchoir slid by the desk, the deputy put down the magazine and went off to bring back a prisoner he had forgotten until just that moment. He wouldn't return for nearly half an hour, though he would later insist it wasn't more than three minutes.

Melchoir walked down the aisle of cells, unseen, unnoticed.

He stopped in front of Frank Dolezal's cell. Dolezal stood in the front of the cell, as if he had felt his Master coming. He gripped the bars and said to the shadow walking before him. "It is time, My Lord?"

Melchoir's shadow nodded.

Dolezal's eyes lit with hope, his lips turning with a perverse joy. The beatings had been worth it. He would become one of the chosen now. One of the blood.

A whisper came from Melchoir. "Take those rags." He pointed at a pile of cleaning rags heaped in the corner of Dolezal's cell. "Tie them together.

Dolezal nodded and did as he was told, making a short length with the rags tied end-to-end.

"Fasten it to that hook, here." Melchoir reached to the ceiling of Dolezal's cell, where a rusted hook projected from the concrete. His arm extended, through the bars, more than was natural, until a pale finger touched the metal.

Dolezal did so, watching his Master with wide eyes.

"Loop the other end around your neck," Melchoir said.

The first flickers of doubt crossed Dolezal's face. Melchoir stared at him and repeated, "Do it."

All the force of hell seemed to reside in those two words, and Dolezal found his hands working of their own accord. The doubt was turning to fear as the rags tightened around his neck. His traitor hands had fastened them tight enough that it was painful to croak the word, "Why?"

The rags were slack between Dolezal's neck and the hook above.

Melchior reached a hand through the bars and rested it on Dolezal's forehead. "Because it is necessary," Melchoir said, and pushed down on Dolezal's head.

Dolezal's legs slipped out from under him and the rags went taut. He clawed at his neck, and kicked out with his feet. He tried to scream, but it only came out as a strangled gasp.

"They will want your body," Melchior said. "Head intact, I'm afraid." He looked down at the struggling form. "Crush the neck long enough, it's as good as decapitation."

No one seemed to hear Dolezal's struggles. Eventually, his body hung slack. Still, Melchior held his hand to Dolezal's head, as if dispensing a blessing.

Melchior stood that way with Dolezal, pressure on the broken neck and windpipe, until he was certain Dolezal wouldn't rise again. When he was certain, Melchior strode from the jail unnoticed by all who saw him.

The suicide of Frank Dolezal marked the end of the official investigation into the Torso Murders. Even with questions about the confession and the bizarre nature of the suicide, even though the case remained officially unsolved, the Cleveland Police had little impetus to continue the case. No more bodies were found. In the eyes of all but a few, it was over.

BOOK FOUR

March 1942—October 1944

THE STREETS OF HELL

1942

1

Sunday, March 1

Times were quiet for Eliot Ness. He was easing toward middle age, his career was going forward, and the press and the public thought he was doing a good job. He had the credit for taking one of the country's most dangerous cities and making it one of the safest.

As he sat in his den, reading a newspaper, and drinking a tumbler of Scotch, his thoughts were nowhere near the string of bodies that had begun on the shores of Euclid Beach Park in 1934. His thoughts were on the paper, on Europe. At the moment he thought of all his men that had gone overseas, how they were doing. A lot of his force, firemen, patrol officers, and a few detectives were fighting. He wondered how many of them would be coming home.

His musings were interrupted by a knock at the door.

He looked up from the paper and at a clock on the wall. It was after eleven. Who would be knocking at this time of night?

He wanted to ignore the late visitor, but his wife had gone to bed early and he was afraid that the persistent knocking would wake her. He put the paper aside as the knocking continued and walked to the door.

Angry at the interruption, he was ready to curse his visitor, but when he saw who the man was, the words died on his lips. The tumbler of Scotch he carried slipped out of his fingers.

Standing on his doorstep was Stefan Ryzard.

"What are you doing here?" Ness finally said.

"I want you to listen to me," Stefan said.

He looked into Ness' eyes, and Ness thought he could sense something in his gaze, something dark and inhuman. Ness tried to shrug off the feeling and bent to retrieve the tumbler. "Listen to you? I should arrest you. Your ex-partner witnessed you at the scene of a murder."

Stefan smiled down at him, and the smile made Ness feel cold, alone, and badly exposed. He began worrying about his wife's safety.

"That must have been a long time ago," Stefan said. "Things have changed."

Ness looked at him, empty glass in his hand. Time seemed to have done well by Stefan. He didn't look any older than when Ness had last seen him. If anything he looked younger. There was an eerie confidence in his face that Ness found unnerving.

"Will you let me in?" Stefan asked.

Ness considered closing the door on his one-time detective. Ness suspected that if he did so, he would never see Stefan again.

He wondered what it was that could have taken Stefan out of hiding. He gestured back into the house, into the den, and said, "Come in, Mr. Ryzard."

Stefan entered, and Ness noticed that he carried a large attaché case with him.

Ness followed him and asked, "What do you want?"

Stefan took a seat and pulled a coffee table toward him. He opened the buckles on the case and said, "I want your complete attention for two hours."

It went much longer than two hours.

"You assigned me," Stefan began, "to gather evidence on Eric Dietrich in relation to the murders of Edward Andrassy, Flo Polillo, and a number of other unidentified people." He spilled the case onto the table in front of him. "I have evidence now, and I am here now because the only cop I trust is overseas."

Ness sat on the other side of the table, mounded high with papers and photographs as Stefan began to tell him about the thing called Eric Dietrich, began to tell him about the creatures of the night. The story was unbelievable, and Ness tried to protest, but every time he met Stefan's gaze, he fell into silence.

All the deaths, every one and more, were either at Dietrich's hands or at his orders. This wasn't a case of a madman murdering transients. Each death was an assassination, with purpose, meant to inspire terror in Dietrich's enemies. In some cases the deaths were followers of Dietrich who dared to defect, in others they were the leadership of Dietrich's main opposition. By the time Ness burned the shantytowns, those shantytowns had been the sole refuge, the remnants of the society that Dietrich displaced trying to leave via the only avenue left them.

When Ness called his forces down on the transient population, he had solidified Dietrich's control of the city.

"Now the only one of the blood here that isn't pledged to him, is me."

Ness shook his head. "You started on this supernatural nonsense before you left. I still don't belie—"

Stefan held up his hand, silencing Ness. As Ness watched, transfixed, the skin darkened and thickened. The fingers lengthened with the sound of breaking bone. Nails grew into black talons as the hand became a weapon capable of tearing Ness' throat out.

"You do not know everything," Stefan said. "Melchior believes he is Satan and destined to rule the Earth, and *he* does not know everything. I have been saved from my fate, and my purpose is only to stop him and his plans. Do you understand? I am here because his darkness hasn't reached you, and his destruction by human forces will be far preferable to the means *I* would have to use." He clenched his demon hand into a fist and it slowly returned to normal.

"Preferable for whom?"

"Every human in this city who would be near Melchior when he dies." Stefan said the words with such gravity that Ness feared for anyone who would be near that event.

"He has prepared himself to regain the kingdom he lost a millennium ago." Stefan pulled a sheaf of documents from the pile and handed it to Ness. "Eric Dietrich is a Hungarian expatriate industrialist. He has become an influential voice in the legislature, in the administration in Washington. He's invisible, but he's taken in thrall major forces in our government. All of this was in preparation."

"Preparation for what?"

"That folder contains an agreement between Dietrich

and our government. In return for his resources, and contacts in Europe, the Allies have agreed to install him as the provisional leader of the occupied German Empire."

Ness stared at Stefan, and then looked down at the folder.

"Melchoir knows who will win this war. He was planning this long before the first shots were fired. Before this century began."

The folder was official-looking, and carried markings from half a dozen agencies of the US Government, including the Army. It was marked top secret.

"Where did you get this?"

"I'm invisible," Stefan said.

It went on, and on, and on. How Melchior took over the rail empire of the Van Sweringens, using it as a network to move his influence across the continent. How the killing ground rode on the rails themselves. How every organized force, human or not, was stalled, subverted, or destroyed if it served Melchior's purpose.

Ness watched as Stefan sifted through the mountain of evidence. Deep into the night he asked, "How did you gather all this?"

"I am alone. No one is left to betray me. He might sense others of the blood, or his own thralls, but my nature has become alien to his. I walk on ground he cannot perceive." Stefan stared at Ness. "Do you believe in God?"

Ness nodded. "Of course."

Stefan frowned slightly, as if the answer came too quickly, too facile. "You should. That is all that can protect you from him."

Stefan watched Ness and hoped. Stefan had worked alone, gathering the evidence of what Melchior had done, what he *was* doing. He hoped he could cause something to happen, stop Melchior short of what would be the ultimate solution. Ness had the forces of the city under his command, and through connections in the Treasury Department he could call on many more.

If Melchior's plans were balked, if he were discredited, Stefan hoped it wouldn't end the way he feared it would. If he could take away the human levers that Melchior used to amplify his power . . .

Ness looked at the pile of documents, listened to Stefan's story, and shook his head, "I don't know what you want me to do, arrest him?"

"Perhaps as a beginning. Even though he is old enough and powerful enough to walk abroad in sunlight, he still relies on darkness and fear. Illuminate him, just a little, and these tangled plans begin to crumble."

Ness gathered up the pages and photographs and told Stefan, "I'll think about what you've said. Look into it. If anything's here, we'll see this guy behind bars."

I hope so, Stefan thought.

2

Eliot Ness spent most of his spare time in the first half of the week trying to independently confirm the evidence Stefan had given him. He couldn't double-check more than a fraction of what he had been given, but what he had checked seem to pan out. The man named Eric Dietrich was many of the things Stefan said he was.

Ness was still far from believing in the supernatural.

But confirmation of any part of Stefan's story was unnerving. Deitrich, or Melchior, seemed the center of his own twisted form of worship. Stefan had given him dark pictures of ceremonies that twisted Ness' stomach. Even if there was nothing supernatural involved, there were people who followed Melchior as if he were the God of his own religion. After two days going over Stefan's papers, it was easy to believe that sacrifice was part of it.

By Wednesday, Ness believed that he might be the one to bring in the Torso Murderer. He might be able to erase the one dark spot of his term as Public Safety Director.

He was in a good mood as he accompanied his wife to one of the parties he frequented. As he danced with her, he felt as if he were just about to reach the high point of his life.

Driving home, his wife asleep beside him, slightly high from the party, Ness imagined the headlines when he would capture Dietrich. It would be a news story of epic proportions, not just here, but all over the country, maybe even overseas.

The night was dark, the roads slick and icy. The headlamps of his car picked out a tiny circle of reality ahead of him on the road, the rest of the world vanished into blackness. Ness suddenly felt a shiver of apprehension and he reached first to touch his sleeping wife, then the satchel that sat in the back seat—

Stefan's evidence followed him everywhere, even to the party. It was too important to let out of his sight.

The road was dead in front of him, the only sound the wind and the engine—

Then, as he rounded a curve, a car appeared in front of him. It appeared suddenly, as if it had been pushed out into the road ahead of him. He slammed into the side of it, his head striking the steering wheel, then snapping back. His car rolled to a stop ahead of the car.

My God, where did he come from? What happened? Ness' thoughts were a haze. He looked in the mirror and saw the other vehicle unmoving by the side of the road, windshield shattered, driver slumped behind the wheel.

Good lord, I've killed someone.

A shadow passed in front of the mirror. Ness looked up to see a figure standing in the darkness between the two cars. Ness wasn't a fearful man. People had often said that he had less fear than was smart. All the threats that followed him throughout his career had left him unmoved—

The figure standing in the moonless night, backlit by the damaged car's headlights, *that* frightened Eliot Ness.

"You broke one of your own rules," Ness heard on the air. The voice was quiet, but as hard and icy as the pavement. "One of your commandments for safe driving. You have alcohol on your breath."

The words slammed into Ness like blows. They left him dizzy, speechless. There was barely time for him to wonder who this figure was, angel, devil, Melchior, or some phantom called up by the blow his head had just taken. All he could think was that his own mistakes had probably killed a man.

The figure stepped up until it was next to Ness' car. Ness couldn't take his eyes away, even though it never became more than a shadow.

It pointed an accusing finger and said, "Your wife needs to be tended to."

Ness looked into the passenger seat, and felt his heart nearly give way. He saw his wife's face as a nearly featureless mask of blood.

He had no time left for thought. He accelerated away from the scene. He had to get her to a hospital. He had driven like a madman for what seemed like hours, but must have only been a few minutes, when he heard her say, "Honey, we need to go home."

Ness turned to look at her and felt a sick wave of disorientation when he realized that her only wound was a scrape and a bump on her forehead. There was no sign of the massive hemorrhage he had seen earlier.

He swallowed and drove home, while through his head he kept telling himself that he had to return to the accident. But he didn't remember exactly where it was any more, and every time he looked across at his wife he felt that he couldn't trust his own memory.

When he got home, he realized that the satchel with Stefan's papers was gone.

When he made sure his wife was all right and in bed, he started calling hospitals to find the unknown man he had collided with. He eventually found him, alive and all right. He hung up without leaving his name.

He knew that wasn't going to be the end of it. He couldn't live with himself if he allowed himself to become a party to a criminal hit-and-run, even if it wasn't his fault. He picked up the phone and called the Central Station.

Afterward, shaking, he walked to the bar in the den and poured himself a drink. He was picturing different headlines now. Eliot Ness stared into the amber liquid and realized that his career as Public Safety Director had just ended.

3

Watching the end of Eliot Ness' career was like watching newsreel footage of a bomber going in extreme slow motion. Stefan read the papers, saw every hit as it landed, read salvos that lasted days.

Ness had been a public hero, but the act of fleeing the scene of a drunken accident was the one thing that would have made the public turn on him. If there had been an accusation of bribery, or corruption, the public wouldn't have believed it. Somehow it was easier to believe in personal hypocrisy, and it was somehow more damning.

Stefan suspected that it had been more than an accident.

He knew it was more than an accident when every move Ness made toward Melchior petered out and eventually stopped. He knew it when Ness resigned.

Stefan sat on a bench overlooking the night-blackened lake and reread the story over and over. There was no choice left. He had spent his time to gather the evidence to support Ness' actions, and with Ness gone there was no one left for Stefan to turn to. The only other ally he could trust was Nuri, and he was overseas.

And Stefan saw that trust was no longer an issue. He could evade Melchior because he was alone. Every time there was anyone else involved, Melchior began to see what he was doing. He had been more than aware of the police and the local gangs, he had manipulated them. Even with a conspiracy as small as him, Nuri and Iago, Melchior had seen through it. Now, the instant he tried to bring some human agency into the picture, the most trustworthy man Stefan knew of, he was removed from any position of authority.

Ness had asked someone the wrong question.

He tossed the paper on the ground, and watched it blow away. He had no choice. The only chance against Melchior was an individual with no one to share his secrets.

It would require more time for preparations, and Melchior's fall would come at a cost that Stefan didn't want to contemplate. He sat and began to pray for forgiveness.

1944

4

Sunday, October 15

Nuri Lapidos walked Euclid Avenue as the night turned to dusk. He was still getting used to being home. More than that, he was still getting used to the absence of half his right foot. He used a cane, but the doctors said that he'd eventually regain his equilibrium. He'd been lucky. The sergeant who'd actually stepped on the land mine behind him lost a more than his foot—some of the shrapnel they'd taken out of Nuri's legs had been splinters from the sergeant's pelvis.

The sergeant had died within minutes, while Nuri spent three months in a hospital fighting off a dozen infections. He had managed to return home a lieutenant, and something of a war hero. He still wore his uniform, as if putting on civilian clothes would deny what happened.

Also, a uniform and a cane gave him more respect than a badge ever did. It occasionally made asking questions easier. That's what he'd been doing ever since he had hobbled off the train, asking questions.

He'd been wondering, since before he was wounded, since he began getting letters from people he knew on the force.

There were rumors about Stefan Ryzard. Nothing concrete, but people said they had seen him. The reports were enticing: stories of Stefan asking questions, lurking around neighborhoods at night. The oddest ones were about people seeing him at nighttime services. He had apparently been at more than one midnight Mass.

When Nuri returned, he felt an impulse to seek him out, to find him once and for all.

What Nuri had found out for himself was more than the rumors. He had followed Stefan's trail all over the city. He had been visiting junkyards and hardware stores, apparently bribing people out of some items collected for aluminum and copper drives. He had paid cash for a ten-year-old Lincoln V-12. Most disturbing was his purchase of a large quantity of dynamite.

From there, Nuri struck a dead end. He found no one who could tell him where Stefan was. He appeared, bought what he wanted, and disappeared again. It took a while before Nuri had an idea of where Stefan might be hiding.

Nuri turned off of Euclid and began walking north on East Fifty-Fifth. He was heading toward the Slovenian community on St. Clair. Toward the unpretentious structure of St. John's. Father Gerwazek had retired, and the Church had decided to close down the building rather than appoint a new pastor to the superfluous parish. Everyone in the community went to St. Vitus now.

But the building was still there.

Nuri stopped in front of it and suppressed a shudder. It had only been shut up for a year or two, but it looked as if it had been abandoned much longer. The paint had peeled away, someone had removed the statue of Mary, and the sign saying "St. John's" had disappeared, leaving a dark spot of unpainted wood on the side of the building.

But a cross still stood, at the peak above the front doors.

A gate stood in front of the church, locked with a rusty chain.

Not knowing quite what to expect, Nuri circled the structure. It was crowded on all sides by turn-of-the-century working-class houses. It hugged its small grounds to itself with a wrought-iron fence that two winters without maintenance had canted at an inward angle, as if it were retreating from the surrounding neighborhood.

Nuri followed a narrow alley, paralleling the fence, all the way to the rear of the church. Another gate stood in the fence, but on this one the chain was shiny, the lock new.

Nuri prodded the weeds around the gate and uncovered the remains of an older chain, the metal still shiny where the links had been cut. Past the gate, Nuri could still see signs of a car passing through—a rut in the weed-shot lawn where the wheel had left the drive.

Nuri looked up at the church, through the bars. There was a large shed that took up almost all of the church's small back lot. The doors were shut and locked, but Nuri suspected that there was just enough room there to hide a car the size of a Lincoln.

Nuri walked up to the fence, shoved his cane through the bars, grabbed the top, and heaved himself over. He barely avoided impaling himself on one of the ornamental spikes on top of the fence, and landed shoulder first into the tall grass behind the church.

He grabbed his cane and used it to push himself upright.

Nuri stood still for a few long moments, waiting for someone to notice him. The church stayed dark and silent, the only sounds distant ones from the neighborhood around him; a baby crying; a dog barking; two children shouting at each other in the distance; a radio . . .

Nothing came from in front of him, no sound of alarm, as if the building was a tomb.

What do you expect? It's supposed to be abandoned.

Nuri walked up to the shed. The entrance was two swinging wooden doors, securely padlocked. The lock and the clasp that held it were both new. Nuri tried to see through the crack between the doors, but the interior was as dark as ink. He couldn't see anything but flat blackness.

He moved around to the side, where a dirty window looked in on the shed. Nothing was visible there either. Nuri stood and stared at the window. Something was wrong with it. The window was covered in grime and cobwebs, but there still should be moonlight leaking through. He reached up a hand and wiped away some of the grime.

The blackness beyond was too flat. The other side of the glass had been painted so no one could see in.

Nuri tried to open the window, but it refused to move, locked, painted, or nailed shut. After shoving the frame a few times he smashed in one of the panes with the head of his cane. The sound seemed deafeningly loud in the quiet space around the church, and Nuri paused and waited for something to react.

Nothing did.

The glass had shattered, but the cane stopped moving an

inch through the window. The cane leaned against something inside as shards of black-painted glass fell by Nuri's feet. Inside was still blackness.

Nuri pulled the cane back and felt through the broken window. The cane had caught on a drape of heavy velvet, dark as pitch. Nuri tried to push it aside, but there was too much of it. It felt as if it covered the entire inside wall of the shed.

Feeling around, Nuri found the latch to the window. After a few tugs, it loosened.

The window frame let out squeals of dry, warped wood as Nuri forced it open. Again, when he was done, he waited, listening if anyone heard him.

Again nothing but the nighttime sounds of the surrounding neighborhood.

Nuri pulled himself through the window, sliding behind the velvet drapery. For a few claustrophobic seconds he tried to find the bottom of the drape. He finally got his hand underneath it and managed to duck through to the other side.

Unexpectedly, the inside of the shed was lit, and brightly. All the walls were covered with black drapery, it was even nailed to the ceiling. But from that ceiling hung a very bright bulb, and a reflecting skirt drove all the light on to the car below it.

Nuri stood there blinking for several moments while he tried to make sense of what he saw.

A Lincoln V-12 was here, in the last stages of some major modifications. Both hoods were open and the doors had been taken off the hinges. The glass on the windshield, the rear window, and on the doors he could see leaning against the wall, were all painted black. Every seat but the driver's had been torn out, and in their place stood stacks of wooden boxes piled to waist height, surrounding a metal barrel that reeked of gasoline. In the trunk was the same thing, a drum—this one sidewise—surrounded by wooden boxes. Thick wire coiled from one box to the next, throughout the whole car.

Nuri walked up to the side of the car and gently lifted the lid of one of the boxes. He wasn't surprised by what he saw. In the box, connected by wires to each other, were at least a dozen sticks of dynamite.

The Lincoln was a rolling munitions dump. He felt the same sick feeling in the pit of his stomach that he'd felt when he heard his sergeant step on a land mine.

The room was no longer silent. Something moved behind him. Nuri turned, raising his cane to defend himself. He was too late. Something slammed into his head and he fell into the blackness of the draperies.

Nuri came awake in a familiar room. A single light burned above him, dangling from a wire in the ceiling. He lay on a dirty cot, still in his uniform. At the moment he wished he'd been wearing his service pistol.

He sat up and looked at the stone walls surrounding him and called out, "Stefan!"

From the other side of the door Nuri heard Stefan's voice say calmly, "There's no need to shout."

Nuri sprang up and stumbled on his bad foot. He limped up to the door and tried to force it open, even though he knew it was hopeless. The door had held Stefan, and Stefan had been stronger than him even before he was claimed by the supernatural.

"What are you doing?" Nuri yelled at him. "Let me out of here!"

"I can't, Nuri." Stefan's voice sounded heavy beyond the thick door. Nuri wished he could see him. "I wish it was possible—"

"Just open the door."

"You saw what I was doing. I could stare into your eyes and tell you to forget, but that wouldn't be enough. You would do something—inadvertently I'm sure—that would alert him. I can't let you, not when it's almost over."

Nuri looked at the door and shrank back, thinking of the modified Lincoln. "You're going after him? Good Lord, you can trust me. I'm not going to warn the bastard after all this—"

"It's not about trust," Stefan said. "I've spent years making sure that I was the one person who knows what is about to happen. You found me here. I don't know what you asked, or who, but it might be already too much. Melchior has ears everywhere. I'm also not sure you wouldn't try and stop me."

"Why would I do that?"

"If you knew what it was going to cost."

There was a long silence, and Nuri thought Stefan had left him. He pounded on the door. "Are you still out there?"

"Yes. It's probably a good thing that there'll be someone left to remember what happened and why."

The way Stefan said it made Nuri freeze. He began to realize that there had to be someone driving the Lincoln when it went up.

"Sit down," Stefan said. "I'm afraid that you'll be here a while. But I might as well tell you, so someone knows."

Nuri tried the door a few more times, then gave up in frustration. He backed away and sat down. He stared at the wooden door, and shivered as the cold began to sink in. He wrapped a blanket around his shoulders as Stefan spoke.

During the whole monologue, something in the tone of Stefan's voice kept Nuri from interrupting.

"You saved me, Nuri. If not for your intervention, I would still be one of his thralls, probably used up and truly dead by now. He could see in me, and through me, but you found his blind spot. My presence here, on blessed ground, blinded him—or gave me the power to blind him. Father Gerwazek gave me the faith to push him from me. I died to him, and I gained my soul back.

"But I knew, even as I walked from this place, my redemption wasn't free. I was saved for a reason. What afflicts me might not be evil in itself, the thirst given me doesn't have to kill—but Melchior is an abomination. He feeds on his own kind. In the end, he wants all the world's flesh bound to his own.

"The war we're fighting in Europe is a result of his desire to rule an empire of men, an empire ruled by those of the blood. If he lives when this war is over, he will gain that empire. He has become part of the industrial sinew of this war. He builds munitions, transports them, feeds our effort in Europe and Asia. He is so tied into the powers of the allies that he will rule what is left of the axis when the war is over. That cannot happen. Compared to Melchior; Hitler, Mussolini, Tito, Franco, they are all angry children.

"I've seen the carnage that supports him and his followers. I've been a part of it. The bodies he left for us, the ones he wanted to be found, those weren't a hundredth part of the blood left in his wake. And what he wallows in now is not a thousandth part of what would happen if he is granted what he seeks.

"My redemption won't be complete until that is prevented. I want you to realize what I am stopping. The cost may be appalling, but what would happen without it is unspeakable. I only pray to God that the sacrifice will succeed."

Nuri grew colder and colder as Stefan spoke. He had been in Europe, and had seen the Nazis' handiwork for himself. He knew what the SS was capable of, and he knew stories of things much darker. Imagining something that might be worse gave him a sick feeling in his gut.

It was a while before Nuri realized that Stefan had stopped talking.

"You can't do this by yourself," Nuri said.

"There's no other way I can do this," Stefan said. "I've left you food. You won't see me again."

Nuri sprang up and pounded on the door. *"You can't just leave me here!"*

"Father Gerwazek will be here to let you out on Friday." Stefan's tone became frighteningly cold. "When he does, leave here as fast as you can."

"What are you going to do?" Nuri said, "What happens on Friday?"

"Melchior dies," Stefan said flatly. "Remember, leave here quickly. Good-bye, Nuri."

"Stefan?" Nuri called.

There wasn't an answer.

"Stefan!" Nuri yelled out, to no response. *"What happens on Friday?"* Nuri called repeatedly, into the night.

That was the last time he ever heard Stefan Ryzard's voice.

5

2:10 PM

After four days Nuri was stir-crazy. He had broken his cane attempting to open the door, his throat was raw after hours of screaming for help, and his head ached from the cold and damp. But the room had held Stefan, and it held Nuri. On the fourth day he looked at the last dregs of the food and water Stefan had left for him and wondered if he would ever get out of this small stone room.

But, just as Stefan had promised, on Friday afternoon, Nuri heard Father Gerwazek's voice calling out, "Hello?"

"In here," Nuri yelled, and then erupted in a fit of coughing. The shout tore at his abraded throat.

"I'm coming," Gerwazek said. In a few moments the door pushed open.

Gerwazek entered, looking older and more worn than Nuri remembered. The priest stared at him for a moment before saying, "Detective Lapidos?" There was the sound of surprise in Gerwazek's voice.

Nuri grabbed his shoulder, "Where is he? What's he doing?"

"What?" Gerwazek said.

"He *sent* you here. You have to know what's going on."

Gerwazek looked at him blankly. "All I know is I got a phone call saying that someone was trapped in the basement of old St. John's, and I needed to come here before two. I didn't know it was you."

Nuri shook his head, and pushed past Gerwazek. He hobbled toward the exit. "He's planned something for him. It's about to happen."

Gerwazek followed. "Who? Who's been using this building? Who locked you in there?"

"Stefan, Father," Nuri said as he pulled himself up through the trapdoor. "I've got to find out what's happening."

Nuri stumbled out into a brisk, cloudless, sunlit afternoon. He stood in front of the church, staring at the sky.

Gerwazek came out after him. "What's happening?" he asked.

"I wish I knew," Nuri said. "He's planning something for today. The way he said it, saying I had to leave here quickly when you showed up, it has to be happening now—but it can't be."

"I don't understand."

"You know what he is. He can't be running around in daylight. I've seen what sun does to them." *He'd have to be as powerful as Melchior to walk in the daylight. . . .*

Nuri looked up at the afternoon sun and whispered, "Or be shaded from it."

"What?"

Nuri ran unsteadily around the church to the shed in the back. It took a few moments for Gerwazek to follow him. When he caught up, Nuri was standing in front of the open shed, looking at where the Lincoln used to be. He remembered all the windows painted black.

"It *is* today," he said, staring into the empty shed. "He blacked out the windows so he could go out in daylight."

"Stefan?" Gerwazek said.

"Yes, Stefan. Father, I need to get to a phone. Stefan's riding a bomb somewhere, and I want to find out where."

2:20 PM

Stefan Ryzard checked his watch and then started the engine of the Lincoln. The powerful V-12 roared into life, vibrating the chassis around him. It was time.

He had parked way back from the site of Eric Dietrich's visit. He hadn't wanted anyone in any security capacity, either Dietrich's, or the plant's, to take notice of the car. The black windows were enough to draw attention.

Even with the windows blacked out, even with only a

sliver of window open for him to see the road, Stefan sensed the pressure of the mid-afternoon sun. The light outside was a numbing presence that he could feel even inside his pitch-black car. Wherever the light from his sliver portal touched the skin, it would go numb and dead. Stefan knew that if such light hit him directly, he would become a pile of dead meat. His recuperative powers would save him from a gunshot, or a broken bone, but they were taxed to the limit by just a thin beam of sun.

It was a measure of just how old and powerful Melchior was that he could walk abroad in the sun, apparently unharmed.

The sun also brought a crushing fatigue that Stefan had spent years learning how to fight. The natural order of things was for his body to shut down while the sun was in the sky. Every motion, every thought, required an inhuman effort to maintain.

Fortunately, while the planning and the secrecy was delicate, the execution was not. All Stefan had to do now was aim the car down two miles of road, and accelerate. When the Lincoln came into Melchior's view, Stefan expected that he would sense one of the blood inside, even though Stefan had purged himself of Melchior's blood long ago. It was the nature of the blood that its people sensed one another. Stefan just hoped that by the time Melchior knew what was racing toward him, it would be too late.

Stefan pulled out into the road, and began flooring the accelerator. He dodged slower-moving traffic as the speedometer crept toward ninety.

On the gearshift, Stefan found a button strapped there with cloth electrical tape. He pressed it down and held it.

There was no turning back now.

2:22 PM

"Look, I know I'm not on the force anymore, I'm asking a favor as a friend." Nuri stared at the phone in front of him. He wanted to beg, to plead—mostly he wanted to tell the officer on the other end what kind of stakes they were dealing with.

"Look," said the man on the other end of the line, "As a friend I'm telling you, we're not supposed to be giving out that kind of information. There's a war on, you know."

Nuri shook his head in exasperation and looked out of the phone booth. Gerwazek was still there, watching him with a bit of concern, but calmly enough that Nuri realized that none of the unease that flooded him had really touched the priest.

The closest phone they'd found was in a little drugstore on the same block as the old St. John's. The white-jacketed pharmacist was busy talking to some old Slovenian lady.

Nuri took a few breaths to calm himself and said, "Are you suggesting I'm a Nazi spy?"

"I'm saying that—"

"I had my foot blown off for schmucks like you!"

The pharmacist and the old lady both turned to look in his direction.

"What do you want from me?" asked the man at the other end of the line.

"I want to know where Eric Dietrich is, right now. He's a VIP, he gets police protection when he's in public, you have his itinerary somewhere."

"Is that all?"

"Yes, and *hurry.*"

"It'll take a minute." Nuri heard the officer set down the phone.

Nuri felt time slide by, oily and slow. The Slovenian lady got what she'd wanted, walked over to Father Gerwazek and started talking in hushed tones, occasionally looking in Nuri's direction. Nuri suddenly realized how he must look. He had slept in his uniform for four days without a shower or a shave. Dirt was smeared all over him, and he must have smelled like the mildewed basement where he'd been kept.

Every minute was marked by an axlike thunk from a large clock above the pharmacist's counter. Nuri stared at the clock, wondering how much time he had before whatever happened, happened. It might be happening now, might have already happened. . . .

The officer came back on the line. "Okay, I've got what you wanted."

Nuri listened with slowly growing horror as the officer told him where the Hungarian industrialist Eric Dietrich was at that moment.

Nuri stumbled out of the phone booth without hanging

up the phone. The old lady stumbled backward like a frightened bird as Nuri grabbed Gerwazek's shoulders.

"What is it?" Gerwazek asked. Some of the fear from Nuri seemed to finally erupt in the priest's face. It was as if everyone could see it, smell it on Nuri. Even the pharmacist stepped out from behind his counter, as if he suddenly felt the sense of menace that had a stranglehold on Nuri.

"He's at the East Ohio Gas Company," Nuri whispered.

"What?" Gerwazek asked.

"Some industrial tour, him, some Congressmen—" Nuri shook his head. "Don't you get it? The natural gas tanks."

Gerwazek stared at him.

Nuri looked at him and said, "Millions of cubic feet of liquefied natural gas, and Stefan's riding a bomb in there!"

The minute hand thunked home. It was 2:28.

2:29 PM

A man in a hard hat led Eric Dietrich and a small horde of followers across the grounds of the new East Ohio Gas liquefication-regasification facility. The tanks towered around them, reaching toward the cloudless sky.

"The first part of the facility," their guide was saying, "was completed in January of 1941. Tanks number one through three." He motioned to a column of spherical structures nested in girders and scaffolding towering nearly sixty feet into the sky.

He motioned around to a different tank, this one cylindrical and somewhat shorter than the others. "Tank number four," he continued, "was built later on, to help deal with the wartime shortages. Despite the fact that it holds a hundred million cubic feet, double any of the others, the design actually uses less material, saving about a hundred tons of steel for the war effort." He looked at Dietrich as he said it.

Dietrich was here in his capacity as a wartime industrialist. In that capacity he had visited innumerable factories and power plants. This was just the latest in a long line. His party consisted of bodyguards and two congressmen who were bound to him by more than party affiliation.

"I am interested in the transportation of natural gas," Dietrich asked. "The feasibility of rail transports is my current concern."

Their tour guide nodded and started to say something when he was interrupted.

The party stood outside and towards the front of one of the buildings of the Number Two Gas Works. From there they could see the three spherical tanks and the cylindrical tank number four. Also, through the fence around the gas works, they could see the street that went by the grounds.

One of Dietrich's bodyguards, and one of the cops with them, both shouted that something was coming.

On the road, shooting toward the Number Two Works, was a long black car. It was topping a hundred miles an hour as it barreled down the street, weaving in and out of traffic. Sunlight gleamed off of its ebony windshield.

Dietrich stared at the vehicle, as if he saw more than a black shell hurtling down the street. Across his face ran an expression of first puzzlement, then recognition.

The car swerved so it was no longer pointed down the street, but angled toward the gas works, toward the group gathered around Dietrich.

Calmly and without passion Dietrich said, "Stop that car."

The cops were still assessing the situation when the triad of Dietrich's bodyguards responded to his command. All three drew their weapons, braced, and began firing. Sparks boomed across the long hood of the sedan. The ebony windshield sprouted spidery cracks. One of the rear tires exploded, throwing its hubcap across the sidewalk and jerking the car off its course as it burst through the fence surrounding the works.

"Stop shooting!" the tour guide shouted, his voice on the edge of panic.

The bodyguards emptied their weapons into the vehicle as it swerved past them. It slid between the massive storage tanks and the main building of the works—its body peppered with holes, the engine spouting steam, three tires flattened.

It was still going near sixty miles an hour as it plowed through the supports of tank number four, grazing the massive tank. The impact slowed it enough that it rolled to a stop about thirty feet beyond the tank.

The incident had lasted less than a minute.

"My God," said one of the cops.

Their tour guide let out a long exhale. "Thank God. I have to go to operations, and get number four drained. God knows what damage that did." He turned to Dietrich. "If there're any bullet holes in our equipment, you have to answer for it."

Dietrich paid him no attention. He motioned his body-guards and told the others, police, congressmen, industrial-ists, "Stay here, I have an issue with the driver of that car."

The tone was so cold that no one, not even the police, objected. No one would look him in the eyes. Dietrich strode the distance to the car. His stride appeared unhur-ried, but it carried him faster than any man should have been able to walk. Every move carried him with a repressed fury that anyone watching could sense.

The bodyguards followed, reloading.

2:31 PM

Gerwazek's response was down-to-earth and sensible. He told Nuri to call East Ohio Gas and warn them. It was his only chance to avoid catastrophe. Nuri kept telling himself that Stefan wouldn't do it, wouldn't ignite the tanks there.

But each time he thought of what Melchior was, and importantly, what Stefan thought Melchior was, he knew what Stefan was going to do.

If Adolf Hitler was in an allied city, would they firebomb the place to kill him? Would we do it if it cost hundreds or thousands of civilian lives?

Nuri didn't try to answer the question. He knew what the answer was. But he was a soldier, and he knew it wasn't his decision, or Stefan's. The people in this city hadn't con-sented to the war Stefan was fighting.

He reached a desk at East Ohio Gas after several tries.

"Hello?" someone said. Nuri heard commotion behind the voice.

"Please listen. I don't think there's much time. You have to evacuate the plant and the grounds around it. There's going to be—"

"You have to speak up, there's a bit of confusion here. An auto accident— What are you saying?"

"You have to evacuate!"

"What?" Nuri heard the voice muffled, talking to some-one else. The voice continued, "No, you've got to be kidding." Nuri heard the phone rattle on the desk, and the voice moving away. Then, distinctly, he heard a different voice say, *"Holy God, Number Four's letting go!"*

Nuri heard running feet, and the line went dead.

The clock went thunk. It was 2:34.

2:35 PM

No one at the Number Two Works who chose to look in the direction of tank Number Four noticed Dietrich or his bodyguards as they strode to the ruined Lincoln. They didn't notice the ruined Lincoln, pockmarked with bullet holes and belching steam from its fiercely idling engine.

What captured the attention of every employee who saw tank Number Four was the cloud of white fog that poured from a crack that started about ten feet above the ground and ran halfway to the top of the tank. The fog looked innocuous under the bright blue sky, like ice smoke or water vapor.

The sight struck terror in everyone who saw it.

The white vapor was heavy, spilling to the ground, rolling like a short cloud, spilling in a circle around the tank. All the employees who saw it began running to put as much distance between themselves and Number Four as possible.

Dietrich wasn't looking at Number Four, or at fleeing employees. He was looking at the Lincoln with an inhuman anger. His bodyguards followed, mindless, following his will.

But when the rolling cloud reached the feet of the rearmost bodyguard, he looked down into the rolling white vapor. He lowered his gun, stopped moving and said, "What the—"

If Dietrich heard him, he gave no sign. He walked next to the Lincoln as its engine finally died.

2:39 PM

Stefan lay inside his Lincoln, his body riddled with a dozen holes. Every strip of flesh seemed in agony as it tried to knit itself together again. He was nearly blind from the sunlight streaming through the holes in the car.

Spots of sunlight fell on his body, and everywhere they landed was a spot of boiling numbness. He couldn't move, and he thought that one of the bullets must have clipped his spine. He tried to force his will into his right hand, which still had a deathgrip on the stickshift, and on the switch he'd taped to it.

However he thought, how much he willed, how much he prayed, his hand would not release the button. What he could see of its flesh was dead and white, washed in a shaft of deadly sunlight.

"God forgive me," he whispered through cracked and bleeding lips.

In response, the driver's side door was torn off the hinges, flooding the inside with the lethal sun. Stefan could feel it searing his whole body, driving the life and the spirit from it.

The last sensation Stefan knew was Melchior dragging him from the car, hissing, "No one of the blood opposes me."

Stefan never even felt the tug of his hand coming free of the stick shift.

2:40 PM

When the being called Melchior tore free the door of the Lincoln, white fog had already crept around his ankles. He didn't notice. All he had focus for was rage, a rage that one of the blood would still oppose him. His form was changing as he tore the door away. His arms and legs distorting with the crack of bone, his head becoming fanged and goatlike. The suit he wore tore away, revealing leathery skin that was tearing and distorting with the pressure to keep up with the changing body.

He reached in for the one who defied him, his hand sinking deep into the chest of his enemy. He knew that this was one of the blood. He could smell it rank in the air, even as his enemy was already dying in the light. His enemy's small will was too fragile to chain the spirit to the flesh when confronted by the sun.

"No one of the blood opposes me," said the thing that was Melchior. He tried to recognize the latest fool who had tried to bring him down.

He pulled the corpse closer, but the name wouldn't come to mind.

As the body came free of the automobile, there was the

sound of a click as a button taped to the gearshift raised back into position.

The dynamite went first.

It threw the goat-headed thing back toward the main building of the Number Two Works, the body still clasped in its hands. The explosion blew the tanks of gasoline into a fine aerosol that instantly ignited a rolling ball of flame that engulfed Melchior as he was still flying backward.

Shrapnel and fire ripped from the car, tearing through all three bodyguards. Metal pierced Melchior in a dozen places before the blast had carried him six feet.

He was still conscious, still alive, his body still repairing itself, when the fog ignited.

Flames shot through the white cloud, and the air around Melchior turned into a searing hell as the natural gas burned. The air itself became fire. Melchior tried to will his body together as he felt the flesh turn to carbonized ash. It was too much. His breath sucked in fire that seared away his lungs. His eyes melted. His flesh was consumed and the bones beneath cracked apart with the change in temperature.

He was dead before his remains struck the ground.

Then tank Number Four exploded.

2:42 PM

The floors of the Union Terminal building shook so violently that people on the platform looked down the tracks for a collision. Along Kingsbury Run, the railroad cop who had found the head of Edward Andrassy looked up as the sky to the east turned red. In the Roaring Third, still waking from the night before, a bartender that had known Flo Polillo thought he saw the sun set in the north before the wind of the blast burned his cheeks and cracked windows around him.

A hellish wind tore through the Norwood-St. Clair neighborhood. Within seconds everything was burning between East Fifty-Fifth and East Sixty-Third. Telephone poles became pillars of fire, utility wires whipping tendrils of flame. The wind turned the walls of working-class houses into rippling sheets of fire. Birds cooked in the air and fell into pools of melting asphalt. Cars swerved off the road as their windows shattered and their tires blew out, seconds before their gas tanks ignited.

In the basement where Tito, Dante, and Aristaeus had played poker, the walls turned red and black-painted windows blew in. In a few seconds, jets of flame whistled through the floorboards. In the corner of the basement where a cot sat, one of Melchior's thralls opened his eyes. He had the briefest time to realize that the chains of blood that bound him were gone with his Master's death. Then a house of flame collapsed upon him.

The walls of St. John's blistered with the heat as the windows blew inside. The black curtains burned where the wind touched them. The cross over the door fell burning to a blackening lawn. In seconds, the dry wood of the storage shed exploded in an imitation of the holocaust around it. The flames spread to the already burning church.

Close to the plant, where liquid fuel had penetrated into the sewer system, rivers of fire followed the streets from the storm sewers and manhole covers. Inside buildings, toilets and sinks exploded and basements flooded with fire, burning houses from the inside out.

High above, millions of burning fragments of insulation from tank Number Four rained down on the neighborhood, igniting what the blast hadn't touched.

Nuri had been trying to get through to the Gas Works again, when the sun rose in the north. Nuri only had time to turn around in the phone booth as the windows of the drugstore blew in. The paper posters promoting the war effort burst into flames. Gerwazek fell across the old lady, protecting her from flying debris and the contents of the shelves around them spilled to the ground as the whole building shook. The clock fell from the wall and smashed to the counter next to the pharmacist.

Nuri pushed out of the telephone booth, into a searing wind that made him feel as if his skin was on fire. Around him the air roared as if the earth itself was dying.

"My God," Gerwazek said. Nuri could barely hear him.

"We have to get out of here!" Nuri said, grabbing Gerwazek's shoulder. "Get her to safety."

Gerwazek nodded, helping the old woman up. Nuri limped to the rear of the store to find the pharmacist.

Nuri found him behind the counter, unconscious, his face

cut and bruised. Fire was rolling across the ceiling as Nuri tried to revive him, and the air was almost too thick to breathe. Nuri glanced around and saw that the rear of the shop was already a mass of flames; it was no use trying to revive the man.

Nuri grabbed the pharmacist's arms and pulled him over his shoulder. Then he began walking to the front of the store. The air was rank with the smell of burning chemicals. As he passed shelves, he could see bottles of medicine melting into bubbling black ooze that dripped flame. Some of it dripped on to his uniform and stuck, burning all the way through to his skin.

Under his feet, the black-and-white linoleum was yellowing, warping, and cracking in the heat. It seemed forever before he reached the entrance and what seemed to be safety.

It wasn't safety.

When Nuri stepped out of the drugstore, he stepped straight into hell. Flames rolled from buildings on both sides of the street, the air choked with rolling black haze, and the light seemed to come, not from the sun, but from a thousand-foot-tall pillar of fire that burned to the north, glowing through the smoke.

Nuri looked around and saw Gerwazek's car burning by the side of the road, and he saw Gerwazek, hunched over with the old woman, running down the center of the street. He was one of what suddenly seemed thousands of people running through the street, away from the towering pyre to the north.

Nuri ran into the street following the crowd, hobbling as best he could on his bad foot.

6

It would be nearly twenty-four hours before Nuri allowed himself to rest. Initially he was a refugee from the blast, but his uniform and his status as an ex-cop made it easy for him to join the rescue effort as safety officials began pouring into the disaster area. He fell to work helping people out of the rubble, rendering first aid, and helping firemen rig a feed from Lake Erie because exploding water mains had cut off water pressure to the blast zone.

Ten thousand people were evacuated from the area, while in the center, eight square blocks burned to the ground. The fires burned out of control until early Saturday morning.

Sometime during that morning, Nuri began finding more corpses than survivors. It may have been stress, or lack of sleep, but as Nuri worked through the night, he suspected that—despite the fact that the whole area was sealed off—the safety workers weren't the only ones searching the smoking rubble.

Many times before dawn, Nuri would see a set of pale men and women digging at a ruined building. Their clothes were ragged and torn for the most part, as if they were survivors of the blast, but none of the safety workers would approach them.

Each time Nuri saw such a gathering, they were retrieving a body from the wreckage, and sometimes the body wasn't quite human-looking. Whenever one of the safety workers approached them, one of the pale ones would stare at the intruder until he walked away. Nuri would always wonder how many of the blood had died in the blast—and how many survived.

By morning, dozens of safety workers—firemen, police, coast guard, and others—had to be relieved due to fatigue. A large proportion of them had small wounds on their legs, wrists and necks . . .

Nuri worked with the effort until he couldn't go any further, and then he kept at it until someone ordered him home. He got home, exhausted, around three Saturday afternoon. He smelled of ashes, and he looked as if he had worn his dress uniform into battle. Nuri collapsed into a chair and opened the *Cleveland News* he had picked up on the way home.

"71 Known Dead in Gas Plant Explosion," said the headline.

It was conservative.

According to the paper, about 250 homes were destroyed, and at least a thousand people were homeless. Nuri scanned the article until he reached the point where the coroner had asked the county engineer for bulldozers to help search for bodies.

Nuri had to put the paper down.

He sat in his new apartment, barely furnished since his return. He felt an odd sense of guilt at having survived. He slowly balled up the paper, wondering if it had been worth it, if there had been anything he could have done to prevent it.

The bodies he left for us, the ones he wanted to be found, those weren't a hundredth part of the blood left in his wake. And what he wallows in now is not a thousandth part of what would happen if he is granted what he seeks.

Nuri shook his head. Nuri knew that Melchior himself was responsible for many more deaths than the explosion had taken. But he kept feeling that Stefan was wrong, that the deaths were wrong.

If Adolph Hitler was in an allied city, would they firebomb the place to kill him? Would we do it if it cost hundreds or thousands of civilian lives?

Nuri knew the answer.

It was yes . . .

. . . but he would never be able to accept it.

Author's Note

This novel incorporates a number of actual events and people from Cleveland's history. Nevertheless, this is a work of fiction, not a work of history, and none of the characters in this book, even those based on historical personages, should be considered as representing actual people. In particular, Eliot Ness, the Van Sweringens, Mayor Burton, and various police and county officials who appear in this book are all products of my imagination.

While a dozen decapitated bodies were discovered in the Cleveland area around the end of the Depression, and while Eliot Ness was Public Safety Director through most of the investigation of the Torso Murders, the investigation as portrayed bears little resemblance to the actual events. I have also taken liberties with the events surrounding the East Ohio Gas Company explosion. And, of course, most of the events portrayed in this novel never happened at all. . . .

C.S. Friedman

The Coldfire Trilogy

"A feast for those who like their fantasies dark, and as
emotionally heady as a rich red wine." —*Locus*

Centuries after being stranded on the planet
Erna, humans have achieved an uneasy stale-
mate with the fae, a terrifying natural force with
the power to prey upon people's minds. Damien
Vryce, the warrior priest, and Gerald Tarrant, the
undead sorcerer must join together in an uneasy
alliance confront a power that threatens the very
essence of the human spirit, in a battle which
could cost them not only their lives, but the soul
of all mankind.

BLACK SUN RISING	0-88677-527-2
WHEN TRUE NIGHT FALLS	0-88677-615-5
CROWN OF SHADOWS	0-88677-717-8

To Order Call: 1-800-788-6262

DAW 18

Tad Williams

THE WAR OF THE FLOWERS

"A masterpiece of fairytale worldbuilding."
—*Locus*

"Williams's imagination is boundless."
—*Publishers Weekly*
(Starred Review)

A great introduction to an accomplished
and ambitious fantasist."
—*San Francisco Chronicle*

"An a...ictive world ... masterfully plays
with he tropes and traditions of
generations of f... ...y writers."
—*Salon*

...ery elaborate and fully realized setting
...or adventure, intrigue, and more
than an occasional chill."
—*Science Fiction Chronicle*

0-7564-0181-X

...der Call: 1-800-788-6262

DAW 45

Tanya Huff

The Finest in Fantasy

To

To Or